ROOKIE SEASON

Jamal Donte Childs

To my family, friends, and the city I will always call home.

CONTENTS

CHAPTER 1
2nd Friday of Mirci

aank! aank! aank! annk! aan-

About a minute after Flip Stokton rolled over and hit the Snooze on his 6:30 alarm, he got a call on his mobile-communicator. After taking a glance at the screen, he wasn't too happy with the caller ID. Letting a few rings go by before sitting up, he groaned out an answer. "Yeah, hello?"

"Flip? You up?" the voice questioned.

"I answered the phone, didn't I?"

"It's too early in the morning for you to be a smart-ass. Let me at least have some coffee first."

"My bad, I thought you called me? What's up?"

"We've got a helluva scene on our hands over here at Pike's Creek. How soon can you meet me?"

"I just got up. Give me two hours, including travel."

"Make it one and I'll get us some food. If you got company, tell her she can't stay for breakfast."

Click.

Flip turned his head slightly because it wasn't just any company. It was Elena Starks, Matriarch of Founding Family Starks since the age of 12. El in her younger years but forever Olga to Flip. She spent the night after pulling a double at the Fountain City Community Center to kick off the clothing drive for the oncoming new season. Flip asked why she feels the need to be in the trenches so much despite being the Director of the place. Her response, in the same Starks efficiency that defined her athletic career, was simply, "I'm no good sitting on the bench." Flip couldn't do anything but

1

laugh.

As Flip told someone he'll be somewhere in two hours, Elena was stirring awake. She had nowhere to be and was hoping to spend the day (or most of it) out with Flip. Preferably in bed, but she'd settle with a nice breakfast somewhere. The look in Flip's eyes immediately told her that neither was on the table, and she turned over slowly.

"Morning, Olga."

"Zzz..zzz..Zzz..zzz.."

"Fake snoring? Really?"

Elena smiled and turned back to face him. "Wanna tell me what the call was about?"

"I would if I could. He just said there's a mess out in East Pike near the Creek. Mind passing me that?"

"Who's h- "Elena stopped herself, she knew exactly who it was. Fountain City PD CaP'rotector Dante Monroe. Although she had no personal reasons to dislike Monroe, she wasn't the biggest fan of him and how he used Flip. During his time working with the Department over the past year, she's grown to tolerate the relationship between the two, but deep down she was convinced she could never be objectively fine with it. Since his two years out of the League, Flip has been able to keep busy heavily in part to working around the Community Center and with Monroe, not that he needed to. Looking on the nightstand to her right, she saw what he was referring to, the joint leftover from the last night. She crossed herself to pick it up.

Turning back to Flip, "You don't want to come over and get it yourself?" a smile curled her lips as she lit and took a hit, letting the bedsheet slide down to her stomach when she sat up further and exhaled. She saw Flip give her a quick look up and down, knowing the mental math he was doing between how much he wanted to stay and knowing he needed to go. She extended her arm, expecting him to take it and start getting ready for the day. Flip leaned over to take a deep hit and sat on the edge of the bed as he exhaled. "Leaving it with me? Quite the gentleman the morning after." With his back still to her he let out a small chuckle. As she took her next hit, she started to feel that the part of the call she didn't her must have been more serious than she thought. This feeling was gladly washed away when she saw him crawl over and kiss her in a trail that started from her neck and made its way downward.

"I reserved a court at the Center for 1. At least call if you're gonna be late." She said, taking another quick pull.

"Mmhmm." Flip mumbled back.

As she exhaled and put the joint back in the ashtray, she let herself bathe in the sunlight starting to fill the bedroom. She closed her eyes and allowed her body to relive some of last night, letting out a barely audible moan as she felt the sheets pull past her waist and the trail lead further down.

CHAPTER 2

Flip walked towards the elevator for the garage of his condo community, Cloud Mesa. Despite being kicked out the UBL at 26 while still in peak physical condition and skill potential, he did all right with his contemporaneous earnings from the League and sponsors. Forgoing college to go pro six months after his 18th birthday, there were some deep financial valleys while navigating his first few seasons, thanks in part due to reckless spending and frequent tandem fines with Elena for violation of the League's in-season Green Leaf policy, something that put his sponsorship deals in jeopardy more than a few times. By his third year, he began connecting himself with the right people and with the Starks' family and his father's investment advice, the following peaks continued to grow.

Being the "Emissary of Fountain", as he was frequently announced, he's seen a lot of people work hard only to finish with very little. In between rubbing elbows with celebrities and meeting people who "knew what they were doing", he saw how some people made fortunes while others lost theirs in what felt like the same day. Some would have little more than their name and the clothes on their back. The Stokton's were a prominent and more-liked-than-not name in Fountain with a long connection to the entire territory itself. With the Starks' ancestral HouseMother Em-June, Flip's great-grandfather Crayton and his brother Randal Stokton were one of the only two *Vi'nnakan* families on the Seven Clans recognized as official founders of the Fountain City settlement after the Great Territory War. In the peacetime that gave way to further, the settlement was later renamed to simply Fountain, though some of an older time still use the proper name. This was something Flip's parents never let him forget while growing up and eventually became a point of pride later in his playing years.

Standing at 6' 4", Flip quickly learned to duck after his first steps entering the garage. He knew the building was old, he just didn't realize how old until his first time stepping into the garage from the residential elevator and almost concussed himself on the ceiling overhang that was two inches lower than the elevator door ceiling. "Historical Buildings" red tape had always been the reason why things like this could never be immediately fixed and it seems like everyone had to grow to learn and live with it.

Walking to the opposite of the garage, Flip reached into his jacket and felt for his keys. When found, he hit the unlock and what responded was a forest green Cabrini Motors SM Coupe named Joy. One of the biggest reckless purchases that made it out his playing days alive, Flip bought it on sight with a hefty chunk of his sophomore signing bonus from being retained by the Redwater Rogues, the de facto home team of Fountain. After he took them to the Men's Division Finals his first year, the following season saw a large salary increase and brand sponsors practically throwing money at him. At the time, people couldn't stop looking at it because it was the first "luxury-domestic" coupe Cabrini manufactured, with the price tag to match. Now, almost 6 years later, they look because soon after the SM release a huge race fixing scandal left Cabrini Motors all but bankrupt and forced them to shutter most of their local factories, depreciating the value but marginally evening out because of its now antique status among collectors.

Ironically, the SM was quite spacious on the inside. It had just enough leg room to be comfortable after seat adjustment, but less than average trunk size. On an open road, though, the SM could feel like driving a two-seated road missile. Aside from the interior bells and whistles, this was the part that exhilarated Flip the most. Starting her up on the first go, Flip whispered, "Good girl." and proceeded to the garage exit.

It was only quarter to 8, but it was already warm. Being Mirci in Fountain, this wasn't uncommon as it was still in the middle of the rainy season. What is uncommon is when it's warm and generally dry, which was the feel of today. Like anyone that knows their hometown, Flip can mentally review the *"Days since..."* timeline in his head on when it last rained and decided they're due for a nice shower in the next couple days. Safe to ride with the windows down, he rolled them down halfway and felt for few more things in his jacket when he got to the red light. First, he checked his wallet and made sure his FCPD Consult marker was in the first fold. He always liked being able to just flip the wallet and flash it when needed, like they did in the movies and recalling how his mother would do effortlessly when she really wanted to look cool. After taking care of business, he fished out the remaining clip of this morning's joint and the lighter that lived in the passenger cup holder. Elena figured he'd need it more than she would considering his meeting with Monroe, something he was still unclear on what the purpose was. Outside of something happening at Pike's Creek, there's not much more to go on. Whatever it was, Flip gave the benefit of the doubt and figured they did a little legwork on their own before calling him at 6:30 on a Friday morning. Sure, he was planning to wake up anyway, but they didn't know that. Just before the light changed green, he lit up, switched the radio to the local station and checked his mirrors.

Looking at his surroundings during the typical Friday morning stop-go traffic in Fountain, Flip gave a little smile. Partly thinking about his Friday morning start with Olga and partly because he couldn't help it whenever he looked at the inner districts. He loved Fountain, and he knew it loved him back. In his 28 years, he had spent them all either living in or playing for this city, even when he wasn't. Even bouncing around the UBL Men's his last 4 years, getting two of his three career championships in the process, he made sure that he always entertained calls from the Rogues if they gave him a call. Had he known his final season ended the way it did, he'd have taken the pay cut to finish his career with the Rogues. At least he would have exited with a more dignity and fanfare. Instead, he had to deal with reporters asking too many questions and even more rumors in a Territory he already didn't care much for.

Close to 8:00, Flip called CP Monroe.

"I'm about 10 minutes out Cap. Where we meeting?"

After a brief pause and indiscernible verbiage, Monroe responded, "About time son, I'm at Ruby's Diner. What're you eating?"

"Don't call me son, but tell Sandra to make my usual."

"Don't call me Cap, and got it... Coffee or tea?"

"What do you think?"

"Got it."

Click.

As if there was a tipoff to get the phrase first, both men simultaneously said, "Fucking asshole."

Ruby's Diner was normally busy around this time of day, especially on a Friday. Today however, there were much more people than usual, immediately noticeable by the number of cars in the parking lot. Flip pulled around the back to "his" space in the employee lot and saw Monroe's car greeting him. Seeing this immediately elicited his second curse at Monroe before even seeing his face. He pulled in next to him and rolled the windows up. After making the Mark of K'd, Flip got out the car, did a quick look around, and locked the car.

Opting to cut through the kitchen rather than walk around the front and deal with the crowd, Flip walked over Carl, the head cook, and went to dap him up.

"Carl, what's happening, man? How's everything?" He extended his right hand.

"What's up, my brother? Ain't nothing changing but the days, man." Carl extended his hand on connection of the two, Flip felt a shock and in the span of a couple seconds saw muted flashes of Carl yelling at a sports event, likely basketball based on the way the audience seating curved, followed by a less fun one of Carl being cornered by two much larger men with bats. Coming back, he took a step back and looked at Carl up and down. Carl noticed the change in demeanor and looked a little confused. "You ok man?" his voice sounded less than previously upbeat.

"Uh yeah, yeah, I'm good. You going to a game sometime soon?'

"Oh yeah man, taking my brother out to the Rogues-Skyhawks game in a few weeks." His face returning to its former jovial look.

"You wouldn't happen to have anything on the result, would you?"

At that mention, Carl immediately looked ashamed. More like embarrassed, actually. He took a half-step closer and spoke in a hushed tone.

"Don't tell anyone, but I put some money on the Hawks to win. Got a tip that boy Akton been dealing with injury on the low and might not play. How'd you know?"

"I didn't, but I suggest you change your bet. Whoever gave you the tip might not be as much in the loop as you think, or they're tryna play *you*." Flip stepped back and started towards the kitchen exit into the diner. Carl looked at him puzzled before going back to the grill. Listening to the sizzle of two patty melts, he hovered his hand over the pocket that held his mobile. His guy always gave him

"Uh, ok cool, Flip, thanks for the tip!" Flip was already out of the kitchen door and behind the kitchen bar.

As he exited the kitchen, Flip saw the back of Monroe as he exited the bar counter, planting a kiss on Sandra's cheek as he passed and lightly squeezed her waist.

"Ooo, keep on playing like that, I'll need you to get a ring!"

"I don't think Elena would be too keen on that, but give her a call. Y'all might can work something out." Giving a her a wink.

"Don't think I won't! Your food will be out in a sec." She turned to take a new order.

As Flip approached the booth Monroe was seated while exchanging greetings with a few regulars, Monroe turned around at gave his trademark eye cut. Following him until he sat down, he looked at him for a few seconds before speaking.

"You been smoking? Ain't even 9 yet."

9

"Barely. Figured I keep my head straight until after this meeting. By the way, good morning to you too, Cap. How's Oleane doing? The kids?"

"It's Mrs. Monroe to you, and she's doing fine. The same with Kevin and Da'na." Looking Flip in his eyes at this point while taking a sip of his coffee.

"Don't call me son." Meeting Monroe's gaze.

A few more tense seconds in silence, now broken up with the arrival of two large plates of food brought over by Sandra.

"O-kay, so I have an Old Territory omelet, extra salsa, for you mister- I mean CaP'rotector, Monroe. As for you, Flip, I have the steak and egg bagel with a jelly on the side. I'll have Penny bring your tea over once it's ready. Anything else?" She looked at both men to study their faces for an answer.

Looking at Monroe and seeing he wasn't going to break first, Flip looked up to Sandra and said, "No, I think we're good here. Penny's here? I didn't see her when I came in."

Sandra looked at Flip as if not convinced by his first answer, but after a second eased her glance and took his word. "Yeah, she's here, I'll have her come over." Walking away, she gave another glance back once she passed Monroe and looked at Flip again. After receiving a thumbs up and a smile, she smiled back and turned back towards the main dining area and walked off. Looking back to Monroe, still in silence he indulged the power move and initiated conversation.

"Seriously, CaP, what am I doing out here? It's almost 8:30, on a Friday, and I didn't intend on working today. This a social visit? You know you can always swing by Mesa."

Taking another sip of coffee and starting to scoop

salsa out onto his omelet. His voice became audibly lower and he leaned in. "We got a call around 5 this morning, couple fisherman wanting to start the weekend early. They reported a body of an embankment of Pike's Creek."

Whatever buzz Flip left immediately upon hearing the words *"reported a body"* and he straightened up. In that moment his gaze became much more focused.

"Seem to have your attention now? That's right, I said a *body*. Now I-"

"I told you already, man, I don't do murders. Too many shades of grey. Plus, I have trouble sleeping as it is."

"I know son, just let me finish. Now I-"

"Don't call me son."

"...Now, I know murder isn't something we call you in for. But this, this feels different than your random homicide. It feels a little more targeted and deliberate. Take a look at this."

Now, Monroe started to reach into the inner pocket of his modified FCPD issue jacket. He took out a twice folded packet of five papers stapled together and placed it on the table in front of Flip. As Flip unfolding the papers and started to leaf through, Monroe started to give the verbal summary in between new bites of his omelet.

"Isiah Shockley, going on 43. Originally from here in Pike's County, but started bouncing around all up and down the East Coast after 22, usually staying in one place no longer than a year or so. Had my fair share of interactions with him during his main time in Fountain due to his career choice. He wasn't much of violent crimes guy, but was known to keep some type of hardware on him. Allegedly, he even managed to get a couple kids out of his time in Fount, but we can't say either way right now."

"By "career choice" you mean being a criminal? I mean, over half of this second page is from Fountain alone. You seem to have his info, last place of address, why don't you bring him in?" Flip took his first bite of breakfast.

"Well, in a way, we did. He's our-"

Another interruption, again by a pleasant face. This one belonged to Penny Adlouw, Sandra's "sister-daughter" as many liked to describe her. While not knowing each other personally during their time at Fountain Fifth District Academy he did know two things; how protective she was of her brother and that she was tall, standing a slender 5' 11", shoes off. Flip always thought she reminded him of a bamboo stalk, slim but sturdy. Penny's twin brother Aron played on the school's basketball with Flip and was one of the top leading scorers in the Redwater, Fountain and further out Monarch tri-city area. Flip remembered him as being a great player, but an even better academic. When everyone thought he was going to go pro with Flip, he blew their collective mind by accepting a full ride to a school out west to study advanced math or science or something like that. Rumors said there had been something going on between him and Sandra, but between hearsay and Sandra not saying much, Flip stopped caring to find out. Whatever it was, it either didn't affect her relationship with Penny or deepened it because since inheriting the diner after her mother passed, she's made Penny Adlouw her right-hand. Initially a shell-shock to everyone, but once seen in action, was received with genuine positivity by everyone who wanted to continue being a paying customer.

Penny herself was good student. She was just a little more "special", as her family would put it, than the other children. By 2nd grade, she was diagnosed with the crude term of being "mentally retarded" despite getting above average grades and skipping the 1st grade altogether with her brother. Being quieter than the other students, for a while people thought she was a mute, which may not have done may favors for her with the doctors, but she spoke just fine when you spoke of something she interests. She wasn't exactly a loner, but letting Aron explain, some social things were indeed tougher for her to grasp, like knowing when to say, "thank you" and "you're welcome", and when to appropriately enter a conversation, but by no means was she the "retarded lil *vi'nnak* girl" people made her to be. At times, she did seem child-like while at the same time exactly her age as she grew into adulthood.

Aron may have been the velvet glove of the family, but Penny was without a doubt the iron fist clinched within it. She received her High Honor in the elven martial art of *Pak'fajr* at 17 (2nd degree at 19), was basically Aron and Flip's emergency mechanic throughout high-school, and on one memorable occasion got into a fight with two opposing fans in the bleachers during their junior year homecoming. The Fount City Titans beat the Second District based Starks High School Marauders in double overtime, but it was Penny was on the front page, photographed mid-way of a movie poster worthy kick to a man's ribs with the headline, "THE REAL FC TITAN?", above it.

The Adlouw's weren't the wealthiest non-Founding Family in Fountain proper, but most people know East Pike is their domain and their name was on the paperwork of almost every major business in one way or another. Even those that didn't know the business savvy did understand they were also a breed from a previous time. Tangle with one, get entangled with them all. The guy at homecoming either didn't get the memo or wanted to test the theory. Either way, Mom and Pop Adlouw got some lawyers that worked magic to not only keep Penny from being expelled but even squeezed a modest settlement and public apology from the instigator. After that, people stopped the name-calling to her face but didn't necessarily stop treating her as if she was what they called her. When Aron left for college the following year, Penny was in a car accident coming home from a tournament that left her with a faded but prominent scar down her left cheek and completely deaf in both ears. Maybe because she didn't talk much to begin with and had grown adept to reading lips, the learning curve for her new communication was shorter than expected, though there were a few slips here and there.

Penny placed both the mug of hot water and tea bag next to Flip's sandwich and proceeded to sign to him. "Hey Flip!" Her custom sign for him being a V and flicking the legs forward. Monroe received a smile and wave hello that was reciprocated with an acknowledging nod.

"Good morning, Ms. Adlouw." Monroe spoke lowly.

"Hey Penny, how's Aron? Talk to him lately?" Flip mouthed and tried to sign the words he figured were universal.

Penny started signing her response and halfway through could tell she lost him. She reverted to a simpler, "He's fine." with a thumbs-up. She then tapped on a gold necklace with her name in cursive block, the shine giving away that it had to be new.

"He got you that? I like it. Very pretty." Pointing and making a thumbs-up. "Must be making that good money."

Now with a huge smile, she quickly nodded her head yes and started to walk away with a final wave. She doubled-backed and had her notepad out with a pen, already writing as she walked. She ripped off the page and gave it to Flip:

Tell Ms. El I can't make it Tuesday for defense class. I'm going to a date.

Knowing what it was supposed to say, Flip let out a small laugh and pointed to the word *date* and looked at Penny. She smiled and shifted her eyes down slightly. Before Flip could say anything else she held her index finger over her lips, accompanied with shaking her head. Flip shrugged his shoulders and said, "Ok Penny, I'll let her know." Misreading his lips as "Ok Penny, thank you.", her response was to sign "You're welcome" and walked off. Gotta love her.

Looking back at Monroe while steeping his tea, Flip glanced at the first page mugshot and asked, "Ok, so you were saying you *kinda* brought Shockley in. What happened? Alibi checked out and you let him go?"

Monroe finished his coffee, "No, we still have him, but he's not talking." and went in for another bite of omelet. Flip went for the bait.

"Because he knows he's guilty, or knows he's not?"

Without missing a beat, Monroe answered between chews. "Neither, because he's not our suspect, he's our victim. We couldn't tell how he died on first sight, but we know it wasn't originally at the Creek. Scene Scanners think he washed down from some point further up but didn't seem sure. He's already back in Fountain for examination."

Flip could only say, "Fuck..." and repeatedly look over the first page of the file. A smirk found its way onto Monroe's face. He can still find creative ways to render his godson speechless with the right pacing. Reexamining the contents of the five pages he was given and working on his sandwich, Flip didn't see the smirk momentarily turn into a full smile.

Taking the last sip of his second coffee of the day, Monroe sat and let him study.

After finishing their respective meals in relative silence, Flip gulped the last of his tea and started reaching into his pocket. Pulling out some scril, he rifled through the bills and put a couple on the table. Before he got a chance to say anything, Monroe beat him to it and reached his hand out. "Don't worry about the bill, I already took care of it."

"Oh, I figured you did, but I've seen how you tip." Flip responded with a smirk of his own.

Monroe couldn't say anything in response, so he just coughed up a chuckle. *Oleane will have a laugh at that one.* He shrugged his shoulders in concurrence as Sandra approached the table. Flip folded the papers into the same pattern he received them, adding an additional one to fit into his interior jacket pocket.

"So, how'd we do today? Y'all need anything else?" Glancing back and forth at them, she half expected there to be a last-minute addition to-go but was glad to hear the contrary from both. It's been a busy day, so one less of an order for her to trickle down to Carl and Penny helped everyone.

"Well, if that's everything, I'll take these over to Penny. Don't feel you need to rush to leave, most sit-ins are at the front. I'll bring you another tea, my treat." With a playful wink, she turned around when Flip grabbed her hand with both of his.

"Thanks Sandra, but I'll take the tea to go. Split this with Penny and Carl and let 'em know the sandwich was great as usual." Upon contact with Sandra's hand, there was a shock and a flash. Similar to what happened with Carl, but aside from the muffled sound of real-time Sandra talking, there was only a single scene; Sandra standing outside of The Watering Hole, a popular nightclub in a sketchy part of the Fourth District called Low Hang. She appeared to be crying and on the phone with someone. Then nothing. He was back.

"-anks Flip. Want me to leave your tea at the register or bring it over?"

Shaking off what he saw, Flip looked at Monroe and back to her and said, "Yeah, just leave it at the front, I'm about to wrap up here in a minute. Thank you, Sandra."

Sandra nodded and walked to the front of the diner. The look on Flip's face told Monroe that something happened. Maybe something bad. He took a chance.

"Saw something, didn't you?" He was sure Flip did.

"Nah, nah. I'm good."

Monroe noted that although his verbal tone was confident, Flip's face wasn't on the same page. To Monroe, Flip was a very emotive person even when trying not to be. The more he thought he was hiding, the more he showed. Ever since childhood, he was always one of those kinds of people. One of the more positive traits he shared with his father. Always have, always will. Forgoing the urge to press further, he changed topics.

"So, you want to look at the scene before heading back. Still got it taped off for you."

Quickly thinking about his mental *"Days since..."* calendar, Flip begrudgingly decided today would be the safest bet while it's still dry out. Pulling out his phone for a quick time check and seeing it to be earlier than he thought, he figured he should be back home well enough in time to change and meet Elena at the Center. Letting out a small sigh he looked back up. "Yeah, let's go. No need for a ride over."

"I don't recall offering. Your license still valid, ain't it?"

Without a word, Flip gave a look and exited the booth. Again, Monroe gave himself a smirk and slowly followed.

Walking towards the counter, Flip noticed the crowd from earlier had died down and the diner started looking like its typical Friday morning appearance. A couple people at the bar table having some morning news with their coffee and eggs; window tables unoccupied. Flip could see the relaxation on Sandra's face while she totaled up her seemingly last to-go order for the moment. He waited until she was finished, and Monroe walked past to leave out the kitchen before he said anything.

"Going to The Watering Hole sometime soon?"

The look on Sandra's face was of shock. This wasn't the first time he's mentioned personal plans she never told him about, but it got her every time.

"I swear you got bugs in here Flip. How'd you know?

With a small shrug he responded, "So, that's a yes?"

"If you must know, yes, I am actually. One of my girlfriends is having her birthday party there tomorrow, and before you ask, I'm already going with someone. I don't think he'll like seeing me show up with a famous ballplayer. I can see to an invite if you and Elena want to come, though. My girlfriend's a big fan of you two." Her tone, always upbeat, gave off that she was serious about the invite part. Sandra can get anyone invited anywhere, no matter how last minute. Flip chuckled and shook his head.

"Might be working this weekend so I'll take a rain check, but thanks. Nah, I was just asking. Are you and this someone getting there together or separately?" Trying to watch his wording to avoid coming off as prying.

"Probably separately, he said he had to take care of something before the party but he'll meet me there around 8. Why?" Her face was starting to change into a look of mild suspicion. She leaned towards him with a raised eyebrow. "You know something I don't?"

"Oh, no, I don't think so." While shaking his head. "I was just going to say don't wait around for him outside too long. It might rain tomorrow night and I don't want you to get wet."

At this, Sandra's face went to a devious smirk. "You sure? I got a nice dress I'll be wearing."

Realizing the double entendre, Flip shared a laughed and kissed her cheek. "Yeah, I'm sure. I don't doubt you'll be looking nice, but I don't want you to ruin your look before you get through the door."

"Mmmhmm, ok. Let me know if you change your mind."

Flip smiled in response. "I will. Really though, don't hold your breath for him. If you do, at least have an umbrella with you. Let me know if you ever want to swing by Mesa, Elena and I would love to have you and Penny over for dinner." With that he gave her a hug and made his way back through the kitchen where he saw Penny and Carl enjoying a well-earned break at the table against the far wall.

Seeing Penny engrossed in a book, he addressed them both. "See ya later guys, thanks again for breakfast!"

Carl looked up from his phone. "Aight man, good seeing you again! Thanks again for that tip, I'm calling my guy after I get off." He then tapped Penny on the shoulder and when she looked up, pointed to Flip. With a big smile she waved vigorously and signed, "Bye Flip!" and immediately went back to reading. Continuing out to the parking lot, he saw Monroe leaning against his car, a bright white Zindew Condor, waiting for him. The Condor was starting to push 10 years old, but the ritualistic maintenance schedule he kept it on made sure it ran as if he just pulled it off the lot. He checked his watch before straightening up to get in his car.

Before getting in, Monroe asked, "Everything ok?"

Hitting the unlock but pausing to turn around, "Yeah everything's cool, just had to talk to Sandra. I saw something back at the table when I was giving her my tip. Wanted to get some context, that's all."

Seeing that the face and tone matched this time, Monroe nodded and opened the door to get in. Before closing he looked over to Flip. "If you want something in a more official capacity, I could arrange it for you, no problem. You'd be a good street 'tec."

"I didn't say all that but thanks." Is what he was met with before seeing the Cabrini patented Sliding Scissor door slide out and up to open. *At least the kid's always had good taste.* He would never say it out loud except to maybe Oleane. With a quick shake of his head, he started his car and lead the drive out towards Pike's Creek.

CHAPTER 3

Pike's Creek was only 10 minutes up the road from Ruby's, but it was enough for Flip to let his mind wander. He thought about his interactions with Carl and Sandra, which snowballed into the love-hate feelings he still harbored for his final UBL season, and how abruptly it came to an end. They kicked him because of It. Two years after his first flash, he still hadn't seemed to get a grasp on the rules It played by, let alone how to effectively describe It. When It first happened, he saw an opposing play that hadn't happened yet, but couldn't explain how. Or why he was confident enough to follow it and counter effectively. It didn't happen again for another three months, but he followed It nonetheless. Either way, he was fine that not a lot of people knew; even better he could count on one hand those who did and still have a finger left. That brought him a certain level of peace. Until he thought about his mother and what she must have seen in her first flash. Pulling up to a safe distance from any remotely swamp-like area at the mouth, Flip sacrificed walking a few extra yards to meet Monroe if it meant keeping Joy clean. He's put her through some shit, but she's a proper lady now. Before getting out, he flipped open the center console and pulled out a small notebook and a pen.

The Creek was no stranger to a dead body. An unforgiving beast with a beautifully murky exterior. Unless you were in a boat, you were as good as gone. When Flip was a child, he remembers his mom telling him war stories of picking someone out almost every other day during the "Wet Summer". This was the colloquial term for the peak of Fountain's drug related homicides due to a new product at the time called Rock. By the time it came to Fountain, it was already a staple of the party scene in the major western Territories. East Pike, while a self-contained settlement for most civil matters, technically fell under Fountain jurisdiction for major crimes, with its western counterpart falling under that of Redwater. The Creek was the perfect grey place to drop someone if you wanted to give yourself a slight head start on the p'rotecs. Growing up in Pike, Isiah Shockley would have known this legend like he did his own name.

Walking towards Monroe, Flip opened the book to a blank page and retrieved the papers from inside his jacket. He wrote some of the main details.

East Pike native

42

Vi'nnakan (important?)

Last time in Pike: age 22 (maybe)

The last note was more of a question that a confident observation. Aside from his time in Fountain, he didn't really see anything else about Shockley that seemed noteworthy. *He's either smart enough to stay out of trouble on home turf or didn't find anything worth the trouble.* Looking back up to Monroe he already had a few questions at the ready. Monroe was a little quicker.

"Where we found him is a short walk up but I wouldn't recommend trying to drive it. At least not in that."

"It's fine. I do feel like there's still more to why you didn't press me to get out here sooner though. What's up?" Before taking a quick time check, *10:05,* with a little relief. *Not too bad.*

"Got somewhere to be?" There little sternness in Monroe's voice.

"Kind of. Gotta be somewhere at 1." Sensing the tone but refusing the bait, Flip put his mobile back.

"No shit?"

"No shit."

"Thought you were off today? Let's go then," Stepping off towards the scene he added, "up here."

Following to reach Monroe's side, "I said I didn't plan to work today, never said I was off. Slight difference."

Stopping about 20 yards from their parking spot, they stood outside of a box of DO NOT CROSS tape that opens out into Pike's Creek. Miniature tents were still there to show where footsteps and other pieces of interest were found. A few minutes passed by in silence. Flip noticed a blackened pool of blood dried on the edge just before the ground dips into the water. Overgrown water weeds and general debris obscuring it. Then the large number of footprints all over the place. He went back into his notebook and started writing.

"Black" blood – Timeline?

"Shockley was human, right? I saw he's *Vi'nnakan*, but...you know?" Flip asked as he wrote.

"Yeah, he's human. Why?" Monroe answered.

Footprints – different sizes. small area, not enough variety

"You're going silent on me. What you thinking about?"

"I don't know, just stuff I'm seein'. Your guys noticed that blood over there, right?" Pointing over to the pool.

"Yeah, they did, but it didn't tell them much. Like I said, the foundation right now is he washed down from further up but so far Wallace isn't too convinced. Unfortunately for him, it's the only place he can really start

23

from."

"Interesting. What about the shoe prints?"

"People still walk this road Flip, there were prints all up and down before we got here."

"I know but I asked about *those* prints." He pointed, slight agitation showing his face now. "Nevermind, can I just go in?"

"I was about to ask you the same thing. They photographed everything and bagged what they needed so you're good to-."

Flip was already straddling the tape and walking the edges of the scene, careful to not get too deep in. Walking along the side parallel to the road he kneeled and started looking at a pair of the smaller prints. After a minute of studying, he let out a sigh and squatted to press an index finger into one of the waffle-cut indents. Nothing. Putting his book and papers back into his jacket, he took his other index and pressed down. Nothing.

Standing back up he looked at the larger prints and noticed they progressively got closer to the edge of the embankment. Not a direct trail but they get closer whereas the smaller ones stop after a certain point.

"See anything?"

"Doesn't work like that, Cap."

Two steps forward, Flip now stood basically directly over one of the bigger prints and squatted. Taking his index finger, he pressed into it. *Flash.* Muted roll showing two scenes with two sets of legs in jeans. The first scene was a straight look facing up the road but only up to the shins, one person a few steps behind the other. Very dark beside the moon overhead. Second scene was a flash cut to one person pacing back and forth with the other walking in the direction of the creek edge. A rolling light coming from the same direction Monroe stood. Flip's view of things still only shins high. Then nothing. Flip stood up and walked to Monroe in the same path he took to leave. Only after crossing back over the barricade did he get back into his notebook.

Two people

Faceless

Jeans

shit.

Closing the book and replacing it into his pocket, he continued looking at the scene for another two minutes before saying anything.

"Wallace he may be right to question the float idea. I didn't see anything but there were definitely two people here at the same time within the past couple days. You may already be on it, but you might want to ask people around here if they've seen anyone. I think someone may have saw them. That's all I got."

Checking his watch, Monroe readjusted his jacket before pulling out a pack of cigarettes and a book of matches. Putting one in his mouth, he struck light and took a pull.

"I'll ask around Ruby's again. Need to see anything else?" Making sure turn his head before exhaling.

"Not from here. By the way, you know those things'll kill you."

"Hasn't so far." Turning around to go back to his car.

"Yet.." Taking a last look at the scene with a smirk before turning to follow. Hearing the quip, Monroe took another short pull and exhaled.

Back at his car, Monroe reached to place his hand

on Flip's right shoulder before taking a final drag. "Thanks for coming out here. I'll talk to Wallace when I get back in town and relay what you said. Keep that file with you. It's not in full but it's the most I can let you see outside the station." Flicking away the butt, he opened the driver door and climbed inside. After starting it up, he rolled down his window as Flip starting walking away.

"I'm serious, I do appreciate you coming out. You didn't have to come in on a day off."

Not fully turned towards the direction of his car yet, Flip put his hands into his jacket pockets and turned back to face Monroe. "Yeah, I know. Thanks for the breakfast."

"Of course, son. Anytime." A tiny smile made its way to light.

"And Cap?"

"Yeah?"

"Don't call me son."

Smile aborted.

Walking back to his car, Flip reached for his phone checked the time again, *11:03AM*. Flip knew he'd have more than enough time to run home and just walk over to the Center. Doing a lookaround, he noticed a dark car down the road he wasn't sure was there when he first arrived. Shrugging it off, he unlocked and got in. He got out his phone and dialed a number. All the while, the owner of said dark car watched Flip pull out and drive off.

Finishing the dishes from her breakfast of one, Elena heard the faint sound of her mobile ringing over the TV; sounds like it's coming from the living room. Finding it between the couch cushions she picked it up and immediately answered.

"Elena Starks." Not paying attention to the caller ID, she was hoping this wasn't a work call.

"Hey, you still at Mesa?" Flip asked.

"Yep. Are we still on for the Center later?"

"Yes ma'am. I'm on my way from Pike's now. Figured I'd park there and walk over. Wanna wait for me and go over together?"

Looking down at her watch, she made a face and walked back to the kitchen. She put the communicator on speaker. "Think we'll have time to stop at my place so I can pick up some stuff? I don't have anything to play in." Raising her voice some to compensate for the running faucet.

"We can do that, or you can check my closet. Your bag is still in there from last time. At least it should be." There was a faint click of the center console closing.

"Shit, that's right. Well did you at least-"

"Yes, I at least washed it. Them shoes might be funky, but I promise I won't tease you too bad." She could hear a chuckle weakly disguised as a cough and couldn't smiling a little herself. Taking a second look at her watch, she finished at the sink and turned around to lean back against it.

"What time you think you'll be here? The reservation is for 1:00."

"I should be there right before midday traffic gets going. See you soon."

"See you here." Picking up her mobile to disconnect.

"Olga?"

Thinking he forgot to mention something important. She stopped herself in time.

27

"Yeah, Flip?"

"I love you." A two-second silence went by before she said anything.

"I know... I love you, too. I'll see you soon, ok?" And disconnected the call. Now off the phone, Elena let out a small sigh and started walking back towards the steps that led to the second floor, grabbing the remote to turn up the TV before ascending. There was a breaking news alert coming on as she walked. There was a body found in the early morning hours at Pike's Creek. Very few details have been confirmed, but the story is being monitored and will be updated as more come in.

Walking up the small flight, Elena started thinking about the last few moments of her phone call. *I love you.* The last two years have been good for them, really good in fact. The first 6 however, have left them both with a few emotional scars that still itch occasionally if given enough air of thought. During their time in the League, Elena and Flip were almost more infamous for the on-again-off-again nature of their relationship than their career fine totals. At one point, their friendship altogether was on the line. She's made her peace with it all by now but that didn't make the memories any rosier. Entering the bedroom, she circled around the bed and opened the closet.

Sure enough, Flip did have her gym bag in a far corner of his closet like he said. Back in the day, she used to leave it on purpose so she could have a reason to come over and (more than likely) spend the night. Now that they're both grown up, the bag has stayed more for the convenience than anything else. *Not like he's strapped for closet space.* Walking a few paces to pick it up, she opened it and again, Flip was speaking out of fact. Her jersey and shorts were folded over and in garment cleaners' plastic. Socks had obviously been cleaned and folded into one of her shoes. Taking out the socks, she picked up her shoes and gave them a sniff. She was met with the relieving smell of what she always felt was the incorrectly named scent "Clean Linen". A quick tip of the shoes caused two Deo-Balls to roll into the heel. Realizing she fell for the tease, Elena looked up and laughed to herself. *Flip Stokton, award winning comedian.*

CHAPTER 4

Flip was sitting at the first red light leading back into Fountain. Looking at the dashboard clock, Joy told him *11:48 AM.* He started for his console-

green light

 then changed his mind. One set of his notes had come to mind:

2 people/1 night?

Partners? First finders? Witnesses?

Jeans

Shoes: different sizes, same print

He had circled that last item. Something about it felt important to remember. Something to talk to P'rotector Wallace about? It made him think about his mother and her many anecdotes from when one small detail helped her crack a standstill case.

"Never discredit anything. If it's worth writing, it's worth remembering"

It was one of her favorite sayings when recounting her tales from work. Likely because of these stories, Flip got into the habit of making these lists during his year working with the FCPD. In the beginning, he was a little embarrassed because of all the jest he got comparing him to "Birdie" Stokton. For a bit, it even made him feel like a try-hard. After a frank off-the-clock talk with P'rotector Wallace at The Watering Hole, those feelings died down and the jokes no longer felt like digs on him but more like they were paying homage.

Lead Homicide P'rotector Joh'nathan Wallace has

always been cool in Flip's book. Being almost 40, Flip looked up to him as the older brother he wished for as opposed to the one he had. Ronald Klima, Jr., and Flip were 12 years apart due to a previous marriage of his father's and didn't appear too interested in being around the new family. Flip saw him every now and then when Ronnie would come and visit his father but not much outside of that. He remembered how one time Ronnie came to hi outside of his usual visit back in sixth grade with Wallace. They were both wearing dusters, the fashionable trend at the time but not as much anymore even among the older generations. Fountain Fifth District Academy was playing Redwater Hill in a heated Rivalry Night game. It was the year Flip made the pre-highschool Varsity despite being one grade under the minimum requirement.

Flip came off the bench at the top of the 3rd to get what was intended to be a symbolic gesture by the coach to introduce his youngest player than to give actual minutes. The stat line showed the young Founder scored 12, and though the night ended in a loss, Ronnie and Wallace still took him out to Ruby's for ice cream as if he had made the game winning shot. After that, the house visits resumed but stopped altogether shortly after Flip's 15th birthday. From there on, most updates came through what his father shared and the rare minutes-long text exchanges. Last he heard, Ronnie moved out of Fount almost 6 years ago to Outer-Monarch. Wallace on the other hand left the area for a while and upon return immediately applied to the Fountain City P'rotectors Department. His arrival to the force gave him enough time to personal witness the chaotic tail end of Fleice Stokton's storied career in law enforcement.

Since starting his work with the department, Flip's learned more about Wallace in a year than he had known his entire life. Being friends with his older brother, that wasn't much. He already knew he at least was originally from the Third District and worked with his mom for a little while. Everything in-between was up for grabs, but the past year has been progressively sealing the gaps. Apparently, he went down south shortly after 20 and moved around for almost two years. *"What were you doing down there?"* Flip recalled asking him.

"Living, man. Just... living." Wallace said after a sip of beer.

After his time in the southern territories, he went more west to help some family and got into "a little trouble" with the law. *"No time or nothing like that. Just running around doing dumb shit with my cousins."* Was his description of that time pocket. After a few years, he moved up to the Redwater area and got into the Private Investigator business.

"Wasn't pretty, but the pay was steady. Steadier than most work I'd had at the time."

"What'd you do?"

"Ehhh, almost anything that came along. The typical: cheating spouses, theft, the ol' 'Can You Bring Them Back Home' situation. Shit, a couple times an actual murder found its way to me. Mostly shit the p'rotecs either closed too quickly or straight-up didn't look into, you know?"

Weirdly, Flip did know. His mom was the Lead Homicide Investigator of the FCPD for almost 23 years before her leave from the force. It was groundbreaking not because she was a Founder, but because she was a woman, a *Vi'nnakan* at that, and the youngest Lead Homicide Investigator to date at the time. Even the first Fountain Territory Sheriff, Randall Stokton, was almost 40 when he was elected to the position.

"It was just something about it, you know? I felt alive a

little more whenever I was working a case. After a couple years I got good at it and registered with the nearby settlement. Did it a little longer and that's when I came back to Fountain and applied for PD. You're looking at the rest of that story."

After that night, he's served as Flip's Case Councilor and Department Liaison ever since. Over the year, he has gotten to know about Flip a bit more too. Through Fleice, he felt like he knew exactly the right amount of what he felt he ever needed to know combined with what he remembered: tall, smart, athletic as all-hell, with a pinch of trouble to keep him interesting. Because of this prior knowledge, he kept his initial meets with Flip strictly work-oriented. Getting to know Flip as a man, especially after everything he went through, he saw there actually wasn't too much they didn't have in common and loosened up a little. What he didn't foresee was that in short time, he'd be a mentor passing along his gems of being a PI, and how to enjoy it, to a Founder.

Finishing his beer with a final gulp, *"Tell you what, though, the cheating cases were always the best ones."* Adding a chuckle to himself before getting up from the barstool. Small head swim but nothing to keep him from getting home.

Laughing a little himself, Flip finished his beer and was about to order another. *"Really?"*

"No shit, brother." While putting his jacket his jacket on and heading to the door. *"Every client used to claim they didn't already know. I'd say about a quarter of them was tellin' the truth."*

Pulling up to the Cloud Mesa's Resident Parking garage, Flip took a check at the dashboard. *11:55 AM.* Rolling past the other vehicles, he tapped on the steering wheel rhythmically as he eased into the corner space. Getting out, he noticed the garage still looked relatively as full as it did this morning. This made him smirk. *Guess if you're living here, you can afford to have three-day weekends* he thought to himself, and then closed the door. Starting to walk across to the elevator he turned around, keys in hand. "I'll see you later, ok?" before pressing to lock. Joy chirped back and locked up. Flip liked talking to his car. He always imagined it's the same feeling people get when they talk to their pets. They have no idea what their owners are saying but it makes them happy all the same. Making sure to duck under the overhang, Flip boarded the elevator and selected his floor.

"Hold the door! Hold the door, please!" He heard a voice call out just as the doors were closing. Pressing the DOOR OPEN button, the voice revealed its owner seconds later. Missy Blaskow-Hermann, aka the "Specter of the Mesa". One wouldn't guess on first sight but at north of 70 years old, Missy was not only one of the oldest and wealthiest residents in the building but also the longest staying among the few decades-long owners. This veteran status has afforded her not only the general respect of Mesa's residents but rumors of being a sort of unofficial member among the even more shadowy management group that handles the building's application process and overall resident affairs. After her 34th birthday, she came in on the 7th floor and every few years, worked her way up to eventually sitting high in the largest of the double-floor units on the top floor. Her last stop on the way was Flip's very unit before skipping residential floors 11 and 12 altogether shortly after her first and only marriage dissolved. Flip respected her hustle, even though he didn't exactly know what it is or was.

"Thank you. Oh! Hi Flip, how are we today?" She's always had a schoolteacher's formal way of speaking. Maybe she was one at some point. Yes or no, Flip never felt comfortable enough to ask.

"Hey Ms. Blaskow-Hermann, I'm doing alright. You?" He took a second to send Elena a text.

"I'm beyond great! It's Friday and I'm alive." Pressing the 13th floor, she turned back to him quickly as the elevator started moving up. "Actually, before I forget! I'm having a get together with some friends and other residents on the rooftop later tonight. You are more than welcome to stop by. Maybe you can finally introduce me to that pretty friend of yours with the fancy car I sometimes hear about. She must be something special to be paying for a second parking space." A smile went across her face.

This invitation came as a surprise. Flip had heard (usually after the fact) about Missy's occasional Friday night roof-parties through the grapevine of other residents. Listening to the way they talk about them, he felt it was either a resident initiation resident or the perfect way to determine whether Missy likes you or not. A few stories have been told to him of newcomers caught on the latter of the spectrum and soon after received letters of how they weren't "exhibiting Cloud Mesa values", and in the most polite wording possible, asked to find somewhere new to live. Considering he's been in this building since he was 23, Flip just assumed that either he didn't fit the demographic of The Specter's normal guests, or she didn't care about him enough to care.

"Oh, um, thanks Ms. Blaskow. I'll uh... I'll have to see what tonight is looking like for us. If I'm home, I'll make sure to swing by." Not exactly sure how to accept a potential one-way ticket out of his home, he sounded audibly nervous in his response.

With a big laugh, Missy threw her head back and knew why. "Don't worry Mr. Stokton, it's not a 'test' or whatever these people like to call it. I like you quite a bit and I know your name is good as fresh-minted scril. I even used to schedule my parties around your games so we could listen to them on the talk-box." Adding a wink to punctuate just as the automated voice announced the 10th floor. "Quite a shame how they treated you on the way out though. For what it's worth, I never believed the papers, but I guess persecution runs in the Stokton family." It was at this point Flip made his way.

"Still in my old unit, I see? Taking care of it?"

"Yes ma'am. It's a nice place." Not sure of what else to say. Of course it was a nice place.

"Yeah, it is, isn't it? There used to be a time I would've called it my favorite." Her voice dropped a touch and she seemed to look past him to the door, "Anyway, have a good Friday and I hope to see you later. *Both* of you." before her smile resumed.

"See you later Ms. Blaskow. Have a good day."

"Call me Missy--"before being cut off by the closing doors. Giving a second before walking off, he half-expected to see the doors reopen and she restarted whatever he felt she was about to say. *Things to plan and people to set up, I guess.* Flip liked Ms. Blaskow-Hermann, but despite being only 5' 5" and maybe 125 on a healthy day, that tiny elf sure knew how to make him a little nervous.

Walking inside, Flip smiled when he saw Elena in the kitchen; back turned, music playing, gym bag on the couch. He slowly tiptoed his way across the floor and into the living room. He got to the couch before,

"Excuse me, Flip Stokton, but what are you doing?"

"Uhh, nothing." he went back to a regular walk and came behind her.

"Mmhmm, ok. Tryna sneak on me?" Giving a small smile and kissing him. "Thank you for this morning." Another kiss. "How'd Pike's Creek go?" Something told her that whatever it was, it wasn't a social call for CP Monroe; wasn't his style. Didn't the news earlier mention something about a body was found.

"Could've been better, but we'll talk about it later." Already halfway out of his head, he almost forgot about the rap sheet still in his jacket. *Don't ruin a good thing with shop talk.*

"Mmhmm." *Don't press it, El.* "You ready to go?"

"Sure." Suddenly snapping his fingers. "Shit, my bag's in the car. Want a ride?"

"How else I'm getting there?" For all her athleticism, Elena was never the one to walk somewhere if it can be helped.

"Funny. Aight, let's go."

Approaching the car, Flip opened Elena's door then went around to the truck. He opened up to check if his bag was still in there. Seeing that it was, he closed it and got in. Once the car was started, he paused and looked over to Elena. "Two things for you." Then started Joy up.

"What's that?" Not sure where this was going.

"Missy Blaskow-Hermann from 13 invited me to her rooftop party tonight. Well, technically *us*."

"Technically? She mentioned me by name?" Elena

started searching her mind of where she could have met Ms. Blaskow. She knew everything she did from Flip's relays but positive she's never met The Specter herself.

"Not exactly. She said 'that pretty friend of yours' so.." He engaged to drive.

"Uh huh. You sure she wasn't talking about anyone else?" At this, Flip turned and saw she was sticking her tongue.

"No, I'm sure she wasn't talking about anyone else." Responding with a tone of sarcasm. "So childish."

Laughing and looking at her watch, she checked her shoes as they approached the garage exit. "I know. Anyway, are we going?" Then stuck her tongue at him again. "Plus, you said there were two things. What's the second?"

"Simple question." Giving a smirk, "You know you getting smoked today, right?" Flip poked her arm.

This motherfu- "Boy, whatever, just drive."

As requested, Flip shifted into drive and pulled out of the garage.

Driving to the Fountain City Community Center from Cloud Mesa, one would have to pass the Fountain City P'rotectors Department – Second District Headquarters. For Flip, this pass-by always brought a flood of memories. Many good, even great. Some, less than. The only constant in the overlap was his mother. Even though his family still lived in the affluent "Founders" Fifth District of Fountain, Flip spent a lot of his time here in the "city". Between his mother's job and coming to hang out after school, he felt more comfortable in the streets of the other Districts and the people he found in it than the sheltered, almost boring open outskirts of his neighborhood. As soon as he was old enough to drive, he started spending more time at the "Triple-C" than the manicured grass-front of Fountain Fifth District Recreation Center; playing with some of the best Fount City had to offer and getting into some trouble with them afterward. Even with a rank P'rotector for a mom, Flip himself got in his fair share of trouble. Hell, at times it almost felt encouraged by her.

"Never trust a slate that appears too clean and never trust a man that doesn't use a mirror."

That was something he remembers her saying a lot. Initially he took it as a weird way she looked at her work, especially the latter. He's had his run-ins with the p'rotecs, but he understood the aces in his sleeve of his name and his mother and kept the run-ins to a minimum. Plus, he knew she'd try to pick him up personally if he ever got into something serious. *Act like an asshole, get caught like one.* She seemed to always have a line ready for him. When the dual Aces dropped to one was a few months after his 18th birthday, where Housemother Fleice Stokton's career already slow burning decline fell into the fire pit that eventually consumed it.

Passing by the precinct, Flip took a quick look at it and sped up. The sudden increase jolted Elena and she glanced at him with minor surprise. She did ask her customary question, almost instinctively. "Hey, you ok?"

"Yeah." A steady gaze looked ahead.

"Ok. Just watch the light."

"I got it, Olga."

Elena understood why Flip initially preferred to want to walk. It gave a few more route options that allowed bypass of the precinct. She also knew he was his own man that makes his own decisions. In his own way, she always felt that going past the building was his bittersweet way of reconnecting to his mom of when she was, as opposed to where she is. Nevertheless, she was glad he did watch the upcoming light and slowed down when it struck yellow. *If he hates them so much, why work with them? Does he actually hate them, or what they did?* This was something she still asks herself every time, just like how Flip speeds up every time.

After a few turns and passes, Flip and Elena pulled into the parking lot of the Community Center. It was barely 12:30 but the lot was already populated. On the outside playground they could see the jungle gym and play area teeming with children. A little beyond that, the older kids and adults at the picnic tables and a few outdoor ball courts. That's when it hit her.

"Why so many kids?" Flip asked while rounding a bend looking for a spot.

"I almost forgot, today starts Spring Break. Kids either got off early or had school cancelled. You heard the Minister make that announcement a couple weeks ago?"

At this reminder, Flip did recall. Newly re-elected Fountain Minister Gerrie Esun made a whole show announcing that the week before Spring Break would be shortened by a day. The stated reason was the noticeable absences or "sick" calls that occurred on the Friday before the weekend of. "Wish they had that when we were in school."

"I know, right? Wanna be cool and use my spot?" Pointing a few feet up to an open space between two cars. This was the employee line. Right in front of the entrance, it was the perfect place, no matter whether you were just pulling up or calling it a day.

"Sure." Pulling up a little in front and backing into the space. "What court we using?"

Grabbing her bag from the floor, she started to open the door. "I forgot about today, so I had got us one of the outdoor courts. You don't mind a fan rush, do you?" Now looking over the car towards the playground area, the only outdoor path to the courts.

Looking over and seeing the amount of already excited kids, he sighed and looked back at her. "Mind if I go change first?" And chuckled.

"Sure. Make sure to see Ms. Ingram." Glad to see a smile on him again. He's always been a little funny about kids. A brief foresight trying to picture him holding a baby was funny to think about.

"Will do." With that, he went to the trunk and got his back and made his way to the front door. Not being the most physically inconspicuous guy, he was already being peppered with distant greetings by a few early noticers.

"Mr. Flip! Mr. Flip!" From a little boy waving.

"Hiii, Mr. Flip!" A group of girls jump-roping in the grass in front of the play area entry gate.

"Hey Coach, coming to ball with us?" Couple of teenagers starting the walk to the courts, basketball in hand.

"Nah man, not today." Shaking his head and pointing back to his car. Elena was already out of her shirt and in her jersey, bag in hand.

"Oh aight, do your thing!" Before enjoying a group laugh with his friends and proceeding on.

As he walked inside, he did a quick look over the front lobby. It looked like it recently experienced a thorough much needed cleaning and repaint. *Green and yellow? C'mon Olga.* Since becoming the Director, Elena's been adamant on "cleaning up" the Triple-C's social position within the city, starting with its appearance. The outside didn't take long. A triple play of additional lights, new play area flooring, and updated outdoor furniture did most of the heavy lifting. The rest came from Elena and her staff working together. It's been on a steady uphill climb, but Flip could still clearly remember when this place was used almost strictly as the neighborhood fight spot, trap spot, with basketball peppered in the mix. It was in that mix that he liked to reside. Here, nobody cared about his name or who his mom was, just his ability on the court. Once he showed that he could run with and outplay the best, that was when they started to care about his outside life. When Chou Deric, the Director before Elena, first arrived a little under a decade ago he did tackle the "trouble" that was attracted to it but soon after made it obvious that it wasn't a big priority of his. Only when Elena was hired as his successor did Flip start coming back around the Center again. He had the time and had already spent most of the previous year staying home feeling sad and angry about his "retirement". He knew a second one wouldn't be healthy for him.

On his way to the men's locker room, he passed the main office. He was only a few paces before a stern, older voice called out to him. "Now, I know Fleice raised you much better than that to not say hi to anybody."

"Oh, hey Ms. Ingram! I didn't see you in there when I passed. How you doing?" Already walking back, arms outstretched, Stokton Smile in tow.

"I'm doing good, baby, and you? Ms. Starks isn't here today but she should be soon. She put a reservation on one of the courts outside." Meeting halfway for the hug followed by a kiss on the cheek Flip had to hunch for. Scarla Ingram went back with Fleice Stokton all the way to when they first met in 3rd grade. Since then, she has been connected to the Stokton family in a way that only Elena and Monroe can appreciate. She also acted as the eyes and ears for Fleice whenever Flip was cutting up a little too much at the Center.

"I know. She's out front while I came in to change." Jostling his bag. "You guys do some cleaning around here?" Now pointing at the nearby walls. "Looks good."

Ms. Ingram leaned in a little and looked around, making Flip dip down.

"It does, but between you me, I'm not a big fan of the colors. Almost *too* bright." She whispered with an added a smile that conveyed jest but with a sprinkle of truth on top. Flip kept his position and looked at her.

"Same here." Matching her tone and smirked himself. They shared a laugh before he said good-bye. As he turned towards his original route, he felt a small grab on his arm. Turning back, he saw Ms. Ingram's face adopted a more sober look. Somewhere between a whisper and conscious monitor of voice, she asked him something that she meant to when he last visited.

"You see your mother lately?" Flip could tell she already knew his answer.

"No... It's been a minute." It had been a couple months. Turning his head down, he felt the gravity of his words as they were leaving his mouth.

"It's ok, Flip, she-"

"Nah, it's not ok." As he spoke, he felt a rush go to his throat.

"What happened, or you not going to see her?" Her face told him that this wasn't a rhetorical answer but he didn't need to respond, so he didn't.

"You're not a bad son, Flip. Never was. Next time I talk

43

to her, I'll just tell her you'll come by soon. Deal?" This time she did expect an answer. One answer.

"Deal." He gave her another hug and a kiss on the cheek. "It was good seeing you again."

"Of course, baby, anytime. Now go on and get changed. I'll have a ball for you when you get back."

Flip continued down the hall and turned left into the locker room.

Stepping back outside, a new energy took over. He was wearing his favorite uniform: a Rogues postseason variant of white and gold with maroon *Rogues* text accented with gold lining. The feelings that bubbled up during his talk with Mrs. Ingram had not only subsided but evaporated completely. He had been meaning to visit his mom, just not sure when. Starting to bounce the ball, he did a couple crossovers as he walked over to the car. Elena tried to look unimpressed as she leaned against Joy.

"Took you long enough. What were you doing in there, *making* the uniform?" responding by mimicking his moves. "You ain't the only pro out here."

"Oh, I know, don't worry. I know."

"You see Mrs. Ingram in there?"

"Yep, she caught me on the way to change. When'd y'all repaint inside? Wasn't like that a couple months ago." Stretching out his hand to escort her to the gate. She accepted and met him at his side, arm in arm.

"We started right after the last time you were here. If you came around a little more, you could've helped."

Her last comment stung a little. He knew it was true, though. Visiting the Center outside his weekly basketball workout with the teen rec team became sporadic over the last three months. Did the fact that it was around the time he and Elena had an argument over his PI work have anything to do with it? Maybe, but maybe not.

"Sorry about that." It was all he could muster. "What's with the colors though? Green and yellow? A bit on the nose, with a Starks is the Director, don't you think?" Opening the gate into the pathway, he let her enter first. That's when the fanfare came. "Here comes the press." she heard him whisper.

"Oooh, Ms. Elena, very pretty uniform." A little girl came over to say. "Hi, Coach Flip."

"Hey, Breona." adding a small wave to counteract the monotone that came out.

"Are you guys playing again today?! Can we watch this time?" This voice belonged to the verbal ambassador of a group on the jungle gym.

Elena shrugged her shoulders and looked to Flip.

"Sure, you can, just make sure to stand outside the court gate."

"Ok! We will!" Then proceeded to spread the word to the others nearby.

As they got closer to the courts, Elena walked to the half-court and took off the laminated RESERVED sign taped to the chain-link door.

"Ready to lose today?" She asked, looking back at Flip.

"I'm ready to play. No crying when *you* lose." He responded with a wink.

"*When?* Oh no, no, no, Love, that's not happening. I need to get you back from last time."

They entered the court and latched the door closed. Soon after, a gaggle of bodies and eyes started to convene along the opposite side. These one-on-ones normally happen in the indoor gym, but inside or out, there's always an audience.

"Wanna make today interesting?" Elena asked while dropping her bag the hoop's base. Flip couldn't help but give her a look over. Elena was a slim 6' even but there was always something about the way she could wear that uniform that could get him going. Always has, always will. *Focus, Stokton. Play now, maybe some play later.* Her pick-up look consisted of a souvenir from her playing days: black and silver Silver City Skota jersey with matching shorts and shoes. Only thing missing is the ring she won with them. That was being kept snugly on the pinky of one HouseFather Khristoph Starks.

"Sure, what you thinking?" Starting his ritual stretches, he did a few arm and body rotations.

"I win, I get to drive Joy for today *and* we have to go to that party. No backing out." Wagging her finger to emphasize.

"And if I win? Also, I don't really know what time it starts."

"Oh shit! Ms. Starks and Coach Flip about to ball." Teenagers and some adults starting to gather from the picnic areas, strong smell of a free Friday following them.

"You *let* me drive Joy today." Initiating first check-up, then lowering her voice, "and anything else you
want *after* the party." before winking and spreading into a defensive stance. "Good with you?"

"Sounds good to me. Let's go, Starks, ball up."

Good weather and better talent on the court. This one's going to be a real heater today, folks!

CHAPTER 5

Around the same time Flip and Elena started their one-on-one, Rac' Tabine was settling into his lunch at Ruby's Diner. Looking across the table, he saw his sister Hana looking at something on her mob-comm.

"What're you looking at?" He forked up a few fries and started chewing.

"The news." She then put it down and started on her fries as well.

"Anything?"

"A headline and the typical 'more details forthcoming' bullshit. Other than that, not much. Looks like we did a good job. They even had to go back for a second look, remember? He had some new guy with him. Must be some street rookie." Satisfied look on her face, she picked up her burger and took a healthy bite, blood and grease dripping to the plate. Licking blood off her lips she gestured, "Go on, try it. You already started the fries without me."

Rac' rolled his eyes. He and Hana were twins, separated by mere minutes, but to a certain point they did everything together, even usually eating in the same order. He picked up his burger and bit in. He had to admit, it *was* good. A little bland, but he could still note that unmistakable fresh off-the-grill aroma. Taking another bite, he shook his head in agreeance.

In the silence that often found them whenever they shared a good meal, Sandra came over with their drinks and her notebook.

"Two sweet teas and two waters, no ice. Need anything else?" She then wiped her hands on her skirt towel and got her pen ready. She swore she heard something but not sure where.

"No." Repeated Rac', voice barely above a whisper, while still looking down at his plate before taking another bite. Hana looking back into her phone. "Thank you."

"I'm sorry, sweetie, can you say that again? I didn't hear you." Taking a small downward lean forward.

"He said no *and* thank you. What are you, *fucking death*?" She had no issue identifying the owner of this voice. Hana was looking her directly in the face and boring holes into her eyes; fast bubbling anger seen rushing to her face. The few people that were inside turned towards the sudden sound and looked towards the source. Sandra's face was one of shock and a flash of anger. Then she thought she saw, fire? Yeah, she swore there was literal fire in this girl's eyes.

"Now, I apologize if I offended y'all, but I will not be disrespected in my own goddamn restaurant. When you finish your meals, I'd appreciate it if you pay at the front and leave. Penny will ring you at the register." With that she turned very quickly and walked, not noticing Hana smiling the same as earlier. That smile was short-lived as she felt a force hit her leg under the table. She looked at Rac' who had a look of anger himself.

"The hell you do that for? She was just doing her job." He said in a measured tone.

"She called you 'sweetie'. I hate that pet name stuff from strangers."

"She didn't mean it like that and you know it."

"I said what I said." She picked up her tea and started to sip.

"I'm not *yours*, Hana." He whispered.

"Oh, is that right?"

Rac' sat silently for a few seconds and lowered his head back into his food.

"You *are* mine." Taking another sip of water before finishing her burger. Her eyes like a bed of embers occasionally catching a breeze. Rac' met them with a smoldering bed of his own.

"Whatever." He put his head down and forked the final few fries and piece of burger on his plate.

Hana's face softened and she reached across the table, resting her glassy-skinned right hand on his left before it left the plate.

"I'm sorry. You know I love you, right?"

Part of Rac' did know. It was true that Hana has always been there for him and would give her life to protect him. She loved him; she just had a funny way of showing it, that's all. Just a funny way of showing it.

"I will always be with you. These people," circling her finger in the air, "will not. It's just me and you. Never forget that." She pulled her hand back and rested it on her lap.

"What about Mama?"

"She's always around us." Taking another sip of tea.

"And *Him*?" Rac' picked his head up slightly to meet Hana's eyes. His said he was scared.

"Fuck..*Him*." the embers came back as a full blaze, "We removed him from our lives, therefore we do not speak of him, little brother." She gulped the last of her tea and then her water and started going for her wallet.

"You act like *Him* more and more, though. I thought you said you'd be better." Rac' did not back down in the shadow of her fire. She went for her wallet and spoke softly.

49

"Are you finished your food?" She pointed at his plate. Basically empty, but one never knew with Rac'.

"Yeah, are we leaving?" He was expecting a response, just not this one.

"No, we're ordering seconds." She laughed while getting up. Rac' looked around the diner. There was something about that laugh. "After you, little brother." Holding her arm out directing him towards the front. "I'll meet you out there." As they separated, she kept forward. She saw Penny at the register like Sandra said. *No way to miss her,* she thought to herself. 5' 4", almost everyone was tall to her; everyone except Rac'. Sure, he was two or three inches taller physically, but they both knew who the bigger sibling was.

As she approached Penny, she was greeted with a frown and a sign that roughly meant, "Mean lady" accompanied with the sign for scril and their bill total. Hana went into her pocket and took out a fold of bills as Penny tapped numbers into the register.

"Please, keep the change," Hana said while sliding the scril along the countertop, *"and could you tell your boss I'm sorry about my outburst. Give her this for me."* Sliding another bill over then turning towards the door. *"Have a nice day."*

By the time Hana Tabine was exiting Ruby's, the color in Penny's face was drained and she was starting to cry in her chair. Later, when her shift was over, she would tell Sandra that it wasn't what the mean lady had said that upset her; it was that she said it without moving her mouth, and that she heard everything.

Hana could see Rac' across the lot leaning against their car. He had shades on and was looking out in the direction of Pike's Creek, specifically in the direction of where

Isiah Shockley was eventually found.

"Hey?" Hana resumed the earlier softer tone.

"Yeah, what-- "

SMACK! SMACK!

Rac' was almost to one knee before he realized Hana swung on him. Soon after, he was lifted back to his feet, even briefly leaving the ground, before being pinned against the driver's side passenger door hard. Hana's face moved so close to his ear; he could feel her breath as she spoke.

"If you ever, and I mean *ever,* compare me to *Him* again, I will bleed you fucking dry. I swear I wi-" Rac' felt heat pool in his face and lower abdomen. Adjusting so she can feel it against her thigh, she spoke in that tone that always makes him feel sick afterward.

"You like it when I hit on you, don't you?"

His breathing was heavy, but he met her eyes. Fire was starting.

"It looks like you do."

"Let me go. I'm not little anymore."

Giving him another hard slap with her right. "You like making me hit you, don't you?"

With that final tap, his defense broke. Two thin red streaks made their way down his right cheek. Cooling a reddening hand shaped heat as they passed over. When she saw the tears come down, Hana eased her hold and stepped back. The fire that was there tampered down but not quite gone. She then caressed his face and kissed his cheek.

"Get in the car." Opening the driver's door, she hunched down before getting in.

"Can I still drive?" It was the least he could do after making her hit him again.

She scanned him up and down, lingering a little before speaking. "I was going to let you, but I changed my mind. Now get in."

Wiping his face, Rac' silently agreed and walked around the trunk to the front passenger. He got in and buckled up without a word. Hana did the same and put her hand on his lap.

"Look at me." Her voice stern and clear.

Penny can now see him looking at her and they caught eyes. Almost like he was staring at her. *What does he want? Did he leave something?* She tried to remember if she'd seen them before. She couldn't.

"I said look at me. Now." Now facing him, the fire was reignited.

He turned to her, bracing himself for another hit. Instead, he was hit with something different. Words. Five simple words.

"I love you, little brother. You know that right?"

He shifted anxiously as he saw the fire.

Say something, before she hits you again. "I know big sister. I love you too."

"Good." The fire died out completely and she kissed him again on the cheek before smiling to herself and starting the car.

Hana turned on the radio and put something in Rac's lap. It was his sunshades. He put them back on as Hana shifted to drive and started out the lot of Ruby's and onto the road back to Monarch via Fountain City. Penny Adlouw watched the parking lot scene in a confused silence. She felt as though she intruded on a couple's private moment in a public restroom. Not intentional but still embarrassing for all parties, nonetheless. She kept thinking about his eyes she saw as she watched the car drive off. Convinced that Hana was fully cooled from her episode and he was safe again, Rac' leaned his chair back as a talk radio segment came from commercial break. He was asleep within minutes.

◆ ◆ ◆

swish

"That, Mr. Stockon, I believe is game." Elena stayed at the 3-point arch to catch her breath as Flip went to retrieve the ball. "You wouldn't have been tryna to see something with that hand check, would you? Very unsportsmanlike." She added with a quick tongue stick. By now, Elena's gotten a very loose understanding of It. At least enough to know to only tease that he would purposely use It to win a simple ballgame. The way he played, every bit of her said he did straight up. She just did something he didn't expect, and it paid off; nothing more, nothing less. Their game tally has returned to its equal balance.

The only slightly smaller crowd still watching at this point were inconsolable. An almost even 50/50 split of people were either celebrating or contesting the results.

"*YAAAY! Ms. Elena won!*" From the lot of younger children who were rooting for their Director to come out on top this time.

Some teenagers, mostly boys, were not as excited.

"Ah, come on Coach! What happened? You had it tied up!"

"C'mon man, how you gonna let a girl beat you?"

Flip immediately turned around and shot the group a look as if they just cursed at him.

"Yo, yo! Drop that shit and put some respect on you talkin' about." He shot back. "She's still your Founder."

"Easy, he's just playing around." Elena walked over and spoke softly to him. "It's fine."

The look on his face said otherwise. For a brief second, the crowd went silent. Some of the younger ones' eyes got a little wide at hearing Mr. Flip yell. Some people quietly giggled at hearing him swear. It then dawned on the boy what his next move should be.

"S-sorry Coach, my bad." A quick eye dash towards Ms. Starks let him know he wasn't finished. "My bad, Ms. Starks. I ain't mean it like that. You be ballin'." He now had a flushed look of embarrassment.

"It's ok Jesse, I know what you meant." She gave him a smile of all forgiven and subtly nudged Flip.

"Just watch it with that kind of talk, aight? One of these girls out here might end up beatin' you one day." Giving him a nod. Coach Flip was cool, even if he was a little touchy about Ms. Elena. They should just get it over with and wed already.

"Nah, you right, Coach. My fault."

"Good man." Flip walked over to his bag and started rummaging around. He pulled out a set of keys and dangled them in front of him.

"I believe those are mine for today." Elena playfully snatched them away and gave him a sweaty hug, "Thank you. Joy better play nice this time." winking before separating. Elena liked driving Joy when she could but noticed it would conveniently start to act funny whenever she took over the wheel.

"Nah, you better," Flip threw a playful jab, "I love that

car."

Now it was Elena's turn to flash some jealousy of her own. "Any-way, what are we wearing to the party tonight? I'm thinking I'd wear..." Flip didn't really hear much after that. Something told him he was being watched. He could almost feel the eyes on them. He looked side to side quickly. Elena didn't know why but she did see the look-around. She stopped talking and looked around as well.

"Did you hear what I said?" She thought she knew the answer already but wanted to hear the reason why.

"Yeah, most of it." He looked uneasy.

"Everything ok? What's wrong?" She walked over to her bag and picked it up. "Flip?"

"Yeah, yeah everything's ok. Felt something, that's all. Ready to go?" He was already walking towards the court door. She followed behind.

"Yep. Let's roll." He couldn't see it, but her face was a little skeptical about his answer.

"After you." He opened the play area gate and extended his hand. She walked in front of him and led the way to the car. As they walked, Flip noticed a black car turning the corner in the parking lot before pulling into a space a few rows from the Employee row. He thought back about when he was leaving Pike's Creek and he saw a car like it down the road. After a few seconds he shrugged it off when the driver didn't exit and continued on. The distance was too far to see details back at Pike's. He instinctively walked over to the driver's side and was met with a palm to the chest.

"Uh-uh, you may forget easy, Flip Stokton, but I don't. Other side, please. Thank you." Gratified look on her face as Elena opened to get in. Flip took a delay to look around the parking lot, specifically at the dark car, and got in. He got his mobile out for a time check and then turned to Elena.

"Olga?" He watched her play with Joy. She was on her second attempt.

"C'mon, c'mon. All these stupid buttons." She said to herself. She expected this to happen. Third time was a charm and Joy woke up. "There we go. Yeah Flip?" She turned to him.

"Good game." Flashing her the Stokton Smile.

She couldn't help but blush a little. "I know." Sticking her tongue out at him before leaning over for a quick kiss. Flip cut his eyes so hard they were practically closed. "Now can you ease up and let me drive? I just got her going." She said before leaning back and turning the radio on, cycling stations until she landed on The Fount City Messenger, Fountain City's number one station for talk radio.

Talk radio? Geez.

She was definitely going to milk this win.

CHAPTER 6

"What's the word?" P'rotector Wallace was sitting at across from Monroe in his office. "He point anything out?"

"Yeah, he said a little bit. Said you might be right that Shockley didn't float down the river. Thinks he may have been put there from somewhere else."

Wallace took a too quick gulp of his drink before coughing out his next sentence. "No shit," *cough* "forreal? He saw somethin'? Or he guessed off the strength?" *cough cough*

"I think he saw something, but he didn't say. He did make the point that two people were up there at within the past few days. Possibly the owners of the matching prints." Monroe leaned back in his chair and sighed. Wallace sat there looking at him and took another sip. He knew the bare minimum about Flip and It, just enough to be fine that the PD is usually on the business end of when it works out. He'd been meaning to ask him about It and Birdie Stokton, he just wasn't sure if he was ready to visit that chapter again.

"Aight, CaP'ro, so what now? Is he on the case?"

"As of now, no, but only because he didn't say yes. He said to keep him updated though. I'll give a day or two. If I think we really need him, I'll try to convince him to help. Anything from autopsy yet?"

"Nothing in full. From the outset they think it's a typical beat and dump. They're running a tox on him though to cover bases. Whoever it was worked him over something good. Dude was black and blue all over." He took another sip and sighed himself.

"Yeah, I remember." He looked at his watch, *2:10PM,*

then back at Wallace. His face told him there was something else.

"You look like you're still holding something."

"I don't know, man, just thinking about something one of the Mages said when they got him out the water." He was looking Monroe in the eyes now.

"Well, what was it? I don't do the suspense films."

"I don't know, maybe it was just some Medi-Mage humor, but sir, they said he was really light when lifting him onto the board. I thought it was a weird thing to say. I'm sure they've had floaters before." He shook his head, trying to get it out of his head. "Like I said, maybe it was a joke I was just outta the loop on. Forget I mentioned it." He finished his drink and let out a belch. Monroe's eyes cut immediately.

"That's just coffee in there, right, Jo'hn?"

"I'll only answer to K'd on that one, sir, all due respect." Wallace met Monroe's gaze. He looked clear.

"Either switch your brand or throw the cup out outside. Don't need the Auditors in here over some bullshit." Monroe sat straight-backed in his chair. If this wasn't his lead P'rotector, he would have lit him up. He knew Wallace didn't drink in the field, anymore. Luckily, he's noticed these office indulgences normally occurred on Fridays. Nothing obscene, just something to jumpstart himself into the weekend he figured.

"Yes sir. I'm gonna go down Ming's for some lunch, want anything?" He got up, taking his now empty cup as he rose.

"No, but thanks for the offer. I had a big breakfast." Monroe was already looking over some files. "You coming back after?"

"Not sure yet, might do a foot around the neighborhood. See how the kids are using their Friday off, y'know?" He picked his jacket off the back of the chair and turned towards the office door.

"That reminds me, Flip did say something else." Still looking at the papers.

"Yeah?" One foot out, one foot in.

"He said we may want to ask around if anyone saw people hanging around the Creek the past few days if you haven't already. I would specify at night. Let Holmb know."

"Yes sir." And he was out.

Monroe simply shook his head as he read over his desk.

Elena made a left at the first light and went down a few blocks. Flip sat up his chair and looked around.

"Where we going?" His voice had a hint of concern.

"Don't come by for a few weeks and already forget where I live? You sure you ok?" She looked at him for a second before back to the road. She was joking, but not really.

"Yeah, I'm good." He leaned his chair back to its former position and looked up. He almost forgotten the ceiling décor; nighttime starry sky with some of the more famous constellations in prominence. *Did I get that or was it standard?* He sure did love this car. That's when it hit him. "Wait, why're we going to your place?"

Elena almost couldn't believe the question but could tell it was innocent. She turned into Ms. Starks for her response, "Last I checked, we don't live together. Plus, I don't have appropriate clothes for a party, so I need to get some options together." She made a right and could see her car and driveway. "*And* I'm hungry, and *we* need to shower."

"*We?*"

"Yes, *we.* You thought my only prize today was Joy and some party with strangers?"

He shook his head and scoffed. "Ok, Ms. Starks."

As they were pulling into the driveway, Flip raised the seat and grabbed his bag. Sitting up, he felt the papers, still in the inside pocket. He waited until Elena got out before putting them in the center console. She was already walking to her front steps by the time he got out.

"Excuse the mess when you come in." She said while unlocking the door.

"Aight."

Flip looked around expecting clothes or unread postage piling behind the door but found neither. The place looked as though it was set for an open house. This was considered a mediocre rush-clean to the Starks' standards of cleanliness. Elena was raised in the Fifth District social ecosystem, and through her parents, the concept of always having a clean appearance was ingrained into her. So much so, that it seeped over into how she carried herself as a ball player. Envy bearing pre-game outfits, clean yet aggressive efficiency on the floor. She put her own style to the execution, but the philosophy was there. He loved it, even though it came off a little close to the textbooks compared to how he liked to move.

Looking back at the driveway, he noticed the car next to his looked different than he remembered. It was a Suban M3. Midnight Blue. Latest model by a year or two. He couldn't tell if this in fact was a new car or a new paint job.

"Yes, it's new. Courtesy of Uncle Starks." Still facing the door and now opening it. "I told him not to, but you know how he can be."

Oh, he knew. Shortly after her mother passed, Elena noticed her father taking more interest in her personal life, especially of her growing basketball "hobby". He wondered, how long she had been doing it? (Almost 3 years now). Did she like it? (She did). He recalled how her mother would read the stat line from the previous night's game over breakfast before work. He loved when she did that. Her voice made the numbers sound like music, especially when she got to Elena. Only when they sounded normal could he tell she must've been having an off night. He wondered, did Elena intended on playing the following year with Flip on the city's rec team? (She did). He's been content with the decision ever since and made sure to support her as much as he could, in any way he could.

"He chose a nice color."

When they entered, Elena went over to the alarm system as Flip closed the door. Aside from a few changed furniture placements, everything looked like the maid service just left.

"I thought you said it was a mess? I'm sure this place looks cleaner than when I was last here." Elena was already headed to the kitchen.

"You're just being polite. I think you left something on the table." He could hear drawers opening and closing but went to the living room. When he sat on the couch and turned on the TV, he found it. Nicely rolled, still unlit.

"Got a light?"

No response.

"Olga? You there?"

Nothing.

"Hey?"

"Right here."

He started to get up and turn when he was yet again silenced by surprise. In front of him stood *the* Matriarch Elena June Starks, heir of the Starks throne and fortune in her toned glory. Her hair out of its usual ponytail now draping her back and shoulders. In her hands were a book of matches.

"I'm going to run a shower. Join me, please?"

Aggressive, he thought. Just like her play. Still hunched over the back of the couch, he could feel blood start to rush as he watched her climb the stairs. "Flip?"

Goddamn. "Yes, ma'am."

Taking his uniform off, he followed. Making sure to stay a couple steps behind the whole time up.

"Flip? What time is this party?" Elena was almost fully absorbed into her closet as she occasionally tossed clothes out.

He was lying in bed, coasting a mellow high and watching the Ritual of the 5 Outfits commence. Next to cleanliness, Elena lived by her own fashion philosophy; one should never have not enough options in clothes. Especially in social settings. *It has begun.*

"I already told you, I'm not sure. Figure we'd head back over after this. I still gotta change, too."

She turned around; face twisted into a mischievous look.

"Ooooh, whatcha wearing? I'm thinking this black one right here, but I also want to have some color." She was holding up the corresponding articles. In her left, a black calf length dress with a slit up the legs. The other, a blazer and skirt combo consisting of intricate patterns colored with bold yellows and pinks.

"If you go with the right, I'll just tell 'em you're auditioning for a reboot of *Torina Vice*." He smiled, already on the brink of eruptive laughter.

"Hilarious." She tossed the blazer at him and pounced onto the bed. "I don't wanna look stupid." She crawled into him for a face-to-face cuddle. "I just want to make a good impression, that's all." She gave him a kiss and turned her back to him, maintaining the cuddle.

"Olga, it's gonna be fine. I don't even know who else is gonna be there."

"Exactly, I don't know who this lady knows." She started rubbing her lower self against his. The softness of her skin was starting to wake him up.

"You remember your name, right?"

She was silent but kept wiggling.

He could hear the TV on the first floor. *Did I leave it that loud?* He shrugged it off.

"So, what're you really tryna wear? I'm sure this will be a casual thing, y'know? It's just her friends and some of the residents."

Elena turned around to face him.

"Yeah, but she's old, isn't she? What if she's still into the whole "suit and tie, evening dress to dinner" look? A girl's gotta be prepared." At that, she sat up and returned to the foot of the bed. Next thing Flip knew, she disappeared into the closet, reemerging with a few more items on hangers. "For real though, muted or colorful?"

"Let's go colorful. Hit 'em by surprise so they'll always remember you."

"I do have something I've been wanting to wear for a little bit now. Check this out."

Flip did check it out. As he did another dress, a multi-piece ensemble, and the Ritual eventually ended.

By the time they pulled into the Cloud Mesa parking garage, it was just after 5pm. Showered and refreshed, Flip had more time for the hard part, finding something to wear. Elena's practice must have rubbed off on him because he found himself occasionally throwing out multiple outfits as well when planning for social engagements. Laying them on his bed, Elena eyed him and his choices.

"You're not serious about *that* one, are you?" She was pointing to an early choice of button down with an abstract black and white design with matching pants. Not "Founder's Summoning" formal, but possibly a little too much for a casual night out. He looked at it then to her.

"Maybe. I really like that shirt. I think you bought it for me."

"I know, Love, but that doesn't mean it's for everything. At least wear the jacket that came with it." The jacket in question was of the same black and white design but the white outlines were replaced with a raised fabric in black. The creator, a conjuror from the mountainous Nidun Territory, said the viewer would be led into an illusion that makes the garments' wearer appear as though entering and exiting the void, especially when every piece is worn together. Elena had it shipped in for Flip around the time she was named Director; when she thought his UBL appeal would be approved for lack of evidence. This would be his first time wearing it.

"Yes ma'am." He had to admit, it was a good combo.

She was wearing one the more colorful options that made it out of the Ritual. Close cut pastel purple pantsuit with a jet-black blouse under the jacket. Matching pastel 3-inch heels on the feet with a thin gold anklet on the right side. Short-length gold choker; "OLGA" written in cursive and outlined with circular cut greenstone just above the collarbone. "What time are we heading up?"

"I was thinking 6. *That* too early?" Something happened to his voice then he coughed.

The look on her face immediately turned into one only best-friends recognize.

"Are you nervous?! Please tell me I didn't just hear that!"

Now it was his turn to feel self-conscious. It was always a weird hitch in his voice when he prepped for things like these. She never understood it; people liked him, and he liked people. If it were up to him, he'd probably trying to actively find a reason to not go. *Remember to ask about Pike's Creek.*

"I think that's a good time. You said these parties tend to go late, right?"

"I said that's what *they* say."

"I think 6 is a good time, leaves enough to stay a while but leave early if you need to. Or want to?"

"I like the way you think, Ms. Starks."

They got off on the 13th floor at 6:05. Flip looked down the hall, towards the ROOFTOP ACCESS door that opens to the stairway, then back to the door of Ms. Blaskow-Hermann's unit. There was a sign taped:

If you're reading this, we're already on the roof. - Missy

Of course, they were already on the roof. For a quick second, Flip thought he'd be able to finally see what the top-level double-decker unit looked like. He didn't plan on moving any time soon, but it doesn't hurt to see a potential option. He then wordlessly walked back to the elevator and hit the UP button. Elena was already taking her shoes off when she tapped his shoulder.

"Why don't we just take the stairs?"

"That's at least 4 flights. Her unit is technically two floors."

She was already walking down the hall.

"My shoes are already off, let's go."

He shook his head and followed behind her.

CP Monroe sat at his desk sipping the remains of his fifth and last coffee of the day. He was wrapping up a few notes before calling it a night and hopefully make it on-time for his monthly date night with Oleane. The kids were each hanging out with friends and would be gone the entire weekend. With Spring Break starting today, he wouldn't mind if they were gone the entire time. He had to miss their date last month because of work and he'd be damned if it happened again with such perfect circumstances like these.

It was while he was thinking about all of this, he received a call at his desk. He was going to let the machine get it until he saw the caller ID.

"Monroe speaking."

"Dante? It's Rizzo. Bad time?"

"Actually, I was on the way out. What is it?"

"Something interesting with that Shockley guy y'all brought it today. Your guys figured it was something drug related, yeah?"

Monroe glanced at the clock and started to get agitated.

"Spit it out, what is it?"

Small pause.

"Well, we found something on him that may go against that. Two things, actually."

"Can you quit the 'riddle-me-this' bullshit and just come on with it."

"Aight, aight man, be easy. We found two small holes on the side of his neck, identical in size and barely noticeable at first. It was only after we cleaned him off that we even noticed it. Initially we assumed he got stuck with a needle twice. Then something told me to go back."

Monroe stayed silent for a second.

"Dante?"

"Yeah, yeah, I'm here. Go on." The edge in his voice dulled out of curiosity.

"Yeah, man, so I came back down here after Diana left and something told me to look at those marks again. I don't think they were done by needles. Too evenly spaced. Ain't no junkie got that kinda handle." His voice was beginning to waver.

"What're you tryna tell me?" Monroe was about leaning on his desk at this point.

"Dante, I... I think these were teeth man. Fucking teeth."

Lee Rizzo was known for two things around the precinct: talking in riddles and elaborate jokes, in and outside the office. Monroe could tell by his voice that neither was at play here.

He was hoping his gut was wrong and asked, "Teeth? C'mon man I know it's Friday, but that one's pretty weak. Stop fucking around."

"Look, I'm not saying that's my final call right now, but I can tell you that this isn't a joke. I did the measurement of the space between them and I'm telling you, give or take a millimeter, these things match the distance of human canines." Rizzo was starting to get a little agitated himself. If it's one thing he doesn't joke around with is his work and his ability to do so effectively.

"You know I wouldn't be calling you like this if I didn't think it was worth mentioning. The tox screen won't be back until after the weekend, but I don't know how much drugs will have to do with his cause of death."

Monroe was leaning back in chair. He started thinking about something Wallace had mentioned earlier today about a joke the Medi-Mages had made; something about him being drained? He had jotted it down on his notebook.

"I hear you brother, and I appreciate the call. I'll keep it in mind and let Wallace know. Thank you."

Rizzo relaxed and spoke easier. "Aight man, I'll let you

know when the screen is in."

"Sounds good."

"Aight, man, I'll call you on-"

"Riz, hold on. Outta curiosity, did Shockley feel light to you when you examined him? Did he seem noticeably underweight?"

"I made a note of it, but you saw he wasn't that big to begin with. He wasn't a big guy, but it's interesting how he hadn't gained much water weight yet, ain't it?"

"Yeah, a little. Any indication on how long he was swimming?"

"Nothing exact yet, but my timeline is no more than 30-32 hours."

Click.

"Teeth?" That was the only thing he could say to himself as he gathered his things and headed out. As he was walking to the elevator for the garage, he tried two unsuccessful calls to both Flip and Wallace.

CHAPTER 7

Flip felt a call come in as he was climbing the last flight of stairs to the roof but let it ring through when he saw it was Monroe. When he got to the top landing, Elena was putting her shoes back on and straightening her still buttoned jacket. Audibly breathing while she did it.

"No regrets on taking the stairs, right Ms. Starks?" He was breathing a little when he met her. Goddamn stairs. She noticed him putting his phone back into his jacket.

"None at all. Who was that on the phone?"

"Just CaP, don't worry. Probably just wants to drop me more about earlier." He felt the short vibration indicating a voice message. "I ain't calling him back."

"You better not, Flip Stokton. I didn't get all dressed up just to turn around. You promise not to call him until at least after we leave?" She stuck her pinky out towards him.

"Yes, I promise." His voice was joking sarcasm but him meeting her pinky was not. He sealed the agreement with a kiss as Rubina no. 5 wafted into his nose.

"Good." She gave a slight smile and breathed out.

"So, Mr. Stokton, ready to show these old people how to have a good time?" Her eyes gave a cool, slick look; her game-day look.

"I think I am, let's go." He brought her close into a quick two-man huddle.

"Aaannd, break."

As soon as they opened the door, they learned that a 6ish arrival was perfectly timed.

"By K'd's Grace, you made it just in time! We were

just about to get the music going. I see you've brought your girlfriend, Mr. Stokton." Their host exclaimed before facing Elena. "Hello, I'm Missy Blaskow-Hermann. So nice to finally meet." She then went for an eager hug to both, almost spilling her drink in the process.

Elena squeezed Flip's hand twice. They both realized that Missy was comfortably under the spell of a few drinks already. They returned the respective embraces and looked at each other briefly. Flip noted a second minor detail, relatively speaking.

Girlfriend?

Elena heard it loud and clear, maybe even louder than Flip. She made the mental note to talk about *that* later, too. After her hug, she introduced herself.

"Hi Missy, my name is Elena Starks. Flip told me abou-"

"Wait a minute," so excited she almost missed her mouth on a sip, "Elena Starks, as in *the* Elena Starks? House Matriarch Elena Starks?" Her smile was big enough to swallow her face.

"Um, last I checked, yes ma'am. Very pleased to meet you."

Now it was Flip's turn to squeeze. He slipped his hand behind her and gave her left buttock two good ones. *Told ya.*

"Well, this must be a special night! I have not one but *two* Founding Families members at my humble little party. As I live and breathe." She took a healthy sip. "Ms. Starks, can I speak freely?"

"Please call me Elena, and yes you may."

"I must say, you sure are tall. You were a baskets player too, if I recall correctly?"

71

Elena laughed. Old people called the game Baskets. It's been a while since hearing that one.

"Yes ma'am, I was. Flip I were both in the UBL."

"I see. This really is a special night. There's plenty of food and drink, and more if needed. It's mostly residents here now but soon some of my friends will be coming by. I'll see you two later." She waved and started back to the group getting the speakers set up. Before completely leaving, she turned back around and walked up to Flip. "Mr. Stokton, I would like to apologize for my remark earlier today on the lift." She now looked like she might start crying. "I didn't find anything funny about what happened to you or your mother's careers and I dare not denigrate the work she did for this Territory, Founding Family or not. I'm not originally from Fountain, but the work she did as an Inspector was by far some of the greatest work I had seen. I just wanted you to know that I didn't mean to come off as malicious, simply misplaced jest."

Flip looked at her for a second. He'd almost forgotten her comment as soon as it left her mouth. He could tell by her face that this was to be a serious moment.

"It's forgiven, Missy."

Her body reacted as if an over encumbrance was lifted.

"I was hoping you'd say that. You don't strike me as the grudge holding type. I don't go out much anymore, so sometimes I say things better left in the head."

"I get it, don't worry." He could feel Elena looking at him at this point.

"By the way, you can just call me Flip. We're neighbors, right?" He gave her a reassuring smile.

"Yes, yes, we are Mr. Stock—I mean Flip. Yes, we are."

She then walked over to the speaker crew.

"Gonna tell me what that was about?" He knew that was coming.

"Later?"

"You better." She stuck her tongue.

"Whatever, let me introduce you to some of the residents." He took her by the hand, which she transitioned into her arm wrapped onto his.

"Since I'm your *girlfriend* tonight, guess I should look the part?" She whispered as they got closer.

When they got over to the small group, Flip introduced Elena to everyone. Turns out she had more fans than she thought due to a couple of them being heavy into following both the UBL Men's and Women's Divisions. Missy explained that although she used to have the Rogues' games on at past parties, she herself was never much of a sports fan.

"That was more of my husband's thing. He was really into it, I myself never really understood how someone could get paid so much for a child's recreational game. Nevertheless, it's one of the nicer habits he left me with that I still engage in."

Flip noticed her face turned for a second into the same as it was on the elevator when she referenced his unit. *Did something happen to him in my unit? Something to her?* He started to think to himself. The file on his unit didn't mention anything worse than a repaired kitchen leak and subsequent 10 years prior to his residency. He looked at the others; nobody seemed to notice Missy's face or tone. Convinced that tonight will end up going well, he went over to a far table and made Elena and himself a drink. As he walked away, he heard a female resident, probably that girl from the fifth floor, give Elena the first of many compliments she would receive on her outfit.

"Ms. Starks, I love the outfit. Very retro, in a *Torina Vice* kind of way. And that necklace too, just beautiful!"

Told ya.

Walking back over to the group, he could now hear music playing all around him. He rarely comes up to the roof, and when he does it's to barely utilize everything that it offers. Ankle-deep "Restoration Pool" on one side, built-in grills along a far wall. This place can actually look good when someone wants it to. He saw Elena, in typical fashion, already getting people she's just met to laugh with her as if they've been lifelong friends. She's always been the naturally charismatic one, his pro years taught him how to grow into his brand. He handed her a drink and sat across on an open couch seat. He could tell she was into a story, he just had to figure out which one. Likely something from her playing days. Elena, much like himself, was a much different, wilder, girl when she was in the League. Flip knew that all too well. He took a sip and listened on.

After a few hours into the party, Missy went over to stand in the pool and called for everyone's attention. Considering how much he's seen her put away, Flip didn't think her choice of location was the soundest. When everyone quieted down and the music lowered some, she went into a possibly rehearsed speech.

"Hi everyone, I just would like to say I really do appreciate you all coming out to another one of my parties."

"We love you, Missy!" Somebody cheered from crowd,

garnering a few laughs and cheers.

"Thank you, thank you. I love all of you too. But seriously, you guys let me get through this. I would like to say thank you all for coming and an especially big thank you to Flip Stokton and Elena Starks for gracing us with their presence."

An applause started that felt genuine. He liked it and joined Elena in a wave to the group.

"Before you all get nervous, this is by no means a closing of ceremony speech. We can keep going until you all decide to go home. For most of you, that's just a matter of getting down the stairs."

A laughter spread among the crowd.

"I just wanted to say thank you for coming. I don't go out much anymore, so these get-togethers tend to be the most outside interaction I allow myself to experience. For that, I thank you all."

A huge cheer and applause erupted from all of the party's attendees. Missy could be seen taking out a handkerchief and wiping at her eyes. She's made a variant of this speech at every party, and every time her guests reciprocate their appreciation like this. And every time, it brings her to tears.

"Now with all the sappy stuff out of the way, *L'vat!* Please, continue to yourselves tonight."

And they did. Good music. Good food. Flip and Elena cleared their heads of the outside and had a social night out together they haven't shared with each in a long while.

They got back into the condo around 1 in the

morning. Enjoying a full stomach and steady buzz, Flip went up to the bedroom. He came back down a few minutes later with changed clothes: lounge pants and t-shirt, and a tray. He found Elena half-sitting, half-laying, on the couch in the living room.

"You ok?" He came over to sit next to her.

"Yeah, I'm..." small hiccup. "I'm good, just really full. Those dumplings were *sooo* good. Reminded me of my mom." She curled up next to him.

"Yeah, they were good. I heard her family's originally from Brijnn." He was starting his rolling process before grabbing the remote to turn on the TV.

"Watch a movie?"

She looked up to him, Smile of the Buzzed on her face.

"Mind if I stay over again?"

"I thought you were my *girlfriend* for tonight?"

She let out an excited squeak while he surfed through until he got to the film channels. She excitedly got up to go change.

"So, is that the case now? Am I your *girlfriend*?" He could hear her call from the top of the stairs.

"Let's start with tonight and see about tomorrow." Going through his options, he chose a movie he knew she'd like that was still in opening credits. Some cheesy action movie from before they were born.

"Deal." She replied. *Typical Flip.*

When she came back down, she stood there and looked at him for a second.

"What's up? Everything ok?" He was just finishing his scroll, swiping his tongue across the seal.

"Everything is fine. I just wanted to look at you."

She gave him an up and down and took it in. It was always good to see that Flip hasn't let early retirement get the better of him just yet. She went back to her spot on the couch. "Please tell me this is just starting."

"Looks like it."

She curled up to him and let herself dive completely into the film. Occasionally shifting herself to smoke and not get ash on the couch. A few minutes in she looked up to him.

"Flip?"

"Olga?"

"We are gonna talk in the morning, right?"

"Yeah."

He took his hit and passed it to her. They then enjoyed the rest of the movie in a peaceful silence before going upstairs and calling it a night.

"Hana? Hana, are you up?"

She felt the shaking before she heard the voice. Laying on her left side, back faced to him, she had no way to know who was. Thus, it triggered a blind response she had to teach herself a long time ago. When *He* used to be a part of their life. Teeth drawn, she quickly grabbed his arm with her left and twisted down. Rac' went from looking at his sister's back to flat on his stomach in less than a few seconds. Hana was on his back, his neck pulled up to her, teeth sitting on the tender of his neck. Ready. Hungry. When she could see clear, she immediately turned her brother over before smothering him with an assault of hugs and pecks. *He* was no longer here to hurt them anymore.

He can never shake me in my sleep again.

"Rac'! I'm so sorry! I'm sorry!"

She hated herself when she had these reactions. It made her feel sick, ashamed, and vile. How could she still act like this?

It's because of Him.

Everything was because of Him.

"I'm sorry! I'm sorry!

He is why I hit Rac'.

He is why I treat him badly.

I'm so sorry!"

He is why I protect him.

He is why I love him.

My brother will not become Him.

I cannot become Him.

This was not the first time, but it was just as scary every time. Rac' only imagined how much of his sister was still trapped in fog of bad childhood memories. Sometimes, he would be able to overpower her and wake her up in time. She needed him as much as he did her. She would never admit it, but he knew it to be true. They both did. When he could tell it was a reflex than intention, he couldn't find anything to say but an apology himself, lest her repentance turned to anger. It was a response he also had to teach himself a long time ago.

It was dark outside, but a peek of the moon was still visible. The grey between late-night and pre-dawn. Monarch was a Territory that wasn't completely rural but wasn't exactly what the average warm-body would consider a city either. The properties on their side of Outer-Monarch were separated of a main road followed by miles of mostly dense woods. The Tabine property rested on 20 acres that bled into a backyard comprised mostly of dense forest of its own. This isolation provided both a scenic blessing as much as it did a curse. Hana hated this place, but it was one of the few remaining she knew Rac' felt truly safe. For that, she stayed when he came home and stayed. For him. She would do anything for him. And with *Him* gone, she was able to fall sleep knowing she wouldn't be interrupted. Most of the time, anyway.

Rac' and Hana both heard his stomach growl loudly, as if it was a beast starting to wake. She smiled at him before a final kiss on the forehead.

"Hungry, little brother?" She said as she laid forward and rested her head against his sternum, listening to his heartbeat steadily slow down and settle back into normal rhythm.

"A little. Can we get something to eat?"

"I'm not really hungry, but you can go get something." She didn't look at him while she spoke, choosing to listen to the music that he held internally.

"Will you come with me?" He asked her.

"No."

"I want you to." He knew what she was getting at, a dominance thing. It was always a dominance thing for her.

"Magic words?" She looked up to him showing an oil-slick smile. It's always a dominance thing for her, even to him. Especially to him. "C'mon, you know them."

He sighed. He hated this part. No matter, he went against tried-and-true better judgement and got ready.

"We're not little anymore, Hana."

SMACK

Not as hard as he thought it would be.

"I'm not going to ask you again. Now say it and I'll go with you. That's what you want right?" She said as she started licking her canine. "Say it. *Now*."

He looked at her. Not with fear, but with a sibling's defiance. He suddenly felt a powerful hold around his throat. He could feel the uneven, eerily smooth texture of her burned hand. He could also feel something else on his neck. A thin, warm, rolling feeling coming from where Hana's nails were digging into his skin. He tensed himself and started to push himself up.

SMACK! SMACK!

"Stay--" *SMACK!* "down! You stay down while I'm talking to you!" She yelled at him.

"You--"

He is why I hit Rac'.

SMACK!

"stay--"

Why I feel to protect him.

SMACK! SMACK!

"down!"

He is why I love him.

On what was supposed to be a final punctuation slap, Rac' noticed that the next hit across his face was coming from a closed fist. He saw a flash when he closed his eyes and fell back. Still mounted on him was Hana, fist raised, letting it hover before firing again. He put his arms up across his face in defense. Seeing this, Hana lowered her fist. Seeing fire, she eased herself.

"Good. Now get out of my room and clean up. You're still hungry right?"

As if sentient and answering for him, Rac"s stomach made another low grumble.

"I thought so. Now get out." She hissed at him as she dismounted, her own fire beginning to subside.

He slowly got up and climbed out of bed. He felt the sides of his neck and then his face. His jaw felt one-sided and hot. His fingers felt wet with blood, but he wasn't sure whether it from one or both. He made his way back across the room to the door.

"Excuse me?" He heard as he opened the door. "Forget something?" She asked while sitting on the side of the bed facing him. Staring at him.

He knew what "something" was. Hanging his head, he spoke the phrase he felt she enjoyed more than hitting him. "I'm sorry...big sister." He whispered at the bare minimum of audible.

"What? I didn't hear you."

"I said I'm sorry!"

"I know you are. Now get out so I can get changed. Unless you want to watch?" She asked as she got up and began undressing.

Silently, Rac' left and closed the door. Did he just slam the door? No, surely, he didn't. She then walked over to her closet, stopping to open the curtains on a nearby window that overlooks the back end of the grounds. As she rifled through, Hana licked her canines as she felt her breasts with her right hand. As she perused her closet for the right look, she tenderly nursed the sensation. It was a dominance play and she won. Again. It was always a dominance thing for her.

◆ ◆ ◆

Half an hour later, Hana came out and found Rac' already at the car. The engine was running, and he was standing on the driver's side. As she came closer, he started walking to the other side before she stopped him.

"Your feed, you drive." She entered the passenger and started going through her mobile. A few missed texts but nothing of importance. Tossing it into a cup holder she looked over to Rac'.

"So, what're we eating?"

"I thought you said you weren't hungry." He said as he put the car in gear.

"First, you wake me up wrong. Then, you ask for me to come. And *now* you don't want me?"

"I didn't mean it like that."

"I'll decide if I'm hungry or not when we get there."

"Ok, chill out."

Rac' made his way off of the Tabine grounds and turned onto the road that leaves Monarch and eventually feeds into Fountain City, First District. He rolled his window down, allowing the cool air to calm the stinging on the left side of his face.

"Junk food kind of night?" She had a hint of excitement in her tone.

He didn't answer her, instead choosing to keep looking forward out into the open and empty road before him. He liked driving, preferring roads like this. Open. Dark. It gave him a sense of knowing. Knowing he can continue forward with no impediment. It allowed him to not have to think about anything else, even if briefly. In the car, it made him feel in control in a way he only felt after he left for the Great War. When it was clear The Queen was willing to sit while her kind were becoming fodder to satisfy The Culling. As he settled into his thoughts, he unconsciously began picking up speed.

They arrived into First District in time to beat the sun waking up. As they drove up First Avenue, he could see potential snacks straggling along. He shook his head lightly in disgust. Did it really have to be this trash? Normally, he would go after something like this for the sport, not the food. They could have these "people" around the house for snacks if they wanted to. At least they'll be cleaned. He continued his creep, turning onto a side street. In most parts of the First, seeing an unfamiliar car making a slow crawl up the street was nothing suspicious. If anything, it's the signal of potential new business, no matter what that business may be. Still moving forward, he looked across Hana and saw it; illuminated by an overheard canopy as if it was placed specifically for him. Light, young, nice proportions, and seemingly alert enough to show she wasn't currently under anything. He couldn't see her face but something about her looked familiar and brought him to the threshold of childhood memories for some reason. He nudged Hana with his elbow and nodded in the woman's direction.

"She's pretty." Hana said to him as she started to feel his shoulder.

He brushed her hand off and parked along the curb a few feet ahead. After a few seconds, the woman walked over. Hana could see her in the side mirror and rolled her window down as the woman got closer.

"Hey honey, a little late for a date, don'tcha think?" She said as she looked up and down the street.

Hana was already talking before he could get a first syllable out. "Hi. My brother here is a little new to this, but he finds you attractive and wants some of your, time, so to speak." She gave a smile. "What's your name?"

"Um, Alexis." He eyes widened. "Wait, did you say that's your brother?! Uh-uh, I don't do that sibling shit. That's nasty!" She was starting to walk away until Hana grabbed her arm through the window.

"Hi Alexis, I'm Hana and this is Rac'. I understand this may not be a typical meeting, but I can assure that you don't need to worry yourself about any of that. Like I said, he's new to this." She said to her, still brandishing a smile.

Suddenly Alexis felt herself as though floating. It was something about this girl. She ain't look much older, or younger, than herself. Funny little accent; can't be from around here. She must be from Monarch or North Redwater. There's something about her eyes. Inviting. Intense. She regained herself and moved back to the window, allowing for Hana's grasp to loosen and then lift altogether.

"On anything right now?" Hana asked.

"Damn bitch, what're you, a p'rotec?" Alexis casually slid her purse up her arm.

The fire was lit, hungry for kindling.

"I won't ask again. You on anything right now?"

"Uh, no. No, I'm good." She started to feel hot and itchy. She scratched her at her arm.

"You sure? My brother doesn't like no junkie bitch." The fire was breathing now.

"No-- I mean yes. I don't like to use when I'm working."

"Smart girl."

Alexis did another lookover of the car. A little dusty at the bottom but otherwise clean. She could tell it was old, but they kept it sounding and looking good. Not the fanciest car she's found herself in, but nowhere near the worst.

"You sure ain't no weird shit gonna happen?" There was something about this girl's eyes. She took another look at the driver. It was dark but when he faced her, she saw it was there too. Not as bright, but it was there.

"I'm willing to pay double, if that sets you at ease." Hana reached into her bag and revealed a thick stack of scril, held together by a rubber band. "I'm sure this is enough."

Alexis took a second to think it over. Only a second. She nodded in confirmation.

"Good girl. Now get in." Her tone let Alexis know it was an order not suggestion.

Without another word, Alexis got into the back passenger seat. Hana looked over to Rac' and nudged him.

"Yeah, I think so."

"Huh?" Alexis asked from the backseat as she deposited into her purse.

"Nothing, just talking to my brother." She responded while Rac' made a U-turn.

They were about 10 minutes out from the house. As light flooded her side, Hana quickly pulled the visor down and swiped it to her right to block it before turning on the radio. The ride was generally quiet until Alexis spoke up.

"We in Monarch?" She asked.

"Yes, we are. That's not an issue, is it?" Rac' finally decided to talk.

"Uhh yeah, it's fine. Y'all should've said we was coming out this far. How'm I getting back to Fount? Shit, we could've gone to the Night for all this."

The Golden Night. A low-budget motel at the end of First Avenue. Rac' made a look of disgust thinking about it but kept looking forward. "We'll provide transportation back and throw in some more for the inconvenience, cool?" He said as he could see the turnoff into the front yard.

"Yeah, I guess so. Just saying, that's all."

As they pulled into the front, Hana got out and opened the door for Alexis.

"Your brother, he don't talk much, does he?" Alexis whispered as they walked to the door.

"No, he talks plenty once you get to know him. You're his first nightgirl."

Alexis felt as if floating again. What was it with this girl? She looked barely old enough to drink, but she feels so old; spoke too formal. And her eyes? There's something there.

When Hana opened the door, Alexis gasped. She's been in some nice houses, but this one sure sit among the top of the list. Clean, almost immaculate. Antique furniture. Surely, all of this had to cost more than a little bit. Tasteful, albeit weird, art hanging on the walls in the side rooms. Portraits of what she guessed were family members lined the stairway wall going to the second floor. *Who the hell are these people? And how in the hell did they get the money for a place like this? Must be some trust babies.* Lost in thought, she jumped when she heard the door close loudly. She then felt an arm around her waist.

"Uh-uh, I thought I told you I don't do girls? You said it was just him." Pointing at Rac'. Seeing them both standing and in full light, she saw she was the tallest. *Twins?*

"I already said you won't need to. I was going to ask you if you wanted something to eat." She was already guiding Alexis towards the kitchen. Rac' not far behind, began to lick his canines.

"Oh, uh, yes please. Long night, you know." Alexis felt her body begin to relax on its own. Her last bump of Rock was already tapering off.

"I know very well. I used to take care of a few girls years ago."

As they walked over to the kitchen, Hana said she'd be right back and went upstairs. Rac' went over to the refrigerator and started looking. He spoke to Alexis. "You eat eggs?"

"S-sure, eggs are fine. Y'all got sausage or bacon or something? Can't have eggs by itself." The hot and itchy feeling was coming back. She scratched again. *What is this?*

"We do." He went over to the stove and turned it on. Getting a pan out and oiling it, he started for a bowl to work the eggs. "Scrambled fine? I'm not much of a gourmet cook"

"Yeah. Hey, so are we doing anything soon? I appreciate the hospitality and all, but I can't be out here all day for a 20-minute date." Hot and itchy.

"Alexis, I don't know your rate, but this ain't gonna be no 20 minutes." He looked at her in a way that told her he wasn't lying. He looked like it too, now that she was getting a good look at him. Nice build. Quiet. A little short, but no dwarf. What's that phrase they say about things coming in small packages...?

"You sure this your first time? Well, if that's the case, you keep the money coming, and you can have me as much as long as you like. Keep it coming some more, I might have to consider your sister up there. I can break a rule or two if the pay's right." She teased. Anything to break the unease she kept feeling at the pit of her stomach.

"I might take you up on that." He responded as he beat the eggs. "She might too."

Alexis then felt a cold hand on her shoulder.

"I can take over from here, Rac'. You should go freshen up." Hana said.

Alexis looked over to Hana. *Where'd she come from? I know I heard her go upstairs.*

As Rac' and Hana switched places, Alexis thought Hana was dressed like she was the client. House gown? Cute, but definitely something her Nana would be wearing. How old is this girl? Pale, but clear complexion. Perfume? What happened to her hand? Maybe why for the long sleeves. *What the hell is going on?*

Rac' made his way upstairs. Alexis slyly shifted in her seat to confirm this time, then turned back as Hana started cooking. Hana licked her canines.

"Like what you see, Alexis?"

There was a small pause. As she was trying to decide if what she heard was in her head or aloud, Alexis could feel something new; being watched. "Oh, yes. Y'all have a beautiful house. You said it's just you and your brother?" The hot and itchy came back in moving spots all over her body.

"Yeah, just us. It's been in our family for generations. When our parents went on, we just felt we should keep it in the family."

Still feeling as though being watched, Alexis couldn't help but look around a few times. *Where the hell is her brother?*

"Well, that's nice." Hot and itchy! She started scratching again. "So, should I go upstairs to your brother?

Or--"

"Are you ok, Alexis? You seem nervous." Hana began cutting thick slices of sausage.

"Nervous? No, I just haven't been to somewhere like *this* before. I mean, I've had some clients that live in Cloud Mesa, but this is the nicest home I've been to in a while. You guys really went in on the vintage look."

"Interesting. Well, if he likes you, you're welcome to stay if you want. He's a little lonely around here so he would appreciate your womanly touch, you could say. You might even grow to like me, too."

Alexis was immediately snapped back. *I said that as a joke. How the fuck did this bitch hear that? Wasn't she upstairs? She--* It was too late. She felt a rushing pressure closing around her throat and a violent pull backwards. As she felt her seat and purse fall over with her, she started to claw at Rac's arm but couldn't get a hold. She was only an inch or so taller than him, but her legs were now out under her and she was at the complete mercy of a closing vice. His muscularity betrayed just how strong a Rotation's worth of time can truly make someone. As she was choking, Hana came over and met her nose-to-nose. Alexis could only focus on the fire that stared back.

"Alexis, *I need you to calm down before you hurt yourself. I can promise you three things: there will be no breakfast for you. You won't die today, but you will not be seeing Fountain City any time soon.*"

She kissed Alexis' forehead and turned to go back to the stove, perfectly timed with the eggs before they stuck and to get a second pan started for the meat. She looked behind her shoulder. *"I'll cook you something if you're still hungry, little brother."*

Alexis was already drifting in and out of when Rac' reached the base of the stairs. As the dark curtain started to close around her, she could swear some of the paintings along the stairwell wall were moving. Surely, they were turning to look her. One of the last things she clearly remembered was how that weird girl never moved her mouth, but she still heard her. The very last thing was her eyes. Fire. In it, she knew what she heard was the truth. Her body was limp before he reached the top landing.

Hana laid the bloody slices into the pan and inhaled the aroma as it sizzled.

CHAPTER 8

Rac' finally descended the staircase after a couple hours. Aside from the occasional scream, Hana also noted that it was quieter than a normal feeding for Rac'. And much longer. *Maybe she gave up. Smart girl.* Rac' was a different person when he was hungry. It excited her as much as would scare her. A long time ago, Hana began to prefer not being in the room when he had his meal, unless they were sharing. She did say she'd decide if she was hungry when they got to where they were going. She decided she wasn't, at least not then. But seeing the still wet blood on Rac's face and shirt, she began to have pangs. She noticed a change in his gait that wasn't there earlier. What's he been doing with her? He sat across her at the kitchen island as she put away her dishes. Smirking now, a small hiccup left him as he sat.

"So, how was your whore?" She asked him while reaching a nearby dish towel to him.

Alexis, if that was her real name, didn't have that same junkie BO the others usually gave off. It was always repulsive to him of how someone could tolerate smelling like that. No, she was clean. Clean-ish. Her perfume smelled a little stale. He had to punish her for lying to him, so she could learn not to do it again. Time in solo-quarters will do her good. Rac' could feel his head buzzing as he wiped his face. He hiccupped again before he answered Hana.

"Better than--," *hiccup* "Better than I thought." *hiccup*

"What does that mean?" She asked. Hana walked around the island and stood front of Rac'. She was too close. A familiar scent came from her. A scent he loved as a boy.

Mama. He unsuccessfully held in another hiccup. Moving even closer, she wrapped her arms around his neck. He could feel the scent fully envelop him even as he began to pull back. *Mama.* "Do you like her or something?" Hana asked with a sharpness to her tone.

"Hana, stop, we just got her."

"You do like her, don't you?" Hana began slapping his face. Light taps initially but grew more intentional as they continued.

"Stop hitting me." Rac' pushed her back and rose from his seat. Hana followed and continued.

SMACK!

SMACK!

"You like that fucking warm-body, don't you?" She was punching him at this point.

"Quit it!"

THUD!

SMACK!

Rac' reacted before he spoke. The last hit made him taste blood and for a moment, he didn't see his sister. In it, he tasted far memories. *Him,* landing punches, over and over again. Two defense strikes to the chest and face put her down. She kept her face away from him. Long enough for Rac' to see the welt. She held her face, the sleeve falling enough to see the burned branches stretch past her wrist, disappearing at the forearm. He knew the full extent of their reach. He caused it, a long time ago, the result of an emotional short-circuit just like this one; just like *Him.*

When she faced him, Rac' saw fire. It was a dying one, but the embers shone brightly. She held her arms up to him and went to her knees. Streaks of tears flowed down her face and stained her gown with small crimson dots, freshly bloomed roses among the faded garden ingrained into the fabric. He knew she was not crying because of pain. She'd never yield herself from something as simple as that. No, she yielded because she had been tamed. He was her equal right now.

"You hit me." Her voice was quiet. She lowered her head.

"I'm sorry, Hana. I told you to stop."

A surge was running, and he didn't like it. He never liked it. Not towards Hana. It felt like *Him*, yet a part of him welcomed it. The power. It untapped a reserve he's controlled since coming back home. Pleasure and shame. He felt them equally. As he took off his shirt, he began to lick his canine's and crack his knuckles. Hana could see the scar that went from the left of Rac's rib cage to just under his right armpit. A wound that should've killed him had not Hana saved him. He owed her his life. Rac' stepped closer slowly. Cautiously. This could always be another one of her tricks. He settled into the surge. Becoming a part of it. Becoming *Him*.

"Say it." He said to her. It was more plea than an order.

Silence.

THUD!

SMACK!

Hana almost fell over on the second hit. Almost. She could see blood to her left on the floor in an irregularly dotted streak. She spat her contribution; a flare of red that branched out like stray rivers, and steadied herself but kept her head down. Rac' began to feel sick.

He did this to us.

"Hana, just say it."

A whisper.

POP!

SMACK!

Alexis thought she heard a fight in the in the kitchen and hoped someone was kicking that weird girl and her brother's ass and would come save her. It was only a few seconds before she went back under with that hope last in her mind. Unfortunately, help wouldn't be coming for her.

It was the sounds of pleasure and shame, as Rac' experienced them equally.

Flip woke up to the smell of burnt waffle and air freshener. He looked around for his phone before remembering it was still downstairs. Rolling himself out of bed, he got to the top of the stairs and called down.

"You good down there, girl?!"

He heard a couple of spritzes from the air freshener.

"Uhh, yeah, I'm good! Come on and eat something."

Shaking his head, he slowly walked down the steps. Each step made him aware of exactly how much they drank last night. But last night was a good night, and it was a Friday he didn't have to work. Nothing better. As he reached the kitchen, he saw his nose betrayed the relief of a scene he found on the table. Two-person plate setup on opposite sides. A stack of waffles on a center plate. Cups of juice near their own plates. Joint next to the waffles. Very formal for a morning-after breakfast.

Shit.

Elena was taking her apron off, leaving her open-robed with little else on under it. Bra and panties, accented by the "OLGA" necklace. He sat, then got back up towards the living room for the lighter. When he got back to the kitchen table, he was about to light up before:

"Uh-uh, not that easy. We'll see after this if we're sharing." She said to him while shaking her finger. "Two things. One, we're going to talk about last night."

"Alright." It was the only thing he felt appropriate enough to respond.

"Two, you're going to try these damn waffles I made with that stupid press. I didn't waste two for nothing."

"Alright." Waffles were not Elena's specialty. They were usually good, but she could be too heavy-handed with the mix sometimes. May be why she didn't make them often. He replaced the joint and put two waffles on his plate. Before cutting into them he took a swig of juice to wash the taste of stale smoke and booze. He then cut a piece of waffle and began to eat. "Not bad, Olga, not bad at all. Still a little heavy, but it's cooked through this time." As he spoke, memories of previous, less fortunate waffles came to him.

Elena jokingly frowned before giving a genuine smile. She could tell he wasn't just being nice. He could taste something was different with this batch. More vanilla? No, probably a few drops of syrup in the batter. Whatever it was, he hoped she wrote it down for next time. He scarfed down the first and was starting on his second when Elena sat and took her first sip of juice. A few seconds of silence passed while they started breakfast, but only a few. Flip looked up from his plate and saw Elena was already looking at him.

"Ready to talk?" She asked flatly.

Working on his second waffle, he started feeling nervous. These talks always did it for him. Even with Elena.

Especially with Elena. He's gotten himself out of some delicate conversations with common girls but never had to with Elena, not in a long time at least. They gave up on the runaround with each other a long time ago specifically around the same time he was "asked" to retire. She didn't know fully what happened at his last game, only what she saw on the floor. What she did know was that the stories she kept hearing at the time weren't true. They couldn't be. When he finally told her what he saw and the other games leading to it, even the losses, she believed him whole-heartedly. That was the last time Flip ever doubted her loyalty.

"Were you for real last night?" She asked.

Flip swallowed a last bite and got another waffle from the center plate. "About the girlfriend thing?"

Elena stifled a flare of irritation. "Yes, Flip, about the *girlfriend* thing. Were you serious about what you said?"

He sat back from his plate. Suddenly, breakfast wasn't as appetizing, and he wished he had simply turned over in bed when he had the chance. Finishing his juice, he tried to play out how the different ways this morning could go. "Yeah, I was serious. These past two years have been good. Being honest, I like how things are now, but it doesn't cut down that I do love you and I think you know that as one of my closest friends. It may sound a little selfish, but I mean that shit."

She did know. The past two years have been a mix of an enjoyable casual dynamic, little fighting, and even declining a few dates to go out with each other. She knew about a couple of his one-nighters; it wasn't like she didn't have a few of her own to speak on. Flip wasn't the easiest man she's been with, but he was still hers. She relaxed her look and continued eating.

"So, you gonna cut to it, or make me force you?" She finished her juice and poured another glass. "Because I don't want to hear no bullshit. I love you and all, but not knowing where this is headed is getting a little tired."

Flip had a feeling she wasn't done and stayed silent. He took a bite.

"I'm not asking to move in. I ain't even asking to wed right now. I just need to know, Flip, am I *yours*? Or am I yours for now? I don't ride the bench, even for you. I think you know I 'mean that shit'."

Damn. It was the only thing he could say to himself. He knew exactly what she meant on that last question. He didn't expect that. It's true, she did catch him a while back with a commoner, but she played it cool. He saw who she was with; some shirt-and-tie shorty waiting at the nearby table. What she didn't know was that after they came back to Mesa, his date became history. Another fangirl for the eternal stat line.

"Elena Starks," Flip put his utensils down and looked at her. After a few chews and a swallow, he proceeded, "House Matriarch of Founding Family Starks, Princess of Territory Fountain, unless there's a shirt and tie your daddy got waiting for you, would you accept my hand, as Rising Patriarch of Founding Family Stokton?" He felt a hitch in his throat as he went to pick up the joint.

Elena went from relaxed to enthused grinning mischief to choked up. She knew those words too well. It was the formal way a Founder initiated courtship. Minus the shirt-and-tie jab, it was word for word what he said when he asked her out for the very first time. When she could tell he was being for real. When they thought they'd be together, forever, and uninterrupted. It was only days after signing his rookie contract with the Redwater Rogues.

"Flip Stokton…" After a second, she got herself together and went on. "You weren't nervous saying all of that, were you?" She asked before getting up for the sink. He was cute when he was nervous. Cute, and genuine.

He noticed she had her "nice" underwear on. Taking in the sight, he put the joint to his mouth. "For real though, you wanna be official again?" Stokton Smile trained on her.

With formalities taken care of, she turned to him and reached behind her back. Her bra dropped to the floor. "Flip Stokton, Rising Patriarch of Founding Family Stokton, Prince of Territory Fountain, I accept. Now, how 'bout you come over here?"

"Yes, ma'am." Flip put the joint back on the table and got up.

He went over, gave her a deep kiss, and turned her towards the window. Lightly pecking her neck and back until she let out her first moan, he pulled her panties down just enough. All the while he held her, tight yet tender. After, they regained themselves and went back to breakfast, gossiping about last night's party and their takeaways, including a comment Missy made about Elena's necklace and exactly what she had said about HouseMother Stokton. Elena didn't find the remark humorous at all. Fuck a "misplaced jest".

It was almost 11am, but when Flip finally checked his mobile, he was greeted with a screenful of notices. Some social media mentions here, some subscription renewal confirmation emails there, and a few missed calls. He knew about the one from Monroe last night but now there was one from Wallace and second from Monroe. There wasn't a voicemail from Wallace but that didn't mean much. Whatever he needed to say was usually in person or if the intended party picked up the phone, especially if it was important. Must be a holdover from his PI days. Flip decided that whatever Monroe was trying to tell him, he figured Wallace knew as well.

"Wallace, speaking." Flip could tell he either just woke up or he woke him up.

"It's Flip."

"I got caller ID on this thing, brother. What's up?"

"You tell me, man. I saw that you called last night. I was out so it wasn't really the best time to talk."

"You good man, I figured whoever it was, she was a little more important than a phone call with an old dude."

Flip looked back to Elena as she put dishes in the sink. "For real, what's up."

"I don't know man, CP hit me last night about some weird shit the morgue found on Shockley."

Flip almost forgot about his early morning visit with Monroe yesterday. All being fair, he didn't say he'd take the case so there was no genuine concern or interest aside from knocking off another case.

"Yeah, yeah, yeah. What about him?" Flip caught Elena looking over at him.

"Riz said he thinks he found teeth on him."

"Teeth?" He took the phone from his face for a second and looked at it. For some reason, he began thinking about his mom and something she said about a case around the time she was getting pushed out. He shook it off and went back.

"Teeth? You sure? CaP aint say nothing about teeth."

"Sorry about that, I meant teeth *marks*, not actual teeth. We saw these two dots on the body when we got him out. Assumed it was needle jabs or something. Figured he got pumped or something before getting dropped off."

Flip was thoroughly confused. Monroe never mentioned any marks on the body, just that they thought it was a simple drug related situation. "Wallace, this a joke? You talkin' about some vampyr shit or something. Come on man, what's real?" Elena made a look behind her but went back to washing.

Wallace was in fact just getting up. He shifted to a sitting position and looked around his small bedroom. Clean, but really needed an update. He still never got around to putting that new paint color on.

"This is serious, man. That's what Monroe told me. Said Rizzo thinks that it was teeth that made the marks and not needles. Something about the spacing being too neat. What you doing later on?"

Flip took another look back at Elena. "Honestly, I don't know. How much later?" He hoped it wouldn't be soon.

"Like later, later. Meet at the Hole?"

The Watering Hole, their usual office venue for case-talk. Flip remembered about Sandra's friend's party, then his vision. He thought quickly.

"Uh, yeah that can work. What time?"

He heard a yawn from the other end that confirmed he must've woken Wallace up and felt a little bad. *It is Saturday*, he thought.

"I don't know, soft 8, maybe?"

"Yeah, yeah that's cool. See you then."

100

"Aight, man."

Click.

Flip let out a sigh as Elena walked over and cuddled up to him.

"That Wallace? How's he doing?" She asked before kissing his neck lightly.

"He sounded fine, just letting me know something about the guy they found out in Pike's Creek yesterday." He pecked the top of her head lightly.

"This have something to do with what the CaP'rotector needed to meet with you about?"

"Yeah."

"Wanna talk about it?"

"Not really. I'm not even sure I'll help out on it."

"Ok."

Flip turned on the TV and went through the channels. He eventually stopped on the news and saw that the Shockley discovery was the topic of discussion. As it played, he broke down and told her everything, from the crime scene visit to his visions with Carl and Sandra to the car he saw as he was leaving the Creek. Then he told her about his call with Wallace and the teeth, or rather, the teeth marks.

"Sounds like you had an interesting field trip yesterday. You still have the papers in the car?" She asked after being sure he was finished.

"Yeah. K'd forbid someone opens her up just to steal a rap sheet that's not even mine. Hard to blackmail a dead guy, right?" He responded with a smile. Elena didn't find it as funny. Taking the hint, Flip got back to being serious. He wasn't sure what to say so he just kept watching the coverage. He noticed there wasn't any mention of the teeth in the report which led him to believe it had to have been either a real afterhours discovery or a withholding of special details. Weird detail to hold but whatever works, works. He felt Elena get off of him and the couch, heading towards the stairs.

"I'm going to go shower and get dressed." She told him as she made her way upstairs.

"Want some company?"

"Not now. Find me after." She responded with a stick of her tongue.

Close enough.

"Yes ma'am" He settled back into the couch and continued watching the TV. The Shockley story transitioned into the more typical Saturday morning news coverage; weather forecast, traffic notices, the latest popular breakfast smoothie recipe or something close to it. When he was sure Elena cleared the steps and made it into the bedroom, Flip went back to his phone and called Monroe. He had a few questions already lined up.

"Monroe speaking."

"It's Flip. Why didn't you tell me about the neck marks?" He was already getting up there.

"Guess you talked to Wallace already? I'm sorry about that, son. I didn't get the teeth thing from Rizzo until later in the day. I tried calling you." His tone was even.

"Yeah, sorry about that. I was out and couldn't really talk."

"Mmhmm yeah, I figured. Gotta keep that Founder sociability meter active. How is Princess Starks, by the way?"

"She's fine. You know, you can always go over to the

Center and see for yourself, it ain't far."

"My bad, son, no offense to her. Honest intrigue, that's all. Send her my hello."

"Will do."

"Y'all been hanging out a bit recently, you two back together?" Monroe said.

"You could say that."

"Hey, good to know, son. Maybe you two can finally come for dinner with the family again?"

Flip had a short flashback to the last dinner he and Elena had at the Monroe household. It was only a few months after he was finished with the League, and he was in a really bad place. Their relationship wasn't doing much better. That night didn't end well. Flip felt a tremor of remorse at how he acted. The Monroe's were only trying to help. "Maybe, but don't hold your breath."

"I'm not. Look, you called about the teeth and I'm giving it to you straight. Yes, Rizzo found what he thinks are teeth marks on the neck of Isiah Shockley. He said it's not a definite yes, but he sounded willing to put money on it. He almost let it go by him if it wasn't for a second look. We haven't even gotten the tox screen yet so at this point, so there's still a chance he's dead wrong."

Flip knew Monroe was telling the truth, unintentional pun aside. He thought back to his mom again, trying to remember what she had said years ago. Something about teeth? He was sure he knew it involved actual teeth, or was it teeth *marks*?

"Stokton? Stokton, you still there? Flip?"

"Ye-yeah, I'm here. Sorry, just got the thinking about something."

"Mmhmm. Well look, I don't have any more to tell you but did feel you should know about this. Let the tox screen come in and I'll get back to you. You decided on if you're gonna join the case?"

"Not yet. I still got the sheet you gave me though."

There was a silence over the line. Flip could hear the traffic in the background. And people. Was he with his family right now? "Alright, guess that's fair. You still want to know about any updates?"

"Either through you or Wallace. I just saw the morning news coverage, they made y'all look like some dummies. Ain't no real info with it."

"Yeah, well, aside from him having gotten beaten to shit, it's not like we had much to go on. I saw that they didn't report on the teeth thing, so we can still trust our delivery line."

Good point. Even if they did decide on the spot that those markings were from teeth, it's still an interesting detail to leave out. Flip concurred with Monroe and got off the phone.

Since he now had plans to visit The Watering Hole with Wallace, Flip had to prepare for the hard part: convincing Elena to go with him. Elena liked the Hole. She did not, on the other hand, care for Sandra too much. He knew that was going to be the tricky part. If they weren't officially together, chances were in his favor he could yada-yada his way into talking her into hanging out with Sandra while he talked to Wallace. Now that he was, those chances slimmed quickly. Elena was a different girl when in courtship with Flip. Aggressive and possessive. *My* Flip. He liked it about her. Hell, he loved it. He couldn't help it. There was something about how a different aspect of her comes to light when she knows she has something she doesn't have to share. Taking his phone with him, Flip made his way up the stairs and hopefully make his meeting with Elena. When he went into the bedroom, he found her naked lying prone on the bed, towel still under her, on the phone. He couldn't tell who she was talking to but figured it wasn't important. He went into the bathroom to run a

After what felt like forever, Elena eventually spoke. "Sure. I'll go."

After explaining his plans to meet Wallace, Flip had asked Elena if she would go along with him for the cover. He thought it'd be more plausible if he told Sandra they decided last minute to come to the club and didn't get a chance to call her. Wallace is timely if anything, so he should be there within a few minutes of them, if not there already; perfect way to break away from the group. The only tradeoff was that Elena had to stay behind. Her agreement sounded like she *wanted* to be in on the scheme.

Elena listened and heard clearly. As soon as she heard Flip talking about meeting Wallace, she remembered what he told her about his phone call and also his time in Ruby's Diner and his vision. She didn't have a personal problem with Sandra, she liked her enough. What she didn't care for as much were the "joke" exchanges with Flip, and on a few drunken occasions, Elena herself. She was flattered of course, though it did feel like they were a little forward. Never crossing the line, but right on it. Aside from Aron Adlouw, she never cared to know the specifics of what made Flip and Sandra so close. No matter, a commoner like Sandra could never make her insecure enough to think she could be a valid threat to Elena Starks.

She went along with his plan because Sandra was expecting a date, so there was nothing to worry about on that front, and because being asked to help Flip with work always excites her.

"You sure?" He said to her.

"Yeah, I'll go. I haven't been there in a while, and it'll be nice to see Hazel again. I could have my own excuses, Flip. Not like I have to actually stay with *them* the whole time." She stuck her tongue out.

"I get you. Thank you."

"Of course. Now what are we wearing today?" She asked while already opening her dedicated drawer, not impressed with the choices she had. She quickly put on her second choice on before taking everything out and put it on the bed.

"What's wrong? Everything's clean." Flip said to her.

"I know, but I wanna change this out. Freshen it up, y'know?"

"Thought you said you didn't want to move in?"

She gave him a look. "Don't get cute. I just want more than just sweats and shorts in here. Some real clothes, maybe."

Flip wisely kept his thoughts to himself. "Uh-huh." He went over to the closet and finished getting dressed. "So, no after-shower meeting today?" He called back to her.

"Ooh, I'm sorry Mr. Stokton. Ms. Starks was supposed to call and let you know the meeting had to be pushed back to six o'clock. That's not too late, is it?" She responded in her Director's voice.

"No ma'am. Tell her I said six is fine." He gave her a wink.

"I'll pass it along." She returned with one of her own and a tongue stick.

"I love you, Olga."

"I love you too."

Back in the closet, Flip couldn't help but smile as he figured out the day's look.

CHAPTER 9

He didn't have an intended target destination aside Elena's house to drop her off. As they walked across the garage, Flip gave a brief run-down of his call with Monroe. She wasn't enthused. When they got to Joy, Flip tossed in Elena's bag of clothes to the backseat. When he got in, he took a quick look into the center console and saw the packet from yesterday was still there, undisturbed. He closed it and started the car. Looking over to Elena, he asked her:

"Hey, so what're you doing after I take you home?"

She looked at him with a mild confusion. "I thought we were just going to drop off the bag and hang out. Trying to get rid of me already? Got some news you need to break to a few girls I shouldn't be around for?"

He pretended to think before shifting into gear and starting to drive. "Nah. I was thinking about going to see my mom and dad for a little bit."

"Oh."

Elena didn't know the last time Flip's went to visit his mom. She thought she remembered him mentioning it a few months ago but never knew if he went through with it. Outside of visiting them and her own father on occasion, he didn't go back to the Fifth District much after living full-time in the metro-area of the Second. Flip seemed to use the family house more as an extravagant storage unit than the multi-level mansion it was. She had the thought to not push it and ask if she could come along, Flip liked to spend the time alone, but something in his mentioning gave her hope.

"Ms. Ingram was telling me on the phone that y'all had talked about your mom yesterday when you came in.

Said she still talks to her."

"Yeah, to both." He responded flatly.

"Everything ok?"

Fleice Stokton was always a touchy subject to discuss, and Elena could understand why. Ever since getting the boot, Flip doesn't like to talk about her unless it was at a time before, and seeing her situation start right after he went pro and was already on the road, those times tended to be from childhood to late teens. Guess he just likes to remember the better times. Maybe the remark from Missy Blaskow hit harder than she realized.

"Yeah, everything's ok. Did you want to come?"

He made his way out the garage and onto the street, starting his usual route to Elena's. *Still no rain* he thought as he crossed the block and got to the first light.

"Do you want me to come?" *Don't push.*

"The original question was 'Did you want to come?'"

"And I asked you if you want me to come. It's a yes or no, Flip, I won't be upset if you don't." *Easy. Easy.*

There was a brief pause as the stoplight turned green.

"Mind if we stop by your place on the way back, then?"

She smiled at him softly and rolled down her window, allowing in the mid-afternoon air of a typical Fountain Saturday. "That's fine with me."

"Cool."

At the next street, Flip checked his mirrors and made a quick right instead of his usual left. A few turns and dashes later, they were on Founder's Way, the most direct route leading from the Second District into the Fifth, colloquially known to those within it as the Founder's District.

Home, sweet home.

◆ ◆ ◆

Eleven years ago.

"Flip Stokton! Come on down here and get some breakfast!" Fleice Stokton called out from the kitchen. There was no response, but she could hear footsteps rushing down the main steps and into the foyer.

"Flip! Come on--"

"I'm right here, Ma." Flip said to her as he entered, kissing her cheek as he walked by. *"Morning mom, morning Ms. Ata."* He gave a small wave as he spoke.

"Good morning, Mr. Stokton!" She gave a small bow. *"Your mother told me you have big game tonight and could use big breakfast. I make special meal for you."*

When he went over to the table, he indeed saw something special. Laid out was a spread that made Flip question if it was still a school day: eggs, sausage *and* bacon, fruit salad, and in the center was the crown jewel. A stack of waffles, already buttered and syruped, was waiting for him. Flip's mouth watered and his stomach spoke up in agreeance. He felt a soft poke in his side.

"What do you say? I know I taught you proper manners." His mom said in a low voice.

"Thank you, Ms. Ata. Everything looks really good." He didn't realize the pause he left looking over the food.

She laughed and bowed, *"Of course, Mr. Stokton."* She gave him a big smile as she opened his chair, motioning him over to sit down. *"I hope you have good game tonight. Your mom said it was 'Coming Home' game. What's that?"* She asked with a puzzled look.

Flip smiled and shook his head and looked towards his mother. Ms. Ata's been head of the Stokton's household staff for two years now, but being only 20 years Flip's elder, and not originally from the Aligned Territories, there were still some cultural practices that flew over her. He remembered having a similar conversation with her over the summer when they used fireworks to celebrate Fountain Founders Day. Fireworks were considered a signal of mourning where she was from, so she was confused why the party guests were dressed and acting like it was a day of fun and not of meditation over their fallen.

"No, Ms. Ata, I think she meant 'Homecoming' game. Remember last year, we had Elena and her dad over for that big cookout to celebrate?"

"Homecoming, that makes more sense. I do remember, now. It was good cookout."

Already sitting and fixing his plate, Flip looked to her and nodded. *"Yes, it was."*

Fleice went over to her chair at the table and sat down with the day's newspaper. Another person killed in the First District to add to the three currently on her desk at work. Fuck. As Ms. Ata walked away; Fleice watched her with a suspicious look as she felt a headache come on. Earlier in the week, she happened to touch Ata's hand and was transported to a hazy, vocal, view of her and Ronald in a living room rendezvous. She could see the TV playing and hear the passion, swears and all. The flash was only a few seconds, but since then couldn't help but think about it whenever she looked at Ata, or Ronald, for that matter. These scenes have started happening more and more over the past 6 months, mostly while on the job. Some she acted on, some she didn't. Either way they came to pass exactly as she saw them. She shrugged it off and went back to her paper but made a mental note to "look into it". When she took her break from the paper to make herself a plate, Flip took his chance.

"Dad's already gone?"

"Yep. Had to get to the office early today, something about an account going belly-up. He said he'll be able to swing by the game though, he's gonna record it so I can watch it when I get in."

He expected it, but it still stung that she couldn't come watch him in real-time. She's been really supportive and actively helped him to pursue and follow his aspirations in basketball, the only thing missing was her. Flip understood it was part of her job. By now, it doesn't faze him like it used to when he was a little kid. Having a mom that with the coolest job in the world has to have some strings attached, and he was fine if that meant she had to miss a few games to put some scumbag in jail. If he wasn't so into basketball and in a good place to make it pay off, he would've considered going into the force like her. Maybe he can still do it in time to work with her, be a kick-ass p'rotector duo like those buddy movies they liked to watch.

"Aight, that's cool. You know Penny Adlouw? She made up another play for me and Aron to--"

"Aron and I." Fleice corrected him in tempo of the conversation.

"Aron and I, to run. It's basically a fancy pick-and-roll, but we've been trying it out at practice and put some more on it." He finished with a smile of satisfaction.

"That's good baby, I hope to see it on the tape. You know, I like that Adlouw girl. She seem a little slow, but she's a nice girl." She looked at him with her own smile. *"So, how many can I expect to see tonight? 15? 20?"* She said as she bit into a piece of

fruit, still smiling and showing now blueberry-stained teeth.

"I don't know Ma it's Homecoming, so I'm aiming for 25 minimum. If Aron keeps shooting like he's been lately, we might have to fight for the last shot." He said as he got a second waffle.

"I can deal with that, baby." She then finished her coffee and got up, gathering a few scoops of salad into the mug. She walked over and kissed his forehead.

A flash happened in her eyes and two short scenes played out. The first was a behind the back view of a guy yelling from the stands, presumably at the players. He could work on the language, there were children around, for K'd sake. Probably a parent from the opposing team. Cut to the next scene the same man and another guy fighting a girl in a hoodie among a big crowd. She could hear yelling everywhere. She could see Flip on the floor, and he was making his way over to the sidelines. Then nothing, she was back. It quick, Flip never noticed her hovering for a little too long. A small chill went up her back causing her to almost drop her mug.

"Alright Flip, I gotta run. Please get to school on time, will you? I know it's Homecoming and all, but I don't need to get a call at work. Deal?"

He looked back at her as she walked across the kitchen and gave a thumbs-up.

"Deal."

"Good. And Flip?"

"Yes mom?"

She gave him a finger-gun and pulled the trigger.

"Give 'em hell tonight. Don't feed into the crowd, they're just trying to throw you off. I love you, baby."

"You too mom. Lock 'em up."

When she left out, Flip went back to his plate. He didn't think about what his mom said until much later that night, when he saw Penny Adlouw fighting two grown men in the stands.

◆ ◆ ◆

They were approaching the main gate to the Stokton property. As Flip typed the owner's code into the keypad, he nudged Elena to wake her up. She got up with a start.

"Here?" She said as she wiped her mouth proactively.

"Yep."

As they approached, Elena let out an audible "Sheesh." She's been coming here since she was a toddler, but the longer intervals between visiting since her adult years made her look at it each time with new eyes. It was a massive two-story building that could honestly be mistaken for a mega-sanctuary from TV if it wasn't for the large gate and statue in the driveway bearing the Stokton Coat of Arms. She looked up and saw the two elongated windows on either side of the front door the stretched to the height of the second floor.

The exterior of the home still looked clean and taken care of; sheet white and shiny due its metallic accents. Mr. Stokton was too old and much too busy to oversee his own lawn maintenance anymore, but this current look is different from the routine cut and trim him and the HouseStaff would do. No, this was a professional service, and it looked really good. On the far end, she noticed a new pathway leading from the roundabout driveway to a fountain, complete with a few chairs and a small table. *That's probably why the yard looks so good* she thought as Flip slowly rounded and came to a stop off to the right of the stairs leading to the front door.

"Was this here last time you came?" She asked, pointing to the pathway.

"Nah, it's been a few months, but dad did mention he was thinking about doing it. Said mom's been sitting on the edge of the fountain to read the paper." He responded.

"How was she then?"

"Eh, she slept most of the time. She was on some new medicine."

"Oh. You ok?"

"I'm fine. You ain't gotta keep asking me."

"I know, I know. I was just... asking."

Elena could hear the edge clear enough to know she was less than a step away from it. She didn't like asking, but she also didn't know what else to ask. Visiting Flip's family now was a bittersweet occasion for her. It's great to see how he keeps in touch with his parents (though not frequent enough for her taste) and that he took these visits seriously. So seriously, they once were over an hour late for a dinner reservation because Flip didn't feel comfortable enough to leave his mom alone before his father got home from the office. That was early on in her situation, when he was more sensitive to it, and still trying to process how to handle it. Now, he's gotten a better grip on it and knowing what to be concerned about when it came to his mother being alone.

When they got to the front door, Flip was getting out his key just as the door opened. Standing there was all of 5' 9" of Ronald Stokton. Looking up to Flip, he stood briefly before giving a single word greeting. "Flip."

"Dad." Flip began putting his keys into his jacket.

Elena started to wonder if coming along may not have been a smart choice. She began thinking if there was something that happened the last time Flip was here that he failed to mention. She stood silently, as did they all. After a few seconds, both men broke into a hearty laughter and went to hug.

"Goddamn boy, still tall like your mother I see. Hey, El." Ronald said as he went to dap Flip.

"Don't act like you forgot." Flip said as he hugged his father.

"Hey, Uncle Ronald." Elena said with and a wave. *Fucking comedians.*

"How you doing, son?" Ronald said as he stepped aside. He shared a hug with Elena and went over to Flip. "Here for your mom? She's actually up this time."

He went over to the foyer table and picked up his pipe and lighter. As he got it started, the smell and smoke of a sweet tobacco blend drifted around the room. Flip noticed a more familiar scent underneath it. "Yeah, just came to see her before Elena and I go to this thing a little later." Flip said as he lightly waved away smoke and closed the door. "You smoke now?"

Ronald gave him a slick smile, The Stokton Smile, and took another puff. "Nah, you know I was never into that stuff. That's a young man's habit. No offense Elena." Exhale. "But your mom was prescribed this last month from Dr. Bollard to counter the sleepless nights. Prescribed a little extra for me 'just in case'. Shit, he was right. Days like this when she's doing alright, I'll put on some TV or the radio and mix it with the pipe blend." He looked at them both, Smile still going. "Good way to spend a Saturday afternoon, huh?"

Flip looked at him with his own Smile, "Nothing better."

"Y'all want something to drink? Something to eat? I

can have Ata put something on." Ronald asked them.

"I'll get something from the fridge, but we actually ate not that long ago. Waffle breakfast."

Ronald's face went to an enthused curious look. He then shifted his eyes to Elena.

"What's the occasion? Y'all pregnant?" He asked.

It was Elena's turn to share a laugh with Flip. She laughed hard. Flip thought maybe a little too hard before she mimed feeling her stomach. "Very funny, Mr. Stokton. No, we're not pregnant, but we do have some news. We're back together!" She said with an excitement in her voice that made Flip think she came solely to be here when the news broke.

"Shiiit, that's good to know. Another try to make him an honest man I see." Ronald took another puff on his pipe. Flip could tell his dad may have also had himself an afternoon drink. He's only this loose with the vocabulary when either mom was out the house, or he's relaxed.

"Well, Mr. Stokton, that's the thing. Your son asked *me* this time." She said, pointing at Flip with a quick wink.

"That right?" Ronald looked to Flip for confirmation, receiving it with a nod. "Well goddamn, good on y'all. Starks and Stokton, back at it. Boy, I wish the UBL went forward with combining the Divisions. Y'all would've made a helluva duo on the floor."

"If they didn't push me out, we may have been able to." Flip remarked.

"Nah you right, you right. They could've waited until after the post-season at least." He then clapped his hands together. "But hey, you still got your money, your health, and now, this beautiful woman back at your side. Shit, y'all both look like you could go out and still put up 20 apiece." He took another puff and after a few coughs, made his way into the living room.

"*Only* 20, Mr. Stokton? Come on." Elena called out to him.

"You're right. You could go for 30 easy, so long as that ankle stay together. Him, I don't know, maybe a solid 25 with a few assists." He said back to her, giving an over-the-shoulder peace sign. "Your mom's upstairs, Flip, in the drawing room. Elena, it was good seeing you again, and congratulations to y'all."

"You too, Mr. Stokton. And thank you." She said back.

They were making their way up the stairs before they heard Ronald calling Flip from the living room.

"Yeah, dad?"

"Car still looks good, nice to see you're still taking care of her."

"I don't plan on letting her go any time soon, I ain't got a choice."

He heard his father laugh over the TV as he continued up.

Elena heard Flip's response and smiled to herself. She knew he was talking about the car, but for a second, it felt like Flip was talking about her too. She then grabbed Flip's hand and walked with him the rest of the flight up. When they got upstairs, they saw the door to the drawing room was wide open. Looking down the hallway, Flip called out. "Mom? You up here?"

He heard what sounded like a crash and ran down the hall. When he got there, he saw his mom standing above a blank canvas on the floor, staring at it.

"Hey Mom, what'cha looking at?" He asked her cautiously.

As if coming out of a trance, Fleice jumped and shook her head quickly. She looked confused, but when she saw Flip, she knew where she was.

"Flip! Baby, how you doing? Come here." She went over to him for a tight hug and a kiss.

"I'm doing alright. I brought Elena with me." He moved to the side.

"Aw, El, how you doing, girl?" She then went over to her and repeated her physical greeting. "Still tall, I see."

"Yes, ma'am. I'm doing ok, you?" Elena responded.

Fleice twitched her head as if she heard something and looked back at the canvas. After a second, she looked back to Elena and Flip. "I'm doing alright. Good days, bad days. You know?" She said before another head twitch.

"Mom, you doing alright in here? We heard something fall." Flip asked her, looking at the canvas.

"Yeah, yeah, I'm ok, just thought I saw something that's all. Y'all look like you got some news on your heads. Y'all back together?" She smiled and then gasped. "No, y'all pregnant, aint'cha?" She whispered, bringing her face very close to them to keep out eavesdroppers. "Bout time."

Flip glanced at Elena in a way that said to not laugh like she did downstairs. She understood perfectly and settled with a chuckle. Flip hugged his mom again. "No, you were right the first time. We're back together, as of this morning."

"Officially? Or is this another one of your little flings?" Fleice asked.

"Officially. I said the whole preamble and everything." He smiled to her. She returned it.

"Oh, that's such great news! I'm so happy, Flip! So happy." She said to him. Her voice was breaking up and she went over to a dresser to get a tissue. "So happy." She kept repeating the phrase as she dabbed at her eyes.

Flip felt hot all of a sudden. He wanted to get out. He didn't like seeing his mom cry, no matter the reason. He also didn't like the fact that her emotions had its vessel more in their grasp than her of it. One minute she can be yelling at Ata because her bread didn't come out the toaster the way she wanted. The next, Ronald could tell her that said toaster was broken and she'd cry like she lost a close family member unexpectedly. It wasn't her fault. She was still here, but how much? He helped his mom into her chair and got two chairs for him and Elena to sit at the easel. Fleice sat and went back to looking at the canvas still on the floor, the blank endless staring back.

"You want me to get a new?" He said after a few seconds of seeing his mother not move.

Snapping back, she looked at him and said, "No, I think I'm done for the day. I think Ata's been in here doing something. Some of my paint's missing."

Flip shifted his seat and looked over at her supply. It looked stocked up in every color she could need. "Why do you say that? You've seen her taking stuff?"

"No, I thought saw her. I was trying to put it on the easel and just saw her leave with something. Then I look over and see you and Elena." She sounded like she might begin crying again. "I don't know, Flip, I just saw her. Didn't y'all pass her in the hallway?"

"We must've just missed her, but it's ok, I'll get you some more. Don't cry. I'll order the fancy stuff."

Flip glanced at Elena and the sadness in her eyes. Mrs.

Stokton was a nice woman, always has been. When Elena's own mother died, Fleice respectfully stepped in to help keep the Starks household together. She helped Elena with her school projects; drove her to games when her father couldn't. When Elena had her first period during a Junior Territory Scouts camping trip, Fleice made the journey into the woods of the Fifth District to avoid her being sent home early. Now, Elena felt like she was looking at a shadow of that same woman. This was a Founding HouseMother, the only *Vi'nnakan* of three women in the Seven Clans with the title. Hopefully, it was just today, but Fleice looked as she was; troubled. Seeing her reminded Elena of the hospital visits she and her father would make after school, and stay well past dinner hour, to mostly watch Rubina sleep under the spell of IV's and the Mages' meditation cycles.

By the sick humor of Fortune, Elena was still young, and it was all over after 16 months of fighting, making a then 12-year-old Elena Starks one of the youngest House Matriarchs in Fountain's history. She couldn't say the same joke was being played on either Flip or his mother. The Stokton HouseMother had been like this for a little over a decade and wasn't getting noticeably "better". She didn't fully understand Felice's condition, but it seemed like nobody did, even Dr. Bollard in all of their brilliance. She just got the gist from what she could see and what Flip told her.

"She just goes away sometimes, that's all."

"She's been seeing stuff but can hear it, too."

"Sometimes, it's nothing and she's back. She's even normal for a few days."

She then thought about Flip. *Is he going to become just like this? What if we're not together? Does Bloss know about it? Does she care?*

Elena excused herself and made her way downstairs to the kitchen. She felt tears of her own coming on and would not dare allow herself to cry as an adult in front of Mrs. Stokton. When she reached the kitchen, she almost bumped into HouseMaiden Ata and the mug of coffee she was holding.

"Hello, Matriarch Starks. How are you?" Ata said after checking her uniform and giving a bow, keeping her mug in perfect balance.

"Hey Ms. Ata, I'm fine thank you. You?"

"I'm fine, thank you. Here with Mr. Stokton?"

"Yeah, you didn't hear us come in?" Something was off. Ms. Ata was always the first one to greet visitors. She always seemed to be in arms reach of the door. She also looked more than a little pale, almost like she was sick.

"Oh, no. I was making HouseMother and Master Stokton's lunch. Will you and Flip be joining us?"

"No, not today. I think we're actually leaving pretty soon. It's good seeing you, Ms. Ata."

"Likewise, Matriarch." She bowed again and walked toward the living room. Elena couldn't help but think about how Ata looked. She remembered her always having a beautiful tan to her complexion, but today looked pale, drained even. Maybe she was just getting over something, the weather had been up and down the past few weeks. She brushed it away but told herself to not forget it.

Flip came down the stairs after another 30 minutes and found Elena sitting at the kitchen table. She was sitting in the same spot his mother would normally sit. He could see three crumpled tissues she didn't have earlier sitting in front of her. When she looked at him, he knew his guess for why she left was right. He couldn't blame her. He crossed the kitchen and sat next to her, one chair shy of his normal placement. Over the next couple of minutes, he held her hand while she quietly cried for the second time today at the Stokton's kitchen table.

When Elena got back from the bathroom, she was sure the tears were done. She came back into the kitchen and saw Flip was gone. She walked to the living room she saw Ronald was sleep. She walked around the first floor and decided to go upstairs. When she got to the top, she could hear mother and son talking in Flip's childhood bedroom. Flip was sounded like he was saying his goodbye, so she felt it was safe to walk in. "Hey, Mrs. Stokton."

"Hey, baby, Flip was just saying y'all about to head out. You hungry? I'll get Ata to make something for y'all to take with you." She was already heading to the door to call her up.

"No, no, Mrs. Stokton, you don't have to do that. I already saw Ata and let her know. She said she was prepping lunch for y'all."

Fleice looked at her with a squint that Flip recognized. It was a look she used to exercise regularly during her police days. The Bird's Eyes. It was her way to analyze an interesting statement. Or investigate how it was wrong. Her head twitched again. "Oh, Ronald and I ate lunch a few hours ago. We wanted to eat early so I can watch my afternoon shows all the way through. Or was it to paint?" She shook her head and shrugged. "I don't know, maybe I wanted to paint, but we did eat early. I'm sure of it." She then reached behind her and pulled out a tiny notebook and flipped through pages. "Dr. Bollard says I should keep writing my notes. Keeps me sharp." She flipped a few more pages then stopped. "Yes, we ate at 11:30. Ooh, says we had pestojc salad. You two missed a good one." She said matter-of-factly and looked at them. Head twitch, followed by a few scratches into the notebook.

Flip felt himself getting hot again. He didn't know what exactly to say but went for it anyway. "Well mom, I think we're going to head out. Ok?"

Fleice shrugged her shoulders and had a big smile. "Ok, Flip. I'll talk to you later baby, ok?"

He kissed her cheek and gave her a long hug. "Alright mom, I'll see you later. You need anything?"

"No baby. I got you, your father, and my mind, that's all I need. No offense, El."

She smiled her first genuine one since arriving. Old girl could still make a decent joke. "None taken, ma'am."

"Alright, Flip-baby, I love you." She said while giving Flip another hug.

"Love you too, mom."

"Oh!" Fleice snapped her fingers. "Ronnie was here a couple weeks ago. He asked about you."

"Oh, ok."

"You talk to him lately?"

"Nah."

"Mmm, ok, well give him a call sometime. He's still in Monarch."

"Aight, I will." Flip knew he had no intention of doing so.

When they separated, Fleice went to Elena and

opened her arms. On contact, she had a flash of a single scene showing a well-dressed Elena yelling down at somebody. She had their arm twisted behind them. Then, nothing.

"Mrs. Stokton, everything ok?"

"Yall going out tonight?" Fleice asked as she was returning.

"We were going to The Watering Hole later. Flip has a work meeting."

"Yeah mom, I told you we were going out, remember?"

Fleice looked at Elena for a few more seconds then snapped back to her earlier buoyancy, "I'm just asking. Try to be a good girl tonight, ok Elena? I don't want y'all getting' kicked out of anywhere."

"Um, yes ma'am, I will." She didn't know why but made the scout's gesture for honor. "I promise."

"I know you do. Alright baby, I hope to see you again." She went to hug Elena again. She then gave Flip a finger-gun salute, which he returned.

"Me too, Mrs. Stokton. I'll see you later." Elena said before leaving the bedroom and heading for the stairs. She looked behind and saw Flip was right behind her, taking another look at his mother while he walked away. She looked as if in her own world; aimlessly walking around Flip's room touching old trophies and desk trinkets with a faraway smile on her face. As if reliving a good memory, or trying to.

Flip wrapped an arm around Elena's waist as they walked down the stairs. She looked to him but the face she saw helped her decide she can wait until they're out of the house. As they reached the bottom landing, Ronald was coming out of the living room checking his watch. He had a pill bottle in his hand.

"Y'all heading out?" He asked as he opened the bottle and tapped out a pill.

"Yeah, we gotta get going." Flip responded. "What time you got?"

Ronald looked at his watch again. "A little after 3. Where's your mother?"

"My room for now. That for her?" He pointed to the bottle.

"Nah, not this one. I think I pulled something in my shoulder at the driving range the other day with Khris and that asshole Charlie Brandton. Bollard gave me a couple of these to dull it out, just gotta take them once a day and he said I should be good to go back out by Tuesday." He walked them to the door and opened it for them.

"I got you." Flip said. He dapped his father and gave him a hug. "Take it easy, alright?"

"I will son. Work is the always easy part, you get me?"

Flip just nodded with a smile before leaving out.

"You take care, Elena." He waved at her.

"You too, Mr. Stokton." She said as she waved back.

Flip was halfway down the front steps before he turned around and started back to the door.

"Dad!"

Ronald had the door half-closed before he heard Flip calling for him. He quickly reopened the door.

"Yeah, what's up? Forget something?" He asked.

"Not exactly, just had a question. Has mom been talking about any of her old cases since I was last here? Something about teeth?"

Ronald searched within himself and thought about the many things his wife talked about on a regular basis. He remembered Scarla Ingram coming by a few weeks ago for dinner but couldn't recall any work talk. Scarla wasn't really into the old work stories like he grew to appreciate. He remembered Ronnie came by later that same week. "Nah, not that I recall. I think the last time she talked about something was when y'all were talking about them robberies a while back. Got a new case? I just heard about this Shockley guy that was found out in East Pike."

Flip kept his father at arms-length about his work with the P'rotectors. He would usually talk shop with his mother. It seemed to be one of the few times she instantly became her old self again. She was normal, or as close to it. Ronald was a different story. Despite being married to a rank member in law enforcement, Ronald Stokton was always little skittish about being too close to the police. He didn't talk much about what he did prior to meeting his mother, aside from having his brother and being mostly into account handling, but he remembered a few encounters in his early days of establishing his own brokerage firm with Khristopf Starks due to rumors of "questionable internal practices". Those rumors plagued him until he started warning of a major Cabrini Motors stock blow-up when everybody was still riding it hard. The news of race-fixing didn't come out for another four months; the stock plummeted month later, after the first of three Cabrini board members went to jail. Nobody could figure out how Ronald knew about the crash, but nobody ever doubted his word or warnings.

"Nah, not right now. Just asking." He reversed course and went back towards the car. "See you later dad."

"Alright." Ronald responded before closing the door.

Forgetting he didn't unlock the car, Flip saw Elena standing on the driver's side waiting for him.

"I believe I'm still driving, right?" She asked him with a smile.

"A bet is a bet." He responded as he hit the button and tossed the keys to her.

"Ha-ha, funny. Not." She stuck her tongue out and opened the door to get in. *Come on, Joy, don't be a bitch.*

Joy started on the first try. Elena gave herself a proud smile and looked over to Flip, sticking her tongue again. Flip adjusted his seat and laid back. Elena got into gear and turned on the radio. The Shockley discovery was being talked about again, only now featuring more theories and opinions from the station hosts than actual facts. There was still no mention of teeth. Flip looked at the dashboard; *3:12PM*, then to Elena, "Thanks, Olga. For coming with me."

"You're welcome." She said before reaching to hold his hand. "Wanna talk about it?"

"Not really."

"Later?"

"Maybe."

As Elena let the front gate open, she could hear a couple of sniffs and looked over to see Flip wiping his eyes. Allowing him the same respect he gave her in the kitchen, she continued to drive back into the city.

CHAPTER 10

Alexis woke up to the smell of food. It was dark in the room, and she had no idea what time it was, let alone what day. What she did know was that she was starving. Looking around, she could see the curtains were drawn closed and feel a pain just below her neck. She felt drained. Her right arm was tied to a bed post with a thick rope and dried blood was all over the bed. If her throat wasn't so dry, she would have screamed. *Is this my blood? All of it?* she panickily thought to herself. That was when she realized her clothes were hanging onto her by threads, and she began to panic for new reasons. She could remember being grabbed from behind in the kitchen, then being dragged up the stairs. After that, things got spotty. She thought about the paintings and how they seemed to be moving. They were looking at her. She could swear the portraits were staring at her. Weren't they? She didn't remember much after that. Except the screaming. Her screaming.

There was a still steaming plate of food next to her and with her free hand, she franticly did her best to eat. She was forced to pick everything up by hand and, barring a few burnt tastebuds, ate everything on the plate, even licking the plate just in case it was to be her last meal. The bedroom was closed but she could hear voices talking nearby, muffled by the door and her distance. When she heard footsteps approach, she panicked and decided to play unconscious just in case whoever it was came in. She could then hear the door open and had to fight the urge to move as the steps made their way to the bed. She heard something being placed on the bed desk and then steps going over to the opposite side, where the plate was. The steps then retreated back to the door. When she heard the door close, she gave it another minute before she felt safe to open her eyes. A cup was on the same side as her bound hand and just out of reach with her free one. Alexis turned into the closest pillow and cried dry tears.

When Hana had closed the door and went back to the sunroom, she held up an empty plate.

"Your whore-pet is up." She said flatly.

Rac' was sitting in his chair focused on playing a video game on the sunroom's TV and didn't hear that Hana spoke to him. Hana pulled up her gown sleeve and calmly walked over.

SMACK

"Hana, what the fu--" Rac' jumped like he was rudely woken up.

SMACK

"I said, your *whore-pet* is *up*!"

"I heard you." He paused the game and looked at her.

"You did a number on her. You sure there's anything left?"

"That's why I gave her the food." He un-paused the game and got back into it.

"Uh-huh, ok."

Without response Rac' focused on his game and kept playing as Hana walked away. Alexis was going to die eventually, just not yet. No, he wanted to see if she learned her lesson first. After a few minutes went by, he paused the game again and got up, leaving the sunroom and walked towards his room. To Alexis. Maybe she learned her lesson after some time and a hot meal.

"Let's go out tonight!" He heard from another room.

He pretended not to hear her as he walked.

"Rac'? You hear--?"

"I *fucking* heard you!" He yelled back before opening the door.

Wallace heard his phone ring as he stepped out of the shower. He didn't know how long it's been ringing and he ran from the bathroom to his living room and quickly scanned the caller ID: D'avid Holmb. Junior Homicide P'rotector D'avid Holmb. Good kid. Intelligent, but definitely had a bit of learning to do about city life. Wallace answered the phone, putting it on speaker.

"Go ahead Holmb."

"You free?" Holmb sounded like he was in a car. Or had the TV on the auto channel a little too loud. Him and his cars. "Something's up."

Wallace paused as he was drying off. He picked up the phone and went back into the bathroom to finish his routine. "Something? Like what?" He asked as he placed the phone on the sink counter. Holmb could hear running water.

"Got me on speaker, sir?" Holmb asked.

"Don't worry, ain't nobody else here. You good."

"Ok. But yeah, something's up. It's Alexis."

Wallace stopped the water and looked at the phone. *Shit, Alexis. Come on.* He thought to himself what it could possibly be. It's only been a month or so since she's been working as a Confidential Informant with FCPD Vice, on the vouch of P'rotector Wallace himself. She was young but still had her looks, considering the severity of her Rock habit she used to have when they first met. He also knew that she was the girl of choice for a mid-level Rock pusher Vice has been trying to nail for a while now. Fucking Luc St. Clair. Only guy to treat mid-level management like he was the CEO. Wallace remembered picking him up for petty theft less than 5 years ago. Now he's become a notable figure in the Fountain drug market. Wallace began to think about one of two realistic possibilities: she was either picked up again for trying to turn a street 'tec, or she missed a check-in with her handler. Or she was dead. Shit, three possibilities. He braced himself for all options and went ahead.

"What about her?" He asked uneasily. *Please don't say option three.*

"That's the thing, Vice hasn't heard from her since Thursday afternoon. Said she would be with St. Clair at some point yesterday and would check-in this morning." Holmb's story hung in the air. "Wallace? You still there?" He asked, the sound of an engine decreased in volume.

"Yeah, I heard you. They got any leads on where she might be? Maybe had a slip and got laid up with someone?" He couldn't help but cringe at his own words, and felt Holmb might have too. "Look, you get what I'm saying. Any reason to why she'd leave town or be layin' low?"

Holmb was quiet for a second before he answered. "No, not from what Agent Valer has said. Apparently, she's been going to those Next Step meetings at the community center in the Third as part of her stips."

Quiet again.

Wallace told Holmb that he'd call him later and asked that he stay in touch with Vice. He directed to start asking around if anyone saw Alexis between Thursday and Friday. They hung up and Wallace continued getting himself together. His gut told him Alexis isn't doing well right now, wherever she was. His experience told him that this wouldn't be the last time he's found someone who was supposed to have gone clean in a drughouse or a bar, relapsed and oblivious to the rest of the world. He hoped that was all it was and told himself to remember to ask Flip if he'd heard about it. Well, after his first beer, he would.

Nighttime in Fountain. To Flip, that's when anyone would see the real Fountain, good and bad. Driving from Mesa to The Watering Hole took almost 30 minutes, but you got a chance to see a piece of 3 of Fount's largest districts; the Second, Third, and Fourth. A shorter route would have taken them on a straight-shot through the First District, but Flip liked the scenic route. Elena on the other hand, wouldn't fare as well. She could handle herself, but he was willing to bet she's never set foot on actual First District land. Not the Matriarch Starks, no. The Triple-C was a respectable compromise; she could still help the children of the First even if she didn't go there herself. As they were driving, Flip looked at the windshield and saw a few water droplets hit and slide down. *Days until rain...0* he thought as he chuckled. Elena looked over to him and touched him slightly on the ear.

"What'cha thinking about that's so funny?" She asked him softly.

He kept driving but noticed her accent was thicker than usual. It's toned it down over the years from traveling and living in different Territories, but she's still a Fountain girl before anything. When he got to the light, Flip looked over to her with a smirk and simply said, "Nothing, just had a feeling it was gonna rain tonight, that's all."

"Uh-huh, you get that feeling from your little visit

with Sandra?"

Flip looked at her again and saw she had a dark smile of her own. She looked good, not now, but especially now. He had half-a-mind to find the first alley and have some fun before they hit the club. It was a passing feeling and he forgot about it by the next light. Flip reached over and played with her necklace.

"Now, you wouldn't be the jealous type of Matriarch, would you?" He said in an exaggerated drawl.

Elena rolled her eyes and playfully swatted his hand away, "Never. Us Starks don't get jealous, whether it's about business or our lovers." before she joined his hand.

"I love it when you talk like that." He responded as the light turned green. *Aggressive and possessive.* Even during their "flings", as his mother would describe it, she didn't act like this. This kind of talk was reserved for when it was for real. As they rounded the corner of 35th Avenue, Elena looked over and saw the Fountain City Third District Library and laughed.

"Fountain City Library. We had good times there, didn't we?" She looked over at him.

"Yes ma'am, we did. Good times if I recall correctly." He continued before crossing over to 36th. "I think that place was the reason your mom gave you that nickname." Pointing to her necklace.

"Why yes, it is. I wasn't going to let them Brandton boys jump you and think they got away with it. Mom cut me a deal and gave me two weeks punishment in exchange of helping our Wards do family laundry after school. Dad taught me a 'proper' right hook." She laughed as she reminisced. "Hey, remember Mrs. Hendrix caught us smoking in the parking lot that one night?"

Flip let out a big laugh and tapped the steering wheel a few times. He never forgot it. It was one of his first times smoking and supposed to be Elena's initiation. "Didn't even get midway before she came out yelling at us. I'll never forget that." He coughed out another laugh as he made a perfect impression. "I swear she ended up smoking the rest herself."

"I know she did. I remember seeing her trying to light it when we got to the other side of the gate. No use throwing away good green."

"But it was terrible." He said while laughing.

"I know." She shared his laughter and cracked the window. She then reached into her blazer. "Speaking of which..." Her voice trailed as they were getting onto Brandton Boulevard, officially entering the Fourth District. Elena could see a clump of traffic further up.

Flip looked over and saw what she was talking about. "Let's wait till we get there."

Elena went back into her blazer before leaning over to kiss his cheek. Rubina no. 5 coming off of her.

"Damn girl, you smellin' good." He said while turning onto a side street to bypass the holdup.

"I know. Now you do too. Why didn't you tell Sandra her date wasn't showing up?"

The hours after leaving his family house were a mix of talking, getting ready, and loving. Twice at Elena's, once more before leaving Mesa. She had her own territory marked plenty. Elena sat back in her seat and played with her necklace some more; feeling the individual stones that lined the edges of the lettering. It, aside from the nickname itself, was one of the last things Rubina left her with.

"Technically, I don't know. He might show up late or

something." He flicked his wrist to look at his watch, the only one he still owned; solid gold with red accents and "*Give 'em hell.*" and the Stokton seal engraved along the curve and center of the back plate. A present from his parents when he won his first championship. *7:52*. Making good time.

"Mmhmm, ok. You know, I really like this necklace. I ever say thank you for adding the stones?" She said to him, necklace still in her fingers.

"I remember you said it to your daddy." He responded with a smirk.

"Thank you, Flip." Elena said softly as she took his hand and kissed it.

A few minutes later, Flip slowed down as they approached The Watering Hole. There was already a line of people at the door, and they could hear the low din of music from inside. The rain was starting to come in at a trickling drizzle. Despite the crowd, there weren't a lot of parked along the street. It was a similar story with the parking lot across from them. Guess a lot of people weren't thinking about rain.

"Where we parkin'?" Flip stopped the car and looked over towards the building.

Elena scanned the street and saw a car she recognized parked across from them in the lot. She pointed over. "Isn't that P'rotector Wallace's car?"

Flip laughed as he looked over and saw the car immediately. A cloud grey dot against the background of nightfall, he could recognize Wallace's Voltijr Landstar anywhere. Nice car. Nothing too flashy, but fitting for a Fountain City Lead P'rotector. Very Wallace.

"Good for me, I hate parking right in front of this place."

"You hate parking in front of *any* place." Elena quipped back.

"When you got a 'tec for a mom, y--" He started.

"I know, I know. *'You can't help but pick up things.'* Right?" She stuck her tongue at him.

Flip wheeled over into the lot and made his way to Wallace's car. "Yes, ma'am" he said as he put Joy into park. He opened the center console to grab the Shockley papers and a lighter. "Ready?" He asked Elena as he closed the console.

"Yep." She responded while opening her door.

It wasn't the Third District Library, but they did share a smoke in the parking lot of The Watering Hole. Getting his umbrella, Flip looked Elena up and down and grabbed her by the waist. "Damn, miss, you lookin' good tonight."

Elena held onto him, careful not to ash on his clothes. Or hers. "Thank you, I'll be sure to tell my boyfriend." She had a giddy smile on her face and took a hit. "I think he forgets sometimes."

Flip took the joint and took a heavy drag, then exhaled. "Girl, if I was yo man, ain't no way I'm forgetting somethin' like that." He took another and passed it back before kissing her neck softly.

"I'll let him know that, too." She pulled, "Hopefully he remembers this time." and exhaled. Elena wrapped around Flip's arm, and they walked the lot and towards the Hole. As they crossed the street, a voice called out from the line.

"Flip! Elena!" It was Sandra, standing next to a group of five and waving. He didn't recognize everyone, but he saw Penny standing pretty much eye-to-eye with one of the men near her. Penny saw him and waved excitedly. They walked over to the rope partition and shared hugs with Sandra and

Penny. Elena could smell the pre-game before Sandra opened her mouth.

"Damn, what'd y'all do, pick it yourself?" Sandra asked Elena with a laugh and kissed her cheek.

Elena feigned a laugh and looked at the others in the group. "Is this the birthday party Flip told me about?"

"That's right, girl, but we're down one for now. Flip! You won't believe it, my date called saying he's running late." Sandra told them. "Guess you were right."

"You at least bring an umbrella?" Flip asked her.

"Yep." She reached down. "Right here. Thank you, Flip."

Elena rolled her eyes. She looked over to the bouncer standing a few feet up from the group and then to the remainder of the line. She saw their eyes and could tell they all recognized her. Out of her periphery, she could see heads craning around to get a look at who this random couple was trying to cut the line. Elena walked over to Penny and made conversation with her and the man she was standing with.

"Oh, Flip, this is my friend I was telling you about. Donna, this Flip--"

"Flip Stokton, I know. I'm sure Sandra told you I'm a *very* big fan of you and the Matriarch. Nice to meet you." Donna reached her hand out.

"Likewise, Donna. Happy birthday." He met her hand and shook it. *Solid handshake, professional tone. Must work in an office or something.*

"Thank you. I thought Sandra said y'all couldn't make it? What made you change your mind?"

"Work, actually. I gotta meet someone here for a little bit. Elena and I are celebrating something too, you could say."

Flip felt uneasy, like he shared a little more than he should.

"That why y'all looking good tonight?" Sandra asked enthusiastically. Flip looked to Elena and for the first time thought that maybe they did dress-up a bit. They were both wearing an all-black ensemble accented with gold. Elena in a cold-shoulder dress with side-slits going from knees to the upper thigh, the "OLGA" of her necklace resting bare, shining in the overhead lights. Maybe not the best choice in hindsight of the rain, but hey, they *were* celebrating. Flip went with denim for the shirt and pants, the blazer from Missy's, his watch, and a pair of custom blacked out Stokton 5's he barely wore out.

"Celebrating what, if you don't mind me asking?" Donna asked.

"Well, we recently got back together." *In for a cent, in for a pound.*

"How nice," Donna said. "I love to hear couples giving it another go. Will you be with us tonight? Maybe after your 'meeting'?"

"I don't know, maybe. Elena's gonna be with y'all more than I will, I'm sure. Actually," He shook Donna's hand again and hugged Sandra. "I should probably get inside. Donna, it was nice meeting you. Sandra, I'll see y'all inside." He tapped Elena on the elbow and leaned in. "You coming?"

Elena stopped her singing and turned to him. "Yep." She hugged Penny again and shook her date's hand before walking with Flip to the front door. Sandra waved one last time while Elena whispered something to the bouncer and nod in response. She then saw Elena walk over and open their section of the rope and wave them out.

"Girl, what you doing?" She asked as she walked out of line.

"Nothing, just letting y'all in before it rains. Happy birthday again, Donna."

"Thank you, Ms. Starks. Who would've thought I'd have some Fountain royalty at my party?" Donna said before giving a hug that lasted a second too long. "I'd would love for you and Mr. Stokton to join us."

"Thank you. I'll meet up with y'all after I say hi to Hazel. Where y'all sitting at?" Elena asked.

"Second floor booth. I hope to see you there. *Both* of you."

Elena pretended not to hear the emphasis. "You will. After I talk to Hazel, I'll head up." With that she closed the rope and walked with them past the large group occupying the front of the line and stopped at the bouncer. "Thanks again, Riko."

"Thanks, man." Flip slipped a couple folded bills into Riko's hand when they shook.

Riko gave a slick nod and responded, "No problem at all, Founders. Have a good night."

Flip waited until Sandra's group made their way to the stairs leading to the second floor. Penny lagged behind and looked at Flip and Elena until she figured they weren't coming with them right now. Flip held Elena's hand and leaned to her ear, "What was that all about with the line?"

"Oh, nothing, just thought I'd be nice that's all." She kissed him. "Now, can we get a drink? I think I'll need one before going to hang out with *our big fan*." They made their way into the main dance and dining area.

As they walked across the main hall towards the bar, Flip couldn't believe how clear the music was. Then again, the smoke in the parking lot was taking hold. Before Hazel could notice them, Flip saw Wallace down the line and they nodded to each other. He then tapped Elena and she exchanged waves.

"Hey y'all!" Hazel Solan, owner of the Hole, came from behind the bar to stretch and double-kiss them both on their cheeks. "Flip, P'rotector Wallace actually just got here not that long ago. I should've figured it was a work thing and not for me." She winked at them and turned on a devilish grin. "Talk to him, would you? I can be very appreciative of my boys in orange for their service."

"Aight, I will. Mind if I get a drink?"

Hazel walked back behind the bar. "What you want? Your usual?"

"Yeah, that'll work." He then kissed Elena. "See you in a bit."

"Or I *will* come looking for you." Elena said as he turned for Wallace.

"Y'all are being pretty lovey tonight, El. Holding hands and shit. Kissing. What's going on, y'all finally engaged or something?" Hazel paused her drink prep and looked at Elena.

"Hell no, girl," she held up her left hand as they each laughed, "you see anything on here? No, Flip and I are back together, *for real*. He asked me, special speech and everything." She arched her eyes so Hazel can grasp the emphasis. Hazel's own widened to point they might pop out.

"Girl, are you serious!? When? Where? I need all the details." She began moving with a vigor and finished the drink. She then got out a glass and two bottles of wine, opening one. Once she poured Elena's glass and gave it to her, she held up a finger, "Hold on, don't start yet, I'll be right back." before walking down the bar and placing Flip's drink in front of him.

"Thanks Hazel." Flip said and slid her a bill.

"Boy, put that away, I hear tonight's a good night for you." She slid the bill back to him.

"She told you already, huh?"

"Nope, but she's about to." Hazel let out an excited giggle and started to turn back.

"Of course. Well look, hold it for me in case someone try to take it." He said, sliding the bill to her.

She folded the bill into her pocket. They've been coming here too long, and she's known El for even longer to treat them the same way she would some office-type trying to impress his date. Hazel gave a small wave to Wallace and walked away as her two barkeeps came from the kitchen and got to their posts. If he would finally take her up on it, he could share in similar perks, and a few exclusive ones. Flip took a small sip before he spoke again.

"You know that she likes you? Like a lot." He said to Wallace.

"Yeah, I know man, but she's a little young for me, don't you think?" Wallace responded.

Flip looked back at Hazel. He had to admit the age difference was something to think about since she was only a few months older than him and Elena. But was she pretty and intelligent? Without a doubt. Surely that makes up something. Doesn't it?

"I don't know, she ain't that much older than me and Elena and I." He took another sip. "She's also the owner of this place, and you come here enough." Another sip. "I don't know man, just something to think about."

"Alright alright, brother, I think you've earned your promo fee." Wallace said back. "She is a pretty girl, though. I'll holla at her before I leave. But before that, let's talk."

Flip was already getting out the Shockley papers and handed them over. Wallace already had Shockley's full sheet memorized but took a look anyway. When he finished, he looked up, "So what you think about the teeth thing?"

"Honestly, I don't know. I mean it sounded weird when CaP told me about it, but he didn't have much to add of his own." Flip could feel himself plateauing and settling into PI mode. He thought back to his mother. He was positive there was something about teeth she had going on in an old case.

"Yeah, it was the same for me when he told me. You ever heard of some shit like that?" Wallace took a sip of his beer.

"Nah, not directly. It did make me think about something my mom may have talked about a long time ago. Couldn't remember if it was an old case or not. Y'all ever have a case involving teeth markings on a body?"

Wallace took another sip to finish. "Yeah, but not like this. If it was something else, it had to have been before I got there. I'll look at some old case files on Monday. How's she doing, by the way?"

"She's good, I went by the house with Elena earlier today." Flip said before he took a sip. "So, what's up man, look like you got something else on your mind."

Wallace was about to go for a sip until he remembered. "Nah man, ain't nothing big. Got a call earlier today from Holmb about a CI that ain't check in yet. You know a woman named Alexis Valer? Nightgirl. Born and raised here in Fount."

Flip took a minute to think about it. He was sure Elena may have mentioned the name before.

"Nah I don't think so. First name sounds a little familiar, but I couldn't say how. Want me to ask El? Maybe she's been around the Center."

"Yeah man. She was supposed to been going to those Next Step meetings in order to keep working with Vice and stay on the outside. They're still trying to get that St. Clair asshole, she was the go-between."

Flip knew enough of Luc St. Clair to know he didn't like him. His only personal interaction was at this very bar, only a few seats closer to the front from where he and Wallace sat now. Luc shook his hand one night two years ago and Flip caught a flash of him tapping something into a glass and then another of a woman drinking it. The next time he came by, Hazel told him that she found a girl passed out in the women's bathroom during closing. After a few days of asking, Flip found out who the girl and visited her in the hospital. She wouldn't say who she thought drugged her but he still offered to pay for therapy whenever she was ready and kept his word. It was one of the first stories Flip shared with Wallace when they started these meetups. He was still kicking himself in the ass for not decking St. Clair on the spot.

"Fuck that guy." Flip punctuated it with a sip of his drink.

"Same here, brother." He got a barkeep's attention and ordered another beer. "He's been moving up in the world since your run-in with him. This Alexis chick was his recreational drug of choice." His beer arrived as he finished speaking. He then took a sip and savored the taste. "Nothing better than a fresh beer."

Flip raised his glass and shared a toast with Wallace. "Nothing better." He said as they clinked and took a finishing sip. "What you think about it? Think Luc's involved?"

"Right now, it's a coin toss for me. Holmb said Vice last talked to her on Thursday morning and she told them she'd be seeing him yesterday. Honestly, this ain't the first time she's missed a check-in, but usually me and Holmb would find her near a fucking Rock house or out working." Wallace took another sip. "This is the first time we ain't heard from her in over two days. She may be a busy girl, but she ain't that busy."

"Think she might be skipping town? Got cold feet and can't do it no more?" Flip asked.

"I thought about that too, but it brought up two things. One, why leave right before check-in? Especially when you're supposed to be with the person of import so soon before. Two, how far is she going? I mean, I'm sure Luc gives her a little bonus to her normal rate, but it ain't like he got her on employee payroll or something. She's still out here working like a lot of girls in the First, you know? Shit, I still don't even know a permanent address for the girl." Wallace took a sip and stayed silent.

Flip was silent. After eating an ice cube, he asked, "Think she's dead?" and took another sip.

"Shit, I don't know. We may have to start thinking about if Shockley and this are related, but I don't think that's the case right now." Wallace let his theory sit in the air and saw that Flip was thinking it over. He let him. Aside from bad timing of the two, Flip couldn't see any connecting tissue between the events. He shrugged his shoulders and slid the papers back to him. "Look, hold on to this and read it over again. Something might jump out. Let know what you decide."

"Thanks man. I'm still not sure, but with this murder and now a missing woman, shit is looking interesting. I'll keep in touch." Flip told him as he folded the papers over and put them in his jacket.

"What was that bit Hazel was talking to you about?" Wallace asked.

"Oh, yeah. Elena and I are back together." Flip sipped, trying to play it cool.

"*Back* together? Man, I thought y'all been like that. What y'all been doing this whole time?" Wallace looked genuinely shocked.

"We been off-and-on the past few years. I asked her this morning, and she accepted."

"Shit man, so when I saw y'all in here a couple months ago with different people, y'all was single?"

"Yeah, man. You were here for that?" Flip felt embarrassment wash over. "Where?"

"Right here, man. I saw you had a lady with you so I wasn't gonna blow you up. But yeah man, I saw that look-down she gave you and everything." Wallace was starting to laugh now.

"What'd you think we was doing?"

"Man, between you and me, I thought y'all was just into some different shit. I know you Founder types be into some interesting relationship dynamics. I been around the Fifth a couple times, man." He was almost laughing at this point.

Flip couldn't help but laugh himself at that one, mostly because it was sort of true. Oddly specific rumors of Brandton HouseMother Drue and Patriarch Charles came to mind. He dapped Wallace again and left him so he can now go upstairs. *How weird is coming to a place like this for Penny?* he couldn't help but think as he got to the front of the bar.

"Want another drink?" Hazel called to him.

"Nah, I'm good."

Hazel nodded and placed a glass of water on the bar. Flip took a sip and she leaned over as she was cleaning drinking glasses. "Congratulations on you and Elena. I like seeing y'all get together. Very cute couple." She winked at him.

"Thanks. Wallace is gonna talk to you before he leaves. Don't forget to remind him if he tries sneakin' out." He told her with a smile and a finger-gun. She shot back with a smile of her own.

Flip checked his watch, *8:40. About another hour or so.* He climbed the steps to the second floor and noticed it must have either been way more people in line than he saw or people really felt like dancing tonight. A small line ended at the stairs' midpoint. Flip stayed to the open side and tried not to fall for the questioning eyes of the waiting partiers. Most of the questioning turned to recognition when they realized who he was, but he didn't know them, and this wasn't a club promo social appearance. When he reached the top, he was happy to see another familiar face.

"What up, big homie?" Flip dapped up Smetty. J'oc "Smetty" Tal, current head of The Watering Hole security and former personal Ward for Flip in his playing days. The two men were relative peers, but Smetty had 3 years and almost 70 pounds of muscle on him. Before security, Smetty was a traveling martial artist, attaining two black belts by 24 and a few major tournament titles to his name by the time the two met. When Flip found out he was originally born in Fountain but raised in Redwater, their first interview was effectively finished right there, and he hired him on the spot. They went from employee/employer to genuine friends over the span of Flip's first two years and continued so even after he left. Smetty was one of the first people to publicly come out and defend his employer's personal and athletic integrity when reporters came to feed.

"What up, coming in?" Smetty was already undoing the rope.

"Yeah, for a little bit. Elena come up here?"

"Yuh, she up here with Sandra and them. The one in the orange is bangin', bro, who is she?" Flip followed Smetty's gaze towards the dancefloor and saw he was talking about Donna.

Laughing along, Flip said, "Man, you better chill, I thought you and Sandra had something going on."

Smetty sucked his teeth, "*Vi'nnak*, we grown out here! Sandra and I be having a little fun, yeah, but if her friend wanna have fun too, so be it. Shit, I know how Sandra get when she been drinking."

They laughed and dapped again as Flip crossed the rope onto the floor of the second level; the actual "club" part of the Watering Hole. This floor had an extended dance floor and multiple booths along both sides against the wall and a second, but slightly smaller bar than downstairs on the opposite wall surrounded by double-stacked speakers. It was also much darker on the second floor than downstairs, aside from the multi-colored lights that flashed in patterns along the walls and floors. Bathed in yellow and blue on the large center stage were The Sirens, the Watering Hole's in-house band, playing an aural string and horn melody while lead-singer Cass' crooned on. Local legend said Cass' and The Sirens have been a fixture of the Hole since it opened, the only change being the gender of whoever was the new Cass'. The story went that they showed up the first week, unannounced, and set up to play. To this day, there hasn't been an owner that's had the courage to ask them to leave.

The general vibe and the décor of the place always gave Flip the feeling of the social houses from Old Territory movies but with contemporary furniture. Purchased from the original architect by the Solan family in the early years of Fountain's founding, the Hole was originally the only real bar to go to outside of the Fifth District. Founders and commoners alike could go as private citizens for a hard drink and a few games of Scratch while The Sirens played or rent a confidential hour or two in one of the "Love Mage" rooms upstairs. Some say the placement of the building was intentional since it sits exactly half-and-half First and Fourth District land, allowing it to circumvent normal operating mandates and Alms charges. They also say it was to make up for the Solan family never being welcomed into the Seven Clans.

Weaving through dancefloor edgers, Flip made his way over to the birthday booth. He saw that Sandra and Elena were the only two. Sandra looked like she had been recently crying. And wet. He looked at Elena as he sat and kissed her cheek. "Hey." Elena's face looked sympathetic. He noticed she had a tall skinny bag next to her. Penny and her date were on the floor with Donna. In that moment it hit him; he's never seen Penny dance a day in his life. Even at their high-school formals, he remembered how she would sit relatively undisturbed with a book at her own table, occasionally stopping to smile and watch Aron have enough fun for the both of them. He took another sip from his water and cautiously waded in. "You ok, Sandra?"

Sandra looked at them both and tried a smile. "I'm good. My date called, and now he's not sure when he'll get here." She shifted. "I don't think he's gonna show. He either comes late, or not at all." She looked like she was about to cry again and dabbed her eyes with a napkin. "How was your meeting?"

"It was alright, you know." Flip took another sip. "Work stuff, that's all."

"Was it about the guy they found out by the diner?" She asked. She knew of Flip's occasional p'rotec work but not how much he could and couldn't talk about. "Both CP and a 'tec named Holmb came by asking questions."

"Yes and no." Flip answered but kept his tone upbeat.

Sandra nodded and looked at Elena before taking a gulp to finish the drink in front of her. The band started a low, booming piano transition into to the newest song by Fountain-born musician FTN BLDHnd. Flip remembered how he played with him in summer rec when they were kids. He wasn't bad, but no real ballplayer. Life started moving a bit faster at that time for the young Cal'oc Truy, but ultimately, he made her work in his favor. "Could we dance? I like this song."

Flip looked at Elena and saw he wasn't the only one caught off guard. He could see Elena's face turn to a smiling flustered. He lightly pinched her shoulder. She bounced and looked at a smiling Flip and then back to Sandra. "Let's dance." Elena responded with a laugh and sipped her wine.

Sandra's face lit up and she excitedly grabbed Elena's hand, straightening her dress as she rose. Flip could tell by it that she was looking very forward to seeing her date, whoever he was. His loss. He then felt himself rise and saw that Sandra grabbed his hand as Elena stood. "I meant both of you. I really like this song." She said with an intentional tone.

When she picked her spot, Sandra wasted no time eking out her frustration about being stood up. Flip looked around and saw they were the only group on the floor in this dance throuple, noticing Donna was now watching and Penny having a laugh at how funny it was seeing two girls dance on each other. As the song faded into another, Flip saw that Sandra's aggression didn't as she volleyed between him and Elena. He then saw Donna walk over as Sandra switched to him.

"Can I cut in?" Flip could barely hear her over the music but saw her take a sniff of something. "Y'all look like you're having fun!" Donna then looked to Elena. "Don't worry, I got something for you too!"

Flip and Elena looked at each other and she shrugged again with a smile. She took Sandra by the hand and brought her close, allowing her to grind against her and opening a spot. Donna took her chance and went over to Flip and danced in synch with the music and his body. This wasn't how she thought their night out was going to go, but Elena had to admit Donna looked good while she danced. She settled into the fun and let Sandra to go to work.

Flip looked over and saw Elena going so far as to slapping Sandra on the ass a few times and how Sandra's face said she liked each one. He scanned the room while he danced and saw Smetty escorting a couple to a roped booth and open it. When they sat, they finished their drinks and the woman started dancing on the male. In the dark, their faces looked alike, but so would a lot of people in the room on an offhand glance. It wasn't until seconds later that he

151

started feeling hot and itchy all over. His eyes went back to the booth and saw the woman of the couple looking at him. She continued dancing without missing a beat and continued staring. Not expecting the eye-contact, Flip looked away but kept moving. He couldn't get a good look at her face, but he was sure that girl was looking directly at him. *Maybe just in my direction,* was the last thing he thought before he flushed it out and went back to Donna and her orange dress.

CHAPTER 11

After another unintended hour in the Hole, Flip and Elena made their goodbyes and went for the stairs. As they walked, Flip took a quick look over to the couple's booth hoping to get a better look at both the man and woman occupying. The woman wasn't watching him this time, she was more focused on her conversation with her date. He did get a better look at the guy and saw that he looked a lot like his date, even noticing they were wearing similar clothes in a "his and hers" kind of way. His thoughts went back to the Creek and the matching shoe prints. He felt a twinge pass through again as they said goodbye to Smetty and walked down the stairs. Flip saw a noticeable change in the amount of clientele and the subsequent change of the overall vibe. Being just after 10, Flip saw some less traditional nine-to-fivers coming in and was glad they were leaving. The Rock Boys, the stupidly named crew of Luc St. Clair, were entering the main room, with some heading for the stairs and others going over to Hazel's bar. Flip couldn't see St. Clair himself but figured he couldn't be too far away. Elena told Flip she was going to say bye to Hazel and he waited by the front door.

As he watched Elena put her bottle bag on the bar and talk to Hazel, he saw two Boys standing close to her and trying to get her attention. They weren't too close, but Flip felt his body energize as they continued their efforts. She said something to the one sitting and Flip saw him try to grab at her necklace. He started walking over to them before seeing Elena slap the Boy's hand and yell at him. The Boy then stood up and started yelling back, even reaching for her chain. His friend looked like he was getting ready to say something too. An internal click went off and Flip ran over, umbrella point at the ready. He saw Elena twist and pin the Boy's face to the bar, arm craned in an upward lock with pressure applied to his shoulder. By the time he approached them, Elena was already yelling as Hazel watched with a slight hunch to her, one arm under the bar.

"--and don't you *ever* touch me again!" Elena yelled, accent in full force. "I *will* fuck you up!"

"Olga, what's going on?" Flip said when he got to them, umbrella tip raised to the second Boy. He looked at Hazel and she looked at him, arm still under the bar.

"Why it matter?" The second Boy said to him with a smug look. His hand was at his waist and lifted his shirt slightly, causing a glint of light to bounce off the metal hilt of either a dagger or shortblade.

"Flip, El, I love y'all, but whatever's about to happen, take it outside, please? I don't wanna have to put someone down on a busy Saturday." Hazel cut in, placing a heavy-bolt crossbow on the bar top.

Flip kept looking at the Boy in front of him and could feel the eyes on onlookers on them all. *These motherfuckers are just kids* he found himself thinking. "Olga?"

"I'm fine, Flip." She pressed down on the other Boy's shoulder. "Right?" She pressed down again, extracting a pained yelp this time.

"Wai-Wait, Flip? Flip *Stokton*? *That* Flip Stokton?" The second Boy asked. His smugness was breaking, and he pulled his hand back.

"You know another one?" Flip asked.

"N-Nah, man. Shit, my bad bro, we didn't know she was with you." He walked over to his friend at the bar. "We ain't know, our bad. Sorry, Miss."

"That *Miss*, is the *Matriarch* Elena Starks to y'all." Hazel said to them. "Now, am I gonna have to put y'all out or will you behave yourselves?" Her arm already replaced the bow and she started cleaning a glass.

"We'll be good, Hazel. We got you." The first Boy finally added in. His eyes had the *oh shit* look to them. "My bad, Ms. Starks, didn't recognize you out of a jersey."

Elena still had his arm in a hold and suddenly remembered Mrs. Stokton's warning, "*Be a good girl tonight, Elena.*" and she let him go with a push. "It's not fine, but I accept. Don't be going around touching on a woman like that again, *especially* her jewelry."

"Yes, ma'am." The Boy said as he grabbed his shoulder. "Won't happen again."

"Good." She recollected herself. "Now, Hazel, I will see you later. Thank you again for the wine, and get these two whatever they want for their next round." She reached into her cleavage and took out a thin fold of scril and placed a note on the bar.

"Yes, ma'am. You two have a good night." Hazel shot a look at the two Boys.

"We will." Elena responded as she waved and went to Flip. "Ready to go, Mr. Stokton?"

"Yes, ma'am. Boys." He nodded at them and the second one reciprocated. The first was busy massaging his arm, and ego. As they walked to the door, Elena wrapped her arm around Flip's and leaned to his ear.

"Get me to Mesa, *now.*" He could still hear the heaviness of her accent.

Flip laughed and unlatched his umbrella. He knew what she meant. "Yes, ma'am." He responded slickly.

◆ ◆ ◆

"Are you hungry?" Hana looked over to Rac'. He couldn't hear her over the music. Hana reached and dug her thumb and pointer nails into the back of his neck and pulled close, causing the top of his beer to spill over. "I said, are you hungry?"

"I'm fine." Rac' responded, looking around to see if anybody was watching. They weren't.

Hana let go of his neck with a push and sat back. She mumbled to herself before taking a sip of her drink. She leaned back over. "He was here." She whispered into his ear.

"Who?"

"Him, the other guy from the Creek. I saw him on the dancefloor."

Rac' took a second and remembered. He didn't see who it was but he recalled seeing a group that looked like they were dancing together. It looked fun, albeit a little weird compared to the standard they grew up under. Plus, he was little preoccupied looking at some of the other women that were coming up the stairs at the time, and uncomfortably looking to see if anybody was watching Hana dance on him. They looked good. "I didn't get a good look at them."

At this point, the measly few drinks it would take someone to get drunk barely registered. After so many years, alcohol became inconsequential in their effect, similar to normal food. She ate and drank because of the taste, the sense of being somewhat normal again. She eased her face and let herself enjoy the music and ambiance. She noticed a few guys from the booth over looking at her and opening wine bottles, waving her over. After a few seconds entertaining their glances, she leaned over and tapped Rac's shoulder. "I'll be back." she whispered.

"Where you going?"

She pointed over to the booth and he saw they were now standing, seemingly having fun with their dates and pouring glasses. His face changed slightly.

"Don't be jealous, little brother. I just want to have some fun. You had yours, right?" She saw his face and smiled. "I promise I'll be right back." She kissed his cheek and got up.

Rac' watched her walk over to the group. Watched her flaunt around like a hired nightgirl for these assholes' entertainment. Watched her take a sniff of something offered and stumble-dance like some loose *fla'ptre*. His face went from disgust to anger and he walked over to the booth and roughly took Hana by the arm. "We're going. *Now*."

"I don't want to." Her voice was slurred but he felt a resistance in her arm.

"Hey homie, fuck is you doing? We just having some fun, bro." One of the guys, probably the ringleader, got up and said, arm going for his waistband.

"You can sit back down." Rac' said, looking the man directly in his eyes as he did, fire starting.

"And if I don't? I ain't scared of you, *vi'nnak*." He lifted his shirt slightly and Rac' could see the large grip of a dagger in the lights of the club. Rac' chuckled at such a child's toy being brandished. By this point, the ringleader's friends were starting to stand up, their respective dates having trouble figuring out what exactly was going on. "We got a problem?" The man asked.

Rac' felt a hard slap and looked at Hana, who was yanking her arm loose. "Let me go!" she yelled at him.

The group now were sharing a big laugh, the leader of

them laughing the hardest. Rac' felt heat rush to his face and began licking his canines.

"Damn bro, you out here getting bitched by your girl? Guess she ain't really yours." the leader said in between pauses to catch his breath. "Get the fuck outta here, *vi'nnak.*" He sat back down as did his posse.

Rac' looked at Hana and saw she had a dull fire going herself. She was fully under the spell of whatever she sniffed, eyes now wide but unfocused. She continued looking at him. "You can go if you want." She waved him away, "Or stay and wait for me." before sitting back down for another sniff.

Rac' angrily walked back to their booth and his beer. He stared at them as they continued laughing, Hana now joining in. He felt the surge starting; a fire breathing to life. After he figured they had their laughs, he finished the last of his beer and noticed one from the group get up and make his way in the direction of the bathroom. Rac' put his glass down and got up to follow.

When he entered the bathroom, he took in that it was otherwise empty besides the most recent attendee who was at the sink, taking a few short sniffs from a vial and looking himself over in the mirror. When the door closed, he looked over quickly and saw it was Rac'. "You still here, bro? Thought your girl told you to roll out." He continued looking himself over and took another sniff.

"Just taking a piss." Rac' responded as he walked over to a urinal. He looked over his shoulder as he pretended to do his business. "What you got?" He asked.

"Some grown man shit, *vi'nnak.* You ain't built for this." the guy responded with a laugh.

Rac' flushed and went to the sink. As he washed his hands, he looked at him from the mirror. He said something under his breath. The guy looked up and saw that there wasn't a second person in the mirror and jumped back. Maybe it was the Rock, maybe it was the drinks he chased it with, but he started feeling his heart pounding and fear run through him. "Yo, what the fu--" He was interrupted by of a quick and deep slash across the neck. Blood pumped quickly out of his neck and onto his clothes. There was another slash across the face that sent him stumbling into an open stall and onto the toilet. He held his neck and tried to yell out. With his free hand, he went for his waist before Rac' grabbed his wrist, twisting and hearing the unmistakable *pop* of broken bone. Rac' slashed him another three times that painted the stall and his own shirt in red streaks. He let the surge pass and he regained himself. He spat some of the splash-back onto the body and left the stall, making one quick stop at the sink to clean his face.

Hana didn't see him leave, but when she looked and saw that their booth was empty, she figured Rac' must've left. Probably going home to play with his whore. She waited a little longer before settling on that he was indeed gone and returned her attention to the leader of the group. She leaned over to him. "Luc? that's an interesting name?" She played up her accent.

"Yeah, short for Lucie. Don't call me that shit though, I ain't no flagboy." His voice was a mix of aggression and annoyance.

Hana reached down between his legs and felt him up. "Guess you ain't." She said before kissing him deeply.

Luc's date looked over and wore shock on her face. "Uh-uh bitch! Don't be touching on my--"

Her words were cut short with a hard slap across the

face. "Bitch, don't *be telling* me what to do." Hana retorted. As the girl held her face, she saw what looked like something flickering in the rude bitch's eyes.

Hana went back to Luc. "What y'all doing after this?"

Luc looked over to his date and then leaned to the table, taking a sniff. "I don't know, ain't your man gonna be waiting for you?"

"Don't worry about him. Your mine's tonight." Hana said as she rubbed him up again, looking at his date the entire time.

"Damn, baby, I can dig that. Yeah, we prolly gonna go back to my place and hang out. Have a little party. You down?" Hana could see Luc's pupils as he spoke. They looked wild.

"I'm 'down', as you say. Is she coming?" Hana asked as she pointed to the date, head down and taking a few sips of her drink.

"She ain't got to." Luc started to shoo away his date before Hana stopped him.

"No, bring her along. I like her. Knows when to be quiet." Hana said with a slick smile as she licked her canines. "She's pretty cute."

Luc's eyes grew big and he looked from his date and then back to Hana. When he looked back, he felt light all of a sudden, like he was floating. Damn, that recent shipment batch turned out good. Real good. He kissed Hana and noticed how cold her mouth felt. He kissed her again. "Yeah, she is, ain't she?"

"I just said that." Hana responded with slight agitation. Luc didn't seem to hear.

"You ain't like my usual girl, but you give her a run."

He kissed her again. Hana cringed at the incoming stench of wine breath and whatever else had been in there. "Wanna get out of here?"

"Sure. You bringing your friends here? I don't mind." She asked, circling her finger around the booth. The other Boys were too busy partying to notice.

"Nah, baby, this gon' be a private party now." Luc responded. He offered another bump to Hana and she accepted. She felt her head rush and a pleasurable wave come over her again. "Good. Let's go." Luc told her when she reopened her eyes. He got up, talked to one his Boys, and led Hana and his date towards the steps leading downstairs. As they left, Hana noticed the Boy that left for the bathroom was still missing. It made her think of Rac' with a tiny smile.

When they arrived at his house, Luc parked in the driveway and stumbled his way out the car. They did a few more bumps during the ride over but Hana decided she should have a clear-ish head for when she got inside. She did feel bad about his date but brushed it off. Sadly, she was to be "collateral damage", as Rac' would have put it. Seemed like a nice girl, even if she had a mouth on her. She didn't have that nightgirl street smell to her. When they got into the house, Hana took a look around. "Nice place Luc, it's larger than it looks from the outside."

"That ain't the only thing, baby. What's your name again?" Luc called back to her with a grin. He looked over and saw his date making a drink. "Babygirl, make two more and bring them upstairs!" he called to her.

"It's Hana." Hana told him.

"I ain't room service! Have your new friend make her

own shit." She called back.

Luc walked over to her and grabbed her by the arm, almost spilling her drink on the floor. "Bitch, I got you for the night, so you whatever the hell I say you are! And right now, I want you to make some fucking drinks!"

Memories of childhood came back to Hana. She remembered how *He* would go off on her mother for perceived disobedience or defiance. Then it was Hana's turn. Almost everything was perceived as disobedience. Every word of defense was treated as defiance.

"Alright Luc, aight! I'm sorry. I'll bring 'em up, damn." Hana heard the anger in her voice but knew nothing would come of it. *Just like me at one point.*

"Good." He patted her face on the same side as Hana's slap and she gave a minor recoil.

Luc led Hana upstairs and into a large bedroom. Hana stayed on the edge of the room and watched him unbutton his shirt in the mirror. He looked over to her and said, "C'mon girl, get comfortable." as he opened a drawer and threw a small clear sack of pinkish powder on the bed.

Hana slowly started with her jacket and tossed it on a chair. When she saw Luc continue stripping down, she saw that he was already at full attention. She continued to her lower half but grew hesitant when it was time for her shirt. She had short sleeves on and knew Luc was already looking at her arm, and the burn that trailed up and under her sleeve. Slowly, she pulled her shirt off so that she was in her bra and panties, the entirety of her scar on display. Luc's face changed to a confused surprise as he also noticed how pale she looked in regular light for the first time.

"Damn, what happened to you?" He asked as he took a bump, pointing to her up and down. "And why the fuck you so pale? You sick?"

"Long story, but I'm fine." She responded, trying to sound calm. The burn had always made her self-conscious. Rac' didn't mean to cause it, but she hated it all the same. Before he could ask any more questions, she went over to the bed and started kissing Luc on the neck and chest, working her way down. As she moved down his chest, she could feel Luc rubbing on her arms. He started focusing his fingers on the glassy patch that covered most of her bicep.

"No, don't do that." Hana paused and looked up to him. The fire was back.

"Aight baby, aight." Luc said as he leaned back. He saw his date at the doorway with their drinks and waved her over as Hana worked. "Hey Cherry, come on over here, baby."

Hana could hear Cherry put down the drinks and felt her join her on the bed. As they were sharing Luc, Hana took her bra off. She moved to Cherry and kissed her neck multiple times as she used her right hand to explore. Once she let herself in, she grabbed Cherry by the hair and controlled her rhythm on Luc, pushing down for more each time. *That's right, whore.* When she felt it was enough, Hana kissed and caressed the under of Cherry's neck and moved up to Luc to kiss him, first on the lips and then on his neck. Suddenly, Luc felt a sting and pushed her back.

"Damn, bitch." He then felt his neck and saw a splotch of blood. "What the fuck?"

"I thought you were a real man? You can't handle it?" Hana asked as she licked her lips before going to kiss him again.

"I can handle it, but calm it down with the bitin' and shit." He felt his neck again and pulled back; more blood.

"I'm sorry, I didn't mean to. It's...It's been a while." She said to him with a smile as she went to take off her panties. She felt herself and knew she was ready. "I won't do it again."

Luc looked at her and waved it off. "Then come here, let me show you what you been missing. No biting this time." He then directed to Cherry. "Aye Cherry, move."

Hana lifted Cherry off of Luc before straddling him. When she got on, she let out a genuine moan and began grinding back and forth, letting out another as Luc became in tune with her movements. Luc felt a sudden stop and opened his eyes to see Hana staring at him. "Did I mention my father's name was Luc?" She asked.

Still in the throughs, Luc didn't register Hana spoke and sat up to kiss and suck on her breasts, taking a more active role by thrusting to his own tempo. Allowing her body to remember the long-lost touch of a warm-body man, Hana felt herself melt. She leaned to repeat herself, "My father's name was Luc. I *hated* my father."

Luc, realizing what was said, looked over to Cherry and saw a dark red pool forming under her neck. He began to panic and went to push Hana off. Hana grabbed him by the neck and Luc felt as though he was now pinned to the bed. She put a hand over his mouth, hearing muffled bits and pieces of questions. As she spoke, Hana slowly resumed grinding on him.

"My father's name was Luc, but I don't think it was short for something as stupid as Lucie. I hated him. I fucking hated *Him*." She changed to rhythmically lifting up and down, switching herself into a squat, changing her tempo as if to the bassline of a song only she heard. Luc's growing sensation of floating intensified as he found it impossible to divert from Hana's eyes. As she spoke, she went into cruise control, "I do love my brother, though, but you

disrespected him tonight. Nobody disrespects my brother."
She kept speed, feeling her carnal ascent with each descent.
"My father, he wasn't a nice man. I can tell you aren't either."
As she felt herself reaching, Hana raised her right arm above
her and made a single swipe across Luc St. Clair's face. Then
again with her left. As she did, Luc yelled through rasps.

"Get off me, bitch!" He said before finding the
strength to slap Hana. She turned back to him with a smirk
and dropped back into to her former straddle. "The fuck you
do to Cherry?" He yelled at her. "Cher-ry! Cherry?!"

Hana moaned as she rocked faster, summit
approaching. She clawed his chest, leaving four deep and
dark red trails. "I'm almost there," she moaned. "I just need
you to keep screamin' for me."

CHAPTER 12
Sunday

Nursing mild hangovers, Flip and Elena decided it might be better to go out for breakfast and drove over to EndZone, a sports-themed restaurant in the Second District with an underrated brunch menu. As they talked about their previous night Flip noticed a scrolling headline on the corner TV that made him stop eating:

BREAKING! DOUBLE HOMICIDE IN 4TH DISTRICT!

Flip interrupted Elena's story with a finger and yelled for the bartender to unmute the TV. Flip's stomach wasn't eased from what he heard:

"*--in the second-floor bathroom. Police have not determined whether these two situations are connected and offered no further comment. This is a still developing story.*"

Everything after briefly became a muffled sound of itself to Flip. He couldn't believe what he was seeing.

"--told me she won't be at the Center on Thursday. Said she got a date. She ain't say with who, but I think it's with that Dom guy. I-- Flip?" Elena tapped his plate with her fork. "Flip?" When he snapped back, he looked over to her and motioned over to the screen. Elena turned around to the TV and gasped. She turned just in time to see the reporter's face cut to the outside of Luc St. Clair's house, fully taped off and swarming with jacketed P'rotectors. As she followed with the reporter, she heard a muffled mob-comm ring and felt for her purse. It was Flip's.

"Cap?" Flip answered. "Yeah, watching it on the news right now."

A few more seconds.

"Now?" Flip looked at Elena.

"Shit. Ok, ok, I'm on my way." Flip then hung up and put his phone on the table. He took a few more forks of waffle and bit down. In between chews, he asked, "Wanna go to a drug dealer's house?"

"Do you have to go?" Elena asked. She knew the answer.

"They're asking for me, but you ain't gotta." Flip wiped his mouth with his napkin. "It might be messy." he burped. "I'm starting to regret eating so much."

"Can I stay in the car? I don't really wanna see inside. Send me the address." As she said it, a text message came across Flip's communicator. It was indeed the address to Luc St. Clair's house. Flip didn't want to see either, but Monroe's request to come there and not The Watering Hole interested him. After a few minutes of discussion, Flip got up and settled their bill while Elena gathered their things, and they made their way out.

"You feeling ok?" Elena asked while checking her mirrors.

"Yeah, just getting myself ready." Flip responded, tiredly, but assured. He laid his seat back into a flat.

"Aight. Let me know if I need to slow down."

"Drive slow, and I won't have to. Please."

Elena was about to respond until she looked over to a smirk. "Whatever." before shifting into gear and driving out of the EndZone's employee lot. As she got on the road, Flip closed his eyes and thought about his previous night. Nothing was out of the ordinary, except that girl and her lookalike date. He thought about the footprints at the Creek and the dark car that was there when he left. Something told him to believe that it was there, watching him the entire time.

◆ ◆ ◆

Flip woke up to Elena nudging him hard in the shoulder and calling his name.

"Flip, wake up. I think we're here." She said nervously.

When he was together, he sat up and leaned over to give Elena a kiss on the cheek. "I'll be back soon." He whispered to her.

"Not too soon. Take your time, I'll be here."

He kissed her again and got out the car. Elena then turned on the radio to a low volume and leaned her seat back. The radio hosts were debating the merits of a recent pastryfood trend in the south. News must not have reached them yet or they already started the show with it. She let them serve as the last likely positivity she'll be getting until Flip came back. Hopefully, this St. Clair situation was simpler than it looked.

As Flip took in everything as he walked. He noticed a lack of evidence tents like at the Creek, telling him he needed to steel himself for the interior. Last night's rain wasn't initially as heavy as he thought but saw it picked up at some point in the night. He also noticed a hell of a lot FCPD Vice agents walking around, mostly talking to the Scene Scanners. Monroe came out as he got to the front steps and closed the door behind him. Flip could see on his face that he was pissed or been thinking for a while. He's noticed they were interchangeable looks. He then saw Monroe unrolling some white gloves.

"Morning, Flip. If you're gonna touch stuff, here.

We're still not 100% on what does and doesn't have residue on it." Monroe said as he held out the gloves.

"I know, I know."

Monroe reopened the front door and let Flip walk in first. "Damn." The house didn't look like your "typical" drug dealer's place. There was a feeling of hominess to it; mature. There weren't a lot of photos. Flip looked over to the living room and saw a photo of what he assumed was an adolescent St. Clair with two women: one maybe in her early 20s and another noticeably older. Flip assumed it was maybe Grandma St. Clair and an older sister, or even his mother. Putting on his gloves, he moved around the room, looking at and occasionally touching items. His mind sent him back to his mother in his bedroom at home doing the exact same thing.

"We got the call in the early hours this morning. Door was closed but unlocked." Monroe called over to Flip. "Wallace is upstairs with the rest. Make sure you got them gloves on too."

Flip waved his hand to show that the gloves were indeed on. He continued tapping on photo frames and nearby furniture. Nothing. After a few minutes, he noticed the other P'rotectors nearby were starting to look at him and touched an antique, waist-high drink cart. It reminded him of one he remembered being in one investigator flick he watched as a kid with his mom. The lead character was being seduced by the wife of the red herring prime suspect while addressing her husband's guilt. He then felt a spark. *Flash.* He saw a really hazy scene of a woman being grabbed by St. Clair, a drink in-hand and two glasses on the cart. St. Clair looked like he was yelling something to her before she responded, and he pat her on the face and walked away. Then nothing.

He was back. The three P'rotectors in the room who noticed Flip Stokton suddenly freeze in place were staring at him, almost like they were waiting for him to say something. Flip walked back over to Monroe.

"Was there a third person here?" Flip asked him quietly.

"Yeah. It's actually one of the main reasons I wanted you here."

"Think the third person was involved?"

"We're still trying to figure it out. No trace of another victim, so it's possible. You ready for upstairs?" Monroe was already walking towards the base of the stairwell that led to the second floor.

"Guess so." Flip responded as he followed behind. "How is it?"

"Make sure to watch your step." As he finished, they were at the top of the stairs and in the hallway, looking into the main bedroom. Flip looked down the hall and saw a group of p'rotecs and scanners in the bathroom. Tents went between both rooms like a parade of miniature camp sites.

Flip let Monroe enter the bedroom first as he settled the fight between him and his stomach. It wasn't the sight of everything, it was the *smell*. The smell hit him, and he could almost taste its metallicity before he walked through the door. When he was able to settle his stomach, he walked in and looked over to Wallace. His eyes were busy looking at the bed. Another pusher and mover killed, nothing to write home about. Except for this one. This wasn't normal. Wallace looked up and nodded at Flip before going back to talking to Vice Agent Valer. Flip stayed on the outer rim of the room as he walked around the room, hands in his pockets this time. As he walked around the room, Valer leaned into Wallace's ear and whispered, "Why is Flip Stokton at our scene? He an undercover now?"

Wallace whispered back, "Nah, he's been working with us for a little bit as Consult. CP's trying to get him onto the Shockley case."

"Uh-huh. Taller than he looked on TV."

"I said the same thing."

Valer broke from Wallace and went over to Flip. He seemed *much* taller now that she stood right next to him. When turned he saw that her hand was already extended to him.

"Flip Stokton?" Valer said to him, hand still extended.

Flip met her and shook. "I thought people normally say *their* name first in introduction?" *Flash.* He saw hazy film over the façade of the Golden Night motel. Wallace's car was in the parking lot. Agent Valer was walking to room 19. Then nothing. Flip returned to see an anticipating look on Agent Valer's face, as if waiting for him to speak. "My bad, we ain't met before, right? I was just trying to place your face."

Agent Valer chuckled. "Funny man. Joh'n told me you're one to joke." He didn't.

Flip glanced to Wallace. *Joh'n?* Flip almost forgot Wallace had a first name, let alone a strange woman using the shorthand of it. "Nice of him, but yeah, my name's Flip. Yours?" This woman was very pretty, even attractive, in her uniform. Like if *Torina Vice* had a female-led offshoot. The FCPD Vice jacket wasn't the most flattering piece of clothing, but Flip could still see by her arms that she had some definition to her. She reminded him of Elena, only a few shades lighter and half a foot shorter, heels off. He looked back at Wallace for a second as he walked to Monroe. He'd never been on a serious crime scene with him before, but he was quieter than usual. *Interesting.*

"Camailla Valer, nice to meet you." She gave her card to Flip. He glanced at it before putting it into his pocket. "You helping the big guy on this?"

Flip stifled and responded, "Haven't made my mind up yet." *She just say Valer? "Big guy"?*

Agent Valer tamed the urge to investigate what she felt was about to be a laugh. She hated when people laughed to themselves; only the crazy and the untrustworthy did it. "Funny way of showing it, coming to a scene like this. I was told you normally help with the pettier stuff."

"Wasn't much of a choice." As he answered, Flip nodded to Monroe, who was walking over to Wallace and another scene tech.

"Well, either way, it was good to meet you, Founder." As she spoke, Valer's comm rang and she left as she answered.

Flip walked around the room some more. Even with gloves on, he was still in a drug dealer's house; bedroom, no less. No telling what he'd see from the most innocent of items. He decided to wait and went over to Wallace and Monroe. "What's up Wallace, or should I start calling you *Joh'n*?" He then looked over and got a too detailed view of what he saw across the room. Luc St. Clair, rising player in the Fountain drug scene, was now victim of a rare outcome of his career choice: death by carnal conduit. Flip also noticed the large pool of blood off of St. Clair's left, and how it was lower than where he would expect to find a romantic partner. Then it hit him.

"Flip, let's keep it at Wallace, or P'rotector." Wallace interjected into his train of thought.

"I thought on the news, they said there was a *double*

homicide. St. Clair's one, the body at the Hole makes two." Flip then pointed to the blood pool. "Reporters get their story wrong?"

"Nah man, they got it right. We have two bodies, but there's a third victim. We found her right there, barely holding on. This girl laying on the bed, huge slash across her neck. Medi-Mages say she woulda completely bled out given another half-hour."

The way Wallace doubled down on the blood loss made Flip unsettled more than he already was. He looked at St. Clair with more observation, doing his best to hold his stomach and nose. He saw the slashes across both sides and the heavy bruises that dotted his face; the much deeper slashes down the chest and how similar they all looked with each overlapping set. They weren't exactly evenly spaced but everything looked similar. If these were done by a knife, the wielder had to have taken their time, and meant to. These looked like they could've been made by hand, by *a hand* specifically, like if a woman let her manicurist to shape her nails into fashionable weapons.

"We think she was a nightgirl." Wallace added. "ID in her purse, couple SoftSheaths, hefty fold of scril. Whoever did this, they had time to take a shower when they were finished. Scanners are sure Luc here at least got a last one out before dying. What a way to go." Wallace said the last part to himself as he went into his jacket his notebook. He wrote something down before ripping off the paper and folding it over, then writing on the new side and handed it to Flip. When Flip read both portions, he didn't like what he saw:

Outside

This one has teeth

Monroe, only a few feet away with a scene

photographer, didn't see the exchange and Flip decided he didn't need to know or already did. He nodded and continued looking over the scene, tapping his jacket pockets as he walked around. *Shit.*

"Need something?" Wallace asked him.

"Nah, just forgot my notebook in the car."

Wallace brought out his and ripped a few pages out and held them out to Flip. "Need a pen too?"

"Yeah." Flip took the pen and paper and wrote immediately.

Vi'nnakan. Again. Other girl possibly too.

"Was the girl y'all found *Vi'nnakan* too?"

"Yeah, why?" Wallace answered back.

"Just asking." Flip went back into his notes.

Fucking Luc St. Clair

Three glasses on the nightstand. Two completely full.

Killed in bed. No mention of break-in. Knew his killer? In bed with her (or him)?

At his last note, Flip looked up from his paper and asked aloud, "You think this was a group thing? Not just him and the girl y'all found? Maybe St. Clair invited the third person here?" Everyone stopped what they were doing and looked at Flip. "Maybe they weren't getting enough attention." He quietly chuckled. "They got a little jealous?" He laughed again.

"We did bounce that around, but it's nothing to confirm. We at least know that the person didn't have to force their way in." Monroe answered him after a second-long pause. He didn't find anything funny about the past few days. First, a body in East Pike on Friday. Now, less than 48 hours later, a double-murder in two places roughly 40 minutes from each other. "Scanners confirmed there was sexual activity but right now it's assumed to be with the girl we found until we know our third party. She's in no shape to talk so we got her over at Fountain Memorial. Right now--"

Flip walked over to the side of the bed where the puddle was. He assumed this was where they found the girl. It was unsettling at how neat it was, but also curious. He looked at how the middle of it still had a shine but fanned out to dried dark-brown edges, no sign of being disturbed or even as violently made compared to St. Clair's wounds. Flip took a moment and went for it. He took a finger and pressed into the wet portion. Nothing.

He cursed to himself and undid the glove enough to free a single finger and went again. *Flash*. For a few seconds, he saw multiple scenes of Cherry and Luc: First, in the club with the rest of the Boys and a few other women. Quick cut to a hand slapping her across the face. Even in the darkness of the section, he could tell the hand didn't belong to St. Clair but he couldn't see the owner. Next, he saw Cherry at the door while St. Clair and another woman were on the bed. There was some talk, but Flip couldn't hear it. He did have a better view of the second woman, albeit from behind. She had semi-long hair, probably no further than just under the shoulder. A little pale. Not just lighter in skin tone, but pale. It was above sickly, but not by much. There was something about her that seemed familiar. He then saw a hand go across the under of Cherry's neck as she had her turn with St. Clair. If only he could see the face of those hands. Then nothing. Flip then felt himself hunching over.

"Stokton? You ok" Monroe's voice was coming in as a loud muffle at first. "Stokton?" As Flip was standing up, the

175

room felt realigned, but he was the center post. A switch turned and he looked at Wallace and made an eye movement towards the door. Monroe called out again, "Hey, you ok, son?" He was already at Flip's side, hand on his shoulder.

"Yeah, I'm good. I just need some air real quick."

"I'll walk him out." Wallace called out before Monroe could respond.

"Take it easy Flip. If you don't want to come back up, it's fine. I'll be in touch." Monroe told him as they went to the doorway. Flip's face told him that he saw something, and a lot of it. It was less than 10 seconds of what looked like Flip was staring at the bloodstain but after a few call-to's, he knew what was happening. Fleice used to look straight ahead like she was listening to someone that wasn't there. There was a small hope he saw the third person. Monroe wasn't sure which would be worse: that it's not the same person who did this, The Watering Hole *and* the Shockley murders, or if it was. The last thing he needed right now was a serial killer setting up shop in his Territory. Fountain wasn't a metropolis by standard means, but it's enough day-to-day bullshit to keep everyone busy as it was.

When Flip and Wallace got outside, Flip saw Agent Valer and Elena talking. Once they were outside of earshot for most of the P'rotectors and agents working outside, Flip finished cleaning his finger and made a slight thumb-point behind him. "That why you're not giving Hazel a shot?" There was little change in Wallace's face but Flip noticed it. In typical Wallace fashion, he kept it cool. Flip put the stained paper into his balled gloves.

"Damn, what you got, birds talking in your ears?" Wallace coolly responded. Typical. Not exactly a confirmation but not a denial either. "Yeah, we had something a little while back. Sometimes, we still do. I actually talked to Hazel before I left. We might do something soon." He had a smile forming when he said the last detail. Flip let him have it.

"So, there's teeth on this one too? You mean the girl or St. Clair?" Flip asked.

"Definitely St. Clair. The girl apparently goes by Cherry according to a P'rotector that's pulled her before on some undercover shit. Responding p'rotec said she didn't have anything aside from the slice across the neck. Aside from that and a reddening on her cheek, she was spotless. Maybe St. Clair got a little rough."

"Or the other woman."

Wallace's eyes went wide for a second, but he kept his face still. St. Clair didn't seem like the type to share his toys with another guy. He only assumed there was a second woman but didn't actually expect it to be true. His going theory was that someone set up St. Clair to take out the competition or settle a grievance. Until he saw the teeth markings.

"You think this other woman was the killer?" Wallace asked as he took off his gloves.

"I don't know, but I'm positive he didn't see it coming. When I was downstairs, I saw that Cherry was making three drinks and then upstairs I saw some more. She was in the Hole with St. Clair and his crew but at some point, somebody slapped the shit outta her. It wasn't Luc and I couldn't see the one who did, but it was definitely a woman's hand. When they came back here, seems like the third party was able to get her turn with Luc. She might be *Vi'nnakan*, but she was pale, almost sick. I think it's the same person that slapped her."

Wallace nodded his head along with what Flip told him and took the abrupt ending as that was all he saw, or the gist of it. He still didn't really get how the whole "seeing" stuff worked. It reminded him of Fleice Stokton when he was her junior partner. The only difference was that Fleice used to speak in riddles when she spoke about it all the damn time, at least Flip was straight-up. By the time Wallace came back to Fountain City, he had only heard rumors Lead Homicide P'rotector Stokton always had way of knowing when something would happen, or exactly how it did. When he had gotten word that she asked for him specifically for partner, he was beyond nervous. He'd been on for a few years and only knew her previous partner was caught in an Internal Audit Fleice herself participated in based on info from a "personal CI", as she called it. At the end of it, she was proven to be right. That Junior P'rotector was indeed on the take, along with five other street-level P'rotectors, and they were promptly thrown off the force. No pension, no benefits. Those sympathetic to the accused felt that the whole thing was unethical and Fleice herself should have been thrown off the force for conducting such an operation against one of her own. Her own partner, no less. Those who simply weren't a fan of taking their directions from a *vi'nnak* woman, Founding Family or not, tried to infect others with the rumor that Stokton was in deep with the corruption, and used IA as a way to not only throw the scent off herself but take down her accomplices in the process. Wallace wasn't sure what to believe until he worked with the woman herself. No way she would be in on some lowlife shit like that, the woman was a fucking Founder.

"Interesting." Wallace said to him. Flip couldn't tell if it was an "interesting" in the sense that that was all or that it was more than Wallace expected to hear. Wallace had some of the puzzle together, but Flip's story helped add a few more pieces. "We still haven't heard from Alexis. Valer hasn't been able to reach her and she's getting nervous. I am too. It's not like her to miss a check-in for days at a time." He reached in his jacket for a metal tube. Opening it, he tilted out the remaining half of a cigar and lit it. After a few quick pulls he resumed. "You know, I've had my share of missing persons, Flip. Sometimes you find them laying low somewhere, but that was the outlier, especially if they were working with Vice 'tecs. 'Tween you me, we might be already looking for a cold one."

Flip looked back over to Elena but didn't see Agent Valer anymore. Elena saw him and waved and jokingly looked at her wrist as if she had a watch on. Flip held up a five. He then went back to Wallace. "You think the person that did all of this is the same who took Alexis?"

"It's still too early to say for sure, man," He took a quick puff. "but I'm willing to lay some scril down that it is." Wallace this time looked over to Elena and waved, before looking back towards the house and seeing Agent Valer motioning him to come over. She was on the phone but her eyes were growing wide and her motioning became more vigorous. "Aight brother, I'll see ya later." Wallace took a final puff, put the cigar back in the tube, and walked over to Agent Valer.

Flip walked across the yard, taking a more observant look around as he did. After tossing his gloves into a trashcan at the field-station, he looked the car sloppily parked in the driveway. St. Clair's car, an impeccably clean late-model and noticeably modified maroon Suban M4, sat silently, patiently waiting for a master that's not coming back. Flip took an extended look at the car and silently thought to himself about if the third woman he saw had left a print on the doorhandle or the car itself. When he got to his own, he stopped Elena from tossing him the keys and went to the passenger seat. When they got in, Flip kissed her on the cheek and leaned back into his seat.

"Bad in there?" Elena asked him as she started up.

"Yeah. Somebody either wanted to make an example or had a grudge. I saw a few things."

Elena knew what he meant but wasn't sure if she wanted to know any more right now. She let the car sit for a few seconds and turned the radio down, looking over to him as she did. "Wanna go home? Maybe talk about it?" Flip didn't cover murders in his work and secretly hoped this wasn't going to be his start. She thought of Fleice and began wondering if her focus in homicide had any influence on her current state. She thought about her next question. "Are you going to take it up?" The question hung in the air like the start of a bad smell.

"I don't know, Olga. Part of me wants to, part of me doesn't. Shit, part of me wishes I didn't even meet up with CaP on Friday." Flip let out a sigh and closed his eyes. "If you want to go home, it's cool."

"And what if I *don't* want to go home? You didn't even ask." Elena heard her response had more bite to it but she stuck by it.

"Do you want to go home?" Flip asked, eyes still closed.

"No. What I *want* to do is talk to you about something interesting that Agent Valer told me and what Penny texted me while you were inside being Investigator." She put Joy into gear and started driving. "Did you know about Alexis Valer going missing?"

Flip opened his eyes and quickly sat his seat up. He

began fishing for the card Agent Valer gave him. "Valer? As in--"

"As in *Valer*, like Agent Camailla Valer, formerly Valer-K'al, yes. She's her cousin on her father's side. Why didn't you tell me?"

"Elena, I don't want to argue. I was going to ask you about it today before I got the call to come here. I just didn't expect a Vice Agent I just met to beat me to it." Flip felt his voice and temper start to raise.

"I'm not trying to argue Flip, I was just asking a question. Alexis hasn't been to her meetings the past couple weeks and now I'm hearing she's been missing for the past couple days. I'm just worried, that's all."

"Olga, I swear I didn't know until last night."

"You said that already. Now, do *you* want to go home or should I just drive around the city until we're out of gas?"

There was a pause before Flip answered. "Can we at least get some gas first?"

"Sure."

The ride to the gas station was in relative silence, aside from the radio. Elena told Flip about what her and Agent Valer talked about, which was mostly about Alexis, and that Penny texted her saying that she saw the mean lady and her brother from the diner at the Hole sometime after Flip and Elena left. Something about them didn't seem right. Elena had no clue what mean lady she was talking about but said she'd mention it to Flip. He asked if Penny gave a description of the lady and Elena answered with a negative. Flip made a mental note to follow-up. What made this lady special out of all the customers she's interacted with before? As Flip pumped gas, he kept replaying the scene he saw while in the bedroom. He couldn't help but think about the other woman and then the woman from the Hole. Was she pale? He couldn't tell, but It said that there was *a* pale woman there at some point. It can't be the same person he saw, could it? There were a lot of people there last night and it was dark. Maybe Penny was mistaken.

As they rode over to Elena's, Flip felt he needed to look over the Shockley papers again. He remembered the portion that talked about Fountain City, and that one of the last charges involved something with kids. Didn't Monroe say something about him possibly having kids. "Hey Olga?"

"Yes, Love?" She kept looking forward, at the now growing Sunday afternoon traffic.

"Any kids that come to the Center with the last name Shockley? At this point they should be at least teenagers. Or anyone that works there?"

Elena was quiet for a few seconds to think about the many kids that come in and out on a regular basis. She knew the name sounded familiar and thought about a volunteer that helped at the Kid's Fair last summer had the last name Shockley. They were about 19 or 20 but she never spoke to them personally. "I think we had a volunteer with that name, but I can't remember. I know we don't have anyone on staff with that name. Want me to ask Ms. Ingram about it?"

"Yeah, you may have to. I think there's something I'm missing. You talked to Hazel today?"

"No but I tried calling her as soon as you went inside." She made a left at the light into a roundabout and got off at the second exit. "She's fine, just really shaken up. She said a bartender found the body just after last call." A few minutes later they were pulling in next to Elena's Suban. She liked her car but never felt the same attachment enough to name it like Flip. Elena looked over to her car as she turned Joy off. It was a nice car, even if it wasn't necessary. She had a perfectly good Suban before, one she even liked a little more than her current, but daddy knew best. He just knew she was going to love this one. It may be a year behind but rode way smoother than the newer model and the color was one of a kind. Elena had stopped protesting his gifts after her 17th birthday when she specifically asked that he not get her anything and instead found her bedroom had been completely redone with new handmade wooden furniture after a late practice. She was more excited about the basketball she found on the bed, two-tone dyed in the Starks family colors with her and her mother's names stitched on and a handwritten note taped to it:

> *Elena,*
> *I figured you would probably enjoy this more than*
> *furniture. You have grown into a young woman that*
> *brings your mother and I great pride. I love you, now*
> *and always, my precious Matriarch.*
> *Daddy*

As Elena got out to go open the door, Flip thought about Penny as he opened the console to check for the Shockley sheet. He needed to look at those charges again. There's got be something there. He also needed to talk to Penny. There's got to be something more to this "mean lady" that made her stick out than a coincidental sighting. It was a soggy Sunday afternoon, and he had no plans to go anywhere, at least not yet, so he figured he could do a little work while he was here. Elena saw him stuff the folded papers in his pocket as she opened the door, "If you're gonna work, you can use the living room." and went inside to deactivate the alarm system.

Walking inside the house, closing and locking the door, he snuck behind Elena and held her by the waist, kissing her lightly on the nape of her neck.

"I thought you were going to work?"

"I can't give you a kiss?"

"Mmhmm, ok." She kept her back to him but moved closer into him. "You sure that's it?"

Flip felt himself waking up but went against it. "Yeah, I'm sure."

Elena turned around to him and kissed him. "Ok. I'll be back in a few." She went towards the stairs and headed up.

Flip went into the living room and sat. He immediately unfolded the papers and went to the page with the Fountain City charges and read them over again:

June's Fire 7, X182 T.U – Breaking and Entering
Plea of No Contest; Sentenced 3 months

OhrsDusk 24, X182 T.U – Domestic Assault
Charges dropped

Decimbjr 3, X182 T.U – Domestic Assault
Plea of Guilty; Sentenced 1 year

Final Frost 25, X184 T.U – Unlawful Posses. of Firearm
Plea of Guilty; Sentenced 1 year; Served 11 months

Augest 16, X187 T.U – 1st Degree Child Endangerment

Plea of Not Guilty; Sentenced 5 years; Served 4 years
Mirci 23, X198 T.U – 1ˢᵗ Degree Child Endangerment Plead
of No Contest; Sentenced 7 years

Flip noticed the next charge started a relatively light peppering of mostly misdemeanor charges in West Pike but homed in on the last two Fountain charges: *1ˢᵗ Degree Child Endangerment*. Somewhere after his second domestic assault somebody was willing to keep kids around this asshole. Flip felt it was the same person who was on the receiving end of the domestic charges. Shockley managed to chill out for a few years before he proved the adage that some people don't change. Flip took a nearby pen and circled the endangerment charges. He didn't serve the full terms, but they were the only two related to children. There's got to be more to it, he could feel it. Flip set the paper aside and continued reviewing the following charges. Mostly breaking and entering throughout Redwater with the occasional larceny thrown in for flavor. No other endangerment charges though, meaning he either stayed away or they went unreported. Based on what Monroe said about Shockley's proclivity to bounce around, Flip bet on the former.

By the time Elena came back downstairs, Flip was in the kitchen raiding the snack cabinet. Now it was Elena's turn to sneak up on him. Flip pretended not to hear and continued looking in the cabinet. He then felt arms wrap around him. "You know, you look a lot like my boyfriend."

Flip smiled and continued rummaging, "Maybe he's got a twin."

Elena had a smile of her own, "Don't think so. His brother don't look that much like him." before turning him around and planting a kiss. "Hi."

"Hi." Flip gave her a kiss of his own and took in her

house look. Even in a sports bra and basketball shorts, she looked as good as ever. "What's up?"

"Learn anything?"

"Nothing new, but something interesting. Two things, actually."

"What is it? Or can't you share?"

They sat at the living room table and Flip showed her the two endangerment charges before telling her about the St. Clair scene. He had his own opinions on how the timing of the murders and kidnapping were almost too close together for two or three people to operate so close together and not be working together. When he talked about the marks Wallace noticed on St. Clair, Elena asked him something that he would've taken for a joke if it wasn't for her tone. "Flip, do you think vampyrs exist? Like for real?"

"Like on some Lord Dra'co shit? Nah, I don't think that shit's real." Flip had to stifle a laugh. He still wasn't sure if Elena was joking or not. She could commit to a bit when she wanted to. A few seconds of no response told him this wasn't a joke.

"I can separate movies from real life, Flip. Before she got sick, my mother used to tell me about this family that moved into her village when she was a girl. They went by the name of Sarin, but my mother said she never believed it. Typical family: husband, wife, a couple kids. She said they lived on the outside edge of the village, not exactly isolation but far enough to have privacy. They were generally nice, just considered a little weird since they usually seen after the sun went down, unless they really needed to come into town. People would keep their distance from the father whenever he came. A year after they arrived, people started noticing other villagers had been going missing. Then two kids disappeared after going into the woods and never came back. A search party looked for them for weeks. As a child, I used to think she just made it up to scare me. One of the last things she told me in the hospital was the full story."

Flip could tell this wasn't a joke and Elena sounded as though she was getting anxious. He got up to prep the kettle for tea and went back to his seat. "What happened to the kids? They ever find them?"

"That's the thing, nobody knows." She had never told Flip this story and didn't expect him to believe her. For years, she wasn't sure she believed it herself, but she did believe her mother wouldn't lie to her on what she knew would be her deathbed. "They never found the kids, just scraps of clothes in a clearing children used to go and play. It was assumed that the children may have been attacked by wolves or something, but when the party began focusing on the Sarin property to question the father, the place was empty save for spoiled food and the furniture. It was as if nobody lived in the house to begin with, except for the cellar." Elena took a pause to collect herself. There was no way her mother would embellish the next part. "In the cellar, they found horrible things, Flip. Bodies chained to the wall. People from other villages crudely buried under the floor, blood everywhere. Against a far wall was a table that resembled an altar with a man's body laid across. My grandfather and great-uncle were in the search party and what they described still chills me to think about. There was a woman, a local that was known to be really sick, barely alive and chained to the wall when they came down there. All she would ask was 'Where is Master? Is he coming back for me? He said that he would.' It was the only thing she would say other than that she was very hungry."

The loud click of the kettle indicated the water was

ready and she got up to make two cups. Putting the tea and sweeteners on a tray, she brought them to the table. Flip could tell there was more to this story and held his questions as he made his cup.

"When they found her and the corpses, they noticed they all had varying degrees of the same thing: two identical marks, mostly to the side of their necks. The dead felt lighter than they should. Mom said the party wanted to kill the woman to put her out of her misery, but her husband was back at the village, and they decided it should be up to him. They brought her home, but she never talked about what happened in that house. She wasn't the same; only coming outside on cloudy days or after dark and walk aimlessly, only once did she make it out and go back to the Sarin house. Her husband was worse. After a while, he seemed to never *not* be outside. My uncle would ask him about the wife's condition and the husband would only look at him and not answer. Three months later, after the bodies were all burned or buried and the Sarin house was torn down, there was talk circulating that the husband hadn't been seen in a few days and their livestock was beginning to dwindle in numbers. The chief Medi-Mage made a house call and found the wife hunched over her husband's body, head to his neck. She looked as if crying. When he got closer, he saw that she was in fact biting into his neck. She was drinking his blood, Flip. The doctor said that when he saw the wife's eyes, he swore that they were on fire. She was feral, like a desperate animal that needed food and would settle for anything. That same day, a group went to the house. They lost a few men but was able to subdue and bind the wife. They kept her in the town hold and by nightfall, a stake was erected in the center of town. She was burned the next morning in front of everybody after being declared a vessel of the Red One."

Elena's voice was breaking up and she took a sip of tea. "That poor woman's final words were what my mom said stuck with her the most. Before they lit the stake, the wife said, 'He promised he would come back. He promised.' and kept asking where 'Master' was. The belief was that her cries weren't from the flames but rather the hurt of knowing she was left behind. My mother said that her skin looked as if being turned into glass. When they checked the husband, he had the same marks, so they burned and buried his body next to his wife outside of the village edge. Since then, outsiders were no longer welcomed." She took another sip and let the story sit in the air between them. Flip had no rebuttal and sipped with her. It was a fruit-mint blend. Not his personal favorite, but wholly unimportant in the current moment.

"Guess that explains why y'all always had so many Marks around your house."

"Yep. Dad figured since they been doing it for so long, there was no need to stop. He liked to always say, 'Just in case your mother was right.'" Elena dabbed at her eye with a napkin. She didn't mean to cry. It's been 16 years since Matriarch Rubina K'Ivana Starks passed, and this was a hell of a way to remember her now. Elena had been through with the tears. Or so she thought. "She wasn't superstitious, but she sure as hell believed in whatever happened that year. I don't think you truly understood how much OhrsDusk used to be a very anxious month for the Starks household." With that, Elena let out a soft laugh, then a louder one at a memory of her mother berating a classmate dressed as Lord Dra'co when Other's Eve fell on a school day and students got to attend class in costume. She continued to laugh as that memory blended into another one of her mother's self-awareness when she and her husband decided to dress as Sanctum Speakers one year. They pretended to "banish" trick-or-treaters dressed as vampyrs. Elena was glad that, now, her mother never had to worry about vampyr again.

Flip continued to sip his tea as he let Elena have her reminiscence party for one. He didn't know Mrs. Starks as well as Elena knew his mother, but he did know she always smelled good, was kind of funny, and could cook her ass off. He spent many a weekend meal at the Starks home, eating a seemingly endless supply and variety of things called vareneyogi. They looked a lot like the dumplings Ms. Ata would make when celebrating her homeland's New Year but with more options of filling. There was a sliced pork dish she used to make sometimes but he couldn't recall the name, only that it was good. Rare was the occasion he would have the same vareneyogi filling two visits in a row.

Hana got in almost a full 12hrs since Rac' last saw her. She was sweaty, tired, and fully flushed of last night's party. After she left Luc's house, she decided to walk home. Luckily, she was able to hitch a ride the last few miles with a nice family going through Monarch to the northern beaches of Saphily. She enjoyed her ride with the family and decided there was no reason they shouldn't reach their destination in one piece, especially when she looked at the children. The father, a slender, older man, was recently retired and the mother was a seamstress opening her first store in Saphily. The son was their biological child, and the daughter was adopted at birth. They were nice people, even offering her a sandwich from their cooler to have during the ride. When asked about why she was walking along the road, Hana told them she was at Pike's Creek birdwatching and her brother forgot to come pick her up. That garnered a laugh from the wife. She thanked the family as they let her out at the start of the trail leading to the house, giving them a few scril for gas and their hospitality. She even waved at the daughter when she turned around to look at Hana through the back window. The little girl waved back with a smile.

When she entered the house, she called out, "Rac'? I'm home."

No answer.

"Rac'?"

Nothing.

She started to explore the first floor, starting with the kitchen. When she entered, she immediately focused on two plates of half-eaten food. The first had a bloody burger with a few straggling fries while the other was much cleaner and relatively emptier with a few empty leaves of spinach and halved baby tomatoes. *A date?* That was when she noticed there were broken pieces of what looked like a mob-comm on both the kitchen island table next to the plates and the floor. She couldn't tell how long it was all there, but her nose said the food had to be somewhat recent, as the faded smell of cooked meat was still in the air. Rac' always forgot to turn the vent on when he cooked. Maybe he allowed that whore a last meal.

Through Rac's door, she could hear a rhythm of grunts and bed noises. Seems like he was enjoying his Sunday with his pet. In between the grunting, Hana thought she could here Alexis calling out, but it sounded dry and forced. Either Rac' was choking her, or this has been going on long enough for Alexis' voice to give out. Hana was pleased and quietly moved her head from the door and slipped into her room, making sure to quietly close the door behind her. She can talk to him later. Almost throwing herself onto her bed, Hana replayed last night through her head as she undressed, fingertips slowly circling her nipples after taking off her bra. She reached into her jacket pocket and sat St. Clair's party bag on the nightstand. Fully nude, she went to the window closest to her bed and raised the window halfway to allow the afternoon air to fill the room with the sounds and smells of a wet spring afternoon.

Rac' smelled Hana come up the steps and approach the door. He couldn't tell how long she was there but thought he heard her door close eventually. Alexis had spoken back to him during lunch and had to be taught another lesson. Her mobile had rung and when questioned about who the fuck Camailla was, made a disgusting retort about Mama. He wanted to kill her on the spot but settled with smashing the communicator. This would serve as a learning experience, and he was going to make sure she got it. A quick slap across the face across the face served as the stamp of his message, but that wasn't enough. He needed to nip her in the bud. She put up a fight, but another slap turned into a hold on her hair in one motion.

Alexis clawed and screamed for help but knew that nobody was coming for her. She then found herself being pulled across the floor and up the stairs. When she realized what was about to happen, she fought with a desperation she's never had to even with her most problematic of clients. On the third step from the top, she managed to get her footing on one leg and stood a quarter the way up before feeling the whiplash of being slammed back to the floor. The landing and speed stunned her, and she felt the fight in her leave instantly. She heard a door open and was picked up and carried to the bed. When she was tossed on, Alexis curled into a far corner post, making her last stand a feeble matter of how long she can scream before Rac' reached her. She clocked in at five seconds before feeling his hand grip and pull her towards him, leaving deep claw marks along her lower calf as she gave a futile effort to kick herself free. This was going to be a learning experience; a necessary one.

When Hana woke, the sun was already beginning to set. The rain had been maintaining a steady drizzle for about a little over an hour now but the room was humid. The songs of the birds in the nearby woods had given way to the insect chorus of dusk. The sun, not completely down but behind the tree-line, made her room darker than the time said it should be. That's why she grown to like this room, the darkness. When they were children, this room used to be Rac's, and after they removed *Him* from their lives, her first night alone turned into three undisturbed days of sleep. She didn't have to think about *Him* coming in, rustling her leg and edging the covers down. Hana was telling the truth when she told Luc their current state was the nicest thing *He* had done for her and her brother, it gave them the power to overtake him and make him pay for the years of hurt, to them and their mother. She had her faults but didn't deserve what came to her.

Hana left her room and noticed how quiet it was in Rac's. Quiet, save for the muffled sounds of crying. She decided to go in. She surveyed the room and took in the damage as well as the smell. Blood was in the air like a morbid perfume. The last bit of sunlight stayed on Alexis' side of the room while Hana kept herself in the dark by the door. Alexis was too busy crying into her pillow to notice she wasn't alone.

"Alexis?" Hana said quietly.

Alexis turned with a start and tried to scream. She had no energy to even feign resistance and for the first time consciously allowed whatever was about to happen and curled into a ball as close as she could to her chained arm. She was scared of Rac' and his brutality, but this girl terrified her. She could barely see Hana in the corner, only the outline. Her right eye was almost swollen shut. Her left wasn't much better, as when she tried to focus there were two figures in the corner. She assumed it was from her tears or blood loss, maybe both, and slowly wiped her face with her free arm. Upon trying to focus again, she started to cry again.

"Please...Please let me go. I promise--"

"You promise you won't tell anyone, right?" Hana quickly cut in.

Alexis didn't respond except with more tears. Hana took a few paces forward into the remaining light and Alexis instinctively flinched. She also could see that Hana was completely naked under her lacework robe and tried to back up more, knowing she was already against the wall. As Hana came closer, Alexis could see the full extent of the burn, and for even in her state, felt a sympathetic curiosity. She knew this was the end, she was sure of it. As she made her peace, Hana walked over to her chained side and sat on the bed with her.

"Please let me go. I promise." Alexis could only manage a whisper. She'd do anything to get out of her restraint, let alone this house. Her body trembled all over, a mixture of Rac's teaching and the throbbing start of Rock withdrawal. If she was still in her heyday, she would've probably tried to gnaw her arm off from the pain of withdrawal alone. Rac's lesson would have been child's play to how it feels when you *need* that Rock. Nothing else mattered. Pain. Pleasure. There was no real difference. Rock beats everything, and until you got it, you'd do anything you had to in order to get it. Anything. No matter with who or how many, even money was a secondary concern, she'd settle up after she had her fix. At 24, Alexis was proud to say that those days were long gone and that she would never go back to that version of her. She just got her six-month token from NA last month, though she still did a bump or two now and then. Nothing recreational, just something to breeze through customers from time to time, sometimes a line to satisfy a big spender like Luc to calm his paranoid moments. Now, faced with what she was sure would be the last conversation she would have on this plane, a part of her wanted to throw it all away for a fat rail and coast into the hereafter feeling good.

As if she was reading her mind, Hana moved up closer to her and whispered. "Would you like a treat?"

Alexis tried to stifle her trembling but couldn't. *A treat?* Her face was a collage of bruises and blood, but Hana could make out the look of confusion. By this time, Alexis has learned the hard way that an offered meal in this house led to anything but hospitality.

"I'm not... I'm not hungry."

SMACK!

"Did I ask if you were hungry?"

There was a hoarse yelp as Hana let her hand linger and hold Alexis' face, forcing her to look her in the eyes. It felt like someone was holding an ice pack to her face. Just like her brother and the coldness of his body pressed against her own; the ice pick that would enter and exit her. She could see what looked like a flickering light in her eyes, and she felt liquid fear leave. Moonlight began to come through the window, and she could see that Hana was now looking towards the bed. She thought she could make out a smile.

"N-N-N-No. Please don't hit me again." Alexis pleaded.

Hana shifted her look back to her. "I'm gonna ask you again, do you want a treat?"

"No." Alexis was positive that she gave the wrong answer once it left her lips and braced herself.

"You sure? I think you'll like it." With that Hana got up and left the room, reentering with a clear sack filled with what looked like sand. She went back to her place next to Alexis and treated herself to a sniff. "Here." She held the bag out to Alexis. It was so close, Alexis thought she was going to force it onto her face. She then realized what it was and who it belonged to. Luc had a unique, floral-like scent to his brand of Rock. He said he would mix grounded roseleaf into the last stage of cooking. Alexis felt her body tremble. No longer from fear, but from want and anticipation. It's been a while since she's seen so much in one place again.

"This is really good stuff. I've never had it until last night, but you can say I like how it smells." Hana laughed lightly. "It really did something to me, so I can only imagine how it feels for you regular people. Especially when it's been a while." Hana continued to hold the bag to Alexis' face. She could see that Alexis' eyes were now more focused on the bag than her. "I saw your little token downstairs. Congratulations."

"N-No. I don't want any." If her voice wasn't so shot, it may have been convincing.

"Ok." Hana looked Alexis over. She looked more like a target sheet. There were bite marks everywhere: her arms, legs, a shallow pair on the neck. Hana got up and patted Alexis' cheek, eliciting a flinch. "Do you want to live, Alexis?"

"Yes." Alexis said back.

"Yes, what?" Hana kept her hand where it was.

"Yes..."

SLAP!

"Yes, *what?*" Hana tried not to raise her voice. "Answer me." She could feel herself growing impatient. "Now."

"Yes... I forgot your name... Please, don't hit me again, I'm really sorry." Alexis tensed in anticipation.

"Hana, but you will call me Mother from now on, hear me? I'm Mother. You're Whore."

There was silence as they looked at each other and then another popping slap came from Hana's right, it was a hard one that caused Alexis' jaw to click.

"Did you hear me? Please, don't make me ask again."

"Yes... Mother." Alexis felt her jaw click again.

"Good girl. Keep it up and I'll fix that clicking." Hana petted Alexis' face again and made her way to the door. Before she opened it, she turned, cloaked in lace and darkness. Alexis couldn't make out her lips, only two orange-red orbs where her eyes should be. They stayed on her for a few seconds.

"Yes... Mother." There was another sharp click.

"Good girl. You'll get some water soon, and maybe we can get you cleaned up." Hana opened the door and left, closing it behind her. She went into the sunroom, where she found Rac' sitting with headphones on connected to his mobile. He was rewatching the news coverage of his work at the Hole. After a few seconds Rac' looked up and immediately lowered his head again.

"Close your robe!" He still had his headphones on and didn't realize how loud he was. Hana leaned over more than necessary and took them off.

"Don't act like that. It's nothing you haven't seen before, little brother." She took the headphones and rested them on her neck.

"Where were you last night? Did you do this?" He turned his phone around to show her the segment talking about drug dealer Luc St. Clair having been found murdered in his home. St. Clair had been the target of a Fountain Vice Squad investigation over the past three years. A second unidentified woman was also hurt and currently in critical condition. As of now, potential suspects have not been publicly identified.

She held up her bag as if it was an award. "Maybe. Did you kill that guy they found at the club?"

"He made fun of me." Rac' responded.

"And so did he." Hana pointed to the screen. "I defended your honor. You should be saying 'Thank you, big sister'."

"I don't need you to defend me. I could've found him myself."

"What kind of sister would I be if I didn't?" Rac' looked into Hana's eyes as she spoke.

"Are you trying to be like Mama? Turn into a fucking *salop*?" Rac' felt his temper raise. Hana saw a breathing fire in his eyes.

"Mama was a shell of a woman that let us take her beatings once we were old enough. Don't you ever compare me to that bitch."

SMACK! SMACK!

Rac' stayed silent but his eyes still shone brightly as he stood over Hana. "Get up, and take it back." He said as he sat back down.

Hana rose to her feet before mounting Rac' and cradled his head. It was maternal-like, and she offered herself. "I'm sorry, I didn't mean that." She pulled him closer. Rac' tried to push away as he started wiping away tears, but she insisted. He did accept and bit into a suckle, immediately feeling a head rush as scarlet milk ran over his tongue. For the next five minutes, there was no exchange between them. Between the sounds of feeding, Hana felt a cold and steady trickle roll down. It was painful, but she forced herself to endure. She deserved it for what she said. It was too far. She loved and still loved their mama. When she felt it was enough, she kissed his forehead and dismounted, helping her brother up. She looked at him as she readjusted her robe. Rac' wiped eyes for a final time and then his mouth.

"Come here." Hana said to him as she opened her arms for a hug. Rac' reticently embraced Hana, feeling his body jump as he stifled another hiccup. Hana giggled and Rac' felt himself ease. He laughed himself and kissed Hana on the cheek. When he did, he leaned into her ear. "Let's keep this one."

She recalled her first pet since coming back was a young housekeeper that had gotten away. She never told him about it, but she was supposed to be for him. After that, she never really cared to keep them. She did get better at Turning, but even better at feeding and discard. She didn't know if Rac' had any pets in his travels after his service, but she was sure he did. She felt he was nice to his pets. He didn't talk much about what he did after leaving the War when he came home, and still didn't, now that she thought about it. She wondered if he had taken on a special woman during his time away. He had grown into a handsome young man and could be very kind. He was always a kind boy. Maybe she was still alive, waiting like a good wife for him to return, or looking for him with their children. In the short years since he returned, he didn't seem to be in a rush to find them. "Do you plan on Turning her? Should I get the basement ready."

"Not yet. She needs to learn how to be good."

Before he left, Hana liked when Rac' found a girl he fancied, she just didn't like his choice of girls. Even as children, he was a quiet boy, but it attracted girls that wanted to take advantage of him. One particular girl learned the hard way to never betray his loyalty. They shared a connection that most people, even siblings, would never experience, but she did wonder how strong it would be if there was someone else around consistently. Someone that wasn't family. When they reunited before removing *Him* from their lives, Hana was everything to Rac': Mother. Sister. Creator. She was everything she needed to be to him, or for him. She saw that Alexis vaguely looked like Mama. Maybe it was some weird complex he had, like that story she learned in school about the guy who ended up doing his mother on accident even though he tried not to. At least Rac' wasn't that disgusting; he just missed Mama, that's all. She shrugged it away and offered a final statement, "I don't care what you decide to call her, but she's Whore to me."

Rac' didn't know what she meant but nodded. He never really thought about renaming his pets. She then glanced over to Rac's closed door before turning into her room, licking her canines as she walked into darkness. She let him have some more alone time and decided to go for a walk.

CHAPTER 13

After an early dinner, Flip made a call to Wallace while Elena was upstairs sleeping off an after-dinner shootaround in the backyard. He wanted to learn more about what happened at The Watering Hole. Outside of similar claw marks across the face and throat like the St. Clair attack, Wallace told him that the attack had to have happened at least an hour beforehand, meaning it's possible that whoever killed at the Hole would've had time to go for St. Clair. The only thing was that there were no teeth on this one. As Wallace continued, Flip asked something he'd been thinking about earlier, "Hey, question, did St. Clair have any kids?"

Wallace let out a hearty laugh. Luc St. Clair and "family man" didn't seem appropriate in the sentence. "Nah man, he got a niece and nephew through his sister, but I last I heard, he put them in nice spot out by Redwater Beach. Why?"

Flip told him about the child endangerment charges in Shockley's sheet and if Luc had ever been brought up on similar charges. Wallace answered in the negative. Flip then went back to Shockley.

"C'mon man, what you expect? Shitty guy outside the home is just as shitty in it. I mean the gap in time is a little interesting so maybe the first few years made him settle down a bit, but man, those kinds of people eventually go back to what they know, good or bad."

There was a pause. Something still felt like it was there. Flip really wished he could've seen that mystery woman's face. He coughed to indicate he was still on the line and looked at his list of notes:

Long hair. Black or dark brown
Vi'nnakan? Lightskin but pale
Very pale.
Burn trailing up right arm
Short. Maybe 5'-5' 3" max
At the Hole with date.

Flip looked over them again. It wasn't much, but it was all he could remember from his vision. It was more than Wallace and Monroe was working with. "Hey, I think I got a description you can work with on our third party from Luc's."

"Hold on a second." There was a brief silence, and then rustling. "Aight, hit me with it."

Flip relayed his notes as Wallace wrote it all down. After a few more seconds of silence, Wallace finally came back. "Aight, brother. Anything else?"

"Not on that, nah." Suddenly he had an idea. "One last thing; was Luc's name short for anything?"

There was another laugh and Flip wasn't sure what he said. He didn't know anyone else named Luc with the St. Clair spelling. After more laughter, Wallace was back. "Yeah man, check this out. His real name is *Lucie*, man, IE and all. Fucking *Lucie*."

Flip laughed. No way one of the biggest dealers in Fountain was a man named Lucie. Oddly, Flip felt a little unsettled learning this bit of info. A man named Lucie in the hard drug game sounds like he's either a pushover or a *really* dangerous guy. From the stories he could remember even before their handshake that night, Luc, or *Lucie* didn't have the rep of being a pushover. Maybe this time, he punched above his weight-class and got hit back.

"Aight man. I think Rizzo is getting the official tox screen done tomorrow. We didn't find anything big at the house, but we did pick-up Rock residue from the bedsheets and dresser in St. Clair's house so we're pretty sure we'll find some in his system. Nothing usable in the bathroom, though. Just dead skin that can't read."

"Aight well, I might have something new tomorrow. Gonna try and catch Penny at work and ask her a few things."

"Penny? The deaf girl that work at Ruby's?" Wallace asked.

"Yeah. Elena said she saw somebody from the diner last night."

"Somebody related to this?"

"Not sure yet. That's why Imma talk to her."

"Gotcha. Let me know if it's anything important."

"Will do, man." Flip signed off and hung up the call.

After talking to Wallace, Flip thought about the possibility that the woman Penny recognized could be possibly linked to St. Clair, the Hole, and even the Shockley murders. If she is, then how? Was she the killer? Was it a simple "wrong place, wrong time" situation? His mother would say it's never that simple. To her, murder was playing a game of degrees and nuance. He got back on his communicator and shot a quick message to Wallace:

Tell Cap to start my paperwork tomorrow.

It was less than a minute later when he got a response.

Marker still valid?

Flip tapped his pockets and realized his wallet was in the car. He hedged his bet.

Think so.

Almost like a game, Wallace sent his own two-worded volley.

Good enough.

It was on that final response that Flip noticed the time. *6:37PM.* He ran off one of the few numbers he'd always know by memory. After a few rings he heard his mother's voice. "Stokton residence, Fleice speaking."

"Hey Mom, it's Flip." *She sounds normal today.*

"Flip-baby! How you doing? Want me to get your father?" He could tell she already was about to.

"Nah, just tell him I'll call him later. I wanted to talk to you. Think I need some help."

"What's wrong baby? Everything ok?" Her voice turned serious. "Is it Elena?"

"Nah mom, It's about work."

"*Court*?! Boy, what you going to court for?! What happened?"

"I said *work*, not court. I'm on a case." He felt bad about raising his voice, but he needed to rein her in before she got too excited. He could tell the effectiveness by the sound of her voice when she spoke again.

"I'm sorry, baby, I thought you said *court* and I got scared, that's all." She was silent for a moment. Flip pictured her having a twitch before she returned, back to her earlier happier tone. "So, what's going on? Haven't heard from you in a while."

"I was just there yesterday, remember? Elena and I came by." Flip was wondering if maybe he should've waited until the morning to call. Evenings can be a gambit on where she was.

"Oh... No, I know that, Flip, I ain't *that* crazy." She

giggled into the phone. She still did have her humor, so she may have been right. "No, I mean *heard from you*, about work. This about that St. Clair murder?"

"Yeah, and possibly the Shockley one. Honestly, I--" He stopped short of adding his additional posit.

"You think it's connected, right? Same person, or *people*?" Flip heard her coming back, her words clearer and Investigator-toned, especially in the way she said "people". She read the papers, and likely had a case file of her own at home already in the works. She knew she hit dead-on and waited before speaking again. "Been seeing anything?"

"Yeah, a little. Once at Pike's Creek on Friday, where I saw that two people were there at some point. I'm thinking it was whoever dumped him. Then twice at St. Clair's house. That's where I saw who I think is connected to everything happening. So far though, no faces to go off of." He then heard his mom laugh away from the phone. She then readjusted the phone.

"I'm sorry Flip, but I was just thinking about when It came to me on a case for the first time. Almost the exact same thing happened to me, baby. All the pieces, just not how they fit. Don't worry, It'll grow the more It visits. Just be careful, baby, seeing too much of this evil shit will do a number on you." Flip heard another giggle.

"So, what should I do? I'm officially on the case starting tomorrow."

"Same as you would on your other cases. Get some sleep and be ready to work. I suggest you talk to the owner of The Watering Hole and check the cameras. Actually... No, they might not let you do that. No... Yeah, try and see if someone noticed something. From what the papers say, there was a lot of blood. Whoever did it couldn't have left clean."

This was the most lucid Flip has heard his mom talk in a while, but he was happy for it despite the circumstances. Whenever she got to talk about work, it's like the vet player still able to give 20 coming off the bench. She was still on top of her game. Flip could only imagine how things are outside of these pockets of intersection; how it must feel for his father. It must be especially tough for Ms. Ata and the other HouseStaff. Half-jokingly, Flip imagined his mom making phony files on random members, with fake or perceived crimes that she would then "solve" for the practice. Flip laughed harder than he should, even though a part of him was scared of the realistic possibility that it was really happening. He thought about Ata and his mom's suspicion of paint theft.

"Flip? You ok?" Fleice answered someone in the background. "Flip?"

Flip was gathering himself from his mental tangent. "Yeah, I'm here but I gotta run in a few." he then smiled. "I love you, mom. I'll talk to you later, ok?"

Unable to see it but feeling it's warmth, Fleice smiled herself. "Alright, Flip-baby, I love you too. Be careful, ok?" She then turned the TV up a few notches and held the phone closer to her face. She felt somebody was listening nearby. Her voice became an intense whisper, looking over her shoulders as she spoke. Someone was listening in. "This is the big leagues, Flip. I know you ain't been in the game that long, but rookie season's up. Trust me, Flip, the Sight won't lie to you no matter what It shows. It may not be a perfect view, but for good or bad, It won't lie to you. Always remember that. I'll have Patriik drop something off at El's soon." She then went back to a normal volume as did the TV.

She swore she heard steps on the foyer's hardwood as she did, but turned to find nobody. "Ok, sounds good. I love you, Flip."

Confused at what had just happened, Flip didn't respond until Fleice repeated that she loved him. When he was about to ask the first of many follow-up questions, Fleice kissed into the phone as she hung up. Flip tamped the urge to call back and just wrote the main points:

The more It "visits", the more it helps

Seeing too much evil?

It will <u>never</u> lie

No matter what it shows

The last line. It made Flip think about a phone call they had years ago. It was about something she "Saw" concerning Ms. Ata and his father. He looked to Elena. He trusted her. He wouldn't need It to tell him something she wouldn't, would he? Would he trust It if it did show him something? He's caught her before, but he didn't need the Sight for that. What would be different now? He mentally shrugged himself off as he felt himself going down the rabbit hole. He unmuted the TV as the local news was covering the recent spate of crimes between East Pike and the Districts, warning citizens to be careful and vigilant should they travel at night. He noticed this was first time he's seeing public mention of the Alexis Valer. Flip then muted the TV again and made his way towards the stairs. When he got to the top, he saw that Elena's door was mostly closed and that it was relatively quiet, save for the soft volume of soft music. Flip knocked twice and opened up, finding Elena asleep on top of her sheets. Flip took off his shirt and joined her, wrapping his arm over her in embrace. She stirred and looked behind her shoulder, smiling at new company.

"Mmm, you know, my boyfriend might be coming by

soon." She kept her back to him but cuddled close.

"That's fine, you can tell him we was just nappin'. He'll be fine." He kissed her cheek. "Shit, we layin' on *top* of the sheets." He kissed her cheek again. This time he tasted salt and pulled back. *Crying?*

"Shut-up," She playfully rapped his hand and laughed with sleep in her voice that hit a certain note for Flip. "I was tired and didn't feel like getting under. What time is it?"

"Almost 7:00." Flip tightened his hold, "Getting up?"

"Not right now, got an alarm for 7:30. Wanna listen to some music?" She held his hand and snuggled into him.

"Sure." He kissed her cheek again. "You ok?"

"Mmhmm, I just miss my mom. She really liked this record." Elena kissed his hand and drifted back to sleep.

As he felt his breathing grow into synch with Elena, he couldn't help but think back to the conversation he had with his mother, her abrupt warning before she hung up, and what she said about the "Sight". It was weird how it came up, but least she had a name for it. Over the years, Flip just called it, well, It. They didn't talk about It much, even when he told her about his UBL incident and how it had been happening the previous 4 months on and off the court. Her response was something he never forgot.

"Flip-baby, if you were jigging, you know I would've been the first to know. I ain't raise no cheaters."

He was visiting more often then and knew she was right. Between Mesa and the occasional date, that first year out of the UBL, he was basically a recluse and spent a lot of time around the family estate, almost afraid to be anywhere that was full of strangers or fans. Even Elena couldn't vouch for him to be anywhere unless he was right in front of her as she showed up. His treatment of her was one of the biggest regrets he had about that year.

That talk was less than three years ago, but already 7 years and into her condition and a year removed since she "resigned" from p'rotec work. At the time, his mother was the only one he had told the real details to. Not necessarily because he wanted to but because he knew she was the only person to truly understand. She knew full and well how it feels to have your fate determined by others, but he knew she would understand what he saw and how. After a breakdown and a shared cry, Fleice managed to talk him into telling Elena and his father everything.

"They need to know, Flip-baby. You'll regret it later."

Her head made a twitch and she looked back at him. His father mentioned she had been doing that more recently. Probably just getting used to the new medicine. *"I know I do at times."* Her voice was sad but she wore a comforting smile. *"I was a few years older than you when it first happened to me. Just means you're a real Stokton."* She had given him a good-night kiss and went upstairs, *"Just keep making us proud, Flip-baby. Kill the lights if you're not staying over."* and with a finger-gun, she went to bed. Flip drove home that night, the whole time wondering what the hell she meant by he was a *real* Stokton.

Elena beat her alarm by two minutes, just as Flip was settling into real sleep. She did her best to not wake him until she felt a pinch from behind. "Guess your boyfriend ain't come home."

"I guess he didn't." She responded.

He always did like their "strangers meeting" bit. It was an interesting touch, but only for when they were *together* together. Initially more of Elena's thing, but he came around.

"I'm sure you have a nice woman waiting for you at home. Any reason, why I found you in my kitchen *and* my bed?"

"Guess you can say she ain't come home either." He flashed a smile. "Think I can lay a little longer?"

"You nap any longer, it'll be a slumber party." She played up her accent this time.

"Think your boyfriend will mind?" Flip yawned and turned onto his back. Elena starting walking to her closet. "I know you Founders are protective about your partners."

"Who said I was going to ask?" She winked before turning to open and enter.

Flip smiled to himself and thought about tomorrow as Elena picked through clothes. "Got any smoke?"

"Maybe. Check the record stand." Elena called back.

Flip crawled over to Elena's side and leaned over to open the cabinet under the record player with care. The player was older than he and Elena and if anything happened to it, she might actually kill him. It's the closest thing to an heirloom and has been directly handed down the family line starting with Em-June Starks. Despite its age, it still played and looked as if kept in a glass case of time. He looked it over, seeing how the greens on the painted flowers and forging still looked like it came right off the assembly line. Flip couldn't say for sure that it wasn't solid gold, but Elena would never confirm or deny. He thought about the possibility that she didn't know either. He just knows she's said it's heavy. He looked at the plinth and how there wasn't a company name anywhere in view, only a plate with two lines thinly engraved across the front:

HouseMother Em-June Starks
May your name bring honor to Fountain and your family be held in K'd's Grace.

The plate was surrounded by an intricate design of flowers and birds. He opened the cabinet door and looked for Elena's stash box and tray. When he found it, there were a few papers and enough to get the job done. He took it out and slowly closed the door before resuming his place in bed. As he started rolling, he called out. "Mind if we finish this?" Elena was already coming to the closet door, two pairs of heels in hand.

"Got some at your place?"

"Yes ma'am." He was starting to grind.

"Well, mister, seeing you've already shared my food and now my bed, please make yourself comfortable." She stuck her tongue and went back into the closet.

"Yes ma'am." Before licking the seal. As he looked around for a lighter, Elena came back to the closet entrance. A third, different, pair of heels in hand along with a similar colored blouse.

"Hey, can you come here? I want your opinion."

Flip put the stick down and walked over. He learned to give the obscene amount of clothes and shoes a pass as it seemed to be a family trait. Whether it her be father and his age-appropriate financier trendiness or her mother's work with some of the world's biggest fashion houses, Elena Starks always had a latent need to be the best-dressed in the room. Even if it's a shirt and sweats, she'll find a way.

"So, I got a meeting tomorrow, and I cut it down to these. What do you think?" She waved over three outfits. The first was a deep teal pantsuit with flowing legs, white button accents on the jacket and a ruffled white shirt blouse underneath. On a stool next to the suit were a pair of chunky white Gerard Lioni "Blue-Bottom" heels. Flip really liked the choice; it was a good Monday color. He looked to the suit's right and saw an old favorite of his; a lavender purple Lioni one-piece jumpsuit bearing an embroidered *RS* in gold-lined forest green stitching on the left chest pocket. Never one without an accessory, Elena had an ascot of matching colors via a landscape printed on the fabric. Looking at the quality of the fabric, Flip didn't want to think about how much it cost, let alone the actual jumpsuit. On its own pedestal similar to the display before, Elena had placed a pair of low-key gold-toned, black-dotted heels. There was a decorative buckle on the front that pulled the whole thing together. It matched a similar buckle on the waist of the jumpsuit. He didn't even look at the third option before he made up his mind.

"The first one." He pointed over to the teal suit and heels. Elena let out a small fist-pump.

"I was hoping you'd say that." She began putting the other outfits back into the mix. "Now I can finally wear these shoes."

"What's the occasion?" Flip moved behind Elena and hugged her, nuzzling her neck.

"Supposed to meet with the Minister and a few local business owners dad works with. We're going to try and get some donations to the Center for some more renovations and program upgrades. We also need new sports equipment. Tomorrow's a test, to see who's really serious."

"Need me to put anything in?" Flip asked. His interest always worked on her.

"Thank you, Love, but it's ok. I've already set some money to be put into the pot once everything is finalized. Should I put both of our names on the "Doner" line? We'll get nice plaques with our names on them put on the wall. One for each, unless you want the line to say 'Anonymous', again?"

"Nah, that's your money, Olga. You get that one. Why don't I just make my own donation?"

Elena smiled. "Because that's a duplicate set of forms I'd rather not have Ms. Ingram process. I'm donating as a private citizen, and it's allowed up to two adults be named for large donations. Also, who do you think paid for the playground upgrade and the outdoor courts? You thought I just kept your money."

Flip didn't think about the timing of his last donation until now. Where was his plaque that time? "Ok, but what's a 'large' donation in this sense?" Flip tensed his ears for the possibilities.

"In this case, anything over 15,000 scril." She kissed his hand again.

"Damn, Olga, 15? You tryna feed these kids sea and field every day or something?" Elena had to loosen him up as she settled into a slow dance in tune to the music.

"Re-lax. At least the money's going somewhere helpful and not in the bank collecting dust. Now, am I putting your name or not?" Elena continued her sway, feeling Flip move in with her. He couldn't argue. The amount was more than he thought she was looking for, but she was right. Scril was the last thing they, or their children's, children's children would ever need to worry about. Now at still under 30, they each had multiple lifetimes of personal wealth outside of their birthright. He let her have the point.

"Yeah, you can put my name. You said we'll both get plaques, right?"

"I said one for each donor. Couples still get a single

213

plaque, but it'll have both names." She turned to face him. "That fine with you?"

Flip kissed her on the forehead. "Yes, ma'am."

"Good." She leaned up to kiss him. "Wanna watch some TV?"

"As long as it ain't the news. Can't do any more of that right now."

"That bad?"

"It might be. It's definitely weird enough."

Elena's eyes stayed on him. Even on the first cases, he didn't talk much until it was either closed or about to be. She took a chance. "Wanna talk before you can't?"

"Maybe after your meeting." He paused. "I'm working the St. Clair and Shockley murders, as of tomorrow morning."

I knew it.

"Can you crack it?" She was happy about him saying he's going to help. Mostly because it sounded like this was his decision. Flip always said he started investigating to help keep the city safe and the people within it. He was still their "Emissary", even off the basketball court. As true as his words may have been, Elena knew it had to something deeper.

"I can only try."

"Fair enough." She kissed him again and broke away. "Now, let's have a nice Sunday night and watch some bad TV like normal people."

"I'd like that." He followed behind her, stopping at the bed briefly before joining her down the stairs. He was still sure he had left the TV on mute before he came up earlier.

◆ ◆ ◆

It was dark, and quiet. Rac' made his way into the kitchen and placed his bag of disc movies and snacks on the island before going to light a candle from one of the dying wall lanterns. He explored the first floor, coming across rooms he couldn't remember last stepping foot in. As he went back to the kitchen, he heard what sounded like a scream coming from below him. Somebody was in the cellar. He went over to the floor-door and pressed his ear to it; only hearing fragments.

"...right, Whore?!"

"...Mother!"

Rac' opened the door and went down the steps. He found Alexis, naked and chained at the wrists forcing her into a half-stand against a black-blood colored obelisk in the middle of the floor, sobbing and trying to kneel, knees just touching the floor but not firmly enough to rest. Hana was standing over her, right hand mid-air in attempt of another strike. She came down hard with a loud *pop*. The sack of Rock was sealed and sitting on the small altar 20 feet behind Hana. He could smell blood.

"No" *Pop!* "drugs" *Pop! Pop!* "Say it!"

In between her yelps and sobs, Alexis repeated. She told herself to fight against Hana's offering of dinner, but her stomach proved mightier than her brain. Hana felt so genuine in her apology. She even helped bathe and clean her wounds, handling her... Like a mother would. Or an owner cleaning their pet. Another slap landed and she could feel a tooth knock loose. She spat it out and looked up to Hana, staring into steady flames. They were calmer than what she saw the very first time.

"I'm sorry, Mother!" Alexis coughed up a phlegmy mix of blood and mucus. "I'm sorry. Please, no more."

Hana lowered her arm, massaging her teaching hand with her left and walked up to Alexis. Raising her by the throat to stand her up. "What was that?" She looked at Rac' and smiled. There was blood on her breath.

"Hana, stop."

"I'm just helping her rid of some old habits, that's all." Hana roughly pushed Alexis' face away as she let go, letting her fall to an abrupt stop. "She had a slip-up at dinner. I making sure it didn't happen again." Walked over to Rac' and held his hand and looked over her shoulder to the obelisk. "Right?"

"Yes... Mother." Alexis responded quietly.

Hana looked back at Rac' and tipped up for kiss on the cheek. "See?" She looked at Rac' with a deceitful innocence. He walked over to inspect Alexis'. In the candlelight, her face was a welted mask of itself. Clean canvas of a body now bruised and cut. He examined her further and her figure, even in its current setting caused a rush to his lower self.

"I'm sorry... Please, don't hit me." It's been less than two days but Alexis felt like the only things she's ever learned how to say was, "I'm sorry.", "Mother.", "Please." and "Don't hit me." in varying arrangements. Too empty to cry, Alexis could do nothing but hang. She felt her arms going to sleep and wished they just fell off. At least she would have a chance to escape.

"Did you get the one you wanted?" Hana was guiding her brother back towards the cellar steps. Rac' took a final look back to Alexis. Maybe Hana was right and she needed to be taught another lesson.

"I did." Rac' finished his inspection.

"Good. I'll get her some water and meet you upstairs." She kissed his cheek and patted his backside. Like Mama used to. "Go on, I'll be up."

He went through the hatch and disappeared, letting the door slam behind him. Hana turned and walked back over to Alexis, standing her back up by the throat. "Would you like some water, Whore?"

"Yes, please." Alexis felt the grip tighten. "Yes, Mother." She met Hana's gaze with her clear eye. There was still defiance underneath the bruises, Hana could see it.

"Good girl." Hana petted her face and left the cellar. She returned a couple of minutes later with a small pot of water. "Open." Alexis did to allow the cool water in. It was plain tap water, but in that moment, it could've been from the freshwater isles of Blandiza and she wouldn't have noticed. She drank it in as the excess ran down the sides of her mouth and run onto her body. After a few seconds, she felt the pot recede and tried to follow it.

"No, that's enough."

Alexis stayed silent and looked at her. Her left side of Hana looked out of focus. Blinking didn't help much.

"What do you say?" Hana held the pot by the handle with her left, prepping for another drink.

"Thank you."

"Thank you, what?"

"Thank you... *salop*."

There it was; that bit of defiance still lingering. Hana slapped her with her right and held her face close. Hana allowed her to drink from the pot before making a sharp chop to Alexis' neck, making her to cough up a lot of what she took in. "Good pets always take some time to break in." There were a few more slaps. "Have you ever owned a pet?"

"Yes." Alexis kept her head down this time. She thought about the puppy her Nana used to have. He was so cute and hyper. For a while, it felt more like another friend than an animal. Then Nana passed and her parents didn't want to feed another mouth.

Hana kissed her on the forehead and petted her hair, "How nice." before placing the pot of remaining water at Alexis' feet. She walked over to the steps and climbed out, slamming the cellar door behind her. It was another five minutes before Alexis tried to go far water again and realized that it was out of reach unless she positioned herself to her lowest allowable point and licked into it like... like... a pet. It was a dominance move by Hana, and she knew it would work. Pets were all about establishing who was the dominant one, even when they weren't around. Alexis came to this realization with fresh tears and a notice of the fire from the candles was dying down, allowing her to feel just how cold her bedroom for the night was going to be. It was another 20 minutes before she finally felt safe enough to let herself fall asleep.

"Is Alexis ok?" Rac' was finishing pouring the last of his snacks into a large bowl: chocolate covered pretzels, buttered air-corn, and those peculiar things called "jellybeans". He didn't know how they got so many flavors, but they've come a long way since the ones he had in his youth. Hana looked at the bowl. Jellybeans always got stuck in her teeth, but she used to like them so much. Mama always brought some home after the market.

"I just got her some water." She sat on the couch

facing the far wall, the main menu of tonight's movie projected onto it. She sat back into the couch and watched as Rac' rearranged a low table to face them, placing two glasses and a bottle of wine in the space between them. Once everything was in place, Rac' sat on the sofa and poured them each a glass and took a handful of his mixture to his mouth.

"I brought a couple other movies for the collection; they had some decent stuff on sale."

"You know I can't eat those jelly things anymore." Hana said after her sip of wine. At least the wine was good.

"Don't eat them, then." Rac' said as he chewed. Hana wrapped her arm around Rac' and brought him close. He took a sip of wine and the remote from his pocket, selecting the "Play Movie" option before setting it and the wine on the table and curling into a snuggle against Hana, resting his head on her lap. As the opening credits started, Rac' lifted to get another small handful. When he laid back into place, he looked up. "Hana?"

"Yes?"

"I love you."

Hana took another sip and placed her glass down. "I know you do. I love you too, Rac'."

They enjoyed their movie night in, the dying lanterns resembling a theatre, joking and laughing along like normal people again.

By the time they finished their second movie, it was just before midnight. Hana felt the steady pace of Rac' sleeping as she herself was starting to drift in and out. She paused the end credits and checked the wine: just below half full. Hana poured herself another half-glass and fitted the cork back into the bottle. She turned off the projector and rustled Rac' awake. "Come on, let's go to bed." She helped him up and they walked around to kill the remaining lit lanterns. As they went towards their respective rooms, Rac' saw Hana stop short and turn to the stairs.

"Where're you going?"

"Downstairs."

Rac' didn't say anything and went into his room, closing the door behind him. Hana made her way down the steps and then to the cellar door. As she opened it, she was met with a cool gust brushing past her. The candles had long burned out and the steps looked like they were leading into a black hole. She walked down slowly and calmly over to the obelisk. As she walked, she heard chains rattle and a small whimper. Even in the pitch black, she could see Alexis cowering against the stone.

"Whore?"

"Water. Please." Alexis seemed to have learned a new word in the past few hours. There was a silence, she was beginning to think that nobody was actually in the room with her. "Please, Mother. Water."

Alexis then felt the pot come to her lips and she immediately opened her mouth. As she drank, there were two low burning orbs looking right at her. She focused on the now ice-cold water.

"That's right. Drink."

Alexis then slowed her pacing to almost a standstill, thinking about her exposed neck. She stopped drinking with two gulps. Hana shook the pot in a circular motion, gauging how much water was still left.

"Finished?"

"Yes, Mother."

"Would you like some more?"

"No, Mother." She couldn't see anything but two orbs.

"Good."

SMACK!

A hard force came across Alexis left and she lost her feet from under her. There were two more before she looked up.

"I didn't appreciate what you said earlier." Hana slapped her again. "You hurt my feelings."

"I'm sorry, Mother! I'm sorry."

"Are you really sorry?" Hana slapped her again.

"Yes, Mother. I'm sorry! I swear!"

Suddenly, Alexis felt hands traverse her body. Slow tears began to flow as she bit her lip to keep from crying out; her only refuge being the obelisk that doubled as her punishment post.

"We'll see."

Hana continued on for what felt interminable. As she kept eye contact, Alexis felt as though fire itself entered her, invading and all-consuming. Her body became hot, not just externally but internally. When she could feel the last of herself burn away, her body twitched, and a pressure released. She no longer looked into fire, she was focused on what looked like a man standing against the far wall. He was watching her. He was tall. Thin. Scarily thin. Unnaturally thin. Alexis saw his face and turned her head away. When she opened her eyes again, he was gone. Alexis tried looking around and saw nobody except Hana. She was alone earlier, but she knew she felt somebody else with her before Hana came in. There was another release as Hana increased her veracity. After another wave as Alexis screamed, Hana slowed to a stop. Alexis could only see white. There was a voice that sounded like her own yelling to stop, but it sounded far away. So far away. Her mind felt nothing as her body experienced everything.

There were no more defenses to tear down, no need to *prove* her dominance. She was a pet. Nothing more, nothing less. She was Whore. As Alexis saw the white bring her back to the cellar, Hana inhaled the essence before wiping her fingers across Whore's cheek and the rest on her own nightgown. Alexis collapsed and her wrists hit a sharp stop as she tried to kneel her legs closed. Her body began trembling as the cold set back in.

"Now, are you truly sorry?" Hana finally spoke, stroking Whore softly by the hair.

"Yes... Mother..."

Hana could hear it in her voice. The desperation, the brokenness. Alexis wasn't sure what terrified her more, what just happened or the man she saw. It no longer mattered. Her mind couldn't comprehend either. "Is this going to happen again?"

Alexis' body twitched and she tried to turn inwards, towards the pillar, the only sure thing she knew wouldn't hurt her. She thought she could feel a vibration coming from the stone as a warm streak slowly ran down her inner thigh. "No!" She instinctively screamed before lowering her voice to a flat whisper. "I'm sorry, Mother. I'm so sorry, it won't happen again. I promise."

Hana could feel excitement rise in her now. "Good girl. We'll see how you are in the morning." Hana then walked back towards the steps, stopping before she opened the door. "And Whore?"

Alexis was slow on the draw, but she did answer, "Yes, Mother?"

"A good pet makes a useful pet, and a useful pet is only good if they are alive. Let's not have this talk again." Hana then climbed up the stairs and closed the door behind her. Alexis held out for less than 72 hours. Longer than Hana expected of streetwalker, but she knew her place now. She would be ready to serve when needed. Hana smiled the entire way up the stairs and to her room, resuming her light touch as she walked up. As Rac' laid in bed, he heard footstep on the stairs and thought he picked up a scent, but shrugged and rolled over, making another attempt to go back to sleep.

CHAPTER 14
Monday

Rac' woke up with his back to the open window, freezing. When he turned, he was greeted by a cloudless sun along with an open window and hastily went to close the curtains, reducing the fan of light to little more than a sliver. He closed the window and looked for his mobile. It told him that it was already 70 degrees and a chance of rain later. Despite its effect, he liked the sunlight. It reminded him of when he was little and Mama would take him on their special picnics to Pike's Creek, back when it was a respectful and desired place to be. They would drive in her big car, a new introduction to the still horse-drawn society. It would just be the two of them and the rushing wind, laughing and singing the entire way. Mama liked to drive fast when she was on her "funny dust", but Rac' never worried. Mama would never hurt him. She could never do such a thing. At the Creek they would sit at a bank edge and have lunch while Mama would sing and watch him play in the water, trying franticly to pick up fish bare-handed. He never could, but Mama always gifted him a handmade shirt for his efforts. He missed Mama. For a long while in his time after the Great War, he used and drank anything he could to try to remember her. Hana tried her best, he knew, but she could never replace her. When he could feel himself fully waking up, he heard Hana's voice. It sounded like she was talking in the hallway. As he went to his wardrobe for a sweater, he heard a knock at his door.

"Little brother, are you up?" Hana called through the door. There was another knock pattern.

"Hold on, I'm--"

Before he could say anything else, the door opened,

and Hana walked in holding a section of chain. Alexis followed close behind, crawling on hands and knees, wrists shackled together in front of her with a connection that led to a collar around the neck. She looked cleaned and wearing an embroidered housedress that went to her calves. Rac' could see by the way the fabric clung to her that there was nothing under it. She kept her head down as she crawled in, only looking up to him once she was beside Hana. Rac' could see in her eyes, or more accurately, her clearer one, that she wasn't the same. She looked defeated. Broken. Dominated.

"Good morning." Hana looked at her communicator. "Or the last few minutes of it. Are you going to introduce yourself? Tell him your new name." She tugged the chain and Alexis spoke. Her voice was hoarse.

"Good morning... Master." She whispered. Her left eye began to look partly cloudy, only a touch more than the overcast outside. Her face, splotched with dark purples and reds, had cuts scattered all over. Smaller ones were closed and healing, those deeper having been cleaned and bandaged. Her jaw was swollen on one side. She spoke the pain again, feeling her jaw click and reset as she did. "My name is Whore." After she spoke, she inched closer to Hana. It sounded as earnest as it was unprovoked. Hana then pulled Alexis up to her feet and ushered her to Rac'. Hana extended her part of the chain out.

"She had some fight to her, but I don't think you'll need to worry about that anymore." She slickly dug a nail into Whore's side, out of Rac's sight. "Isn't that right?"

"Yes, Mother."

Rac' reached for the chain but pulled back. "Is that Mama's gown?"

She looked to Whore. "Where did you get this nice

gown? It's ok, you can tell him." She dug in again.

"You, Mother." Alexis kept her eyes on Rac' and he saw her hide a wince. "You gave it to me. Thank you." Her voice was a hoarse monotone. He reached for the chain again and Hana let him take it.

"I would never dishonor our mother like that."

He nodded. He wasn't hungry to feed but felt himself lick his canines. Hana took a few steps back towards the door and saw Rac' looking Whore up and down. It had been long time since he's had a pet. He didn't get to enjoy the last one like he wanted, having to leave her in the cover of night. She played her part very well.

"Want some breakfast?"

"No, I'm not hungry." He was still looking at Whore. She had a faraway look. It was as if seeing through Rac'. As if looking at something else behind him, or for someone else.

"You sure? Don't want to see if your pet knows how to do anything except cry and scream?"

Like activating a sleeper cell, a flash came across Whore's face and she spoke up, her attempt at a normal volume coming out just above a loud whisper. "I can cook. Please, Master." She sounded like she was telling him more than asking him. "Can I cook for you?"

Rac' didn't care for the title of "Master" but he did like the surge that untapped when she said it. It reminded him of when he first heard it in Hana and how in times of supposed privacy, he would hear her call *Him* Master. He didn't realize why until years later when she found his camp. Whore didn't appear to be leaving any time soon. She was a different person now. Less than a week ago, she was Alexis Valer, a recovering addict and active nightgirl, living life on her own terms and wanted desires. She was a daughter, a sister, and at one point, even a Sanctum attending young woman battling personal demons like her fellow parishioners. Now, she was Whore. No family. No story. No past, only present circumstances. She had no selfish desires, except to extend her credit of borrowed time.

"Hana?" He looked over and saw she was starting to smile.

"I can eat."

Whore felt two holes boring into the back of her head and knew Mother was looking at her. She shivered despite the steady breeze of warm afternoon air coming from the shuttered open window. She then looked at Rac' and saw how pronounced his scar was. It was unsettling as it was, but against his paleness, was more detailed than she previously thought. *Will that happen to me?* She thought as he walked her over to the door. Mother was already gone. Whore anxiously looked around while staying close to Master as they walked downstairs. When they got to the kitchen, Mother came down shortly afterward, wearing wide-leg jeans that were a few decades removed and a band t-shirt that looked a size bigger than it should be.

Hana sat at the kitchen island and silently watched as Whore was led around the kitchen. First the fridge, then the freezer. She forgot that Whore wasn't exactly used to every part of the house yet, not in the way she's going to be from. Hana's stomach grew more vocal. "I'm getting hungry."

Whore had a new pace about her movements. She fumbled with the frozen meat and in her nervousness almost dropped a slab of meat. She tried to determine what kind it was but couldn't tell. It looked like beef, but didn't have the same marbling to it. It didn't have the same smell either. She caught it on the first attempt when it bounced on the counter and looked behind her shoulder before resuming. "I'm sorry, Mother."

"It's ok, I just get a bit impatient when I'm hungry." Hana watched as Rac' helped his pet make breakfast. She liked how fast Whore seemed to acclimate herself with her new life, and how maybe it'd be nice to finally have a pet around the house. Her last one was a man almost 20 years her elder. He was intelligent; tall. He was one of the nicest men she knew then, but had a mouth on him. He spoke himself to his downfall. This would be the first one for both her and Rac', and it felt nice. Maybe this will be a good change for them.

Around 1pm, Penny Adlouw felt her pocket buzz as she was taking an order. It only buzzed once, so it wasn't a phone call. She finished the request and made her way to the kitchen to tell Carl. There was another single buzz and this time she took her phone out to see what was so important. Sandra didn't like her being on the phone outside of the kitchen. She says it's distracting and looks rude. She glanced at the screen and immediately put her phone down. She didn't recognize the number but felt from the Fountain area code that it had to be someone she knew. Once in the kitchen, she opened the messages and smiled:

Hey Penny, it's Flip. I got your number from Elena

Are you working today?

Flip! Penny thought Flip was a nice guy and was happy he and Elena were together now. She knew they always liked each other. They kiss and hug too much to be just friends. She then thought about herself and Dom. They kiss and hug a lot to be just friends, too. Penny giggled and replied.

Hi Flip!

Flip was waiting in his car for a second message to come, but soon realized he shouldn't. He sent a two-piece volley:

Hi Penny.

Are you at work?

After a few minutes, progress was made. He started his car as he read the return.

Yeah, I'm at Ruby's! We're open!

It's not crowded if you and Ms. Elena want to come for lunch!

He sent a message off and tossed his phone into the center console with his notes and house keys before shifting into gear and backing out of the driveway.

I'll be there soon. We need to talk about Saturday night.

Saturday night.

Penny thought about the mean lady with the scary voice and what happened in the bathroom. She came in as Penny was washing her hands and occupied the sink next to her. It took a second, but Penny recognized her when she looked over. She didn't see that hers was the only reflection in the mirror. The lady turned and tried to hug her; Penny's body went on autopilot and she slapped her arm away defensively and took a quick step back into a fighting posture. She only had a couple drinks but was coherent enough to not be in the mood for funny stuff. The lady then spoke to her, *"Hey! You're from that diner. Penny, right?"*

Penny nodded her head and slowly lowered her hands.

"I thought so. My behavior yesterday was unacceptable. I'm really sorry for that."

There was a hot and itchy feeling on Penny's arms as she heard the lady's voice; her mouth wasn't moving again. She grew scared and felt her body needing to go again. She resisted the urge to run and instead signed "OK". She proceeded to shift around slightly as she tried not to wet herself. Penny was a big girl, and big girls didn't wet themselves. She wished Aron was there to help her.

"Can we hug it out?" The lady was already walking towards her. *"I've always been a hugger."*

Penny stiffly embraced and then felt a small but strong pull. The hug was tightening. Now, she really needed to go, right now. As soon as it happened, it was over. The lady hugged her tightly again and wished her a good night. Penny immediately rushed into the stall next to her and barely made it. She didn't like how the lady could talk to her the way she could. It was scary. Her voice made her scarier. Penny felt bad that she was scared. The lady had been nice to her, but something wasn't right. *Was she like me?* She went on to try with Dom when she returned to the booth. It didn't work, and she was too embarrassed to tell his confused face what she was doing. Tears were starting to form when she realized that she couldn't talk to Dom the same way the lady spoke to her. She quickly wiped her eyes before taking her drink and finishing it in a single take, washing it down with a full glass of water. After that she slowed down her consumption of everything; she really didn't want to go back to the bathroom if she could help it. The weird lady may not be as nice next time.

There wasn't a response after Flip's last text but by the time he noticed, he was already on the road. Midday on a Monday meant traffic was little to non-existent; he'd be at Ruby's in less than a half-hour. He saw more kids than usual out and remembered Elena telling him about Spring Break. Hell of a time for a killer, or killers, to get active. An unsettling thought creeped in and made itself comfy in his head, *Is it a coincidence, or intention?* And he now started to think about what the worst-case scenario of either option. They both led to the same place: a front-page news story about a kid having gone missing or found dead by brutally violent means. Marks on the neck; body feeling as though having been drained out. Now, he thought about the story Elena relayed about the family from her mother's village and how they never found those kids. He got to the light and said to himself, "That shit ain't real, man." He wasn't sure why he felt the need to say it aloud, but it didn't help him shake the uncertainty he felt after. He hoped the timing of the break had nothing to do with these recent murders. Nothing so far tipped him to think that a child would be involved, and he wanted it to stay like that. For the entire drive to East Pike, he kept telling himself that this vampyr stuff was blowing a few ill-timed scenarios a little out of size, but the more he said it the more unsure he became.

Sandra heard Carl and Flip talking while she rung someone's order. Soon after, she felt a soft poke into her side.

"Hey Sandra, Penny around?"

"You ain't come for me? Even after Saturday?" She asked.

"Nah, not today, but thanks again for letting Elena and I join. Penny still here?"

Sandra could hear in his voice he was serious. Penny told her about the rude bitch from Friday just this morning after she clocked in. She was so pissed she didn't tell her the night of, she made a spatula bend out of shape from hitting it against the wall. She scanned the front dining area and didn't see Penny. Then she remembered, "Oh, you ain't see her taking the trash out? If she's still out there, tell her she can take an extended break. I think she thinks I'm mad at her." She felt that Penny genuinely thought weren't friends anymore because of how upset she got. She could never be that mad at her.

Flip didn't recall seeing her on his lookaround but went back into the kitchen and outside. He found Penny tossing a black bag into a far dumpster next to the diner. When he got close, he saw that she had earbuds in, he couldn't tell what was playing but Penny seemed to bob her head in a rhythm. She noticed a hand waving and turned quickly. When she saw it was Flip, she eased her face and signed her greeting. He signed back and let her know they need to talk and turned to go inside. "Sandra said you can take a break if you want." He waved over to a small table and sat. Penny sat across from him. She was visibly fighting back tears and wiped her eyes before writing again. She slid the paper back over.

She was scary, Flip. She talked to me. I heard her.

"Penny, you could *hear* her?" He teasingly poked her arm. "You telling me you been actin' this whole time."

Penny smiled wide despite her head shaking no. Flip was a funny guy sometimes. She took a new sheet and wrote:

No, not hear her with my ears. She was in my head. She acted nice but her inside voice was so scary. I think she was on drugs or something. Drugs are bad.

Flip couldn't believe what he was reading but put a mental pin in for now. He needed to know something. "Nah, you right, drugs are bad." He accepted a cup of water from Carl and took a sip. "You remember what she looked like?" He reached into his back pocket and pulled out his notebook and pen and slid them over.

Penny looked at him a little confused. Why was he asking about the music? That's weird, but she figured it was important. She tried to recall the basslines to as many songs she could remember and wrote them down. She had a good memory. Flip leaned over to find names and waved his hand. "No, what'd the lady look like?" He swept over his face hoping it'd drive the message home. Penny kept her eyes on his mouth. The next paper that came back still had more than he expected but it had what he needed:

much shorter than me but REALLY strong! Like HeroMan strong!

young, but talks very proper like gramma

pale or reeeally light. She looked kinda sick (I think from drugs)

VERY pretty. (don't tell Dom!)

Accent. Definitely not Fountain or Redwater.

He looked over the list a few times before it was ripped away. Penny was writing something else at the bottom. She didn't think it was important but thought Flip should know anyway. She didn't want him and Sandra to be mad at her. When she was finished, she slid it back over and tapped a finger on it.

She has a brother. I didn't see him that night but he was here with her on Friday. They're twins. Did you know there was a murder at the Hole Saturday night?

Flip's eyes went into tunnel vision on the words *brother* and *twins*. Suddenly his stomach started to do somersaults as he thought about his vision and notes from the Shockley scene and went back to them.

Two people

Faceless

Jeans

Shit. He ripped a blank page from the back and wrote on it before handing it to Penny. His mind went to that girl staring at him while dancing on her date. Her lookalike date.

Did they have matching clothes on Friday?

Penny needed only a second to respond.

Yeah. It was a little weird. Aron and I didn't even do stupid shit like that.

Flip laughed softly to himself and gave a thumbs up as he pointed to her line about Aron. She was right, Penny was too cool for some dumb shit like that. Aron loved his sister to death and would do anything for her, but he wouldn't be caught dead matching his outfits with his little sister. Then again, they weren't identical twins.

Flip checked his phone and saw it was almost 2. He was sure he kept Penny way longer than the extended break Sandra intentioned for her. He made his goodbyes to Penny and Carl, hugging Penny tightly and thanking her for the help. She didn't see his mouth and instinctively thanked him verbally for the hug. Her voice sounded like a croak, but

Flip could make out what she said, chuckling that she must not have saw what he said. Gotta love her. She then started making steering motions with her arms and went back to the paper. She was very excited as she tapped the table.

I saw their car on Friday. It was nice. Maybe nicer than yours.

Penny had a teasing grin. She gave a description of the vehicle, and the shorthand of the parking lot scene she witnessed before the twins pulled out after their meal. Penny admitted that she didn't think anyone else was paying attention to them after they left, but she was sure in what she saw. She thought these two were a little too close, in a way that went further than matching clothes and lunch orders.

Flip went to the front and ordered to-go for him and Elena: Flip's Breakfast Sandwich and a Pancake Platter with sausage substitute and fruit salad. After a brief Q+A about what she remembered, Sandra pecked him on the cheek as he left and said she put a little extra in the Matriarch's order, a thank-you for being there for her on Saturday. She still hasn't heard back from her date. Flip expressed his apologies and made his way out. When he got to his car, he made a call as he got in.

"Elena Starks speaking."

"Damn, you ain't got my number saved? Your boyfriend caught on that I be calling?"

"I think he did. Maybe I shouldn't be talking to you. Now, how can I help you today?"

"Share some lunch with me? Got some pancakes with your name on it."

"You must be something special to know I haven't

235

eaten yet. How soon can you get here?"

"30ish if traffic's light. That good?"

That's perfect, my boyfriend should be showing up in 45, maybe an hour from now."

He wasn't sure what she meant but liked it. Her meeting today must've been successful. He started the car and hung up, immediately making another call, and placing it on speaker.

"Wallace speaking."

"It's Flip."

"What's up man? I'm talking to Ms. Solan here at the station. We're trying to track down the bartender that called Saturday in."

"I hear you. I got some stuff on our third-party."

"No shit?"

"No shit. Meet me at the Community Center when you're finished there. I'll call you when I get there."

"Aight, brother."

Flip pulled out and started his way back into Fountain. He thought about how Mystery Woman was at the locations of two murders in the same night yet was sure she didn't do both of them. Her brother had to be involved somehow. He didn't know whether she ran into Penny before or after the men's room attack but should be lucky to be alive either way. He turned to go down the street of the precinct and saw a number of news caravans parked on the street and a large group of reporters talking to someone. *Shit, is that Wallace?* Flip slowed down but maneuvered himself through the vans. He'd find out in a little while what it was all about; probably just the typical nosy reporter bullshit for the St. Clair story.

◆ ◆ ◆

"Damn, how much food she put in here?" Elena asked as she opened her container. Traffic was lighter than intended so Flip was able to make it in time for the food to still have warmth.

"She said it was a thank you for Saturday. Guess she was really beat up about her guy not coming through. Still ain't even heard back from him."

"I'm surprised she could remember Saturday. I wouldn't be surprised if she let Smetty take her home. There was an interesting mention of him just before we started leaving."

"Maybe." Flip could hear the gossip motor revving.

"So, is she seeing Smetty *and* this other guy?" Elena cut a few pieces of pancake and ate a forkful.

"I don't think so, at least based on how he told it. I don't even think he knows she's seeing someone else. He says they 'have a little fun' from time to time." He fed her the gist of his conversation, self-editing the mention about Donna's "bangin'" dress and Sandra's tendency to be adventurous after enough drinks. After seeing her in action Flip figured that it was something innate. Maybe she just knows how to acknowledge beauty and alcohol just makes her more appreciative. No harm, no foul. Flip dug into his sandwich.

"What'd ya get?"

"Breakfast sandwich."

"Of course. You didn't get me any custom meal?"

"Go there more often and order something not on the menu. They'll eventually catch on." Flip looked up from his container with a teasing Smile. Elena rolled her eyes and continued to eat.

"Want some coffee?" Elena asked as she was getting up from her desk. She began walking over to her coffee station.

"I'm fine. How'd your meeting go, and are you finished for the day?"

She turned around. "It was.... Awesome! I'm serious Flip, Daddy really came through with these guys. They like what we're trying to do, especially the owners of EndZone. Did you know they originally started just outside of Redwater? Everyone was so nice and they were really happy to hear that you were also part of the 15,000 in seed money. They were practically pledging their children at that point." She laughed as she checked the water and replaced the holder. "Looks like you'll be getting that plaque, Mr. Stokton."

Her trailing tone let Flip know she wanted him to come over. As Elena's coffee dripped into her mug, Flip kissed her as he held her by the waist. They made-out until the ding of the coffeemaker went off. Elena leaned her head back and said, "I'm done for the day with meetings, but I'll be here for a little while doing other work. I've also been talking with Agent Valer today. Still no word on Alexis."

"Yeah, same here. Wallace hasn't mentioned anything about her. He thinks she's likely dead at this point. I don't know if he's said it to Valer yet." He still held her by the waist but loosened his hold. This was definitely not what he expecting, at least not right now. Maybe in 30 or so minutes, when Elena's boyfriend would arrive.

"If I didn't know Alexis, I would think so too, but she's a good girl, Flip. She's been coming to her drug meetings and has talked about leaving her working days behind. I know she still does it from time to time, but I can't make her do anything she doesn't want to. I've tried." Elena thought about one the last times she talked to Alexis. It was more of yelling at her because she saw Alexis and a man come out of the women's restroom after an NA meeting. The most obvious thing she could tell was that they both were clearly on something, maybe Rock. Everything else she inferred from appearances but withheld accusations. She knew the man as Robert and at the time was still new to NA. She kicked him out of the Center immediately. Alexis, on the other hand, she took into her office and chewed her out over glasses of water for them both, not just to try and sober Alexis but to calm herself down as well. By the end of it, they had both cried at least once, and Alexis appeared remorseful. Whether it was for cheating NA or getting caught for it, Elena never knew, but Alexis seemed to be on the steady for every meeting after that night. She admitted that she still cheated, but got herself to using less at a time, only indulging herself whenever Luc came around for her. He paid more when she partied with him. Ms. Starks was nice enough to not look up her sponsor and snitch. Alexis had no plans on screwing that up, she knew her cousin would kill her if she found out she was still using.

Flip didn't know Alexis and indeed did feel more comfortable with the sad possibility that she was dead. The only thing he wasn't as convinced on was that St. Clair didn't have anything to do with it. Being mixed up with people like him, one never knew where he may have had eyes and ears, even when they thought it was safe. Even then, he still thought the time window between her going missing and him murdered seemed to be too tight be an "A got B and was then got by C" kind of equation. He pulled out his notebook and wrote a few things down as he spoke.

"Olga, how old was Alexis? Did she talk about St. Clair

at all during her meetings?"

"She was a little younger than us, like 24. Camailla mentioned her birthday was coming up later this year. I don't know details of what Alexis talked about in her meetings, only that she kept to them fairly regularly. I'll have to ask Ms. Ingram which one of our volunteers has led more of her meetings."

"Thank you, Love. What she look like?" He prepped himself.

"She's about average height, about the same as Agent Valer, give or take an inch. I think part-*Vi'nnakan*, and from the few times I've seen her, I think she might have some elf in her. Naturally pretty, but she wore make-up a lot. Last time I saw her though, I don't recall her having make-up. Maybe she just does it for work because whenever I saw her, she always had the natural look going on." She shrugged her shoulders. "Maybe I just caught her at the right times. Flip," She put her hand on top of his book, pushing it down, "you don't actually think she's dead, do you?"

Her face said she really believed Alexis was alive. She saw on Flip's that he wasn't as optimistic.

"Flip, no. No, someone would've found her by now."

"Elena, I don't know. If St. Clair caught on to her work with Vice," He took a pause and let out a sigh. "it's very possible we may not find her again. I would say it's damn likely." He let his voice drop as he edged closer to the end.

Elena let out a sigh of her own. She sensed that he was going to say that but was still shocked at how seemingly easy it was for him to say. Flip was more of a realist, likely a byproduct of having a homicide investigator for a mother that didn't shy away from talking about the details of her work. She liked that about him, kept her leveled when some of her more enthusiastic ideas got the better of her. Sometimes though, she wished he would knock off the moody, private eye shtick; only she knew it wasn't a shtick. It was his first (and hopefully last) major crime he's on, but she can see that he's taking it seriously. Working break-ins and street stick-ups gave more opportunity to joke around, mostly at the stupidity of the perpetrators. She still kept a certain distance when they talked about it though. If it didn't involve her, or her children, she preferred to stay out of it. One less of a headache for both of them.

"Aight, Love. Thanks." Flip closed his notebook and got out his phone. "Wanna hear about what Penny told me before I call Wallace over? Can't tell anyone though."

"Deal." She sealed it with a kiss and a pinky promise. Then another kiss.

"Cool, so check this shit out." He opened his notebook to the pages he used while at Ruby's and pointed out some of the things that Penny wrote that seemed to match some of what he wrote from the Shockley scene. He told her about how Mean Lady apparently has a brother and possibly had a Monarch accent. He told her about the car and as he was describing it, had a realization that may have otherwise slipped him if he wasn't currently at the Center. "Oh, fuck!"

"Flip Stokton." Elena was caught off guard by this sudden eruption.

"I'm sorry, but I think I've seen this car a few times. I swear it was at Pike's when I was with CaP but I think it rolled by here too. I don't know how, but I swear this car's been following me." He was pointed at the description Penny gave him. In the back of his mind he thought about the TV, and how he was sure he left it on mute.

Cool car! Black but almost too black. Scary-faced

car.

Old model Exum Golf 4-Door. Not the most popular model but has vintage appeal.

Old people's car. Maybe they got it from gramma and grappa

No plates on the front or back

They both chuckled at Penny's less than fact-based observation of the car being an "old people's car" but it being either borrowed or inherited could make sense why these two were driving it around. The Exum went out of production long before either of them was born. No tags on it also provided a perfect cover added with a very non-descript look and if they don't come into Fountain enough for people to notice it. Flip went to his first page of notes and wrote two words:

TWIN KILLERS.

He didn't need his mom to tell him that one. Flip got his mobile and went to the sink and then the coffeemaker.

"Wallace speaking."

"I'm at the Center." *Ow!* Splashback from the water.

"Aight, be there in a sec."

"What was up with the reporters?"

"Tell you when I get there." Wallace hung up. He didn't sound happy.

❖ ❖ ❖

Eight years ago

Bzzzz...bzzz...bzzz.bzz-

"Hello?"

"Flip-baby?"

"Hey, mom, what's going on? It's a little late. Everything ok?" Flip reached and turned the stereo down. Elena stayed in her book.

"Flip, I think something's wrong with Ata."

Flip quietly sighed. A recurring conspiracy that was almost worth a TV movie. He glanced at Elena. *"Mom, she's not hav--"*

"Flip, don't start, I know she is. I haven't caught them, but I know." Fleice said with a resigned assuredness. *"Anyway, that's not the point. I think something's wrong with her. Something serious."*

Flip was sitting up by now. Ata hadn't shown up for work a few weeks ago for almost a week with no word. Fleice gave her the benefit of the doubt and withheld searching her quarters in case she was as sick as another HouseStaff said he was told. Sure enough, Ms. Ata had showed back up for work as if nothing happened. She had a few noticeable bruises and small cuts, her only explanation be that she fell one night while out and was home healing. Ata lived in the HouseMaiden Quarters, a small two-floor home on the far-end estate near the Staff Quarters complex and HouseWard home. It was far enough for some earned privacy but was still Stokton property, rendering it fair game for ordered "wellness checks" and searches when deemed necessary. A HouseMaiden or Ward who suddenly doesn't show up for work for days at a time was a perfect reason when considered within it. Personally, Fleice wanted to leave it at Ata having met a really nice man one evening, until he turned out not to be so nice and was now in need of a major ass-kicking. Professionally, she felt something much darker happened. Fleice pressed her to know what happened, but Ata never talked.

Despite the bruising and the voluntary four months of therapy, she never talked about it with Fleice and resumed her duties like she was never gone. She eventually got back to her upbeat and normal frequency of talking along with a new level of zeal for her position within the staff and ensuring the well-being of her Founding HouseMother. She'd give her life to protect her. She had shown K'd she was willing to. Being bestowed the title of HouseMaiden or Ward came with an understanding it's a traditionally lifelong position. They were given a practically free house and a healthy paycheck, but no real retirement clause and no realistic chance to raise a family of their own. If they were Released, it's as good as dead in the Founders' society. Ata returned with a new feeling she'd be with this family for a long time. There were a few odd new habits that came back with her, however. On more than one occasion, cook staff would say they find her hanging around the meat chamber every now and then. They nicely described the look in her eyes as hungry. Ata's response for each run-in was that she was "just inspecting" the inventory, but they always noted the smell of raw meat on her breath.

"Ok mom, what's up then? What's wrong with her?"

"She's pale. Like really pale."

C'mon mom. "Mom, for real? Call Dr. Bollard if you think she's sick."

"Flip, I mean it. What if she's infected with something?"

"Mom, you been watching too many movies? Infected? Think she's gonna eat your brains in your sleep?" He really hoped this was an elaborate joke. It's been 2 years and change, but he was still getting used to her condition. Maybe elaborate gallows humor was a side-effect.

"*Flip Stokton, you watch your damn mouth, I ain't that fuckin' crazy! I'm only a few years off the force, and you know that was bullshit. That whole thing was bull-FUCKING-shit! I still can't believe that fuckin' Monroe. That coward mother--*"

"*Mom, mom, I know. I'm sorry, I thought you were joking, that's all.*" Elena looked up from her book and over to Flip, worried. It's been a while since he told her how his mom was doing, only that she's been having migraines recently or something like that. *Who were they talking about? Infected?*

There was a silence for a second and then a sniffle. "*I'm sorry baby. I know, I just got a little excited. But Flip, I think she might be really sick. I felt her hand the other day and she was freezing cold, Flip. I'm worried about her.*"

Flip was intrigued but felt way out of his depth listening to his mother explain everything. He reached onto the nightstand for the joint; where there's smoke, there's still fire. He managed to start it up a few short pulls could resuscitate it and he passed to Elena. When he exhaled, he still wasn't sure what else he could contribute that he hadn't tried already. "*Mom, can you have Bollard check her out? Just to be sure whatever she has isn't contagious.*"

"*I already did, but she wouldn't allow him to do much. She got all defensive about it when he came to the house for her. He said she was fine, physically at least. The bruising on her face and arms were healing quicker than he thought they should but she seemed ok. It was when he needed to draw blood when she got dramatic and hysterical. I could only see what she did Flip, and I been tryin', but I know something's happened to her. I know she's still fucking your father, Flip. What I don't get is what Ata is hiding. She knows she can talk to me.*" Assured in her belief, Flip could hear that he wasn't going to talk her off this hill tonight, but maybe he could get her to think about it.

"Mom, it might be a little hard to talk to someone if you know they think you're sleeping with their spouse. Even more so if the offended party is an employer. Sorry for my language." Elena had already put down her book and was looking wide-eyed at Flip. *They talkin' 'bout Ms. Ata??? With Mr. Stokton?*

There was another silence. "Maybe, maybe. But still, I can put that away for now. I'm not some slimy ass HouseMother like that slippery bitch Drue Brandton. I swear she goes through Wards like her husband does them cheap-ass cigars. Right now, I need to know what's wrong with my Ata. I can't lose her."

"Mom, maybe she's just tougher than she looks. You can't solve every case. Some things just can't be solved. I mean, what exactly would you do if she either confessed to an affair or told you where she was and what really happened? What if she had to kill in order to escape? Would you let her go? Or keep her around and not trust her again, on top of harboring a suspect regarding a killing? Justified or not, you'd be charged as an accomplice after the fact, especially if they think you knew about it. You thought they railroaded you before, now they'd have you dead set." Flip felt the sting of having to use his mother's work-speak against her. He also stood by it.

Fleice adjusted the landline set. "I refuse to answer that right now, Investigator. Ata has come to mean a lot to me, and I just hate having to think she'd hide something so big from me. I'd like to know about the cheating from her own mouth, sure, but it happens, and I know it's been going on. Right now, I want to about the wellbeing of my Maiden and if we need to tell Monroe about another possible attack, especially if Ata's attacker is focusing on Maidens in the Fifth. I'm a HouseMother of this Territory, and my duty still is to protect everyone in it, P'rotector or not. I can deal with her and your father's indiscretions after."

"Maybe she's afraid. Rightfully or not. You've seen that plenty, right? A witness who saw something but won't initially talk." He could hear laughter on the other end.

"Flip, I swear if it wasn't baskets, you'd be a hell of a p'rotec, baby. Have me outta a job." She laughed some more. *"We'll go your route, Investigator. I'll ease up and see if she opens. If she doesn't, then so be it, but I'll still be watchin' her..."*

Flip laughed himself. *"Aight, cool. Thank you. Let her sit for a little and see what happens."* He felt Elena's hand under the covers and thought of a transition to get off the phone until a question came to him. It's been about four years since the start of this cheating conspiracy theory arrived and he's tried hard not to fall into it. His father was a good man. Maybe a little grey with describing some of his business, but he wasn't some criminal. He admired him, and in many aspects strove to be like him. Him cheating on mom never entered his mind as something he'd lower himself to do. It would be less than a year later that he learned first-hand how easy it can be to hurt someone you loved like that. Flip placed his hand on top of the sheets to capture Elena's. *"Mom? What about dad?"*

Without letting a beat pass, *"I love your father. He's the only man I've been with that I can say I truly loved with my all. He's given me you. He's not leaving, and I'm not either. If I really was up to start over, the chance escaped me a couple years ago, when I was still right."* she laughed. *"If he and Ata are doing something, at this point, it'll take more than a fling to really upset me. Just know that I will not acknowledge what may result from it, should it go that far. Your father and brother aren't Stokton blood, but you are, and you will be the HouseFather of this family. There is very little he can do to change that, unless he's not the man I've come to know and love."*

Silence. She ain't have to get all formal and stuff. Flip took a turn on the joint and came back. *"Aight mom, I was just asking."*

"Don't worry about your father. We're going to sit down like adults and have a nice talk. Anyway, you got a game in a couple days, right?"

Flip loved to tell his mom about his games. *"Yeah, we play Oak City. I'll be starting."*

"Why else would I watch it? I'll talk to you later Flip-baby, ok?"

"Aight mom. Love you."

"Love you too. Give 'em hell."

"Always do." And he hung up. It was weird to him how blunt she was talking about his father's possible affair. She had never mentioned seeing kids in her visions. What if it did go there? *Now I'm falling into it.* He shook away all notions and focused on what was happening now. Elena's hand resumed its trek and settled into a very comfortable stroke.

"What you doing, Ms. Starks?" He looked to her.

"Oh, nothing. My boyfriend's out in Redwater and I'm a little lonely." She stuck her tongue at him. *"Mind occupying my time until he gets back? Tell me about your phone call?"*

"Later." He leaned back as Elena tore back the sheets and started to kiss him softly. First on his cheek. Then his chest. Then his abdomen. Then lower. She took him in as she stroked, giving him control and making her go as deep as he wanted, as rough as he wanted, enjoying it all. He came back from his four-game road trip with some interesting new things he wanted to try. He deserved every bit of herself she could give him, including the right to testing her bodily limits in a way no other man could ever dream to with a

Fountain Matriarch. It'd be less than a year later she would see how easy it is to give an acquaintance the same level of access, the result from a mix of deeply hurt feelings, more than a few wine-soaked texts, and an afternoon of lonely smoking.

"Flip? Flip? Stokton, you there?"

Flip didn't even realize he was daydreaming. He shook himself out and looked at his mobile. "Hey, yeah. Sorry, I was thinking about something."

"Aight man, had me going for a second. Yeah man, I'll be there in a few minutes."

"I'll be here." Flip looked at Elena as he hung up. They met eyes. He doesn't remember seeing Ms. Ata when he was at the house. That was very unusual. "You see Ata at the house?"

"Yeah." Then her mental note came back. "Yes! I meant to tell you I saw her when I left to go to the kitchen while you talked to your mom. Something was off. I swear she looked the same as when I last saw her. I mean almost exactly." She became visibly excited as she spoke.

"Ata's always had a young face, you know that. Anything else?"

Elena took a pause and thought back to Saturday. There was something else about Ms. Ata that didn't seem right. Something about her uniform? The way she looked herself over when she saw Elena. "There wasn't anything specific, but she did look a bit lighter than usual. Almost like she was pale. Was she getting over something recently?"

Flip thought about his daydream and how that was

a long time ago but similar description. He couldn't recall seeing her the last time he went home by himself either. *Still pale.* "No, I don't think so. I was there a few months ago and dad didn't say anything. I don't remember seeing her, though."

"Oh! That was it!" Elena dropped the excitement and got up to walk towards Flip. She stood a few paces from him at the coffeemaker and leaned against the counter and held his hand. "Love, I think something's happening between your father and Ata. I don't know what it was, but when I saw her--"

"I know. Well, not really, but you know." Flip cut in. He swore he had told her about Mom's longstanding theory about an affair. He forgot that him and Elena never got around to much talking that night eight years ago. Elena's mouth dropped open.

"Flip, are you kidding me! What do you mean 'but you know'? Does your mom know?"

"Olga, calm down, she's the one who told me." He went into how Fleice had long suspected that his father and Ata had been messing around and expressed it to him just before fully succumbing to the worst her condition. She never did tell him if she cracked the case. Flip wasn't sure if it was because she chose not too or couldn't bring herself to believe the findings. Ms. Ata's was among the few staff to be there to first-hand witness the downslide, and among the fewer that chose to stay. Whatever happened during those missing days, it changed Ata. "I did think it was a little weird about the lunch mix-up. I don't think mom would write something that didn't happen, but I don't know. Either way, it's old news, Olga. I thought I told you about this." He saw on her face he was mistaken.

"No, you didn't. Are you ok?"

"I'm fine." He took a quick sip from his tea and thought about his mother's straight talk about something that most would find devastating. If her frankness wasn't a holdover from her clear days, it would've shocked Flip. Elena asked him again. "I said I'm fine. Even it was or still going on, I can't judge from a clean slate." There was a knock at the office door. "Plus, he's still my father." He left Elena at the coffeemaker and walked over to let Wallace in. They dapped each other and Wallace made greetings with Elena as they sat at her desk. He passed on the offered coffee, opting for a bottle of water. He didn't notice Elena's look of concern.

"Do I need to leave, y'all? I don't mind." She asked as Flip got out his notebook.

"Did you see anything Flip isn't about to tell me?"

"I don't think so. I kind of know the missing Valer girl. Alexis? I didn't know she was Agent Valer's cousin."

Wallace looked to Flip. Flip shook his head lightly. Wallace turned back to Elena. "Well, Ms. Starks, unless you want to hear some boring back and forth and be willing to say I asked you a few questions, you're free to go."

"Thank you, P'rotector Ladies Man." Elena walked over to her desk and opened her change drawer. She scooped a handful of coins, "Agent Valer called you *Joh'n* during our chat. What's the story there, P'rotector? She's pretty cute." and walked over to the door. Wallace didn't expect the questioning and stumbled over a backstory. "Sure. Anyone want some Stim? We just got a new machine."

"Yeah, and please get a decent flavor this time." Flip teased.

"Thank you, Matriarch." Wallace responded.

The surprise on Wallace's face was completely worth it. She didn't really need to know the story, but his facial expression said there *definitely* was one. If he didn't tell, Flip would. On the way to the vending machine, Elena stopped into Admin and knocked on the desk. "Hey, Ms. Ingram? You in here?"

"Back here, Elena!" The direction of the back office, intended for a second assistant but effectively an extended space storage area for surplus office supplies and the smaller indoor rec equipment. Elena walked to the frame of the entrance.

"Hey Ms. Ingram," She looked at her watch, *3:04.* "can you do me a favor before you leave?"

"Yes, ma'am, what'cha need?" Ms. Ingram was doing her routine of tidying up the storage area. She usually picked the slowest times to clean. Now that she thought about it, it did seem like only a few kids in here considering its Spring Break. A few kids in the gym but nowhere near the expected weekend tally.

"You hear about Alexis Valer?" Elena lowered her eyes as she spoke, she felt bad for not taking more notice when she hadn't seen her around. Alexis was a nice girl, but Elena understood she couldn't make every meeting. Untraditional work carries untraditional hours. "It's been a few days."

"Yes, ma'am. I saw it on the news last night. Alexis was a nice girl." Ms. Ingram signed the Mark of K'd and bent her head momentarily. "K'd be with her." She said to herself.

"They'll find her, Ms. Ingram. She'll be ok."

"I don't know, there are rumors she's sometimes with that St. Clair boy. I remember when he used to run in and up outta here when he was a kid." She Marked herself again. May K'd be with Luc. He was a good boy that just went the wrong way. "What'd you need me to do?"

Elena was surprised at the trivia. Her transition was not the smoothest and some formalities had to be sacrificed for the sake of workflow efficiency. A formal introductory meeting with the core staff was one of them. The previous regime was not accommodating and bordered on sabotageable intent. She knew Carla had been here since she began coming around right before high-school, and thus trusted her read of the kids that's been in and out since. Everyone seemed to respect Ms. Ingram, even the kids she knew that didn't like her. Ever since that first week, it felt like a new breadcrumb of how things were prior to Elena's arrival would fall. Elena knew she'd been here for a long time, but not *that* long. She thought about who else Ms. Ingram watched grow up.

"Can you pull the last two months for me and bring them to my office when you get a chance?"

"Sure thing. Anything else?" She was still focused on her cleaning.

"If you want, you can leave early today. It's not too busy that I can't handle, and I feel like I might be here a while." Elena made her way across to enter the hallway. "Thank you, Ms. Ingram!"

"I'll be over soon!" Ms. Ingram called back.

Elena walked to the gym and stopped at the closed doors to look through the window. A few groups of kids in the bleachers. A couple halfcourt games going on each end of the floor. Elena smiled to herself as she watched the only girl playing set a strong pick before receiving a no-look pass for a left-handed layup. Elena held up a thumbs-up even though she knew she was way too far for the girl to notice. She had never seen this girl before and made a mental note to introduce herself to her the next time she saw her, and to ask Ms. Ingram if she knew her.

Roughly 15 minutes after Elena left her office, she was back just as Ms. Ingram was walking up and about to knock on her door, thin filing folder in-hand. As she handed it off, she saw Flip in the door window and knocked. Flip was facing her and waved as she did.

"Wanna come inside and say hello? He's just talking to P'rotector Wallace."

"Oh, no Ms. Starks, that's ok. Fleice told me y'all came by the house. She sounded so happy."

Elena smiled at the happiness she heard in Ms. Ingram's own voice. "Don't forget to leave early. Just let me know before you close the office."

"Will do." Ms. Ingram responded and went back to the Administration office. If the Center could look like this all week, Ms. Ingram doesn't need to be as on-time for the next couple of days. It's Spring Break, for K'd's sake. She walked in and took her laptop off the desk and across the room to the sofa. Being in the room during this type of info exchange was against protocol, but Elena was no stranger to occasionally being in the room and having to at least look like she wasn't eavesdropping. She actually wasn't most of the time, but Wallace didn't know that. After a few times, she saw that at least looking like she wasn't in the way was good enough. Wallace was a nice guy from what she personally knew of him, just a little mysterious. She liked him enough, he could smile a little more. Reaching into her blazer inside pocket and taking out her earphones, she got cozy on the couch and dug into emails and online videos.

◆ ◆ ◆

"What you think mom left?" Flip checked his mirror as they were turning down her street. He thought a car was making a few too many similar turns to be just coincidence. It pulled into the grocery store lot three turns ago and he never saw it again. It was still a little weird. As they came down, Flip noticed a car parked in front of Elena's house and a man with a noticeable streak of grey in his hair leaning against it. He also noticed he had a box in his hands. He pulled into the driveway and cut the engine.

"Honestly, I'm afraid to guess. When was the last time she's had something sent into the city?" Flip couldn't remember. Elena was more surprised somebody took Birdie serious enough to actually come into town for what could've been a simple overnight parcel. She then remembered Mrs. Stokton also distrusted courier services unless it was her own making the delivery. She walked over to the man with Flip.

"Patriik, how you doing, man?" Flip stuck his hand out.

"Master Stokton. Matriarch Starks." He met Flip's hand and shook with his characteristic firmness before bowing to Elena. Patriik had been with the Stokton family years before Ms. Ata arrived and has always taken his position seriously. Officially, Patriik was the StaffMaster, the youngest in Stokton employee history and helped Ata with executing the day-to-day directives of the larger estate staff. When Ata's predecessor was Released, he was the first to be offered position of Complete HouseWard. He respectfully declined, being mature enough to acknowledge he was much too young at the time to wield that level of authority

255

effectively over many Staff that were older than him. After that "interview", Patriik saw that he began making HouseWard pay even after the gap year before Ata's arrival, and his entrusted duties and privileges greatly expand, now including some requests delivered behind closed doors or sealed notes.

Flip always remembered a specific memory of interaction with Patriik: He and Elena cut afternoon classes to hang out at the house when it was expected to be empty. His parents were both at work and staff was light around the house. Their meeting in Flip's bedroom was more than a little awkward for everyone involved. Later, during a three-day break before his next home game, he asked about why Patriik never told on him. Patriik only responded with a laugh, *"Mr. Stokton, what my employer does with his fellow Founder is of no concern of mine to share. I also appreciated the return of discretion regarding what you saw between Maiden Ata and I. Count us even."*

"This is from your mother." He extended out the box. Flip saw it was more of a case. Rectangle in shape with crimson suede and gold lining, complete with a latch-style keylock.

"You know what's in it?" Flip took the case and asked. He felt it wasn't light but wasn't heavy either. The case felt padded or tightly packed.

"Not officially, sir, but she said I was to witness you open it. Mind if I have some coffee, Matriarch?"

"Sure, come on in." She led them both up the driveway and to the house. "Cream and sugar?"

"No, just honey. Thank you." Patriik answered as she opened the door.

"Interesting order."

"Yes, ma'am. An old habit from my Arms days." He answered quickly but respectfully.

"I hear you. Coffee, black with honey. Flip?" She made her way into the living room and then the kitchen.

"Nah, I'm fine." He and Patriik moved into the living room and sat at the table. Flip was inspecting the case as Elena sat with them.

"It'll be ready in a sec, Patriik."

"That's fine, thank you Matriarch." Patriik nodded his head and went back to Flip. "Mr. Stokton, I think you have the key already."

"Interesting." He got his car keys out and went to one of the few others on his hold-all; his house key. Flip inserted the key and turned until there a *click* and the latch popped. Flip laughed loudly and picked up the folded papers on top of the item inside. Elena let out a loud gasp as Patriik watched silently with a tiny smirk. The kettle indicated it was ready. Elena stayed where she was.

"Don't worry, Ms. Starks, I'll get it." Patriik excused himself and went into the kitchen, where he found a mug and the honey jar already on the counter. He made his coffee and came back to the table, noticing Elena's silence. "Is everything ok?"

"Mmhmm." Her eyes were still on the case.

"You sure you ain't know this was in here, Pat?" Flip asked, still looking over the owner's title and registration papers, and then back over the pistol. It was nice. And very clean; like just polished clean. Surrounded by a felt the same color as the case sat a Tojke T45 L.E.O Compact; semi-automatic and custom colored body in the Stokton family color, accented with engravings of both the Stokton crest and Fountain flag on either side of the handgrip. A deep, strong matte finished crimson with reflective gold for the engravings, magazine release and hammer. On both sides of the slide was a name engraved in fine cursive: *Birdie*. Flip could see his mom asking for something like this, especially when he read this particular model was only for those in law enforcement, but it was a bit away from her sense of aesthetic. He imagined his dad taking enthusiastic liberty to edge his wife away from her favorite colors of black, grey, P'rotector's uniform yellow, and Standard Issue. Next to it was a single magazine, nuzzled in its own mold. Flip picked up the gun and held to examine it. Its size felt small but very comfortable in his hand as he wrapped his finger onto the trigger.

He couldn't forget his parents' small array of "personal defense" built up over the years. Flip could remember the first time he saw them shoot as a young boy. It was amazing and scary at the same time. He came outside in time to see Patriik launching ducks across the backyard as his father shot them down with a single-bolt longshooter. Mom had a weird thing about birds, despite her nickname; but his father? He thought his father loved animals. Through the lens of a child's eye, Flip didn't realize the ducks he saw in the air were not frozen and real, but only vividly decorated clay, and was in tears about his father being a duck murderer. As the only staff member closest to Flip in age, Patriik was tasked with having to delicately explain the scene as Ronald's appointed counselor.

After a "thorough investigation", conducted by the obvious unbiased choice of In-House Investigator Fleice Stokton, Ronald Stokton was deemed an innocent man and even curried an interest in Flip with knowing how to shoot. It became a bonding hobby between father and son. Over the years, target shooting gave way to Flip's bigger interest and budding skill in the kind of shooting intended to leave only riddled egos. Ronald's enthusiasm and want-for-knowledge in guns continued but took a big hit once his wife's condition revealed itself in full. He then decided to move them all, except the handcannon he kept in the bedroom, to the large shed in the backyard. He loved his wife dearly and trusted her impulse control, he just wanted to move them, just in case, that's all.

"No, but I had my suspicion. She had been cleaning it earlier in the day yesterday. I believe it stemmed from your talk on the phone." Patriik took a sip and then a pen out of his pocket. He clicked and passed it across the table. Flip read the owner's title again. It was the original document and only 6 years old, still having the old Fountain City emblem as the watermark and dated a month short before it was updated. He scanned the title again, focusing on the bottom.

Firearm: Tojke T45 Law Enforcement Official Compact

Original Purchaser of Firearm: Ronald Stokton, House Patriarch, Founding Family Stokton

Authorized Registered Party: Fleice Stokton, HouseMother, Founding Family Stokton

Then he saw something a lot more interesting.

Clandestine Carry for Law Enforcement Official: Approved

"Why'd dad get a gun for mom? She don't go nowhere, and already got plenty." Flip looked back to Patriik. "Did she tell you she Saw something?"

Patriik sipped again. "Your father got it as an anniversary gift for your mother, though the night he presented it to her, she couldn't seem to remember asking for it. She passed all of the physical and mental checks and Dr. Bollard signed off that she could legally own it, but strongly discouraged it. As for our meeting tonight, I was explicitly told not to tell your father. Also, when the last time your mother told you when she's Seen anything?"

Flip took the registration papers and scoffed the question. It had been a really long time since mom's admitted to knowing something due to her Sight. She's so used to talking in riddles and cloudy warnings. Among the stamps and seals of verification, there was a line that was blank underneath his mother's signature. The "Date" line was blank, but he could tell it was recent by the tweaked second 'e' he'd been noticing over the past year in her letters.

Original Registered Party: Fleice Stokton,

HouseMother, Founding Family Stokton

Authorized New Registered Party: Flip Stokton

Rising Patriarch I, Founding Family Stokton

Authorized Transfer of Registration: Approved

Transferring a gun? Flip thought about his visit and the incident with the canvas, and then about Ms. Ata. Those two didn't mix well. Ata was a lot of things, and a thief was not one of them. As he looked down the barrel again, he swore he felt the T45 vibrate for only a moment, causing his hand to jump from surprise. Nobody registered the hand movement. Flip took the pen and signed his name and the date and returned it. In the indoor light, Flip saw that Patriik's eyes had an almost unnatural reflection to them. They looked, cleaner? Had they always been like that? Patriik took another sip and asked, "Should I get the other box from the car? She said it was dependent on your initial acceptance."

Flip nodded and Patriik got up for the door. He saw Elena's face as he rose and decided he should take his time looking for that second package. "Flip, there's a gun in my house." Last she knew, Flip hasn't been to a range since his playing days. He told her about the end of his call last night and how his mother sounded concerned.

"Maybe she knows something I don't yet. You heard Pat say my dad doesn't even know about this." There was a hitch in his throat. "Mom doesn't need a gun right now anyway, Olga. She doesn't go out unless Ata or dad is with her."

"So, what she think you 'boutta do, huh? Have shootouts in the street like it's a fucking Nite Owl comic?" Elena's accent was full bore, going to sit next to him, she calmed her voice as her words came out measured and stern. "Flip, is there anything about this case you haven't told me? Are you in danger? Am I?"

"No, I don't think so." He put the gun away and closed the case, twisting the latch until he heard it *click* to lock back into place. The TV came to mind and he looked over to the living room for a second. "There might be some silence going forward until this case is closed or solved, but right now, you know everything. It is still a murder case, but I promise to tell you what I can."

Elena looked at him before Patriik conveniently entered during an extended period of silence. He was carrying a bigger, slate-black attaché box by the handle. When he came over to the table, he gulped the last of his coffee and requested another for the road as he unlocked and flipped it open. "I promise this won't take too long."

"Mmhmm." Elena responded as she walked to the kitchen, switching between standing at the entryway and the kettle as it reheated.

Flip knew staying over was out of the question, and indulged Patriik on a brief explanation of the T45 and the goodies his mother sent from her personal collection. Patriik placed his own standard T45 on the table for size comparison and demonstrated optimal ways to carry the compact model for a smooth retrieval and concealment. Among the goodie box were crimson matte-coated extended and standard magazines and a single magnification reflex scope. The lens is said to be infused with augmented redstone and will outline any heat source within 10 yards. The optimal distance for accuracy was five or less. Patriik de-constructed the T45 and after a short inspection, reassembled it in a few seconds. He then took out boxes of both live-rounds and practice ammo along with two holsters: a dark brown leather one for the hip and a black tactical one fitted for the thigh. Flip dug the thigh holster, he just hoped it would fit.

"You remember how to load a magazine, right, Mr. Stokton?" Patriik asked with a smile. He was already reaching for a standard magazine and opening a box of ammo. Flip saw how smoothly Patriik transferred the rounds from box to column. "Want an extended? You got 4 here." There was a sound of restrained eagerness in his voice.

"Just one. I'll do the rest at home. As for shooting, let's say I might be using that practice ammo before anything." Flip took two of the standard size mags and loaded them with practice and live rounds respectively. "Your blade lessons are much closer to mind."

"Understandable. Your father's been expanding the range at home in anticipation of the summer. He wants to do something very special for your mother this Founder's Day." He was barely looking at what he was doing but his rhythm never went away.

Elena liked Patriik a lot without knowing much of his personal life before Fountain. She enjoyed how seriously he took his job and service to the Stokton family. She knew he was in the Territory Arms before coming to serve the Stokton family. Even for a wood elf, he looked young. Almost younger than her and Flip if it wasn't for his persistent stubble and the streak of grey in his tastefully unkempt brown hair. She hoped the hairstyle was intentional, playing even more into his general air of laid-back professional. She then thought about a funny memory of him walking in on her and Flip on their first time. He apologized profusely and with a quick smooth-back of his hair, closed the door. By the look of his face, she wasn't sure which one of them was more embarrassed. "I apologize again, Matriarch, but HouseMother did feel this would serve Flip better than it is her. She is only looking out for his, and your, safety. I do hope this eases your spirit." He looked at her and nodded. They both understood that she wasn't truly upset at him. She also couldn't be truly upset at Mrs. Stokton for wanting to keep her son safe.

"It's fine, Patriik. I've just never been a big fan of guns, that's all. If she wanted to give it to Flip, I can't stop that. I'm sorry that she feels she shouldn't have it. Would you like another coffee?"

Patriik finished loading a standard magazine and carefully arranged everything back into the attaché before closing and locking it. He took out an envelope and a small drawstring bag from his blazer. He placed the envelope on the table in front of Flip and put the attaché key into the bag. He then looked to Elena. "Yes, please. Do you have a cup I can take with me?"

"I'll do you one better." She snapped her fingers and went into the kitchen, disappearing into the pantry. After a short search, she returned with an open box and pulled out a tall plastic container with a screw-top. "Have you heard of these RoadMugs? You can stretch a couple days out of it before having to wash it or throw it out. I'll give you the rest of what's in the kettle, ok?" She was already placing it on the counter and beginning to pour.

"It'll only be an hour drive, but thank you, Ms. Starks. I'll save the rest for tomorrow and test your claim." He coughed out a laugh as he spoke to try breaking the veneer of tension. He couldn't understand how the same girl that used to come over to the house and watch action movies with Master Stokton was the same woman in front of him with such an aversion to the very thing that supplemented her entertainment. She's even practiced her bow shot on the family range; good shot from what he recalled. He then placed his finger on the envelope. "I truly don't know what's in here, Master Stokton, only that your mother said to open and read it before you decide to start carrying." He shifted his eyes to Elena. "And Matriarch, my father used to tell me a leng is most effective when their handler is judicious. I'm sure you and your other Founders understand this philosophy regarding your own Maidens or Wards. I don't see Master Stokton playing 'Tecs and Robbers with his life or yours. He is but only one man." Elena saw a tiny smirk come across. She noted the interesting use of "their" when referring to an inanimate object.

"Thanks Pat." Flip put the sack into his pocket and picked up the envelope. He'd read it when he got home. He then walked Patriik to the door and they shook hands a final time. When he saw Patriik enter his car, Flip closed the door and turned to find Elena holding the gun case. "I'll be leaving in a few myself. I'm really sorry, El."

Elena knew he was. "It's ok, Flip. If she wanted you to have it, I can decide for you if you keep it. I just don't know why she told him to bring it here. You know I don't mind them dropping stuff off, but what if we didn't show up when we did? Would there be a gun sitting on my front porch all night?"

"I don't know, Olga. I doubt it," He walked back over to the table and stood over the attaché. "something tells me Patriik had additional orders to wait as long as he needed to. But look, I'm putting it away, aight? Mind handing me that?" Flip could almost hear the tension during the short pause that followed his request. "Don't be like that, you saw me lock it up. For K'd's sake, you actin' like you ain't shot before." He wasn't sure where this was coming from but Flip was starting to get a little tired of the scared act, real or not. The damn thing wasn't even loaded.

"You know that was for Scouts, Flip. I had to get that fucking merit badge before camp was over." She couldn't believe how stupid that sounded out loud, but this wasn't the same as archery. Her father has gifted her a few bows over her childhood years and even an ornate longbow for her first UBL Women's Championship, but it stayed in the attic unless she had time to practice. This gun, as beautiful as it was, could make the most spineless person feel like K'd Herself if put in the wrong hands, and that wasn't appropriate for mortals. At least with a bow, one still needed Her hand to guide their aim, and heart. She breathed in slowly and exhaled, trying to get centered. Monday evening fighting was not the way to start a week. But neither was having a HouseWard, or anyone for that matter, deliver a gun to your house in the cover of dusklight. "If you want to sleep over tonight, *this* needs to sleep in the car." She was pointing at the gun and attaché. "I'm serious."

"Fair." He locked the T45 case and envelope into the attaché and put the ammo key into his pocket. Then he reopened it and took the envelope out. It was still early in the evening; he might read it before bed. He noticed something slid inside the envelope as he placed it on the table. After locking up again, he went and put the attaché into Joy's trunk. *Maybe she's right. Then again, three people are dead and one's missing.* He thought as he walked back to the house. It was darker out than he thought it should've been and he checked his phone; *6:57PM.* He was walking in as an observation came to him; *all the murders been at night.* As he closed the door, he found the dining room empty and went towards the kitchen.

"Look at this!" Elena called him from the living room. He found her standing at the sofa, eyes fixated on the screen. When he walked over to her, she grabbed his hand. According to Fountain City News, the unidentified woman found at the St. Clair home had woken up an hour ago. She was currently sleeping but is confirmed to be otherwise responsive. It was a still developing story. Flip was pulling out his phone and making a call as Elena asked him something he didn't hear.

"P'rotector Wallace speaking."

"Watching the news right now?"

"I got it on, yeah."

Flip thought that was an odd way to answer but shook it off. He thought he could hear music in the background. Not like a club or bar, but soft and contained. Like he was home.

"This a bad time? I can wait until tomorrow if you need to talk to Holmb first." Flip felt he may have jumped the horse a bit by calling. He felt Elena break hands and went to the couch, laying across but still watching the coverage of the miraculous recovery.

"No, I got a couple minutes and I actually do need to talk to you. Vice and Homicide are going to be working together on this St. Clair thing. Seems like Luc may have had a few more strings that tangled than we initially thought. Basically, you're not *officially* on the St. Clair murder, but CP and I were able to have a contract made for the Shockley and Watering Hole murders, which is fast approaching the bottom of the priority queue for lack of suspects or new evidence. Sorry, man." There was a rustle. "Hey, Flip? I gotta run, man. Let me call you back."

"Yo, Wallace, hold up!" He caught him just in time.

"What's up?"

"Say, I got a gun. It's legal and registered. Anything I need to know?"

"No shit? We talking some real hardware or some fancy crossbow?"

"Any difference?"

Flip could hear the click of a lighter. "Nothing changes. You're still a PC, just now carrying a tool on you. I ain't even know you shot like that, man. Hopefully, it's as good as your court action."

Flip felt the dig and chuckled. It's been a couple years since he last shot for target. Maybe longer than that with a pistol. "Aight, thanks."

"Yep." Then an abrupt hang-up of the call. Whoever was there with Wallace was probably giving better incentive to get off the phone than Flip was for him to stay on. He thought about the possibility that he was with Hazel, or

Agent Valer. As he lifted Elena's feet to sit down, he put his mobile on the table and leaned back, watching the coverage.

"You think Wallace can cook?" He asked after a minute.

Elena laughed and sat up some, "I think he knows a lot about food and has better taste than the average 'tec. Why? Was he cooking?" After the Valer reveal, she wanted to know more gossip about the p'rotector.

"Nah, just curious. Apparently, I'm on the Shockley case and that guy who was got at the Hole. Wallace said Homicide and Vice will be working together on St. Clair."

Elena got close to Flip, draping an arm around him and to play with his hair. "Flip. Please be careful with this, ok? This is murder a few times over, Love. I don't like the feel of it."

"I know." He turned to kiss her hand before resuming his attention to the TV. "I don't either."

"Hey, tell you what. Get Birdie and meet me in the dining room." She kissed his cheek and climbed over the sofa, making her way for the stairs. He left for the car and returned to see her standing with her K'd talisman in-hand and her Sanctum Veil. He rolled his eyes.

"Can't we do this in the morning?"

"Why put off for the morning what can happen tonight?"

He put the suede case on the table and opened it. The light allowed the *Birdie* engraving and Stokton family crest to glow brightly against the deep red of the frame. Ever since a burglary suspect tried to stab him during his first case, Flip made sure he kept a dagger on him when he was on official business but never found the need for anything else. He had no problem with K'd, if such a being did exist. His mother and father raised him to respect the teachings from school and live an honest life, they just weren't the most orthodox of practitioners. They were a High Holidays and Sanctum social obligations kind of family by the time he got to high school. Up to their high school senior year, Flip and Elena already went to school mandated Sanctum three times a week. Elena's family was slightly better, her mother having more than enough belief in K'd to cover for her husband's personal disbelief and making sure they attended Sunday Sanctum at least twice a month. Elena was always jealous her father only had to go at least once. He allowed Rubina to practice Its ways within their home, and credits it for the woman that Elena grew to be. When everything was set, Elena lit two candles on either side of the gun case.

"Ready?" She asked him, talisman still in hand.

He nodded and she began her blessing. It was a personalized Prayer of P'rotection for Flip set to the tune of K'd's Oath followed by a Prayer of Arms passed down from Elena's maternal grandfather for Birdie and the dagger. May it strike down the enemies of K'd and Its children. May it protect its owner and those of His import. May K'd guide the hand so it will strike justly and lead to glory. In K'd's name, *Anum.*

"*Anum*" Flip repeated silently.

"May K'd be with you, Flip." Elena looked up through her veil and saw a closed-eyed Flip in his personal reflection. *Can't take the Sanctum out of the boy.* K'd loved all of Her children, no matter how infrequent the visits.

"And K'd be with you, Olga. Thank you." He lifted his head and blew out one of the candles.

"You're welcome. I noticed you ain't been getting in

any more trouble since I been doing this." She stuck her tongue. Flip rolled his eyes, then he saw a backpack on the floor.

"What's this?" He pointed at the bag "Going somewhere?"

"Your place, if you quit rolling your eyes." She put her arms around Flip's neck, bringing him close.

"Ain't you got work in the morning, Ms. Starks?" He held her by the waist.

"I do, and I promise to be out before your girlfriend comes home." She stuck her tongue again. "But seriously, I do have work tomorrow. I'm leaving early in case we have more kids come. I'll drive over with you." She kissed him before putting the candles and talisman away and went back upstairs. When she returned, she had a t-shirt and joggers with a pink and purple windbreaker.

"That jacket new? Shit looks nice, girl." Flip eyed the jacket.

Elena smiled coyly and did a turnaround. "You like it? Remember I went to speak at AC Poorsmith? They gave me this as a thank-you in lieu of payment."

"Looks good on you."

"I know. You say so every time you see it." She giggled as she saw the short embarrassment rise on his face. "It's ok, Love. I know I don't wear it often." She stuck her tongue. "Ready to go?"

"Yep."

She made sure everything was turned off, got her keys, and turned on the security system before leaving and walking to her car.

CHAPTER 15

As Elena was leaving her house to enjoy a calm night, Whore was picking herself off the floor for the second time of the evening. In a private moment, she asked Master if he could let her go home. Two slaps told her that was a hard no, and she was verbally told that she was already home. Maybe she was home already, and everything from the previous days were all a really bad, vivid dream. It was just some *really* bad Rock; she'll be waking up sometime soon. Her body told her that was impossible. Mother had to hit her earlier, but it was understandable, she had overpoured the dinner tea and it burned her legs. Whore was sorry, and agreed that no dinner was an appropriate punishment. At least the hits didn't come as often, now. She was far from the perfect pet, but she was learning.

Rac' stood and watched as she got up slowly, the length of chain from her wrists sliding across the floor as she held her face and stood up. She kept her head down and quietly apologized. Loud enough for him to hear but soft enough for only him. He looked up and saw Hana standing at the banister, trying to see what the commotion was down there. "Nothing. Don't worry about it." Rac' called to her. Hana turned back towards her room and went inside. When he heard the door close, he went for the length of chain. Alexis flinched until she saw he was only holding it in his hand.

"Need to use the bathroom?" Rac' asked her.

"Yes, Master." Her voice was coming back but it was still nowhere near its original smoothness. It had a hoarseness now but was still attractive to Rac'. It reminded him of that red-headed theatre actress that was really popular when he was a teen. *Something-something Bricke.* He even had one of those adult "postcards" with a full-body nude of her for a few months in the Arms, until he lost it in a drunken game of Scratch one night against his Commanding Officer. He hoped that at worst, this would be Alexis' new sound. She just needed stop fucking screaming all the time.

Rac' led her to the first-floor bathroom and opened the door. When Alexis entered, he threw the chain in and turned around. The next sound he heard was the steady run of relief, then the toilet flush. When he turned around, she was at the sink washing her hands and her face. Aside from the patches of red, the bruising and swelling has decreased greatly. Hana was feeling very nice after lunch and tended to her in the kitchen before disappearing upstairs. She thanked her; even kissing Hana's hand in gratitude. Hana coldly petted her on the head and left soon after, not coming back until just before dinner. Rac' noticed that she didn't eat much on her plate beside the meat and a some of the vegetables. She even left a practically full glass of wine when she excused herself and asked Whore to make some tea.

Rac' looked at his watch and saw it was only quarter to 8. Another hour of free time before it was bedtime. He turned and asked Alexis what she would like to do for an hour.

"What?" She was instantly scared, sure that this was a trap of some kind. This is the first she was *asked* of anything of her own will. She didn't know how to proceed and kept her head down.

"I said, what would like to do? Watch TV? Read a book? You *can* read right?"

Whore was still positive there was something else

but nodded yes. She looked at Rac', her left eye still visibly cloudy in the upper corner but hadn't expanded to the whole eye.

"Hello? You hear me?" Rac' called to her. *Her eye's gonna stay like that, for sure.*

Whore jumped and thought this might not be a trick. "Can we go outside?" She instinctively tensed herself. Nothing came.

"Sure." He held the chain as they walked to the door. He then turned and yanked at the chain, pulling Alexis just a few inches away from himself. He placed a firm grip on the section that held her wrist bracelets and leaned in, "Please, don't do anything stupid. I really don't want to have to hurt you." before opening the door and letting the cool air enter the main foyer. They then stepped onto the porch.

"Yes, Master." She gave up any intention on running a long time ago, she didn't even know *where* to run. On the ride out, she didn't see what looked like a house anywhere. She breathed in deep as the cool, rain scented breeze entered her lungs, making her cough aggressively at the taste of fresh air. When she regained herself, she found herself crying. The emptiness of the yard confirming she was indeed at her final home. Rac' let her weep and sat her on the porch couch, choosing to sit next to her, chain still in-hand. After a few minutes, Rac' walked with her around the front yard, doing more talking to than with Whore about music trends that were long dead, his already muscular frame only more intimidating in the isolating darkness of the openness.

When Hana heard the front door reopen and close, she was leaving the sunroom and coming down the stairs with used bowls and cups. She saw from the sunroom window that Rac' was walking Whore around the yard. She was learning; quickly at that. Last night's scorched-earth strategy was effective. Rac' taught her that sometimes the most savage tactic is often the most effective in getting a point across. She felt *Him* last night, so much so that she thought *He* may have even been in the cellar with her.

"Good walk?" Hana asked as she gave the bowls to Whore.

"Yes, Mother." Whore answered with her head down.

"Not you." She looked back to Rac'. "Was it?"

"Yeah. Got some fresh air. It feels good out. Not too warm but comfortable enough for no jacket."

Alexis felt her ear twitch hearing Master's assessment of the weather. *Warm?* She would've preferred a jacket if she knew she was going to go outside tonight.

"I might take a stroll then later." She looked back at Whore. "Mind helping me clean these?"

Whore nodded as Hana took the leash from Rac' and turned towards the kitchen. Rac' followed them and sat at the kitchen island, looking at Hana and Alexis go over to the sink and start the water.

"Have you been online tonight?" Rac' called over to Hana.

"No. But I'm guessing that the girl woke up?"

"Yeah. Did you Turn her?"

"No," Hana stopped and turned to him. "I just had a taste, that's all." Hana started on the last cup. "You pull on me enough, little brother. A hospital can be a bad place to Turn without proper care. Or the perfect one." Hana turned off the water as she and Whore finished drying the last bowl. "If she's Turned, I'm interested to see how they explain her 'odd' cravings and behavior. Or why they had to kill her." She laughed to herself and winked to Whore. It was returned with a meek smile and averted eyes. "Everything ok, Whore?" She shifted the leash into her left hand. Whore became very nervous. Her leg started to lightly twitch as if revving up.

"Yes, Mother. I'm fine." Whore was unsure whether to look Mother in the face or at the floor. She did both.

"I didn't ask that." She took a step closer. "I asked is everything ok?" Mother had a calm look on her face. A little too calm. She had the same look when she tended her. She seemed relaxed. Sedated. Drugged. Drugged?

"Yes, everything's fine."

Hana smiled, "Good." then made a quick finger across her cheek. It wasn't enough to break skin but Whore felt it like a papercut. She didn't flinch. She was learning. If Mother wanted to hurt her, she would have.

Rac' partly stood. "Stop it. She's been good."

"I was just asking." She then held Whore's left hand in her right. "I can trust you to be honest with me, right?" There was a flicker in her eyes.

"Ye-Yes, Mother. I swear." There was a *pop* on her left cheek. She did flinch back this time.

Rac' got up and walked around the island. He snatched the leash out of his sister's hand and pulled. "Stand down." Hana caught one of the wrist shackles and held Whore in place.

"Either you're scared or lying, but I don't like that little stutter. It has interesting timing of showing itself." She picked up the dishrag and started to wring it. "If you're still scared of me, I promise I can be good, but how can I keep my promise if I think you're lying?" The rag was neatly splayed on the edge of the sink to dry.

"I promise, I wasn't lying. I promise, Mother." Whore saw another flicker and then nothing. The fire was out. Hana smiled at her before pulling her down to kiss her cheek. It was almost right on the surface of the scratch. As she pulled back, she saw Whore's cloudy eye twitching.

"I'll try not to be so scary from now on, ok? Just keep being a good girl." Her voice went almost playful.

"Yes, Mother." Whore lowered her head. She quickly looked back at Master.

"'I'm going to take a walk." She kissed Whore's cheek again and heard a faint growl from her stomach. "Good night, Whore." She tapped her on the stomach. "I'll cook you a nice breakfast tomorrow. You've earned it."

"Thank you, Mother."

Rac' led her out and down the hall, towards the cellar door. He wanted to have a snack before he retired for the night. Alexis followed behind him and began to anchor herself as they got closer to the floor-door. She tried planting her weight to resist his pulls, only grunting in effort as she thrashed her wrists.

"No!" She dropped into a ball. "No!"

Hana stepped just outside the kitchen and saw Rac' tugging on his length of chain. She leaned against the threshold post and put her hands in her pockets.

"Get up." Rac' pulled her up and planted a swift punch just below her ribcage. Alexis felt like she deflated. He caught her before her knee could hit the floor and as he put her on his shoulder. He caught a glimpse of Hana looking at them. "What?"

"Nothing." She stood up and went back into the kitchen.

Whore was 0-3 with staying on her feet when it mattered. Master carried her down the stairs and to the center of the cellar, towards the blood-red obelisk. The dark made him barely visible, and he stayed silent, only exhaling as he absorbed her blows. She was doing her best to hit and kick until she felt a hand grab her ankle and a sharp sting into her calf. She covered her mouth as a yell left her and she was thrown against the obelisk. Then she was pinned against it. Master was really angry, his fire told her everything she needed to know. His grip on her neck punctuated it. The floor started to feel as though it was falling from under her. She was floating. Alexis allowed her body to go limp as she closed her eyes.

POP!

"Open your fucking eyes."

POP! POP!

She did, and felt her airway constrict as her breathing thinned out. Her heart was beating in her head. After a few beats, Master let her go and she dropped to her knees. She clutched at her neck as she coughed herself into a fetal position. Master reached down and tore at Whore's gown, ripping away a large portion of the left sleeve. He then started to take off his shirt. And then his pants, standing over her in only his briefs in near pitch-black. There was a heat radiating from him despite the perpetual cold of the cellar.

"I thought you were learning." Rac' securely wrapped his left hand with his t-shirt and lifted Whore by the wrists. She could feel him fumbling around with her lock until she heard a *click*. She then felt her shackles release and fall off. Stillness. There was a *thud* on her right cheek and she fell back. She straightened herself and immediately went for the center of the room, towards the obelisk, and into a fabric-headed backhand. "Put your fucking hands up, Alexis." came a growl left-center of her position. Obeying her command, she raised her hands in front of her.

"Yes, Master."

Two orbs of fire burned as hands came from the darkness and adjusted hers into a fighting posture.

She's tastes cleaner now, Rac' thought to himself as he climbed the stairs. Alexis put up a better than he expected from her. There was a solid punch somewhere in her. As he approached the top, he could see flickering light coming from of the sunroom. He slowly walked down the hall.

"Hana?" There was a sniffle.

When Rac' got to the sunroom entry, he saw the furniture was the same as it had been for movie night, but tonight's feature was a real deep cut. A sepia toned silent film of a beautiful woman making a dress, with descriptive text "chapters" describing each stage of the process. At one point, these instructional videos were a white whale within the garment and commercial fashion industry in their time. In Monarch, they were only made by a single woman. Now, any warm-blooded nobody can make a "tutorial" in their unkempt bedroom and be taken seriously as a fashionista. Rac' was stuck to the projection screen. He hadn't seen this one in a long time.

"How'd you get this done?" Rac' was still looking at the screen.

Hana sniffled again and sipped her wine. "Mr. Frost from the library has been working on it for a while. He called me just before lunch to pick it up." She sipped again. "This one was always my favorite. I love how she dyed the fabric."

Rac' heard the bottle as it emptied into Hana's glass. "I miss her, Hana. I miss her a lot." He broke his trance to look at his sister.

"Me too, little brother, but she's better now. We'll see her again in time. Can you throw this away for me?" She pointed at the coffee table and a sack on the table. Rac' picked it up and went back towards the doorway. The sack still felt heavy.

"You done any more?"

"No, I've been too busy fucking crying, nosey." Hana adjusted herself into a sitting position. Rac' saw she only had a short sweater on. "Wanna taste test me?" She pulled a sleeve up held her arm out.

"No." Rac' turned to leave.

"Good. Should I cook for three tomorrow?"

"Maybe."

There was a part of her that *really* wanted to hear about the cellar. He had been down there for a while. She moved her hand under the blanket and traced herself. Maybe it'd be better she didn't know; more exciting to imagine what he did and how. How he broke her down. There was a feeling Rac' wanted to try Turning her soon. Very soon. "Can you stay here a little? It just started over a few minutes ago." Hana asked.

"Not tonight, I'm tired. I'm going to bed." Rac' called back. "Good night, Hana."

"Good night." Hana teased herself with a final touch

and went back to her wine. She loved her mother, through all of her faults, and promised herself and Rac' she wouldn't fall into the same vices. Rock made Hana feel nicer, but so did Mama's "funny dust". Sadly, it also allowed *Him* to get away with his more egregious brutalities. C'elia Tabine was a tiny but strong woman, but even as a child, Hana recognized she was also a broken woman. She was broken a long time ago, probably before Hana and Rac' were even thought about, and when Hana was Turned, she could understand how. *He* almost broke Hana too, but since then, she refused to ever put herself in that position for anyone else. She watched her mother's tutorial video another two times before she drifted asleep. There was a tiny pull, like something was siphoning from her, but it was far away. Nothing to think about right now. Things might end up being a very interesting in Fountain tomorrow. Especially for those working at Fountain Memorial.

CHAPTER 16
Tuesday

Flip was practicing some early-morning jump shots in the Center's indoor gym. It's been a little while since he's ran solo in here, but it was still the best place. Working out in the best facilities around the country couldn't compare to true home-court advantage. The first month or so before he went dark, he would have some of the kids pick anywhere before the half-court line and he'd throw one up for them. Most of the time, it went in with no problem but sometimes, he'll goose one so the kids can gossip with their friends and parents how Coach Flip missed a shot. After a few behind the arch corners, he saw Elena knocking on one of the open double-doors. She had a mobile to her ear. It was his mobile.

"Flip! Flip!" Elena was waving him over.

His first thought was his mother. Then how he hadn't read her note yet. He let a fadeaway fly from the top of the arch. There was short roll around the rim, but it fell in. "What's up?" He asked as he got closer, already reaching for the phone.

"It's P'rotector Holmb. He needs to talk to you right now."

Flip put the phone to his face as he accepted a towel Elena bought with her. He wiped his face as he spoke. "P'rotector?"

"Mr. Stokton, I know you're not on the St. Clair case, but I ask that you come to Fountain Memorial as soon as possible. Ms. Shockley is awake. And talking."

Flip paused. *Shockley?*

"Mr. Stokton?"

"Yeah, I'm here. Did you say *Shockley*?"

"'I'll have to fill you in when you get here, unless I need to meet you somewhere."

"Nah, it's cool. I'll be there in a few." He hung up and wiped sweat again.

As he entered Elena's office, Flip placed his bag down and sat across her at her desk. She was on the phone, and by the sound of it, taking care of business. After a few minutes, she wrapped up and looked at him. She didn't look happy, and he knew why. He had Birdie with him. Technically, it was in the car since weapons of any kind were forbidden within the Center, but Elena didn't see the difference. "Everything ok?" He asked.

"Yep. What'd Holmb want?" Elena had a sting to her when it got to Holmb. When Flip had started his consultant work and he met Holmb, he realized he was the shirt-and-tie Elena was meeting that awkward run-in that night in the Hole. He later learned that nothing came of it. Holmb wasn't sure of how much Flip knew, but he still kept it professional once they made acquaintance. This was the first time either man would be working with the other directly.

"He said the girl at Fountain Memorial was up and talking. He said her name was Shockley." Flip saw the change in Elena's face probably more than she felt it. He began to change his shoes. "Can I use the showers real quick?"

Elena's face eased as curiosity took over. "Yeah, sure. Did he say a first name? Also, here." She handed him a thin folder. "These are from the past two months of Next Steps. I highlighted the days Alexis was there." Flip took the eased look as an opening.

"I should hire you as an assistant. Thank you." He said

as he took the enclosed papers and folded them over and put them into his bag.

"If it means another delivery from your folks, I'm fine." She went back to her laptop. "P'rotector Stokton." Flip heard her whisper. She looked at him and stuck her tongue.

"That tongue's gonna get you in trouble, girl."

"Won't be the first time." Elena responded and stuck her tongue again. "Now, I think there's a shower with your name on it, Mr. Stokton. Hurry up before we open."

"Yes, ma'am." Flip gathered his bag and made his way to the door.

In his car, Flip opened the center console and was glad he brought one for the road. He placed the joint in his mouth but held off on lighting. Founding Family or not, drugs on the grounds of the Center was still punishable by Fountain law. He then got out the envelope from his mother. As he started Joy, he took in dry pulls for flavor. Nice and fruity, perfect for the morning. He opened the envelope and took out the tri-folded paper inside. As he unfolded it, a small plastic rectangle fell out onto his lap. He picked it up and saw it was a stamped and sealed pocket-sized version of the registration for Birdie. His name had already been signed as the registered owner. No tweaked letters, but he could tell his mother's handwriting. How far back did she know he would accept her present? With the paper fully open, he read the accompanying letter.

Flip-baby,

I'm sorry I didn't tell you the other night, but I thought you'd do better with this than I would. Think of it as me always being there with you on your cases. No good PI is ever without need for backup. Give 'em hell and trust your Sight.

I love you,

Mom

P.s. Tell Elena I'm really sorry about having a gun delivered to her house, I know how she feels around these things. I thought she came from military stock? That girl needs to stop playing proper.

After reading the letter a second time, Flip looked into the console and at the holstered T45. Before pulling out of his space, he took his windbreaker off and threw it into the front seat on top of his bag. It was a muggy and cool this morning, but the jacket felt like too much. He put Joy into reverse and slowly backed out to leave the lot. As he did, he saw a Fountain City Florist delivery van pull into the lot. He got out his phone and called Elena, putting her on speaker as he drove past the van.

"Miss me already?"

"Maybe. Come to the front door, I think you got something being delivered."

"Oh, um, ok." He could papers being arranged and movement. After a few seconds, heard a gasp. "Flip, what's this?"

"I don't know. What is it?" He exchanged his phone for the cup holder lighter and began to ignite. "Olga?"

"Flowers, from HouseMother Fleice Stokton. Flowers and a big plush hummingbird with a card." Another second of rustle. "'I'm sorry I had a gun delivered to your house. I love you, El. Love, Aunt Fleice." Flip heard loud laughter as he got up the street. "Guess she couldn't find a more decorative way to say it. The arrangement is quite beautiful, Flip. She had them set in the shape of my family's crest, colors and all. That also explains the plush, I guess. Should I call her? Is she up right now?"

Flip exhaled and stopped at the light, "Call the house. She's probably up or about to be soon, but if she doesn't answer, Dad or Ata should."

"Ok." She took a pause. "And if they don't?"

"Not funny." Flip heard the edge. He took two quick hits and let it rest in the passenger cupholder.

"I swear I wasn't trying to be, Flip." Elena's voice was quiet and even toned.

Flip exhaled. "I know. My bad, I just don't want to talk about that." As he spoke, the light changed and he continued on, making a turn and onto the same street as the precinct building. He sped past and took a straight shot to the next two block and turned, entering the Third District. "If she wants him to go, she'll go through with it. If not, then she won't. Either way, I'm sure Ata will still be there. Honestly, I'd prefer not to know. I still love my father, Olga."

She understood Flip's position but didn't at all. How could he be so centrist about the possibility of his father's infidelity? Then she thought about her own past indiscretions, and how she hasn't told Flip about all of them. She was sure he had some of his own she'd prefer not to hear about, especially now. "I know you do."

"It just doesn't have anything to do with me, that's all." Flip continued driving, looking over to the park and seeing a few kids playing around. He let the phone stay quiet as he took another hit. He ashed out and replaced it in the cupholder.

"Flip?"

"Yeah, I'm here."

"How long you think you're going to be out?" Elena's voice went to its normal tone.

"Not sure. I may have to run back out to East Pike depending on what this Ms. Shockley has to say." He saw the top of the hospital from the light he was driving through. A few more blocks and he's there.

"Well, if you're still out and want some company for dinner, come by the house."

"Ok, cool. I'm pulling into the hospital now. Call you later?"

"Ok, I'll talk to you then. Love you."

"Love you."

Flip still had at least three blocks before he was at the hospital. When he hung up, he opened the console and got out his notebook and Birdie. There was no need for a shooter in a hospital. That made it the perfect place to get used to having a gun on his thigh. It wasn't heavy but the new weight was foreign to him. He practiced a walk last night with the hip holster for Elena and was laughed out at how he looked like he was in an Old Territory film. After a few more attempts with each holster, Flip was glad the black tactical felt the most comfortable. Not as one-sided feeling as the hip holster, and still able to be relatively hidden when put with the right outfit. Unfortunately, today's outfit of sweats and old-script *Redwater Rogues* crewneck was not the best choice. As he approached the hospital, Flip could see Junior Homicide P'rotector David Holmb standing out front waiting. He pulled against the curb and let the passenger window down.

"Morning, P'rotector." Flip called through the window.

"Morning, Mr. Stokton." Holmb responded.

"Wait here while I go park?"

"That's the plan."

Flip rolled the window up and drove off to the guest parking lot next to the hospital. After a lookaround and lock-up, he walked back to the main entrance, notebook in hand. A dark 4-door drove ahead slowly as he walked but was too far to tell if it was an Exum. Holmb was still out front and extended his hand for a shake. Flip met him and noticed Holmb's eyes lower toward his thigh.

"Don't worry, it's registered." Flip went for his wallet and pulled out his registration.

Holmb took a quick sniff. "I wasn't concerned about the paperwork, but thanks. Under the influence of anything that could affect your ability?"

"Nah." Flip put his wallet away.

"Sure. Need coffee or anything before we head up?" Homlb led the way to the door.

"I'm more of a tea guy."

"Same here. Allergies." Holmb gave a laugh as the automatic doors opened. "Just know, I should've clarified on the phone earlier. Ms. Shockley's *trying* to talk."

"Yeah, about that," Flip followed him to the elevator as he hit the call button. "you said her name was Shockley."

"Cheryl Shockley by day. Cherry to her friends and after-hours. Works an office job, but I guess you could say she 'dabbles' in ways to make some extra cash. I've had a small run-in with her, but she's otherwise a nice girl."

"Right." Flip said as the chime of an incoming elevator sounded. He wondered the nature of that "run-in".

When they got on, Flip saw that Holmb hit the 8

287

on the elevator pad. One floor down from the start of the Psychoanalysis units. Already not a good look. "How does she look? Physically speaking?"

Holmb looked at him with a half-smile. "Weird place to look for a date, don't you think, Founder?" Flip's face told him everything. "Sorry, just some dark humor." The elevator was at 4. "She's looks fine, considering. A little pale but doctors said she should come back in a couple days..." The elevator was at 7. "She lost a lot of blood though. I still can't believe she's alive." Holmb sounded like the last part was more to himself. Flip couldn't tell if he was saying it as a positive.

There was a *ding* and the elevator opened to the 8th floor. He let Holmb exit first and followed until they were side by side walking down the hall. When Holmb stopped at a closed room, Flip saw a P'rotector sitting sentry. "The hell is this? Is this girl a suspect or a victim?"

Holmb placed his hand on the handle and turned to him. "Just a precaution. We don't know who did this yet. Considering we haven't mentioned her name publicly, we suspect that if the perp intends on eliminating possible loose ends, they'll be looking to pay a visit. Even more if it happens to be the same that did the other Shockley. As for your earlier comment, pay attention to her mouth. Doctors said her top canines are longer than the average. We're still waiting on her dentals for comparison."

"Ok." Flip responded.

When they went in, Flip could still see but the blinds were down and at half-slit to allow little sunlight. Cheryl was sitting up and watching the daytime circuit of talk show TV. There was a thick wrap of gauze around her neck and a large notepad on her food table. Flip looked around and thought about the girl from The Watering Hole a couple years ago. As Holmb closed the door, Cherry looked over quickly and started shaking her head "No".

"Ms. Shockley, I need you to talk to somebody. This is Flip Stokton, he's a consultant working with us on your uncle's murder. He's here to help." Holmb made his short introduction, "I'll be right outside." and excited just as quickly, closing the door behind him. Flip felt there was something else he failed to mention. He sat in the chair next to Cherry's bed, turning it so he could face her.

Cherry shook her head again and instinctively tried to speak. Her face showed it was painful went for her notepad and pencil.

Flip Stokton? You're a tec now? Wasn't your mom

"Just Flip is fine, and no, I'm not a tec. I work with the PD occasionally. Mind if we talk for a little bit? How're you doing?"

Cherry nodded her head this time and went back to her pad.

I'm fine, except for my neck. My teeth feel a little weird. The doctor said it will be a while before I can speak normal again. I already talked to P'rotector Wallace and the other lady with him.

"Ok, I get that. Whatever you tell me, it'll stay between you and m-- you and I." He got his notebook out. "I'm going to take notes while we talk, ok? Also, should I call you Cherry or Cheryl?"

Cherry nodded again but didn't write anything.

"Mind if I let some light in here, it's kind of dark."

Cherry shook her head no and started to write.

No, it hurts my eyes when the light comes in.

"My bad." He reached to her indicating a handshake, seeing if he could focus in. If this wasn't a good time, then when would? "Manners, you know?" It was a gamble that paid off and Cherry shook his hand. He felt a shock. *Flash.* He was inside the Hole. There was no sound but even in the dark ambiance of the second floor, he could make out St. Clair clearly and saw they were sharing a booth similar to the one he and Elena shared with Donna. There was another woman under St. Clair. She was very light. Her head was down as she took a sniff of something off the table. *Flash.* Now the woman reached over and slap Cherry. It looked like it hurt. He also got a look of the woman's face. She looked older and somehow younger at the same time. There was an exchange between her and St. Clair but no way to tell what about. The woman took another sniff. Then nothing. He was back in the hospital.

Cherry retreated her hand and wrote on her pad before lifting it up to him. She looked at him with a raised eyebrow.

You ok?

"Yeah, sorry about that. How're you related to Isiah Shockley? Your father?"

Fuck no, and I'm glad I never met him. He was my uncle on my father's side.

"Got it. Did you dad ever talk about his brother?"

Not really, but I could tell he was a bad guy. He broke my father's arm once when they were little climbing trees. My dad always said it was an accident, but I think he was just sticking up for his big brother. He didn't talk about him much. I don't think he liked him.

A lot of past tense. "Cherry, is your father still alive? Any way I can talk to him directly?" Flip had a feeling of the

290

answer, but it's never good to assume about a witness. His mother always said something about it making an ass out of all parties. The answer he got was so blunt, Flip could hear it as if spoken.

No, he died almost 12 years ago.

"I'm really sorry about that." He didn't exactly know how to segue but did his best as he wrote. "I need to talk to you about the other night. Can you tell me anything about the girl that was with you and Luc at the Hole? The girl that slapped you?"

There was a noticeable discomfort as Cherry adjusted her posture. She felt at her face, specifically the cheek that had been slapped. She never told anyone that part. Flip held his hands up. "Cherry it's ok, be easy. You're safe." He set his notebook on his lap. Cherry went to her pad.

Something wasn't right about her. Her eyes didn't seem right. Too clean. Luc called her over from the booth across us. She was originally with some guy that looked like her. Luc got into it with him when he came over and told her he wanted to leave. She slapped him too. She was kinda cute, but her clothes looked old for her. When we got back to Luc's, she said something about how the guy she was with was her brother and how Luc disrespected him. She was very aggressive with me.

Cherry stopped and gave the pad to Flip before putting her hands under the food table. She looked uncomfortable. Not from fear this time, but possibly embarrassment, and even shame. After Flip read the blurb, he put the pad back on the table. He saw Cherry's face and made another gamble.

"You can leave out those details, but I need to know everything you know about the woman. Did she say anything else?"

Cherry hesitated but began writing again.

She said her name was Hana and she had an accent. I remember her saying something about Luc having her father's name and how she hated her dad. I think she was enjoying it all. Like, THAT kind of enjoying it. She cut my neck with her nail and bit me Last thing I remember is hearing her walk down the stairs.

Flip wrote his notes and closed his book. He felt himself getting wavy. "Thank you, Cherry. I hope you continue to full recovery." He was about to get up before Cherry reached out. She didn't touch him, but it got his attention. There was more writing and a request.

Flip, I don't know if you can do this, but do you mind watching some TV with me? I haven't had any company beside the doctors and 'tecs. I don't even know if my mom's heard yet. She lives in North Redwater.

Flip quickly checked his watch and saw it was 20 minutes to 10. He could spare a few minutes, even if it was for talk TV. He never understood how people could sit and watch other people talk about mindless shit. At least with the sports talk channels, someone could learn something interesting. He put his notebook in his pocket and sat back down. Cherry's smile showed teeth, and Flip saw what Holmb was so nervous about. Her canines weren't abnormally large, but anyone that looked at her face on like he was now would be able to see them clearly and would rightly feel uncomfortable about being in the same room alone with her. This girl had fucking fangs. As the talk show went off and into a commercial break, Flip made his departure and left his contact information in case Cherry remembered anything else. He knew where to find her if he needed to. She ripped off her written page and handed it to Flip, flashing another appreciative smile. Her fangs were the only thing Flip could focus on as he left; doubling back only to offer his assistance for any therapy she pursued. He swore this was the same room as the other girl.

Thank you, Flip, but that won't be necessary.

Something about the wording didn't feel right with him. Nor did the fact that he Saw what happened to her previously.

Outside of the overwhelming hospital smell, Flip had to shake himself off. He took out his notebook and sat on a bench at the outdoor patient pick-up area. He went back and forth between pages from Penny's talk and Cherry's paper. As he read, Holmb walked over and sat down. He went into his pocket and took out a pack of Stik-O-Stim; bringing it to his nose to bring in the aroma. He tapped it twice against his knee and unwrapped. He took out the first stick and tapped it on Flip's arm. Flip looked up from his papers. When did Holmb sit down?

"What flavor?" Flip closed his notebook.

"Mint Ice. My dad always says it's good luck to offer someone else the first piece." Holmb kept his offer out. Flip took it and saluted him before he unwrapped.

"Thanks." Flip said after a few chews.

"Of course." Holmb unwrapped his own piece and ate. "Can I ask you something? Two things, actually."

"Yeah," Flip straightened against the bench. "what's up?"

"First, did you learn anything from Ms. Shockley?"

"Did she tell you the name of the woman that did it?"

"Only a first name."

"Then, nah." Flip had a feeling he didn't know about the brother. He kept that card to himself for now.

Holmb crossed his right leg and draped his arms on the benchback. "Ok. Second, is it true you and Ms. Starks are now involved with each other?"

You're joking. "Uh, yeah, we are. Wallace told you?" *Involved?*

"He mentioned it." Holmb continued looking forward. The sun was trying to peek through the cloud cover. It was enough for Holmb to get his shades out. "Congratulations. I'm still new to this side of the country, but it's not common that Founding Families to parlay romantically, is it?"

Flip went from mildly amused to slightly annoyed. *What's he getting at? I knew the paste was a sneak.*

And the ball is being brought up by Stokton. Looks like Holmb declined first possession at the check and is staying back until he crosses the half. Dangerous game for both if anyone's careless. Stokton: 0 / Holmb: 0

"It's not against any rules, if that's what you mean. Founders tend to mess with each other a lot, but it's not really common for leading members to marry, in order to maintain the 'Seven' in the Seven Clans. Rising Patriarchs and Matriarchs are 'Destined' to one another damn near at birth, but nobody really sticks with it by the time they're old enough to decide on their own partners. You know, you should check out the Fifth sometime. A lot of the younger women love them 'inner-city' boys, even the non-natives. We can hang out sometime."

Looks like Stokton's reading for options. Holmb's holding strong with a solid defense. Will the size difference prove too much?

"I'm well aware, but thanks the offer. I might take you up on it."

A cross-over and solid pump-fake. Holmb stutters for it but doesn't jump. Stokton takes the opening and goes for the mid-range.

"Cool. Not like I got anything else to do." *Well aware?* Flip laughed, more to himself than for comradery. Holmb laughed with him. His inflection was enough to tell Flip he didn't quite get what was funny.

"Good one."

Good one?

And it's good! Stokton: 1 / Holmb: 0

"Interesting. Mind if I ask you something else? I hope I'm not being to forward." Holmb kept his gaze, focusing forward on nothing in particular.

Holmb's bringing up the ball now. He's moving cautious as Stokton locks in.

"Shoot."

Looks like Stokton is easing his defense and dropping back, almost daring him to take the shot.

"Are you and the Matriarch Starks 'Destined', as you put it?" He shifted himself so he could look at Flip.

Holmb's going for the drive. Let's see if he can capitalize on the size mismatch. He's crossing the charity stripe. Stokton's moving up and looks like he's gonna go up with him, folks. Holmb goes for the lay-up, Stokton with him. This might be a too-easy block.

"What you gettin' at, P'rotector? You said you

wanted to talk. Don't get on with the interrogation bit."

"Not getting at anything, Mr. Stokton. Just curious. Like I said, I'm still new on the rules and social culture of the Families. I don't know how familiar you are with Blak'rin, but we don't have any 'Founders' as you would call them."

"Fountain's kind of a big place." Flip responded. He felt the Stim kicking in as the paste began to disintegrate and spat out a bright green wad. "You been liking it here?"

There's a bounce off the glass...

"I have. Y'all definitely have a better selection of cars here. Horses are still the best way to move back home. Us dwarves tend to stick with the old-fashioned stuff for as long as we can." P'ro. Holmb chuckled as he took out another piece of Stim and ate. "Speaking of which, that Cabrini you got is pretty nice. Looks like been taking good care of it."

Another bounce onto the rim.

"I try to. Sometimes it feels like she takes care of herself."

"Flip, I don't mean to intrude on your personal life, I just didn't want there to be any friction regarding this particular topic, seeing as I'll be your main contact while Wallace works with Agent Valer and Vice." He extended his hand. Flip joined him. He noticed this time Holmb's grip was slightly tighter.

"P'rotector, I don't really care about what you and Elena may have done or how long ago you did it. It's none of my business."

It rims out! Always the worst for such a promising drive.

"Understandable. I like you, Mr. Stokton. Looking forward to working with you."

And with that final play, this game is over. Stokton: 1 /

Holmb: 0

"Same here. Mind if I get another piece?"

"Sure." Holmb got up as he went into his pocket. He took out a piece and gave it to Flip.

"For later." Flip said as he put it into his pocket.

Holmb tipped his shades and opened his communicator. After a few seconds, he looked back up to Flip. "I've got a few things to follow up on, Mr. Stokton. Is your marker activated?"

"Yeah."

"Cool. If you ever want to test that out." Holmb pointed to Flip's thigh. "Let me know. We can let off a few at the range. What kind is it?"

Flip unholstered Birdie, making sure to check the safety. Holmb let out a whistle as he now could see its full body. "Tojke T45 LEO Compact." He put Birdie back on his thigh. "It was a gift."

"Nice piece. And holster." Holmb unholstered his LEO Standard. "I like the standard, but I was always more partial to the compact. Much easier for concealment. Those are some interesting engravings. Nice touch against the red." He then re-holstered. "Name it yet? I call mine Hawk."

The name was almost laughable, not that Flip's was much better. "Yeah, kinda. Birdie."

"Birdie?" Holmb chuckled.

"Like I said, it was a gift." Flip gathered himself and stood.

"Yeah, I understand. My grandma gave me my first bow. She called it Sugar." Holmb chuckled. "Hawk and Birdie. Anyway, it was nice seeing you again, Mr. Stokton." He was already turning around and starting to walk. "K'd be with you."

"You too, P'rotector."

Holmb raised his hand in a wave as he walked down the block. Flip shook his head lightly and chuckled. Holmb seemed like he was a good guy, awkward questioning aside. Flip remembered something about Wallace telling him how Holmb was scarily intelligent and the youngest to make Junior P'rotector of the FCPD. Based on Holmb's build and look, he wouldn't have taken him for the intellectual. Especially if he hadn't heard him talk. Standing just over 5ft, Holmb easily had an additional 50-60lbs pounds on Flip. He wondered how Holmb would fare against Smetty. He also couldn't help but laugh at the imagined sight of him and Elena. Flip checked his mobile: *10:13AM*. He then placed a call as he walked over to the parking lot.

"Elena Starks, speaking."

"Ms. Starks, did you know it was against the rules for Founders to 'parlay romantically'?"

There was a burst of laughter on the other end. Flip could hear something being placed down. "Flip, what are you talking about?" There was more soft giggling. "What the hell is 'parlay romantically'?"

"Something your young, strapping friend P'rotector Holmb brought to my attention a few minutes ago."

"What'd he tell you?" The laughter was gone.

"Nothing, unless there's something you done left out. He was asking about Founding Family customs and the other bullshit. Wallace told him we were together." He crossed over the elevated planter and walked the potter's decline to short-cut into the lot. Once he hit the unlock button, Joy chirped from the next row over and he went over. "Anyway, I need something."

"Oooh, is that right?" Elena's voice got quieter. "And what would that be?"

"Hazel's number, I'm gonna run over to the Hole real quick."

"Oh," The accent was gone immediately. "that's it? You know you could've texted me that?"

"And everything I just said? That's too much through text." Flip got closer to Joy and unlocked the trunk. When he opened it up, he undid the holster and placed it in. Once he was in the car, he felt a buzz.

"I just sent it. I feel horrible, Flip, I haven't talked to her since the weekend. Let me know how she's doing."

"Will do. I'll text you when I leave." Flip hung up and started the car. He then pulled out and left the lot, already starting his next call.

Hana and Rac' kept their word and made a very big breakfast. Pancakes, toast, fruit, eggs, the works. There was some rare-cooked meat on the menu, but after her first serving, Whore declined any further helpings. Aside from a slap for eating without permission, she had been a good girl today. She was even able to clean the dishes by herself. As Hana walked down the stairs, she heard the dull dragging of chain as Whore tried to turn around. Hana was already next to her by the time she got a good angle. "Everything ok?" Hana looked at her and stroked her hair. The dirt was tangible, and parts were beginning to feel matted.

"Yes, Mother." Whore responded. Hana could see that aside from a fading red spot and that damn eye, she was slowly reverting to how she did when they first met due to her healing. There was a scratch here and there but nothing major. She was still pretty. Pretty enough. "Can I use the bathroom, please?"

Hana got in front of her and lightly pressed her hand against the lower of Whore's stomach, forcing her into a vice of the blood-red obelisk and herself. "Of course, you *can*." She pressed in a little more, "Do you need to use the bathroom?" as she took a step closer, carefully pressing her weight against her hand and adding the pressure. She did her best to not panic dance. She could hold out, but not for long.

"Yes. Please." Whore felt another step and knew she was entering the danger zone as felt a couple warning drops run down her thigh.

"If you piss yourself and ruin my gown, the bathroom will be the last thing you'll need to worry about." There was a small ease of pressure. "Now, how do we ask for things?"

"*May* I use the bathroom, please? I really need to go." No more external pressure.

"Of course." Hana went over and got Whore's leash. She then undid the overhead shackles and let Whore stand and shift around. Hana took her time putting on Whore's shackles before walking her to the stairs and out of the cellar. Occasionally tugging at it. "Keep up." Whore was keeping pace but started second guessing. She made sure to be practically parallel with Mother.

"Yes, Mother."

A tiny smile came across Hana's face. At the bathroom, Hana let Whore enter and close the door to a crack, letting her length of chain serve as a doorstop. When she could tell she was finished, Hana opened the door with a calm smile. Whore could see her canines peeking from under her upper lip and started to feel hot and itchy. As she started scratching at a constantly moving itch, Hana came close and cupped her chin, tilting her head down.

"You've been a good girl the past couple days. A little hiccups, but you've been good."

"Thank you, Mother." Whore still felt hot and itchy.

"You deserve a treat. Come on." Hana let go and tugged at the chain as she opened the first-floor bathroom. When Whore was finished, Hana led to the stairs. Whore kept pace and followed her upstairs and towards a room at the end of Hana's side of the floor. When they walked in, Whore was amazed at how clean and bright it was inside and how large. There's no way a bathroom could be this big. The large curtainless windows allowed so much light through the red-glassed window in that it bounced off the pastel blue floor tile and mirror-sided shower walls. She looked at the large tub positioned against the window and then over to the sink where she found a tray of vials with different colored liquids in them. There were small pastel-colored circles and shapes that she assumed were soaps. Hana closed the door behind them and went over to draw the bath. Whore went to the sink without hesitance and stood patiently.

"Master had to leave after breakfast, so I thought we can have a spa day." Hana said as she let the water run, occasionally touching it for temperature. She went to the sink for a vial and let a few drops into the water. Steam was beginning to come from the spout and the base of the tub as water began to rise. "Is this too hot?" She walked over and picked up the chain, pulling it for Whore to come over. She placed her hand into the rising water.

"No. It's fine. Thank you, Mother."

Hana let the water run a little longer and then cut it off. She then pulled on the chain hard enough for Whore trip into her.

Whore looked into Hana's face and then glanced at the corner shower with the mirror sides. She didn't see Hana. It was only her, standing in a dirty and partially torn, calf-length house dress in front of a large bathtub. Never having left Fountain except for a few adolescent trips to Redwater, she used to hear rumors about vampyr that lived in Monarch. It used to be the dumbest thing she had ever heard. Vampyr were only in the movies. Right? Hana could hear whimpers.

"Hey, it's ok." Hana stroked Whore's face softly. "Hey!" Before a *slap* and the attention was back to her. "I said it's ok." She reached into her pocket and pulled out a key and set it on the built-in soapdish of the tub. "I'm going to take this off. I can trust you to be good, right?"

Whore nodded. "Yes, Mother. I'll be good."

"Show me."

Whore tried to step back but was pulled her back in place. The last time Mother asked her to prove her obedience, she was known as Alexis. That felt like a long time ago, but her body remembers. Whore stood stock-still as she waited for her command.

"On your knees. Now." Hana kept the chain coiled and stayed in place.

"W-What?"

SLAP!

"I thought we talked about that stutter. Kneel."

Whore saw embers flash and pop. There was a small feeling of her moving but knew she wasn't. Her body kneeled as if on its own.

"What's your name?"

There was no answer.

"Answer me when I'm talking to you." Hana let the chain drop and she began taking off her sweatshirt. Whore kept her eyes to the floor. "Now, look at me."

Whore looked up, the red light illuminating her face and hitting her cloudy eye. Mother wasn't wearing anything under her sweatshirt. Looking up at her allowed Whore to see the full branching of Mother's burn. She wondered who did that to her, and why.

"Now, what's your name? Don't make me repeat myself." Hana was already lightly tracing herself with her right hand.

"Whore." It came out quietly.

"Say it again." Hana demanded, savoring the display.

"Whore. My name is Whore."

"Good girl." Hana traced herself. "Now get up. I'm going to take these off, ok?" Hana let Whore to her feet.

"Yes, Mother. Thank you." Whore kept her head down as her shackles were unlocked and fell to the floor with a loud *clang*. She raised her hands as Mother helped her out of her dress. She could see that Mother was very skinny. It would have been concerning if not the small definition of abs and how clear her skin looked. Eyeing her up and down, Whore darted her eyes. She didn't deserve to see Mother full-bare. Nor did she dare ask what the scarring was from. The largest of it encompassed her entire pubic area and in the shape of a symbol. The texture was faded but looked the same kind of glassy as on her arm. The symbol almost looked like the Mark of K'd but perverted, and maybe even upside-down. Who did that to Mother? Why? The smaller but cruder scars over it told her for some reason that Mother might have made them. They were clearly cut into her, as if trying to erase the brand. It all looked gruesome and very painful. Whore wasn't sure which was worse to endure.

"What's wrong, never seen a kitty before? I personally like to shave, but one day want to try that fancy technique people on the TechAir rave about all the time. I hear they use some kind of wax. There used to be something like it back when I was younger, but it wasn't too popular. You ever tried it, Whore?"

"I think so." Whore felt at her wrists. She felt naked without them. She felt vulnerable.

Hana laughed. "You *think so*?"

Whore tried to think. Small details like that were hazy and seemed too far away to catch. "I... I don't remember." Whore's voice started to break. "I *can't* remember, Mother. I'm sorry, I'm so sorry!" She stood there, sobbing. Hana held her close. This wasn't how their day was supposed to start. "Please don't be mad at me. I'm sorry. I can't remember." Whore stood with her wrists together in anticipation of being cuffed and led back to the cellar.

"It's ok. Come on, let's take a bath." Hana went for the tray on the sink. She placed it across the opposite side of the tub just before the faucet. "Come on, now. There's more than enough space." She stepped into the tub and settled in, before motioning to get in. Being enveloped in the water eased Whore and she found her tears easing and eventually stopping completely. Her earlier cleaning was little more than a once-over and first-aid to her wounds. Now, she hoped that this bath could wash away everything. "Can you hand me one of the soaps? You can pick which one." Hana asked after they were both settled in.

Whore reached and picked the soap she liked best. It was star shaped and smelled like fruit. She passed it back to Mother and laid into her bosom. Mother wasn't lying, this tub was spacious. And deep. The water was now just under her neckline.

"Do you trust me, Whore?" Mother's lips brush the curve of her ear as she spoke.

"Yes, Mother. I trust you."

"Good." Hana gripped a handful of hair and forced Whore's head below the water. After a few seconds, she raised it back up as Whore gasped and coughed up water. Hana went for a second dump and held her down longer this time. Time felt like it stood still underwater. When she came back up, Hana let go started to lather the soap bar and mix it into her hair. "Your hair is filthy. You're a pet, but you don't live in the woods like an animal." As she lathered and hand-scooped water, a mix of dirt, sweat and dried blood began to mix with the water. After the first rinse, Whore's normal hair color was coming back. She continued to work on the hair, occasionally dunking Whore back under, holder her down longer each time. Whore resisted less and less each time. She trusted Mother. If she really wanted to hurt her, she would have already.

"We weren't always like this, my brother and I." Hana lathered again but now let her hands drop from Whore's hair to her neck, stroking nails along her throat as she massaged her neck. She tapped Whore's shoulder and pointed to a vial of green oil. "We used to be regular kids. A little stronger and faster than most warm-body children, but regular just the same. I don't think father liked that about us. After our 16th birthday, Rac' escaped to the Great Territory War a couple years after The Culling and moved all over the place. Father Turned me soon after. I thought he was only an angry man, but that's when I knew him for the man *He* really was. *He* thought he owned me, just like he did Mama. Luckily, I found

Rac' before *He* found me. I moved around with Rac' and his men for a bit, helping as a Medi-Mage, but we went on to live our own lives when Rac' left the Service. The Culling made him angry, but the War changed him. He didn't even know I came back home until he saw the car." There was what sounded like a sniffle accompanied with a scoff. "My only regret is that we couldn't get back in time to save Mama. She was a good woman. She made me want to be a mother. When Father caught me with a boy at the creek, he made sure I couldn't be a mama of my own." A single red drip fell into the bath water. Then another. Hana quickly swished with her hand to blend it before cupping water to her face. She made a fresh froth of shampoo and continued on.

Whore wasn't sure if this story was for her or Mother but didn't want to interrupt. Mother began to massage Whore's shoulders before reaching her right hand under the water's surface. She brought her left hand to Whore's neck, two claws pressing into either side of her throat. "I won't hurt you this time, I promise." She continued her stimulation in silence for a short while before entering. "You'll grow to like us, maybe even love us. I think I'd like that. My brother really seems to like you, too. Do you like Rac'?"

When Mother switched to a full choke, Whore couldn't tell if the warm running on her neck was either bathwater or blood. She was too afraid to open her eyes and check. She trusted Mother. If she wanted to hurt her, she would have. Her answer came out in constricted gasps, "Yes...Yes, Mother."

Mother held her chokehold and continued. She could hear the servility in Whore's voice. Everything was hers. *Everything.* Hana paused and leaned into her ear again, "But I promise you, if you try to take him from me, it will be the last thing you ever attempt." She could feel the submission grow with her excitement as she held her grip. Whore couldn't see the fire in the reflective sides of the shower when she finally opened her eyes, but she knew it was there, looking back at her. Mother was in control. Her grip on Hana's arm tightened enough to break skin and she felt a release from her. She didn't fight back. If Mother really wanted to hurt her, she would have done so already.

It was just after two when Rac' got home. One of the wide fridges at the butchery went out last night and until it got fixed, he found himself with a half-day off and a surplus of assorted meat to take home. As he opened the front door, he called out for Hana and got no response. He called for Whore to come help with the bags. Same response. Moving the bags from the door to the kitchen, he could hear laughter from the second floor. The air smelled vaguely floral and he began arranging the food into the refrigerator. Now, he could hear a second voice. He went upstairs towards Hana's room and her door closed and music playing. Standing against the door, Rac' pressed his ear and listened.

"You can come in." Hana called out.

Rac' opened the door and was hit full on with the smell of perfume. The window near Hana's bed was raised and the curtains were open, allowing the light to filter through the clouds and cover Whore in a new glow. The music playing was coming from Hana's record player. It was a popular dance number that from almost 90 years ago. A "one-hit-wonder", as the later years designated. A year or two after it came out, the lead singer of the band was found in a hotel, dead from an overdose. A real one-hit-wonder. After that, the band could never capture their original sound and eventually disbanded. Rac' saw his sister dancing and Alexis trying to match. He was sure this was the first time she's tried dancing to some real music, not the digital trash being made today with half-decent vocalists.

"Dance with us, Rac'. I'm trying to teach her The Spin!" Hana then went through the multi-step routine that was "The Spin"; raising her arms in the air and spun around before clapping twice and rolling her fists around each other to her left and right as she swayed her hips. "This is my favorite part." The conclusion was two claps and a final spin. Hana always was a good dancer, but she didn't dance a lot. Well, not anymore.

"I'm fine. You were always better at that stuff." Rac' came in and sat against the windowsill. "Mrs. Klima gave us a lot of meat to take home. One of the freezers went out so they let most of everyone go home for the day."

Hana kept trying to get Whore to dance. She tried to keep up, but the wrist shackles proved an issue when it came time to the fist rolling. Rac' noticed that she would occasionally glance at him, averting her eyes to the floor whenever they met. She looked fully bathed this time. The gown she wore was different but still ankle-length. As the record finished and began giving off the staticky silence, Rac' went over and lifted the needle. Whore took a small step in Hana's direction and spoke softly.

"Hello, Master." Whore kept her eyes to the floor.

"Been a good girl? Look at me when I'm talking to you." Rac' went to her and stroked her hair. A minty breeze flowed to him and he sniffed lightly.

"Yes, Master."

"She's been a very good girl. Isn't that right?" Hana followed up. She was in a good mood. A little too good of a mood. He knew he flushed that trash last night.

"Yes, Mother."

"You're home early today." Hana looked to Rac'

"We had a freezer blow out, so Mr. Klima sent most of us home. I told you we started working with the Condent family a few weeks ago, remember? A lot of their stuff was in the freezer."

"Steak and wine lunch?" Hana excitedly went over and held his hand. "Or an early supper?"

"I had something before I left work. Are you hungry?" Rac' pulled his hand free and put it into his pocket.

"A little. I was going to eat earlier, but thought to wait." She glanced over at Whore and winked.

"Right. Well, I can put something on if you want."

"Would you, little brother?" She watched as he went to the door. "Thank you." Then she focused on Whore. "Well, looks like our girls' day is at an early end. Unless you wanted to do anything." Hana looked at Whore with an inviting look.

"Can... Can I walk outside? Master let me last night."

Hana pretended to not know about her evening walk. She twisted her head in confusion and asked what she was talking about. Whore took a pause before she answered. She did go outside last night, right? Was it all just a dream? She knows she felt the grass against her ankles, the cool air against her skin. The soggy dirt of the driveway. Was it all her imagination? She started to panic and thought about if she's been dead in the cellar this entire time. Even in death, she would be stuck in this house.

"Last night." The walls of her thoughts were beginning to close on her. "You met us when we came in." Whore was beginning to believe she was dead in the cellar, and the feeling was bitter-sweet. At least she didn't actually experience everything her body remembered. That also meant she didn't actually have her spa day today, and that she hadn't been a good girl. "Don't you remember, Mother?"

Hana's face went into a big smile and she took Whore by the shackles. "Of course, I remember. I was joking." She brought Whore close to her. "Let's go outside. Get some fresh air." She led the way to the staircase. Walking down, Hana did notice she was in a chipper mood. She like being Hana again, but it also meant that she was weaker. Her power was being spread thin. That Cherry bitch either needed to live closer, or not at all.

Flip was rolling up at the kitchen when he heard a text message come in. As he lit, he checked and saw it was Smetty. He opened the message on the inhale.

Hey bro, Haze told me you came by earlier to check the tapes. I'm working tonight if you want to come through and talk.

Flip sent a quick response and went back to his notebook.

Cool. I'll swing by tonight.

After his earlier trip to the Hole, Flip hung out on the roof of Cloud Mesa and made small-talk with residents about their weekend. He hadn't told neighbors about his PC work and wanted to keep it like that. Let them think he just was a basketball player in retirement earlier than he should. Aside from a drink with Hazel, where he inadvertently learned she was the one with Wallace the other night, his trip to the Hole seemed useless. That was until Hazel said she briefly interacted with the "date" of Mystery Woman, or Hana, or whatever the fuck her name was. He was muscular, but

310

short; barely taller than Hazel herself. Very light in skin tone, but handsome, in a "young classically handsome" kind of way. Hazel didn't see his date but did rent the man a booth for two for the night.

Since it was an on-the-spot rental and not a reservation, she didn't need ID but didn't remember the name he gave. It started with an "S", though. After Mr. Classic paid for the booth, he gave her a hundred scril to cover their drinks ahead of time. Hazel couldn't remember seeing him for the rest of the night but remembered he had a cute accent, maybe east of Redwater or even Monarch, but she's never met anyone personally from there. It wasn't much, but it did give a general idea of where these people may live or at least were from. It also gave an idea of the red tape for Cap that would come up if these people were crossing borders for their crimes. If it did involve Monarch, there was going to be a lot of tape.

Feeling himself lift-off, Flip closed his notes and shot off another text before going to his sofa. Surfing the channels, he stopped on the 24-hour news and saw that the Honiwell geyser in Fallsmith finally erupted, keeping in line with its tradition of erupting every 15 years. After surfing channels for another couple of minutes, he settled on the Wildlife Channel in the middle of a desert animal documentary when his mobile chimed.

Hi Flip, I get off at 7! What's up? I got a new phone today :D

Flip took an inhale and thought of something.

Awesome, Penny.

I need you to meet me at the Hole. I'll need your help.

He exhaled as a brown-belly dirt rat was being scooped up by a Bomber's eagle and being carried into the air.

Homie was about to be baby food. *Ding!*

Sure! Can I bring Dom? He thinks your nice! :D

Flip shook his head and smiled. Emotisigns now? Gotta love Penny. He took a small inhale.

Did he see anything?

A single message came back quickly.

I don't think so :(

He had a feeling that was going to the case. Exhale.

Sorry Penny but we can hang out after I'm finished this case. You two can double with me and Elena.

It felt wrong to make an open invitation like that with Penny. He intended to honor it; he just wasn't sure when that would be. Another chime sounded as the eagle was returning back to her nest, presumably to serve lunch.

Ok! I can be there after work. How's 8-8:15?

Perfect.

Sounds good. See you then :D

He didn't expect a response but laughed out loud all the same.

Flip watched the rest of the documentary as he smoked and thought about everything so far. By half-way through the joint, a second program came on about insects and the similar roles among three different groups. Insect stuff creeped him out. He clicked over to the sports channel and watched a few highlights and general commentary. The big topic was the upcoming Rogues-Skyhawks game. It was going to be the second of four regular-season meetups and the Rogues were 1-0. Flip took a few final pulls before ashing out and planned for the evening. The cameras were a dud, but Saturday's staff wasn't there. Specifically, the bartender that found the scene wasn't there.

One name, two people. "S" something.

Better not be Sarin

His mind floated as he thought back to his notes from Cherry. Both her and Penny said "Hana" had an accent, possibly Monarch. Aside from his brother, Flip didn't know anyone personally that lived in Monarch and couldn't remember the last time he was out there. He remembered he was supposed to play a game there during his West Coast days, but it was cancelled a few hours before tip-off for unclear reasons. It was cool and all, but something about the place always creeped him out. The people always looked like they were hiding something. Monarch wasn't as cooperative as Redwater was with Fountain City when it came to law enforcement. He remembered his mom telling him about a back in forth she had to do with the Monarch and Fountain courts to get the paperwork approved to extradite a killer operating in both locations over the course of a year. Whoever was in charge was fighting to not share evidence that would have connect him to two specific murders Fleice had him dead-to-rights on. It wasn't because they didn't agree with the findings. They fought it on the basis that he was originally from and lived in Monarch. Something about "dealing with their own". Fucking weird. That type of "home justice" was still common in the southwestern Territories. Flip blinked the daydream away. He felt it was still a road to go before suggesting Cap and Wallace get their good suits ready. He continued watching highlights and analysis before letting himself drift to sleep.

P'rotector Wallace was approaching the Golden Night motel when Agent Valer finally spoke again.

"You think Twiggy was telling the truth?"

"You asking as a friend, or a colleague?"

She took a pause. The fact he had to quantify his response told her everything she needed. Being honest, Joh'n could be a little too blunt sometimes, especially when it came to his work. Being more honest, it was one of the things she liked about him. It was an attraction for her. He was about his work, and it tended to shine through all aspects of his life. In their time knowing each other, there's been many phases and phrases that could be used to describe their relationship, professional or otherwise. Bullshit wasn't one of them. She wished her ex-husband would've taken note. She looked over at the Golden Night as it brought back memories.

"We used to have some good times in there, didn't we?"

Wallace laughed quietly. "Yeah we did, until your husband found out. Then things got a little less fun…"

"Or *more* fun, depending on how you look at it." She placed a hand on Wallace's thigh. "So, how 'bout it? Help a girl take her mind off a few things."

"Come on, we're still on the clock."

Valer noticed that he didn't move her hand in spite of his answer. She let it travel and felt that something wasn't too concerned about what time it was. Wallace shifted his eyes. "Camailla, what you doing?"

She continued. "Nothing, P'rotector, just a standard contraband search. I think I need to do a full-body." She leaned over into Wallace's ear, "Come on, we got time." and kissed it lightly. She knew what he liked.

When the light turned green, Wallace checked his watch and drove up another block before making a U-turn.

Valer smiled slightly and leaned over again to kiss his ear and then his neck. Initially, it was purely a physical and a vocational attraction; someone else at the top of their game who fully understood the world she worked in. He was a good man. Sure, there was some innuendo here, a few drinks there, but it was nothing to bring the Auditors in on. But then it happened. And then again. And again. As she got to know him more, there was a different kind of satisfaction. It also didn't hurt that he did a few of the things her ex-husband used to hesitate on. After a year and a half, S'ant K'al reached peak suspicion due to some drunk gossip by a few beat p'rotectors one night. The way they talked about a motel "stake-out" didn't sound like real work talk.

That suspicion led him to his own stake-out at the Golden Night, specifically, room 19. When he finally knocked on the door, he found his wife in a bathrobe and clearly expecting other company. Less than 5 minutes later, he met said company, filled ice bucket in hand and also not dressed for any official p'rotector work. Wallace was declining to press assault charges as the then married Camailla Valer-K'al and her husband drove out of the parking lot. Going forward, Wallace and Camailla decided that they should keep things professional. Mostly. Camilla and S'ant decided they keep things in separate homes and separate lives.

Wallace rolled the windows down as he drove. It's been a while since they had a "stake-out" and Camailla was right, they had plenty of time before having to check-in. He wasn't sure why he still listened to Twiggy and her "tips". It was either too old information, or a person or two removed from the source. As he entered the lot, he scoped a far space and went over to park. He got out and went to the main office to get the key for short-term lodging in room 19. Going towards the stairs for the second floor, Wallace did his trademark lookaround. He didn't see anything and proceeded, key in-hand. Upon entering, he put everything on the nearby table and went into the bathroom. Agent Valer entered the room as he was coming out and locked the door behind her, chewing a piece of Stik-O-Stim and putting her service weapon on the table next to Wallace's.

"P'rotector Wallace, is your body search going to be willing?" She was unbuttoning her VICE jacket as she walked over to the second bed. Role-playing, even work related, was something her husband never found appealing. She actually liked the "naughty architect's assistant" game they played once. After laying it across, she did the same with the rest of her clothes until she was in her bra and panties. Her badge on a thin chain that swayed lightly as she walked over to him.

Wallace began undressing and laid his clothes as well. Camailla helped. "I don't know Agent Valer, say I get a little rough?" He pushed her on the shoulder.

"I can handle rough." She pushed back.

"Mmhmm." Wallace looked at her before stepping forward and quickly grabbing her by the waist and pushing her onto the first bed. Upon landing, Camailla smiled and turned over, facing the headboard and arching herself into the air. She could feel the Wild Ice flavored Stim was activated and she swallowed the paste for a head rush. Wallace went back to the second bed and got a pair of cuffs. "Agent Valer, I think I'm actually gonna need to search *you* for contraband. Don't make me rough you up."

Camailla raised to a kneel put her hands behind her back. "Like I said, P'rotector, I can handle rough." She looked back to him. "Search all you want."

Wallace ignored his ringing communicator as he put the cuffs on Camailla and gripped the back of her neck, pushing her into a prostrate. After ripping her panties off, he started his inspection face-first as she let out a loud moan and buried her head into the pillow, allowing the smothering darkness to heighten the sensation.

Across town, CaP'rotecter Monroe was deciding against leaving a voicemail for Wallace. He was probably still out with Agent Valer. A far-off memory came to mind of having to show up at the Golden Night in the middle of the night because of a fight between two men and possibly a woman. One of the men in question was none other than his leading homicide investigator, having been attacked by a civilian; the husband of a Vice Agent working undercover. Monroe knew the story he was fed was bullshit at best but let it run. He didn't need to know details, just if Wallace wanted to press charges.

Monroe closed his mobile and went back to the report in front of him. Shockley had quite a bit of residual Rock in his system when he died, but it wasn't enough to suspect OD. It wasn't even enough to say that he took any the day he was killed. Either way, they were working in the deficit. It's been almost a week since they found him and aside from an estimated time of death and a visible thorough beating, they had nothing of major value. They still couldn't identify where Shockley's been living the past six months. Based on rumors, nobody's seen him much in his usual Fountain hangouts. There was a possible tip about Redwater, but the source was known to be less than trustworthy at times. He put down the report and made another call.

Flip woke up still laying on the couch and a low-volume sports report, Alexis Valer's Next Steps attendance next to him on the table. He checked his phone for time and saw he still had a bit before meeting Penny. After making a cup of tea, he went to shower. He was taking a gamble on the bartender being in tonight, but something told him it was a good bet. They must have seen something on Saturday before the bathroom find. Maybe they served a drink to an "off" patron, particularly a patron that claimed it was already taken care of. As he picked out his evening look of practically all-black save for the bits of color in his shirt, he tossed a holstered Birdie on top. He got himself dressed and rolled two more before going back downstairs. At the couch he saw a recent missed call from Elena and a text from Monroe.

Tox screen's in but nothing helpful. Shockley is officially LF as of tomorrow morning.

He couldn't do anything but shake his head before going to call Elena. The toxicology info was a little surprising but putting the case on cold wasn't. He didn't have anything solid either; only two people and a single first name. As the phone rang, he lit up and inhaled. He thought about the camera footage earlier. Whoever did the bathroom was conveniently outside of view. That didn't sit right.

"Elena Starks, speaking."

"Hey." Flip exhaled as he spoke, putting the phone on speaker as he got up to go into the kitchen.

"Hey. You coming over for dinner?"

"Nah, I'll swing by after. Gotta go by the Hole to check something out. Penny's meeting me over there."

"Penny?"

"Yeah, she saw the girl that went home with St. Clair on Saturday and there's a bartender I need to talk to that may have seen her date."

"Interesting. Need me to come by?"

Flip took a pause to drink some water. "Nah, I think we got it. I'll call you when I'm leaving out. Shouldn't be too later."

"Oh, ok. See you later?" Her voice dropped a little.

"Hope so. Love you."

"Love you too. Be careful." And she hung up.

Flip finished his joint and went to the news. Shockley was already out of the cycle and by the low-level coverage, felt the murder at the Hole was on its way out as well. As he ashed, he thought about asking Hazel if she had seen Alexis recently. After a few minutes of getting himself together, Flip headed out and went to the garage. Before pulling out, he sent a text to Penny and made his way.

Driving into the lot across from the Hole, Flip was met with another surprise, the lot was almost at capacity. That made him more curious than disconcerted. It was a Tuesday night at a place that just had a violent murder occur in one of the bathrooms, who'd think that it was still the perfect place to relax and get a bite to eat? Flip checked his phone for time, *8:05PM*, and sent a text to Penny. As he walked across the street, a car stopped abruptly before him, its owner looking between their phone and him. When Flip made out who it was, he waved at Penny before motioning to the lot. Penny drove up and turned in. She thought Flip looked cool, like he was out of an early *Nite Owl* comic, when he used to wear regular clothes instead of armor. She noticed there was something strapped to his thigh. When she realized what it was, she rethought why he asked her to come out. Was the killer here? Should she have brought her dusters?

Penny met Flip in the foyer and hugged him tepidly. She patted his thigh and he had to give the extreme shorthand. His story sounded straight out of her comics. Nite Owl's father passed onto him what would become his most signature weapon, an auto-firing crossbow called Talon 1. She made a drinking motion.

"Sure, what you want?"

Penny shrugged. Flip nodded his head.

"Let's find Hazel." He took her by the hand and led her across the foyer and into the main dining area. It was a packed first floor and clientele looked lively on a Tuesday night. He walked with a tunnel-vision. He was zoned in. Work mode. When they approached, Flip got the attention of the first bartender he saw.

"Hey, how're you doing? Can you tell Hazel that Flip is here?"

"Sure thing," the bartender looked young, but in a "still new to the job" kind of way. Flip also took in how short and stocky and was reminded of Holmb. It was like he was using a footstool just to look over the bar. The bartender took out a notepad and a pen, "anything I need to tell her? Or just that you're here?"

"Just that I'm here. I'm sure she'll come out."

The bartender closed his empty notepad. It still looked fresh. He told Flip to wait a few minutes and he'll be back. Before he turned, Flip called him over again.

"You know who was working upstairs on Saturday?"

"Who was working, or who found the bathroom?"

The bartender's response wasn't exactly rude but had a certain tone to it.

"Both, if you know." Flip sat down and got ready to listen. Penny watched the bartender's lips.

"Yeah, I was working that night, but T'cKall was the one who found the scene." He pointed down the bar to a pretty, or handsome, person pouring a beer and handing it to a customer. From the haircut to the body-build, Flip couldn't tell if he was looking at a slender man or a woman. He looked back at the bartender.

"Ok, thanks. What's your name, man?"

"O'an." He extended his hand.

"Cool. Flip, Flip Stokton. Nice meeting you." He met his hand and shook, feeling a small spark. *Flash.* A quick scene of O'an taking money from a customer and putting in his pocket instead of the register. It was dark and the lights display told him this was happening on a busy night. A few more seconds to see another pocket transaction, then nothing. He was back. Still holding O'an's hand but now being met with a look of suspicion.

"Uh, I'll let Hazel know you're here, Flip. Say, you wouldn't be Flip Stokton, would you? The basketball player? Used to date Elena Starks?" O'an was retreating his hand as he spoke.

"Yeah, that's me." Flip nodded slightly.

"Cool, cool. I'll go get Hazel. It was nice meeting you." O'an turned and went down the bar. He tapped TcKall and they leaned down. O'an said something into their ear, holding them by the waist as he did. After O'an went through the kitchen entrance, T'cKall turned towards Flip and Penny to wave. Penny waved back and tapped Flip on the arm to show him they were being hailed over. She walked ahead of

Flip and sat directly in front of T'cKall. There was an issue of understanding, so Flip had to clarify and handled the drink order. After introductions and a few sips, Flip got to it.

"T'cKall, O'an told me you found the bathroom situation." He took a sip and grimaced to himself. Spiceroot didn't belong with beer. He looked at Penny and saw he wasn't the only one who thought so. It must be a new brand they were trying out. T'cKall looked uneasy and made a glass of water. Then two more for Penny and Flip. After a gulp she began talking.

"It was horrible, Mr. Stokton. I'd never seen anything so violent."

"I'm sorry about that. Did you ever serve anybody unfamiliar? Somebody that may have been off?"

"Look around, Mr. Stokton. We get new people all the time, especially on the weekends." T'cKall waved her hand around. "Are you a p'rotector or something? I already talked to a man named Holmb." There were two more drinks now in front of them, clear but definitely not water. "Sorry about the beer. It's a new brand Hazel's trying to get rid of. Spiceroot and beer. Sounds like some shit an amateur 'artisan brewer' would come up with." She shook her head as they all shared a laugh before Penny asked for a pen and pad. She began writing until T'cKall placed her hand on the paper. There was a signing that she could understand Penny and was met with a smile.

"Nah, I'm not a tec, I just work with them when they need me from time to time." He got out his wallet and flipped her his PC marker. Penny was signing and T'cKall responded. She didn't see the mean lady, Hana, at the bar or generally. She barely left the bar area aside from going to the bathroom, but she didn't cross paths with her. As Hazel came through the kitchen door, Flip remembered that he saw Smetty escort the couple to their booth. He took Penny to the side. "Hey Penny, I need you to keep T'cKall talking. See if she knows anything else. Order whatever you want to eat or drink, but don't pay. I'll settle up with Hazel."

Penny made a quick nod and they separated. She went back to the bar with T'cKall and they began talking in silence. Flip made a comment about O'an that shocked her and walked over to Hazel. They went to the opposite end of the bar.

"Hazel, two things; I think you'll need to retrain to your boy O'an about ringing drinks sales before you open back upstairs. Two, have you ever seen an Alexis Valer in here in the past couple months?"

Hazel's face went to a disconcerting calm. El told her a little bit about how Flip seemed to know about things he shouldn't, and how he was usually right. She exhaled. "How much he been taking?" The edge in her voice told Flip this may not the first time she's heard about it.

"I can only verify two drinks worth, but my mom always said, 'With crime and mice, when there's one, there's more'. You don't have any personal connection to him, do you?"

"Not at all." She was moving her arm toward the bottom of the bar. She started looking towards the end of the bar. "T'cKall in on it, too? I hired her around the same time."

"I don't know. Unless she's really good at Shank, she seemed surprised when I told her. What's up with them?"

"They haven't been here that long, but I'm sure they're already fuckin' or something. The way he talks, I wouldn't have taken him for liking a girl with the 50/50 look. She must look more convincing outside the uniform." Hazel brought her hand back to the bar. "So, you said Alexis who?"

"Alexis Valer. Working girl. Early to mid-twenties. Said to be really pretty." Flip didn't even realize that Hazel was already putting his drink in front of him as he spoke. Hazel snapped her fingers and pointed.

"Oh yeah! Yeah, I know Alexis. She's dead, ain't she?"

"Officially, still missing. You see her lately?"

"I talked to her about a month ago. She wasn't working, just coming in for a few drinks. Her looks ain't alleged, Flip, that girl is *fine*. I mean, way too pretty for the streets. I think she's mixed with elf or something. She woulda made some real money layin' it on them old-money pretty boys down in Ca'rtek." Hazel told about her last conversation with Alexis and a funny story about how they first met a little over a year ago during an ill-timed bathroom break. A discussion of terms and a handshake sealed their agreement that Alexis can pick up clients at the bar as long as real business occurred somewhere else. Their last talk was a general catch-up and an offer of a hosting job. Alexis already had a few and nonchalantly brushed off the offer. It wasn't rude but it was clear the offer was unwanted. Hazel didn't take it personal. She's seen some of the people Alexis would leave with from time to time. A night in her shoes surely brought in more scril than even a double-shift's worth of hosting tips. Hazel could respect the business angle, moralities aside. She later felt a bit patronizing in her approach. She wasn't trying to extend pity or nothing like that.

Flip let the stories sink in and wrote in his notepad. He thanked Hazel for talking.

"Sorry I couldn't help more." Hazel said.

"It's cool, I had meant to ask you earlier today.

Where's Smetty?"

"He's somewhere around here. Check upstairs with the other staff. We won't open the second floor again until next week so right now it's just a big ass break room. You can go on up. I need to talk to O'an."

"Can you tell Penny to meet me upstairs? Don't rush it with O'an, just double-check the count after your next really busy night. It might be after you reopen upstairs."

Hazel's eyes were questioning, but she trusted the sureness in Flip's voice. She let it rest for now. "I got you. Thank you, Flip."

Flip made sure nothing was in Hazel's hands before leaving the bar and made his way back to the main foyer. When he looked to the staircase leading upstairs, he could see Smetty talking to a female staff member. Flip walked up as she was leaving and dapped him up. They went over to a nearby booth. It was the same one Flip saw "Hana" and her date, or brother, occupied. A small shiver went through Flip as he sat down. No static.

"What's up, bro? Want a drink?"

"Nah, I'm good. Work night."

"Guess that's why you strapped up?" Smetty chuckled. He knew about the break-ins and lower crimes Flip sometimes helped the p'rotecs with. "What they got you on? Serial purse snatcher on the loose?" He laughed some more; just some teasing between homies. "Nah man, I'm just playing. Hazel told me you're working on the guy Teek found in the bathroom."

"Teek?"

"Yeah, man, T'cKal or however the hell she says it. Most of us just call her Teek."

By the time Flip and Smetty got into his description of what he saw on Saturday, Penny came up and sat next to Flip, bowing to Smetty fist in hand before she did. He stood to return her greeting and continued talking. He respected Penny a lot, particularly regarding her martial arts background and wondered if it was how she got that scar on his cheek. Sandra never told him the story of it but he thought it made Penny distinguished, and kinda cute, in badass movie chick kind of way. Outside of the High Honor, she wasn't really his type, though. She was smart, but a little childish. Penny liked Smetty a lot too, but in a student-teacher kind of way. He had belts and experience in styles she only dabbled in and that made him potential sparring partner material. Personally, she felt he ran around too much with the ladies, Sandra being one of them. That made him strictly off-limits. Plus, she had Dom, and he was turning out to be a really nice guy. She smiled to herself as he thought about their upcoming date.

"Hazel said that the dude gave her a hundo to cover their drinks for the night?" Flip asked.

"Yeah, she texted me while they were still in line that they took care of the booth and drinks with her. She had someone bring up their drinks. Weird people man. They even looked alike, bro. Either they related or into some *really* kinky shit. The dude was kinda cool, though. He slipped me a nice tip when they arrived, but that chick was straight weird, bro. Something about her felt dangerous."

"Did he give a name?" Flip asked.

"Nah. Like I said, bro took care of everything with Haze. We ain't need to talk about anything else."

Penny had been intently watching Smetty's mouth as he spoke and shook her head over and over when he mentioned that Mean Lady felt dangerous. Flip wasn't surprised by Smetty's assessment, he's been the beneficiary of ones like it in the past and because of it always made it home. Penny made a writing motion and Flip gave her a pen. She wrote on a nearby napkin and slid it to Smetty.

Scary lady! Did she speak to you too?

"Nah, she didn't say much. It was her eyes, Pen." Flip forgot Smetty's liking of nicknames for people. He also saw Penny trying to hide she was blushing, pretending to now seem more interested in her new phone. "*Their* eyes, actually. There was something in there. Something bad. Like I said, the guy was nice enough, but they were killers, bro. Especially the girl. She looked like the hair-trigger type." Smetty took a final gulp of his water. "I feel like the dude was in the military, maybe some Dark Ops shit, but he looked way too young to be in that. He kept looking around, like he was taking note of the room before their first round came. My cousin used to do the same thing for a long time after coming home from the Arms."

Penny wrote about her interactions with Hana in the bathroom and the diner. Flip added his story of how Hana was looking right at him as she danced on her date. Smetty read Penny's further description that Hana's escort was her brother and was visibly uncomfortable about the implications he was mentally forming. He thought about his own older sister. She was pretty and all, but never in even the most confusing moments of pubescence did he think about her in that way. They talked for another half-hour about much lighter topics before Smetty had to go back to work downstairs, letting Penny and Flip hang out with the other staff on the second floor. They talked with a few other employees about Saturday before Penny said she wanted to go home. Flip walked her down the stairs.

"I think we found out everything here we're gonna get here. Thanks for coming out, Penny. I appreciate it." He hugged her and kissed her on the cheek when they reached the landing. Penny hugged him again but tighter this time. Flip reminded her so much of Aron, it sucked she didn't get to see him a lot. She held her hug an extended beat before letting go. She wiped her eye quickly.

"You good to drive?" Flip asked.

Penny made an "OK" and nodded her head. She went for the door before turning back. She wasn't exactly sure how to ask what she wanted delicately and went with a mix of signing and the rare verbal supplement. "Can I help out again, Flip? On this Investigator stuff?" Her voice came out quiet, but she looked hopeful.

"You know, I was thinking about that when I saw you talking to 'Teek'. You did good tonight, so let's make a deal? I close this case, I'll give you a cut of my payment. I might also have a job opening for you afterward if you're interested." He stuck his hand out. "For now, just let me know if Hana or her brother comes back to Ruby's, or you hear about anything else. Deal?" Penny was already shaking his hand vigorously by the time he said 'Deal', adding a verbal "Deal." of her own and another quip.

"Remember, even Nite Owl had a sidekick." She signed after tapping his holster.

"Ha-ha, very funny." Flip adjusted his jacket. "I'll go handle our tab with Hazel. See ya later, Penny. Get home safe."

He began to feel self-conscious he was likely the only other person beside Hazel armed. It was concealed by the jacket well enough, but still, Penny spotted it immediately. She also had a point: Nite Owl did have a sidekick. Granted, his first sidekick was a teenage street kid that met a violent death, and not a deaf, (mostly) non-verbal 2nd degree High Honor martial artist, but her point stood. He was serious about his offer, Penny played tonight cooler than he expected. As he walked over to the bar, he thought about the St. Clair home. If Hana was the type, there's a chance she'd at least drive by the house to relive something. When he got to the bar, he gave a sizeable tip to T'cKall and thanked her for the info before settling his amended bill. She asked about Wallace and how she hadn't heard from him since Sunday. Flip told her he was sure he'd call soon, he's been busy working that St. Clair situation, that's all. His mind blinked to what he saw with Agent Valer and room 19. He shared a shot and a water with her and left.

Walking across the street to the parking lot, Flip got the hot and itchy feeling he felt on Saturday and went for Birdie. He looked around and couldn't see anybody, but swore that Birdie was lightly pulsating in his hand. Gun at his side, he looked at the cars still in the lot but couldn't see anything that matched Penny's description of Hana's car. After a few seconds, he felt Birdie stop and the itchy feeling pass. When he got into Joy, he called Elena to let her know he was headed over.

CHAPTER 17

Rac' was rubbing his hand as he and Hana led Whore down the stairs. She got a little too comfortable with Hana's day of hospitality and addressed them by their names. Hana opened the cellar door and let Rac' lead. She was excited, mostly for him. She had never seen him Turn anyone, but he had for many in his absence. There were usually no pomp displays like this, unless the particular culture of his location called for it. A lot of them initially occurred in dark alleys or one-night stay lodges but he rarely stayed around long enough to see if it was successful. The lack of constant blood from battle left him with a need that felt almost addictive when he left the service. As they entered, the room was just above freezing, but felt thick. The blood-red obelisk now reflected black against the candlelight, as if it knew what was coming to it. It was ready. It was hungry. An aura emanated from it in a rhythm that felt akin breathing. Rac' walked as though he was being willfully led towards it by invisible hands. He had never felt this before, but he liked it. The obelisk was beckoning him. The Red Master commanded him forward.

Hana held back a few steps, allowing the aura to enter her. At one point, the obelisk was a point of scared hatred. When it was under *His* control. Now, she learned to understand what it wanted; what it needed. She felt that same tiny pull as she did earlier. It was the same with that damn housemaid. Only this time, she wasn't sure that Cherry would keep her silence. She was sure that she's already talked to the p'rotectors at minimum, and maybe even that mystery man that she keeps seeing. She'll pay her vessel a visit tomorrow and find out. For now, it was Rac's night. She took a small, thick and well-worn book from her back pocket and walked to the altar as Rac' began to lock Whore in place.

"Take the gown off first. Preferably without ripping, this time." Hana said as he lifted Whore's arms. She promised to keep her input to a minimum, but Rac' has ripped two of her gowns already. One was to the point of unrepair. She passively put her hands up to show she'd back off when he shot her a look. She went back to her book and opened to a blank page.

Rac' took the suggestion and applied it to his own shirt as well. After Whore was in place, he let himself be engulfed in the aura. He could feel the pulse and how its rhythm became one with his own. Even the bloodlust from battle couldn't do this to him. He felt feral, but never more in control. The obelisk's aura was becoming one with him. Whore could see a steady blaze in his eyes; a fire constantly being fed fresh tinder.

Hana picked up the book and walked over to the obelisk. "Alexis, do you trust me?"

Whore looked up. "Yes, Mother."

"Do you trust your Master?"

"Yes." She was now looking at Rac'. The fear was gone in her eyes. In its place a blank awaiting.

Hana smiled, "That's a good girl." and slashed Alexis across the chest with a single nail. A thin red smile showed itself just under the collarbone. "Now, open your mouth."

Whore did and kept her mouth open, her eyes facing the flames looking back at her. Hana let a few drops fall onto the page where it then seared itself into the ink of a thickly drawn symbol. Whore couldn't see was that her new name was above it. Hana didn't care for it, but Rac' liked it a lot. She still couldn't get the pronunciation based on the too simple spelling. Whatever; his pet, his name. Hana then took Rac' by the arm and drew blood, giving Whore a true taste of what it meant to be owned. She then repeated the process with herself. "Good girl." The obelisk came to life as the room's atmosphere grew thicker. Whore thought she could feel a low heat from the stone's surface.

"Whore, would you give your life for Master?"

"Yes, Mother."

"Would you for me?"

"... Yes."

"Do you think we would ever hurt you?"

"No, Mother."

Hana backed behind Rac'. The obelisk was as hungry as she was beginning to feel. She could practically smell the hunger from Rac' when she kissed his cheek. "She's yours." She whispered and sat on the altar to watch as Rac' fed. There were only pained yells this time, nothing like the screams of the other night. She's learned that making a scene only makes it hurt more.

The little bit of light of the cellar was growing into blackness as Whore's nerves ignited. A steady run trailed down in a warm streak against the cold of the room, dripping onto the chiseled path at the base of the obelisk. The pain transcended into something much more as the room grew darker. There was no pain, only the numbing feeling of a fire spreading with haste. Just before full dark, Alexis thought she saw a third face, in the same spot as last time, watching her. Only this time she didn't see leering hunger. Hana noticed Whore's legs struggle to keep her up and walked over to Rac', patting him lightly on the shoulder. Whore slumped into a hanging stand, motionless, as the obelisk pulsated with the taste of new blood dripping onto its base. Hana said as she put two fingers to Whore's neck. Faint pulse. Slow, but she was alive. Hana licked her fingers again. "She'll be fine." She then walked towards the cellar steps. "Come on."

Rac' stood over Whore, breathing heavily as the surge went through him. He experienced the contentment as he felt his own blood rush. The real thrill was how close he could bring his target to The End and not go over. He realized how much he liked it in his time after the War, choosing to live among the warm-bodies and their willful ignorance. The feeling of killing in honest battle was one thing, but this, this was something entirely different. He made a red smile of his own, licking his canines and savoring the taste. It's been a while since he's felt this. It's been longer since he Turned someone for personal enjoyment.

Hana extended her hand as he began climbing the steps. "I'm proud of you, little brother. Want something to eat?"

"Not particularly." Rac' took her hand as he climbed, feeling the skin of her burn; smooth and glass-like.

"Well, I am. Come with me, I need to tell about our errand tomorrow." She started walking towards the kitchen as Rac' climbed out and closed the floor-door.

Flip laid in bed while Elena showered. The detour over to the St. Clair house was a dud. As he thought over the last couple of days, he was beginning to think that he may have been in over his head in signing onto the cases. Something wasn't right about these murders; they weren't normal. His thoughts drifted to Ms. Ata, and then what Elena said about her run-in with her at the house. Then they briefly melded into the thought of her and his father. Grabbing his mobile off the dresser, he called home. The phone was answered on the first ring.

"Stokton residence."

"Evening Ata, it's Flip."

"Mr. Stokton! How are you? You sound so much like your father over the phone. Should I get him? Your mother?"

Flip wished his daydreaming didn't muddle the compliment as much as it did. He brushed it off and continued. "I'm fine. I actually need to talk to you." Even over the phone, Flip felt the mood change on Ata's end.

"Oh... I'm sorry, Mr. Stokton, I don't follow."

"I need to talk to *you*. Can you meet me at your quarters this evening? When will you retire for the night?"

"Mr. Stokton, I don't- That's not very appropriate, no?"

"Ata, c'mon, don't play. It's for work. It'll stay between you and me."

The call was still, but there was no *click* of the landline. "Ata?"

"Yes, I'm here."

"When will you be done for the night?"

"Will Mrs. Stokton find out?"

"I already said that. Did she ever find out about the time with Patriik?"

Flip didn't realize how scared Ms. Ata was at what he was asking. She could only think about two things her employer would want to speak to her about in such a private setting, with only one of them being remotely connected to his work. She just wanted to get back to her life. In her native country, abductions of young women were not uncommon, and one was faced with only two options; escape, or don't. She worked hard to push herself past what happened to her that night, especially when she realized what she was left with. Her father used to talk about how he came across a group of nomadic people similar to her captor during his travels. Since arriving in The Aligned, she's had no family, having left them all behind in a beautiful land but no prominence. The Stoktons helped her become somebody important and respected, entrusting her with their lives and everything in it, including their only child. They were people that loved her as her own family did, which was why it hurt so much that she couldn't bring herself to tell Ms. Stokton about her sickness. There were fictional creations to scare children, but any talk of vampyr being real was met with hushes or house-calls by the local Spirit Mage.

It was only when she arrived in The Aligned that she saw how casual it was to make a real and dangerous affliction the subject of entertainment. It was also a weirdly comforting juxtaposition to her enjoyment of said entertainment. She particularly liked the more dramatic and emotional films. The characters seemed to speak to her through the complexity of its focus characters and their struggle to control the inevitable. That Lord Dra'co character always came off as more comedic than scary with his cape and funny haircut, though. He could use an update; make him a little younger with better hair.

Ata said her good-bye to Flip and hung up the phone. It was still a couple hours before she would retire. She quietly left the living room and rejoined Fleice in the kitchen as she was finishing her dessert and writing something into her notebook. She spoke without looking up. "Was that Flip?"

"Yes, ma'am. He passed along his love." Ata sat down

next to her and took the empty plate. "Did you enjoy dessert?" She noticed Fleice twitch before she looked up.

"I did, and you've done it again, Ata! It was an amazing. Interesting to use sweetspice with vanilla."

"Thank you, HouseMother. It was in new *Home Oven* magazine. I added in sweetspice to recipe." Ata resumed her silence and watching of Fleice. Within the last couple of hours, she felt very hungry all of a sudden. Her stomach grumbled lowly.

"Hungry again, Ata?" Fleice looked at her watch and saw it was only quarter to 10. "Why don't you take something home from the fridge. We have a lot more meat around since this new diet. Speaking of, can we still throw in some actual meat again? I miss your cute little steak cubes, and that substitute stuff ain't cuttin' it for me. I know it's supposed to soak up the taste, but it still tastes funny and's a little too chewy for me."

"Of course, HouseMother. How about twice a week? You can pick days."

Fleice smiled. She loved trying to negotiate with Ata. "Counter: three times a week. We move dinner up to 6 and I skip dessert on those days."

Ata made a smile of her own. Fleice noticed two points peeping from under her top lip. "Three times a week but you *must* eat main course of vegetation. Meat on side. We keep dinner at 7 but that is 'final offer'." She made a wider smile and her canines came into view. "You still have dessert, but only if you eat main course fully. Dr. Bollard will not know."

Fleice sat and pretended to think over the terms. "You drive a hard bargain, as usual," She reached her hand out. "but you have a deal." She knew Ata wasn't cutting dessert.

She was tough, but she wasn't a monster. Ata gingerly reached her hand out and shook. Fleice went back into her notebook.

"Everything ok, Ata?" She was writing her new diet agreement, passing the book to Ata for her signature of mutual agreeance.

"Yes, everything's fine." Ata's face went back its base state of a welcoming cold before hugging Fleice tightly but very unexpectedly. "I love you, HouseMother. As both employer and person. Thank you for allowing me to work for you and family. It brings me great honor to serve you."

"Aw, thank you, Ata. I love you, too, but you're making me nervous. Don't make me interrogate you, now. Are you in trouble? Talk to me." Fleice kept an upbeat tone, hoping she was reading too much into Ata's post-phone call behavior and silence. What did Flip and her talk about?

"No, Mrs. Stokton, I don't think so. I promise to tell you." She hugged again, softly inhaling the smell of Felice's hair, then made a sharper sniff. "Mrs. Stokton, did you not wash hair? It still smell like tennis."

"That's right, Ata. I was going to be late for dinner, so I rinsed it in the shower. A full washing and doing up would have been a whole thing." Fleice waved her hand in front of her face. "I was going to wash it before bed."

Ata squeezed Felice's hand and got up from the table for the kitchen sink. She proceeded to clean it and the silverware before cleaning the sink again and running fresh water. Fleice watched her leave from the kitchen to the hallway and then heard what sounded like footsteps for the stairs. When she returned, she placed a few towels on the sink counter with a clear bottle containing a thick light purple liquid.

"Ata, no, I was going to shower again. I'll wash my hair then."

"Nonsense, Mrs. Stokton." She took a tall chair from the high-table and placed it right in front of the sink. "Please." Ata tapped the cushion of the chair twice.

Fleice sighed and got up with a smile. Her head made a twitch. "You twist my arm." She walked over to the sink, noticing a smell of purpleaf and spiceroot. "New shampoo?" She took off her over-robe and climbed into the chair, leaning her head back as Ata helped her hair into the soapy water.

"My father's recipe. It help grow hair to be healthy and very long, like mine." Ata let the building water grow to just below the lip of the sink basin before turning it off. "It's also a good conditioner."

"I think my hair is long enough already. It's already to my shoulders. I don't know if I like it too much, but I'm afraid to cut it again. I think Ron's on the fence about it, too."

"No, this is still first phase, it never looks good in the beginning." This coming from someone who's unfurled length landed right below the mid of her back.

Fleice took the compliment. "I don't know..." She sighed again and twitched. "Ata, can I ask you something?" The warm water and Ata's massaging felt so relaxing, so comforting.

"Of course, HouseMother. As you say, 'shoot'." Ata poured water over the soapy hair, avoiding her eyes from focusing on Fleice's exposed neck. It was so close; so, tempting. She pretended to cough to cover any sound that escaped as her stomach rumbled again.

There was another sigh and a pause before Fleice spoke again. "Ah, nevermind, I forgot what I was going to say. Please, continue."

"Yes, HouseMother." Ata continued with her last duty of the night, occasionally holding conversation with Fleice about whatever she brought up. A show she couldn't remember the name of she saw earlier today. A playful dispute about a call from the second round of their tennis game. The week's weather forecast. Whatever it was that Fleice was going to ask Ata, it never came back up.

Flip knocked on the door of the HouseMaiden Quarters a second time. He could hear at least one person inside and put his hand to his right thigh.

"Easy, you sure she's home?" Elena asked. She wasn't comfortable with Flip coming out here alone. It wasn't misplaced trust in Flip, it was the not knowing how and why a Patriarch would give in to his Maiden. She'd known Uncle Ronald all her life to be a good man.

"I can hear somebody. It may be the owner of that car." Flip pointed to a car parked under the large awning on the side of the house. In the dark, it looked only vaguely familiar, but it wasn't the same one Patriik drove into the city.

"Maybe she's got company. Isn't she single?"

"Yeah, but company or not, she knows I need to talk to her."

He went to knock again as Patriik opened the door, unrolling his shirt sleeve.

"Master Stokton. Matriarch Starks." He bowed.

"Oh, shi- Hey, Patriik. Is Ata in?" Flip gave a him a look-over. He was either stopped in the middle of something or was about to kick it off. In normal circumstances, he would've turned around and let him to it.

"Yes, sir. She's just cleaning up." He moved to the side of the door to allow Flip and Elena entry. "Would either of you like something to drink? Tea, Mr. Stokton?" Flip took note of Patriik's look, like he needed sleep.

"Patriik, you ok? You look a lil tired." Flip sat at table in the living room portion of the large one-floor home, Elena sitting next to him. Ata had an interesting design aesthetic contrast to the retro-modern build of the home. Very eastern and cultural, with a Mark of K'd on almost every wall; Flip assumed the décor choices was reminiscent of Ata's home country. The way she's arranged the furniture really prioritized maximum floor space among the many bookcases that lined most of the walls. She was either an aggressive reader or a kleptomaniac for literature. Patriik was in the kitchen space turning on the electric kettle and grabbing a paper towel for his arm. Before Flip could ask about the blood he saw against the white, Ata walked out of the bedroom in a revealing sleep-dress and over-robe. Elena averted her eyes. This was the first time seeing so much of Ata out of her HouseMaiden uniform. Flip felt uncomfortable about how Ata looked even younger now. She should be in her mid-40's, but she looked barely a day over when she first came to work for the Stokton family.

"Good evening, Master Stokton." She came over and sat at the table.

"Hey Ata." Flip and Elena greeted almost simultaneously. Elena glanced at Flip then to Patriik.

"Patriik, are you handy with cars?"

"I know enough. Is something wrong?"

"I don't know if it's wrong, but my car makes this weird click as I turn it on. Do you mind looking at it?"

Patriik poured Flip's tea into a mug and brought it over to the table. "Of course."

"Thank you." Elena and Flip said simultaneously. She looked over to Flip as she got up, "Hex." and stuck her tongue. Flip rolled his eyes as he steeped his tea. He waited until they both left out before taking out his notebook and wallet. He flashed her his marker.

"Ata, like I said, this is between me and you." He met her eyes. There was what looked something burning behind them. "I gotta know about what happened to you."

Ata nodded and sighed heavily. Even though she never saw her captor again, she intended to go to the grave with her secret. Yet now, her Maiden duties obligated her to follow her Patriarch's wishes. She composed herself and began.

"I... I was taken. By a woman. We talk shortly but I know she was not of Fountain. She hit me hard, and I wake up in her house. It-" Ata sniffed and pulled a tissue out of her robe pocket and dabbed her eye. Two tiny red splotches met her when she finished and she stuffed it into the pocket of her robe. "The woman was young. My age at time, or younger."

Flip nodded and sipped lightly. He'll get to that tissue shortly, and Pat. "Did she ever say her name? Was there anybody else with her? Maybe a young man that looked like her?"

Ata shook her head, "No, Mr. Stokton. She was strong, didn't need help. She said something about a brother. Never said name but he had birthday coming up. I was to be gift should he come home. She hurt me bad, Mr. Stokton. She would break me for brother. She *took* me against will. I could not fight her off, she was too strong."

Flip heard the emphasis and closed his notebook, causing the statement to hang in the air as a concentrated mass over the table. "I'm so sorry, Ata." Flip went to his mug. "Is there anything else? How'd you get away?"

"I escaped. Father always told me and my sister if we were taken, to talk and keep talking. Talking keeps you thinking. Thinking keeps you alive. I prayed that K'd bring me home." Ata had a somber smile. Her father was a smart and experienced adventurer. Her favorite bedtime story was about a funny young boy that escaped capture from sea pirates by responding with farm animal noises whenever he was spoken to. Eventually, the pirate captain got annoyed and let him off at the nearest port. When she was older and away from home, Ata felt the young man's story was true but nowhere near as humorous as her father told it. He was a great storyteller, but he took on a certain air whenever he told the tale of The Boy and the Pirates. "There is something else, Master Stokton. I have broken law of Fountain." She lowered the left shoulder of her robe and moved the collar of her gown to the side, slightly leaning her head. There were two small dots that could've been mistaken for moles. Looking closer, Flip saw that they were healed bite marks. Ata then curled her upper lip in so that he could see her canines in full. They were similar to Cherry's, only a little shorter but somehow sharper. He imagined she also had two perfect moles on her neck. Ata cried into her tissue, staining it with a growing red. "She gave me the Hunger."

Fuck.

Flip made some notes and casually rested his right hand under the table. This was Ata he was talking to, not some random lead he's tracked to a dive bar. She wouldn't try hurting him, would she? "The what?"

"In my home, it is the Scarlet Hunger. It make you sick and want to kill. People act like it's just myth but it's not. It is Dark Master, you call him Bad One here in Territories. When you have the Hunger, you are His servant."

Flip hushed his voice as Elena and Patriik walked back into the house. "I'm sorry Ata, but it sounds like you're talking about vampyrs." He wrote vampyrs in big letters at the top of a new page with a question mark. So far, a lot of these cases can still be wrote-off as being done by a couple crazies that think they're in the movies. That didn't settle the fact that all of his first-hand accounts said a lot of the same things. "If you're sick, Dr. Bollard can help you."

"With respect, Master Stokton, I don't think he can. I have read much, yet I find no cures. Even on the TechAir, I find nothing." Patriik was walking over to the table. He stood beside Ata and rolled up his arm sleeve, revealing two small holes in his forearm. The bleeding subsided but Flip could tell this wasn't the first time they've been made. Then he looked into Patriik's eyes. They were the same color, but without the same fire as Ata's. He straightened his posture and his hand dropped below the table again.

"Please, Master Stokton. You're safe here." Patriik calmly spoke.

Flip kept both hands in sight. "Did you know about this?" He then looked at Ata. "Does my father know, Ata?" The tone of his question told her what he meant.

"Flip!" Elena called out as she walked over to the table.

"Your father does not know, and he is no longer risk of being like me. I cannot tell HouseMother. I tell Patriik three years ago. He stopped temptation to do something very bad." Ata was close to crying again. "I didn't want to hurt anybody, Master Stokton. I am not dark servant."

Patriik left to go towards the bedroom. Presumably to clean his arm, Flip leaned in. "I know you're not, Ata. Do you remember anything else about the girl? Anything about the house?"

Ata sat in thought, dabbing at her eyes from time to time. She took Flip's notebook and pen.

I think we were in Monarch. I stayed in the woods the first day then hitchhiked back to Fountain. The girl had an accent. Well-traveled. I think she's been alive for a long time, Flip. She knew a lot about the body. I know I wasn't her first one. I could tell she was hurt, on the inside. Someone treat her really bad.

Flip saw from his periphery that Elena was following along with Ata's writing. He leaned over to her and spoke into her ear, "Can you check on Pat?" before going back to Ata. "And no name?"

No, but Tabine keeps coming to my mind as I try to picture her. I do not know that name.

"Got it. So, is Patriik also..."

No.

"Does he know how you became vampyr?"

No. He cannot. I gave my word to her.

Ata sniffed and went for her tissue again. She loved Patriik, but did he know what he was getting into when he let her feed from him. Did she? Did he truly love her for what she is? He says he does, but who would *choose* to live around one with the Hunger, knowing they could be a victim, or meal, themself? Flip asked how Pat factored in.

I was hungry and he gave himself. He kept me from doing something bad. Raw meat helps fight the pangs now but it was the first time. My body was in pain. I was ready to hurt. Ready to murder. My mind said it was the only way. I'm better now, though my hunger is always there. But so is Patriik, as I am for him.

"So where does that leave-"

Your family is safe, Flip. I mean you or the other HouseStaff no harm. If I were to let the Hunger take us both, your line would end and likely the Matriarch's. I am the same person, just stronger and faster. Most of us don't want to hurt people. It's not Other's Eve movie-thon all the time.

Flip smiled and looked at Ata before quickly turning to a new page, thinking about how refined Ata's written word was to her spoken. Elena and Patriik were coming out of the bedroom, with Elena holding a roll of gauze and antiseptic. Patriik had a short-sleeve shirt on and a half-eaten oat bar in-hand.

"I apologize for the casual look, Mr. Stokton. Thank you, Matriarch, for the assistance."

Flip nodded to Patriik and looked back Ata. "Ok, Ata, I gotta ask you something."

This was the second time of the night where a Stokton's had to preface they were about to ask her something though they were already in conversation. "Yes?" She asked.

He closed his notebook and put it and his pen in his jacket pocket. "Off the record, how does it feel?"

"How does what feel?"

Flip looked at her with a knowing mug.

"Ah, being vampyr? It's not like your films, Master Stokton. Not completely. I don't explode in sun. The brightness hurts and is very cold, so I must wear sleeves or

345

stay inside. Nighttime is warm." Ata went over to the kitchen counter and filled the kettle. She walked back over as it warmed. "When I got back, a power come over my body. Hot, like with fever. Couldn't leave house, had to live in darkness." Her voice broke before continuing. "I had to hurt animals at night, Master Stokton. I was so hungry." She made the Mark of K'd. "I am free from her, but I feel her power. This power was given to me to live for and to protect this family. To protect your mother. K'd blessed me for my devotion. Now, I can live to protect like Him. Father was right about talking, yes?" She went to prep her tea and continued, "When I feed from Patriik, I feel my own power. It's stronger the closer we are together." She looked away slightly as she spoke, "I feel most powerful when he loves me." and giggled to herself.

"Patriik, are you ok?"

He sat at the table in front of Flip. "Yes, sir. I've trusted Ata this long and find no reason to stop now. We have a system in place for her cravings. I think we'll be fine." He leaned closer and lowered his voice. "We will be fine, won't we, Master Stokton?"

"Yeah, man I trust you two. No reason to stop now, right?"

"Thank you, Master Stokton." Patriik bowed his head in gratitude. "You always had good discretion." He shared a dap with Flip.

"I will not protest Release, Master Stokton. I will turn myself over to P'rotecs." Ata spoke with her head down. She hid her stained tissue.

"Of course not, Ata. Please, just continue to keep my parents safe and we have no problem. Nobody else needs to know about this." His mind remembered an earlier sentence and he took out his notebook. "Ata you said, '*most* of you don't want to hurt people'?"

"Yes. In my travels with your parents, I speak with many people we come across. I learn that the Hunger goes by many names and has many victims. Some just small children." She poured her tea and immediately sipped, unfazed. "Many were nice. There were places full of them living *with* the living like you and I. Those that were not honorable were revoked of their blessing. Scarlet Hunger takes different for different people, Master Stokton, but Hunger is always there. With many, temptation to do bad is too strong." She concluded by coming back to the table and sat next to Patriik, completing the four-way stare between all parties. The air still felt tense.

"Is there something else?" Flip shifted between Pat and Ata.

"It is a matter of asking." Ata responded. "It regards your mother."

Flip realized why it was so tense. "Is something wrong?"

"Thankfully, no, but with your permission," Ata smiled. "I think I can help her."

Elena's eyes widened as she thought Ata was about to say. In normal circumstances, a HouseMaid, or any Staff, wouldn't be the appropriate candidate to volunteer radical health treatments. How did Ata even--.

"Nope." Flip didn't need to think about it. Sure, there was a chance that "turning" her could heal mom and even bring her back to normal. There was also the reality that it could also not do anything and maybe make it worse. Then, he'd have a vampyr mother to worry about on top of her current state. What if she found her way off the estate and out of the Fifth altogether? He's seen risky plays pay off for him, but that was mostly basketball. This was his mother. Fleice Stokton was still regarded as the best modern-day Homocide P'rotector the FCPD has produced. He wasn't going to risk ruining her honor. "No, Ata." Flip stood up. "What if it doesn't work? What about my father?" He was starting to raise his voice.

Elena reached up and held his hand, massaging it slowly. "Easy," She whispered. "hear her out."

"Ata, what about my father? What happens when he realizes his wife isn't aging while he is? When she's holding *his* hand on his deathbed while she continues through life?" Flip kept his eyes on her as she looked back down to the table. "Right. Now, what if she fucking kills someone, even by accident? I don't expect for you to be the one to put her down."

"*Flip Stokton!*" Elena clamped his hand. "You *will not* continue speaking to her like this. You will hear what she has to say."

"No, Matriarch. Master Stokton can speak freely. We are still 'off record', yes?" Ata looked back to Flip. "Am I correct?"

"Yeah." He calmed his voice and tried to speak. "Look Ata, I appreciate the earnest, but my mother has led a great life. When K'd calls her, I want her to pick up. Get what I'm saying? I'm really sorry I blew up like that."

"Then I have said all I must, and I accept apology. You are angry, but I respect decision as Patriarch and will abide." Ata made the Mark of K'd and bowed.

"Thank you, Ata. All I ask is that you keep her safe and her diet in line with Dr. Bollard's recommendations. From what I see, you're doing both perfectly. Now, if you want to reevaluate your service with our family after mom, we can talk about that when we get to it. You too, Pat."

Ata looked at a smiling Patriik. "Thank you, Master Stokton."

Flip nodded.

"Would you mind having a seat?" Patriik himself was getting up and went into the bedroom, returning with a large dark glassed decanter and four glasses. He set them up and poured each a shot's worth of a red-tinted liquid. "Would you share a drink with us? Ata didn't say when you were coming by, but it's the least I can offer while I'm here. My cousin sent us a few bottles of her newest homebrew. She's a uses flowers from her shop in her recipes. I think she said this one has roseleaf and pink sunfruit. Can we end tonight on a good note, sir?"

Flip sat back down and looked at Elena. Ata already had both of their glasses in-hand and was walking from the table. Elena thought Ata was floating and looked at her feet on the way back. It looked like she was walking, but in a single motion. When Ata got back to the table, Flip thanked her for helping with his case. Elena sniffed the liquid and had to hold in a sneeze. The four of them toasted and enjoyed the late hour. Flip made hand contact with Ata and got a flash of what had to be an intimate moment between her and Patriik. That was when he decided he and Elena should be heading out.

"So, did your HouseMaid tell us she's killed people while on vacation? With your parents?" Elena asked as she drove.

"Technically no, but only technically. Even mom wouldn't have enough to bring charges." Flip leaned back in his seat. He reached his hand up and played with Elena's hair. "Olga?"

"Yeah, Flip?"

"What do you think about all this?"

"I think you should trust Ata. You gave her an order, and she has to obey it."

"Yeah, but what if she doesn't?"

Elena stayed silent for a few seconds. She knew he was going to ask, but it didn't mean she had an answer. "Do you think she won't?"

"No..." Flip stopped.

"Ok then. I mean, she had a point; if she wanted to hurt somebody, she has ample opportunity. And if she's as devoted to keeping herself in check as she looks, she wouldn't hurt her anyway." Elena did her best.

"Yeah, but she doesn't view it as hurting my mom, she thinks it would be helping her. That's the part that worries me."

"I think you should trust her. Shit, you should be glad she even asked you for permission as opposed to an apology. We may not have been driving ourselves home, in fact." Elena continued driving through the Fifth District backroads in relative silence. She felt Flip's hand return to her side and go back to her hair. He felt calm.

"I do trust Ata, I just needed to make sure I wasn't alone." He continued winding and unwinding hair around his finger. "And thanks for coming out here with me. Your daddy did good with this one, it's a nice ride."

Elena took his hand and kissed it. "Better than Joy?" She teased.

"Can't nothing ride better than Joy. She's built a little

different." He softly laughed.

"Nothing?" Elena made a turn to bring them back onto a main road.

"Almost nothing." Flip kept his eyes closed.

"Oh, ok." She kissed his hand again.

Flip then settled and closed his eyes again; trying to not fall asleep as the radio played on.

CHAPTER 18
Two winters ago

S'uan Park felt her visitor's presence before she saw her. She watched from a short table as the woman was let into the playroom. She started coming shortly after her seventh birthday and would return every few months over the following year. She was scary at first, but after a few subsequent visits yielded gifts, S'uan felt she could trust her. Her parents used to bring candy at first, Redwater Ocean Rubber-candy, but they didn't visit anymore. They even missed her eighth birthday last month, but not the woman. She must really be her aunt; how else would she know her birthday? The woman gave S'uan a hug and sat down at the table, placing a small bag underneath. She looked funny in the kinder chairs, like the giant in her storybook whenever he sat down with his human family for dinner; he could be so silly at times. The woman said that same book used to be her favorite when she was a little girl herself. By the feel of it, S'uan felt that was a really long time ago.

"How are you today, little one?" The woman went into her jacket to reveal a clear bag filled with Redwater Ocean Rubber-Candy, the foil stamp of authenticity reflecting the ceiling light. She watched as S'uan's eyes grew and brought a finger to her lips. *"I believe these are your favorites, yes?"*

"How did you know?" S'uan excitedly accepted the bag and undid the twist-tie. She opened a rubber-candy and sneakily put the bag in her hospital robe pocket. Outside food was not allowed to leave the playroom after visits were over, but S'uan knew she'd want another piece after dinner. She can put the bag in the hidey-hole she made in her room. The woman reached over and replaced the bag on the table.

"I hear you are partial to the blue ones." The woman took a yellow candy from the bag and ate it. *"I was always such a sunfruit. Not the most popular flavor when I grew up, but that just meant more for me. My older sister also liked the blue ones."* She shared smiles with S'uan as they ate a few more pieces of rubber-candy and talked about their past few weeks in a one-sided silence. As S'uan spoke, the woman went into her bag and pulled out a hairbrush and a vial of a green-yellow oil. She situated the child's seat to face the window and began brushing, occasionally pouring some the oil into her hands and massaging it into S'uan's scalp. This was the first time the woman took physical interest into her appearance. The smell of the oil hit her nostrils with a cold sting and tingled her scalp.

"That feels funny." S'uan said with a giggle.

The woman stopped abruptly. *"Does it bother you? How rude of me, I should've asked before if you had any sensitivities. Dr. Lesli didn't mention any prior allergies."*

"No, I like it, it smells good. It tickles my head." S'uan turned around to face the woman. She looked so young but spoke very proper, like Nana Ronin. Maybe this lady was just as wealthy.

"Very well." The woman turned the girl's head back towards to window. The snow was falling in big clumps. Dr. Lesli said it was too cold to go to the 5th floor courtyard today, but she promised the kids would tomorrow after lunch.

As she massaged and brushed, the woman began to softly sing. S'uan couldn't understand what she was saying but heard her as if she was saying it right into her ear; her voice was so beautiful. In the time it took for the woman to begin braid S'uan's hair, she was already dozing off until her mind heard the woman's voice again.

"Have you thought about my offer, little one?" The woman's voice was low yet inviting.

S'uan jumped in her chair, *"Huh?"*

The woman kept her pace. *"Are you ready to come with me?"*

"Um... I don't know. What about my friends?"

"Do you really believe these other children are truly your friends? You would be free to make all of the friends you desire at my home. You would be welcomed and treated as if you were my own, and you could have your hair done like this every day. In fact, I have another child that would enjoy the constant presence of a loving peer. He is kind and looking forward to meeting you." The woman allowed a few more drops of oil onto S'uan's scalp.

S'uan thought about the woman's questions. The KinderPsych Unit has been her home for the past four years, and she loved Dr. Lesli like her own mommy. Aunt or no, she couldn't imagine living somewhere else; with someone else. Aunt or no, this woman has also been very nice to her. She didn't dare ask who the really tall woman was that always came with her aunt. She was really scary. She also had really long hair. *"Would you still do my hair?"* The woman's hands were light and slim, yet she never felt more protected in them.

"If you wish it, little one. Take your time to decide, I am patient. A new life can be a regretful decision for the unprepared."

"But mommy and daddy said I shouldn't go with strangers."

"Yet, you have allowed me to feed you, and now tend your head without the slightest resistance. You have told me many things about yourself of your own will, so tell me this,

when was the last time your parents have visited you? I do not recall seeing them on your birthday." The woman stopped to go into her bag. She took out a doll and sat it in S'uan's lap. The splotched and far faded colors showed it was clearly very old, yet the stitching was straight from the sewing line. Even without pupils, S'uan felt as though it was looking directly at her. *"He was my comfort as a child. I feel he will be the same for you."*

"I miss mommy and daddy. Will they be able to still visit me if I leave? What if they can't find me?" S'uan asked. She heard the woman sigh.

"I am sorry, but they could not appreciate the gifted child they created. They will no longer be coming to visit." The woman stopped to hug her arms around S'uan, feeling the real meaning hit her. Under the quiet crying, she knew this child was beyond her more damaged peers. It would only be cruel to continue allowing her to stay. It would be worse to force her into leaving. She worked hard to gain Dr. Lesli's trust and, more importantly, S'uan's love. The woman kissed the back of S'uan's head and audibly spoke for the first time. *"I am so sorry, S'uan, but it was by His Will. In time, you will understand. Your grandmother has already given me her blessing."*

Through finished tears, S'uan could only look at the doll and his funny hat. It gazed back. It was kind of cute, and really soft. She nuzzled it against her face before leaping from her seat and running behind the woman, hiding in a crouch. *"He spoke to me."*

"I had hoped he would. It means he likes you. Can I trust that you will keep him safe? He will do the same for you." The woman turned around and lifted S'uan onto her lap. The woman did not look as strong as her movements said she was. *"Do not be afraid of him, little one."* She hugged S'uan and

nuzzled her cheek. Her nose was really cold, as was the rest of her. *"Can I trust you?"*

"Why can't you keep him?" S'uan asked, keeping her face in the woman's jacket. She smelled cold. She was cold.

"Because I am no longer a child, and I know he will return home eventually. Only you can control whether you will be there when he does." The woman responded.

She looked into the woman eyes. They were so pretty; so scary. There was a low flicker behind them. She wanted eyes like her aunt. *"Does he have a name?"*

The woman smiled, *"His name is Mr. Pits."* and guided S'uan back to her own chair. She replaced the doll on S'uan's lap to face her, *"Now, let's finish your pretty hair. I was told you all are having a party tomorrow. Happy K'dsthajh, my S'uan."* and went back to softly singing as she continued braiding.

"Happy K'dsthajh, Auntie." S'uan responding after giggling. Mr. Pitts was really funny.

◆ ◆ ◆

Wednesday. Present day.

The 8th floor of Fountain Memorial was generally quiet during the overnight shift for Medi-Mage Benjk. There were a lot of p'rotecs coming in and out in the first hours but eventually it became a changing rotation of the same three officers keeping watch over the chick inside room 8-18. He looked at the desk clock, *4:00AM,* as he a small figure walked down the hallway, clad in a junior hospital gown with a pair of jeans peeking underneath. Her head was down but Benjk knew exactly who it was. The slap of bare feet against the floor tile echoed down the hall to MedStation 8-2. As usual, S'uan Park from the KinderPsych Unit made her 4am arrival, but this time empty-handed. As usual, Benjk was glad that at least the hallways were well lit during the late hours, especially when S'uan came.

"Where you going, Little Miss Park?"

"I can't find Mr. Pits." She wiped at her face followed by a sniffle. "I can't sleep without Mr. Pits. It's too dark. It's too dark."

"It's ok, we'll find him. I'll call upstairs. Stand over there for me, Susie, ok?" He pointed to a few feet away from his desk as he picked up the internal phone and dialed for the KinderPsych Unit. S'uan Park was one of the younger residents in KPU, but the girl was scary. It was something about that "Mr. Pits"; it didn't look right. S'uan was aggressively attentive to it, like she was listening to someone talk. As the line rang, Susie stood in place by the desk. After a few seconds, she began to sniff. There was a bad smell in the air. As Benjk was receiving the news that Ms. Park lost her privileges with Mr. Pits until Friday because of an, accident, at dinner with another KPU patient, he failed to notice that she was looking in the direction of Cheryl Shockley's room, now sans authorized FCPD P'rotector.

Benjk hung up the phone after a minute on the phone with the attending Mage upstairs. "Susie, you can hang out here with me for a sec. Dr. Lesli is gonna come down to help you find Mr. Pits. She said she thought she saw him upstairs."

S'uan looked up at him. "But I looked everywhere for him. Where did he go?" Her voice cracked.

"Maybe he went to the bathroom?"

S'uan smiled and let her brow relax. "That's just like Mr. Pits! He did have a lot of water at dinner. I told him it was too much, but that meanie Gradon went and hurt his feelings about it. It wasn't really nice. I thought it was good to like water? Mr. Pits says it's good."

"It is, S'uan, it is." He could hear the distant chime of the elevator down the hallway. A thin elderly lady stepped into view and turned toward MedStation 8-2, walking at a calm but consistent pace. She was holding something tiny in her hand.

"There's something in that room." S'uan said as she pointed down the hall. "Something bad." She started to tear up again. This time from fear, and she backed up further from the MedStation desk. "Where's Mr. Pits!" She started to dart her head around and curled to the floor against the base of the desk. Dr. Lesli was running up the hall. "Mr. Pits! Mr. Pits! Help! Mr. Piiiits!!!" S'uan continued calling out until Dr. Lesli got there and placed the cup she was holding on the desk.

"Do you have a compression kit back there?" Dr. Lesli asked.

"Yes, ma'am." Benjk was already reaching under the desk.

"I need it."

Benjk opened a case containing a reinforced blanket and bottle of water and came around the desk. He wrapped S'uan in a Level-1 embrace as Dr. Lesli got the tiny cup of the desk and opened the water.

"Where's Mr. Pits! I need Mr. Pits!" S'uan cried out. She was starting to flail in dull thuds as the blanket wrapped around her. "Mr. Pits! Help me!"

"Mr. Pits is on a trip, remember? He left you some candy, but said only if you were being good." Dr. Lesli held out the cup to show her three small circular tablets: one white, one green, the other a pale pink. "We can write Mr. Pits a letter that you miss him when we get upstairs, ok?"

S'uan looked from the wall and down the hall towards 8-18. Mr. Pits never told her when he had to leave on his "trips", but the stories he told when he came back were always amazing. He was such a good storyteller, even mimicking the voices of the people he met. Knowing he made his way out again helped her calm down enough to not drop her candy. He always left her candy before he left. She liked it, but it made her really sleepy, especially the green one. She accepted Mr. Pits' gift and got close to Dr. Lesli's ear, "There's something in there, Dr. Lesli." speaking into the doctor's ear. Dr. Lesli looked to Benjk.

"Where's the P'rotector that's supposed to be at 18?"

"He said he was going to check on the girl and then go to the restroom." Benjk then thought about when he last saw the officer and realized that had been almost 20 minutes ago. He relayed his estimate to Dr. Lesli.

"See about the patient. I'll handle S'uan and call downstairs."

Benjk walked down the hall, instinctively looking into every other window as he got closer. The door to 8-18 was slightly open, but it was enough to see it. That hue of red was unmistakable. How didn't he hear anything? He called down the hall to a Dr. Lesli still on the phone. "Call the p'rotecs! Doctor, call the fucking 'tecs!" His focus went back to the door and the dim darkness it led to. The hall window curtains were half-drawn and gave no viable preview at what to expect. He tapped the door open and looked into the shadowed room, the dim all-lights illuminating the bloody mass in the middle of the floor. Benjk hardly moved for the light switch when there was a *knock* and a piece of bloodied paper slid under the door. He bent down to pick it up. When he turned to look through the hinge-gap, two low burning coals met him. He read the message before him:

Don't do that

"Ms. Shockley, is that you? What happened to the p'rotec?" As he yelled for Dr. Lesli, a second piece slid from the door.

I didn't mean to. The light hurt too much. Please don't come in.

Benjk quickly closed the door and called for Lesli to hurry the hell up with the p'rotecs. As he kept his hand firm on the doorhandle, another note slipped through. It was the name and number of former UBL Men's champion and Founding Family Rising Patriarch, Flip Stokton.

Medi-Mage Benjk was the first person Flip saw when he and P'rotector Holmb got off the elevator. Holmb wasn't as in on the vampyr theory Flip pitched and wasn't going to circulate it around the other p'rotecs without more evidence; if there was such a thing. Once they stepped foot into the hallway, Benjk was already talking to Flip. His recap of the last few hours matched Holmb's but with the additional detail included that he was specifically asked for. He found it interesting that part wasn't mentioned in the elevator. Flip shook Benjk's hand and thanked him for the call.

"Don't turn on the light." Benjk words sounded more of a warning than suggestion.

Flip nodded and walked with Holmb to the door of 8-18.

"Need me to go in with you?" Holmb asked him. His hand was already on Hawk, ready and waiting.

Flip shook his head. "Just stay at the door."

Holmb nodded and walked over to the still half-blinded hallway window as Flip walked in. In the dim all-lights, he could see Cherry sitting on the bed to the window that overlooked some of the parking lot. Flip silently closed the door.

"Hey, Cheryl, it's me, Flip. Mind if I open the blinds over here some more?"

"Just...don't turn on the...lights." Cheryl kept her back to him but her voice was breathy.

Flip walked more into the room after pulling the interior blinds up to allow Holmb to view in. After avoiding the blood pool, he saw the visitor's chair was still where he left it and pulled it further away from the hospital bed and sat down in front of the interior window. He thought he felt that same pulse from the parking lot of Hole. "What's happening, Cheryl? I see you're talking again." He tried keeping his tone upbeat and his eyes off the body.

"I... don't know... Flip. Something's wrong. I shouldn't be... able to... talk right now. The doctor's... said it would be... almost...a year." Cheryl finally spoke after an extended silence. Her voice sounded like a hoarse croak. "Something's...really wrong. It's not just my...eyes. Or my throat. It's the light. The light hurts everything." She adjusted herself and turned to profile. In the all-lights glow, Flip could see that at least part of Cheryl's had what looked like a major burn already in the first stage of healing over.

"Did the lights do that to your face? Is that why you killed P'rotector Vin?" Flip moved his hand to his right leg. There was a now a heartbeat rhythm pulse coming from his thigh.

"I promise I didn't... mean to. You have to... believe me. I... I just asked him to turn off the light. I... told him it...

hurt."

"I believe you, Cheryl." Flip stayed calm but kept his hand at his thigh. He silently unfastened the holster. "The Medi-Mage told me you asked for me to come."

"I didn't... know who... else to call. The P'rotectors... wouldn't... have believed me." Cheryl turned to Flip and in the dimness and outside light, he could roughly make out the full extent of the burn. The streaks near her eyes resembled tears that seared as they fell.

"Cheryl, what'd you do when Vin turned on the light?" Flip reached and held out a tissue. Cheryl's response came through tears as a bloody hand reached out to accept. Flip stayed silent and then there was sobbing. "I went for the light... and scratched him. Some blood got into... my mouth and... and... I couldn't help it. I was drawn to it. It calmed... the pain. The... heat. My body reacted... on its own. I couldn't stop myself. It... wants more."

The more Cherry spoke, Flip could hear the increase in effort it took. His thoughts were rushing to what Ata and Patriik told him just hours ago. *Ata said it was days she had to stay in the dark.* He looked back at Holmb, unsure of how much he could actually see on the other side of the glass. Flip stood up and backed away from the chair, retracing his path to not to step into what's now evidence.

"Cheryl, I think the girl who bit you was a vampyr. I believe you're going through the first stage of the Scarlet Hunger." Flip kept his right hand at his side. "I don't know how long it lasts, but if you live through it, you'll become one yourself."

"Vampyr?" Cheryl asked through her tissue. Flip saw it fall and how it was now completely dark. Cheryl felt herself get up. Her body was burning up again. Even from across the room, Flip could see an increasing glow where Cheryl's eyes were supposed to be. They reminded him of the low-burners on his oven.

"I know, I thought it was fake, too." Flip stood in front of the door with his left hand behind him feeling for the handle. He noticed she was getting closer. "Cheryl, I need you to stay where you are. I can get the Mage in here, just stay on the bed." She didn't go back to the bed, she actually looked to be inching forward. He couldn't tell if she was actually walking.

"Let me get P'rotector Holmb real quick." Flip hoped he had said it loud enough for him to know to open the door.

She hunched down and ran her fingers across the pool before bringing them to her mouth. It was old now and the blood tempered the heat like spit would a campfire. "I.... need more, Flip." She took another dip and tasted before baring her teeth, her canines having grown more since their first meeting. Flip pulled Birdie out and trained his line on Cheryl. The pulse was undeniable at this point, and had now sped to a singular constant vibration. He pulled the hammer back and measured his breathing.

"I'm... so sorry... Mr. Stokton. It just.... hurts... too much."

"Cheryl, please, just move back towards the bed for me."

Flip saw her take what had to be two quick steps forward. He couldn't say he actually saw her lift her feet.

Through the glass, Holmb couldn't see where Flip's

exact location but was able to hear his request for Ms. Shockley to move back to the bed. He saw her hunch down into what he thought was the blood of P'rotector Vin. Then a second request and the sight of a gun being leveled on Ms. Shockley. He couldn't tell exactly when she charged at Flip, but he heard a final call for her to stop. The next sounds he heard were the distinctive *pops* of a compact-model T45 LEO and a heavy thud against the door. He dropped to the floor after the second shot. The last shot sounded to have gone through the exterior facing window. *"Shots fired! Shots fired! Get down!"* He yelled as he crouched under the hallway window.

Benjk had ran for the MedStation while a five-man team of armored p'rotecs all drew their weapons and went into a coverage formation facing the door. The timelapse before the door to 8-18 opened could have been less than a minute, but enough shoot-outs taught Holmb the silence is more indicative than the battle. He didn't hear Flip or Ms. Shockley and tested the handle. There was a resistance against it on his first attempt to open, but he felt it lessen once he stood and tried again. Getting a small opening, he leaned into it and called out. "Stokton? Ms. Shockley?"

"I'm here." Flip called out.

"Are you hurt? Is Ms. Shockley alright?"

"Yeah." Flip responded. The door pushed back onto Holmb as Flip got up. When the door opened fully and Flip walked out holding his face, Holmb saw the blood flow between his fingers. Seeing all of the p'rotecs with their weapons drawn and aimed, Flip raised both hands in the air. A steady flow went down the left side of his face and dripped onto his shirt. His cheek stung along multiple lines but the worst, and largest, of it was along the center. The heartbeat from Birdie had stopped as soon as Cheryl hit the floor but his own was in his throat. He felt sick. Holmb called for everyone to stand down.

"Are you ok, Mr. Stokton?" Holmb asked while he brought Flip to the sentry chair. Flip sat down, free hand back to his face but didn't respond. He stared forward and replayed the last 20 minutes. "Mr. Stokton?" Nothing. "Founder?"

"I'm... so sorry..."

Flip's talk with Cheryl Stockton came to him in spots. Her description of how she felt. The pain he heard in her voice. The change in her face that went against what she was saying. The fire he saw grow brighter as she jumped at him. Her teeth. His eyes saw the armored p'rotectors and the colorful diagrams on the wall behind them, but his mind was still in the hospital room behind him.

"Mr. Stokton, if you can hear me, I am attempting to remove the weapon." Holmb slowly reached down and grabbed Birdie. *"Ach!* Fucking thing's still hot." He tried not to drop it as he replaced it to Flip's lap. Flip couldn't focus on anything but the excruciating stinging in his cheek. Benjk came over with an open medbox. After cleaning the blood away, he examined the slashes and grabbed a roll of gauze and tape. Elena's story came to mind and Flip thought about the woman burning in the middle of town. He wondered how many men fell in effort to subdue her.

"Mr. Stokton, you're gonna need stiches for this. And you're going to have to stay at least 24 hours for observation."

Flip tried to contest but it took too much to try and talk. Benjk caught on and said he would talk to Dr. Lesli about getting an amended 12-hour observation but stopped short of a guarantee. He applied a stinging patch of gauze and walked Flip to the MedStation desk. After a standard trauma assessment, he endured the pain to give a full relay about his talk with Cheryl and why he fired on her. As Benjk stepped away to call Dr. Lesli, Flip leaned to Holmb. "Burn the body, Holmb. Burn it." It hurt like hell to move his mouth, but he needed to make sure Holmb knew what to do.

Holmb looked at him like Flip grew another finger. "All due respect, Founder, but what the hell are you talkin' about?"

"I just told you, *vi'nnak,* shit!" Flip winced and lowered his voice. A few responders looked over at the use of such a derogatory word, by a *Vi'nnakan* Founder, no less. "She was becoming a vampyr." There were now three Mages running down the center hallway following a woman wearing what looked a pajama pantsuit. He went back to a whisper. "You need to burn the fucking body, Holmb. I'm serious, burn her."

"Alright, alright, relax, I'll talk to Wallace. You get yourself cleaned up. You look like shit." Holb tried a smile. In another situation, Flip would've appreciated the joke. "Need me to call anyone?" He asked. Dr. Lesli was walking through the Mages and approaching the desk.

"Nah, I got it." Flip responded with another wince. He felt the wet pooling under the gauze.

"Founder Stokton, I presume?" Dr. Lesli asked. Her eyes went to his cheek and the slow spread that was forming.

"Yep."

"Let's go to my office upstairs. I'll bring you back for your observation, unless you want to stay on the KP floor?"

Dr. Jan'e Lesli introduced herself with a bow and offered a handshake. "You have quite a following up there, but some of your neighbors can be a little excitable when they experience new environmental changes, for good or bad." Flip shook her hand and agreed to come back to the 8th floor. Walking down the center hall to the center-hall elevator in relative silence, Dr. Lesli asked a single question before Flip got out his mobile.

"That room, it was Ms. Shockley's, correct?"

"Yes, ma'am." As he walked, he felt the adrenaline wearing off and the real pain came over him. Every step sent a shock directly to his face. He checked the time, *6:07AM*, and dialed. Dr. Lesli pressed the call button as Flip was hearing the last ring before Elena's voicemail. "I don't know when you'll get this, but I'm still at FM. I'll try to call later." He immediately went to dialing again. The phone rang as he was walking onto the KPU floor and he got his mother's mobile outgoing message. Dr. Lesli turned down the hall towards MedStation 9-2 and waved at the Mage keeping post. "I'm ok, but call me as soon as you get this." Flip whispered before hanging up.

Flip tried Elena again during the walk to Lesli's office. When he got to the third ring he hung up. They were walking a hall of sleeping children, most with their room doors half open. As they walked, the hallway was dimmer than the all-lights in the patient rooms. Flip couldn't help but look at the artwork and cheerful decorations on the walls. He noticed a few posters of himself and Elena in a little girl's room. One of his was a picture of him mid-air going for a layup against a defender, hers was an action shot in the middle of a likely a cross-and-shoot. He remembered his game specifically. It was one of his last in the League. Post-active playing, posters like those became uncomfortable to look at. Too many memories of what used to be. Probably why mom never came into the city much anymore.

"Have you ever been on the 9th floor, Mr. Stokton?" Lesli asked as they approached the door to her office. *Dr. Jan'e Lesli, MD, PSYCH.* She took out a set of keys and unlocked it.

"Maybe once when I was still playing. Mental cases are a little close to home for me." Following Lesli into her office, he couldn't believe that it was more studio apartment than doctor's office. He saw a section towards the back that was half-closed off by a partition wall. Flip assumed that was the bedroom. Lesli went to her tiny kitchen/dining room section, complete with a circular table with chairs and humble decorations. It was sad to think that this woman lived here in the hospital and wasn't a patient. She spoke as she went into a wall cabinet. Flip sat at the table. The top layer of gauze was beginning to feel wet.

"We do not refer to our children as 'mental cases' but I will forgive your candor as I'm familiar with the story of your mother." Lesli pulled out a heavy medkit and brought it over to the table. "How is she?" Flip held his cheek and didn't answer. "I see." Sitting down and unzipping her kit, she pulled out multiple pools and a pack of needles followed by a bottle of antiseptic and a much smaller bottle of clear liquid. "Would you like a drink? The numbing agent creates a mildly unpleasant taste." She then took out a syringe and injected it into the lid of the small vial, drawing enough to fill it quarter-way.

"Sure. Thank you..." Flip responded with a wince. Lesli went back into the kitchen and picked out two glasses and a half-full bottle of Castain's Bay Sweetwhisk before washing her hands. Granted that she didn't have a plethora of cabinets above her small stove, Flip still found it funny that she kept her liquor in the same one as her medical supplies. When she sat, she poured them each a glass and toasted to a good day.

"Now, would you like a particular color? We normally use red, but I think you've seen enough of that already." She chuckled.

"If you have green or purple, that's fine."

"Ah, give an old woman a challenge. Let's do both."

Dr. Lesli went to work. First, slowly taking off the bandage and recleaning the wound, allowing herself to see the full damage up close. "This big one is going to leave a nasty scar, but I promise it won't take away from your handsome face. Are there any other injuries I need to know about before we start? Did she bite you?"

Flip thought that was a specific question to ask, but let it sit. He felt Cherry go for his chest somewhere between the second or third shot but she didn't make it. He couldn't tell which was the one that hit her in the face. Flip declined and Lesli administered the clear liquid to multiple areas of the cut, and he relayed the story of what happened as best he could through a mostly still mouth. Lesli listened silently and readied the needlework. Flip poured himself another glass and drank quickly which elicited a small laugh from Lesli. She was right about the taste, but "unpleasant" was a major undersell.

As she began, Lesli told Flip about herself and her work. Chater and Jan'e Lesli were an accomplished and respected couple from their private practice before working at Fountain Memorial. Working with children provided the perfect audience to utilize Jan'e's minor in Visual Art (painting specifically), and her husband Chater was regaled as transcendent in how he handled those deemed "too broken" by their trauma or imbalances. Shortly after the KinderPsych Unit was completed, Chater died in his sleep exactly a month before his birthday and Jan'e became the lead psychiatrist of Fountain Memorial but chose to stay on the 9th floor with the children. After Chater's death, the hospital allowed a conversion of the Lesli's offices into a remote live-in office. In the beginning, she couldn't go back home for weeks at a time. It was simply too much. For a long time, she lost her love of painting to the bottle. Since then, she's better managed her time between the office and home but noticed that she slept better when she was at the office. As she spoke, she smoothly threaded the torn flesh together. Flip couldn't feel anything in his face and continued listening to Dr. Lesli. She felt she was ready to try sleeping at home in a real bed again.

When she was finished, she poured herself another glass and drank to a job well done. She took out a small mirror and passed it over. Satisfied with the result, Flip and Jan'e walked to the elevator.

"Doctor Lesli? How long do these children stay here?"

"As long as they need to or until they turn 14. If they require further inpatient treatment, they will be moved to the East Wing of the 9th floor with the other teens until they are 17. Should a more long-term or aggressive approach be needed, they're moved to the 11th after their 18th birthday. Unfortunately, there are two up there I don't think will ever know life outside of this building again." Lesli waved her hand for Flip to enter the elevator first.

"Do you work with any of the adults?" Flip hit 8 as Lesli walked in.

"Not much. I host an art class with the older teens once a week, but I let doctors Samble and Graff work with them and the adults. They're very good and capable at what they do." She got off first and led the way back to MedStation 8-2. When approached the desk, Mage Benjk and Holmb were talking with one of the responding Mages from 8-1. Wallace was with them. "Benjk, I need you to find Mr. Stokton a room along the East Wing. Mr. Stokton, how do you feel?"

The numbness was still in full force. At least he could talk without too much pain. "Still numb but I think I'm fine." He looked to Wallace, and they met eyes for a second. "How long will I need to stay?"

"SOP requires you to stay at least 24 hours. I'll sign off on an amended half-day observation as your operator. You can leave any time after 2pm, just talk to Benjk before you do." She extended her hand. "I need to get some sleep. We have a birthday party later for one of the children. I hope to see you under better circumstances, Mr. Stokton. You should visit the children one day, when you're ready, of course."

Flip gave his thanks and shook the doctor's hand. Feeling static, he was transported back to the KinderPsych floor. He was in what looked like a multi-purpose room or the communal playroom. There were birthday decorations all around. In the silence, a little girl called out to a boy before grabbing her plastic fork and rushing at him. She was saying something as she ran, holding a doll with a flat-top hat and pitch-black beads for eyes. The next thing he saw was Dr. Lesli cleaning her hands in a bathroom. She was washing off blood and icing. Then nothing.

"Are you sure you're ok, Mr. Stokton? Benjk, can you revert the observation to 24 hours?"

Flip blinked a few times and found himself in his chair at MedStation 8-2. "No, I'm fine. Just a little tired."

"Mmhmm." Lesli walked over to Benjk and grabbed a

bottle of Waterlyte. When she came back, she took two pills from her jacket pocket and held them in her hand, one green and the other a pale blue. After giving him the water, she pointed to the pills, "Blue to dull the pain, green for good dreams. In that order." and turned to leave. Flip took the blue pill first and signed a piece of paper. Before the doctor was a quarter of the hallway, he got up and walked to meet her. He gave her his signature and told her to give it to the little girl with his and Elena Starks' poster on her wall.

"Why thank you, Founder. I'm sure Ms. Park would love to see this. I'll have it framed and give it to her after the party."

That's when he quietly told her about what "might" happen at the party and described the boy and girl.

"Interesting. Maybe I can show her beforehand incentivize good behavior. We had to take 'Mr. Pits' because of an incident between her and Mr. Bond earlier today." She carefully folded the autograph and put it in her house-jacket pocket. "Professionally, I find him to be very disturbed but one of our more treatable kids. My unprofessional diagnosis is that he has become infatuated with Ms. Park and unsure how to show his emotions in positive ways." They shared a smile and Dr. Lesli excused herself.

Flip walked back to MedStation 8-2 and was escorted to an empty and isolated room on the East Wing, Wallace and Holmb in tow. Benjk took a wellness check and allowed the men privacy. When it was deemed safe to talk, Wallace and Holmb proceeded to take a witness report about what happened in room 8-18. Wallace let Holmb take the lead while he recorded. When they were finished, Wallace said one thing to Flip before getting up to leave: "For what it's worth, 4 outta 5 hits is good shootin', brother."

By the time everything was over and he finished his statement, Flip saw that it was almost 9 o'clock. He opened the blinds and saw the sun was still waking up, took off his shoes and laid back into the hospital bed. He took his pills and turned on the room TV. News channels must be the default in hospitals because he was greeted with the Fountain City News morning lineup. He was awake long enough to learn he wasn't explicitly named in the story about a shooting at Fountain Memorial. The sole witness of the St. Clair murder, Cheryl Shockley, had been gunned down in self-defense during an assassination attempt on a Founding Family member after killing her sentry, seven-year FCPD veteran P'rotector Kalo Vin. As of the reporting, the FCPD could only confirm that the Founder was a Rising Patriarch and in stable condition. It was still unclear on the motive of the attack and Ms. Shockley's connection to the Founder. At the time of the report, Ms. Shockley had still been considered a witness to the St. Clair murder and never a suspect. Flip was asleep before he could hear that there was no mention of Cheryl exhibiting signs of vampyrism. FCN would continue to report further details as they became available.

Flip groaned awake. His cheek was only a dull throb as the sound of soap-opera dialogue made its way to his ears. He opened his eyes and went for Birdie. There was nothing there. A hand clasped over his mouth while he felt two points on the soft under of his neck as he was pinned to the bed. The pressure of four claws dug themselves into his left cheek. Hana lowered her face into his.

"I don't want to hurt you, Founder." She kept her grip. Hana still felt a struggle and dug in deeper. Flip could feel the sting of air against his cheek. He stayed still and looked next to him. Birdie was sitting on the bedtable with the magazine, a single standing bullet, and his opened wallet. He noticed this girl wasn't moving her mouth, but he could hear her, just like Penny.

The fuck? How'd she get in here?!

Flip saw the branches of a burn peeking from the low-cut shoulders of her shirt. This was the girl he and the FCPD have been looking for, and he was about to be her next victim. Hana eased her grip and continued. *"I've seen you before. You were out at Pike's Creek last week, right? And The Watering Hole with that cute girl. You and my brother like 'em tall."* Her hold turned softer, tender even. She lightly trailed her index fingernail against his cheek as she spoke. *"You used to play baskets, didn't you?"*

Flip nodded.

"I thought you looked familiar, now seeing you up close. You're an Investigator now? Interesting." Hana stopped and stared at him. She couldn't sense the fear in him she expected. Hana lowered her sunglasses. No fear meant the will to fight. Her eyes squinted as she smiled at the thought. Flip heard a soft erratic vibration against the surface of bedtable. Whether it was real or not, Hana didn't acknowledge it. She continued her tracing, applying a little more pressure. *"How'd you know Cherry? Were you asking about me? Maybe about a girl named Alexis."* Hana saw his eyes go wide and clasped harder. This time she dug enough to draw blood. She leaned down into his ear and verbally spoke, taking in his aroma. "We have what we want. Please, leave us alone." She let go of Flip's face. He wasn't expecting that.

"You and your brother are wanted. Homicide and kidnapping." Flip moved up and kept his hands visible. He couldn't tell how long Hana planned to do nothing. "Why don't you stay a bit? The 'tecs should be back soon. You can plead your case with them."

Hana smiled again as she looked to the door. "You're funny, but I've been here a while already, so I think I'll head on out. I thank you for saving me a messy visit." She walked to the door and rested her hand on the handle. Flip watched through the window as she exited and sped walked to the right instead of the left for the elevator. There was a stairwell at the end of the hall. He moved to catch her, and his head went heavy. After loading the magazine back into Birdie, he ran to the door and wobbly aimed in the direction Hana went. The stairwell door was still closing but Hana was already out of sight.

Flip lowered and holstered Birdie as a headache was coming on. He thought he was going to drop. When he looked down the hall towards 8-18, he saw an empty MedStation and a single p'rotec outside of the elevator, talking to a Scene Scanner. Before he could think the worst, a voice called out to Flip.

"Mr. Stockton! Mr. Stockton!" A p'rotec was jogging from the stairwell door with something in his hand. He held it out as he approached. "Is this your communicator, sir? A young woman said she just found it in the stairwell." The p'rotec handed him his mobile. Flip opened it to see he had five missed calls and almost a dozen texts. There was also a messaging app he's never used before loaded onto it, already with a single message from user *JenniC78* that was followed by a photo.

It was so nice meeting you! Alexis says hi!

The photo was a full body nude of a woman. She was taller than Hana. Her appearance and build matched the bits of a description that Flip remembered of Alexis. He could see healed and still healing bruises on her body that went mostly from the torso up. There was a large tub next to her and the shine on Alexis told him that she must have gotten out of a bath to take the photo. The woman's face said she was more likely made to get out. Flip noticed the look on her face; a meek smile and the eyes of scared animal. He closed the app and thanked the p'rotec. "Did you see where she was going?" The p'rotec shook his head shamefully before accepting another thank-you and walked toward the MedStation. Flip went back to his room and sat on the edge of the bed. Hearing approaching footsteps, he went back to his weapon, only retreating when he saw Elena's puffy-eyed face enter the doorway. Fleice and Ata came in behind her. Elena collided into him with a tight embrace.

"Rough morning for you, too?" Flip coughed out. He heard a sniffle and looked at his mother and Ata.

"Shut up." Elena said into his chest. "I'm sorry I didn't pick up. I'm so sorry." He could feel her crying and held her.

"She only got your face?" Fleice asked. *twitch* "You look alright to me. The news said she tried to *assassinate* you."

"Thanks, mom." Flip broke away from Elena to hug Fleice. She hugged him tighter than expected then froze. "I'm alright." This was the first in a long time since he first-hand saw his mother off the estate. It was good to see her cleaned up and out of the house, let alone the Fifth District, though coming to see him in the hospital wasn't his ideal location. It hit him that she had yet to come by his place in Cloud Mesa since the day he first moved in. She also looked like her wardrobe's been updated. Still casual and subdued in color, but a definite divergent of her normal comfort of sweats or jeans and FCPD sweatshirt. Likely the work of his father, with some persuading from Ata.

"I know you are, Flip-baby. Heard you dropped that bitch pretty good." Fleice kissed him on the cheek and hugged him again, whispering into his ear. "I knew you would." He felt her put something into his back pocket. "Thank you for lunch." Flip looked his mother before greeting Ata. "Is Patriik here?"

"No, I told him to stay with your father until we knew what was going on. When Elena called, I had Ata drive us in to meet her. Nobody told us much until we got here."

"Sorry about that. After I got stitched up, Dr. Lesli gave me some meds and I was out until a few minutes ago. I--" He stopped. Ata snapped to his direction. She knew the aura she picked up wasn't from Flip. It was strong but fading fast. "Master Flip, you had another visitor, yes? Did they make scratches?" She tapped her right cheek.

"Uh, yeah, they did, but I'm ok. Comes with the work. Right mom?" Flip looked back at and saw she was looking him over with suspicion. Elena came over and looked over his face. He checked his phone for the time. "Look, I got at least another hour before I can leave, so I'm gonna try and get some more sleep." He went over to his wallet and opened it; of course, everything was there except his scril. He went into his pocket and gave Ata one of the five 100 scril notes Fleice slipped him. "Go get some lunch, I'll call you when I'm heading out. You should check out EndZone, they got a good brunch menu." Fleice looked at him with a teasing smile and head twitch.

"Actually, baby, Ata and I have a tennis match this

afternoon. We need to properly rout our last match." *twitch*
"That ball was in, Ata, and you know it. That Linda doesn't
know how to call."

"Linda is best HouseStaff tennis player in all of
Fifth, HouseMother." Ata retorted. She smiled as she spoke.
Keeping the competitive spirit in HouseMother kept her
from slipping away too fast.

"Don't mean she know how to ref." Fleice responded
curtly. She had a tiny smile of her own. Tennis always looked
dumb to her, but after a few weeks, she learned it can be
fun. Ata was the perfect person to develop and hone her
skills against. She was much better than initially thought;
much more athletic her stature gave off. The power behind
that backhand swing was unreal. "Flip, thank you for the
recommendation, I'm sure Ata will find something good on
the menu."

"Of course, HouseMother." Ata put the money into
her purse. Unless there were more vegetarian options, she
knew this "EndZone" to have mostly unhealthy and likely
greasy meat-centric food options. Maybe it wouldn't hurt to
stop by; the owner might be persuaded to make a unique dish
for a HouseMother. "Thank you for recommendation, Master
Flip."

When they left out, Flip turned to Elena in the visitor
chair. She shifted to get up.

"Olga, I--"

"Flip, don't talk." She hugged him again. No tears this
time. She looked him in the face and kissed him, bringing her
hand up for a soft hold. She turned his head back and forth
to look at the cuts, focusing on the fresher ones. "Who made
these?"

"She did."

"Who?"

"Her. Hana. Had all my shit on the table when she woke me up." Flip looked away as he spoke. "She could've killed me, but she didn't. She could've taken my damn gun if she wanted."

"So, what now?"

"First, I need to talk to Wallace or Holmb. I'll figure something out after that." He then kissed Elena, "When's the last time you been to Monarch?" and went to the bed. Elena pulled the chair closer, rolling the food-table towards the foot of the bed.

"I don't think I've ever been." A mobile started ringing and Elena went into her purse. "It's daddy, hold on." She got up and walked to the hallway.

Flip let himself relax for the first time since being woken up. He surfed through the channels and settled on a rerun of a long-finished sitcom. It wasn't a favorite, but it would do for the next 40 or so minutes. As he watched, his stomach made a loud growl and Flip realized he hadn't eaten since getting back from Ata's. As Elena returned, Flip patted for his keys. He tossed them to Elena.

"Mind driving me around for a little bit today? I'm on some strong shit right now."

"Good thing I rode with your mother. Hungry?"

"Very..."

"Ok, Love. Get some sleep." She took his hand and kissed it. She held his hand until he fell asleep to the sounds of sitcom laugh-tracks. Elena let him sleep as she looked him over. She couldn't see any bite marks on either side of his neck. She watched the rest of the sitcom until a courier silently came into the room with a card and flowers.

They were from Minister Esun on behalf of the citizens of Fountain, thanking Flip for his courage and physical sacrifice in what she was sure was a template used for wounded servicemen returning home. She couldn't believe he didn't come down and thank Flip in person. Elena made a note to ask her father to rethink his Founder's Vote of Confidence when election season came around.

Two hours after dozing off, Flip woke up with a start and saw his hand was already on a holstered Birdie. He swore Hana came back for him; even feeling her nails against his skin. The window blinds were up and the sunlight shone through and into his eyes. His head felt only a little lighter clearer and he wasn't as groggy when he moved. The pain in his face was there but it didn't hurt when he moved his mouth. When he turned to where he last saw Elena, he only saw her purse. Getting up, he moved slowly and went to the bathroom. As he washed his hands, he heard his room door open and then close. He opened the bathroom and saw Elena with two plates of cake.

"You're up?" She held out one of the plates to him. "Dr. Lesli came down while you were sleeping earlier. She said they were having a birthday party for one of the kids but had to end early. Some little girl stabbed a boy in the arm." She forked a piece of cake with a chuckle. "She sounded disappointed, like she knew it was going to happen. You wouldn't happen to know anything about that would you?" Flip took a bite of cake.

"I may have told her something might happen." He went to the outside sink and turned on the mirror's overhead bar-light. Setting the cake on the countertop, he carefully undid the tape of his bandage, wincing as the adhesive peeled away from his skin and matted blood. He could hardly see Hana's scratches once the blood was gone.

"Fuck." He whispered to himself. His eyes went to Elena and shook his head. "Nah. Is the boy ok?"

"Yeah, he'll be fine. Dr. Lesli said he was more scared than anything." Elena said back.

"The girl? You know why she did it?"

Elena's eyes went down. "She's fine. Lesli said she was 'tired of Garrod teasing her and Mr. Pits all the time'. Have you seen that doll, Flip?"

"Nah."

"Don't. Whoever gave her that thing has a sick sense of humor." Elena shook herself free of the photo Lesli showed her of "Mr. Pits". Even cleaned, that doll didn't look right. It was definitely not something she would've asked for as a little girl. Flip told (and hesitantly showed) her what Hana said about Alexis and Cherry. She felt the photo was old and Alexis wasn't alive.

"I know Olga, but why come here if Alexis was already dead? There was nothing that connected her with Alexis' disappearance. She even said Alexis is still alive." Flip took another bite of cake but thought about the party again. He put it back on the sink counter. "The shit she was talking about Cheryl is circumstantial. With this, I got something solid FC can use to get her on kidnapping. She wanted me to know they have her. If Alexis was dead, I think she would've told me." He could see Elena wasn't convinced. "Olga, I've played guys like her and I know you met some chicks that were the same. The type that'll try to big-time you by saying what they'll do even when they don't have the ball yet. I fucking hated guys like that, even if they were that good."

Elena had a small smile on her face and she got up to walk over. "Mr. Stokton, you seem to have a fire behind those words."

"I coulda been killed twice today, I think I got the right to."

Elena checked her watch, *3:16*, "I wasn't calling you out." and pecked his better cheek. "It's kind of cute. I take it that means you're staying on these cases?"

"I don't think I have much of a choice. You ok?"

"I am, now. I'm so sorry I didn't pick up the phone." She hung her head. "I... I was asleep."

"Stop it, just be glad it was me that called and not Holmb or Lesli." He kissed her forehead. "Now, can we go, please? I'm hungry and need to change."

"Let's get you fed first. I'll let you change later." She stuck her tongue at him before leaving the room and going to MedStation 8-2 to perform check-out paperwork and try to catch Dr. Lesli.

The cellar door creaked open and was proceeded by footsteps. Rac' could see the body still chained to the obelisk, but heard nor saw any movement. He continued to walk over until he was a foot away from Whore. Her body was shivering on its own as she slept. Rac' squatted down and inhaled her scent. He took another sniff and tapped her face. After a few raps, she came to as if being brought back from under water. Instinctively, she looked up expecting Mother and found Master. They stared at each other in silence.

"Get up. Now."

She did as was told with haste. Her body felt like it

was in the worst days of her Rock withdrawal. She tried to stabilize herself as she stood up and realized her arms were asleep to the point that they felt they had been removed at the shoulder. Her footing fell from under her and her throat was in the full grasp of Rac's hand. He clenched as he raised her to stand.

"*I said get up.*" Rac' forced her up and held her there. Her wide eyes weren't fearful, but held a low burn. A campfire was starting.

"Master... I'm... hungry. Food... please." Whore choked out. "I'm... hot."

Rac' looked into his eyes and squeezed tighter. The fire in her eyes grew to a steady simmer. He held longer until he couldn't hear her trying to breathe and then let her go. Her fall to a standing-kneel made her feel a sharp pain run down each of her arms, followed by the pins and needles of waking limbs. "Master, please. I'm hungry. Please..."

Rac' took a bottle of water and a small heavily wrapped item from his back pocket. As he unwrapped, Alexis' stomach started growling at the scent. It was a raw flank cut, ready to eat. He held it out in front of her, waving it back and forth so that the aroma can waft over in small waves. "Hungry?"

Alexis tried to move forward to snap at the flank. Rac' stepped back once and watched as the fire grew. She was hungry, all right. He ripped a piece off and resumed his original place, holding it just inches away from her lips. The smell was too inviting. Too tempting. She opened her mouth and bit into the cold meat. It didn't taste like steak or pork, but she didn't care in the moment. She waited for a second piece as the fever-heat took a tiny dip before rising up again. Rac' ripped another piece in silence and fed it to her.

"Thank you, Master." She refused her third piece and lowered her head, her stomach unable to accept her meal's aftertaste anymore. She then turned as much as she could manage, so that her back was to him. She then pointed herself out towards him in offering. The thinness of her gown's fabric clung to her curves and forged an outline. Rac' thought he heard her say thank you again. He dropped the flank and grabbed her hair.

"Enough…" He pulled again and a quiet whimper left her. What he didn't expect was for her to go with his pull willingly and put herself against him, feeling him on her backside. She had reverted to a submissive instinct.

Rac' yanked her head back again before turning her to face him. He stared at her before slicing his palm and holding it to her face. "Drink."

Whore sniffed once and fed in earnest. As she consumed, she felt her body cool down and the fever subside little by little. It hit her better than the purest of Rock. The rush was calming and stimulating. After a few gulps, Rac' tried to pull his hand back. She bit down and latched. A hard left-hand across the face told her to let go.

"How," *SLAP!* "fucking," *SLAP!* "dare," *SLAP!* "you?!"

Rac' pulled back for another hit but stopped himself. He saw the fire going in Alexis' eyes. It reminded him of himself when he went through his Turn with Hana; having to stay in his tent for over two weeks before he was back better than ever, fighting with a new fire of his own. Hana never left his side, even in face of concerned eyes and the start of talk about how this "friend" that tracked to an active warzone may be more than just that. He thought back to when Hana fed him for the first time and how she had to teach him not to be so greedy, just like he needed to teach

Alexis now. He clenched his right hand and grabbed her by the throat with the other. Even her cloudy eye had an ember behind the fogged glass.

"You will not do that again." He slapped her again.

"Yes, Master." Alexis responded softly. She knew she did bad. She couldn't help it.

"Speak up!" The sudden raise of his voice caused a flinch.

"*Yes, Master!*" Alexis scared herself at how loud she responded. "I'm sorry."

Rac' walked away without another word and went towards the cellar stairs. As he walked away Alexis licked every drop she could reach around her mouth. Every bit helped with the fever-heat. She heard the cellar door open before she called to him.

"Master? Am I still a good girl?"

She didn't hear anything. No footsteps. No closing of the cellar door.

"Master?" Nothing. "Master?" Her voice was anxious. She learned that he was very good at moving silently in the dark. She started looking around, even trying to maneuver her view around the blood-red obelisk. "Please, Master, am I still a good girl!? I'm sorry I bit you!" She heard steps and then the cellar door slam. She continued to lick around her mouth as the fever-heat and shudders began to come back, as well as a surge of power. He tasted so clean, and her body reacted. Pieces of her old life came to her in violent flashes. Master was right. Master and Mother was right, she wasn't going back to Fountain. They gave her a new one with two people that loved her; that cleaned her. It was no secret that she was trying to leave her old life. The secret was that she didn't want to. The money let her live how she wanted. Being

385

under new people gave her a comfort and bodily satisfaction. The many perks were often free but short-lived. Her life had been painful and going nowhere of note. Mother and Master made her feel *secure*. Terrified, but secure. They would keep her. Protect her. All she had to do was be a good pet. A good pet was a useful one.

Maybe it was Flip's recaps of both Cheryl Shockley's death and his meeting with Hana. Maybe it was the early-morning call from Wallace. Maybe it was the vulnerability she saw in his eyes as he talked during his lunch; something even different from he talked about his mother. Between that and her already heightened emotions from today, it made Elena's passion skyrocket. She had to resist the urge to kiss his lips and face too much but found there were more exciting ways to compensate.

By the time they made it to the living room, Flip had heard "I love you" so much that he was wondering if a ring would make an appearance. With every "I love you, Flip" and "don't leave me" he heard them less as words of passion and more as statements of fact and instruction. Elena held him close as she climaxed a final time, Flip followed her soon after. They held each other in sweaty silence as they laid on the couch, Elena kissing his neck and chest softly over the low volume of the TV.

"I love you, Flip. You know that, right?" Elena didn't have to look up for him to know she was close to crying.

"I think even your neighbors know."

That got a laugh, and she wiped her eye. "Flip, shut up and tell me you love me."

"I love you, Olga." He kissed the top of her head. "I'm

not going anywhere."

"Can I ask you something?" She kept their face-to-face.

"Go ahead."

"If asked, would you honor your obligation to your Destiny to Bloss? She's still unmarried."

"Come on now, so are we. Yeah, she's unmarried, but she ain't single. Last I talked to her, she went back to that art dealer that's supposed to be 'helping her career'." He curled his index and middle fingers on both hands for emphasis. That five-year-old conversation did not go the way either one of them had expected, but the night still ended the way it was planned. He always got a slimy feeling whenever he thought about Bloss'... whatever the hell he was. It was something about the tone he took about Bloss when she was out of the room. He seemed to be more enthused about her being a HouseMother than she did. "Plus, she ain't really like being around ballplayers. Wasn't her scene."

"But you ain't in that 'scene' anymore," Elena repeated his gesture, "and she likes you, a lot. You shouldn't believe everything you hear."

"Listen." He kissed her again. "I know you don't have to worry about your Destined, but the only person I'm destined to be with is the woman I'm layin' with right now. We've been through a lot." He kissed her again. "I had my times with Bloss, but that's all they were. You and I both know she's always been a nice girl, but *I* know she doesn't love me like that, Olga. I love *you*, not her."

"Ok." Elena kissed him and climbed over the back of the sofa, heading to the dining room. Flip enjoyed the view.

"Plus, she can't put it down like you." He said to himself when she disappeared behind the half-wall.

"I heard that!" Elena called back with a melodic sarcasm. She came back into view with two glasses of ice and poured their juice from lunch into them. "Now, let's clean up and get ready for P'rotector Wallace. I need to call Ms. Ingram. How're you feeling?"

"Better than earlier."

Elena smiled and nodded. "Good. Let me run you a bath."

Flip rolled his eyes. He didn't care for baths; the concept of sitting in a bowl with your own dirt. He accepted his glass and finished it in a few gulps before getting up and followed Elena upstairs. As he bathed, they talked about what's going to happen in his meeting with Wallace. Her interest piqued when he told her that it wasn't going to be like their meeting at her office but dampened some when he explained it'd be at the FCPD range. Elena negotiated that she'll come so long as she can bring her bow, she could use the free practice. As he bathed, Elena applied a salve-laced bandage to his cheek. Being so close, she was able to see in detail that the scratch started much further up than the sutures told, and that the sutures were double layered. There was a thin break of skin that started at the base of his tragus. She wiped along the trail with an alcohol wipe and Flip winced slightly.

"She apologized to me, Elena. Right before she jumped." Flip adjusted his posture and sat up. "I could hear the pain in her voice."

"I know, Love, but you had to defend yourself." She applied a thin layer of the ointment to the thin trail. "It's ok. You did the right thing." The eyes that met her said she and Flip weren't on the same page.

"Did I? I don't know she really wanted to kill me, but

I know she didn't want to live. I think she saw my gun and charged, *hoping* I pulled the trigger in time." Flip sniffed and wiped his eyes proactively. He could only think about the few times his mother told him about having to "put someone to rest" but she had yet to tell him about her first time. Vampyr or not, did he really do the right thing? It was him or her, right? She already killed a p'rotec by the time he arrived and made it clear that she was willing to kill him too. His mind told him that Elena was right, but his gut told him that he was too. Cheryl wanted him to pull that trigger. She knew her body was giving in to something it couldn't have known how to control. It just wanted to calm the fever. Flip thought about the picture of Alexis and wondered if it was taken before or after her own change, if she was still alive. He didn't know which was worse. Part of him wanted Elena to be right that Alexis was dead already. It would be easier to stomach and move on.

The ride over to the FCPD building was in relative silence. They still didn't know how Hana was able to make it into the hospital and find Flip, on top of leaving with no problem. Elena decided they should take her car. The wider frame also made placing her longbow case in the backseat easier. As they drove, Flip thought about Hana and how she was able to disarm and lift his wallet without waking him. Of everything she could've taken, she only took a thousand scril in notes. Hell, she had a perfectly good gun at her fingertips and all she did was eject the clip and clear the chamber. She wasn't going to kill him, despite what he thought in the moment. No, what she did was a power play. A show of dominance. He remembered how when he first got to the league and the most veteran player on his team would foul harder than necessary during scrimmages to get into his head. He was even the biggest player on the roster, but he made sure to establish who ran shit.

Flip recognized that same mentality in Hana, only she wasn't just trying to get into his head. She was the one to be feared. It didn't matter, because even the most obnoxious of veterans came to respect him on the court, especially when they saw him collecting rings and Top-Star appearances while they were struggling to get their teams into the last spot of the playoffs. The same is going to apply to this chick and her brother, who was still the wild card in everything. It was curious that he didn't come with her to the hospital since they seem to have been spotted pretty much everywhere together minus the St. Clair house. They may be twins, but Flip wondered that maybe they're not as connected to the hip as it appeared.

When they walked into the precinct, Flip didn't expect CaP'rotector Monroe to be the first person to meet him. There were other p'rotecs walking around, many with sadness in their eyes and faces, but almost everyone within eyesight came over and personally thanked him for his valor and for not letting P'rotector Vin's death by that Shockley bitch be in vain. Receptionist P'rotector Cur even kissed him on the lips and thanked him for doing what he could. When he held her hand, he caught a short flash that implicated that she and Vin were apparently an item and had plans to go somewhere nice. Flip comforted her with the thought that although he could not be there for Kalo, he didn't go down easy. Flip couldn't help but think that it was the complete opposite, that Vin was a dead man when he touched the lightswitch. Monroe escorted them into his office and sat them at his desk. Elena placed a large forest green case bearing the Starks family symbol on the floor next to her.

"Flip, how're you doing?" Monroe closed a file as he spoke.

"I'm ok; cheek is still sore, but I'll live. I already made a statement with Holmb and Wallace."

"I know, son, they've briefed me in full. We're just talking right now. I wanted to check-in with you before I left for the evening. By the time I got to the hospital, you were gone already."

"It's cool, I was sleep most of the time anyway. Do I need to turn in my gun for evidence or something?"

Monroe shook his head. "Multiple witness accounts and her first-strike offensive showed a clear case of self-defense. You took a big risk putting yourself in there by yourself, but we're all glad you're ok. If you don't hear it from anyone else, I'm proud of you. You really lived up to your duty as a Founder." Monroe's eyes showed that he was being genuine through all the 'tec-speak. He walked around and embraced Flip. "But, I do have some bad news for you." He sighed when they separated before continuing. "Alexis' kidnapping and the Isiah Shockley murder are going cold at the end of the week. I know you're still working on them, but with Cheryl Shockley's death, it doesn't leave us with much else to go on regarding viable suspects. Unless there's been a break on your end?"

Elena looked over to Flip and was preparing to speak before Flip beat her to it.

"You firing me, CaP? I'm going to solve this."

"I know you will, but Esun's been on my ass hard about this string. Officially, you're still on the case and your contract is still valid, but after Friday, it's going to Limbo Files. The tip we got about Redwater was a fucking goose chase and waste of resources. If it's any consolation, he's considering giving you a Star for what you did at the hospital. I know it's not your style, but expect your name to pop up tonight on the news." At that, Monroe looked at his watch and saw it was approaching 8:00. "He was probably already on the phone with reporters the night of once he learned what happened. If you still want to work 'em, that's fine. You'll be on your own, though. No liaison, no on-call backup. You'll be in open water, son, especially if it takes you to Monarch."

Flip sat silently and took everything in. He's had a case go cold on him before, it was one of his first cases. A series of violent home break-ins over in the First District that abruptly stopped after a month of starting. There was a robbery of an alleged St. Clair stash spot somewhere in the mix. A few weeks after that hit, a flash directed him and the FCPD to a man and woman were found dead just outside of Fountain on a road leading to Redwater, their car riddled with bullet-holes and arrows. Despite the most obvious suspect, no charges ever materialized against St. Clair due to lack of evidence. Wallace chalked it up to a case of 'the enemy of my enemy' and the force didn't press it further. Elena looked at Flip and then back to Monroe. He didn't want to have to tell Flip this news but was doing it as a professional courtesy instead of seeing it on the news. Flip adjusted himself and spoke.

"CaP, how much were the Valer and Shockley contracts worth?"

Elena looked at him in shock. "Flip?"

Monroe answered as if she wasn't in the room.

"Before Friday? I think 10, but mostly because of Alexis and her connection to Vice Agent Valer. After Friday, we'll still give the usual 30 percent based on your report of work thus far. Word has it that Camailla Valer has opened a Blood Bounty for whoever brings the kidnapper alive, but I haven't seen any paperwork on it."

"Could you talk to whoever handles the pay and make the check for Penny Adlouw?"

Monroe had a look of questioning. "Ms. Adlouw? Why would I do that?"

"Flip, what's going on?" Elena asked.

"Good question. I'm going to need to know why I'm giving a P'rotector's Consult check to a private citizen of East Pike. At minimum to explain it to the Auditors if they come sniffing." Monroe added.

"Can you do it?" Flip asked.

"Care to explain?"

"I made her a couple promises I plan to hold. If I don't have anything by Friday, make the 30 percent to Penny."

"If I can't do it directly, I'll have it made to you. You're free to do whatever with it you see fit."

Flip nodded and checked his phone, *8:00PM.* "Wallace still here? I'm supposed to meet with him."

"Yeah, downstairs." Monroe got up and started to get his things together. Flip and Elena followed suit, picking up her case and leaving the office. Monroe stopped Flip just before he got to the doorway. "Everything ok with Elena?"

"Yeah, she's just not keen on Penny's want to help me, that's all."

Monroe nodded and left it at that. He put his jacket on and walked Flip out before making his way to the elevator.

Flip found Elena standing at the reception desk talking with P'rotector Cur, arriving just in time to hear her apologize for her reaction to seeing Mr. Stockton. The emotion of meeting the man who risked his life for Kalo got the better of her. Elena was too sympathetic to have taken it personally. She joked that if Vin had made it through, she wouldn't have been so understanding. Cur tried to laugh. It was the first time the entire day she's been able to feel a positive emotion. Elena gave her a contact card, in case she ever needed to talk, before excusing herself and walking with Flip to the elevator. "What was that about Penny?" She asked once the doors closed.

"She went with me to the Hole the other night. I told her I'd make sure she got paid for her time."

"That's a lot for a one night of asking questions."

"She asked a lot of questions." He gave her a smirk. "And you know I don't do this for the money. Like you said, we have more than enough to worry about, and Penny could use a vacation or something. I don't know when's the last time she'd seen Aron."

Elena didn't think about a new aspect of everything until now. Why *didn't* this Hana chick kill Penny when she had the chance? By the description of her work so far, she had no problem with murder, so why not Penny? Did she have something bigger planned for her? The thought unsettled Elena. What if Hana planned on doing whatever she's done to Alexis to Penny? She was a grown woman but at times could be considered the same level as a large child to the unfamiliar. The right person, or the worst one, could find a way to play her to their advantage. "I guess you're right. Have you talked to her since?"

"No, but she wants to keep helping me. I don't know

how I feel about it. I don't want to outright tell her no, but if anything happened to her, I don't know if I could handle that." Flip pressed the button for the basement level. "Aron would probably come back home and kill me his-damn-self, fuck a Blood Bounty. Shit, Sandra might even help him dig the hole." He scoffed at his imagining of the scene and the ensuing headlines.

The elevator chimed to indicate the Shooting Floor. As they exited, Elena turned to him, "Was she that helpful?"

"She helped get info from a witness, and I can tell she's got a certain way with people. Must be all that work in the restaurant. I also kinda made a deal with her that she could keep helping me in the future."

"Then why you asking me, Love?"

"Second opinion."

"Want me to talk to Sandra about it?"

Flip curved an eyebrow. "Think she'll go for that?"

"I'm sure we can have a civilized discussion."

As they walked to the door of the shooting range, Flip pressed his marker and waited for the beep sequence letting him know the door was unlocked. As they entered, Wallace was in the middle booth unloading on a target sheet. By the sound of it, he was shooting something much larger than his standard issue weapon; probably something from his personal collection. Flip and Elena grabbed ear covers from the first two stations and walked down to meet him. As they got closer, Wallace emptied the shells and rested his gun in front of him. He turned and went into a dap.

"How you doing, brother?" He brought Flip in for a hug before repeating with Elena. "Ms. Starks. Y'all doing ok?"

Elena answered for them. "Doing better, P'rotector."

395

She looked down the range as Wallace brought the target up to change it out. "Nice shootin', Ace." Elena laughed at her own reference.

"Ace?" Wallace didn't get it.

She shook her head, "Nevermind, it's from a movie." before lifting her case onto the table in the station to Wallace's left. Wallace saw the size of it and whistled.

"Damn girl, this range wasn't setup for long fire. Handshooters, bolts and short-range automatics only. Long range and heavy caliber is next door." He saw her unlatch the case and open it. When he saw what was inside, he couldn't help but admire the craftsmanship. "Nevermind. It's been a while since I've seen someone with a longbow in the field. Don't wanna step into modern times?" He reloaded his shooter and offered it to her. Elena was already putting on her hand guard and testing her bow string. She loaded a bolt and took aim.

"Not when it comes to shooting. I'll leave you and Mr. Quickfire here to that." She quietly breathed in and let the arrow fly. The next sound heard was a rip in the aim followed by a loud *pop* of the target paper. She let another fly and there was another *pop*. She hit the buzzer to bring the sheet up. If it was an actual person, they would've been useless after the first shot.

"Show-off." Wallace teased. Flip chuckled and came up behind Elena, kissing her on the cheek.

"Nice shootin', Ace." Flip said to her.

"All in a day's work, Starbuck." She kissed him back and smiled.

"Aight, aight, enough with the cute stuff. Ms. Starks, replacement sheets should be next to you. Use as many as you want. Flip?" Wallace holstered his weapon and grabbed his box of ammo. He led Flip four stations down the row and loaded another target sheet. As it made its way to the end of the range, Wallace saw Flip load a sheet of his own in his station and unholstered Birdie. Wallace put his hand out and rested it on Flip's right shoulder. "You're a little quiet tonight, man. What's up? Still shaken up from FM?"

Flip let the target sheet go the full length before placing Birdie back on the station desk. He sighed and looked over to him. "CaP told me everything's going into Limbo on Friday."

"Figured that's why he was staying behind. I was gonna tell you when you got here. I--"

Flip let four shots go. Three landed. Individually they would have incapacitated their target; added together, the target was lucky if they could crawl. He adjusted his aim and fired two more, hitting the outline twice in the neck just above the collarbone. He thought about Cheryl Shockley's face after the last shot that hit her. He put Birdie down and leaned against the desk, looking at Wallace.

"They still have her, Wallace."

Wallace's looked over. "Alexis? She's alive?"

Flip shook his head. "It could be bullshit, but I think she is. I've seen a photo of her that looks recent. My gut tells me no more than a day or two. I think they're keeping her for something."

"Well shit, man, how'd you pick that up?"

Flip paused before he answered. And tapped his pockets before grabbing a blank target sheet and turning it over. "Got a pen?" Wallace went to his pocket. Flip wrote down the username and application that was loaded onto his phone when the p'rotector at the hospital returned it to him. "Can you get one someone to look up this username for this app?"

"Don't hold out on me, brother, how'd you get it?"

Flip picked up Birdie and aimed, "I met our St. Clair third-party today at the hospital. Woke me up with the bitch standin' over me. Even had my weapon and wallet sitting on the desk." He pulled the trigger until Birdie coughed empty. Five shots to center-mass, four hits. Individually, they each would've killed their target; together was simply overkill.

"Homegirl got the drop on you, huh? She hurt you?" Wallace took aim and fired the final two in his chamber. Two shots, two hits, man down. In the ensuing silence, the sounds of a bow release and the popping rip of paper echoed. "You know, if you need to talk, you can go to Dr. H'al'a. He's a mentalist that works with the department, and a damn good one. Normally, a debrief session is mandatory for all shootings in the field. Consultants aren't usually given access to those kinds of resources, but CaP talked to H'al'a and he was more than happy to offer his service. He wants to talk to you. Especially with all the vamp talk Holmb told me you were on."

Flip nodded. "He work on the weekends? I might have to head out to Monarch soon." He saw the surprise in Wallace's face. "Following a lead."

"Shit that's better than what we got. That tip Camailla and I got was had us sending men out Redwater for nothing. As for tracking this user, it won't be before Friday before we run it down, but I'll try to push it as much as I can. If you're lead is taking you to Monarch, be careful, brother. They're more than a little finicky about that jurisdiction bullshit when it comes to 'one of their own'. They're weird as hell out there."

"I've heard. I think Ronnie still lives out there,

though." Flip looked at Wallace for a confirmation. Wallace only shrugged.

"I don't know, man, I ain't talk to Ronnie in a while. Shit, man, I can barely remember the last time I seen him. It had to be a few years ago when he was talking about opening a butchery or something like that. You know he got married a while back, right? I think it was to the chick he was with at the time."

"Nah." Flip answered coldly. He didn't hate his brother or anything; he just didn't feel he knew him enough to care about what happened in his life. The last real conversation they shared was when Ronnie came by the house and congratulated Flip on deciding to take up professional ball. After that came the slow tapering semi-normal routine of birthday texts and "checking in" text exchanges. At least he wasn't like some of the people who called themselves "old friends" that came crawling around after he got drafted but disappeared when he was booted. Ronnie had decency, he could give him that, even if he wasn't too interested in being around. By Flip's third season, the absence didn't bother him, but had he known about Ronnie's efforts to open a business he would've been happy to invest some seed money to get him started. Always good to see another *Vi'nnakan* running an honest business, especially if it was family. Wallace left it at that before checking his watch, *20:40*. He offered his piece to Flip.

"Wanna try it out? It kicks a little harder than that pocket rocket you got there."

"That doesn't look department issue."

Wallace holstered his weapon. It had the bulk of a six-shot but the look of a crazy post-modern build. Must be a custom piece. "Cause it ain't, man. Gift from one of my first clients from the PI days. I still like to take her out from time to time, though, keeps her young."

Flip nodded, "Maybe next time." and dapped him up again. When they separated from their hug, Flip noticed Elena taking her bow case off her station desk and gathering her target sheets. He knew she was going to want to compare scores. As she started towards them, he lowered his voice. "You believe in vampyr?"

"Honestly, I don't know, but I trust you, brother. Look, Limbo File or not, keep me in the loop of what you do, especially if you're crossing borders. I'll let you know what we can get on that username."

Just before Elena was with them Flip asked, "You're still fucking Valer, ain't you?"

Wallace shrugged again but didn't verbally answer the question. He didn't need to. "She's single, I'm single." He looked at his watch again. "I gotta roll on. Need to be somewhere in 20."

Flip smiled and nodded. "Yeah, you right."

They fist-bumped just as Elena came over and stood next to Flip. She kissed his cheek as Wallace made his way to the door. "What'd you say to him that got him going like that?"

"Nothing, Love. Guess he had to be somewhere to be."

She looked at Flip for a second before giving him her target sheets. Based on the progression, she got into a groove by the third one; almost every shot would have proved fatal. The last sheet was for fun, exhibited by the deliberate circle in the ring before bullseye. "How'd you do?"

Flip rolled his eyes and went back to his station. He called his target sheet to him and took it off its hangers, examining the damage. "Pretty good for one clip, huh, Ace?" He handed it to Elena. She looked at it and whistled.

"For someone who doesn't shoot often, looks like you still remember how to aim."

"I could say the same. I thought you didn't go out much yourself."

"I don't, but the tree in the backyard is good enough when I'm feeling lazy and don't want to go all the way out Redwater for HiPoint. Ready to go?"

Flip took the case from Elena. "Yeah, let's roll."

"Wanna eat?"

They walked to the range entry door. Flip didn't expect the bow case to be as heavy as it was. "Nah, not really. I got food at home if you are though. Unless you wanted to pick something up." He opened the door for her and they left out. They decided to pass on dinner but agreed to pick up ice-cream on the way back to Mesa. As they made their way through the station, Flip noticed a p'rotec bring in a handcuffed young man that looked familiar. It was one of the Rock Boys from their night out on Saturday at the Hole. Flip shook his head as he walked on. Before they got to the front door, Elena stopped and went back to the reception desk to speak with P'rotector Cur one last time. Flip saw her writing something down before shaking Cur's hand. When she returned, Flip asked what that last talk was about.

"Her and P'rotector Vin were set to go on a trip in a few weeks. I just wanted to make sure that it still happened, that's all. Your generosity with Penny inspired me." She teased with a stick of her tongue.

"Whatever." Flip teased back. "I heard Roland's can deliver now. Wanna get a movie going and try it out?"

"Oooh, look who's feeling fancy after almost dying. We can try, but I swear if it's melted, we'll have a problem."

They got over to Elena's car and he put the bow case into the back seat. He still couldn't believe how heavy it was; it had to be reinforced because he knew the bow itself wasn't heavy at all. In fact, it was built with the intention to be lightweight; but it being a one of a kind, it's smart to have the strongest case available just in case. He closed the door and went over to the passenger side. Elena checked her mirrors and backed out. On the way to Cloud Mesa, they talked about Flip going out to Monarch. Elena made the decision that she was going to join him whether he liked it or not. No way she was going to let him do some undercover work, in Monarch of all places, by himself. It wasn't like he was going to Redwater, where he's loved probably more than he is in his own hometown. This was Monarch, the black sheep of the tri-territory family of it, Redwater and Fountain. There were always longstanding rumor of it being a home for vampyr, but never any first-hand confirmation or denial. Everyone seemed to know a friend of a friend that's been there, but nobody could confirm what they claimed to have seen. By the time they arrived to Mesa, Elena looked over and saw Missy Blaskow-Hermann being escorted to the front entrance by a well-dressed, noticeably younger gentleman. She tapped Flip's shoulder and pointed, and they shared a humorous exchange of theories as Elena entered the garage and parked.

CHAPTER 19

Cold. So cold. Hot. I need water. Master. Mother. Why don't they help me? Why don't they kill me? They must love me. My life is theirs. I am theirs. I can be a good girl. I must be a good girl.

Whore woke up from a standing slumber and felt herself spinning. From the cold of the cellar to the fever running through her, she could feel her already weak hold on her remaining mental slipping away. She couldn't help but continue to tongue her enlarged canines, despite the previous bites that stung every time she did. The bit of blood that she could taste lowered the heat for a fraction. How long was she going to stay down here? When could she see Master again? Where was Mother? Would he tell her about how she bit him? Was Mother going to punish her? She whimpered in the cold silence and scanned as much as her restraints allowed. She was alone, but knew she wasn't. Something was in here. Some*one* was watching her. She heard what sounded like a footstep and stopped searching. That's when a hand wrapped itself around her mouth from behind. By the soft and eerily smooth texture, she knew it was Mother. She smelled good, like she did on spa day. Maybe she didn't know. Maybe she's earned another treat. Whore realized it's been a while since she could feel her arms.

"Been a good girl?" Mother asked.

Whore hesitantly shook her head and she felt the hand tighten.

"You wouldn't be lying now, would you?"

Fearing that Mother already knew, Whore shook her head again, slower this time. Mother loosened her grip some.

"Don't cry, it's ok." Her words had the opposite effect and made Whore release unstifled tears as she walked around the obelisk. "I said--"

"I'm so sorry, Mother! I didn't mean to do it!"

Mother slapped her hard and leaned in, holding her by the hair with her left. *"Stop your fucking crying right now!"* Whore could hear a voice in her head she never heard before from Mother. "My brother told me about your, overindulgence. I was going to tell you I was proud of you, until you decided to lie to me." She sucked her teeth. "I thought we talked about lying. I thought you said you'd be a good girl?" Mother turned around and walked to the altar, she bent down and came up with a length of chain with a single large cuff at one end. It squeaked as she opened and closed it.

"I will. I promise I'll be good." Whore pleaded. She didn't know what was in store for her but didn't like the look of that cuff. Mother continued opening and closing the latch.

Mother walked over and opened the cuff. She fitted in onto Whore's neck and latched it closed. "Now, be a good Whore and stand still." She then dropped the length in her hand before unlocking the overhead wrists. Whore's arms fell and she felt pins and needles running through them. Her head fell with them before Mother lifted it up and looked her in the eyes. The fire was there but it was dull. The glow in her clouded eye was a dim pearlescent. "You know, I'm sorry about your eye, but it starting to look good on you. It's almost cute."

Whore smiled faintly at the compliment and whispered, "Thank you, Mother."

Mother smiled back, showing fangs.

SLAP!

"Don't you *ever* lie to me again. Last warning."

Whore tensed for another hit when Mother went to stroke her hair. She allowed her to do it again and backed up against the obelisk.

SLAP!

"You lose your voice?"

"I'm sorry, Mother, thank you." Whore fought through the pins and needles and slowly started to raise her gown. "It won't happen again." She continued raising until it was mid-thigh and closed her eyes. "It won't happen again." Her legs inched apart.

Mother watched Whore as she raised the bottom of her gown. At least she knew not to try and bite her. She looked at her in silence for a few seconds. "Don't insult yourself. Drop your gown and get on the floor. Right now."

Whore let her gown fall back to her feet and kneeled on the floor. Mother tugged the chain upwards. "I said *drop* your gown. Don't make me ask twice." She pulled the chain up, bringing Whore to her feet. She cut a small slit in the shoulder. Holding the other sleeve for her, Whore inched her left arm and let the dress fall to her feet. The cold magnified that she was shed of her only layer.

"Good girl. On the floor. Hands and knees."

Whore went to the ground. Mother picked up her end and walked in the direction of the steps. There was a resistance after a few steps. "Come on, now."

Whore began to crawl again until she was at Mother's side. "Yes, Mother." When they got to the cellar steps, Mother walked up and opened the door. Whore followed without resistance. When they were in the main hall, Master was in a chair in the sitting area next to the kitchen, watching them walk over.

"I think someone has something to say to say to you." Hana pulled on the chain to bring Whore closer. "Isn't that right?"

"Yes, Mother." She raised her head to look Rac' in the face. "I'm sorry, Master. I didn't mean to bite you."

Rac' looked at her as he unwrapped his hand, the bite now non-existent besides two faded dots. Whore's cloudy but focused eye looked back at him. There wasn't any fear, no indication of deceit. What he did see was her searching his body, gauging the scars, that covered him. Her eyes traced the largest that initially grabbed her attention.

"Whore, do you love your Master?" Hana asked. She kept her eyes on Rac'.

"Yes."

"Do you love me?" Hana asked with a sinister smile. She kept her eyes on Rac'.

Whore realized that outside was full-dark. Her jaw also didn't click as she spoke anymore.

What day was it? How long have I been here? How long will I be here? Will they get tired of me?

Her thoughts were interrupted by Mother's face, now next to hers, and the sharp entry of fingers. "You can be honest. I'll understand if you don't." The sensation came over her and Whore found it difficult to keep her arms steady. She was ready to rest on her elbows and allow Mother to do what she wanted. She would let her. She deserved her punishment.

"Yes... Mother... I love you." She whispered.

Hana kissed her cheek and removed her fingers, "Good girl." and wiped them across Whore's cheek. "Little brother, can we talk in the kitchen?" She extended her length of chain out to him. Rac' looked at Hana and then back to Whore, and her cloudy eye. The last time he saw Mama, she was beginning to develop a tiny cloud of her own and didn't drive as much. When he blinked, he was transported back to all those years ago, to the last time he saw *Him* hit Mama across the face. *He* found out about Rac's plan to leave for the War and made her pay for it. Rac' tried to hit back and was beaten worse than he ever had. By the time *He* found them, Rac' knew it was too late for Mama. At least he still had Hana; the only other enemy of his own. In so many ways, she was exactly like Mama back then. She was kind. Funny. Caring for others. But since they split up, he can see she's become more like *Him*. *Her* temper. *Her* brutality. *Her* anger. He knew it for certain when he came back and found that the obelisk still stood in the middle of the cellar.

He made her into this.

He made us into this.

"Master?"

When Rac' blinked again, he was back in his seat. Whore now at his feet, the chain that held her clinked and dragged as she curled against his leg.

"Master? I'm sorry." She said as she looked up to him. Rac' could see a dull glow under the cloud. "I love you."

"Whatever." And he got up quickly. It was so quick that she curled into a ball, tensing her body in anticipation. He left her on the floor with her leash and walked into the kitchen. "Stay."

"Yes, Master." Whore did as she was told. Rac' didn't see her looking at the door as he walked away.

When they entered the kitchen, Hana sat across from him and went into her pocket. She pulled out 1000 scril in assorted notes and placed it on the table.

"What about it?" Rac' picked up the scril. Of course, they had money. *His* money, but money just the same.

"I found it in the wallet of the man looking for us. He's a P'rotector's Consultant, and the one who killed that girl at the hospital. You've seen him plenty." She looked over Rac's shoulder and saw Whore was still where she was told to stay. It was nice to see Rac' command her with such authority. She placed her hand on Rac's before flipping it over and lightly tracing his heal. "It's Flip Stokton."

Rac' tried to steel his look of surprise. Why was Flip Stokton, a Fountain Founder, working with the Fountain City P'rotectors? It couldn't have been the money, unless he's fallen into the same trap that most ex-star athletes find themselves in trying to still live as if another multi-million deal was just around the corner. His last memory of Flip was taking Hana to what was supposed a Monarch-Redwater game and enjoying one of the best athletic displays he's ever seen since Monarch native Bor'is Bledso won the men's singles tennis tournament at I'Tacha 44. Instead, the game was called off for unknown reasons. Hana acted like she didn't care, even though he knew she was interested to go. Mr. Klima had a photo of Stokton at the shop. Rac' had always assumed he was a fan since he was originally from Redwater.

"I know right? I was a little surprised too." She winked at him. "I'm surprised you didn't see him last weekend when we went out. He was with that tall chick and that bitch from the diner. Looks like you two have something in common."

"Interesting. How much does he know?"

Hana weighted her touch. "Well, he knows about you but thinks he's just looking for me. He's not a problem."

"Not a problem? Or not a problem right now?" Rac'

closed his hand into a hold. He used his other hand to trace along the burn. The permanent result of a child's temper tantrum. Hana never let him say he was sorry for it. *He* didn't care whether he was or not. "We need to start thinking about moving."

"Do you trust me, little brother?" Hana looked past Rac' again and called out. "Whore, what'cha doing?"

The sudden acknowledgement caused her to freeze in place. "Nothing, Mother. I promise." Whore called back. Rac' was about to turn around before Hana swiftly grabbed his face and turned it back to her.

"I'm still talking to you. Do you trust me?"

"Yes, now let me go." Rac' answered back before yanking himself away.

"Ok, fine. Then no, we don't need to leave yet." She leaned back onto her stool and sat down.

"What was she doing?" Rac' turned around and looked over at Alexis.

"Nothing. She's been eyeing the door since we came in here, though. I was just making sure she wasn't about to do something stupid" Hana saw a small ember ignite in Rac's eyes. He gave a simple order; to stay where she was. Nothing difficult. He never tolerated disobedience. Disobeying direct orders can get you killed, whether on the battlefield or as a thrall. Hana pulled him close. "Don't worry, she's being punished as it is."

Rac' turned around and saw Whore still on the floor. She didn't even try to get into either of the empty chairs. He slowly licked his canines as he watched her try to get comfortable sitting on the hardwood. He decided it was indeed punishment enough for giving in to her new urges. He turned back as his stomach growled.

"Hungry?" Hana asked him.

"A little."

Hana called Whore over. Being the good pet, she crawled over into the kitchen and stopped next to Rac's chair.

"Stand up." Hana commanded. When she stood, Whore was told to hold out one of her arms. It was spotted with healed bites. In actual light, Hana had to admit she still looked good.

"I believe Master's a little hungry." Hana flicked on a stove burner and went for the main hall. "I'll be back in a sec." She then left and started for the stairs.

"Can I cook something?" She turned to Rac', her arm still stretched out to him.

"No, just stay still." Rac' said before grabbing her arm with both hands and was already biting into it before Alexis could react. His mind drifted to memories of previous thrall and those he Turned: exotic nightgirls, fellow war vets that sided against their own kind but had little to live for when the fighting was over. He even found children living in situations that reminded him of himself. Hopefully, they put their new gift to good use. He felt his arms tense and flex as he could taste just how close Whore was to the peak of her transformation. She was so close. As he gave in, he couldn't hear her pleas to stop. He didn't hear anything until Hana was in his head.

"I think that's enough, little brother."

The sudden sound of her voice made himself pull away with a start. She was crying and holding the edge of the island as if anchored to it. Rac' let go of her and wiped his mouth across his forearm, feeling Hana's arm around his shoulders pulling him away. Whore retreated to the floor as she sobbed. When she looked up, he could see he fed longer than he intended. Hana went to the sink and got the dishrag, wetting it before placing the metal rod she now had over the open burner. She walked back over to Whore and dabbed at her wounds, occasionally using her finger to wipe blood and taste it. When she was finished, she looked Alexis in her eyes and saw the dull fire from earlier had grown. The pearlescent grew to a full moonbeam with some flickering underneath. She brought Whore to her feet.

"Did I do something wrong, Mother?"

"No, you were a good girl."

Whore smiled through tears and began crying again. Hana looked at the stove and then back to Rac'. "It's time for her Mark."

Rac' took the rag from her and wiped his mouth and arm. "She's not finished yet."

"She just needs something to push her over the edge. She might even like it." Whore was still sniffling as she calmed down. "Shut it up." Hana slapped her once and held her face in her hand. The fire grew. Something seemed to respond to being hurt. Rac' felt the base of his neck and rubbed over the thin scarred outline of his own Mark. The last night of his Turning, lying face down on his cot, bound and biting onto a padded metal rod, Hana slowly carved the Master's Mark into his neck, solidifying his entry into the cursed blessing that was his new life while also guaranteeing he would always live to see another day and another battle. He had men that were counting on him; they needed their General. He looked at the island top where Whore had latched onto and saw spiderweb cracks in the stone surface. He looked back at Hana and then to the stove, noticing a red glow at one end of the rod. He didn't realize it as child, but Mama had the same brand on her left breast, right where her heart would be. She never wore it exposed except in her most vulnerable and private moments, like their day-drives and picnics by the creek. It was her symbol of belonging to another. *He* wore it on his arm like a badge of honor. He remembered when Hana revealed her own and was disgusted and angered at how depraved the conditions of home had grown in his absence. He was angry at himself for leaving Hana and Mama behind to bear the brunt of his choice. He was angrier when she said she understood. At least one of them had to get out; she would've done the same.

"Why do you still have that? You said you'd never use it again."

"I said I would never use it on you. This is your pet. You Turn her, you Mark her." She looked back at Whore before leading her over to the sink. She then turned her around aggressively so that she was facing Rac' again and swept her hair over her shoulder. The brand was a bright orange-yellow now. Rac' got up and walked around the opposite end of the island as Hana walked around to face Alexis. It felt all too much like their first interaction. Hana picked up the leash, wrapped it once around her hand and curled into a fist. "Stay still."

Whore answered with a single word. "Yes."

Hana smiled and used her free hand to tap the tabletop. She made a quick look and for the first time noticed the spiderweb fractures on the edge. "Hold on with both hands right here, ok? You'll be a good girl, right?"

"Yes, Mother." Alexis held her arms out and held where Hana tapped, having to bend over and lean across the tabletop. Her bites had already stopped running and looked like they were in the beginning stages of closing. "Did I do something wrong?"

"No." She pulled the chain closer to her, forcing Whore to stay in her lean. The cold stone was a shock to her skin, causing her to flinch and almost let go. She told Mother she wouldn't and would not disappoint her or Master. Instinctively, she spread her legs and waited as she closed her eyes. He stood behind her, using his own legs to block hers from closing. At least he was nicer to her than Mother. When she opened her eyes again, the only thing she could do is wish that he had planned to take her.

"Stay still." That was the last thing she heard Master say.

First was the heat. A sudden sting that started from her lower back and sprouted throughout her body. Then came the sound. Then the smell. A guttural, inhuman yell left Whore that was more fit coming from an animal. It didn't even take a second for her mind to catch up to her body and she began to thrash and clench down on the tabletop. Hana wrapped the chain around a second time and pulled down, forcing Whore's head against the stone. As Rac' held the brand, pressing down evenly, the house was filled as the screams continued.

"*No! Stop, Master! Please!!*" She screamed out. "*Please! Mother, help!*"

Mother looked down to stroke her hair. "It's almost over. Don't fight it, just let it pass." For the first time, she saw Hana's face soften and a small, somehow sympathetic, flicker in her eyes. She had no way to know those words were almost verbatim what Mother herself had been told to a very long time ago. The deep buried but still familiar scent of burning flesh drafted into the air and she thought about when *He* made her receive her Mark. *He* wasn't nearly as civilized about it as she was now.

As the pain went through her, Whore felt something else awaken. It climbed past mere hurt to knocking at the door of a numbing euphoria. She was no longer in the kitchen of the Tabine manor. There was only white. She no longer felt the pain. There was only a freeing detachment that felt good nor bad. She felt Master dig into her skin but could not comprehend the shock. Her mind took over her body and went away. There was no Mother. No Master. No chains. No kitchen. Just white. Then nothing.

Rac' saw Alexis go limp and released the brand. A clean smoking stamp sat in perfect placement at the small of Alexis' back. She was theirs now. She was his. He turned off the stove burner and replaced the branding rod as the stamp lightly smoked and began to cool. Hana checked for a pulse. She was still alive, just unconscious. She went upstairs and came back with two small jars and a roll of clear wrap. She walked over and after a few minutes mixed the contents of the jars together in her hand and carefully smeared it over the symbol. Whore came to with a scream as she was wrapping the clear over. Her hands were still in a vice grip of the edge of the island. Hana yanked her up by the hair. "You did good." She threw her head away and looked to Rac'. "You too."

Rac' backed away from Whore and let her collapse to the floor into a fetal position. She was rocking back and forth while crying silently as the remnants of pain and the numbness slowly faded. Hana made her way to leave the kitchen. There were a few drops on Rac' shoe. He sniffed and learned it wasn't urine. Maybe Whore did enjoy her Marking.

◆ ◆ ◆

"Hel-" *cough* *cough* "Hello? Stokton residence,

Ronald speaking."

"Hey, dad? It's Flip." Flip looked over at the clock. He didn't realize it was so late.

"Hey, what's up? Everything ok? It's kinda late for a social call." Ronald laughed softly. "But no, really, everything ok? How're you holding up?"

"Yeah, yeah I'm fine. Elena and I might roll out to Monarch to check a few leads. I might try and see Ronnie while I'm out there."

"Yeah, guess you haven't seen him in a while. I can't remember his address, but his shop is in City-Monarch. Klima's Kuts. Unless he changed locations, I think it's walking distance from the Monarch Arena. I'll send you the address."

"Don't worry about it, I can look it up."

"Of course. You sure you ok? I'm sorry again I ain't come with your mother. Pat said it might be best to stay behind until we knew what was up."

"I told you it's all good, but we'll talk when I get back, ok? Love you, dad."

"Be careful out there. Them *vi'nnaks* are some funny folk."

"I've heard."

"I'm for real. Just make sure to come back, ok? Your mother lost her shit when that Wallace cat called about the hospital." Ronald made a dry laugh. "Broke a few good plates and then some. We really thought you were gone, Flip."

"I know, dad, I know. I ain't going nowhere except Monarch."

Ronald laughed. "My man. I'll talk to you when you get back."

Click.

Flip looked over to still sleeping Elena and hung up the call.

"What'd he say?" She asked with her eyes still closed.

"He's gonna send me Ronnie's address and told me the name of his shop. Klima's Kuts, I'm sure with a K."

That got a laugh, and she opened her eyes. "A little cheesy, but it's catchy. We gonna check it out?"

"Yeah, prolly. Hopefully he's one of those owners that works his own place."

"Mmm, maybe." Elena leaned over and kissed his cheek. "You don't sound so excited. When's the last time you seen him?"

"It's been a few years. Maybe right before or after my first season with Redwater."

"Oh." She kissed him again in lieu of not knowing the most appropriate response. Flip always spoke of his brother with a certain distance. As far as she knew, they hadn't had any major falling out or event to give reason to seemingly not care about each other. "Well, let's get some sleep, aight?" She rolled over and moved closer to him.

"Aight." He rolled over and embraced Elena, taking in the scent her after-shower oil. He should've been thinking about the upcoming deadline but his thoughts went to his brother and then how he felt about seeing him again. It was a mix of hopefulness with an equal measure of reticence. What were they gonna talk about? Latest hobbies? Work? His wife, if he was (still) married? Did he have kids? Was their meat any good? There were so many things that bounced around that eventually, it was too much. Another hour went by before Flip fell into a floral induced slumber.

◆ ◆ ◆

Thursday

Still holding onto his thoughts from the night before, Flip packed his duffel bag in mostly silence, mentally getting himself together like he was in the locker room of an expectedly tough game. This was a game to beat the clock, and part of him said he was too far behind. Elena watched him as she packed her own bag. She didn't like that he was so quiet at breakfast but understood why. Trying to help him see a silver lining in the past week, she contributed that at least he wasn't looking for child-killers. The possibility that any of her children from the Center could've been victims in the same manner as the recent victims was too much to think about over pancakes and sausage.

The plan was to keep their time in Monarch casual but be back by Friday night at the latest. Apparently, the Minister wants to give Flip his Fountain Star in person on Saturday. Flip was sure Esun set the day because he knew adults and children alike would have no excuse to not come and, in his mind, score at least one definite Founder's Vote of Confidence when he campaigned for re-election. Many can say what they want about Minister Esun, but they'll all admit the motherfucker knew how to earn his salary.

Personally, Flip didn't have any major issue with him or his management of Fountain City, he just didn't care for his outward demeanor. There was always something about him seemed a little off; a little too personable. That aside, he listened to the Founders to the point when he should and knew when it was ok to take liberties with how to apply their "suggestions" on most public-facing policy. As a Rising Patriarch, he kept up with what was need-to-know, but until it was time for him to truly lead the Stokton Clan, those two things were all that mattered to Flip in the moment.

Elena made him promise that he'd attend the ceremony, if only for the appearance aspect. Flip agreed, primarily because he knew he wouldn't hear the end of it if he didn't. Fleice always hated that "slick sonofabitch" Esun, but if you're being honored by the highest public leader of your Territory, you set aside your personals, accept it with a smile, and give the man a solid handshake. Flip intended to do exactly, and only, that.

As they finished, Flip let the appropriate parties know that he'd be out of town for a couple days and tried another call to his mother. She came to the phone with heavy breathing.

"Hey, baby, gotta make it quick. Ata and I are in the middle of a match."

"Who's winning?"

"30 all, for now, but I think I got her."

All this tennis play made Flip wonder if more sports were coming down the pipeline. Maybe he can get her into playing basketball. She had the height for a decent wing guard. "Aight, then, I just wanted to let you know we're headed out. I'll talk to you later and good luck."

"I don't need it, but thank you, Flip-baby. You too." Her breathing calmed. "Say hello to Ronnie for me."

"I will. Love you, mom."

"Love you too."

Flip hung up and finished packing. An earlier talk with Wallace let him know that it'd be smart not to carry his piece out in the open, meaning the thigh holster would sadly have to stay behind. He packed the hip holster and an extra magazine, throwing in two extended magazines and the scope for good measure. Now he really felt like a Nite Owl impersonator. Elena looked over to him as he zipped it closed. "You shootin' it out with the whole town?"

Flip made a sarcastic laugh and picked up his bag. "You ready?"

"Whenever you are." Elena picked up her own and made her way to the bedroom door. Flip followed her and cut the light off before heading downstairs. As he left, Flip got a text of his brother's address in City-Monarch. He realized that he's been in the area before, it wasn't far from the one place in Monarch his coach at the time said to go for dinner, an upscale restaurant he went to with his team called Queen's Landing. He remembered the food being damn good and the people a little skittish but relatively hospitable. Maybe Ronnie had a supplier's arrangement with them.

Erring on the side of caution in case either of the siblings made his car, it was decided that they would take Elena's car for the trip as long as Flip paid for gas. In exchange, she arranged for a Ward to fill Joy up and take her home, rolling her eyes when he insisted to talk to said Ward personally so that they knew which grade of fuel to use. After three rounds of "Are you sure you got it? I'm serious, bro.", he returned the communicator so Elena could talk to her father again. She hung up before unlocking the car and put their bags in the trunk.

"You dropping this off before we go?" He pointed at the longbow case as he placed his bag.

"No offense, Mr. Stokton, but I think our target practice last night showed it'd be good to have some backup." She stuck her tongue at him.

"Your boyfriend gonna mind you skipping town with a strange man?" He reached down and gave her a squeeze.

"Oh, I think he'll be ok. I'm sure he's got a nice woman to keep him company." She winked and moved closer, letting him get another pinch.

"Fine by me."

Once buckled in, Elena started up and got into gear. They exited the lot as the young man escorting Missy Blaskow-Hermann was exiting the front door of Cloud Mesa, in the same suit from last night but now holding a small decorative bag. "You get it, Missy." she whispered.

"What?" Flip looked over to her.

"Nothing, Love."

Elena activated her navigator as she approached the Redwater-Monarch border and set it for Klima's Kuts. Sure enough, it was almost 15 minutes walking from Monarch Arena, a very convenient spot for a gameday sandwich, and the only other location that showed on the illuminated map. As they turned onto the strip of road into what felt like town center, "What the hell?" Elena tapped Flip to wake him. For a midday Thursday, it was busier than she expected considering the cloudiness of potential rain. The sun was poking a few holes along the beachline of Redwater, but as soon as they entered Monarch, Elena could only see a faded glow. There were looks at the dark sedan driving down Monarch Main, some of the following eyes sitting behind dark sunglasses as they walked their horse or rode by slowly. Every so often, she saw pairs of official looking figures clad in all black, sunglasses included, idly trotting along. Every pair she rode by instantly turned their head towards the unfamiliar vehicle and eyed it for a few seconds. "Did your dad mention anything about horses?" She pulled into a curbside parking spot, slowly, to not scare the horse two spaces over. She could see a few cars parked further down. Flip tapped his jacket for inventory of where everything was. There was a low rhythm coming from the interior pocket.

"Not at all, but I don't think he's actually been here." Flip felt eyes from all directions. A familiar hot and itchy sensation felt like it was jumping all over him.

Monarch had the atmosphere of a Territory that was stuck in a long-dead time. It was modern enough, but the number of horses threw them both for a loop. Even though it was older than both Redwater and Fountain, it didn't explain why it (so far) looked almost intentionally like a slightly modernized Old Territory movie. Flip walked down the sidewalk looking around for anything familiar, only finding the top of Monarch Arena a short distance away. Shaking off the sleep from the car, he opened the door of Klima's Kuts for Elena as the overhead bell announced the arrival of entering customers. As the door closed, a sun-touched woman made a clean cut to a rack of ribs with a single *shunk* before the now half-rack onto the counter scale. She called out, "0-8-4?", and an older, hunched man got up from a table against the façade window holding a yellow ticket. He placed his ticket on the counter as the woman carefully wrapped his selection in a thick white paper.

"Need anything else, Tak'rii?" The woman asked as she reached over the counter.

Flip was looking around the shop in silence before he felt a poke in his side. He turned to Elena, and she pointed over to a wall off to their left. There were more tables and a couple that were eating and chatting. Under the overhead TV were three rows of photos, most of the ones Flip immediately recognized being actor and musician friends. The first photo of the top row was a photo he hadn't seen in a long time; a calm-faced him in a #5 Redwater Rogues jersey suspended in the air attempting a three-pointer in his very first game as a Rogues starter. The shot rimmed out, but the nationally ran sports channels couldn't help but show the play over and over again and reserving their analytical critiques for at least two days. The picture even made the top three of Aligned Territories Sports Network's 15 Best Photos of the Week.

"Don't think so, this is just to balance out the flanks and links from the other day. Y'all still coming to the feast, right?" The man took his parcel and walked over to the cashier's counter and went into his pocket.

"We haven't missed it yet, have we?" The woman smiled as she responded. Her eyes shifted to the new entries and grew wide. Flip thought he saw something in them. They had a striking hue to them.

The old man laughed and took out a sack closed with a drawstring. Flip thought about how his grandmother used to have one just like it. "No, no y'all haven't." He extended his hand before it was interrupted.

"Ron said this one's on us, as a thank-you for using us this year." Hol looked back at Flip and then to Elena. "I'll have him call when he gets back."

Ron? Ron Klima. Guess it does have a certain ring to it.

The old man looked behind to the couple Hol was eyeing before looking over at the photo wall. He made a slick double-take at the photo and back to Flip. He thanked the woman for the ribs and promised to give a little something the day of the feast. Comped food or not, a man never leaves a bill unpaid. She feigned resistance and said a few bottles of

Father's Spiced Tea should be enough to settle it. He nodded and turned to leave, giving Flip another look as he passed by. When the door closed behind him, Flip and Elena walked up to the counter and asked for Ronnie.

"You must be Flip, and you must be Elena Starks. Welcome!" Instinctively, the woman reached her hand out and realized she still had her cutting gloves on. Her hand jumped back, and she made an exuberant smile. Her eyes went to Flip. "I don't keep up with basketball, but I've heard quite a bit about you two. I'm more of an Auto-Race girl, but Ms. Starks I have to admit, I haven't seen many games but I'm a big fan of yours. Can I get you two anything?" She felt herself going and paused. "I'm sorry, I can babble on when I get excited. Ron didn't tell me you two were coming."

Flip spoke first. "It's cool, he doesn't know. We're gonna for a little bit and thought to visit. It's been a while since I've seen him." Elena noted the use of "thought".

She took off her gloves and set them on the chopping board behind her. "Ah, I see. Well, my name is Hol. Short for Hol'ly, but everyone always seemed to like Hol better." She stuck out her hand and shook both Elena's and Flip's. There was a small spark. *Flash.* He couldn't see who was doing it, but someone was branding a symbol onto the top of Hol'ly's hand. He could see her screaming and crying red, the same as with Ata and Cheryl Shockley. The symbol looked like the mix between a symbol and initial. There was a few more seconds of watching pain and he was back. Hol didn't seem to notice the extended handhold, but Elena did and casually nudged him. He Saw something, didn't he? Hol continued on. "Ron should be back in a few, had to pick up a few things from the house. Y'all hungry?"

Elena answered, looking at her watch. "I could eat,

but I wanted to know if I need to put anything in the park meters out front because I don't have any change."

Flip looked Hol over. She reminded him of Ata with her appearance. If she was like Hana, she probably was older than all three of them put together. He focused his eyes to her mouth as she spoke. "I can tell y'all don't come out here often, but no, you're fine. Those meters haven't worked in a long time. It's pure decoration at this point since most of us have been moving back to the horse. That, or the queen thinks it's a waste of money to get them all removed since they're all over the place. They say she was very enthusiastic about the car trend when it made its way here. Apparently, one of the first owners in town was a lady that lived out in the woods, and it sparked a little jealousy." She laughed again and pointed to an empty table. "Let me call Ron and get you two some food. Grab that table and I'll bring it over."

They did. The male of the couple sitting behind them looked behind his date and met eyes with Elena. He then lowered his head and said something, causing her to turn around and smile with a wave. Elena couldn't tell if it was from recognition or local courtesy but waved back. She saw that they both had a dark amber color, not exactly matching like those of family, but only a mere change in ratio of brown and hazel. She saw something else, breathing like freshly lit fire. It was intimidating but strangely beautiful. Elena tilted to Flip, who was casually alternating between watching the door and back at the counter. "I guess pretty eyes are also a side-effect, huh?" She whispered.

He kept his response short. "Guess so." That was when he felt the pulse inside his jacket was still going. It was light enough, but it was constant. He wasn't particularly worried about being inside this place, but they were surrounded. He had yet to see anyone else like them since entering town. As he was beginning to warn Elena, Hol came to their table with two thick cold-cut sandwiches, two empty glasses and a bottle of wine.

"So, he's a few minutes away. I didn't tell him you were here, but I think he'll enjoy the surprise."

"Thank you, Hol." Flip couldn't recall a time Ronnie was the recipient of a surprise party, but hopefully, Hol knew her husband a lot better than he did his brother. He heard the couple behind him get up and saw them go for the door, the girl of the couple waving again as she walked by Elena. She nodded back and wished them a good day. Once they were gone, Hol came around Elena and sat in the chair next to her.

"I don't mean to be nosey, but can I ask what happened?" She looked at Flip and traced her left cheek.

"Oh, some lady scratched me the other day. It's ok." Flip acknowledged his bandage with his hand. "It's all stitched up."

"Wow, she must've been pretty mad, or hungry." Hol and Flip shared a one-sided dry laugh. "I'm sorry, being a butcher's wife and leaves you with a stain of dark humor." Flip tried to watch her mouth but couldn't help but look into her eyes. Even in daylight, her eyes reminded him of an even cleaner version of Ms. Ata's. And Hana's. "What brings you two out here?"

"Mostly work. Checking a few things out." Flip answered back. He wasn't sure how much his brother knew of his Investigator work, or what he may have passed along in the "much" he told his wife.

"Oh, that's sounds interesting. Guess real estate runs in the family." Hol responded as Flip bit into his sandwich. Could've used some spiced mustard, but it damn good.

"Not exactly," Elena opened the wine and poured her

425

and Flip a taste. "Flip's a consultant with the P'rotectors in Fountain."

Hol's eyes widened again with interest as the entry bell dinged. "Anything you can talk about? Or is it like on the TV where it's all, 'can't talk on an open investigation, ma'am'?"

"A little of both, actually. I got a few things to ask you and Ronnie later." Flip winked at her before looking to the door and saw his brother carrying double-stacked wooden crates. They met each other's eyes for a moment. "Excuse me." He got up and walked over to Ronnie and held the door for him. Elena started to ask something to Hol but he didn't hear it. "Hey, Ronnie." He said as he held the door open.

"What's up? You ain't been here too long, have you?" He continued to walk by. "Mind grabbing the other one from the trunk?"

"I got you." Flip walked out and to a car that was a few spaces over from Elena's. He didn't know a butcher's salary in Monarch, but it must've been nice. In front of him sat a hulking black and white Terra UV-1K, complete with an extended storage bed, elevated suspension and large *Klima's Kuts* decals along each side of the bed. Either Ronnie's been saving up, or had a solid hold on the meat supply market here in Monarch to have the biggest car he's seen here. As he walked to the back, he could still feel eyes all over him. He used the drawn stepladder to climb up and bring the remaining crate down. When he retracted the ladder and closed the door, he saw Ronnie at the door waving him over.

"C'mon, we gon' put these in the back."

Flip walked behind Ronnie and followed him around the front counter and through a heavy set of double-doors. The temperature drop was drastic. "Cold enough in here for ya?" He quipped.

"Yeah man, gotta be so that everything stays as fresh. We don't use that pre-frozen bullshit you find in some of the indoor markets. No offense to them, but we get and keep our shit fresh." He went over to a large metal door with multiple dial readers and a thermometer that ran along the bar handle, "Hold this open for me." and pulled it open before going in to place his crates along a row of hanging beef slabs. He motioned for Flip to slide the third crate inside and walked it to the opposite wall.

Flip took note of his brother's appearance. If he didn't know in advance, he wouldn't have taken his brother for a butcher had they met on the street. He looked like he put on some muscle since he last saw him, but in a farmer's natural development kind of way. As always, and like their father, he stayed relatively clean shaven except for the long mustache connecting goatee. Ronnie always went for the longer chin hair than their father, but he still looked like a perfect younger copy. If they lived in a sci-fi movie, he'd probably be the evil clone trying to take out the original. He also had a lot more tattoos than he last remembered and seemed a lot more easygoing. Looks like the married life loosened him up a bit and fit well. Flip didn't know what to expect from an office in a butcher's shop, but Ronnie's was cleaner than anything he assumed. Aside from the papers on his min desk, nothing looked out of place or order. He looked around and saw on the wall behind what was likely Ronnie's actual work desk a line of framed Fountain newspapers. The front pages were all headlines of situations that Flip helped solve. With their hands free, Ronnie reached out his hand. "What's up, man? It's been a while."

Flip met him and was brought in for a hug. "Nothing much, it's good seeing you. Dad told me about the shop, so I thought we'd come by while we were in town." They separated and sat in an open chair in front of the main desk. Ronnie sat in his well-worn chair.

"Yeah, man that's cool. He mentioned a while back that you're an Investigator now. You still doing it?"

"Yeah, something to pass the time, really." He pointed to the newspapers. "What's with the papers?"

Ronnie laughed and turned in his chair. "You tell me, man. Dad sends these out here. I got the reading of the articles, and something told me this was your work, since they all mention the help of an anonymous 'consultant' working 'in conjunction with the FCPD'." He chuckled again as he turned back. "Forreal though, I can dig it, man. Guess if it ain't about ball, you don't want your name in the papers, huh?"

"Something like that. Enough people know what I do, but I don't need *everyone* to know." Flip's face changed little as he took in the organization and cleanliness of the room. The floor smelled recently wet-cleaned and three metal racks along the wall next to him held labeled boxes neatly aligned on their shelves. Flip wasn't sure whether to be impressed or grow suspicious. He did smirk when he saw a single lockbox occupying its own shelf on the last rack: *Bullshit*.

"I feel that, I feel that. You working on something now?"

"Yeah, but we can talk about that a little later when you're off. It's a bit heavy." Flip reverted his attention.

"C'mon man, what's up?" Ronnie's face took a serious look. "And what the fuck happened to your face, man?"

Flip went into light detail about the situation in Fountain and the real reason he and Elena were in Monarch. It felt better than he'd thought it would talking to Ronnie about what he was doing. It almost felt like a kid bragging to his older brother, but that didn't seem to bother Ronnie. He looked more interested than anything. They talked for almost a half-hour before Ronnie looked over to a clock on the wall.

"So, all these cases, you just go off of *hunches*? Come on, brother, there's gotta be more to it. Who's your source? Got a lil Scanner shawty tippin' you off?"

"Nah, man, I'm telling you, I get a hunch and just follow it. I really couldn't explain it to you." Flip smiled. Technically, he was telling the truth.

"You really are your mother's child. Dad used to say the same thing about Fleice when she was still a P'rotec. She'd get these strong ass 'hunches' to the point she could almost see the shit happening."

It was then that Flip realized his brother truly didn't know about him or his mother. That made him start to wonder how much his father actually knew and whether he was in the dark or playing coy for Ronnie's sake. Ronald, Sr was an intelligent man, but what if mom never told him the complete truth about the Sight? What if she had, and his father was in denial, choosing to accept the more comforting belief that it was an early arrival of unfortunate genetics? What did he think really about Flip when he said he was Seeing things? He returned to the moment. "Any good places to crash around here?"

"There's a B&B not too far from here. It's still in City-Monarch so you'll be able to get around town pretty easily if you need to." Ronnie was already lifting the desk phone off the hook. "It's a little expensive for the tourists." He added with a smirk.

"C'mon man." Flip smiled in return and made the

gesture for holding scril. "I'm good for it."

"I got you. I'll let 'em know you'll be checking in. One room or two? I see you brought the Matriarch out with you. She your assistant or something?"

"Damn, bro, you moonlight as they receptionist?" They shared a loud laugh and Flip confirmed one room was fine, and no, Elena definitely wasn't the assistant type. Ronnie told the other end that he had some family coming to stay for a day or two. His face indicated he heard some good new and he hung up after a thank-you.

"You're set. Ask for Tak'rii or Luna and they'll set you up."

Tak'rii? The old guy from earlier?

"Thanks, man." Flip leaned over and dropped his volume. "Hey, quick question, did Hol'ly suffer a burn or something on her hand?" Ronnie's face changed.

"Ye-yeah, man, how'd you know? It's faded to hell, but she still uses makeup to cover it up when she goes out. She tell you about it?"

"Nah, man, just a hunch." Flip leaned back and gave a Smile. He saw that that was something else they shared.

"Fucking hunches. Look, how 'bout you and Elena come by the house later once you're settled in? Have a proper dinner and see the farm." Ronnie reached under his desk and opened a drawer. When his hand returned, he pulled out a bottle and two glasses. He poured himself one and titled the bottle to Flip.

"Just a little bit, Hol gave us some wine to have with our lunch." Flip pinched his fingers together as Ronnie poured. They clinked glasses and sipped.

"Yeah, she's something, ain't she? We been married

going on 4 years now, together almost 7. Her folks are the real hippy-dippy types, but they're good people." Ron leaned back as he spoke. Flip felt like he was speaking reflectively to himself than to him. He just nodded his head and finished his glass. "I don't know much about that burn though. Shit, it was almost two years before she even showed me and even then, still ain't tell me who made it." Ronnie chuckled. "Maybe you can ask her about it when y'all come by, just know she can be a little sensitive about it."

"I think I will. Thanks for the heads-up." Flip got up from his seat with Ronnie and went to the door as his mind conjured pieces of the flash he saw. When they left from the back area and walked through the double doors, they found Elena and Hol'ly laughing at something they obviously had to be there for. They walked over to the table and in the empty chairs across from them. "Having a good time, I see."

"Yes, Love. Hol was just telling me about some of her time out west. Turns out she lived in Silver City the same time I was playing out there. Her boyfriend at the time was really into basketball and took her to a few games."

"Nice."

"Hey, so I invited Flip and Elena over to the house later on." Ronnie reached over and held Hol'ly's hand. Flip saw it was the same he Saw getting branded. She placed her other hand over his and began to softly stroke it. Her nails were well manicured, but undoubtably clawed.

"That sounds fun. It's been some time since we've had company." Hol'ly looked at him happily. "Even longer for family."

"Hol's family is originally from a small town outside of Silver City, we haven't seen them since the wedding." Ronnie added.

Elena took a final sip of her wine and began to get up. "Flip, ready to head out? We still gotta find somewhere to stay."

"Don't worry about that. He already got y'all a room at Queen's Lodge. It's just past the Arena by about 20 minutes, just look for the large blue and white house." Ronnie looked over to Flip. "You still smoke?"

"What's up?" He couldn't remember ever telling Ronnie he did.

"I'll have something for you when you come by the house. If you brought anything, tell Ms. Luna you want one of the balcony suites."

"Will do." Flip got up and shook Ronnie's hand and then Hol'ly's. He didn't See anything this time, but something about her face made him wonder if she did notice their earlier shake. This time, she looked like she was expecting it. He made his way to the door and tried to open it.

"Didn't mean to lock you in." Hol'ly unlocked the door and opened it for them. "We'll have a car pick you up around 7 if that's fine."

"Sure, thank you, Hol. It was a pleasure meeting you." Elena responded before leaving out.

"Likewise, Matriarch. It was mighty fine to make your good company."

Flip let Elena in and went over to the driver side. Once inside he started the car and let the silent rumble flow through him. It really was a nice car. He set it in gear and looked over. That wine must've been good, she had that look.

"Have a good time?" Flip checked his mirrors and started to back out.

"I had a good *wine*." Elena giggled and kissed his cheek.

"Ok, jokey, let's get to this lodge and get a nap in." Flip shook his head before tapping the navigation panel. Queen's Lodge was right on the edge of City-Monarch.

"Mmm, is that all?" She leaned over and kissed his cheek harder.

"We'll see. If you can stay awake on the way there." Flip chuckled and kissed her hand. "I ain't tryna carry you *and* the bags."

"Deal."

Elena went into the glove compartment and pulled out a pair of sunglasses. The early afternoon sun felt good. She leaned her chair back and laid quietly; falling asleep almost instantly. Flip looked into the rearview as he backed out and laughed to himself. As he drove up the street towards the Monarch Arena, he noticed a tall woman in all black looking in his direction as she unhitched her horse from its post. He couldn't see her eyes, but he felt their focus until he made the first turn available.

"You think sweats are appropriate for tonight?" Elena called from the bathroom. The Lodge's rates were a little more than Flip expected, even with the given "friends and family" discount, but the quality of service has been worth it so far. The Queen's Lodge only had 15 rooms, but based on the size and lack of guests, it was clear that they were staying in one the best rooms if not *the* best. Ms. Luna really came through, even though she kept calling it the "Honeymoon Suite" once she saw Flip's company and threw in a bottle of wine, per first-timers custom, of course. She made a concerning look at Flip's bandaged face when they first walked in but once Elena started the check-in process, she eased her stare when she realized that he was the family that Ron Klima had referenced. Her memory was also jogged of the recent assassination attempt being whispered about. Surely, this couldn't be the same young man, could it? She apologized profusely for her initial wariness and insisted on carrying their bags herself. Flip appreciated the sweetness but privately mused she'd probably have fallen over if the front door closed too quick and generated enough wind.

"You bring anything else?" He responded. There was a pause before he heard an answer.

"No."

"Then I guess they're appropriate enough."

"Whatever." There was another pause and a spray of perfume. "It was nice seeing your brother. You two seemed to get along well."

"Yeah, I guess so. He seemed happy."

"What'd y'all talk about in the back?"

"Nothing important. I told him a little about the case."

Elena stepped out the bathroom and looked over. "Really?"

"Yeah, nothing too heavy, just enough to get his mind prepared to answer some real questions. They've got to know at least one of these siblings." Flip got up and put on his shirt before checking his watch; *6:40.* "I'm sure he's been here long enough to have run into them or at least know their family. You ready?" He put on his shirt before hearing his communicator chime, indicating a message. He looked over at the ornate wooden dresser and saw something he wished he hadn't; *JennyC78* sent another message with an accompanying photo:

I heard you're in town! You should come hang out with us. Alexis would kill for an autograph!

It was another nude photo, but this time Alexis didn't have that awkward half-smile like the last picture. This one was disturbing in multiple ways. Alexis was on the floor and had what looked like a collar on connected to a long heavy link chain. Flip looked into her eyes and saw it. It was the same thing he saw in Cheryl Shockley's eyes. He studied the photo closer and scrolled up to the first photo. Alexis was lighter. Not just skin tone, but almost like she herself was faded. He looked at how defined the chain stood out against her and rubbed his screen. His eyes weren't fooling him, and it made him think about the camera footage back at The Watering Hole. Maybe Mr. Classic was onscreen the whole time. He heard Elena talking but couldn't tell if it was to him.

"Olga." Flip kept his eyes to his screen.

Elena continued talking. "--Hol'ly seems nice, but she definitely gives me small-town-girl vibes. I--"

"*Olga*." Flip raised his voice. "She knows we're here." He held out his mobile to her as she walked over. She took a look and went silent.

"Flip, we just got here less than 8 hours ago. We've only been to the shop and here, how would she know?" She then thought about the couple in the butcher shop. "You don't think she was in the shop, do you?"

"Nah, but the couple behind us did leave a little soon after we arrived. As did Tak'rii."

"So, what do we do?" There was a call on the room's bedside landline. Elena went over and picked it up, doing her best to mask her uneasiness. "Hello?" It was Tak'rii. Their car was out front if they were ready. She looked over to Flip. He only nodded and put his mobile back into his pocket. "Thank you, Tak'rii, we'll be down in a second." She made her way to the door with Flip not far behind, grabbing his jacket off the back of the main room sofa as he walked past.

"Whatever happens tonight, I need to find out if Ronnie and Hol know this girl and if they've seen Alexis. You locked your stuff up?"

Elena nodded and they walked down the stairs.

Getting information from Hol'ly and Ronnie initially felt like pulling teeth, but after a few rounds of casual talk, the couple got into the wine and felt more comfortable opening up. He told them more about Cheryl Shockley and saw there was an exchange of looks between Ronnie and Hol as he went towards the talk of vampyr. Hol'ly knew Hana through an almost strictly social lens but wouldn't describe their dynamic as "friends". She talked to her at social events in town or the rare stop by the butchery, but after an uncomfortable and concerning dinner at the Tabine home, decided that should be the length of it. Ronnie, however, was visibly upset to know that Rac' Tabine, one of his hardest working employees, was the prime suspect for a murder and with his sister for murder and kidnapping. He had just saw him at work earlier that week and everything seemed fine. He was a generally quiet guy, sure, but maybe there was a misunderstanding? You know, wrong place, wrong time kind of situation. Rac' was a fucking war veteran, for K'd's sake. Surely, Flip's seen mix-ups as an investigator? Flip conceded that, yes, from time to time he has but it wasn't often, especially when he followed his hunches. In this case, he couldn't see how that was possible. His jury of one was still out on which of the two did Shockley in but he was sure they were both there to dump him. When Flip excused himself to the kitchen, Hol'ly followed soon after. Flip didn't know he was tailed until he heard the sliding door close a second time.

"How did you know about my hand, Flip?" Hol'ly stood a respectable distance from him but kept her voice low. "Hunch, or whatever you want to call it, or not, there's no way you would know about something like that."

"Hol'ly, I know we just met today, but you'd be surprised how much I can learn about someone I meet for the first time." Flip cut himself another slice of cheese and took a bite. It was both sweet and smokey, contrasting from what he expected based on its deep red color.

Good evening to this Thursday night late game, everyone. The air is thick and both players look ready. Fountain versus Silver City. East versus West. The ball has been checked with the visiting team having won first possession. Stokton's taking his time, taking it easy. We might have a slow burner on our hands.

"I don't think I would." Hol answered. Flip watched her have her fair share of drink but judging from those green eyes and lack of slur, she looked and acted like she'd been drinking water the entire time. He could also see something underneath them, something growing, breathing even. Fire. Her eyes began to look as if made by crystal. "But there's something to it beside pure perceptiveness or good guesswork. There's something more." She wasn't asking.

Klima's making a soft-press. Notice how she's not going directly for the ball. She's either got a play going or a bit naïve on her read of this particular opponent.

Flip turned and leaned against the kitchen counter.

"Hol, if this is something you don't want to talk about, I get it. Ronnie told me it's a bit of a sensitive subject for you."

"No, that's just the thing. The fact you *did* know about is why I don't mind. It was almost two years into us dating before I showed Ron the naked look of it." She rubbed the top of her right hand, feeling the glassy tracks of her brand through the thin layer of foundation. "There's only one other person in my life who used to know stuff the way you do: my father. He used to always say it was just a 'good guess', but even with a clean face and hands, he'd still know you went into the cookie jar." There was a laugh as she thought about a childhood memory. She took a step closer. "He sometimes used to 'go away', as my mother would say, kinda like how you did when we first shook hands. Yours was less noticeable and shorter, but I got the same feeling from the way Elena looked over to you. Does she know enough to explain to the less familiar?"

Flip's brow raised some. *She notices a lot.*

Stokton dribbles around, trying to find an opening. Klima's sticking on him hard. Looks like she's trying to force a turnover.

"Do you know how It worked for him?" Flip asked, sidestepping the Elena question. He didn't need to answer.

"No and I never asked, but he used to hold me and my cousins' hands and tell us everything we did that day. It was so cool when we were kids, we thought he was magic. He used to make it a game with us during family get togethers, every detail he got wrong, he'd give us a coin of scril apiece. Let's just say he'd find an excuse to still give us some. Mom used to say he was blessed by The Father. Some people in town thought he was a nosey prick. As for this," She then stuck her hand out, palm facing down. "I met a young man

438

who was like me. He was a handsome lil rich boy from the south with the accent to match." It was barely visible, but he could see an outline. The skin was similar to Hana's in its smoothness but had a subtle shine to it that hers didn't.

Looks like Klima is...yes, she's actually moving to the side and giving space to the lane. Stokton continues the dribble, wary of a trap.

"He was nice for a while. We were both young, it was my first time so far away from home, and it was exciting, even fun at some points. I knew he was wrong for me, but by then, things weren't so fun anymore. I tried to love him still, but I knew if I kept trying..." Hol'ly seemed to be looking away before she hiccupped and giggled. "But that was a long time ago, well before I met your brother. Sorry about that, I told you I ramble when I'm excited. Or drunk." She moved fast and was already around him for a hug. "Don't be afraid of your gift, Flip. My father became an unhappy man towards the end, and turned a lot of people away, almost including Mom. You're still young, but I see you makin' tracks down that road already." She let him go and grabbed the bottle behind him, taking a swig straight from the lip. She motioned it to Flip, and he did the same, laughing at seeing how much it stung going down. This was definitely not the same wine they had outside. He looked at the bottle and saw it wasn't wine at all. He didn't even know sweetspice liqueur was a thing.

Klima is in fact letting Stokton get an open lane, and he's taking it. He's driving..going for a layup..and it's a dunk! Stokton slams it down with solid one-hander! Not quite the high octane we were expecting, but you can always count on Flip Stokton to put on a good show. Good night, everyone, and get home safe. Final score: Stokton: 1 / Klima: 0

"Now that all the sentimental stuff's out the way, mind escorting your sister-in-law back outside before our dates start asking questions." Hol'ly hiccupped again and turned to walk away. She walked a few steps, before looking over her shoulder. "You comin'? Or should I tell them you couldn't hold your drink?"

Flip laughed and started moving, "Nah, I'm coming. Just cutting me another slice."

They walked together to the sliding door leading to the balcony until Hol'ly stopped him. "If the Tabine's are as dangerous as you say, just know we'll be there to protect you and help however we can. Ron's only a man, but he has a very strong woman right behind him." It was then that she flashed him teeth with her smile. "Your brother is one of the very, *very* few to live among us as a respected citizen, and I promise to keep it that way. I don' know personally, but rumor says that the Tabine children had a very cruel but prominent father. If what you suspect about them is right, I guess some fruit doesn't stop too far from the tree once it falls, no matter how much it wants to continue rollin'." Hol'ly opened the sliding door with a fitting movie reference and took the bottle from Flip. She resumed her seat next to Elena and took another swig. "Flip tells me you're a cine-girl. Think you can handle me in a game of Quotes? I promise to not go too far back."

Elena sat up in her chair and looked at Flip and Ron excitedly before going back to Hol. Flip's seen those eyes, usually before a game. "No help, right?"

"We each can get a single hint." Hol'ly looked excited as she let a hiccup escape. Flip saw the same light as he did in the kitchen.

"Bring it on, girl."

There was a tap on his arm and Flip looked over to his brother, and what he was offering. "Homegrown. A little hobby I picked up last year during the down-season. Let me know what you think." He chuckled to himself and got comfortable. Flip lit up, tasted a mild floral, and allowed himself to enjoy the moment, knowing that good company aside, he still had a long night and incoming day ahead of him. He reached over to his tea and took a sip. After a few rounds of Quotes, the game was called to a solid draw and the women shook hands, acknowledging the other's recall. Everyone shared another joint before deciding to call it a night.

Having gotten back at the Queen's Lodge well after 10, Flip sat at the bedroom desk over his notebook and wrote about the conversation in the kitchen with Hol'ly. He thought about what she said about Hana and Rac', or Raj, or however the fuck it's pronounced. He thought about what she alluded to in their upbringing and how much is being enacted onto Alexis. Looking at his open notebook, he stared at the only note he deemed important enough to take down, a loose description of where to find Tabine house. Outer-Monarch was a sprawling heavily forested area that surrounded its "city" counterpart and dotted with personal properties both expansive and miniscule. Even Ronnie's farm was technically in Outer-Monarch, but close enough to not be considered in the middle of nowhere like some much further out. Elena recommended going out and searching for the home, or at least call Holmb or Wallace. Flip countered that he didn't have an actual address, just a description that could be apt for any property in Outer-Monarch. The Klima ranch could even fit some the description if it wasn't so damn big.

Just before 11, the room-phone rang. Elena leaned over and answered before calling Flip over. Tak'rii said there was a call for him that sounded important. When he told Tak'rii to pass along the call, he realized he was much mistaken.

"What's up Ronnie?"

"Founder Stokton." It was an unfamiliar voice on the other end. "I heard you were looking for me."

Alexis? Alexis!

"Is this Alexis? Where are you?"

Elena shot up at Alexis' name.

"I'm... I'm home. With Mother."

Home?

"Home? Back in Fountain?" Flip didn't know who Alexis lived with, but word-of-mouth didn't portray her the type to say "Mother". "Where are you? Can I talk to 'Mother'?"

There was the sound of movement and another voice came on the line. A familiar voice.

"Hello?" Another sound of movement made him think he was on a speaker. Suddenly, there was a lack of background noise.

"Where is she?" Flip asked.

"She's safe, so long as she stays being a good girl. Isn't that right?" The question was louder, likely toward Alexis. He was sure she was still Monarch. "You didn't strike me as the bed and breakfast type. Enjoying Monarch?"

"Hana, where is she?"

"I told you she's safe. Did you see my message earlier?"

"I did."

Elena stared at Flip as he held the phone in silence. How did Hana know to call here? Then again, how many other places in Monarch host tourists? She tapped Flip's shoulder and pointed before getting up and walking into the living room and picking up the other landline slowly. Childish mischief taught her how to be covert. Her dad was a much different person on the phone when business was involved. Him yelling would've been frightening if it wasn't so funny hearing him swear. This call was devoid of all humor.

"Tell your bitch to get off the phone." Hana hissed into the phone.

Flip looked over and nodded his head. Elena smiled and pressed a finger onto the hook but didn't hang up. "It's just us, now."

"Good. Now, my brother and I are taking a vacation of our own soon. I think Alexis is going to join us. She's been a good girl lately and we could all use some time away."

Whore?

"How 'bout you leave Alexis behind this time? I'll bring her home and y'all can still take your trip, just tell me where she is."

Hana laughed and Flip raised his finger. Elena released the hook and covered the bottom half of the phone right before Hana came back.

"You're funny, Investigator, but sadly no, I don't think I can do that. My brother seems to really like her and it'd be cruel to leave her behind. We--" She paused. "Is that bitch back on?"

"Nah, it's still you and me."

"Ok, cause we *really* don't like liars. I don't want

someone to get hurt for what you said." Flip could hear what sounded like the sound of a chain rattle. "Anyway, it was good talking to you. I'm sorry we didn't get to hang out. You're really cute, and so is your bitch, I hear." Hana hung up before Flip could answer back. He immediately dialed the front desk and asked Tak'rii what was the number of the call he forwarded.

"I'm sorry, Mr. Stokton, but we don't have Caller ID on our desklines. Is everything ok?"

"Did you recognize the voice of the woman that called?"

"Woman? It was a man that asked for you. He said he was a fellow Investigator from Fountain with an update on your case. Is everything ok?"

One sets the pick, the other makes the play.

"Thanks, Tak'rii. Any other calls come in, just say I'm not available, thanks." Flip hung up and went to his mobile. He called Wallace and then Holmb, having to leave a message for both. He sent them a text before calling Ronnie.

"Hey, Flip. Leave something at the house?"

"Ron, is Rac' scheduled to come in tomorrow?" There was a level of tenseness in Flip's voice.

"Nah, he's got the weekend off. Why"

"He's going to call out for an extended leave sometime soon. Can you let me know when he does?"

"Yeah, will do. What's up, man?"

Flip thought about his next move. She already knew they were here, no need to dance around. "I just talked to Hana. They're leaving town soon, like possibly tonight. Can you tell me when you talk to them?" He heard Ronnie curse away from the phone and then return with a sigh.

"Yeah, man, will do."

Flip hung up and tried Wallace again. This time he got a familiar voice, just not one he expected.

"Hello?" It was Agent Camailla Valer. *Fuckin' A.*

"Valer, I need to speak to Wallace. *Now.*"

There was a shuffle and then Wallce was on. "Yo, what's up? I was in the--"

"Alexis is alive and here in Monarch."

"You've seen her?" Wallace moved Camailla to the side as he spoke. "Where in Monarch? Where are you?"

"I'm at a B&B, The Queen's Lodge. Hana just called my room. They're gonna leave town sometime soon, and they're taking her with them." Flip was getting agitated as he spoke. "Have you pinned down that username yet?"

Wallace explained that they haven't but did learn that whatever mob-comm Hana had was likely stolen from a Jenn Cilia of Redwater, Jenny to her friends. The few people they could track and talk to said they haven't heard from her in a few months, but that wasn't uncommon due to her job for a commercial garment manufacturer. As of now, there's no missing persons reports on file in Redwater but the 'tecs there will open an investigation. If the siblings were blowing town, Flip could pretty much guarantee they're going to ditch the mobile, and eventually the car. Flip told him he'd keep in touch before hanging up.

"Flip?" Elena didn't really know what else to say.

"I knew she was alive. I fucking knew it." Flip punched into a pillow. Then again. And again. Elena went over and wrapped an arm around him. "If they leave Monarch, we may never see her again."

"I know, I know." She held his hand soothingly. "Now,

what do you want to do?"

"Find her." Flip turned to look Elena in the eyes. She nodded and turned to get her keys off the bedroom desk. A few minutes later, they were headed out the door of the Queen's Lodge.

16 MONTHS LATER

CHAPTER 20
Fountain Founders' Day

Ironically, Redwater was named for the deep pink hued sands of its renowned Redwater Beach. The water was so clear that the color gets intensified and causes it to take on an almost blood-like appearance. An early rite of passage among native children was to wade out until the red turned into a murky burgundy and one couldn't see below. In spite of the aquatic appearance, Redwater Beach has always been the premier place for vacationing families, or couples trying to have a romantic getaway. For Flip, today's trip was a mix of both. Ronnie's directions had him and Elena driving around through narrow trails and backroads for almost two hours with nothing to show for it except an empty house with a nauseating smell radiating from it. He met Wallace and Holmb at the Lodge the next morning and told them the bad news, receiving the formal declaration of Alexis' case status in return: Closed, pending new information. The day that followed contained a widely attended Day of Honor where, he was presented the Star of Fountain, the highest civilian award given by the Founding Families for acts of valor and/or honorable actions for the betterment of the Fountain and her people. The next two months comprised of testifying and re-testifying his written Account of Effort to the Fountain High Court judge and the Minister's Panel, CaP'rotector Monroe and Dr. H'al'a's offices for formal debriefing, and a private, barely lit, short one-on-one meeting with the current Ruler of Sovereign Territory of Monarch, Queen Sata III.

Sata looked much younger than he expected her to, given her title, but Flip's short time in Monarch told him that age was mostly a matter of appearance and relativity.

He found it interesting that she seemed to be more upset about the news of the kidnapping than that of murder, but even more when she didn't appear surprised at hearing either charge. The Tabine children used to be nice and happy children even though they were not born "True". Around town, however, their outward was thought to be a front for what went on behind the doors of their home. Their father was spoken in whispers to have been a really bad man to his family despite his public image. At the end of their meeting, she gave Flip her permission to enter Monarch as he pleased, as she did for Ron Klima, though she was still puzzled as to why a Fountain-based an ex-ballplayer-turned-Investigator took such an interest in the well-being of a Redwater transplant and his vampyr wife. Whatever his reasoning was, she allowed to keep to himself for now; her allowance stood. In Flip's case, his only payment in exchange her kindness was an autograph, of course. She always found it fascinating how one can hone their body to a such a peak condition and engage in competitive sport for a career. She also found Flip's warm-bodied naivete laughable when he pulled out his pen.

Summer in Redwater was a lot more forgiving than Fountain, even when it's still the dead middle of it. Having an assortment of both natural and man-made bodies of water helped when you add in the elevation changes that put parts of the land well above sea-level. After that fateful week, Flip and (mostly) Elena felt it'd be best that he took a break for a little bit to clear his head. When the word came to him that Alexis was officially put into the Limbo Files, he found himself in a dark, and angry place. He was angry at himself. Angry at the Sight. Just, angry. He found himself at the Community Center almost every day, but not to help out. Outside of leading unenthusiastic workouts with his team, he kept himself in a cycle of running old plays, solo, in the gym and mentally going over everything that happened that long week on replay over and over again, studying it like old game tape and where he could've done better, where he should've done better. There were nights he and Elena would argue over just getting him to go home because she had to close up, only for him to stifle tears as he eventually got his bags together and walked her to her car. He fucked up. He fucked up bad. Elena tried her best to understand, and she did come around, but with a game plan of her own. She wasn't going to let him sulk around and operate on a hair trigger with everyone. He could do that with her in the privacy of their respective homes, but he for damn sure wouldn't be like that around her children. His nights in the gym turned into their nights in the gym and slowly, he was coming back to her. She could almost see the stress of courts and the anger shed from him and that they could still have a night where he was himself. She was happy that her Flip was still underneath.

Keeping his word, Flip signed over his 30% to Penny. Elena convinced Sandra that Penny should be able to try her hand at other potential careers, even if it's temporary. Over the course of a single drink and some alone-time with Penny, Sandra agreed to Elena's reasoning if, and only if, she could guarantee Penny's safety and keep a respectable paycheck. She wasn't letting her go only to wonder if Penny was going to need to decide whether to pay rent or get dinner. Elena put her and Flip's lives down as collateral against the terms and called Flip to tell him the good news of having a new (and first) employee. Flip promised to convert his living room area into an actual workspace. Elena's guest bedroom was cleaned out and given to Penny should she need somewhere stay on the fly due to her new job. Penny happily agreed to keep their sleepovers to a minimum; she really liked Domoni'c's new West Pike apartment and "grown-up" decor. It was much bigger than her place and she liked to have their "private nights" there. This divulgence was yet another reminder to Elena that despite her outward demeanor at vocabulary at times, Penny was very much a grown woman in her own right.

Flip lit up as he watched his mother and father walk along the tide, talking to each other. They looked happy. They looked... normal. As he exhaled, he brushed ash of his Rogues jersey and watched Ata and Patriik walk, keeping a healthy distance from their HouseMasters and a professional closeness between each other. They weren't technically on the clock since this beach trip was to be a vacation day for everyone, but a competent Ward or Maiden understands that one is never off the clock when in their Masters' presence, vacation day or not. They were willing to work together if it meant the rest of the staff could have a day to themselves. Ata had a large umbrella and windbreaker on over her uniform. Patriik went with a thin jacket of his own and a pair of stylish sunglasses, sporting a slick combat-casual aesthetic under his StaffMaster jacket. He even wore his hair out, grey streak hanging in front of his face and all. Flip was sure that the jacket was more for the dual daggers he was wearing than actual chill cover. He looked across the way to Flip and exchanged nods. Ata was saying something but kept her face mostly forward with watchful eyes on her HouseMother, paying particular attention to a couple coming a bit too close as they asked for a picture. Flip took another hit and reached his arm out to pass it over.

"They make a cute couple. Think your parents know yet?" Elena asked as she reached across the mini boothtable between them to accept.

"Don't know. It's not like they'd be breaking any written rules or anything. I highly doubt they know that they're living together, though."

"Yeah, but I know my father would lose it if he knew his HouseMaiden and StaffMaster were involved romantically, let alone living together. I hope Ata and Pat are being smart about their movements." Elena looked over and saw a large man coming from Flip's blindside. A little boy was walking beside him holding his hand.

"I'm sure they are, Olga."

Even through her shades, he felt Elena was looking past him and turned his head. He laughed as he recognized who was walking up and rose from his chair. "Klin Fjr, what up bruh?" He reached out and dapped the man up. Elena went back to people-watching and took a hit.

"What's good, Flip? Matriarch?" Klin bowed to them both. "Brought the little man and the mister out to the beach while the house is getting cleaned. You remember Saimon, right?" The man tapped the boy on the shoulder. "Go on, now."

Saimon looked up to Flip. "Mr. Stokton, could I have an autograph?"

Flip laughed loudly and nodded his head. "Of course, Saimon, anything for you." He went back to his seat and fished his notebook and pen out of his bag. A second later he ripped out a page and handed it over, "Here you go, little bro." and high-fived him. Saiman lit up as he looked over the autograph. Flip chatted with Klin for a few minutes as Saimon went over to Elena. She gave him an autograph too. Big day for Saimon Fjr and his impromptu trip to the beach. He would go on and relay this day to his own children as one of his fondest childhood memories.

Once Klin and Saimon left, Flip went through the pages of his book. He wasn't looking for anything in particular but stopped when he saw a note that chilled him. It was the only one from his last conversation with Hana:

She's still alive, so long as she's a "good girl"?

Talking about her like a pet.

He paused and grew tunnel vision. There wasn't any news about Alexis' whereabouts and the general consensus around Fountain was that she was dead. A vigil was held outside of Fountain Library and a tearful Camailla Valer thanked Flip and the FCPD for their efforts to bring her cousin home. She personally felt that Alexis was still out there, somewhere, but she didn't want to think about a reality that her cousin was still being held captive; still begging for her life and freedom. It was easier on her heart to believe she went out fighting. If it was one thing Alexis was all her life, she was a fighter. She could say that she was still proud of her and prayed she found herself in the Other World reunited with her sister and nephew, sharing a good drink, and making amends for all the things they missed in each other's lives.

Flip closed his notebook and went back to trying to enjoy his day at the beach. He looked over and saw his father talking to two children making a sandcastle and playing with action figures, sure that he was giving them tips on how to fortify the structural integrity against the incoming rising tidewater. He was probably also telling them how they could increase their castle's aesthetic value if they "acquired" the smaller one three children a few feet away were working on, or they could join together and find a way to connect the two. Even on a vacation, Ronald Stokton could never pass up a chance to give a piece of real estate advice when he saw an opportunity.

Elena looked over to Flip and back to the crowds of people along the tideline. The sun was out and the breeze off the water was comfortable. She reached over and they held hands in silence as they shared the rest of the joint. She noticed that Flip stayed in his mind a lot now, watching everywhere and everyone. She felt he was still looking for Alexis, maybe Hana, too. Today was the first day in a while she could say he looked genuinely relaxed. Quiet, but relaxed. She kissed his hand. "Everything ok? You been a little quiet today. I know we ain't smoke *that* much." She chuckled, hoping to get a smile.

He scoffed and sipped of his iced tea. "Yeah, I'm fine, just tryna remember the last time I been out here. It's been a while."

"Maybe we can make it more of a thing. We can use it as a celebration for solved cases."

Flip looked over to her with raised eyebrows. "So, you're cool with me keeping on?"

"I know I ain't do all that talking with Sandra for nothing. Hol told me about what she said to you about her father, and I don't want you to turn into that. I'm at peace that you may end up like your mother, but I want you to be like her. Happy, mostly coherent, but most importantly *here*. You know I'll be right next to you. I always have." They looked at each other's shaded eyes in silence.

Flip continued his gaze for a few seconds before speaking again. "I love you, Olga. You know that, right?"

"I love you too, Flip." They clinked glasses and drank before leaning in for a kiss. "Now, can we get some ice cream? It's hot as shit out here."

Flip scanned the beach for his parents and found

them having a doubles rock-skip competition with Patriik and Ata. His father was still the best skipper he'd ever known. It had to be that funny wind-up he had.

As if reading his mind, "They'll be fine, now come on." Elena called to him.

"Yes, ma'am." Flip took another sip of tea and followed her.

The night brought in a calm, chilly ocean breeze through the open window of the Redwater Cabana hotel. Once Patriik and Ata left with his parents back to Fountain, Flip extended his reservation so that he and Elena can truly have the well-deserved and long overdue vacation they both needed. They decided to capitalize on their time in Redwater and allowed themselves to live like they did in their playing days: a lot of smoking, a few club appearances with old friends, and a lot of fucking. Elena didn't mind that Redwater was Flip's town. He had a universally ardent fanbase here, sometimes more than the people back home, and they never shied from showing their love. Redwater didn't care that he was royalty of Fountain. They didn't care that he barely came to town, but when he did, they made sure to show their appreciation for helping put their Territory in the same sentence with "championship caliber". Even after he was traded and his retirement, the high-level of talent and draft picks that was attracted to play for the Rogues became constant. It seemed like everyone from the east wanted to say they played on the same team as *the* Flip Stokton.

She never understood how Redwater seemed to hold him down stronger than people who've been there to see him grow up, leave, and actually want to come back home after everything was said and done. Part of her secretly wondered if he would've come back if she wasn't already in Fountain after her own injury-induced premature retirement; no way she was going to be reduced to second team because of a stupid ankle slip. She didn't like to think about like that, feeling a tinge guilty at how selfish it sounded to think that of all the reasons he would want or even need to come back home, *she* was the top reason. Despite her interest, she never asked him directly why he chose to come back. It didn't matter; he came back. That was the important part. He was back, she was here. Now, they were back together, officially, and she was happy. They were happy.

Clicking through the TV channels, Elena looked over to him. "What we watchin'? You'd think for the money, they'd have a better selection."

Flip turned his head to exhale and put the joint into the ashtray, "Whatever you want." before he reached his hand under the cover, between her legs.

"Mmmm, come on now." She spoke between waves. "I think my boyfriend should be back anytime now."

"Tell him to walk the beach or something," He pulled the covers back, exposing her bare skin to the incoming breeze. "you're a little occupied right now. He'll understand."

He climbed over her, and tenting her legs into a spread, kissed her stomach in a trail downward, making sure to go off course and show some attention to the fully healed Founder's Seal tattoo on her lower ribcage. Had he known where she wanted it placed beforehand, he would've rethought his agreement to matching with her. There were a few soft kisses until she felt herself become warm. The explosions onscreen were only a visual of what she felt every time Flip stuck his tongue into her. She let the remote fall to the floor as she tried to watch the movie and allow Flip to lick at his own rhythm, synching the arches of her back with the valley topography he knew very well. She felt herself swell in anticipation. The swell grew as he started alternating between suckling and lapping her nectar.

"Don't stop..." Elena's moans filled his ears until it took over the sounds of the TV. There was something else said but he didn't hear it. He kept his rhythm with his fingers as he went back to suckling her.

"I'm about to..." He felt Elena's hands run through his hair, bringing him closer to her. The short gasps she always made before the moment never lied.

"I'm...coming. Flip...Flip, I'm coming!" Elena screamed out as she couldn't hold it back any longer. Hearing a deep moan, he suckled tenderly as she dug nails into his shoulders.

A pool of wet formed under Elena; shockwaves twitching through as the ocean wind chilled her back into reality. Outside of this week, taking a vacation wasn't the only thing that was long overdue. The mutual frustration exuded through in their games; both playing against each other harder than they should have, like they each were actually trying to beat each other. There were hard fouls, some dubious footwork from Elena, and even a particular occasion where a check-up felt a little too aggressive. She may have thrown stuff, but she's never raised her hand to him, on the court or otherwise.

"Throw the ball at me like that again, and I will knock you the fuck out, just go'on and try me! Now check the ball like you got some damn sense."

He knew she wasn't going to swing on him, but in the moment, she didn't. He checked the ball, with sense, and they spent the next two minutes in a scoreless deadlock filled with pushes, undercuts, and suffocating defenses. Neither one of them realized that the other wasn't keeping score anymore, so they both played as if they each needed a basket just to keep the game tied. Keeping in line with a taught mantra since Kiddie League, they left whatever it was that would possess them on the court, on the court. All of it. No matter how rough they played, they walked back to whoever's car hand-in-hand. Anything to make sure they both went to bed content, even it wasn't with each other.

Flip held Elena in a cuddle as they watched a *High Price* rerun, kissing her head every so often. She would kiss the top of his hand in return. Every time he kissed her, she experienced residual murmurs. Even the way he finished and let her put underwear on told her she didn't need to do anything for him. Every now and then she'd shiver, explaining it away with the wind coming from outside.

"Flip?"

"Hm?"

"Unless we *can't* be together, let's not have another spell like this again. Promise? I was beginning to think you ain't like me no more." Her voice taking a childish mimic.

"Promise. I missed you, Olga. I like you just fine." His voice holding a sincere tone.

"I missed you, too." Elena kissed his hand again.

They kept watching the show before Elena turned to face him and softly ran a line along his face. His slashing healed up cleanly and fast but left him with a single long scar with two shorter ones along his left cheek. Hana's superficial cuts were on the right, but one had to look hard, or be up close, to notice the faded line. Their fineness unsettled her because of the amount of control she assumed was taken. Hana could've done anything to him, yet she didn't. Why? Maybe she was serious about only coming to warn him. Putting herself in Hana's sickening headspace made her think of the retort: Why not? She only wanted to warn him, not hurt him. When the stiches were finally taken out, Penny made a joke about how her and Flip were now twins, only admitting the story of Flip's was much cooler. Elena continued tracing. "How's this been?"

"It's alright, but itches from time to time. I still sometimes dream about that night, you know? I still see her face."

"I know, Love, but you did what you had to do. She was going to kill you if you didn't."

"Yeah, maybe." Flip went silent and shifted his eyes to the TV for a second. Elena could remember the last time he jumped awake from a nightmare of that night at Fountain Memorial. He woke up gasping. Fortunately, she never was there for the times when he would yell himself awake, Birdie already drawn from under his pillow, aimed and ready to shoot at anything he thought was moving when it shouldn't. There was only one time he actually fired until the clip was empty, only to find himself waking up for real.

"I know, but sometimes I wonder, was it the right thing? She didn't choose to be what she became. She couldn't control herself." Flip kept an even tone as he thought about the argument, with Holmb and Dr. Rizzo, that Cheryl's body needed to be burned as soon as Rizzo's report was finished. A private, more civil, conversation with Rizzo drove the point home that *vampyr* needed to be in his official filing. Initially, Rizzo cut the difference by stating, *victim was believed to be of vampyr*, but quickly amended once he found fleshy pieces of what felt and looked like glass among the ash.

"Flip, it may not feel like it, it may never will, but you didn't do anything wrong. If you didn't shoot, you wouldn't be here. We wouldn't be here. Cheryl would've got you like she did P'rotector Vin, and possibly continue until she was shot down anyway by Holmb. Your Day of Honor would have been one of Remembrance." She kissed him. "And because of the work you did, our people aren't in the dark as much about vampyrs. They may not fully get it yet, but now they know it's a real thing. As a Founder, you truly exhibited your responsibility to your citizens, and they will never forget it."

Flip smiled and kissed her forehead. "I guess you're right."

"I know I am." Elena smiled back at him.

Flip heard the room landline ringing. A few people knew where he was, and they all had his mobile number. He got up and walked across the room, grabbing a fresh joint of Ronnie's homegrown and the book of matches off the main table. He picked up the phone and spoke as he lit up.

"Mr. Stokton, you have a call requesting to be transferred. The caller says it's important."

"Did they give a name?" Flip took a small pull to get the burn going and exhaled into the window opening.

"No, she refused to, but says it's imperative that she speak with you."

She?

He immediately thought back to the last phone call he took in a place that asked permission to transfer an "imperative" call. Adrenaline started to pump into his blood, and he suddenly didn't feel like smoking.

"Send it over."

"Yes, sir."

A brief silence and then Flip heard the distinctive click of an open line.

"Hana, the fuck you want now?"

"Flip Stokton? Rising Patriarch of Founding Family Stokton?" The voice was female but wholly unfamiliar. It had a sound of old-timey sophistication to it. Definitely not Hana. Or Alexis.

"Who is this?"

There was another period of silence before another voice took over. "Flip?"

"Yes?"

"I understand that you're currently on holiday and I apologize for interrupting. How's Redwater this time of year?" It was Queen Sata III of Monarch. She sounded much different on the phone than she did in person; much older than her physical appearance. How did she know he was in Redwater? What did she want?

"A little hot, but I'll live."

"Interesting. Are you preoccupied right now? I also understand that the Matriarch Elena Starks is with you." She paused as if expecting a response and took his silence as a no, or merely a non-admission. She continued. "It will not last long, but I request your presence. By the time we are finished speaking, there will be a caravan outside waiting for you. I ask that you not keep me waiting."

Flip was on the phone for almost another 20 minutes, speaking in mostly hushed tones. Elena wished there was another room phone so she could listen in. What if it was Hana, calling to taunt again? What if it was Alexis, having finally broken away, and in need of help? Were either of them in Redwater? By the way Flip returned and began to get dressed, she deduced that neither was the case.

"I'm being summoned." Flip said to her as he put on his thigh holster and jacket.

She knew exactly by who. Since their trip to Monarch, she'd gotten in the habit of talking to Hol'ly casually, mostly serving as a listener. Occasionally, they would talk about the rumored habits of Queen Sata, and her particular one of requesting face-to-face meetings. She had quite a few with Ronnie soon before and after he agreed to move with her from Redwater to Monarch, but he always said he couldn't repeat the details of what was discussed. According to Flip, the (in)frequency of talking to his brother hadn't changed at all, but the talks moved from texts to actual calls, and lasted a few minutes longer each time. Despite being a respected couple, Hol'ly still struck Elena as a girl with very few friends and wanted to change that. They weren't the wealthiest by any means, but one prominent woman should always have others in her network. She kissed Flip and took over the now free space on the bed, letting his scent envelope her. "Be careful, Love."

He promised he would and should be back soon. Elena reveled in the now extra space and changed the channel. She stopped on the news and watched the ongoing coverage of a series of deaths in the Territory of Torina. Before suddenly stopping almost a week ago, authorities had not been able to confirm whether these were murders or a result of the recent bacterial breach in the lead water supplier's filtration system as all victims had varying levels of toxicity in their blood. Elena watched the coverage as a sinking feeling in her stomach began to build. She tried not to assume the worst, but she her gut said Flip should have stayed behind a few minutes longer.

◆ ◆ ◆

Friday

It had been a little over a year since the Tabine estate has had occupants. 16 empty months, to be exact. As much as they hated the place, Rac' knew it was the only one he and Hana could call home. The night was warm and through his windbreaker he could feel the first beads of perspiration form. He opened the door and swept for intruders or squatters, finding none and everything in its same place as when they left. He motioned Hana into a wing position and went inside. Hana told X'i to grab their food from the trunk before she came inside and to get it prepped while they cleaned up for an early breakfast, tossing the car keys to her. X'i caught them and felt her stomach rumble. Her stomach was killing her.

"Yes, Mother."

The woman in the trunk thought she heard X'i call someone Mother.

As she opened the trunk, she heard the woman's muffled yelp and looked into the frightened eyes of the hitchhiking couple. They met the two along the highway just outside of the Pase settlement, a little over 50 miles outside of Torina. Almost as soon as she looked into the male's eyes, she lurched over and momentarily dry heaved as her body was rejecting the nausea from the smell of urine that rose into her nostrils, allowing a split second for him to go for an attack. X'i saw it coming and tossed him out of the trunk onto the ground, hearing a *crunch* as she stomped onto his bound wrists. Through the layers of rope, she could hear a pained yell come through. As he writhed around in the dirt, she went back to the woman and spoke softly.

"I'm so sorry, Shuun, but fighting only makes it worse."

Shuun, silently looked into X'i's eyes, and saw them breathing on their own with a glow. It reminded her of a fireplace for some reason, and they were a beautiful hazel-indigo. She focused on the cloudy eye that had caught her attention when they first met, and it told her that X'i was telling the truth. Looking at Ni'col's example, she needed no further demonstration. She nodded and allowed herself to be lifted out of the trunk.

"Can you walk?" X'i asked her. By this time, Rac' was coming back outside and walking down the porch steps.

"What's taking so long?" He asked as he came behind her.

"Nothing, Ra—Master. He attacked me." X'i pointed.

Rac' knew Ni'col was going to be a problem. He sensed it from the way he would make sly suggestive remarks to his sister when he thought he was being clever. He looked back at X'i and studied her face. She was lifting Shuun to her feet and stabilized her when she stumbled. Her and Nic had been almost exclusively in the trunk for the past four days. Rac' bent down and tapped Ni'col's hands where he saw a dusty footprint. Ni'col yelled through his gag and recoiled. He tapped it again harder and held the pressure. "He'll be ok. Good girl, X'i." Shuun saw X'i try to hide the tiny smirk face and her heart began to race faster. She looked like a schoolgirl that was finally complimented by her secret crush. Rac' landed a punch on Ni'col's face with such force that made Shuun jump. "On your feet." Hoisting Ni'col over his shoulder like a sack of flour, Rac' called behind him. "Hurry up with her."

"Yes, Master." X'i responded and locked arms with

Shuun, escorting her to the house. "I'm so sorry, Shuun. I actually liked you a lot. You were nice." She whispered into her.

Mother? Master? Only days ago, she knew these three as Hana, Rac' and X'i, coming back from an extended vacation. Sure, Hana seemed a little too close with her brother sometimes and she heard X'i ask for permission to go to the bathroom a few times, but they were gracious and naïve enough to offer their home to her and Ni'c. Now, she's hearing them addressed as "Mother" and "Master" by who she thought was their traveling assistant. What kind of freaky shit were they into? She hoped that this was an extended and ultimately unfunny joke. As she walked, she began to mumble to herself. X'i' turned and put a finger to Shuun's lips. "There is no K'd in this house." She whispered.

With that declaration, Shuun stopped her prayer and could feel tears running down her face. K'd wasn't at this house, she could feel He hadn't been in a long time. Something else lived here. She could sense it as soon as she stepped inside. Shuun took one last look behind her to outside before watching Rac' close and lock the door. She saw Ni'col laid across one of the sitting room chairs, jaw slacked in an unnatural alignment, but still breathing. Looking around the house, she was struck by the same feeling of amazement that struck X'i when she was first brought here; how elegant everything looked under the dust. Hana had said they'd been gone for a few months, but with a house like this, why would anyone leave? Between the car and the appearance of the occupants, she thought these were some new money rich kids playing around with their trust fund. It was to be a simple in and out job, so long as her and Ni'c could play the long game and hang out with a couple of weirdos for a few days; and if it came to it, the isolation was a perfect setting to put a few spoiled kids down with no worry. It was a break in one of their rules to stay with a target for so long and not get anything, but these kids played their money close to the chest and they were already on the way back home. What was the worst that could happen?

Hana stood at the top of the stairs in fresh clothes. She told X'i to take Ni'col and Shuun into the cellar before Rac' cut in.

"No, leave him up here." Rac' looked up at his sister. "Let X'i have her own, she's been good."

"Got something in mind, little brother?" Hana started to walk down the stairs. When she reached the base, she walked over to X'i and held her face momentarily. She still had her looks. "Think you can handle her, X'i?"

"Still remember how to track?" Rac' pulled a large knife from his ankle-sheath and proceeded to cut Ni'col's binds.

"Yes, Mother." The fire grew double in X'i's eyes as did Shuun's fear when she looked to her. "I think so." She lowered her eyes, feeling undeserved to look at Mother directly, unless *she* wanted her to.

Hana smiled and slapped her on the bottom. "Good girl. Eat up, and we'll have a spa day. You'd like that, wouldn't you." She saw a spark in X'i's eyes.

"Do you promise?" X'i asked hopefully.

"Have I ever broken my promises to you?" She patted X'i on the cheek. "I promised we'd have a nice trip, didn't I? I'd say Torina was quite nice. And all the places we went before that? I only had to punish you once, but we had fun. Right?"

"Yes."

"Good girl, now go and have breakfast. I'll see you a

little later, ok?" Hana patted her bottom again to send X'i on her way.

"Yes, Mother." X'i walked away with the restrained giddiness a child going to their room to play with a new toy. She was practically pulling Shuun along. Hana and Rac' watched as she went towards the cellar door and opened it. Shuun resisted being led into the darkness but a violent yank on her hair told her it was useless. The cellar door was then slammed close.

"Guess I need to change my clothes, again." Hana turned back towards the stairs, stomach growling from impatience. Rac' went back to Ni'col and tried to wake him. After a few slaps, he saw that he was beginning to stir. Rac' put his knife to Ni'col's chest.

"Get up. Now."

Ni'col was then led outside and told to run, run hard and far. It was 10 minutes before Hana came back down in changed clothes and two wallets in her hand. She opened them up and showed that each had multiple ID's for both Shuun and Ni'col, all of different names and photos of people that passingly looked like their new owners. "These were in their bags." She knew there was a reason she didn't like these two, especially Shuun. When Rac' decided it was time, they casually jogged in the general direction that Ni'col had ran. When they got to the tree line, Rac' started to sniff the ground and pointed out where they needed to go. The hunt was on.

Flip got back to the Cabana just as Ni'col had been told to run as hard as he could. Trying his hardest to not wake Elena, he put his given bag down and quietly undressed and crawled into bed next to her, using the remote to lower the volume a few counts. Elena's body moved close to him and curled inward. She could smell what she thought was wine on his breath.

"Good meeting?" She drowsily asked. Flip almost wished her voice always sounded like that.

"It was interesting. Shit wine though." He kissed her cheek.

Elena cuddled into him. "Tell me about it in the morning?"

"Sure. Good night."

"Night." Elena drifted back to sleep. Flip followed suit about 20 minutes later, after he finished thinking about the contents of the bag he was given before exiting the caravan that brought him back to Redwater.

Breakfast at the Redwater Cabana more than made up for the quality of channel selection. Tired of paying for room service, Flip and Elena decided to see how much better it was if they just got it straight from the kitchen. Over their stacked plates, they talked about Flip's late-night meeting with Queen Sata III of Sovreign Territory of Monarch (after a few glasses of Bloodwine, she was comfortable enough to allow first-name address), who was in her third "rotation" as Monarch's ruler, but still considered a young enough woman in her overall lifecycle. She grew tired of expecting the Tabine children to return home and thus called off her routine checks on the house, choosing to leave the children to their fates. They were lost causes and she was sure the girl they had with her was long dead or Turned. Either way, the children were still native citizens of Monarch and, more importantly, part of the people she took a Ruler's Oath to protect from outsiders, warm-body Investigators or otherwise. She made clear that whatever happened to them outside Monarch's borders would not be met with retaliation, even if their ender was from a neighboring territory. On risk of dishonoring her name or post, she ensured that her citizens know that Flip was to be considered a friend to the people of Monarch as the personal *ha'kiet* to their Queen. While most of Outer-Monarch had no official addresses, she did confirm that the Tabine house was in the general area of where Flip and Elena drove out to and showed him an identifier to look for next time: a door knocker bearing the symbol The Father. There were only two in that area. By his reaction, she could tell he had seen it before.

When Elena brought up the news report about Torina from last night, she could tell Flip had already known about it. That was also something discussed in his meeting. Looks like Sata had been keeping up with the major coverage of the contamination as well as a few less reported deaths that were a more in the grey but seemed to be the handiwork of her kind. Flip had also been secretly keeping up with reports of outwardly seeming random deaths down the eastern coast with Penny's help and had been noticing a pattern: victims were mostly drifter types, found on mostly on wooded roadsides or along bodies of water. Until Torina. The ongoing bacterial situation muddied the stat line on what could be unfortunate deaths or intentional ones, but from the homicides he could get info on, nothing stuck out except the demographic of the victims; homeless and/or recorded sex workers. No kidnappings and no major spike in any particular Torina satellites, then as of a week or so weeks ago, nothing. Bacteria doesn't discriminate the way those deaths did. He knew they moved on somewhere, but not knowing exactly where to was what disturbed him. Not knowing if Alexis was being forced to witness or even participate in the crimes was what scared Elena. Something in her said that Alexis was still very much alive, but what if she wasn't? What if Hana and Rac' were gone for good and Flip was truly hunting ghosts? How long could he keep it up? How long would he? Even some of their favorite movies didn't have settled endings for the hero.

"But what if she isn't? What if she's still with them?" Flip asked her.

"Flip, have you thought about if she's *one* of them by now? Like seriously thought about it? If she's one of them, are you still going to try to rescue her?"

Flip looked at his plate in silence. He had thought about the possibility. Alexis could possibly be a vampyr by this point. If she was still alive, he thought it was even likely. It's been over a year, and there's been nothing that come of his search for her. No sighting, no pictures, nothing since that night at the Queen's Lodge.

Alexis would kill for an autograph.

Even in the moment, he knew that Alexis was likely Turned by that point, and he knew he was hunting three people instead of two. He just wanted to hold out hope, like he did when he held his gun on Cheryl. He hoped that Camailla was right, that Alexis went out fighting, but in his heart knew that as a Vice Agent, she's been in the game long enough to know that even the strongest of hostages can break with enough force. He was at peace with knowing that if Alexis was alive, he'd do what was needed.

"If it comes to that, it does." Flip could feel an itch on his cheek but resisted scratching.

Elena studied him before going back to her food.

There was a touch in his voice that told her he was settled on what he was saying, and that he meant it. She admired that he couldn't let this go, but it troubled her just as much. She questioned if there was a catalyst case his mother couldn't solve that set her on the path she found herself on now. He was still young. There would be more cases; more people he could help. She didn't want this to be something that jumpstarted a life of looking over his shoulder and seeing a reality only he could. Fleice seemed level enough because she still had so many people around her, but what would happen to Flip once he got older and the family around him started to move on to the Other? Would Ronnie suddenly step in and help out? Would the other Families? For the first time in knowing him, Elena seriously pondered on what would happen if they had children and started raising a family. Would she spend more time with Ata and the kids as she taught them how to ride bikes, or take them to school? Sure, Flip would be there, but not like he deserved to be. He's worked too hard, and they've been through too much together. It wasn't fair to him, or her. She changed the topic to something she hoped was lighter and could get a good laugh out of.

"So, what's in the bag you came home with? I noticed you still haven't opened it, meaning you either already know what's in it, or you don't want to." Elena stole a piece of waffle from his plate.

"Eh, mostly this weird fire infused ammo. As much as she talks about wanting to catch and deal with these two herself, Sata seems very indifferent to me looking for them. She seems to be more 'new school' to how things are done in these situations." Flip ate his last piece before Elena got any bright ideas.

"Oooh, addressing her by her first name now, are we?

Got yourself a new girlfriend, Mr. Stokton?" Elena took a sip of her drink and stuck her tongue. She thought about Flip's description of Sata after his first time meeting her. He made the mistake of jokingly asking for her mother when she first walked in, thinking she was a young woman scouting her mother's guest as she got ready. Sata didn't find it funny at all and promptly informed him of just how much older than him she was and who she was. That let him know that their first meeting was going to be played straight, at least until the Bloodwine was brought in. Then she was all jokes, but of a darker variety. It almost seemed like a social call until she abruptly shifted gears and got back to business. He could see what she meant by still being considered in her youth despite being centuries old. She was enjoying her time as the young queen and ruler of her "Sovereign Territory" until she was going to eventually have to start making real decisions about her heir. She's entertained suiters, and lovers, from many lands, but she didn't seem interested in them the same way. Maybe it was just the wine, but she kept bringing that detail up quite a bit during their talk, to the point that Flip began to wonder why he was really called for in the middle of the night. At least she didn't ask for another autograph. "Ok, so you *do* have a new girlfriend." Elena chuckled. "Do I need to start considering calling her when we go out? Send her my schedule so we split our days up?"

"C'mon, Olga. It's just--"

"It's just business. I know, Flip." Elena took another sip. "I've heard that one before." She heard that one quite a bit back in the day, actually. Sometimes it was, sometimes it wasn't.

"She ain't looking at me, so don't be jealous. It's not a good look on you, anyway."

"Mmhmm, ok. But you do seem to attract, and entertain, those I'd least suspect."

"I could say the same for you, My Matriarch." Flip retorted with a Smile. Elena almost choked on her drink before coughing out a hard laugh.

"Well played." She offered her glass. He wasn't lying. Fucking Holmb. What was she thinking?

"Got to be quick when I'm around you." He met hers and they clinked before sharing a sip. "But forreal, I'll see if you can come with me next time. That place she lives is a fucking maze. She had guards and servants everywhere."

"Interesting. How did she know we were here?"

"Wouldn't say. Her guards got a little antsy when I asked a second time, so I didn't press it. I think they had us pegged as soon as we drove into town. A couple of strange *Vi'nnakan* come to town and go to an establishment run by one of the few humans there, then leave a day or so later after asking questions about her citizens? I'd have people looking into us too if I was her."

"Even more interesting. Should we be worried about her?"

"She said not to be." Flip went back to his drink and finished it.

"Mmhmm, we'll see." Elena finished her own and her plate. "So, what we doin' today?"

"I was thinking of testing this ammo. Wanna come?" Flip brushed across his waist as he reached behind him.

"Not what I expected, but sure. Should I mail a thank-you note before we leave?" Elena winked as she got her things together.

"Funny." Flip answered back sarcastically as he took

out his wallet. He left a few scril on the table for decent tip as they got up to leave. When they walked past the desk, a server stopped them to ask if they were finished with their table. Flip felt a tiny but undeniable pulse as he said they were. The server thanked them and went straight for the empty table to clear it out and prep it for the soon arriving lunch window. Before being taken away as he entered the grounds of Sata's compound, Birdie was bouncing on his thigh to the point that it was almost a relief when the guards took it off of him. He noticed the guard that handled it was doing his best to hide that it pained him to hold it. Maybe Birdie was the one he should be worried about being jealous and not Elena. He sent a text to Penny letting her know he'd be back in town tomorrow and called the HiPoint shooting range to ask if they still had the outdoor gallery.

P'rotector Wallace was reloading his service shooter when he got the call. He removed his earcovers and answered quickly when he saw the Pase area code.

"Wallace speaking."

"Yo, Wall, remember that car you told me to look out for?" It was Pase Chief Defender Sutone.

"Yeah, Su, what's up?" It's been over two months since he told her about the black Exum. Flip wasn't the only one still leading an investigation.

"We found it." Sutone paused. "Well, technically a few teenagers found it, a few miles past settlement limits in a clearing off the road. Burned out to shit." She paused again.

"What else, Su? Sounds like there's more."

"Two bodies with it. Possibly a male and female."

"How long ago?" He was already holstering and headed to the range door.

"Can't say yet, but's cold. Kids say they found it last night but by the looks of it, it's been here for a while now. Our guys can barely get anything off of it."

Wallace was in front of the elevator, mentally trying to force it to arrive faster. After months of nothing from their suspects, now their car shows up, with them in it? Something didn't feel right about it. Especially since there's only two bodies.

"Alright, keep me in touch with what happens."

"Will do."

As soon as Wallace was off the phone and immediately shot a message to Holmb and then Flip. He got off the elevator and started for CaProtector Monroe's office. Tapping a few times before opening the door, he saw that Monroe was on a call and gestured for him that it he needed to talk to him. Now. Monroe put up a finger but motioned for him to enter and grab the chair in front of his desk. Wallace sat and listened to an out of context jab to Minister Esun before Monroe hung up tensely. "What is it?"

"Everything ok?" Wallce took out a piece of Stik-O-Stim and chewed. He offered a piece that was accepted.

"Yeah, just Esun being an ass. He gives Flip a damn Star and's been thinking he's running this department personally now. Fucking assho--" He realized he was about to rant and pulled back. "What is it?"

"The Tabine car's been found outside of Pase. Burnt out, two bodies in it."

"Our suspects?"

"Not sure yet."

Monroe asked for another piece of Stim and chewed hard. He didn't care for the slimy part, but it was better than cigarettes. "You tell Flip?"

"Not yet, I just found out."

Monroe nodded. "Well, we can't really do much unless there's anything to go with. You said it was only two bodies?" Wallace understood where he was going.

"Yeah, they think it's a man and woman. Car's been burnt out for a while, likely the two with it."

Monroe looked at his desk and thought it over. "What do you think?"

"To be honest, CaP, seems a little curious. I mean, we couldn't find these two while they were active and now, we find not only their car, but them in it as well? Almost too convenient. You see that report about Torina on the news?"

Monroe nodded his head and sipped his coffee, his second for the day. "I did. I take it you don't think they're all from the contamination?"

"Kind of. Interesting how the frequent ones within the city seemed to have tapered off, yet the system is more concentrated there compared to the beach-facing neighborhoods, don't you think?"

"I get where you're going. Let me know what comes of the car."

"Yes, sir." Wallace got up and went for the door.

"And Wallace?"

Wallace turned. "Yeah?"

"Don't call me CaP, I got enough people calling me that already."

Wallace smiled, "I got you, sir."

"Close the door behind you."

Monroe hoped that the two people in the car were in fact the Tabine siblings and he could put an end to their thin file appropriately. He could stomach that Alexis was dead and not going to be found, he's seen similar situations before. Two murderers that managed to slip away from him, that was the part that ate at him. Dead or alive, he needed to be able to say that they weren't still out there terrorizing another Territory, or worse, living and blending in like nothing happened. Since Flip's hospital shooting and the original Shockley murder, he's tried his best to get more educated in this affliction called Vampyrism, among many other names, and how it affects its hosts. He's even been going back to Sanctum to consult his Speaker on the subject. It still looked too much like something he could turn on the TV or go to a cinema and watch rather than something he could be around at any moment and not know it.

In the beginning, he could admit he may have gone in hot, diving headfirst into what he could and found himself spending more time debating with Oleane on what was fact and what was fiction. He did see Monarch pop up a lot in his research when he would look into the tri-territory area, but even then, it was never anything coming from Monarch directly. Everything was more or less a think-piece or educated conjecture featuring second-hand accounts that sounded vague at best. Some things he did find, like the fact that Monarch was one of the oldest Territories on the east coast and they instituted a clause of non-engagement in the Great Territory War, was stuff he already knew. He shook his head and sipped his coffee again. The quicker he can get rid of this Tabine headache, the better. For some reason, he had a flashback about Fleice Stokton and the time he tried to talk her into applying for CaP'rotector. She said she'd think about it. He wished he could call her up and pick her brain about this whole thing. After a long internal debate while holding the landline, he decided some bridges were better left destroyed than risk rebuilding on damaged foundation. She didn't deserve what happened to her, and he couldn't forgive himself for not doing more to protect her. He wouldn't repeat the same mistakes with Flip.

Flip couldn't believe what he was reading, as in, he literally couldn't believe it. There was no way that someone got the drop on the same girl that *chose* not to kill a sleeping target and escape without issue. No, that just couldn't happen. He sent a vaguely adverse response and was glad to see that Wallace was on the same page before telling Elena. She made a joke about maybe Flip should be tracking down whoever did it and thank them, or maybe he should call his *girlfriend* Sata and ask her if this was her work. Maybe she was already keeping secrets so early in the relationship. Flip hoped Elena wasn't actually growing jealous of a 200-and-some change-year-old woman; so what if she looked only a few years over Ata? He was glad she never saw Hana.

"You really think Sata did it? Track 'em and burn 'em outside of her Territory? I told you she's pretty hard about that whole 'Monarch punishment on Monarch land' shit." Flip asked as he sat back into his chair, taking a sip of tea.

"She tracked us down, didn't she?" She responded.

"True." Flip took another sip. "I don't know, it doesn't match up with all the talk she made about *their* execution of justice, whatever that is. Roadside car burning just doesn't seem her style."

"I know, and I don't actually think she did, but you

did say she seemed more 'new school'. Maybe she's more 'organized crime boss' and less 'prim and proper protocol' kind of royalty?"

Flip took the idea but shook it away, "I don't think so. Wallace said he'll let me know if anything comes of it This was a diversion, Olga, and a pretty decent one. From what I seen, Pase ain't super far, but it's still short a full week away from here with *constant* driving."

"Think Alexis may have had enough and managed to get away? Caught 'em slippin'?" Elena asked.

He hadn't considered that. Wallace did say that there were only two bodies, and even though it's assumed it was Hana and Rac', he didn't think about that maybe they got too comfortable and let their guard down. Alexis may have still had some fight in her after all. Thinking about it, he didn't like the implication that Alexis could be in the Pase outskirts wandering around, hurt, lost and in need of serious help. His gut still said that wasn't the case; the car was a distraction, pure and simple. If Alexis was found, he would've heard so by now. Elena concurred but still suggested Flip talk to his "Monarch girl" about her recon activity, even if to fish around on if she's even heard about this new development. He agreed that he would the next time she reached him, which he felt would be pretty soon. In the meantime, he was going to operate with the assumption that everyone was alive.

Walking through the halls to the elevator, Flip anticipated a call by Sata, telling him to disregard the news about a car found outside of Pase. She already said her search is done, but he didn't believe her. The active search for them was probably finished; sitting on the house, sending people into unfamiliar places to ask questions, maybe that stuff was done. It was the watching of the news, or whatever she used for information outside of Monarch, he was sure that was still going strong. Riding the elevator down to the lobby he held the case and grew curious about how these "pyrounds" are going to look in action. Elena gave the valet her ticket and a few minutes later saw her M3 pull up, humming patiently as she walked around to the driver's side and got in. Flip promised the valet he'd get him next time, when he had some scril on him, and the valet silently nodded with a smile; he'd heard that one plenty of times. Then again, this was Flip Stokton. Surely, he was good for it. Flip closed the door and went straight into his bag, taking stock of the magazines he was given and began fitting one into Birdie as Elena merged into traffic. It felt heavier now; full even. He felt a hum emanate from his hand but after removing and replacing it, couldn't feel it again. He looked over to Elena to see if she noticed, but didn't say anything, hoping it was only in his head.

Hana saw X'i sitting in the rocking as she and Rac' were walking across the front yard. The early afternoon sun was beaming down with not a cloud nearby. X'i saw that Ni'col was nowhere in sight, sure that the splashes on Master's clothes would be last she would ever see of him again. Unlike Shuun, she didn't like Ni'col, and the way would look at Mother sometimes. It was like he and Shuun knew something they didn't. She found out exactly what their plan was and sat, fidgeting in her seat as she waited to relay. "What?" Hana asked as she walked up the stairs, taking her bloodied hunting blouse and skirt off, standing bare in her underclothes, freezing. X'i averted her eyes as she accepted the bundle.

"Shuun told me something." X'i looked to Master as he took his shirt off, choosing to keep his pants. "They wanted to hurt us, Mother. They were going to steal from us." She kept her eyes on him. "Ni'col really wanted to hurt you, Master. Really bad. They've hurt a lot of people already." There was a glaze over her cloudy eye as if she was about to cry. Rac' nodded and handed his shirt over. Hana began licking her teeth, cleaning them off.

"Interesting. Well, don't worry about that anymore. Ni'col's not hurting anyone now." Hana said as she raised her hand to rub some blood off X'i's cheek, noticing a flinch. "And Shuun?"

X'i looked into Mother's face and smiled, "She won't hurt anyone else either."

Hana looked into her eyes and saw a growing inferno, brightening the dull pearl that was her left eye. She imagined Shuun hoping that maybe if she confessed her and Ni'col's plan and past crimes that X'i would let her go. The silly bitch.

"Good girl." She said to X'i, kissing her cheek. "Wouldn't you agree, little brother?"

"Yeah." Rac' started for the door and went inside. "I'm taking a shower."

"Soak the clothes and I'll get a bath running for us. I'm freezing out here." X'i started to take her jacket off before Hana interrupted, "What did I say?" and walked to the front door. "I'll be right back. Stay." She commanded.

X'i didn't answer and replaced her jacket, and stayed on the porch while Mother went inside. When she returned, she had a large wooden basin and a white chalky sphere. She explained how to get water from the pump out back and let the soap do everything else.

"Don't take too long, or I'll have to come find you."

Hana's eyes started to flare as she spoke. X'i nodded and took her items with the promise that by the time she got back, Master should be out the shower and she'll have their bath going. X'i was excited, as it's been a long time since a spa day with Mother. Their first one was unpleasant, but X'i came around to knowing that she was simply unappreciative of Mother's kindness. They went to a real spa in Torina, but it didn't feel the same being touched and massaged by complete strangers. It felt uncomfortable. It felt wrong. Walking around the back of the house, X'i was already mentally picking out which oil and soaps she wanted to try, causing her to happily pick up the pace.

Rac' sometimes wished he could look himself in the mirror again. Not because he necessarily missed his own reflection, but it made remembering his mother easier. He and Hana were always told just how much they were splitting images of her growing up, even if it meant they also shared *His* temper. Since he came home the first time after the War, he found it harder and harder to remember what Mama looked like, let alone himself. He partially envied X'i for at least still being able to see a faded remnant of herself, knowing it was only a matter of short time. Hopefully, she takes it as well as Hana seemed to; finding the state of non-reflection and no longer having to worry about how her make-up was set freeing. Hana never really needed make-up, but he thought about how she used to play in Mama's when she was a little girl. She would pat and smear until her face was more of a canvas hosting a moving abstract painting. Mama would get upset but she never let it out on her, choosing to laugh it off and lightly tease Hana until she decided to wash it off. *He* didn't find such things as funny and made sure she knew it. She needed to learn that a person's property was *their* property.

Looking into the blank, he went to the bedroom window and continued to dry himself off until he felt another's presence. He turned around and saw X'i, unsure of when she came in since he didn't hear the door open. Without a word she took his towel and resumed where he left off slowly and thoroughly.

"Mother said to check on you." She said to him quietly, not looking at him directly. She continued to pat at his upper body before dropping to her knees and working on his legs. When she got to his thighs, she lingered before using a non-clothed hand to touch him, not breaking her towel rhythm. She would switch hands when she switched legs.

"You don't have to do that."

"Mother told me to." She continued to work his legs single-handed. Her other hand wasn't feeling a reaction, so she tried with her mouth.

"And I'm telling you that you don't. Thank you, X'i, but please leave me alone right now." He backed against the dresser, pulling her off by the hair and taking his towel back.

"Did I do something wrong?" She looked up to him. "Should I hit you first?"

Rac' looked her in the eyes. He didn't see any fire and observed their true color. They were more indigo than true-blue, with a hint of light brown. He hadn't seen a *Vi'nnakan* with those eyes before. Even her left eye had a faint tinge of blue to it. She was still beautiful in spite of the faded cuts and...and that eye. He almost felt bad for her earlier treatment.

"No, X'i. I'm- I'm just not in the mood, that's all. I'm a little tired." He wrapped the towel around himself and used his thumb to smear away a splotch of blood from her mouth.

"Get ready for your bath. I'll see you after."

X'i got up and crossed her hands. Looking down to the floor, she lowly responded, "Yes, Master." and walked out, returning to the bathroom. She found an already soaking Mother pouring the contents of a dark red vial into the running water while a pungent but sweet aroma filled the bathroom. The darkness of the red liquid gave the water a thicker appearance. The vial that contained it sounded heavy from the way it clinked against the tile.

"Get in while it's still warm." Hana adjusted from her slouch to make room. X'i had a flash of her first cleaning; how Mother put her underwater. How she thought she was going to die. How she hoped she did. Surely, Mother wouldn't do it again this time, her hair wasn't as dirty this time. No, Mother wouldn't do that this time. She trusted Mother, just as she did that first time. She trusted her with everything.

"Yes, Mother." X'i responded as she undressed. She paused before lowering her underwear, "Can we try the mint shampoo this time?" and proceeded.

"We can't if you don't get in. Now come on."

"Yes, Mother." X'i did as she was told and entered the tub. Mother was right, the water was still warm. It was perfect. She settled in.

"So X'i? How was breakfast?" Hana asked as she worked a soap bar into a lather.

CHAPTER 21

It was dusk when Flip and Elena got back to the Cabana. Their time at the range wasn't as exciting as he had hoped and after a quick call to Sata he found out why; pyrounds only did their intended effect when they interacted with organic material, and they weren't given to him to be wasted on target practice. From what she knew of, he was a good shot already. They spent the rest of the day making good on Flip's word of going shopping and doing their best to blend in with the Redwater commoners. When they got to their floor, Flip was the first of them to notice the tall woman, fully clad in an almost too black longcoat, standing in the hallway near their room. Telling Elena to keep casual, he moved his hand to the thin pulse on his thigh and unhooked his holster.

"Flip, who is that woman?" Elena whispered as they walked down the hall.

"I don't know, but she doesn't work here." Flip had Birdie in-hand within his kilt pocket, keeping his breathing calm in contrast with the siren going off in his head and his hand. The woman looked familiar in a passerby kind of way. Walking up to the woman slowly, he saw that she was still looking straight ahead and easily had at least 30lbs on him. Now he remembered; she was at Sata's compound, but he never spoke to her and Sata never made introduction. She was also the woman staring him down from their visit to Ronnie's shop. Being eye-to-eye with this woman, he couldn't understand how she addressed them so timely. The opaqueness of her eyes made her pupils appear non-existent, as if she never had any to begin with.

"Good evening, Founder Stockton, Matriarch Starks. Her Highness is waiting for you." The woman said to them as she looked forward. Flip heard the formality in her voice and realized this was also the same woman he spoke to on the phone the other night. She looked much older than him, but somehow younger than Ronnie. He wondered how many "rotations" she's been through already. Her head tipped down to his pocketed hand. "I mean you no harm, Founder." After showing she was unarmed save for a sheathed shortblade within her coat, she opened their room door and let them inside. Flip expected her to follow, but saw that when the door closed, she wasn't behind them. When he turned back, he found Sata sitting at their kitchen table, enjoying a glass of wine. Two glasses sat in front of other empty chairs along with a small black case in the middle of the table.

"Good evening. I hope you don't mind I let myself in. Well, Te'rfreir let me, but she didn't damage the lock." She took a sip of wine. "Her hands are much more adept than her stature implies." Sata briefly smiled before continuing. "Are you familiar with a settlement by the name of Pase?"

"I am. Guess you heard about the car already?" Flip saw the flash across Sata's face as he and Elena sat down. She didn't expect for him to already know. Apparently, his laid-back demeanor betrayed the assumption of his work ethic. She was pleased to learn this.

"Bloodwine, Ms. Starks?" Sata tipped the bottle towards Elena. She poured a glass for Flip without similar preface.

"I'll pass this time. Thank you, though." Elena held up a hand and watched as Sata poured a taste's worth of wine into her glass anyway.

"Do not be intimidated by the name, Ms. Starks. It's

mostly an old family recipe based on a dessert wine in my kind's royal culture. Fermented cherryroot with a few spices, and an important secret ingredient." Sata poured into her half-empty glass.

"Do you mind if I ask what that ingredient is?" Elena rose her glass to her nose and felt it tingle. She calmly circled her glass before taking a sip. It was a bit too sweet but thinner than she expected based on the dense color. It also went down almost too smoothly. Not as bad as Flip made it out. Sata watched and poured Elena a full glass.

"I do." Sata took a sip. "You and your fellow Founder are an inquisitive couple."

"What's with the trip, Sata?" Flip asked. He looked her in the eyes and felt like he was being pulled but staying in place at the same time. He noticed the sensation during his meeting at the compound the first time he consciously looked at her eyes and was met with low glowing embers. He saw those same embers now. Birdie's frequency was growing.

"Since you already know about the car, let's play a game. You tell me what you think, and I'll tell you if I agree?" The embers in her eyes grew slightly. Flip gingerly took a sip before he spoke. It was still shit wine to him.

"The Tabine's aren't dead, and they're either staying relatively close or coming back to Monarch. If they're not already back. From what I've heard, the car's been burnt for a while now."

"Interesting theory. Ms. Starks, would you agree?"

"I don't know where or how, but I do believe they're alive. Alexis too."

"Ms. Starks, I hear the optimism in your voice, but it is misguided."

Elena didn't say anything in response. Deep down, she knew that Sata was being bluntly realistic; Alexis may be alive, but she was no longer human. Cheryl Shockley was changed after a chance encounter with Hana, let alone what 16 months of being held by her and her brother would turn someone into. The three of them continued to talk about what to do next; Sata reiterating that though she could and would never place a monetary bounty on any of her people, her Children, as she called them, she swore on her proper title that not only will Flip have the gratitude of The Father's Council, she would personally thank him with something much better than a Star and ceremony if the Tabine's and their Thrall were neutralized. Elena cut her eyes at Sata's tone and looked to Flip, finding him unfazed.

Flip sat back in his chair when Sata was finished with her promise. He wasn't sure what was this Council was, but he imagined that having a good word put in for him could be beneficial down the line. It never hurt to have someone, or multiple, owe him a favor or two. Every time he locked with Sata's eyes, the pulling sensation took over and he felt light. He declined an offered second glass of Bloodwine and got his smoking kit, propping open the door to the balcony on his way back. He rolled and proceeded to light up, getting it started before passing to Elena. She took a hit and instinctively offered it to Sata. By the time she declined, saying that the scent was more than pleasant enough, Te'rfrejr was already inside and locking the door before walking over.

"Your Highness?" There was something in her voice. It was a mix of concern and... fear? "Is everything ok?"

"Yes, Te'rfrejr, we're ok. Why don't you come take a break? I believe we're finished with business." She looked at both Flip and Elena. "Do we have an understanding,

Founder?" They both nodded, not sure who she was addressing.

"Thank you, Your Highness." Te'rfrejr responded and went over to the couch and started to "watch" tv after an initial fumble with the remote and a quick scan of the channels. Settling on a reality show, she lowered the volume to two counts above a whisper, crossed her leg and looked forward. After a few seconds, Flip heard a quiet laugh and looked over. *Are you fucking serious?*

"Mr. Stokton, this is Te'rfrejr. She was my mother's *ha'kiet* and has served my family faithfully. I like her a lot." Flip and Elena noticed a slur in Sata's voice and began to wonder if her informal assessment was from a personal or professional lens. "When my mother was collateral damage to a power struggle within the Council, Te'rfrejr was the one to comfort me and serve me as she did my mother. She's seen me through a lot, even helped at times, but she doesn't judge me or my actions." Her voice took a less somber tone when she called out. "Isn't that right, Terfie?"

"Yes, Your Highness." Te'rfrejr kept her head forward.

"She prefers to act as though she doesn't like 'Terfie', but I know she does." Sata had lowered her voice. "Watch." She raised it back to original volume. "Isn't that right, Terfie?"

"I am blind, Your Highness, not deaf." Te'rfrejr kept her head facing the TV.

"Love you, too." Sata smiled and looked back at the couple. "See how she didn't say no." This got a silent chuckle out of everyone at the table. Te'rfreje laughed too, but that could've been from the show. Flip wondered how she imagined what the show's cast looked like based on their voices.

"Your Highness, what's in the case?" Elena tapped the small rectangle on the table, acknowledging the tiniest elephant in a room if there ever has been.

"Matriarch, it's our first meeting, but please, Sata is fine enough. And It's more pyrounds. Mr. Stokton, you now understand how they are to be implemented, correct?"

"Yeah, organic material only."

"Good. I have faith in you. A good ruler must have faith in their *ha'kiet*."

"*Ha'kiet*? I'm not familiar with the term." Elena said to her.

"I wouldn't expect you to, Ms. Starks. Old vampyric 'lingo', as they say. It is a title only bestowed by royalty to those in the closest of their trust or employ. Considering the nature of your relationship, I would say it's appropriate to extend that title to you too in time, but we will see. Would you like to make an exchange?" Elena saw a faint glow in Sata's eyes. The hazel color now appearing a bold and heavy red. Like fresh blood.

"Exchange?" Elena questioned.

"More of a favor, actually. Could I get an autograph? I'm something of a collector." Elena saw Sata's fangs as she smiled and how she played her tongue along them. The red in her eyes glowed as if softly breathing. She could've swore she was looking at two small fires.

"That's it?" Elena asked for a pen before Sata took her by the hand and held it in her own, tracing tenderly from palm to pointer finger.

"Ms. Starks, for such a beautiful and intelligent woman, you share the same naivety as your beloved. I can forgive you for that. Te'rfrejr, bring me a notepad, please."

"Yes, Your Highness."

Flip didn't hear when Te'rfrejr rose from her seat, but she tracked down the complimentary hotel stationary pad and had it on the table before he could raise objection.

Right before midnight, Sata decided the vacationing couple should enjoy their last night in Redwater alone, despite her too keen an interest in what they had planned. Te'rfrejr apologized for her Queen's inappropriate line of questioning. She can be a little invasive after a bottle or two of Bloodwine. Elena laughed it off and exchanged cheek-kisses with Sata, making the half-promise that she and Flip would come visit the compound outside of "business". Flip rolled his eyes but hunched down to also exchange kisses. Sata promised to call if there were any developments in Monarch but cautioned that if the Tabine's did come back home, they'll get hungry eventually. She drunkenly giggled to herself as Te'rfrejr escorted her out of the suite and bid the couple a good night. When he was sure that they both were gone, Flip let out a sigh and took Birdie out of his pocket, placing it on the kitchen table.

"Your girlfriend seems nice. Think 'Terfie' is gonna mind you being around her." Elena finally said to break the silence.

"I don't know. She seemed to have taken a liking to you, too." Flip responded.

"You ever act up on me, I might let her." Elena stuck her tongue at him, and they shared a laugh. "We're still checking out tomorrow?"

"Unless you wanted to stay longer. Check this out, I texted Penny to check on her, she texts back saying she

491

beat up that purse snatcher she's been working on. Caught him in the act tryna rob a lady at an outdoor market in the First." Flip scoffed and shook his head. "She's somehow been enjoying working with Holmb, but I don't know about having her work whatever this one is going to turn into. I know she'll want to, but I can't risk her getting hurt again."

Elena nodded her head. She thought back to what was supposed to be a low-level case Flip and Penny had worked soon after his Day of Honor to find a dealer selling laced Rock; with a lot of the most recent victims being teenagers. Flip let her take the lead on most of the investigative route while he used his Sight to help keep her in the right direction. One night he got a text from Penny saying she found out where the dealer was hiding out and that he was "much smaller than she thought he'd be." Despite warning to wait for him to meet her, Penny was radio silent for more than 30 minutes. By the time he arrived with Holmb, Penny was waiting outside the stash house with the suspect on his back with a broken leg and two of his guys tied together. The whole thing (now laughable in hindsight) looked like it was pulled right out of a comic book panel. Only when Penny winced as she was waving them over did he realize that she was actually hurt. Flip was upset at her going solo like she did, but he couldn't help but admire the courage and the look on her face as she waved. She didn't look scared. She didn't even look hurt until she started waving. Elena remembered seeing her face when she visited her the next day in the hospital; damn proud for what she did. Penny was treated for two cracked ribs and the story made its rounds throughout the First District (with more embellishment the more it circulated the other Districts) and gained Penny something of a superhero mythos around the First.

"I know, Love, but she ain't a kid." Elena brought him

over to the bed and sat him down. "Besides, you could use a good teammate like her. She can prolly kick the shit outta that Hana."

Flip laughed loudly and pulled Elena over to him and into a straddle, "Yeah, maybe. I'm interested to see this Rac' though. I remember Ronnie saying he served in the military. He might be the real one to need a good kickin'."

Elena took her shirt off before leaning down to kiss him. "Mmm, maybe. But can we talk about that later and figure out what we gonna do tonight? It *is* our last night."

"What you tryna do, Matriarch?" Flip held her by the waist, caressing the pleasant curve of her hips.

"Something that's out of the room. Isn't that lounge-club on the 5th floor 24 hours?"

"I think so. Hang out and people-watch?"

"Meet me in the shower first?" Elena went to kiss his neck, biting it lightly.

"Yes, ma'am."

Flip let her get up after another kiss. When he heard the shower running, he took his time undressing and checked his communicator. Since his meeting with Hana, he grew to the habit of checking it more often, just in case she wanted to send any more messages. He kept the app she used on his phone but hadn't heard anything since the message she sent before telling him they were leaving town. Weirdly, he almost hoped she would send him something soon, if only to know whether Alexis was still alive. Seeing nothing important, he went for the bathroom.

Saturday

There was a dark cloud-cover at 11 in the morning. The rain hadn't come down just yet, but it was fast approaching. Flip casually shook his head when asked by the receptionist about any unpleasant experiences during his stay. The week away by Fountain was fun and exactly what they both very much needed. Flip texted Penny to let her know that they'd be at Mesa in a few hours and to meet him there after her debrief with CaP. She texted back with a smiley Emotisign. She sent another long message: she saw a woman earlier that morning leaving Ruby's Diner while she was driving back from Dom's into Fountain. She didn't get a good look at her but driving by, she looked familiar. By the time Penny turned around, the lady and the car she entered was already gone. Flip told her they'll talk about it when he got back but to write down everything she remembered. Penny already talked to Sandra. She didn't know who she was, and the name was a single letter: Z. The woman was pretty and smelled nice but had a bad eye and a few facial scars. Sandra said something was off about her, though. Z kept looking behind her a few times as she paid and waited. She picked up three call-in orders. Flip said they'll definitely talk when he's back. He'll let her know when he was close. He relayed the story to Elena.

"Think it's her, don't you?" She asked him when they were in the car.

"It might be."

Elena shifted into drive and pulled out from the Redwater Cabana. Word being kept, Flip made good and left the valet a sizable tip. He was quite appreciative and invited the couple for a return visit soon. Once on the road, she tried to restart conversation.

"So, what now?"

"Maybe try and find where she's staying, and with who. Orders for three? At least two other people she's with?"

"What if it's not the two you think?"

Flip looked over to her. "Meaning?"

"You know what I mean, Investigator." Her voice took a formal tone. "A lot can happen in 16 months." Elena shook her head and shrugged. "I don't know, I'm just guessing. Technically, y'all were only looking for Hana. She may have left them behind so her brother could come back home." Elena merged onto the highway. "Would it change anything if Alexis was a mother now?"

Flip took a few seconds, "Nah." There was a calm in his voice. "If Sata's right about her, she ain't like us anymore. Cheryl was ready to go after a couple days. Rac' is still fair game, too. Ain't nobody say he was cleared of suspicion."

Elena turned her head slightly at his last statement. A lot can happen in 16 months, and with Flip, when he was back, something came back with him. He was quieter. Not callous, but more distant and objective, when it came to work now. And life. Killing Cheryl Shockley affected him to a level in a way that she felt she was still peeling the layers to. He wore Birdie on him pretty much everywhere he went, even keeping it under his pillow sometimes when he would stay over. Their week in Redwater was the first in a while that she didn't notice him looking over her shoulder, or his. Then again, he didn't wear his sunshades that much this week. Letting him explain it, Birdie was like a metal detector. He claimed he felt it jump the night Patriik brought it to her house, but since her Blessing, it would react in the presence of vampyr, only changing in frequency based on its own barometer of threat. She didn't understand it, and it never "jumped" when she would hold it, but trusted Flip's words and judgement. He was in right enough mind to not do anything inexplicable, and according to comparison of Fleice, he still had plenty of good time before they needed to have serious talks. She went back to the road and continued on, rubbing an itch on her right pointer finger against the steering wheel.

Hana took in the smell of the cellar. Even with the door open and a thorough cleaning, there was still the smell of blood that wafted around the first floor of the Tabine house. Rac' played her in a game of Catch the Fox with X'i to settle who would clean and who would bury. Same as they were children and played with Mama, Rac' won; and as he did in childhood, he chose the less tedious task. Hana swore X'i was in cahoots with him and let him catch her, but it was fine. She did quite a number on Shuun, or whoever the limp husk she found at the obelisk's base was. Hana couldn't tell which IDs were the originals, but was convinced that "Shuun" and "N'icol" was not their given names. She could see X'i took pleasure in her meal, as a good pet should. As she finished cleaning and brought the mop and bucket upstairs, there was a loud knock at the door. Nobody knew they were back. Right?

KNOCK!

KNOCK!

KNOCK!

X'i came running down the stairs by the same time Hana got to the door. She gestured to stay and opened it just enough. She was surprised to see Ron Klima standing on the front porch.

"Oh! Hey, Hana. I saw the car in your drive and wasn't

sure if someone new had moved in." He saw a chilling stoic on Hana's face. She looked like she was sizing him up. "New car?"

"Sort of, Mr. Klima. Rac' and I have been on a long holiday, and we just got back, I thought he had mentioned it to you." Hana stepped out onto the porch, "The car was a birthday gift." and closed the door behind her. "Can I help you with anything? We're actually doing some housework right now. I think something got into the cellar and died while we were away."

Ronnie sucked his teeth, "Shit, sorry about that. Nah, I didn't need anything. Like I said, I saw the new car on the way back into City. Guess y'all been saving your scril. V'ago's ain't cheap, last I heard." before he looked at Hana's clothes. There were a couple splotches of blood on her gown.

"You could say we got a really good deal on it. Mother and father's money has been still working for us, so the cost wasn't a big deal. I'm not a particular fan of white cars, but Rac' really liked it." She held a hand to the side of her mouth as if anyone else was watching and lowered her voice. "I wanna repaint it, between you and me." Hana smirked as she took a step closer. "Would you like to come in? I can get Rac' if you wanted to talk to him."

Ronnie kept his ground but now caught a whiff of Hana. Under the cleaning solution was the same smell from his slaughterhouse. It smelled too fresh for her to just find a dead critter. It was way too much blood, too. "Nah that's fine, I won't break your flow. Tell him to swing by the shop if he wants me to cash his last check, but I gotta redo his paperwork if he wants to come back to work." He turned for his truck. "Good seeing you, Hana. Don't forget to tell Rac' I stopped by."

"Will do, Mr. Klima. Have a good day."

Ronnie didn't say anything back but felt like Hana was watching him the entire walk to his truck. When he got in, he looked over to wave again and backed out of the driveway. She watched as he drove away and stayed on the porch for another 20 minutes. 15 minutes into her wait, she saw a second car coming down the road. Maybe it was coincidence, but what were the chances? It felt convenient, almost too much so. She didn't buy the was just stopping just because he saw a new car. In Rac's entire time of working at Klima's, she could count on a single hand how many times him and his wife have been to their house. She went back inside and found X'i standing so close to the door she almost walked into her.

"Being nosey, are we?" She started rubbing her right hand. Being taller than Hana, it was funny to see X'i shrink back.

"No- No, Mother, I promise."

"Mmhmm. Will you get my brother and tell him to meet me in the kitchen?"

"Yes."

"Good girl." Hana moved from the door and waved her hand, sending X'i on her way. A few minutes later, she was in the kitchen waiting for the tea water to boil. When she poured herself a cup, Rac' walked in, dirty, sweaty, and shivering. She poured him a cup and let him take a few sips of his own. Her stare told X'i to get lost.

"Your boss came by." Hana moved her cup aside. "Did you tell him we were back?"

"No. Why didn't you get me?" Rac's face change was subtle. Why was Mr. Klima coming by their house?

"Because I wanted to see your face. You wouldn't lie to your big sister, would you?" She reached across the island and placed her hands around his, claws first. Rac' didn't move.

"Hana, cut the shit." His eyes ignited and he demanded she let him go. He was telling the truth. She let him go and began kissing the tops of each hand.

"I know you wouldn't do something like that. I trust you."

Rac' slowly pulled his hands back with his mug and sipped from it. Hana explained the other car she saw soon after Mr. Klima and how it didn't sit well with her. To Rac', it reminded him of when he would have a soldier or two serve as a distraction and divert the enemies' attention while he and the rest moved into striking position. Mr. Klima may have been an innocent visit, but whoever was in that second car was supposed to be seen. Then again, why would Mr. Klima still have a check ready to be cashed after so long? It's less than two days since they've been back, but the Queen always had ways to know when her Children were home. Whoever Hana didn't see was who they needed to worry about. If she's learned that they're back, Mr. Klima won't be the only visitor they should expect. They managed to leave once without Questioning; he was sure they couldn't do it a second time so cleanly. Then there was the situation with that Investigator. He wasn't positive Ron and he were related, but they must be good enough friends for Mr. Klima to have his picture on the wall *and* close shop early the same day he and a Fountain Matriarch came to town. If they were as close as Rac' thought, the Investigator would know about their new car pretty soon. If he was better than Rac' thought, he already did.

"Interesting." Hana took a sip of her tea. She finished it in silence and poured another cup. "Please be careful if you go into town, little brother. Her Eyes are sure to be everywhere."

After a long recap of their respective weeks, Penny left Mesa to go home. A few hours after, Sata called with info about the Tabine's new car. A white Torina V'ago. She also relayed that they were back and staying at their familial home. He didn't care to ask how she found out, figuring she wouldn't tell him anyway. When he ended the call, he texted Penny and let her know they can focus back on Monarch, he had info the twins were back. Penny sent a thumbs-up and left it at that; she was probably with Dom, or Domoni'c, or whatever his name was. He still didn't know much about this Dom, nor had he still met him, but he was happy that she was still with him. He seemed like a good guy from what Penny said of him. Then again, he was sure that Elena had been telling her teammates that he was a good guy, even in their worst of periods when photos of him with other women made it to the public. He remembers telling his teammates the same about her. He promised Penny that the next time they go out socially she can bring Dom. In fact, since they agreed to meet again later in the evening, she can bring him over for dinner. Flip took the no response as a positive, sure they both saw the invitation.

Flip studied the Map of Aligned Territories spread on his desk. It was already full of circles and connecting lines of multiple colors in places like Fountain and Monarch but as of today had larger ones around Torina and Pase with notes about the most recent developments. He needed to get them before they got another idea to leave town again because they may not come back. While he looked over his map and his notes, a call came in. Flip answered it on speaker.

"Hello?"

"Hey, you busy?"

"Nah man, what's up?"

"Rac' and his sister are back in Monarch. I only spoke to Hana but Rac' was with her at the house. Said they were doing 'housework'." Ronnie took a pause and lowered his voice some. "She had blood on her clothes."

Flip thought back to the car in Pase. "How long they been in town?"

"Couldn't tell you for sure, we were on the porch and she closed the door pretty soon into the conversation, but Queen Sata came to me late last night and asked I stop over there."

Why was she approaching Ronnie about this?

Flip shook his head, "What'd she say to you?" He didn't like the fact that Sata had Ronnie involved.

"Something about sensing their presence, or some shit like that. She thought that since I knew Rac' personally, it might not raise too many alarms if I went by the house."

"Did it?"

"Don't think so, man, but I don't know. Shit, I can barely keep surprises from Hol before she starts acting weird."

"Did she ask you to do anything else?"

"Nah, man, just stop by the house to see if they were there. Nothing else. Rac' might stop by the shop at some point though."

"Why?" Flip's voice grew interrogative.

"Initially, it was a throwaway invite until I got a whiff of Hana. Girl smelled like she just came out the damn killhouse, but they ain't got livestock out there. By then, I didn't want to risk changing anything up." Ronnie sounded away from the phone again before coming back. "Hey, Flip, I gotta go. It's been a little busy today."

"Aight man, let me know if either of them calls or come by."

Ronnie hung up without response. He wondered if the idea to have Rac' come by was really a throwaway or a plan set by Sata. With all that *ha'kiet* talk, he always felt like something was always left out whenever they talked. He wouldn't have been surprised if she knew since her visit that Hana and Rac' were back but spent the time to come up with something. Ronnie wasn't a lottery selection, but he had to trust that she wasn't simply using him as bait. Resisting the urge to immediately call Sata and know exactly what the fuck she was trying to pull, he opted for something more pleasant.

"Where are you?" Elena's voice sounded urgent.

"Home, why?"

"Hol just texted me saying she saw Rac' driving by their shop. He had a different car, but she knows it was him. There was a woman in the passenger seat, but it wasn't his sister."

"Ok, ok, calm down. I literally just talked to Ronnie. Sata had him stop by their house earlier and he told Hana to tell him to come down there. Did Hol say anything else? Was there anyone there with them?"

"A few employees, but a couple of something called 'Queen's Eyes', were in regular clothes to blend as customers.

She thinks that's why he didn't stop and come in."

"Ok. Tell her to call if Rac' tries to come back. I'll call you back soon."

"Ok. Should they be worried?"

"I don't know. I'll call you back."

"Ok."

Flip gave in and called Sata. Her orders to Ronnie were that he simply go to the Tabine house and confirm her feeling that the siblings were back in Monarch. Yes, she had her people in place, but there was no talk of inviting the Tabines to his place of business and she resented the implication that she would be held squarely responsible if anything happened to him. Ronnie was a warm-body in Monarch, but aside from the shared humanity, she was curious why he was so defensive of a brother that until a little over a year ago he didn't seem fond of, considering he had never set foot in Monarch since his cancelled baskets game just under a decade ago. Flip felt like she kneed him in the groin.

"When'd you find out?"

"What makes you think I never knew?" Sata's voice turned from its usual quasi-flirtatious to something he hadn't heard from her before, legit anger. "Your brother has been living among us for a few years now, something I personally approved solely because of his wife being a True Child. Besides, what difference does it make? Understand that you are a Founder of Fountain, Mr. Stokton, not of Monarch. I have the right and duty to know what I need to about those in my domain, and when I saw that your father was his broker, I couldn't afford to be ignorant of why a Fountain Patriarch was conducting business here. My family has been Monarch's leader since before your family line was started, seen settlements take months, if not years to flourish but only mere weeks to dissolve and be forgotten to time. I wouldn't task a new money warm-body as yourself to fully understand my level of control, but do expect for you to fully appreciate." Her voice was raising by this point. "It was my family that helped your Territory rise from the ashes of what it was before The Great War. I was there to celebrate the establishment of the Seven Clans, specifically to see who the *Vi'nnakan* were that were being allowed to hold such prominent positions. Your brother is in no less of my protection as he would in his native land, and *I WILL NOT* let you insult my ability to do so!"

There was a silence over the line before Flip heard an exhale and words in a language he didn't understand. By the sound of the veracity, he was sure they were curses. "Mr. Stokton?" The anger had dissipated as soon as it came on. "Flip?" Now, her voice went soft. "Flip, are you still there?"

"Yeah."

"First, I would like to apologize for my outburst. My feeding schedule has been off today, and, in my age that can make one dangerously short-tempered. Second, Te'rfrejr will personally watch over your brother for 24 hours. After that, I will ensure someone is always near him and his wife as we determine the threat. You are still free to address the Tabines should your hunt bring you here. It hurts my heart, as I tend to remember them as the result of an abhorrent and long-dead practice in our culture, but it was not their fault. Should they be felled, I do pray that they find peace in The Father's embrace." There was a sniffle over the line. And then another. No matter their faults, Sata had a soft spot for her citizens. Even the Untrue. Especially the Untrue. "Flip, I've explained what I can and will not do, but in case I was not clear before: should you see them," Sata voice cracked, "by my order, Queen Sata the Third, Ruler of the Sovereign Territory of Monarch, you may execute them on-sight." Her voice returned to a steady track. "That is all, and again, I'm very sorry about my previous language. It is no way to speak to a *ha'kiet*, or Founder. I am sorry for my disrespect." Flip heard the softness return. "When this is over, I would like to invite you to the compound, so I can properly show my gratitude."

"We'll see. I know we're not close, Sata, but he's still my brother."

"Flip, I am very familiar with mixed feelings towards siblings. I've had to put down two of my own when I inherited the throne. It was not a pleasant decision and still weighs on me today, but at the time, it was a 'necessary evil', as your people tend to say. I only say it was necessary, to ensure the honor and continuance of our family." Sata spoke with a faraway tone. "I loved them dearly, and it is one of the few regrets in my life thus far."

There was another silence before Sata had to break away for "supper". Flip agreed to contact her when he intends to travel into Monarch. Sata returned the courtesy, saying she'll let him know if they decide the threat to his brother was imminent and required in-kind action. For now, let her worry about Monarch and its safety and he on the siblings. Then she was gone, with what sounded like the start of a woman's scream abruptly cut short by the *click* of a landline. Flip needed to get a plan together for when Penny came back that evening. After a short text exchange with Elena, he went back to his desk and started working after a loud string of his own curses.

Domoni'c looked like a good match for Penny, and it was as entertaining as it was heartwarming to see them interact with each other. He was quiet in the beginning of dinner, but once he realized that Flip should be seen as more like a second brother to Penny than her boss, he relaxed and opened up. It was funny to see how he was clearly the silent and observant type, letting Penny tell Flip more about his job as a risk analyst than he did, only pitching in to clarify the finer details that she blurred in her explanation. There was also an interesting tic had when he got enthusiastic in discussion: he would tap the table in double beats every so often as he spoke. He had a good sense of humor, albeit dryer than most would consider tolerable. The one thing he did seem to take great pride in were the Sonicaides he brought Penny a few months after his promotion to Senior Analyst. They were by some designer tech company that operated out of a small valley settlement in the midwestern Dal Territory. Penny wore them to dinner but was clearly not used to them and how clear they picked up sound, evident by the occasional jumps when someone talked or laughed too loud.

They seemed to really like each other, though it was still way too early to assume anything like an engagement was approaching soon. Flip made an aside to Dom that if he was looking that far ahead, 7000-scril aids can jump him ahead a few steps. He wasn't sure how Penny felt about the concept of marriage but was sure he would the longer her and Dom stayed together. Something told him that Dom wasn't the type to mess around for too long, nor the type to try taking advantage. Keeping his side of this meeting mostly dry, Flip focused his Sight and flashed that Dom liked to play around with overseas stocks. He was going to take a bad beat, thanks to that outbreak in Torina, but it wasn't anything that jumped out to Flip as a sign of bigger problems.

By the time Elena arrived in time for dessert, she found the dinner party in a fun debate over which *Nite*

Owl storyline would translate into the better movie. She wasn't into the comics as much as Flip or Penny was but knew enough to hold her own in conversation. Flip stood strong in his offer of when Owl gave up the mantle for a few issues due to a botched hostage rescue that turned out to be a setup. Dom countered that it clearly would be how his gained his first, and honestly the best villain in his rogue's gallery, Caretaker. Penny found herself in the middle giving points for each storyline but contributed her personal favorite: when Nite Owl had been brainwashed into thinking that his second sidekick, Fro'st and the other Owls were all sleeper agents of The Nine Families. It also revealed that his civilian-life frenemy and off-and-on love interest, Isa Hall, was the mysterious villain Clock Stopper. Both men completely forgot about how crazy that arc got, especially in issue six when the panel perspectives would change between what Nite Owl thought he was seeing and what was actually happening. In the end, it came down to Elena giving the tiebreaker, where she safely agreed that all three were better than the bullshit film made solely to soft launch the even worse animated show when they were kids. Being a few years younger than everyone else, Dom was luckily less familiar with the show due to a childhood rule regarding TV, but he knew enough from the reruns he used to catch on the weekend mornings.

After a bit more entertainment discussion, Flip excused himself and Penny to go to his "office" and talk business. Penny gave Dom a peck on the cheek and even waved as they walked the 15 feet to the workspace. Elena couldn't help but chuckle at the affection and how cute it looked. As the Investigators talked, she reintroduced herself and caught up on what she missed from dinner.

"Penny, I may have asked before, but you ever been to

Monarch?" Flip asked as he uncovered the desk with his map and diagram with notes.

Penny shook her head and signed, *"Not since I was little, but I couldn't tell you why. The people are funny there."* She held her open hand palm-down and shook it.

Flip scoffed and nodded, "Yeah, they're pretty funny. Well, the Tabine's are back home."

The mean lady and her brother?

"Yeah. They've hurt more people but seem to be laying low, kind of."

Penny slammed her fist into her hand before reaching for his notebook.

Should we get them?

Flip shook his head again, "Yeah, but not yet. Sata is helping us out and keeping an eye on them."

So, what do we do?

"For now, lay low ourselves, and plan. She said to take them out on sight."

Aside from her personal interactions with Hana, who for a while she thought knew speech-magic, Penny's learned that The Mean Lady and Her Brother were something much worse, and much more dangerous. Despite this knowledge, she wasn't afraid of them, not anymore. She studied Flip's face and wrote again.

You're hiding something.

"Rac' worked for my brother at his butchery. Apparently, he drove by earlier today."

Will Queen. Sata get them?

"She can't do much beside arrest and 'Question' them, whatever that means."

Is Ms. Sata mean too? Will I get to meet her?

Flip shook his head, "No, she's not mean, but she is scary as hell. I'm sure that once we get these two, she'll want to meet my partner."

Penny's face beamed at the title "partner" and nodded. Most of the time working for Flip, she wasn't sure exactly what her official title was. When they would walk around on the street, she felt like a bodyguard, which was cool, but it wasn't what she signed on to be. In her assessment, Flip was already a smart fighter, and he just wasn't as efficient in using his height to his advantage as she would like. He was more proficient in his bladed weapon usage than she expected, however. Before accepting her position, she made him agree to being taught *Pak'fajr*, from the white rope level; never too old to start from the basics. It also meant he wouldn't need to always reach for his shooter or expect to always have a dagger on-hand. Now, thanks her aggressive training and advancement criteria, he's become a dangerous, and efficient, yellow rope over the course of a year. She promised she wasn't going to let Flip down with this case, she liked the work too much. It was waaay better than waiting tables.

They continued talking and decided that they would take the week to monitor what happens in Monarch and maybe go ask around. As if she didn't already, Flip told her to keep her mob-comm handy and to possibly have a bag packed and kept in her car should they need to leave at a moment's notice. With the logistics taken care of, Flip shifted the conversation into new territory.

"Penny, you keep any weapons on you when we go out?"

He saw a shift in demeanor in Penny's face. She

looked embarrassed, like a child finally caught doing something they grew used to doing. She got up and went back to the kitchen table to get her purse. When she returned, she dug in and pulled out two gunmetal tinted knuckle dusters. She put them on and mimed a few punches, letting Flip imagine how much he wouldn't want to be on the receiving end. They weren't as bulky as the average pair tends to be, leading him to guess they had to either be not that heavy or custom-fitted. Based on the money of the Adlouw family and how fiercely they cared for Penny, he went with the latter. His assumption was confirmed when she took them off and handed them over. He held them for a few seconds, examining them and the engraving of "Penn Adlo" spelled out across the inside in the fingerholds.

Flash

Flip was transported back to the night of Penny's one-man raid on the stashhouse. He saw the main guy they were looking for take out a knife and lunge at her before catching a swift roundhouse kick and a duster punch to the outside of his held outstretched left arm, just above the elbow. He couldn't hear the pop but the dropping of the knife and the dangle of its owner's arm let him know Penny wasn't giving out love taps. When the other two guys they found tied up entered the fray, the bigger of the two showed that he was the one to land the hit that cracked her ribs. That was the only hit that either of the two would land the entire fight before getting wrapped up. When Penny went back to for now running leader, she made quick work of his legs and got on top of him when he fell over. She started punching him in the face and chest. He held his good arm up to take a swing and looked like he was trying to say something, but she hit him again. And again. And again. The last thing he saw before coming back was the silently screaming and bloodied face of a drug dealer that realized too late who he was messing with. Then he was back in his living room.

When he saw Penny staring at him, he briskly shook his head and returned the dusters. Penny put them back in her purse before signing he Saw something, didn't he? The look of mild embarrassment turned into one similar of a child fearing of incoming punishment. She went back to the notepad.

I only keep them on me out of habit. I used to only bring them to Ruby's when I knew I'd be working late at night. Sandra said it was ok.

"I did." Flip let himself ease back into where he was. Getting better with the Sight came with the trade-off that it brought him deeper into what he was looking at. He still couldn't hear anything, but it was just as vivid. He swore he could even smell the filth of the house; feel the weight of each hit. Since he and Holmb arrived and found all three men still breathing, at least it meant that at some point Penny relented and decided to bring them outside and make a call. "I saw you beat the hell outta some wanted men. It's aight Penny, just don't ever scare me like that." He stuck out his hand in a high-five and she met it with a huge smile. Flip's always been so cool, he should've gone into movies. When they rose to rejoin the still chatting Dom and Elena, Penny gave Flip a strong hug and a quiet verbal "thank you". Flip nodded back kissed her cheek before letting her go to re-cover his desk. Seeing them up-close, the Sonciaides did look pretty slick, even with the shining dot of green light.

Sunday

"Aww, so you two had your first fight already?" Elena

rolled over and snuggled up. "Was she worse than our first time?"

"Nah, not even close." Flip watched as the summer rain slapped against the bedroom window. "We weren't in a hotel room, so she couldn't throw anything at me."

"I told you I was sorry about that." She kissed his hand. "You know I didn't mean it. And I replaced that damn vase, didn't I? Ain't like it was yours."

Flip let her kiss him again and continued looking out the window. It was a little shocking to hear how hard Sata came at him. He thought about how she would've reacted if he asked his intended next question of why she never mentioned it before. Realistically speaking, the whole exchange made him ask himself the same question. They were brothers, but it's not like Ronnie had any left-field claims to being a Patriarch, let alone HouseFather, over him. No matter his feelings toward their relationship, his brother's life may be in danger. He just trusted that Sata would keep her word. That was really all he could do right now.

"Thinking about Ronnie, ain't you?" Elena asked, noticing the length of silence.

"Yeah, kinda. I think I should call him."

"Think he knows about his new security detail?"

"I'm sure he knows about Te'rfrejr by now, she's not the tiniest of people. I don't know about how much more he'll know going after today."

"Seriously, do you trust Sata?"

Flip turned to face her, "I couldn't tell you by how much, but I trust her more than I don't."

Elena continued to hold his hand and looked to the

window. It was really coming down today.

"Alright, your turn. What's up?"

"Nothing, just watching the rain with you."

Flip turned back to the window. They watched in a mutual silence.

"Did she really say she was there when our families were made Founders?" Elena continued watching the window.

"Yep, said she was 'there to celebrate' our families being named in the Clans."

"Interesting." Elena kissed him on the cheek, "There couldn't have been that many people cheering with her for three *Vi'nnakan* to achieve such standing. I think I just might like your new girlfriend, Mr. Stokton."

"You sure you ain't jealous?"

"I'm sure. I don't mind if she looks around the store, as long as she doesn't touch anything." Elena kissed his hand again and squeezed it. "That fine with you?"

"Yes, ma'am." Flip turned to kiss her. He wondered if her tune would change had he mentioned the offer of "proper gratitude", whatever that meant.

They watched the rain, occasionally talking about a different moment from their in-house double date with Penny and Dom. Elena liked him, though was honestly surprised to see that they were still together. In hindsight, he didn't seem like the type to go to clubs any more than Penny was to long-term relationships. Now that she thought about it, she never knew about anyone Penny's been with lasting more than a few dates. Based on her telling, they all showed themselves to be after one thing, and she wasn't some First District nightgirl. Sometimes they would just stop calling; a few times Penny's had to scare them off. This Dom must be doing something right, or Penny just *really* likes him and been rewarding him quite generously for his efforts. Sonicaides that cost 7000-something scril; that's not something you buy on someone you're taking a chance on, that's a fucking investment. Flip had better take note, he might learn something.

"All you gotta do is ask, that is if your father doesn't read my mind and beat me to it."

"That's true. Think you can buy me some shoes for my birthday? There's some Lioni's I been hearing about."

"Why I gotta wait until that long? Let's get 'em now."

"Cause they won't come out until next year, smarty. You ain't getting off that easy."

"Then ask me again next year and we'll see." Flip kissed her again and found himself being pulled. Things were beginning to heat up before a call from Wallace came in.

"What's up?"

"The Valer case is back on. Got a tip that Alexis may have went to Ruby's recently."

Penny didn't say she told anyone else. She said Sandra didn't recognize the chick that came in. "Who made the tip?" Flip was sitting up in bed at this point. "Was it Sandra? Penny?"

"Nah, man. Guy requested staying anon but said he recognized her. Big time kind of dude. Wife, kids, a fucking dog, all that shit."

"Got it. Think I can talk to him?"

Elena looked over with a raised eyebrow.

"Doubt it, he was nervous enough when he came in to tell us. Said he sat on it because he couldn't say for sure that it wasn't. The hair was longer, but this girl had the same general look."

"Did he see anyone else with her? Penny said she got in a car when she left but wasn't the driver."

"Penny saw her too?"

"Yeah, but not enough to know who she was. Sandra told her about some strange chick with a cloudy eye coming in to pick up 3 orders a few days ago. We don't know if it was her, though."

Wallace stayed silent for a few beats. "We're gonna have posters go up again starting tomorrow between here and East Pike in case she shows up again. Camailla's already running hot on this."

Flip nodded, "Got it. How long we got?"

"Too early to tell. I'll hit you back."

"Gotcha."

"Be careful, man." Wallace hung up and Flip relayed the news to Elena. She was more surprised that someone felt confident enough in their recognition skills to call it in. She thought about Agent Valer and couldn't blame her. If it was her cousin sighted after a year of being considered dead in the public eye, Elena would be kicking down doors herself to make sure it wasn't bullshit. She could only picture how much of Camailla's life was derailed by the news.

Flip decided that he's sticking with his plan of to wait for Sata's assessment of the situation in Monarch. He had a gnawing feeling that despite her efforts, Ronnie was in trouble. As far as he knew, Ronnie hadn't tried to contact Rac' since he left town and seeing they were back when he went by their house. That was when it hit him; if either Rac' or Hana pieced together that they were related, that would make Ronnie the perfect target and a loose end should they try and leave, or decide to stay and take the offense. That thought branched out into all sorts of possible realities: Hana could come back into the Fifth with help and go after his parents, they could even do a little more digging and come after Elena. Whatever their plan, a couple days might be giving these siblings too much time. Flip went back to his mobile and dialed.

"Stokton residence." Thank K'd, it was Ata.

"Ata it's Flip. Where's Patriik? I need to talk to him."

"Ah, Master Flip, he's with your mother. They go into District for groceries. Your father is here, should I get him?"

"No, tell him I'll talk to him a later. As soon as Pat gets home, have him call me immediately."

"Yes, sir. Is everything ok?" Ata's voice grew concerned.

"For now, yes. I just need him to call me."

"I will tell him."

"Thanks, Ata."

Flip was rewiring his gameplan when a dark voice creeped into his head. It told him to mechanize a trap, with Ronnie as the crux. If he could take out even one of the siblings, it would dismantle the way they worked. Even from their only meeting, Flip could tell Hana was protective of her brother. They appeared to be a tight unit, meaning it'd likely throw Hana off and even make her sloppy if he was taken out unexpectedly. It didn't even sound like his own voice, it was something completely different. Was this the Sight personified? Was this what his mother heard on a daily basis? Did she listen to it? Should she? There was so much that started running around that he didn't know what to grasp at first. He continued staring at the window, watching the rain that now seemed like a cruel joke from K'd pour down in streaks. After asking Elena if she could bless Penny and her dusters, he sent a text to Penny, telling her to have that "in case" bag packed and ready if it wasn't already because they were going to Monarch sooner than they planned.

A prompt response came back: a single smiley face.

CHAPTER 22
Tuesday

X'i listened in from outside Mother's room. If it wasn't a walk-in during their time in Torina, she wouldn't have realized just how much a resemblance she had to Mama. Master beat her severely for walking in on his alone time with the portable video player and told her to sleep in Mother's connected room, alone. That night was when she actively listened to them for the first time. Up until then, X'i had only assumed that their closeness went past talk and close touching. Now, Mother's room sounded just like as it did that night in Torina, and again, X'i couldn't pull herself away from the door. She continued to listen at the door until there was an abrupt silence, followed by footsteps. X'i was halfway to the sunroom when she heard Mother whispering.

"Being nosey, again?" Hana stood in the half-open door. There was no color in her eyes, only fire. She licked away some running blood from the corner her mouth.

"No, Mother." X'i answered back.

"Look at me when I'm talking to you."

X'i turned around slowly. Mother's inside voice was as scary as it was overbearing. "No, I wasn't." She spoke up.

Hana continued looking at her with fire and there was an uncomfortableness in X'i's stomach.

"Good girl. Get us something to drink, would you? We'll be finished soon."

"Yes, Mother."

X'i couldn't hear much by the time she got to the kitchen. As she walked back up, she saw Master exiting Mother's room for the sunroom. She continued up and went to Hana's room, where she was thanked and then told to sit, Mother needed to talk to her about something important. If she wanted to stay with them, she needed to be a very good girl and do exactly as she told, her first order being to clean herself up and await Rac' in his room. He wanted to apologize for how he acted earlier. Her next direction was to never leave his bed unless he wanted her to.

By the time Penny got to Elena's house, everything was set up. Elena had her veil on with the candles lit and in place. Penny giggled when she saw the veil, having never seen this getup before, and found it a little silly but kept her thoughts to herself. She read Elena's lips as she said her prayers, both for her, Flip and finally her dusters. When she saw that Flip was taking this whole thing seriously, she respectfully bowed her head and her closed her eyes, turning on her Sonicaides. Once everything was finished, she watched as the candles were blown out and picked up her dusters, putting them on and half-expecting for something to happen. She signed asking why didn't it, and Flip simply responded that it didn't work like that. Penny disappointedly shrugged her shoulders and replaced them into her purse. The Adlouws weren't a religious family, so things like this were always a curiosity to Penny. They shared a light lunch and Flip explained why he's bumping up the timeline of going to Monarch and that she needs to be ready to leave tomorrow. Penny left after lunch, excited about her upcoming trip to hunt vampyrs. Dom was going to be so jealous.

"Flip, please don't make me regret doing this. I'm serious." Elena said to him after Penny walked out.

"I promise, you won't." He sipped from his tea.

"Can you promise you or Penny won't get hurt?"

"I can only promise I'll do my best."

Elena looked him in the eye. She trusted him with this plan mentioned yesterday, even though he wouldn't tell her in full what it was. She wondered if he even told Penny what it was, and hoped that if he didn't, he would have the decency to tell her on the way. It was fine to keep her in the dark since she wasn't going to be in Monarch with them, but Penny was his partner and needed to know, special "plans" notwithstanding. Flip finished his tea and held Elena's hand in silence. He still was trying to stomach the fact that he was putting Ronnie in the middle of him and Rac'. Talking to Patriik wasn't an absolvent of ethics but hearing a decorated former Territory Armsman commend him on the tactic helped a little, though he warned that if Rac' really was in the Dark Ops sector, the elements of stealth and surprise were his specialty. He called Ronnie to let him know he and Penny would be there first thing tomorrow and they'll work out the specifics after they arrive. For now, he needed to keep Hol'ly away from the ranch for a few days and stay armed at all times until they got there. Ronnie confirmed he would and told Flip he kept seeing the same car popping up almost everywhere he went over the weekend, but never the driver. Flip told him not to worry about it as long as it wasn't a V'ago.

"Come on." Flip took Elena by the hand and led her into the living room. He sat her on the couch and got next to her, turning on the TV and taking a joint from his shirt pocket. Elena curled into him, and they began to smoke, not feeling the need to talk, but knowing that if they didn't, they might not get a chance to again.

"Flip, I love you."

"I know you do. I love you too, Elena."

"Just come back to me still breathing, please? I can't lose you."

"I'll try, but I'm only human." Flip said back with a smile.

They smoked as the midday news played onscreen. The rain was forecasted to continue on for the next few days over the tri-territory area, with a major storm slated to hit by the weekend. Flip told himself he needed to be back before that storm came in, with at least one of the Tabine siblings taken down. Maybe he can make the assist for Sata to come and clean up the other one for "Questioning". He thought about Alexis briefly, and how he may need to have a tough talk with Agent Valer when he got back. When he realized Elena was asleep, he finished the joint and let himself doze off.

Ron Klima sat in his living room watching TV, when he thought he heard a tap against the balcony door. He hadn't slept well the past few nights, and his recent diet of mainly coffee and Stik-O-Stim wasn't helping. His last check-in with Hol confirmed she was still safe but anxious to come back and be with him; the baby was finally kicking. He heard the tapping again, but now it sounded more like a dragging against glass. It sounded close. He lowered the TV volume for a second time, forgetting it was already at zero.

T-chiiik

T-chiiik

Ti-tik-tik

Ti-tik-tik

Tik-tik

Tik-tik

It was unmistakable; someone was here. The dragging played out again and he reached for his longblade before getting up from his chair. As he got closer to the balcony door, he could see a black mass at the base. It was a woman's body, clad in a ripped longcoat with the Queen's Sigil on the shoulder. He didn't recognize her, but by the look, he'd have a hard time identifying even if he did. In the rain-cooled night air, steam emanated from the deep slices across her face and neck, visible in the balcony's overhead light. A dark pool had already began forming. When Ronnie looked up from the body, he saw a young woman standing a few feet away looking at him, face streaked in a heavy red. She was beautiful, but the way the light bounced off her left eye scared him, as did the fire that was clearly visible in her right. This had to be the young woman Hol'ly saw riding with Rac' the other day. Ronnie felt very hot and itchy all of a sudden.

"Mr. Klima?"

Ronnie turned around at the voice. It was Rac', standing before him in the dim kitchen, his face and shirt both stained heavily with red. His eyes shone in a way Ronnie recognized, but never from Rac'. He's never seen him so much as raise his voice.

"R-Rac'? Hey, man, I didn't hear you come in. What's goin' on?" Ronnie knew he had locked the front door and would've heard it open from the living room. He triple-checked it less than five minutes ago.

"Why was a Queen's Eye patrolling your home?"

Ronnie didn't know there was one. "We had a break-in at the shop recently. We asked to have a look-out there, just in case it happened again, y'know? I ain't know someone was watching the farm."

"Does that explain why you feel need to walk armed in your own house? Were you expected danger?" Rac' stayed in place as he spoke, and Ronnie looked into the fire that stared back. "Mr. Klima, I respect you greatly for what you've done for me, but a man with a pregnant wife shouldn't engage in deceit. How far along is she now?"

"Rac', I know you and your sister are still in trouble in Fountain, but the Queen *will* protect you from their courts. You're still Monarch citizens."

"So, you coming by the house was by chance, and they happened to follow you there unseen?" The following silence told Rac' everything he needed. "What's your relation to the Fountain PI that came to your shop last year? You have his picture up in the shop."

"Oh, Flip? We did some business back when he was still playing in the League. Seed investor before Hol and I moved out here, that's all."

"So, it's just business?" Rac' took a step forward.

"Y-Yeah man, you know, people with that kind of money put it all over the Aligned. He's young, but he ain't stupid." Ronnie clenched the hilt of his blade and slid his right foot back, putting a slight bend to his knee, "Rac', if you need to clear your name of anything, I'd vouch for you. I'm sure everything in Fountain was just a misunderstanding. Wrong place, wrong time, it happens to people. Flip's an important man back in Fount, he might can take the target off your backs if he knew the whole story." before raising it into a defensive stance. "You were one of my best employees, Rac'. You're still a young cat, and got a lot ahead of you. Shit, you and your sister are friends to me and Hol, but please, let me at least *try* to help you out. C'mon man."

"I appreciate your words, Mr. Klima," Rac' took a calm and deep inhale and let it out slowly. He never knew Mr. Klima to be a bladesman but wasn't surprised given his occupation. It was his stance; much more refined than should suit a backwoods butcher. This wasn't an attempt to scare. He had been taught; from the way he drew his blade to how to keep his breathing measured. Rac' couldn't even He'd been trained, and trained well. "I really do, but I don't think anything you've said has been the truth outside of not hearing me come in. I've already been in here for 15 minutes." Rac' whistled and there was a *CRASH* as X'i punched the balcony door. Ronnie moved and was able to get a deep X-strike that cut across Rac's chest before nicking the side of his face.

"*Raaaac'!!!*" X'i screamed.

Sliding past Rac', Ronnie turned around and came forward with a lunge until the woman lifted him by the throat and slammed into the kitchen floor with such force that he felt the floor tiling buckle under him. He heard the clatter of his longsword but was unable to reach; only able to frantically grasp for it. Rac' was back on his feet as X'i sent a claw flurry across Ronnie's face that made everything he saw become tinted red. She delivered two blows to his chest that sent a shattering wave through his breastplate and collarbone. A muted *POP* reverberated through Ronnie and he soon felt a painful numbness course his chest.

Rac' walked over while holding his chest. He picked up the longblade and looked it over, finding the Stokton family crest burned into the bottom of the hilt. "Great craftsmanship." He went into his pocket and tossed a photograph next to Ronnie's face. It was of him and an elementary school aged Flip in a Fifth District Academy Kiddie League basketball uniform; the only photo he had of the two together. He couldn't stay for the game, but their father said he went on to make eight points. The coach even said he was going to vouch for Flip to tryout for the pre-high school Varsity team next season. "Are you sure you and Mr. Stokton are just business partners?"

Managing only to cough out a harsh wet gasp, Ronnie didn't see who made the slash that made the floor under him hot and wet; only able to focus on the raging fire in the eyes of the young woman. For a moment, he felt like he was floating before everything funneled into darkness.

Packing his bag, Flip included more hardware than actual clothes. In between his underwear and socks were spare magazines and a box each of regular and pyround ammunition. Like a bow placed on a gift, he placed the short scope on his clothes and zipped the duffel bag closed. Before calling it a night, he called Wallace and Holmb letting them know about tomorrow. He fell onto his bed with a feeling that something wasn't right. Maybe he was jumping to get out to Monarch. Flip tossed around for a few minutes before he picked up his mobile. He stared at the screen, *3:03AM*, and opened it to call home.

"Stokton residence, this is Fleice." His mother answered as if it was the middle of the day.

"Mom? It's Flip."

"Flip? It's pretty late, everything ok?"

"Yeah, yeah, I'm ok. I might to be in Monarch for a few days after tomorrow."

"I know you didn't wake me up just to tell me that. What's wrong?"

He didn't know. It was vaguely about Ronnie, but he didn't know what it was. He wanted to know if she heard voices. Sometimes she did, but usually she didn't. The only thing she trusted was what she Saw; anyone can tell you anything. She wanted to know if he's seen anything unprompted yet. Not yet; still only when he touched stuff. That was good; meant he didn't have to worry about anything yet. She asked about the reopening of the missing Valer case and if going out to Monarch was because of it. She said something about not trusting that Queen they had. The name escaped her, but she was always the one to stonewall her with the courts. Allegedly a nice girl, but in her opinion was a conniving bitch, even when she wasn't in the room.

"You know her, Flip?" Fleice asked.

"Kinda." Flip kept his answer short and sweet. "Mom, was the guy you were trying to get a vampyr?"

Fleice went silent before answering again. "Officially, no. He was just a disgusting serial murderer. CaP'rotector Toj'kin didn't want to have the PD or Territory spooked."

"Unofficially, what do you think?"

"Based on the evidence, it was no question. Vampyrs are nothing new, Flip, but its practices are strictly prohibited in Fountain and never to be brought up in the Territories. Rumor has always been that Monarch's supposed to be some kind of home for them, or one of them, but I always took it at half-value. That Rubina Starks used to be terrified at the mention of them. I never understood why until that fucking case. The last girl we found still sticks with me. I saw it all, baby, and I think he knew we were closing on him."

Flip thought about what he was hearing. No wonder she never talked about that case or the subject of vampyrs in general. It was no wonder that nobody really did. She let him watch movies and shows with no problem, but the whole time, she knew that shit was real. He took an inhale and went for it. "Mom, I got to ask you something. It's very important, but I don't want to scare you."

"It's about my HouseMaiden, ain't it?"

!!!!!!!

"Yeah, I know about her. Had my suspicions for a few years now. Soon after she came back, I couldn't See anything off her for a while, but then I could only See stuff from her past. I'm sure by now, you've learned there's only one reason to see the past on someone. And then the girl started keeping them neck ribbons on. She ain't never done no pretty shit like that until then, so that was the first thing of interest." Fleice sounded like she took a pause to drink. "At this point, I'm convinced she is. I'm willing to bet my head on it, actually."

".... Did she tell you?"

"No, but I'm a little upset she seems to have told you. Shit, I'm the one who sees her ass every day. But no, it was that damn shooter your father got me. When the paperwork came back, I had Speaker Fau'lk bless it as I would my service weapons. After that, it would start hummin' whenever Ata was nearby, so I knew something was up. I know I'm off, but I ain't crazy enough to shoot *my own* HouseMaiden." Fleice laughed softly into the phone as she thought about when she got the call about the hospital shooting. "You used it much faster than I thought, though. Rightfully so, but still..."

"Mom, I thought I was crazy or something because it did the same thing to me. Elena blessed it the night Patriik brought it over." Flip felt a mix of relief and confusion at the news. "I didn't know what to think. I thought it was starting." He felt tears forming.

"No, no, Flip-baby, you still got time. If I'm still here

when it does, we'll just be crazy together. We ain't the first, and if you and Elena can get a move on, I'll be happy knowing we won't be the last. Unless you and that Bloss G'oh got something going I shouldn't know about?"

Flip laughed as he wiped his eyes. "Nah, we don't." He still needed to know something; why didn't she do anything about Ata if she knew?

"Baby, Ata came over here with no family and has been the best damn HouseMaiden to serve this name. Her indiscretions with your father are negligible compared to how she's making this point of my life easier to handle. Shit, girl even got me into playing fucking tennis, of all things. I couldn't ask for a better Maiden. What she is now, it doesn't change that. What happened to her wasn't her fault, and I refuse to hold it against her. That ain't right, Flip. It ain't decent."

"Does she know?"

"Hell no! She'd probably request to be Released her-damn-self, and as selfish as it sounds, I wouldn't do it. Where's she gonna go? On paper, being Released is being Released. Nobody gives a shit on the reason why."

Flip thought about the HouseMaiden before Ata. She was nice, but too shifty. Her prior experience was similar to Ata's, but during his adolescence he remembered staff asking him about things going missing. Ms. Kuemer always professed innocence, but when an heirloom *K'dsthajh* ornament was found in her Quarters, her claims were null. Fleice ordered Patriik to personally escort her off the grounds that same night and to shoot on sight if she tried to return. As far as Flip knew, she never did.

"Now, I got something for you, Investigator." Fleice had her gossipy tone. "Bet'cha don't know about her and

Patriik? Did you see them at the beach?"

Feigning surprise, Flip laughed along with his mother and spent the next half-hour talking about the little things they saw go on between their HouseMaiden and StaffMaster, including the handholding as they looked out to the waves. Flip wouldn't risk blowing her mind by telling her about Pat's part in Ata's situation; too much for one night. Then again, she might already know.

"Mom, what you mean by 'we're not the first'? I mean, was our family always like this? Was grandma like this?" Grandma Stokton was gone way before Flip came around, and aside from being a single mother, he didn't know much about the woman. Mom didn't talk about her too much.

"That's a lot to unpack, but let's just say the Seven Clans didn't let the only two most prominent *Vi'nnakan* families in out of the goodness of their hearts. Your great-grandfather was too 'knowledgeable', we'll say, of other people's affairs to *not* be seen as an asset, and that Em-June knew how to make too much money through too many ways. You close this case for good and I'll see what I got around here that ain't in the library, deal? I been meaning to find those old photobooks Ma left us. I'm sure there's enough photos of her from her better days."

"It's a deal." Flip wiped his eyes again.

"Don't forget to hold me to it. Give 'em hell, Flip-baby. I love you."

"I always do. Love you too, mom."

Flip went to bed much calmer and more receptive to his pillow. The voice was below a whisper but restless, still saying Ronnie's name. Either he got too tired or the Voice did, because just before dawn, Flip found himself enter the neutral of sleep.

◆ ◆ ◆

Wednesday

Forecasting must be a sweet gig; make a guesstimate about a phenomenon like the weather and if it's right, the reporter is hailed. If it's wrong, people might be upset but will ultimately brush it off and adjust. It's likely one of the few jobs that never gets hate-mail. The storm slated to come by the weekend showed up almost three days early. Flip didn't know how long he slept but it was deep. There was a thundercrack and he jumped awake in a sweat. He looked out to the window; bright enough to say the sun was out but barely morning. There was someone yelling downstairs. It was a woman's voice. Flip turned over, sure that he was dreaming. It was still another two hours before he and Penny were to be on the road.

"Flip!? Fliiip!"

It sounded like Elena. Now, he heard running up the stairs. When he heard her reach the top, he realized it wasn't a dream. Her voice sounded far away, but this was no dream.

"Flip! Wake up!"

The scared look on Elena's face helped him. Then he saw Penny coming up the stairs.

"Flip, did you talk to Ronnie last night?" Elena asked panickily.

"What's going on?" Flip yawn-spoke his response.

"Hol said she tried to check-in with him, and he hasn't been answering the housephone or his mobile. When was the last time you talked to him?"

"Yesterday. I called him to let him know Penny and I was coming out there. What's going on?" He got up and looked around for his clothes.

"I don't know," Elena hugged him tightly. "but I think something's happened. Nobody can reach him."

Flip held her for a second before breaking away to get his mobile from the dresser. He saw that just an hour before, Sata called him. He made the return call and put it on speaker. It was picked up before the first ring was finished. "Mr. Stokton, have you talked to your brother recently?" Sata calmly asked.

"Not since yesterday. What's going on?"

Sata was silent for a moment and Flip took her off speaker. Ronnie's appointed Eye didn't report in and was found on the second-floor balcony of the Klima home. Te'rfrejr determined she had to have been taken by surprise on the first level but placed at the balcony door, likely as a decoy for Ronnie. There was a lot of blood in the kitchen, mostly Ronnie's. A Stokton crested longblade was found on the floor a few feet away, mostly coated in vampyr blood, as was a single photograph. The skywindow in the master bedroom was found open.

"Sata, where's Ronnie?" He was now pacing as he spoke.

"I have people in City-Monarch and will be heading to Tabine Manor shortly. As of now, we have not found him, but his shop looks to have been disturbed."

"Where is Hol'ly?"

"She is here with me, and safe. For her and her child's safety, it was agreed that she would stay under my personal observation the past few days."

"Her what?" Flip asked before looking at Elena.

Sata calmly repeated herself before Flip hung up and

grabbed his bag, "Penny, give me five and meet in the garage." He was fully awake now.

"Flip--" Elena started.

"Elena, did you know Hol'ly and Ronnie were pregnant?" Flip's voice was cold and even toned. He looked her in the eyes and took a step forward. "Don't lie to me."

Elena met his stare and held his hand, "Yes, but Flip, we-"

He yanked his hand away as Penny tapped him on the shoulder and signed that they should get going. He changed in the bathroom and followed her out and down the stairs, walking past Elena without a word. Elena stayed in the bedroom as she heard the front door slam before breaking into tears. She agreed with Hol that Ronnie should be the one to tell Flip about the baby when he was ready. It was supposed to be a fun surprise.

It's been a few hours since Rac' and X'i came back from the Klima farm but Hana knew they had a fast-closing window still open if they wanted to escape. Warm-body or not, killing a fellow citizen was enough to warrant Questioning *and* Judgment, even without a dead Queens Eye added on. They would likely never be able to return to their home, but that was just fine by her. Homes could be made anywhere, but *He* made her grow to eternally hate this house. She packed Mama's videos and a few bags and sat them by the door. They may to need to get rid of the V'ago. She really hated the color but enjoyed the fancy feeling she got riding around in it. It reminded her of Mama's open-top autorider and how they would cruise into City to the market. *He* made her hate this place, but Mama was why she stayed longer than she should have. Knowing her spirit was around here somewhere was why she came back. Despite her attempts, she was afraid Mama was trapped within the seals and stone of the obelisk in the cellar.

"We need to go. Get Rac'." Hana called out.

"Yes, Mother." X'i went back upstairs to finish packing and get Master.

Maybe they can go south. The family that ran Tar'Kuur were relatives from Mama's side of the family, and they would do anything to keep her. Tar'Kuur would also be a good change in scenery; they wouldn't be so isolated in the woods. *He* likely chose this place because of that. Nobody to interrupt his "work"; no neighbors to run to for help. The only "neighbors" they did have were miles away, but the first to feel Hana's anger when she returned. As she looked out of the ajar front door, there was a pained yell from Rac's room. She ran up the steps and rushed X'i, pinning her against the wall by the throat. *"What did you do?!"*

X'i dropped the bloody gauze in her hands and pushed against Hana's arm, feeling the closing pressure on her windpipe. She weakly slapped against Hana's face. "Moth...Mother! St.."

"What did you do?!" Hana's eyes were an open furnace. "Answer me!"

"Hana, let her go!" Rac' got up and locked Hana's free arm in a twist until she was forced to release her choke. X'i fell to her knees and clutched at her throat, gasping and coughing for air as she kept her face looking at the floor. She knew not to look Mother in the face when she was angry. Rac' kept his hold until he could feel Hana calm down. "I told her to take the bandages off, that's all." Rac' let her arm go and turned her face to look at him. His cuts were still red from healing but had long stopped bleeding. Hana hugged him and kissed his cuts. She looked past to the drained and bloodied remains of Ronald Klima. She then focused her attention back to X'i, still on the floor but now breathing semi-regularly again. Hana crouched down next to her and held her chin to look her in the face. She saw that her eyes were breathing with hers.

""Do you still want to come with us? I'll understand if you say no."

X'i looked at Master. His face was stone. "Yes, Mother."

"Come here, I'm sorry." Hana opened her for a hug. She could feel tears through the shoulder of her gown. *He never said sorry for the things he did, until it was too late. By then, his apologies were nothing but words. She wasn't going to be like that. X'i was a pet, but for saving Rac', she earned something. Maybe she'll like Tar'Kuur. It'll be cold a lot, but the scenery is worth it and everyone wears jackets anyway.*

"Good girl." Hana kissed her cheek and stood. "Now, do what you were told and meet me downstairs."

"Yes, Mother." X'i gave another look to Master before Mother left the room.

"Close the door." Rac said to her as she walked out.

Hana did, after taking a long look at Rac', and his wounds.

Flip pushed Joy to her absolute limit once they hit the straightaway leaving the First District. The rain wasn't letting up and forced them the treacherous connecting roads of Outer-Monarch. Not having actually seen the Tabine manor, he had no way to know how close he was had he stayed on the straightway. By the time they arrived to Klima's Kuts, the overcast was so heavy it made the mid-afternoon dark as an early nightfall. Sata's caravan was parked in front of the butchery, and he rolled into an open space. His mobile rang less than a minute after parking.

"If you are ready to follow, we can go. There is a dispatchment already in place waiting for us." Sata calmly spoke to him.

"Let's move." Flip responded.

The caravan was put in reverse and pulled onto the road, back in the direction which Flip had just come. They drove at an even speed until they were almost an hour back into Outer-Monarch, eventually coming to a large two-story house that Flip found foggily familiar. The now muddy driveway was empty, but Sata was able to sense at least one presence nearby. Before Te'rfrejr got out, Sata reached over her seat and held her shoulder. "Only herd, Te'rfrejr. May The Father protect you--"

"As He guides. Thank you, Your Highness." Te'rfrejr finished the prayer before exiting. She closed the door and walked over to Joy. She hunched down and tapped the passenger window. Flip lowered.

Te'rfrejr made a curt sniff, "This is not Ms. Starks." Whoever this human was smelled of something different, almost ethereal. She smelled powerful; familiar. She smelled like a man she knew a very long time ago. A man she loved at one point.

"No, it's not. This is my partner, Penny Adlouw. Penny, meet Te'rfrejr, the Queen's Right Hand."

Te'rfrejr heard no sound but felt her hand being shaken and yanked it away. Penny signed that she had really pretty eyes, but didn't understand why there wasn't a response, or reaction. It wasn't until Te'rfrejr didn't flinch when she waved her hand in her face that Penny realized her pretty eyes were because she was blind. Very blind. Blush came over her face out of feeling foolish. Under lighter circumstances, Flip would've found the situation would have been TV worthy.

"Te'rfrejr, were you the one driving?" Flip asked with shock in his voice.

"Adlouw? Of the Adlouw family in East Pike?" Te'rfrejr questioned, disregarding his inquiry. She ticked her head slightly towards Penny.

"You know them?" Flip asked. Penny was confused as she watched the woman mouth "Adlouw". She's never met this woman before; no way she'd forget a woman as tall as Flip.

"I'm... familiar, with the name." Te'rfrejr said.

Flip looked at Penny and saw that the odd response didn't fly over just him. He questioned if anyone was home and was told that at least one person was still in the house, somewhere. Flip nodded and got out the car with Penny following and turning on her Sonicaides. As they walked towards the house, Flip saw a man sitting in a chair on the front porch. He trained Birdie on him until he felt it wasn't reacting. He continued walking until he recognized who it was, "Ronnie!" and ran over. By the second call, he knew Ronnie couldn't hear him. He couldn't hear anything. Flip searched his brother's crumpled body as Te'rfrejr opened the door and drew her longblade. The actual blade shone as a silver-red in the light. Penny ran up and seeing a small resemblance between the two men, knew this was the brother Flip told her about. She wondered why he never talked about him before.

Examining his brother, Flip could feel where he was broken. The blood on his face had long dried and made it look more like a grotesque mask. He touched the marks on his neck and was flashed into the Klima kitchen; seeing how Ronnie was attacked by both Rac' and the woman he suspected was the same from the butchery, and Ruby's. Alexis. Flip never knew his brother to be a bladesman. He saw how Alexis choke-slammed him to the kitchen floor and made the largest of the slashes. Another flash showed him a single scene: Rac' making the killing blow with a final swing of the longblade. Then he was back, not realizing he was crying until after a few seconds and he felt the weight of tears.

The surrounding storm filtered back into his hearing, and he felt Penny tapping his shoulder. When he turned around, he looked into her teary eyes as she told him they needed to back up Te'rfrejr. Flip collected himself and went to the threshold of the door, seeing Te'rfrejr a few feet ahead. When he looked at the open door, he saw the door knocker Sata had told him about. The Mark of The Father, the Bad One, the Dark Master. Before he walked in, she used her arm to stop him and pointed to the floor before making a circular motion with her finger. The house was completely dark. "Oil." Te'rfrejr told him after a few sniffs.

Flip couldn't smell anything initially but saw in a lightning strike there was a gloss to the wooden floor. Once he made eye contact, that's when he could notice in waves the subtle smell of lantern oil. He looked around but noticed the candles lining the walls were all out and stepped in cautiously, telling Penny to keep the door open. The light that could come through was keeping them from pitch black. Once all three of them were in the foyer, Te'rfrejr yelled out in a calm authoritative tone. Flip took out his mobile and activated the flashlight.

"Hana and Rac' Tabine, by order of Queen Sata the Third, Ruler of Sovereign Monarch, you are wanted for Questioning before The Father for the murder of Monarch citizen Ronald Klima and the Queen's Eye of the name Skein. Surrender your will and reveal yourselves. You will not be warned again."

In the silence that followed, Flip could hear her mumbling to herself. She was holding an amulet that hung from her neck and speaking in a language he didn't understand. It reminded him of Sata when she cursed him out. When she replaced the amulet into her jacket, she made a gesture that reminded him of the Mark of K'd. Who would have thought that vampyrs prayed? Flip followed her example and said a Prayer for K'd's Shield over himself and Penny. Te'rfrejr continued sniffing as she walked, making her way down the end of the hall. She tapped her foot down in multiple spots, and Flip shined his light all over the first floor as he followed. Playing the light over the stairwell leading upstairs, he thought he saw the portraits along the wall looking at him. Maybe it was the light, but he was sure their eyes were on him specifically. Penny had her light out as well and was going into the living room.

Te'rfrejr was tapping on the same spot now, noticing it sounded hollower than the surrounding area. She hunched down and began to sniff, "There's something under here." then knocked on it. She started to feel around until Flip reached down and lifted the floor-door. Once open, a rush of wind wafted up. A dirty, decaying smell was brought up with it. She turned her head slightly. There was another presence in that cellar. "I'll check here. Be wary of the live one." She sheathed her blade and made her way down the steps.

"Be careful." Flip said as she made her way down. He noticed Birdie's pulse quicken.

"As The Father guides me, Mr. Stokton. May He be with you." She responded. The pulse in Birdie was now a motor at its highest setting.

With Birdie drawn and aimed, Flip double-backed with Penny to face the front door. It was half-closed now. He didn't hear anyone move or come down the stairs but whoever it was, they were on the first floor with them. He tapped Penny to check the bathroom nook that was under the stairwell, and she flung it open. Empty. Flip saw a shadow cross the door and the whole floor was shadowed, save for the faint outlines of the furniture and the fans of light from his and Penny's mobiles. Staring back at him were the same eyes he saw in Cheryl that night at the hospital, only these had a fire that was used to being fed. They weren't as bright as hers, but they were just as piercing. Flip looked into them from down the hall and tried to study their owner. He was short but had a large and clearly muscular frame. This had to be Rac'; Mr. Classic. From his position, Flip noticed that he was taller than his sister, but it had to be no more than a few inches. He was the "little brother", but only in title. Flip could relate, he was taller than Ronnie by just as much himself. Thinking about Ronnie, and everything they would never do, brought a raw feeling to his throat. He pushed it down and slowly stepped forward, Birdie at the point of jumping out of his hand. He kept his aim through the scope but saw no illuminated outline.

"Rac'? Rac' Tabine?" Flip called out as he took a last step, calculating roughly 10 feet between them. Penny moved to Rac's left but kept the same distance. She wiped her dusters on her shirt, and got into a fighting stance, bouncing on the balls of her feet softly to a rhythm. For what he's done, Rac' didn't deserve a bow of courtesy, or respect. May Gramma and Grappa watch over her. She was sure they were proud for her new job, especially Grappa. He was so happy when she got her High Honor rope; to have another one in the family. Te'rfrejr came out of the cellar wiping her hands onto her jacket. She didn't want to see what her hands showed her. "Where's your sister, Rac'?" Flip asked.

This is going to be quite the showdown, folks. Stokton and Adlouw against one member of the powerhouse Tabine duo. It may be uneven from the outset, but this one looks to be street match. No fouls, just straight-up play. The ball is already in check, but it looks like Stokton has placed it on the floor and slowly rolling towards Tabine. Will he bite? Get your snacks and get settled, y'all, this game might go the distance.

"They're gone, Investigator. Long gone." Rac' said back. Flip could see the flames move from him to Penny. Then he saw another one being held just below Rac's face before it went away with a clicking sound. *Click.* It was back.

"They?" Flip asked.

"Our pet is with her." Rac' then focus his look on Penny. "Is this one yours? I know she takes orders well."

Both teams are steadily eyeing each other. Adlouw's already in place, ready to make a play.

"This motherfu--" Flip fired off three shots. Rac' moved so quickly that Flip couldn't tell which direction he went for a second. He heard all three shots land in the door before dropping his mobile and going towards the footsteps. Te'rfrejr ran in front of Flip and into the sitting area to open the door, allowing a grey light in. "Penny!?" Flip could see Rac' and Penny fighting and for now, missing each other in fast exchanges. "Penny, duck!"

Tabine made light contact, but Stokton steals and scoops

the ball, passing it over to Adlouw. Seems like Tabine anticipated the pass and is already all over her in a close and rough defense. This one truly is going to test the limit of "no fouls". Adlouw is holding her own against the much larger Tabine, but for how long? Stokton's calling for the ball as he's moving up.

In between kicking and moving, Penny felt a rush come over her. When she heard Flip tell her to duck, she dropped and heard a shot ring from behind. Rac' ducked with her and grabbed for her leg, clawing her deeply. She rolled back and popped up in time to see Rac' charging at her, fangs exposed. She threw a right that landed just below Rac's eye and felt something give, causing him to yell out. There was another *pop* and a pyround skinned Rac's cheek, searing as it went across.

There's a textbook pick from Stokton for Adlouw. Tabine doesn't fall for it and moves past to stay with Adlouw. She goes for the short-range, Tabine up with her...and IT'S GOOD!!! Penny Adlouw with the first score of the game while suffering a hard foul in the process. Stokton-Adlouw is at 1. Tabine still scoreless but still giving these two a run for their money. Let's see what he does on the next possession.

The punch didn't drop him, but Rac' began to pat at his face as a thin trail of smoke lifted. Flip took the chance and holstered, running past Penny to tackle Rac' with his dagger in-hand. He managed to get him off of his feet just enough to slam him into the wall along the front door frame and went at the kidneys. Rac' dug into Flip's own sides and clawed to force an escape and then swiped at Flip's face, causing him to fall back. Flip felt heat running down his face and the inside of his shirt. Te'rfreir went for Rac' and was met with a hard gut punch and leaping claw, sending her crashing back onto the sitting room sofa to avoid contact. When she got back up, she swept her hair back and drew her blade a second time. Herding was over; Her Highness please forgive but understand her disobedience. She licked the blood from her lips and mumbled something.

Tabine is driving the ball up at full speed. Stokton runs up to meet him, Tabine holding his own despite the size difference between them. There's a steal attempt from Stokton and Tabine makes him pay for it with what would be a flagrant and is now going for the basket. Adlouw guarding solo. Stokton looks a little rattled but he's running to get back on defense.

As Flip scrambled to get up, Rac' punched him square in his face. He felt his nose *crack* and he fell over, causing the dagger to fall with a dull clatter against the hardwood. Penny screamed as she ran over before Rac' could finish him off. Flip felt like he was just hit by a brick, and his nose ran accordingly. He couldn't see anything but white for a split second. Now standing over Flip, Rac' anticipated Penny's right-hand punch and grabbed her arm, twisting outward violently at the wrist. There was a loud *crunch* followed by a scream. She hit him with a roundhouse kick to his front leg thigh and hopped back just in time as Rac' went for her face, barely missing the overhead claw and coming down across her shirt. She didn't feel it as blood began to reveal itself in some of the larger tears as she landed a second roundhouse kick to the outside of Rac's knee, momentarily forcing it to a bend.

Stokton plays catch-up as Tabine goes for the basket. Adlouw stands her ground and ready to take the freight train coming her way. Stokton comes around to help but Tabine's already off his feet. He's up...and... It's GOOD!!! By K'd, Tabine managed to slam it home after going through both defenders with ease. The game is now tied with both teams sitting at 1.

Flip backed up and drew, letting off two more shots.

The first shot hit the floor, burrowing into the wood with a splintering crater. The second shot found a home in Rac's bent leg, and Flip learned exactly what pyrounds did when they hit organic material. The flash of lightning came through the open doorway and illuminated the foyer for a brief moment. A thunderclap that followed sounded as though K'd rattled the house Himself.

Ball is back in play with Stokton and Adlouw coming up. Looks like they're taking some tips from Tabine and running full-bore, none of the fancy shit. Stokton is limping up but still handling the ball smoothly. He fakes a pass to Adlouw, displacing Tabine's foot placement, and goes for the longshot. He goes up a bit uneasy... It bounces off the rim, and to the backboard...but it falls in!! Flip Stokton with the off-balance 2-pointer. Tabine looks like he can't believe it! In one play, this game just went from a hard 1 to 1 to now a comfortable 3 to 1 for Stokton and Adlouw.

Rac's left pantleg caught first. Then, the smoke rose and Penny saw sparks fly. The scream that came from Rac' was enough to put a pause in everybody. Flip looked into Rac's eyes and saw something that was beyond even vampyr. It was the look of unfiltered rage, but something else. In his gut, Flip could tell Rac' Tabine had no intention of being taken alive. This was another distraction, a final one.

One to set the pick, the other makes the play.

One to set the pick, to let the others get away.

Through the fan of light, he saw streaks of blood were coming from Rac's eyes as he furiously pat at his leg. He ripped his shirt off and used it to smother the sparks. Even with his injuries, Rac' moved with a speed that caught Te'rfrejr ears off-guard, managing to dodge her first strike and start the lighter on the first attempt.

What the...? I don't believe this, folks, but it looks like Rac' Tabine is taking the ball and leaving the court! He's practically running for the sidelines. I can't believe what I'm seeing right now.

Te'rfrejr snapped her head to the click she heard and swung her longblade down with a savage scream. The cut was deep and surgical, going across the face to the inside of Rac's right arm, spraying blood onto her jacket. Her next strike upwards across the chest sent blood across her face and now created a large X in part to a similar length scar already made. As she swung, she yelled a string of what had to be words.

Looks like the audience is confused as they are angry about the sudden departure. A woman in the second row just stood and launched her ale mug at Tabine, hitting him right in the face! She looks like she's yelling. That... something, something, coward sonofa—you know what, can we take the camera off of her? For the little 'uns watching at home, ask your parents to transcribe. For the parents, good luck.

Rac' threw the lighter as he continued to back away from under the porch cover. The oil revealed itself to be trailed all over the sitting room and spread out along the first floor. Penny ran and kicked the lighter outside before grabbing Flip with her good hand to pull him along. Fire began to spread in branches around them as they went for the door. Flip saw Te'rfrejr now stuck in place, sniffing incessantly as thin red streaks flowed from her eyes.

"Te'rfrejr! We need to go!" He reached out to grab her hand, still clutching her blade tightly. He could feel them shaking. She was scared. "Terf, let's fucking go!" He tried to pull her but found her planted; too terrified to move. When he touched her bare hand, he felt a shock, but had let go before he could see anything. "Penny, get her out of here!" He ejected his magazine and uneasily loaded another. Rac' was already a few yards away, but Flip couldn't risk anything. Between his face and his body, blood was leaving him fast. In the distance, he thought he saw cars speeding down the road in the direction of the house from his periphery. No time to lose focus, he had to keep running.

Like every good soldier, Rac' knew when it was time to retreat. A soldier couldn't fight if they were dead. He's seen men play hero and fall too soon because of their pride. Rac' taught his men there was no shame in having to retreat, it could be the difference between living to regroup and strike back or dying an untimely death at the hands of a fighter who was just as scared as they were. In his time, only selfish leaders preached that retreat was "never an option". It's always an option, especially when you had something to come back to. During the War, it was Hana. Until she found him, he had no other family and spent a lot of his time off the battlefield looking over his shoulder in case *He* came for him. Mama never got to see him after the War. She never got to hold his medals. She never got to hear about his valor and how he and Hana fought for their kind during The Culling. She would have been so proud of them. The beating she likely suffered to sneak him away wouldn't have been in vain.

"Rac', stop! *Freeze!*" Flip screamed out. "Don't make me do this, man." he whispered. He focused his eyes and breathed in. His mind flashed to Cheryl Shockley before giving a few steps for compliance.

POP!

POP!

545

Rac' could see Mama. She was getting closer and was just as beautiful as she was when he was a boy. She was in his favorite dress of hers: light blue, floor-length, with handstitched roses and the The Father's crest on the stomach. He didn't know why he liked the emblem as a child so much despite not knowing what it meant, only that he liked it. It was cool. The more he ran, the closer she got. He just had to keep running. Being with her meant he wouldn't suffer Questioning. It meant he wouldn't have to give up his sister. He's given her a fresh chance to prove she would not become *Him.* She just needed a proper vessel. He gave her X'i. His shirt had come undone by now, and the area where the pyround hit had already singed a large circle of his pant leg away and created a spreading patch of burning, hardening skin. The rain wasn't helping.

THUUNK!

THUUNK!

First, the bullets burrowed. Then, the heat set, and his internals caught fire. Rac's screams came out blood cloaked as Mama got closer. Fearing of turning away and losing her, he couldn't see that Flip was less than five yards away and steadily trailing. At this point, he didn't care. He did his job, his duty, in protecting his big sister. When he fell forward, Flip eyed a tattoo on the back of his neck and turned him over. It looked a little like the door knocker, but with the addition of what looked like an initial within it. He saw an old scar that stretched from abdomen to underarm and surrounding wounds of varying lengths and ages under the blood of his newest ones.

Looking up, Rac' saw Mama off to Flip's right. She sat on the grass, looking over him and stroking his face, letting him take in her scent; mint, with a sunfruit undertone.

Mama looked healthy; she didn't have the bruises that wouldn't go away. She looked calm. She didn't have the start of the cloudy eye. She did reach into the bosom of her dress and took out a tiny drawstring pouch. She sniffed a bump of its contents from her pinky fingernail.

"Where's your sister, Rac?" Flip asked. He saw the fire was still there, but Rac' wasn't looking at him. His gaze was just off-center, as though on something else. He glanced next to him to be sure he was alone. "I thought you two were always together?"

Rac' heard Mama ask him the same questions. "She's gone." He answered, before yelling out from the spreading fire. The sun sat behind a smokescreen of clouds. Flip saw smoke exit from Rac's throat as he spoke. A thunderclap rang out. "I told her to...to leave. She didn't want to."

"Where's Alexis? I know she was with you." Flip's sight was doubling but looking at Rac' now at his mercy, it lit an anger that wasn't there before.

Rac' shifted his gaze and looked Flip right in the eyes. In the center of his chest was a flickering glow, like a fire inside of a tent. He didn't say anything. His skin was beginning to look like heated glass. The smell was of long dead burnt flesh.

"Why my brother? He ain't have shit to do with this. Why Ronnie?" Flip didn't expect an answer but instinctively felt the need to ask. Criminals tended to admit a lot in their final hours, or seconds.

Rac' writhed in the muddy grass and screamed out as the fire spread through him. Mama leaned down and kissed his forehead before lifting a fingernail to her nose and sniffed sharply. Smoke was beginning to pore through Rac's skin as it took on a glass-like smoothness.

"Let's go for a picnic, honey. We can go to the Creek." Mama kissed him again. *"I got me a fancy new car. You can drive as fast as you want."*

Rac' only looked at Flip. Smoke and blood came out in coughs and spurts. The two looked at each in silence as the rain continued. Flip thought he could hear his name being called but didn't avert his stare as the pulse of a racing heartbeat began to drown everything out.

POP! POP! POP!

POP!

POP!

After a tough game, and a once in a lifetime ending, this one is a win that you need to write AND call home about! This one will have highlights running for a very long time, folks. Have a good night, and please, be safe getting home.

Final score: Stokton-Adlouw: 3 / Tabine: DNF

THUUNK! THUNK! THUNK!

THUUNK!

THUUNK!

When Terfie exited the van, Sata had instructed Mrs. Klima to close her eyes, and to not open them until told otherwise. Over the darkness, Hol'ly heard everything: the first two shots, the screaming, and then nothing; only rain and thunder. There were more shots, but no subsequent screaming. Everything was silent until she heard Sata open the car door and get out. When Hol'ly opened her eyes, she saw Elena crouching over Flip with two men she didn't recognize, yelling for him to get up. Sata stood with Te'rfrejr as she carried another young woman covered in blood with an oddly angled right hand as her arm dangled limply. The Tabine house was smoking heavily from the door and windows. Hol'ly realized that she didn't see Ronnie anywhere until she saw a third body on the ground near Queen Sata. The rain beat against the window as she cried, watching Elena shaking a still-bodied Flip, and was sure that the Stokton family tree had been cut down, the remains only a bloody stump on non-native soil. Red tears fell from her face and onto a photo of a younger Ron and Flip in a Fountain Academy Kiddie League basketball uniform. Neither one's smile felt genuine to her, but she knew this was the only photo Ron and his only brother and hoped the slow trek of the past year was the start of changing things between them. As she sobbed loudly, she felt the baby kick again, this time in synch with a thunderclap.

Friday. 10 days later.

Elena sat at the edge of the large ornate bed. She's been at the High Monarch Royal Compound for almost a week watching over Penny and Flip, cutting her time between the Community Center and their bedsides. She was sure that she had a nap recently but couldn't remember sleeping outside of two days ago. Talking to Ronald Stokton last Saturday turned into an argument that ended with Elena calmly explaining not to come until Ronnie had been properly prepared for his funeral and Flip's recovered, per Queen Sata's respectful request. She assured him that seeing either of his sons then would be much easier to stomach, playing light on the seriousness of Flip's injuries. Ronald took it extremely hard but passed along his gratitude and said for Sata to take as long as she needed. Fleice begrudgingly conceded to her husband to call the shots concerning his first-born but had a lot of choice words when it came to Flip. Neither had been able to get in contact with Ronnie's mother yet. Elena watched as Flip's chest continued to rise and fall in a steady rhythm. Across the room, the door opened slowly and Te'rfrejr walked in. Elena was so focused she didn't hear anything until a hand rested on her shoulder, causing her to jump and turn in her seat. Te'rfrejr was dressed in what she must've considered casual non-uniform clothes but was still covered in black from head. A cute look, even with the shortblade hanging from her hip. Elena glanced at the resting hand and could see numerous faded scars.

"Matriarch, you should rest. There is a bed next door for you. I assure that it's much more comfortable than the chair." Te'rfrejr spoke in her default calm tone. The previous gash on her face now barely visible. "I will watch over Founder Stokton while you rest." She had towels in her other hand.

"What if he wakes up? I want him to see a friendly face." She looked up at the forward staring Te'rfrejr. "No offense, Te'rfrejr, I didn't mean it like that."

"None taken, I understand the sentiment very much. Such is a similar belief in our culture when a child is born. It is a good omen to both the mother and child. It means that the family will always be loved and protected." Te'rfrejr sniffed the air twice and offered the towels again. "Might I recommend an opportunity to bathe? No offense." She smirked. Humans were known for their welcome of levity in times of extreme grief. She was sure she got it right.

Elena smiled but couldn't tell by Te'rfrejr's face that she was either joking or not. After a quick sniff test, she accepted the towels and got up, promising to be back as soon as she got was dressed. Te'rfrejr nodded and felt her way into the chair. Elena took a final look at Flip's bandaged body and left for the room prepared for her. When she opened the door, she found Sata sitting at a desk, her chair turned to the door. There was an empty chair opposite to her. Elena saw two glasses and an unopened bottle of bloodwine on the desk.

"Are you finally coming to bed, Matriarch?" Sata asked. "How is Founder Stokton?"

"I'm just coming to bathe. Te'rfrejr said she'll watch Flip." Elena responded. She felt an itch in her right pointer finger. There was a hitch in her throat as she thought about Flip. "He's still asleep."

Sata lowered her gaze before opening the bottle, "I see." and pouring them each a glass. "Ms. Starks, we have not spoken to each other much during your visits, and I am sure you are as angry at me as you are scared for your fellow Founder. I ask that before your bath, you have a seat, and we have a conversation."

Elena thought about the request. She wasn't angry about what happened to Flip, she was beyond furious. Rageful would be a more apt term. To a small degree, she could understand Sata's position and adhering to rules that may seem archaic and not in-step with the current time. Founders have a lot of outdated rules and customs they must abide by in part of their stance. Being Destined was one, and a fleeting thought of her seconds long phone call with Bloss G'oh entered her mind as soon as it exited. Did she need to tell her about what really happened to Flip? Did she already know? Elena went over to bed and sat at the foot, close enough to Sata but still keeping a comfortable distance. She accepted her glass of wine and sipped, still holding her towels in hopes it indicated for Sata to hurry up and say what she needed to say. Sata took a healthy sip before speaking again.

"I would like to formally apologize for what happened to Flip, but I do not regret my decision to allow him to hunt the Tabines, considering their connection to your Territory. Seeing the sacrifice that both he and his 'partner', Ms. Adlouw, made on our behalf, I would not wish that on any human. Now--"

"Sata, I--" Elena leaned to cut in.

Sata held up a finger, "Ms. Starks, I am not finished speaking, and would like to 'put it all out', as I believe the saying goes." Elena resumed her posture and returned the floor. "Thank you. Now, while I do not regret my decision, I do see the effect that it has had on you. I can see the magnitude to which you love Mr. Stokton dearly, and I see why. He is strong. He is braver than most warm-bodied men I have encountered. Terfie credits him, and Ms. Adlouw in particular, for saving her life when the Tabine home caught fire. Former acts by your kind have left her with an indelible fear of fire that goes further than our normal aversion to its effect. I say all of this as a plea for your forgiveness."

"And if I don't?" Elena questioned. She didn't expect Sata to be the forgiveness seeking type.

"Then so be it." Sata sipped from her glass. "I take full acceptance of my actions, Matriarch. All I ask for is what I have already said. I hold no ill-will should you decline. I have found myself without such capacity when I was in a similar position."

Elena sat and sipped. This was a different Sata that she's come to know. It didn't feel like a shallow play at cordiality. This was real talk, Matriarch to Matriarch. Even if this was to be the only time, she knew a show of vulnerability when she saw it, though she did wonder if things would be different if she or Flip weren't Founders of a bordering land. She finished her glass and began.

"Sata, I would be lying to you if I said I wasn't angry. When I saw him collapse, I couldn't help but think about our last words to each other. He was angry, at me. Hol'ly and I decided that Ronnie should've been the one to tell him that they were with child. We thought it would be the perfect way to really bring them closer. It was selfish, yes, but we thought it would be nice. Before he left, I didn't get a chance to explain. Whether you meant it or not, it felt manipulative to bring it up when you did. He left out without a word and when I saw him on the ground, I was sure I lost him forever." Elena voice broke as she dabbed at her eye before speaking again. "Look, I know you don't know much about us, and you may not care, but we've been through a lot together. We've hurt people we were with for a night of satisfaction. We've hurt each other for the same reasons, but he's my still best friend. He will always be *my* Flip. I pride myself on not holding grudges, and as much as my head tells me to make an exception, my heart won't allow me to start with you. I can forgive you Sata, but I swear, before K'd and my title, if you *ever* put him into a situation like this again, I promise that I *will* come after you. From one Matriarch to another, I ain't above it to hurt a bitch. Respectfully speaking, Your Highness." Elena placed her glass on the desk with a quiet *ding*.

There was an ember in Sata's eyes as the hazel color took on a reddish tint. Nobody, especially a warm-body, had spoken a threat to her like that and lived in a very long time. It was as refreshing as it was exciting to see this facet of the Matriarch Elena Starks. She could now why Flip loved her so. She smiled, drank from her glass until it was empty, and poured herself another. "Ms. Starks, I would expect nothing less. You strike me as a woman to not make promises she knowingly cannot follow through on. Please, let us drink to the hope that our relationship never comes to you having to make good on it. I too once had a gentleman I was madly in love with and had hurt many 'a bitch' for, excuse my language. He spoke my name with his last breath, and as beautiful as it may sound, I assure you it is not. I hope you do not have to experience it prematurely." She poured into Elena's glass and the two shared a toast, neither breaking eye contact as they drank. After a second sip, she rose from her seat, "I thank you for this conversation and hope you enjoy your bath. I personally curated a fragrance palette I'm sure you will enjoy." and walked out of the room, leaving the bottle of wine on the desk.

Once the door was closed, Elena took her glass, wine and towels into the bathroom and drew her bath. When the water was at the right temp, she eased her way in, and once she mixed a few oils, took a stinging gulp of wine, and allowed herself to purge herself of the tears she's been holding in the past two days.

Penny woke up just after 2pm with a jump. The last thing she clearly remembered was having to shove Te'rfrejr to walk through fire to leave the Tabine house, and then, nothing. Now, she didn't know where she was or how she got there. She woke up in a similar way a few hours after the car accident. The headache started to intensify. Was she still in Monarch? Her hand maintained a steady throb of pain and was heavily bandaged along with her whole upper body. When she found a mirror, her first instinct was to laugh at how she looked like an unfinished mummy costume, but it hurt too much. On finding her mobile, her calendar showed it's been over a week since she left with Flip out to Monarch. It also showed Dom had messaged and called almost 40 times.

The look of her room told her she in a very, very old building. They didn't even have regular lights, just a whole bunch of candles on the wall and few windows. Her Sonicaides were on the sink counter, sitting on a strip of purple fabric bearing the emblem of Monarch. She tapped them once and placed them into her ears, more relieved to hear the *chime* indicating there were ready than how they looked undamaged. Vampyr hit pretty damn hard. When she awkwardly washed her face with one hand, she saw her eyes looked a little different. They looked a little cleaner, if that was such a thing.

She one-handedly messaged Flip and asked where he was. She didn't know what happened after everything went black, but she knew he lost a lot of blood. After a few minutes of no response, she got anxious and texted Dom, but didn't know what to respond to first. Her brain told her to answer each one separately, but some of them contradicted each other, especially the ones that got closer to today. His last message was that he already talked to Elena. Did Ms. El know where she was? Was she here with her? Did she know if Flip was ok? She felt tears forming as she tried to process everything and could only manage a message to Dom that she was awake, but didn't know where she was. She thought she was safe. The next message she sent was to Elena: *Where are you? :(Where's Flip?*

It's ok, Penny. We're at Queen Sata's compound.

It eased only a little of Penny's anxiety, but it also

didn't answer her question about Flip. A few minutes later, there was a knock at the door and then a creak of it opening. Penny immediately turned around and got into a wince-inducing fighting stance, only relaxing when she saw that it was Te'rfrejr and Elena. Penny ran and collided into Ms. El with a big hug, almost knocking them both over. Ms. El smelled really good.

"Hey, girl." Elena chuckled. She could tell Penny was scared and had to pry her off after a few seconds. When she did, she noticed something seemed different about her face.

"How are you faring, Ms. Adlouw?" Te'rfrejr asked.

Penny studied Te'rfrejr and her Friday look for a second and proceeded to try and sign that she felt ok, but her right wrist hurt a lot. Elena relayed the gist.

"Yes, Ms. Adlouw. During the arrest, your wrist was dislocated. The current pain is a signal our treatment is working but will wear off over the coming days. Now that you're awake, we can fortify the bandages. I apologize in advance, it will hurt." She pulled a pencil and notepad from her kilt pocket and held it out. "Please, use this in the meantime, should a translator not be present." When she felt a tug on the notepad, Te'rfrejr clasped her other hand on top of Penny's. "Ms. Adlouw, I do not know how much you can hear me, but I also want to express my gratitude. Fire resurrects... painful, memories for me as I have lost much because of it, my vision and family among it all. I thank you, Ms. Adlouw, for saving me. My life is in your debt." She let go and bowed. This child may have been an Adlouw, but she was more of the man she knew than the rest of his ilk.

Penny only looked at her and then hugged Te'rfrejr just as hard as she did Elena. She didn't know this lady, but she liked her, and her hair. How did she grow it so long? No doubt she sits on it by accident a lot. Long hair, powers, *and* swords? Penny wrote on the pad, finding it to be easier than signing. She tilted the pad to Elena.

"He's ok, just sleeping. Wanna come see him?"

Penny nodded and followed Elena out.

◆ ◆ ◆

"Where's your sister, Rac'?"

"Te'rfrejr! We need to go!"

"Penny, duck!"

"Rac', stop!"

"As The Father guides me, Mr. Stokton."

"They're gone, Investigator."

"Why my brother?"

"Ronnie!"

POP! POP! POP!

Flip awoke wide-eyed. He could feel semi-cool patches of sweat throughout his bandages as he tried to move.

"Flip?"

The voice came to him foggily. When his sight adjusted, he saw Elena was right next to him holding his hand, bathed in red light, as was everything else in the room. Penny and Te'frejr were with her until Te'rfrejr hurriedly exited.

"Flip, it's ok. You're ok." Elena started kissing his hand as her eyes watered. "You're ok." She repeated. "It's ok."

She saw the wild look in his eyes and could tell he still wasn't quite back from where he left. He was gone to the world for over a week; enough time for the news to openly question his whereabouts before giving way to the more pressing question: what's been going on between him and the Matriarch Elena Starks? Frequent sightings over the past year hint at a possible relationship again. Though the public statement by the Stokton family was that Flip was ok and just being treated for a recent spate of migraines, the rumor mill was already up and running. Elena's overheard a few theories from kids and adults alike, ranging from that he killed that Tabine asshole like that Shockley girl to he died protecting Ms. Starks herself and the family just doesn't know how to announce it yet. The more perceptive of children spoke in hushed tones of seeing Ms. Starks crying in her office sometimes.

He had his defenders, but after the 3rd and 4th day, they started to come around that maybe Coach Flip really wasn't going to come back. Only when Ms. Ingram brought questions to her that surpassed mere curiosity did Elena feel relieved to not be the only one bearing the weight of knowing how bad it got. *He's not blood, but I love that boy as one of my own,* she remembered her saying during an after-hours talk before Elena left for her lonely and quiet commute back to Monarch.

When his eyes focused on Elena, he moved for a hug and found his body screaming the contrary. His ribs hurt when he breathed and he couldn't even feel his face, just the bandages wrapped around. He felt them and noticed the side with his cheek scar was padded. He felt a smaller padded area on the other cheek. He couldn't tell if any of it hurt or not.

"Easy, Love. Don't move." Elena spoke softly. Te'rfrejr mentioned something about him being sensitive to light and sounds if he woke up. "You're still hurt."

Seeing a smiling and also extensively bandaged Penny, Flip eased slowly into a slouch against the headboard. He waved weakly when she wrote "Hey Flip!" on her notepad. Looking at Elena's face, he could tell that he looked worse than Penny. He looked himself over and noticed his entire torso was wrapped as well. "It's that bad?"

"A little." Elena smiled; her first genuine one in a few days. "You made the news."

"Forreal?" Flip kept his responses short.

"Forreal. Wallace made sure to keep your name out of the public reports, but eventually they started asking your family and me real questions. Your mother was ready to say you died if it meant they would leave her alone. She settled on you been having at a clinic." She saw there was something with Flip's eyes. It was the same as Penny's. And Ata's. Sata didn't say anything about bites among their injuries.

"True." As he spoke, Sata and Te'rfrejr entered. Sata formally introduced herself to Penny. She was told that Penny was very much like Terfie in their overcoming of perceived deficiencies and voiced her gratitude for her bravery and willingness to shed blood for her people. Penny would be properly honored before leaving for home. Her and Flip both would, during dinner. When she finished her invitation, she studied their faces, specifically their eyes, before requesting Penny to sit on the bed and allow Terfie to perform a check-up. Almost immediately, Te'rfrejr had gloved hands tapping and taking her pulse before requesting she open her mouth. Penny stiffened at the request and found it very odd. If anything, she should be asking Flip to open *his* mouth, he's the one that got punched in the face. Twice.

When Te'rfrejr felt resistance, pulled her hands back. "Ms. Adlouw, this is the final but most important part." Penny relented and opened. Looking just next to her, in a way that looked like she was watching Flip, she felt at Penny's canines, "Interesting." noticing a familiar curve to them. "Thank you. I apologize for the invasiveness." She then removed her gloves and took out a new pair from her kilt. When she snapped them on, she stepped in between Flip and Elena, "Pardon me." and began her check-up. It felt like how one would inspect a sick animal, but he wincingly opened his mouth when it was asked.

After a short feel she felt his mouth move and then a sharp prick on her finger. When she pulled back, Flip saw a look of wariness on her face and a small blot of red within the puncture of her glove. Te'rfrejr walked over to Sata as she rubbed her pointer finger and thumb together and mumbled something into her ear. Sata then walked over and looked him directly in the eyes. He instinctively licked his tooth and tasted blood. A short rush followed and forced him into a fit of coughing. When it subsided, Sata then held his hand and softly caressed it. Te'rfrejr reached out and made her way behind Elena's chair.

"Mr. Stokton, I have already asked for Ms. Starks' forgiveness today. Now, I ask for yours."

Flip didn't like when Sata spoke in riddles. "For what?"

Sata breathed in and exhaled, "Terfie?"

In a single motion, Te'rfrejr drew her shortblade and leveled it against Elena's throat. Penny immediately jumped into her fighting stance before taking a step forward, mentally calculating how to disarm Te'rfrejr without hurting Ms. El. It was going to be tricky, but she could do it, she was sure. Flip jerked himself forward, but Sata tightened her hold. His eyes told him everything she needed to know. There was a fire breathing, but it was tame. It was a bright and low heat, but she was not mistaken even in the hue of the room light. Sata reciprocated their intensity, her eyes turning into a bold red-hazel. She smiled and relaxed her grip, then looked over to Penny and saw they were the same as Flip's but not as focused.

"Sa--" Flip's head pounded as he jerked forward, "Sata, this ain't funny." and yanked his hand away in attempt to get up. His ribs were screaming, and he fell back. Elena could practically feel the cold emanating from the metal of Te'rfrejr's blade against her throat. There was something else there, in the thin gap of air between flesh and steel. The air itself was vibrating, as if beckoning her to move.

"Thank you, Terfie. It's ok." With that, Te'rfrejr sheathed her blade as quick as she drew it. Sata sat on the bed, only turning her head slightly towards Penny. *"As admirable as your protectiveness is, I implore you to stand down, Ms. Adlouw. Threat of imminent violence to a Ruler is of fatal consequence, for friend or foe."*

Penny looked at Flip and he nodded. When she looked at Elena, she saw her eyes were closed.

"Sata, what's all this?"

"Mr. Stokton, The Father has thanked you both for what you've done for his Children here in Monarch. Had He found you undeserving, you would be with your brother right now instead of us." Sata said evenly. "Unlike Ms. Adlouw, your injuries were mortal, and had we waited any longer, you would have succumbed to them. I apologize for such a dramatic test, but I've learned that the most drastic move is often the best way to find real results." Sata rose and took Te'rfrejr by the hand, "I will explain more at dinner." and led her to the door. She turned in time to catch Flip trying to casually feel the sides of his neck. "Flip, you've seen too many movies. I'll have someone come for you when dinner is ready." When they exited, Elena jumped out of her seat and went to Flip into an embrace.

"You ok, girl?" Flip asked her. Elena saw his eyes dim to a low simmer and realized what Sata was talking about. Movies or not, she's seen enough to know what Sata was (not) trying to say.

"No." She buried her face into him for a second. When she looked into his eyes again, they were normal, but with a new clarity to them.

"Penny?" He couldn't tell if she was wearing her Sonicaides and made a thumbs-up. She nodded and reciprocated the sign and pointed to her ears. She then walked over and hugged him tight. Flip felt a tinge of pain from the compress and tapped her shoulder. "Guess you were out for a while too, huh?" He chuckled as soft as he could to avoid pain. "What day is it?"

"Two months since the Tabines." Elena answered softly.

Flip shook his head in shock. "What?"

Elena chuckled. "Just kidding, but it has been a week and a half. You've been out since we brought you here, Love. You and Penny." Elena held his hand and looked to Penny. She leaned into her ear and whispered something. Whatever it was, it made Penny stand and head for the door, giving a final wave to Flip as she walked. As he waved back, Elena took the vacant spot on the edge to Flip's left and sat. "Flip, I'm so sorry."

"About what?" The previous week has been coming to him in patches that were only starting to sew themselves together. He remembered the last conversation he had with Elena. He stormed off. He wasn't proud of how he acted.

"No, I understand. I'm not going to sit here and say 'Oh, I wanted to tell you', because at the time, I didn't. It was a made decision brought to me that I happily agreed to. Hol'ly only told me three months ago, but she's already approaching six. She said Ronnie wanted to tell you himself when he was ready."

He was going to be an uncle? Yes, he was going to be an uncle. Flip had an uncle that lived further north but didn't talk to him much. Shit, he couldn't even remember the last time he saw him. Fleice's condition caused Randall's side of the Stokton line to keep their distance. Fleice always said it was jealousy from not having the Sight. It didn't keep some of them from occasionally asking Flip about tickets when the season would start.

"You talk to Hol'ly since we've been here?" Flip asked.

"Yeah, but she's barely holding on, Flip. She wants to see you."

That's when it hit him; where's Joy? Was she still at the Tabine house? Elena let him know she was safe and sound here. Sata had a couple "domestics" clean the remaining mud off her once the storm passed. She did take Birdie with her, and presumed it was still in her possession. Maybe she'll give it back when they left. After more idle talk to catch up on what's happened in the past week, Flip moved over so that Elena could lay next to him. He commented on her new fragrance. By the time Elena was getting to tell him that it was courtesy of their host, he was already back to sleep.

CHAPTER 23
Friday night

The first course of dinner was...interesting. Sata accompanied the first course with a traditional combat display featuring Te'rfrejr and three other Queen's Eyes- two male, one female. Before everything started, Sata led a prayer to The Father in honor of Skein, the Eye that was found at the Klima ranch. She was just in her first rotation and showed further potential. Every Eye in the room made a salute and lowered their head for their fallen comrade. May The Father reward her for her service.

Sata then said a prayer for Rac' Tabine, as he was still a citizen of Monarch and one of her Children, and His. May his troubled soul finally have found peace and The Father mete His discipline justly. She finished with a prayer for Ronald Klima, Jr. May he continue his watch over his wife, and guide their child to bring honor to the Klima name. Almost as soon as the last syllable of this was spoken, every Eye in the room made another salute as Sata praised Ron's will to fight and protect his family.

Once everything was done, Te'rfrejr bowed in the general direction of one of the Eyes as the other two appeared to glide into attack formation Trident-2. When the leader of the trio let Te'rfrejr get into her stance, he made two directions with each hand and the other two stepped in. Te'rfrejr held an arm out and balled a fist.

"Terfie, are you ready?" Sata asked from her seat, overlooking the floor. She had a small child in her lap and was softly bouncing them on her knee.

"As The Father guides me, Your Highness. Yes, I am

ready." She responded.

She sniffed twice, and then a third time, before moving a few stray locks of hair from her face. She changed her position to stance three, something more agile and made to defend against multiple opponents. Penny noticed it looked a lot like hers but with a further back leg. Sata looked over to a far wall and tipped her head. An elderly woman then rung a tiny handbell and all three opposing Eyes moved simultaneously. The leader of the group struck first and caught Te'rfrejr across the face in a way that Penny felt was intentional because of the way she went with the momentum and turned the impact into a grab to wrench the arm behind the man's back. At the same time of her grab, the other two went in for a clawing duo and hit only air. Te'rfrejr let go with a push and backflipped into her previous stance. The second Eye ran forward with a closed fist. Te'rfreir moved her head to the left a few inches and made a one-two palm strike to his chest and face before kicking the crook of his knee, forcing him to a kneel as she twisted his lead hand at the wrist and held it. He tapped the side of her hand as a sign of yield. She knocked him to his back just as the third was about to rush. The bell rung again and the remaining two each pulled out daggers. Elena tightened her hold on Flip's hand when she saw the glint of metal and the third Eye quickly crawl to the far wall to spectate.

"Watch and learn, little one." Sata whispered into the child's ear.

"Yes, Aunt Sata." He was mesmerized. Aunt Sata never let him watch Te'rfrejr fight, only let her lead his combat training when she couldn't herself. He liked to sneak in so he could watch some of Te'rfrejr's solo training. Her movements reminded him of dancing. Seeing it in action was awesome. He hoped she would teach him how she does it.

The main feast table was full of the first of many courses that were brought out and placed in front of Flip, Elena, Penny, and Hol'ly, among other eating and spectating guests. Under his long houserobe, Flip kept the bandages around his torso but was convinced to go with a somehow more unaesthetically pleasing but less speech impeding clear face mask. He knew a few guys that used to play with them on, even when they didn't have broken noses, but he never got how they could manage. They looked so uncomfortable to play in. Having to wear one himself, he kind of saw why: they felt better than they looked, unless it was just this one.

He dug into some steak but after a few bites found himself feeling nauseas. He ate in small pieces, forcing himself to swallow and keep it down. After a few bites, he sipped from a tea that Sata had made for him and Penny that was said to help with any, "uncomfortableness", they may experience since waking up and couldn't help but gag at the metallic aftertaste. Taking another hesitant sip, he watched Te'rfrejr pull an upset and plant the leader of the sparring group flat on his back with a hip toss and his own dagger pressed against his neck. He tapped against her hand as a sign of yield. Once he joined Eye 3, a final bell rang and two offside domestics ran over, each with unsheathed longblades in their hands. As they passed over the blades, Flip felt a tap against his arm and Penny's notepad being slid over from his right.

Are we sure Terfie's really blind?

Flip covered his mouth as he chuckled and winced. With longblades in their possession, both Te'rfrejr and the third Eye backed up two paces and faced each other. In the candlelight, perspiration shined off of them like oil. Flip slid Penny's note over to Elena, eliciting a less hidden but respectfully quiet scoff and a shrug.

"I no longer sense your hesitancy, or unguided anger. You have grown as both a pupil and an Arm of The Father. Your sister would be very proud of you, Hait'een, as I am right now." Te'rfrejr said breathily.

"Thank you, Ms. Te'rfrejr." Hait'een responded.

"Let us begin." Te'rfrejr pushed her hair back and lifted her blade into stance two and sniffed. Stance two focused on direction and power, more effective in armed combat than hand-to-hand. She couldn't believe Rac' Tabine survived a stance two strike enough to run as far as he did.

Hait'een made a sharp yell but instead of moving up, side-stepped to the right, and swung for Te'rfrejr's neck. Te'rfrejr charged her strike forward, glancing Hait'een's blade up and throwing her off-balance. She couldn't help but smile to herself, she personally taught Hait'een that shouting tactic. One must always be aware of their opponent's limitations use it to their advantage. Taking advantage of her opening, Te'rfrejr went to catch Hait'een's blade with her own and trail it back to the floor, but only cut air. Hait'een had dropped into a crouch and went to sweep Te'rfrejr's leg, forcing her into a single kneel. Before she could raise, Hait'een already had her own blade against Te'rfrejr's neck. A smile of her own creeped across her face. She's never gotten Ms. Te'rfrejr into a yield position in exhibition combat.

"Please yield, Ms. Te'rfrejr." Hait'een kept her blade against her.

Te'rfrejr stayed. She had to admit the sweep was a very novel idea. No matter the opponent, one must always take advantage of their limitations. "Ms. Hait'een, your anger is gone, but premature hubris still plagues you." In one motion, Te'rfreir swung her blade up and knocked the pressed blade aside with enough force to cause the unsuspecting Hait'een to drop it, and struck under the chin with her palm. The clanging against the stone floor echoed enough to tell her it was at least a couple feet away and she struck Hait'een again to create more distance. Now standing, Te'rfrejr stepped to put herself between the two. She dropped her own blade and stepped forward with her hands up, firing a barrage of punches and palms, all directed to Hait'een's body. Hait'een put up a guard but knew she couldn't stop them all, she just needed to stop the right ones. Swatting punches away and landing some of her own, the two engaged. Te'rfrejr felt two punches land and turned against Hait'een, putting her back into her. She then elbowed Hait'een's stomach and grabbed her right arm into a hold that turned into an over the shoulder flip, putting Hait'een on her back. Te'rfrejr used the momentum to land in a mount and held three clawed fingers in a choke against Hait'een's windpipe.

"Please yield, Hait'een. I am proud of your development, as you should be as well."

Te'rfrejr didn't feel anything for a few seconds and pressed in. "Ms. Hait'een, allied combatants do not draw true blood. Yield with honor. Your Queen watches, as does The Father."

Hait'een raised her hand and tapped. She was so close. So, fucking, close. Te'rfrejr rose to help her up and brought her in for a hug. She heard sniffles and lowered into Hait'een's ear.

"No tears, Hait'een, no tears. You have done well, and Skein looks on you with pride. May she always be with you as The Father illuminates your path." Te'rfrejr whispered before kissing her forehead and hugging her again. When she released, Hait'een backed up and they bowed to a loud applause. Eye 1 came behind Hait'een and tousled her hair as she and Eye 3 high-fived. Te'rfrejr felt around for her blade and held it for retrieval before then excitedly being brought a towel by the child from Sata's lap.

"Aunt Terfie!"

She followed the voice through the sound of applause and bent to pick up its source, a concerningly skinny little boy barely reaching above her knee, "Viium, is that you?" before getting attacked with kisses. "Shouldn't you be in bed? Have you eaten yet?"

"Aunt Sata said I can watch you if I was good today. And it's Friday, remember? I can stay up late."

"I take it that you were a good boy today?" No matter what he did, she knew Sata would say Viium was a good boy. He was her special boy.

"Mm-hmm." Viium nodded.

"Mm-hmm? Or yes?"

There was a pause as Viium looked at the table's guests. "Mm-hmm." He repeated.

Te'rfrejr smiled, "Good enough." and carried him over to the main table after bowing to the still applauding Feast Hall. "Are you hungry?"

"Unh-uh."

Flip watched Te'rfrejr interact with this child and couldn't believe the duality. A week ago, he saw her fight a wanted murderer of her own kind with a killer's calm. Now, he was watching what felt like a completely different person. Even her manner of speaking felt more relaxed.

"Is that right? What did you have?" Te'rfrejr asked.

"A bad lady. Aunt Sata said the Father found her guilty."

"Then you have done His work." Te'rfrejr began to feel the air for him before playfully patting him all over the face, "Now, where's Viium? I can't find him. I'm sure he was just here." pulling a hearty laugh out of him. "Why excuse me, little boy, have you seen my Viium?"

"I'm right here!" The little boy took Te'rfrejr's hand into both of his and rested it on his face. "I'm right here!"

"Ah, of course! There you are." She kissed his forehead. Holding him to face the others, Te'rfrejr picked up a small carrot and held it up to Viium, "Candy?" who accepted happily and ate into it. His face twisted.

"This candy tastes weird." Viium said between chews. "It tastes like vegetable." He giggled.

"Not weird, Viium, special. Special candy for special boys. This one helps you see better." Te'rfrejr smiled and kissed his cheek. He was her special boy. "Can you say hello to our honored guests?"

This chick even got jokes, Flip thought to himself as he ate a piece of leek.

"Hello." Viium said shyly, looking at Flip but addressing everyone. Flip waved with a full mouth and Elena said hello for both of them. "Are you the one who saved my aunt, mister?" Viium kept his eyes on Flip. There something about this human. He was only a few shades darker that Aunt Sata, yet his eyes were the same as hers. Aunt Sata said he was the one that stopped Mr. Rac' from hurting more people. Flip saw a large, jagged burn in a slant across his face and down his neck. It had the same glassy smooth texture as Rac's did when the pyrounds took full effect. The same texture as the burn on Hana's arm.

Before Flip could answer, Te'rfrejr corrected Viium and said that Ms. Adlouw was technically the one who saved her from the fire before succumbing to her injuries. Viium pretty much leaped from his aunt and ran around the table to the stranger, climbing onto her lap for a hug. "Thank you, Ms. Adlouw!" He buried his head into her chest and Elena looked over in time to see Penny blushing. Something told her that Penny wasn't too used to being around children outside of her self-defense classes at the Center. Over the soft rise of acoustic music, she looked back over to a Te'rfrejr who took the seat across from her. She sniffed at each platter as she made her plate.

"Who's the child, Te'rfrejr?" Elena asked.

"Honestly, Ms. Starks, we don't know, as he was only a few years old when we found him. He is quite the anomaly, but he is a True Child of the Father, as we all are. Minus the domestics. They are of your kind." Te'rfrejr answered matter-of-factly. "Her Highness and I were away in a small settlement when we were told of an orphanage that was supposed to be a safe place for vampyr and warm-body children alike but was only a place of cruelty. After deep prayer, The Father deemed the 'parents' unworthy of such a beautiful child and we freed him and the other children into more appreciative homes. We ensured the owners would never hurt another child again." Te'rfrejr cut into her food and began eating. Elena looked over to see Viium talking and laughing with Penny. He was excited in meeting a warm-body that was nice to him, even if she didn't talk. He was more intrigued by the man sitting next to Ms. Adlouw. He must be the same Mr. Stokton from the autograph Aunt Sata gave him last year. Even in his seat, he looked tall. He had to be as tall as Aunt Terfie. Viium caught the eyes of the lady next to him; that must be Ms. Starks. She was really pretty. They waved at each other before he noticed the veiled woman in all black at the far end of the table and frowned. He didn't like seeing people sad, especially Ms. Klima. She made the best sandwiches.

The music began to liven, tacitly signifying the main course of the feast. In perfect timing with Sata who was across the room, Te'rfrejr also rose from her seat, "Mrs. Klima, could you follow me? Mr. Stokton and Ms. Adlouw, you should be ready to come soon." and turned to walk effortlessly through dancing guests before they cleared a path for the woman that trailed her. Looks of previous joviality faded away as the visibly pregnant Hol'ly Klima walked between them. Many made the Mark of the Father as she passed by; others respectfully bowed their heads. In many ways, every guest in attendance knew Ron Klima and how much he loved his wife in spite of their fundamental difference. Walking down the short steps from her throne, Sata held out her right hand and rested it on Te'rfrejr's shoulder. When she reached the landing, she took Hol'ly's hand into hers and looked her in the eyes; into the fire. It was all encompassing. Sata couldn't tell if it was fueled by rage, or sorrow. She could empathize with either one.

"Mrs. Klima, I am thankful you decided to stay here with us for the remainder of your pregnancy. You are welcome to stay here as long as you want or need. It will be of no burden to accommodate your presence." Sata had a handkerchief in-hand. "Though Mr. Klima was not one of us, but he was a revered citizen within Monarch proper all the same. He was one of my Children, as will the one you will bring into this world." She dabbed at her eye and Hol'ly saw a spot of red.

"Thank you, Your Highness. It's been very tough without Ron. Between the baby and managing the shop, it's been hard keeping everything together. I've been trying to keep me stress down like the doctor recommended but

—I'm sorry, I'm... I'm starting to ramble. Ron would've already pinched me." Her laugh came out uneven but sadly authentic. "Thank you for your hospitality, Your Highness." Hol wiped her eyes. Sata used her handkerchief to softly wipe the smears of blood and hugged her, causing a loud sob to erupt from Hol'ly. Onlooking guests began to either silently cry or keep their heads down, likely to also hide their own tears.

When Hol composed herself, Sata told her that Ron would be ushered to the Other World according to royal custom. Flip looked on as Hol'ly accepted Ronnie's now cleaned longblade. Listening to Hol talk about how just the past week has been for her was painful; even more so when he thought about the coming weeks. Months, birthdays, holidays, the birth of their first-born; Ronnie won't be there for any of it. He only wiped at his eyes and continued to watch on in silence, feeling Elena's gaze on him.

"Mr. Stokton. Ms. Adlouw. Would you join us, please?" Sata called over to the main table, making eye contact with Flip. She could see he was trying look tough, but his eyes were the same as Hol'ly's. They both got up and Viium went over to the pretty lady that sat next to Mr. Stokton, climbing into her lap as he did Penny. Elena looked around but was met with welcoming faces. She lightly bounced her leg as she saw Sata do. He seemed to enjoy that. As Flip and Penny approached closer, Sata snapped her fingers and two domestics came, both holding a small box.

"Mr. Stokton, do you remember when you asked what a *ha'kiet* was?" Sata asked as her servants walked over.

Flip did, though now it felt like a long time ago. "Yeah."

"Well, though the literal meaning has been lost

to time, your recent actions have proven why you were bestowed the title. You and Ms. Adlouw risked your life for the people of Monarch, and despite not being one of The Father's Children, he has graced you into his Family." Sata then looked at Penny and held her hand in silence. Penny nodded her head. Sata then verbally said that they will speak again, in private. "Flip? Penny? You have been healed because The Father found you worthy. You are still human enough, but it would unfair and belittling of Him to say you are still completely. The Stokton and Adlouw clans are now Blooded Brothers, to Monarch and her allies. As you have shed blood for me, I have done the same for you, through His Will."

The weight of Sata's revelation hit them much differently. Flip looked behind him and over to Elena, still bouncing Viium lightly. She saw his eyes when Sata did her "test" earlier; they shone like torch tops. Across the room, she could see it was the same now. Thinking back to when she walked into Penny's room, she knew it was the same thing. Even through the vagueness of Sata's words, she understood the message perfectly.

Sata looked behind him and saw his target. "You do not have to worry about the Matriarch, at least not regarding this."

That made Flip turn around. "What you tryna say? Quit the riddle-speak."

Te'rfrejr heard an edge in his voice and slowly moved her hand to her waist. Either The Father instilled a necessary temper into this warm-body, or he enhanced it. Sata held it in place and squeezed lightly. "Mr. Stokton, I speak to you as a friend. I am only vaguely familiar with the extent of your clan's bloodright, but I am aware of what its effects have done to your mother, and that it is possible you will be the same.

My own father was a sickly man, ironically of sick blood, and mother and I thought that it would take me as well. So far, it hasn't. I can empathize with trying to look further than one can see, that's all."

They looked at each other for a few moments before Sata snapped her fingers and the two servants stepped in front of her, putting themselves between Sata and her honorees. They opened the boxes and revealed their contents: Birdie in his thigh holster and Penny's knuckle dusters. Birdie looked pretty much the same except for a tiny black switch just below the rear of the barrel. Joining it was a new dagger only marginally wider than a standard pencil; engravings along the hilt leading to the symbol of Monarch at the base. The dusters looked well cleaned and shined now with a new red tint in the candlelight. There was an intricate design engraved onto them, with small spikes expertly welded onto the front of each fingerhold.

"My Chief of Arms had some initial trouble handling but managed to take a small liberty with your weapons. Are you familiar with an auto-shooter, Flip?"

"Of course."

"Have you seen it in a handheld?"

Flip raised his eyebrows to question. He's heard of auto-fire handguns, but most Territories he last checked had regarded them highly illegal to carry around, Fountain being one of them. He didn't think his mother had even handled one before. Even as a Founder, he didn't think he could talk his way out of it if he was questioned.

"Not in person."

"My Ward says that switch will let you shoot three rounds at a time. Switch it forward, and it's back to one. I could not find any prohibition against this kind of modification in Fountain, but I'm sure it won't be an impediment for you if there was." Sata said with a smile. "Ms. Adlouw, your gauntlets needed serious cleaning. You could say Terfie put a little of herself into the re-gilding of them. They will always hunger for the taste of battle, and as you feed them, the more powerful they will become. It is the same for your dagger, Mr. Stokton. May The Father be satisfied of your use." Sata's smiling face turned a touch darker. As cool as it sounded, Penny didn't feel right about the implication. Nevertheless, she accepted her box happily and closed it. Flip did the same and they bowed to Sata. She returned their bow and every guest in the hall applauded loudly. Penny tapped Flip on the shoulder and pointed back at their table. Viium was clapping hard with a huge smile as Elena watched, teary eyed and clapping along with him. Sata then announced that the main ceremony was now over, and the feast can resume before saying a final prayer for both Penny and Flip.

As they walked across the floor, a roughly 10-second return became almost five minutes. Everyone wanted to talk to the warm-body *ha'kiet* and his partner. They needed to know what it was about these two humans The Father found worthy of His grace. By the time the crowd finally let them go back to the table, Hol had already beat them there and was standing with Viium hand-in-hand. Elena ran over to Flip and, careful of his facemask, kissed him. Flip kissed her back and for a moment, felt they were the only two in the room. He heard the sounds of Viium giggling as Hol'ly walked over.

"How're you feeling?" Hol'ly asked him, eyes bloodshot.

"I'm ok. I really wanna take this damn mask off, though."

577

Viium giggled again. It was funny to hear people swear, especially Aunt Sata. She tried not to do it in front of him, but she slipped, especially when it came to a "guilty" Judgment. When he saw the *ha'kiet* looking at him, he moved behind Hol'ly's leg. His masked face was kind of scary. It was scarier to know this robed human was vampyr slayer.

"Hey Viium." Flip held out his fist. It was met with an open palm.

"Close enough. How old are you?"

Viium held up two open palms. He liked telling people how old he was.

"10? That's cool." *That's cool?* Flip wasn't sure what to respond with. Small-talk with kids wasn't really his forte, even with the ones he saw on a regular basis. This Viium didn't look like he'd be ballin' anytime soon. Then again, even a dwarf can make a decent point guard.

Viium laughed. "Aunt Sata says I'm special."

Flip did his best to hold a straight face and looked at an unfazed Hol'ly. Something that Ata said to him and Elena rose the surface about vampyrism taking to people differently. This had to be the anomaly that Te'rfrejr spoke of. He couldn't already be 10 at his size.

"Oh, awesome." Flip weakly spat. He was flailing.

"Hey, Viium, do you want to go back to Aunt Sata?" Elena came in with the escape rope.

Looking around and not seeing Sata anywhere, he shook his head, "Uh-uh." and reached his arms up.

"Ok, let's go find her." Elena bent down to pick him up. She looked at Flip long enough for him to mouth a thank you. When they left for the main floor, Hol'ly stepped up to Flip and asked to speak in private. He took his box and followed her out into the hallway, the music now muffled behind the heavy door. Flip saw that she had Ronnie's longblade strapped to her side.

Hol hugged him tight. He grimaced at the pain. "Flip..." Hol'ly sniffled but couldn't let herself cry again. She's cried enough for one day. "I'm so sorry."

"I guarantee you were closer to Ronnie than I ever was, Hol. I should be the one saying sorry." Flip's voiced tweaked. "He died, because of me. I got him involved in all of this."

Hol'ly released and looked up to him. "Flip, he was your brother, and I know he loved you a lot. Ron didn't tell me much about you two growing up when we first got together, only that he had a little brother in Fountain." She went into her dress and pulled out the photograph. "He didn't tell me exactly who you were to him until he opened the shop and put your picture on the wall, and that was going on year four." She laughed weakly. "I thought he was just a really big fan of yours, and in some ways, I'd like to think he was. He showed me this after you and Elena's visit. When your father began sending him the papers with the cases, he made sure to get them framed for his office to remind him of home. After the third one, I think that's when he realized you were the 'anonymous PC' that kept popping up." She then held the longblade out to him. "Flip, I want... I want you to have this. Ron taught me a little of how to use it, but I know he would want it to be yours after all of this."

Flip couldn't hold it in any longer. Hol'ly brought him to her, and felt he was crying harder into the embrace. Everything came to him at once: the long memories of seeing Ronnie coming to the house to visit their dad. The fewer nights he'd come to a school basketball game. The night he and Wallace took him to Ruby's for ice cream. The hate he used to have for him as he grew older, not knowing whether his brother actually cared about or loved him. The confusion as to why he never felt they could actually connect. The acceptance the may never would. The underlying truth that despite all of it, he was still his brother at the end of the day and they shared blood. His anger felt so selfish and trivial now; so petty. It was too late to go back on any of it. Shit, the last time they saw each other was because of work. The tears ran until they decided to stop on their own. Hol'ly patted him on the back and told him it was fine; it was ok to feel as he did. When they released, Flip looked Hol'ly in the eyes and then down to the blade.

"Hol, I can't accept that." He inched the blade back to her. "Ronnie may want me to have that, but it belongs to *you* now. It belongs to your child. Ronnie may not have been of the Stokton clan, but he was family. I'm sure my father gave that blade to him for a reason." Flip swallowed the lump building in his throat. "I wouldn't feel right taking this piece of him away from you. Eventually, your child will ask what happened to their father, and when you tell them, you can show what he used to protect his family, as any mother would."

Despite the promise to herself, it was Hol's turn to cry. She retreated the blade and fastened it to her waist without another word of debate. In her heart, she knew Flip was right. Ron taught her enough of how to use it for her to be competent in a real-world situation. She could learn it well enough to then teach her child. Her son. Their son. When both were calmed enough to rejoin company, they reentered the hall. Flip opened the door, allowing Hol to walk through first. Before fully entering, she looked back and cradled her stomach. "It's a he, Flip, and I will be a good mother to him, as

I expect for you to be a good uncle in turn."

"You have my word, Hol'ly."

Hol walked over the threshold and back into the hall. Flip followed behind and they walked to their table in silence, ready to enjoy the rest of their night as much as they can. They each hoped that they cried enough tears to compensate for Ronnie's funeral. Flip felt something in his pocket poke against his thigh. Reaching inside, he felt a slick, folded piece of paper.

◆ ◆ ◆

Saturday evening

This was her first night funeral, and it was quite the experience. She couldn't understand any of the singing, but it was inhumanly beautiful. She was surprised that Flip had enough words to follow his father for a eulogy of his own. When everything was finished, Fleice Stokton sat, lit candle in hand, as her husband said his final goodbye to his first-born before igniting the cremation structure. Next to him and tossing her candle onto the growing flame stood Blest Klima, now Sous, holding his hand and crying. She had her differences with Blest, but Fleice refused to let them cloud the sympathy she felt. If things went even the slightest bit differently, she would be joining her at the structure lighting a second pyre for her own son. Looking past Ho'ly and down to Flip and Elena, she couldn't stop herself from picturing the alternate reality. It wasn't as vivid as her flashes, but that didn't make it hurt any less. After a kiss, Ronald motioned for his family to join him.

According to Monarch royal custom, the first fires should be delivered from those closest to the deceased, as their light will shine brightest in its guidance to the Other

World. Fleice locked her arm into Hol'ly's and walked with her up to the burning altar. One by one, Hol'ly, Flip, and Fleice all placed their candles at the base and watched as the flames combined. As the flame grew, a floral smell did with it. One by one, they all made their way back to their chairs until there was only one person left: Hol. Through her veil, she silently watched the flames grow to wrap itself around Ron in its guiding embrace. She held her stomach as she watched the wrapped body lay motionless. In the back of her mind, the part that still couldn't believe that it was Ron underneath, hoped that he would suddenly jerk awake, cursing up a storm for someone to put him out and get him a sandwich. Fleice looked at the rows of people behind the family line and got up again to walk over, using an outreached hand to pre-empt Hol'ly that she wasn't alone.

"Come on, baby. People are starting to get nervous." She wrapped an arm around and escorted Hol'ly back to their seats. Whether she forgot her handkerchief or simply found it useless, Hol'ly's face was streak with red. A short, fully greyed, man wearing a floor-length robe flanked by a woman with a candle came to the front. As he was reciting a final send-off hymn, signifying the ending of the ceremony, the fire behind him raged as the smoke floated upwards. As the guests slowly made their way to leave, they all made sure to give their final condolences to the Stokton/Klima families before stopping at the altar a last time for their own Prayer of Guidance. Flip found it weirdly comforting to see that vampyrs were so established in their faith; in this "Father". The movies must have found that aspect not as entertaining for viewers. It reminded him of the night he was at Ata's quarters and how fervent she was about her belief that K'd was the one that led her to escape capture. He wondered if her personal studies lead her to this "Father".

Ronald and Fleice were the first to get up, with Blest in tow. Ronald shared a long, silent hug with Flip and promised to call when they got back into Fountain. The look on his face didn't necessitate to ask if he was ok. He couldn't bring himself to accept the photo of Ronnie and Flip after being asked twice, finding that Flip would appreciate it more, even if it wasn't right now. Fleice asked Flip if he was ok and was already hugging him before he could answer. He cut the difference and responded, "I'll be ok, mom." He told them he was going to stay in Monarch for another day or so before coming back; needed to finalize a few things for work. Fleice looked at him with squinted eyes and took his hands, feeling a tiny pinch in her head. When the pinch subsided, she released his hand. Ronald and Blest had already walked away.

"Let it rest, if only for now, baby. You got your man."

"I can't. Hana's still out there, I just need to need to see if I can find out where."

"And then what? Gonna run 'er down like a fucking dog? Your father can't lose another one, and I for damn sure can't lose my only."

"Mom, I just need to See what I can, that's all. I'm not leaving again. She's one of Sata's people, and if I can help them track her, I'm going to. I need to make sure she's found."

Fleice looked at him, seeing that she wasn't going to change his mind. She recognized the look that reflected back. She wore it too many times to count when she started on the force. All the hard work of investigating a suspect and gathering evidence to put them away just for it blow away because of someone else's lack of due diligence. She smiled and kissed his cheek. "You know you get that stubbornness from your momma?"

"I know." Flip responded as Elena walked up. "I'll let

you know when I'm back in town." He then leaned into her ear, "Do me a favor and make sure Wallace knows to look for a white Torina V'ago with two women. I hope to have more when I come back."

"Ok, baby." She kissed his cheek again. "Elena, please take care of my boy."

"I try, Mrs. Stokton." Before hugging and watching her catch up to Ronald and Blest. She looked to Flip and held his hand, "You ready?"

"Yeah. Where's Penny?" Flip looked around the dark field. "And Hol?"

"I'm right here." A quiet voice came from what felt like it was directly in his ear, causing him to turn around with a start. Hol stood, her veil still draped over her face and her eyes burning with a fire that rivaled the altar; the aroma still strong as it wafted around them. "You two can go on, I think I'm gonna stay here with Ron for a little bit. He kept putting off on what he wanted to name the baby. I figure now's the best time to get an answer before he leaves." She laughed softly. "Penny took Viium inside with Te'rfrejr. She's going to go home tonight after talking to Sata."

"Ok. Will you be ok out here?" Flip asked.

"I think so. It's the first time I've seen him since...that day. There's a lot to catch up on, and my last check-up showed the baby is growing fast and healthily." She stopped herself. "Elena, you especially have been a big help with everything, and I appreciate it greatly. I love you both very much." Hol'ly bowed slightly and went to a chair in the front row that was center-facing the altar. When she moved the chair to get closer, she lifted her veil and sat in silence, matching the pyre's flames with her own.

"Come on, let's leave her alone." Elena led Flip across

the field to the compound. It was approaching 9pm and by now the night sky was full-dark and covered with stars. If it wasn't such sorrowful circumstances, it'd be a romantic setting for a tender night. Looking at Hol and her silent conference with Ronnie, she thought about how this would be the last night the two would share together. They walked inside and followed the passageway until they reached the main structure.

Elena looked over to Flip as he snorted, a current side-effect of his healed nose and removal of the mask and cringed at seeing him swallow whatever had collected. He still kept his bandages around his torso, but felt it was more of a precaution that actual necessity since the worst of his bodily injuries had closed. "Are you really going back?" They walked, trying to navigate themselves the route they thought they remembered from the procession. Luckily, they remembered correctly.

"You ain't gotta go, Olga."

"I didn't say that. I asked was if you were really going back."

"Yes, I am," He stopped in front the door to his room, "you goin'?"

"I am." She didn't need to think about it. "Plus, we need to talk."

Te'rfrejr overheard Flip's plans to revisit the Tabine house. Sata must not have told him about what she had found in the cellar, that sick perversion of reverence to The Father. The faint smell of disinfectant couldn't cover the horrors that dungeon had seen. And that pillar in the center of it all. The inscriptions. It was certain that the Tabine children were not capable of constructing such a thing so powerful; it had to be the work of their own father. It was never known what happened to him when he left Monarch, but she knew deep down that the siblings had something to do with him not returning. She wondered if what became of them could have been avoided. Being born Untrue was not their fault. They were treated all the same by their fellow citizens. Sadly, that same love did not reach their home. The sole comfort she took was that one of them was in the Other World, hopefully at peace. The Father was all benevolent, he didn't engage in holding grudges for the corporeal sins of his Children, but that did not mean they got a free pass. Even in His Grace, His discipline was just. She stood until there was the sound of a door opening, then closing. After determining that both Elena and Flip had gone inside their room, she went to find Queen Sata.

"You heard of a place called Tar'Kuur or Dar'Kuur?" Flip asked when he came back, still holding an uncharred and bloodied piece of bedsheet. He Saw a lot more than he needed and shivered in recoil at the thought that Alexis and Rac' found time to indulge themselves after murdering an innocent man.

Elena was just outside of the bedroom door. "I don't think so, why?"

"I think that's where Hana's headed." Flip looked around the room again, noticing for the second time his eyes were able to make out almost everything relatively clearly in the dark.

"I see. Can we go now? This place is creeping me out."

"I said you didn't have to come."

"Flip, shut up."

The drive over was nothing but talk, and even going across Monarch from the compound, it still felt unresolved, mainly because there were questions posited that he half an answer for: Was he in danger of an urge to "feed"? Was she? What if it came out into the public? What would happen if they had children of their own? What about Penny? All of these were met with an exasperated "I don't know". Despite their voices being raised at a few points, they agreed to leave it at that, for now. Picking around the bedroom a little more yielded nothing other than the bit of a lead he Saw. The driveway only told him Hana and Alexis were gone hours before their meeting with Rac' based on the light rainfall. The attack on Ronnie was planned. "Aight, you ready?"

"Yes, I said that already."

"Olga," He looked at her and decided against finishing his intended mirror request. Elena saw a dim burning where his eyes were supposed to be. "be careful on the stairs."

He followed behind her as she turned without response and cautiously tested each step as he walked down, only glancing away to look at the heavily burned and smoke dusted portraits. His eye caught the gaze of one in particular that he wasn't sure he had noticed before. It was of a woman, not young but hard to say if she was old in the traditional sense of the word. Her eyes, intense and appearing to be the only ones clear and uncovered, made him feel as though she was looking through him; into him. Her eyes, as intense as her gaze was, gave off as though relieved. Before he could ask for a second opinion, he felt the step under him give and rushed the last few steps. Pushing off, his foot dipped into the charred step, and he barely escaped having gotten caught. At the landing, he saw Te'rfrejr standing in the now open doorway with someone else. Getting a better look, he saw it was Hait'een.

"Is that you, Mr. Stokton? I take it Ms. Starks is with you?"

"Yes, it's us, Te'frejr. How'd you know we were here?" Elena asked.

"I... overheard... you and Mr. Stokton, speaking in the hall. It was not intentional, but Sata thought you should still have accompaniment." Te'rfrejr responded. "Have you been into the cellar?"

"No, mostly upstairs since everything down here's burnt to shit. How'd the fire not do as much damage upstairs?"

"I do not know, as there was not as much oil outside of what must have been his own room. The rain did a lot of the extinguishing for us while Sata transported you and Ms. Adlouw to safety. We found the remains of your mobile in the ashes. I'm sorry, but it was beyond salvage."

Flip looked towards the cellar floor-door. "You were saying something about the cellar?"

"There is something at the compound you should look at. It is the only thing we removed from the home."

Flip looked back towards the cellar door and back at Te'rfejr. "Are you sure there's nothing else in there?"

"Nothing that you, or Ms. Starks, should ever see. I will not stop you if your curiosity bests you."

Curiosity was indeed tapping him on the shoulder, but Flip let her pass by. "Then let's go."

"Have you been down there, Te'rfrejr?" Elena asked as they walked towards the door.

"I have, Ms. Starks. It is an unholy room, a blasphemous guise of dedication to The Father. It is such no longer, but the souls it has claimed are doomed to wander these grounds. I sense you are a strong woman, but that room will break your fortitude."

Elena needed no further explanation to make her pick up the pace. She walked past Te'rfrejr and Hait'een and to her car. Hait'een walked to meet her as Te'rfrejr grabbed Flip's arm. Her voice was barely above a whisper, "Mr. Stokton, may I ask you a question?"

"Sure, go ahead."

"You are gifted, yes?"

Flip paused, "Gifted?"

"I'm sorry, let me clarify. I spoke to your mother at your brother's funeral. When she held my hand, I felt something shock me, and she stopped talking mid-statement. It was not long, but I could tell she was not here. When she was back, she complimented me on the beauty of my family home. I had not mentioned anything of my family prior and have not seen my home in a very long time."

"Shit," Flip muttered under his breath. "Te'rfrejr, I'm really sorry about that. She can be a little too straightforward about things. She's been dealing with her, situation, for a while now. I'm sorry about that."

"An apology is not what I seek, as she helped me remember what home looked like to the detail. It was comforting. I felt the same thing here with you, during the fire. Am I correct that you are the same as her?"

"Short answer, yeah. I'm still tryna figure it out though."

"I see." She let his arm go. "Then I pray you think hard on if you really want to see what has happened in that cellar. My eyes are not as yours, but I know you will see that the Tabine children were not the worst to have set foot in there."

◆ ◆ ◆

Sunday, pre-dawn

Flip sat up in bed. He couldn't sleep, not after what he had seen. From the broken chunk of the red stone, he was away for what he knew had been the longest time he's ever flashed. With a father like theirs, he couldn't help but feel something for the Tabine siblings. He thought about the portrait of the woman he saw in the house. It was their mother, and seeing her demise was too much to handle. It was too vivid. For the first time, he was glad to not be able to hear the sounds of the visions. He looked over to a sleeping Elena. He thought about how someone could do that to the one they claimed to love. The mother of their children, of all people. He thought of Hana's branding and began to feel nauseas. She looked like she was just barely older than Flip when he left for the League, if that. Shit, she may not have even had her first time yet.

When he commented to Sata that the Tabine parents looked a little too similar, she elaborated on her mention of the union that created them: their parents were cousins. Even in her time, inter-familial relations became an antiquated practice and all but forbidden. Their children were not born True but had certain traits. She couldn't recall the mother's name, but she knew of her to be a remarkable seamstress and good mother ahead of her purported vices. In fact, Sata was sure she still had a dress or two somewhere around the compound the Tabine mother made for her own. She also suspected that the father had something to do with the children being Turned, specifically Hana.

Flip hoped for Sata to know about Tar'Kuur and she

didn't disappoint. It was a settlement roughly the size of Fountain in the southwest, outside the domain of the closest family on The Father's Council, and thus subject to their own laws and ruling practices. She speculated that the Tabine family would be reticent about sending back one of their own for formal Questioning and subsequent Judgement but will talk with the family of the Vyxt Territory about keeping an eye out should Hana enter their land. The current ruler of was close to Sata's age, reputed to be very handsome and, Te'rfrejr personally thought, had an eye for Sata. As cute as he may be, Sata claimed to not trust him outside of the performance of his royal duties. He had a reputation for enjoying the comfort of warm-body women more than that of his own kind. Carnal pleasure was of one's personal taste, but Sata did not see herself as the sharing type with her real love, the current exception being her little Viium with Terfie. He was their special boy.

Leaning over to reach for his new mobile, another gift from Sata, he checked the time: *3:48AM.* It was still a few hours before first sunlight, but the point of trying to sleep was lost on him. Tired of fighting the horrible TechAir signal and a dual toothache housed acutely within his canines, he decided to get up and take a walk, careful to not wake Elena upon leaving bed. As he walked through the halls, he observed the masonry of the walls and that every so often there were names inscribed. There were no birth or death dates with the names, possibly to honor those that have passed on. He continued on and felt himself becoming relaxed with each step, at least until he felt someone watching him.

"Can't sleep?" Sata asked, holding a half-glass of something dark. She was less than six feet away.

"Not really?" *How'd she get so close?*

"I see you are taking in some of the family memorials. We weren't the type to have a huge graveyard or anything like that. Too depressing."

They looked at each other in the hallway, seeing a dim fire was in each other's eyes. "I feel like you got something else to say." Flip finally spoke.

"I could say the same for you, Mr. Stokton." Sata responded without missing a beat before taking a sip. "Would you care to join me?"

"Maybe. You got any smoke? No offense, but I can't really get with that wine."

Sata smiled and took a final sip to finish her glass. "This isn't wine, but I understand it is an acquired taste. Have you had spearflower?"

Flip couldn't help but laugh. "You mean like mint? Nah, I ain't never tried that shit."

"Within Our culture, spearflower is highly revered for its medicinal versatility and sometimes, philtering, uses once dried and cured. My parents grew it frequently and were known for crossbreeding it with purpleaf. Would you like to try some?"

He thought about the offer, a little wary. *Philtering?* "You tryna pull something, Sata?"

"Not at all. I have enough respect for the Matriarch than to hide behind such underhanded tactics. If I want you, or her, I'll *have* you. No, I can tell you want to talk and can't sleep. I am not asleep and would be happy to entertain your thoughts." She held out her hand and Flip felt a force move his legs for him. "Come, we can go into one of the halls."

Flip walked and took her hand, still feeling that pull until his hand met hers. When they did touch, he felt a shock, but there was no flash to go with it. They walked until they reached a tall door. It looked like the door to the hall of their feast. Upon entering, Flip was surprised at how much smaller the room was than he expected. They sat in the middle seats of the only table and Sata took out an already rolled joint and lit it using the candle on the table.

"I thought you ain't smoke?" Flip said as she got it going.

"I don't, though I did in a previous life, when The Deviant's flowers weren't as sophisticated and refined as I see today. My lover and I indulged in it quite often. Things were very violent among the domains of the Council, especially after my mother was killed, and it was the best way to calm my mind while placating my more hurtful impulses. My father's blood had already claimed him by then, and so everyone was a suspect when my mother joined him, even my siblings. Sadly, they became casualties of a tactic we learned from our parents: eliminating suspicion eliminates the problem. They were Questioned, and The Father deemed them not innocent. My first duty as Queen was to personally render His Judgment." Sata pulled and exhaled. Flip found the use of "not innocent" interesting wording. "For G'jon and I, 'weed' made going into battle feel insignificant and enacting brutality little more than a child's thought." Sata passed to Flip. "Spearflower is not a frequent indulgence for me outside of certain social settings or a particularly satisfying Judgment, but it is a more pleasant one. The purpleaf allows me to envision my lover as though he were still next to me. I can close my eyes and be with him again, if only for an hour or two."

Flip noticed the dull embers in Sata's eyes all but go out, allowing him to see their natural hazel color. "He must've been a good man."

"He was to me." Sata responded before going to get a new bottle of wine from the wall rack. "He was always good to me." She whispered to herself.

Flip pulled and the spearflower hit him in a way that made him cough uncontrollably. A freeze rushed through him while his lungs felt like they were thrown into an oven. He continued coughing until tears streamed from his eyes and he had to place the joint on the table to hold his chest.

Sata quietly watched in mild amusement. "The first time is usual the most painful, as they say. The second allows the real pleasure."

After his fit subsided, Flip brought himself to take another hit. His lungs felt like they expanded as a chill went through them and his body began to feel like the gelatin he and his parents would make when he was child. He was always a fan of the green one. Apple? Or was it green sunfruit? It didn't matter right now. "Fuck, that's strong."

Sata only eyed him with a smile on her face, holding back laughter.

"Oh, yeah, I'm ok. Thanks for asking." Flip said between coughs. Sata couldn't hold in her laughter. "I thought you said this was relaxing."

"It is, just give it time to pass."

As he did, he listened to Sata talk about her deceased boyfriend, G'jon of H'ar'iktan (pronounced Harkton), and a short history lesson about his family and their domain of what would later become Redwater. Despite his nickname "G'jon the Changeling" for his often violently mercurial nature, he was always an open book to Sata. He was simply a misunderstood young man and didn't handle their arranged betrothal well in the beginning. He didn't know who he loved, but grew to love her, and she came to understand both

594

him and the reason behind his mood changes. Their love was extremely passionate in every way it could. They have spilled blood together, and at times, for each other. The success of their relationship was the pride and joy of their respective families and the main reason why Monarch was allowed to be formed and ruled separately of H'ar'iktan. No matter how bad his temper was some days, even when he couldn't explain it, he never laid a hand on her for a cheap relief. When G'jon was lured into what would be his assassination, Sata arranged the "sanitization" of the bloodlines of his conspirators, leaving the actual murderers for last. For her. Now, she's quite content with the occasional love-meal or the tenderness of Terfie. In the grand scheme, it didn't matter, as she would be with G'jon again when her time came.

"I believe, as the saying goes, I've shown you mine, Flip. Your turn."

He started with his time in the League, professionally and personally, and what led to his retirement. He filed an appeal but was convinced that if he was still receiving his pension, he wasn't coming back. He talked about his parents and the few in-person memories he had of Ronnie. Finishing with Elena and their history, he could feel the spearflower kicking in and his breathing came almost too easily. The gelatinous feeling firmed some, but he was still making sure that he didn't slide out of his chair. Eventually, he felt he worked his way enough to a new center topic that's been on his mind.

"You and Te'rfrejr talk a lot about this 'Father'. Is he like, Lord Dra'co, from the movies and shit?"

Sata poured herself another glass with a wide smile that showed stained canines. "Your curiosity is aggressive in the late hours." She took a sip before continuing, offering the bottle to Flip who sipped respectively. "He is the one from which We have all came. Some of the more elderly Council members have spoken claims of having seen Him, but old people tend to say a lot. I believe your kind is more proprietary and liberal in interpreting His teachings, a flaw that led us to what you prefer to call the Great Territory War in your history books, while we refer to it for what it was, an attempted culling of our people. Your kind is also more partial to His more benevolent alias. You are a Child of K'd, no? I have seen the Matriarch pray over you, is fair to assume you are as dedicated to your maker?"

He almost choked on his little bit of wine, "You telling me K'd is responsible for vampyr? Be forreal, Sata."

"I will not tell you what to believe, but The Father has gone by many names over the years. By your teachings, K'd gives many times over, yet asks for nothing in return." Sata sipped again. "But I ask you this, if your belief is in K'd having made you and everything around you, is he not responsible for me, and my kind? Like K'd, The Father's presence is always around Us. He has blessed my kind in many ways, but He is not the simply giving type. There is always a ledger that will be settled when He deems it time. He demands only two things: adherence to his teachings, and His blood-reverence. Many take it to a radical place, something your films portray exceptionally, but as His Rulers, we are tasked to ensure that both things happen within our lands with the respect it deserves."

"So, what happened with the Tabine family? Why all the 'perversion' talk?" Flip took another sip and grimaced. It helped defrost the chill only slightly, but it still tasted like sweet shit. It did sooth the throbbing in his mouth. Sata chuckled.

"Because, what we found in that house *was* a perversion of Father's Grace. The father of those children was outwardly a nice man, generous even, but there was always talk about the things he would do behind closed doors. Rumors of dark practices committed by he and his wife."

Flip watched Sata sip and felt a change in the room. "Why didn't you stop them?"

"Stop what, rumors? We found nothing that warranted Questioning and therefore knew nothing about that cellar until Rac' Tabine's arrest. If we are guilty of anything, it is that we did not rescue those children while they could be saved. I hold that burden squarely on my crown, as I had only just inherited the throne. I let my personal matters and losses cloud my judgement and my ability to perform my duties effectively, a dereliction that I rightly deserve resentment from the Tabine children and many others for. When I learned Rac' had left, it was right after The Culling had started, and we hoped he had taken his sister despite our stance of non-participation. Only soon after did we see that Hana stayed, willingly or not."

"You know what happened to him, the Tabine's father?"

"I only know that he left to 'find' his children and bring them back home. They each came back, in time, but he never stepped foot onto our soil again. That corrupted ebonstone was but a single piece of a horrid affront to our teachings. A false monument to the Tabine patriarch disguised as an offering to The Father. It will never be cleansed of the evil it holds." She sipped. "The mother's fate was more certain, and I could tell that you saw more of what happened to her than what we found. Terfie told me about the interaction she had with your mother at your brother's service and that she had the same feeling with you. Are you ashamed of your gift, Flip? Seeing what has befallen your own HouseMother would drive most to deny their bloodright, surely." The fire was returning to her eyes. "Maybe you are afraid of it? You can't control it, therefore believe it will eventually control you." She took a sip and placed her glass down as she saw the reaction she hoped for. Flip's eyes were breathing in a way that was either from exposed vulnerability or anger. She could sympathize with both.

She watched as he took a hit of spearflower and inhaled the smoke through his nostrils, just like how G'jon used to. If it was good smoke, he liked to "taste it twice", as he would joke. Down to the height, it was scary to her at how much of Flip and his mannerisms reminded her of him. If he was as good a man as her G'jon, Matriarch Starks was very favored to have such a man by her side, warm-body or not.

"I ain't ashamed of anything, Your Highness." Flip said to her, his voice devoid of familiarity.

"Mr. Stokton, I wasn't saying that you were, I only ask. If is not shame, then that leaves you with fear. You shouldn't be afraid of what you've been given. From what I know, your mother utilized it to aid her already fabled career as a Homicide Investigator."

"And look what happened to her."

"Yet you appear to chase her shadow."

Flip didn't answer. In a way, Sata was right, he was afraid. How much longer did he have before he woke up and the world he went to bed in wasn't the same? Before he started having his own conspiracies about those closest to him? Before he couldn't trust Elena? It wasn't the Sight he was afraid of; it was what came with it. He took a few more hits in silence, letting the chill take hold and a new wave of sedation ride over. He then thought about the quip his mom made when they last talked on the phone, about crazy running through the family, presumably starting with Fountain City Deputy P'rotector Crayton Stokton himself. Sata wished she could know what he was thinking.

"How long has she been the way she is?"

"A little under a decade, but honestly, who knows. She says the Sight started while she was still on the force but only got worse after she resigned."

"Interesting..." Sata drank. "Yet, she goes normally through her days? I found her to be coherent during her time here, though we did have quite the talk. I can see where you get your fire from."

"Ata, our HouseMaiden, keeps her active and intact but there's still days where it's best to leave her alone. They don't happen that much, but still."

"Is that all she does? Your HouseMaiden?"

He didn't get what she was trying to drive at, "Yeah, she's basically with her all day, damn near. She wasn't at the service, but she's devoted to my mother, more so after her own 'Turn', as y'all call it."

Sata sat up in her seat. Her ears had to have mistaken her. "You have a vampyr maiden, Flip? Yet, I thought you knew nothing of our existence?" She asked with a smirk.

Flip scoffed. "Yeah, a little while after she started with us, she was kidnapped but managed to get away. She only revealed the whole story to me during my investigation into the Tabines. She gives credit to K'd for her escape, and for her new life."

"Interesting."

"Meaning?" He took a hit and passed the half back to Sata, who turned two strong hits and let the smoke emanate from her.

"Meaning, I find it interesting. Those who have been Turned under such traumatic ways often do not view it as a positive and lash out. This Ata reminds me a lot of Terfie in her trust of the Father, as she feels her blindness and defilement was not forced onto her without a higher reason. I would like to meet this Ata at some point. If what you say about her is true, it is of no rush." Sata laughed at her joke and saw that it was welcomed. "Did she tell you who her captor was?"

"The description of the house and girl sounded a lot like Hana Tabine. Took her right out the Fifth District and brought her to Monarch. Said she was going to be a 'birthday gift' to Rac'. Guess she didn't know he wasn't ready to come home yet."

Sata eyes focused when she heard Hana's name. She didn't know of another Fountain citizen having been held on her land. Whatever Hana had planned was likely what happened to that girl that Flip was searching for when they first became acquainted. She took another hit and exhaled. "Then it is good that K'd lead her from that house. You would have had to look for a new Maiden."

"Would you believe me if I told you my mom knows?"

"I would. She strikes me as very intelligent, contrary to her blunt-force vocabulary. Not like how they show in the movies, full of bluster, and lacking in what you would call 'book-smarts'. Entertaining, yes, but a disservice in portraying to the truly competent, and honest."

They shared a look at the mention of honesty was intentional before Flip saw that it had only been just over an hour since he had left his room. The spearflower had now proven at least one of its medicinal claims, having quelled the throbbing points to a dulled murmur. He then asked about Viium.

"He was a small unnamed child when Terfie and I rescued him, and he will never need to worry for another home. His burn was much worse than it is now, and I believe it to be the major cause of his... delayed, development." She then sighed, "G'jon was taken from me unexpectedly, and we had only conceived once prior. We even had a name picked and everything. It is by The Father that Viium was put into our lives, and I have loved him as though he is my own. His youth has given me a proper chance to be a mother."

"So why the 'aunt' stuff?"

"Because it makes it easier to bear that he is not of my own bearing. Whether he knows we share no blood or not, he still loves me with his all." Sata answered flatly. "The Father may have forgiven me for not trying again with G'jon, but I have not."

"Are you planning to have children of your own again, Sata? You really shouldn't be so hard on yourself." Flip accepted the pass and took a hit.

"Is that an offer for a night of your time?" She laughed loudly and drank. "No, I do not believe so. I feel I can mold Viium into a strong Ruler that will lead and protect when I am gone. He may be a child, but he is intelligent, he is finally accustomed to the royal ways, and he obeys The Father's teachings without question. We have seen that he is prone to violent mood swings, like my G'jon, but his heart is still tender. It is a beautiful trait, but a common one shared among short-lived Rulers. If He deems that Viium should not take my place, there is a girl his age whose path will lead her from your Territory to mine. She is of your kind, but in time, The Father will show me when she is ready, as will she."

"Who's the girl?"

"Why does it matter?"

"If she's a citizen of Fount, I need to know, preferably *before* a missing girl comes across my TV screen or ear."

"What I have with her is not of import to you. I will not force her away like Viium, but she knows I can provide her a better home than her current residence. Try as you might, you will not stop her, or His Will. I hope you still here when it is time to meet her." Sata's tone, and eyes, let him know that was about as far as that topic was going. "Are you thinking about having children, Mr. Stokton?"

"Kinda."

"Go on." Sata finished her glass.

"I think, no, I *know* Olga would be a great mother, but--"

"You are worried what they may inherit through their bloodright."

Flip didn't respond.

"I do hope you reconsider your hesitancy--"

"It's not just that," Flip went into explanation about the Destined clause of the Seven Clans and how unlike Elena, his arrangement with Bloss G'oh is not so cleanly decided. The rules of being Destined are simple but must be respected. That leaves the hypothetical Starks/Stokton children's legitimacy in a gray area should he have to wed Bloss but already has children with Elena, unless they themselves marry, and even that would create a lot of persistent headaches.

"Interesting. Would you like for this Bloss to be out of

the picture?"

"No, I'll figure it out. We all grew up together, and I won't gain anything from an assassination." He wasn't sure if that's where Sata was going, but how else would one remove a HouseMother completely?

"Assassination is simply a means to an end, I've learned. Whatever you should decide, I caution you on your hesitancy. Do not repeat the mistake G'jon and I made." She paused. "We put off a second chance at children. We put off getting married. We were in no rush, until we had nothing to rush to."

"Olga won't let me be that complacent. Especially after all this."

Sata adjusted in her seat. "You refer to the Matriarch as 'Olga'. I've heard you say it a lot in your extended slumber. Why is that? Is it related to the Revered Queen Olga of Brijnn and the story of her slain king?"

"Yeah, her mother was from a village there. When we were kids, I got jumped by these two brothers from another Family behind the library. A few days later, she was right there with me getting them back. After that, her mom was calling her Olga to tease, but as we got older, it sorta just stuck. Now, she only lets me call her that, and maybe her dad, but I ain't never heard him."

"Ah, I see. Like Olga of Brijnn, Ms. Starks defended your honor. There is a similar tale of vengeful love in Our lore. Scor'h, Guardian of Matrimony, Royal Eyes, and widows-slash-widowers. He was also my father's namesake." Sata rose from her seat, reaching her hand out. It wasn't as strong as before but Flip could feel a pull bring him to his feet and he took her hand into his. "Do you need an escort you to your room?" she asked, looking up to him. His cheek scar made him the splitting image of Deputy P'rotector Crayton in the dim of the candlelight.

"Nah, I think I can manage."

"Very well," She held his hand until they reached the hall door. Upon exiting, Sata broke away and turned, "I bid you a restful sleep, Founder. The next few weeks will be the roughest for you."

"Rough?"

"The Father will test you, as he does all of his new Children. He did with your HouseMaid, and I hope she did not commit anything she cannot live with. Be strong, and do not give in to the dark temptation. Good night, Flip." Sata bowed and walked away before he could say anything back.

Flip waited until he was out of sight to use a sconce to restart the rest of his joint. When he entered his room, he found Elena sitting upright and on her phone. From the sound of it, it had to be highlights from a recent game. How the fuck was she getting a signal out here? Flip pulled and exhaled as he climbed into bed next to her, kissing her on the shoulder lightly.

"What the hell is that? It smells like burnt mint."

He relayed what Sata told him about spearflower and watched Elena's face.

"Is that right? Lemme hit."

Flip hesitantly passed the remaining bit over and watched Elena go through the same coughing he did on the first hit, having a small laugh just as Sata did. Elena ashed the joint and put it on the bedside, turning to cuddle to him. He could feel her shivering.

"You ok?"

"Mm-hmm." and then she kissed him. Then again, and again. With each kiss, he felt the shivering subside. They made love until the sun's first light came through the bedroom's massive, red-glassed window. Their sounds filtered past the door as just above a muffle, but those that walked by made no mistake identifying what they heard, and thus let the queen's guests enjoy their morning privacy undisturbed.

Sunday morning

Sata, Te'rfrejr and Viium walked the couple across the front field to a large two-story barn. It was a fittingly bright Sunday morning and they all wore jackets. Opening the doors, Sata allowed them to walk in first. Flip got out his keys but looked over the fleet of cars that sat next to Joy and the horse stables across the room. The cars were both foreign and domestic brands and varied from trucks and caravans to 2-door sports cars.

"You ever find the time to actually drive all of these?" Flip asked, walking over to his car.

"Only the ones I still like. I like to ride the horses with this one, but like I said," She bent to pick Viium up. "I collect a lot of things. I hope to pass along the ones he likes, once I teach him how to drive them, of course."

"I like the red and green one, Aunt Sata!" Viium shouted excitedly and pointed to a sleek, low sitting car. It had three large wheels and a dome covering the triangularly arranged seats. Flip's never seen a car like it, nor did he recognize the logo emblazoned on the front hood. He wasn't even sure the word "car" was an appropriate description.

"I know you do, little one. Once you are a master of the horse you can see, you will be ready for the many you won't. You are still my first passenger when I decide to drive it." She then kissed him on the cheek and whispered into his ear, "My special boy."

Viium pouted, "You said that last time." He slapped his palm twice with three fingers. Flip didn't know what that was supposed to mean but it instinctively felt too specific to mean nothing. Maybe this was part of the mood swings. "Can I at least sit in the front?" He never got to sit in the front. Aunt Terfie always said it's because Aunt Sata drove as though for sport and not recreational leisure.

"Only if Aunt Te'rfrejr doesn't mind sitting in the back."

Te'rfrejr looked in the direction of the voices. Feeling Sata and Viium looking back, she responded, "Only if you are a good boy."

"I promise!" Viium called.

"We shall see." Te'rfrejr answered with a smile. "The Father does not look kindly on empty promises from His Children. Nor does he on little boys who use profane gestures in front of their queen." Viium embarrassingly turned his face into Sata's neck.

"It's ok, he's just excited. I did make the same promise last time." Sata calmly said as she rubbed her nose against his cheek. Te'rfrejr stood quietly.

"Where's Hol'ly?" Elena asked, sitting against the hood of her car.

"She needed to go back into town for a few things. She has decided to stay with us until the baby comes. I was told you two were a little, preoccupied."

Elena and Flip shared a look to each other.

"Please, do not be embarrassed." Sata put Viium down to kiss them each on the cheek. "I bid you safe travel home. Mr. Stokton, your teeth are coming in quite nicely, I must say."

Te'rfrejr prayed for their safe drive home and bowed. As they pulled out of the barn, Viium waved. Unbeknownst to the other, Flip and Elena called their parents and informed them of their return. Flip was told by his father that they would hold a feast at the house to celebrate his recovery and as a proper repass for Ronnie. He didn't get a chance to tell him at the funeral, but Ronald really was proud of Flip and he shouldn't hold his death against himself. Ronald didn't. From what he was told, Ronnie didn't go out without a fight, and Ronald took humorous solace knowing that all that money for blade training back in the day didn't go to waste.

When he turned onto the straightway to go through the center of City-Monarch, he slowed down to observe a CLOSED sign on the front door of Klima's Kuts but Ronnie's truck parked out front. He turned into the space next to it and parked, seeing Elena do the same to him a few seconds later. He got out and went to the door and tried it. Locked. After a few knocks, Hol'ly came from the back, waved, and walked over to open up. "Hey, Flip, everything ok?"

"Yeah, everything's cool. Elena and I are headed back to Fountain and I saw Ronnie's car. Everything ok here?" He could tell from the faint cheek smear that she had been crying.

"Oh, yeah I'm ok, just getting a few things to do some paperwork from home for a few days. I'll reopen later this week."

"Do you need any additional help? I can see if a few Wards can come out here for you?"

"Thank you, but Sata's already got it covered. I'll have a few people to help keep the house and farm together in between my stay with her. Hopefully they're of the domestics, those Eyes scare me. Especially Te'rfrejr. I still can't understand how she can drive. And for all their strength, I don't think most of them are cut out for farm work." She said with a chuckle.

"Neither do I. Aight, well I ain't gonna hold you. My dad said they're gonna have a feast at the house."

"I'll be there, your mother told me about it yesterday."

"I see." He hugged her. "I'll see you later, Hol. I'll need to set up my communicator when I get back home but call Elena if you need anything until then."

"I will. Bye, Flip."

He stopped over at Elena's car and tapped the driver window. When she lowered, he leaned down.

"How's she doing?" Elena asked.

"She said she's fine, but she's been crying. She's gonna be working from home the next couple days before Sata sets her up with some domestics. Did my parents tell you about a feast at the house?"

Elena's face answered for her, "Nope, daddy just told me now."

"Did he tell you when it was? Dad didn't give particulars."

"No, but I'm sure he knows."

"Ok. Following me home?"

"Want me to?"

608

"Kinda."

"Then I guess I am. I'll need to stop at the Center first, but you don't gotta wait."

They kissed and Flip got back into his car and pulled out. Continuing on the straightway, he watched the dark butchery hoping to see Hol again. He felt nervous for her, but had faith she'll be back soon. He didn't have a lot of close friends his age that were married, so trying to read the layered emotions of a recent widow was a foreign practice. Nevertheless, he determined to keep in frequent contact with her as the due date approached. He drove on in excited and equally reticent anticipation of the welcoming he could expect returning to Fountain; his home. He was going to do his best to put everything that's happened behind him, but it wasn't going to slow down his work. He felt the box holding Birdie and thought about the modification made to it. Hopefully there's a "work capacity" loophole he can utilize, but he'll cross that when he gets to it.

EPILOUGE

CHAPTER 1
Thursday. Three days ago

A clean, black Torina V'ago drove across the border-marker that began the start Tar'Kuur. Hana was surprised she could remember the rights roads to take to get out of Monarch unseen, but moving before the enemy's expectations fortifies chances of a plan going in one's favor. Rac' taught her that one. He taught her a lot. After a few hours of already being the road last Friday, that's when it hit both her and X'i. She was driving, and then a wave went through them both, causing her to almost crash the car into an embankment on an elevated portion of highway.

She knew what had happened. It happened when that fucking Founder killed Cherry. It happened when she and Rac' killed *Him.* She pulled over to keep X'i from getting sick in the car and wept. Rac' was gone. Her brother. Her best friend. The only Turn that mattered to. Gone. She wept because she left him behind. She wept because he was going to face Questioning for both of them. It didn't matter that he ordered her to; she left him.

X'i took over the driving for a while, fighting back tears herself. Master was kind to her in Torina. He took her out for nice beachfront dinners. He let her go out with Mother. She was sure he loved her. Now, knowing he won't be coming back, she found herself hoping that she was carrying a piece of him. After two days of driving and sleeping in the car, they drove into a shabby one-road-in-one-road-out settlement that was unfortunate to be in the middle of the desert, a minimum of hours away from the nearest sight of people in any direction. After topping off their fuel supply, they checked into one of the nicer buildings in town, a 16-

room nameless inn.

They started slow, picking the settlers off one by one until by the time people were getting concerned about the connection between the new visitors and disappearing citizens, it was far too late. Hana was willing to offer as many people as she felt she needed to the Red Master if it meant that Rac' could come back, even allowing her rage to lead her to X'i herself. This wouldn't have happened if it wasn't for her. As X'i fought back, Hana came to and remembered why she needed to keep her. She hoped Rac' finally reunited with Mama. On the second morning, they swept for survivors and moved on, leaving fate and time to return the settlement to the sand from which it rose.

As she drove through the wide streets of Tar'Kuur, Hana took in the once familiar sights and smell of her mother's home. Most of the businesses she remembered from childhood visits were no longer in sight, but the buildings still stood and were homes to new things. X'i looked over the people walking by on the sidewalks, some with what looked like leashes connected to them, and caught some glancing at what stranger was driving a fancy new car like a V'ago; must be someone important for the Tabines. Hana drove until they made it to the residential areas and cut through a few neighborhood streets she knew was close to her uncle's place.

"Have you been this far from Fountain, X'i?"

"No, Mother." X'i answered as she looked out the window.

She made a right turn. "My own mother was born here, you'll come to enjoy it. I won't have you wearing a leash, though. I think you know I'm much better than that."

"Yes, Mother. Can I still wear one?"

"You're one of us now, X'i, but if you want, that's fine with me. I'll have a special one made, just for you, ok? You deserve it."

X'i continued looking out the window with a smile, taking in the sand-blasted suburban homes. Her thoughts about the future were interrupted by the sharp digging of nails into her thigh. X'i winced and turned to Mother. There was no fire behind the dark lenses that looked back.

"I'm sorry, Mother, thank you."

"Good girl." Hana pulled her hand back and readjusted Rac's sunglasses. A quick check of her rearview made her realize why he liked wearing them so much. They looked slightly oversized on her, but she liked the movie star vibe that met her.

As they pulled into the driveway a colorful four-story house, there was a portly, older looking man standing in the front yard wearing stained overalls next to a raised sedan with the hood open, parts and tools on the ground around him. He turned and saw a car pulling into the driveway slowly and tossed down his even more stained spill rag. There was a glare in his eyes, and he slowly reached for his toolkit sitting in the driver's seat of the car, wrapping his fingers around the hilt of an ebonstone dagger. He let go at once when he recognized the young woman that got out the driver's side.

"Well, shit, ain't this something? *Haan-na Ta-been*, that you, girl?"

"Uncle Rac'i!" Hana was already running up the driveway. She crashed into her uncle with a tight hug. She turned to the car and motioned for X'i to join her, feeling the return of her half of the power finally settling in.

"Damn girl, you lookin' just like your mama. Seein' how we're talking tells me you're now more like her than just looks." He looked over her shoulder warily, "Who's your friend?" He couldn't help but look at the friend's clouded eye first.

"This is X'i. She's been with Rac' and I for a little bit now, you know?"

"I do." Uncle Rac'i answered with a knowing coldness.

"X'i, get the bags." Hana snapped her fingers.

"Yes, Mother." X'i went back to the car, opening the back-passenger door and taking out their bags two at a time.

"Damn, got her trained up real well. You prolly let her sit at the table when y'all eat, don'cha?"

"Well, it took some time to break her in, but she's a really good girl now."

They shared a small laugh before Rac'i looked back over to the car. "Where's Rac'? Last I heard, he was in the Territory Service."

Hana's face instantly lost its cheer. "He's... He's with Mama."

"Was it the Queen?"

"Someone else, but we'll talk about it later. For now, I'd like to see my aunt and then be alone, if that's ok."

"Of course, honey. Your aunt's prolly in the kitchen. I'm tryna install this new attachment into cousin Elvo's piece of shit here. I'll tell him you're here when he comes by."

Hana picked up her bags, "Thank you, uncle, but I'd prefer you didn't for now. X'i, come on."

Rac'i called behind him as she walked away, "Listen,

I don't care what kind of shit you tracked down here, but we ain't sendin' you back to that uppity bitch Sata, y'hear?" He went back to into the car's hood. "Y'all can use the guest house as long as you want. Need me to look at that fancy carriage of yours?"

"You can, but it's been running smooth since refilling. There's a housegift in the trunk." Hana dropped the V'ago keys on the roof of Elvo's car.

"I hear and thank'ya, little missy." Rac'i spoke in his always spot-on Old Territory character mimic, "Now, git'on and say hello to yer aunt. I know my sister ain't raise no rude kin." and gave a dark smile before going over to the V'ago. He knew he was smellin' something good under all the oil.

Hana walked up the stone trail until they reached the front door, continuing inside and instinctively going in the direction of the kitchen. Aunt Tali was one of the best cooks Hana had known, still able to remember the taste of her first warm-body steaks when she was a small child. She hadn't yet known what human was supposed to taste like and she didn't know that's what she was eating, but it was good as all hell. Mama brought her and Rac' out here almost every winter in their youth, but coming back after so long, a flood of memories broke from the dam they were held. Sure enough, the aroma of active cooking led Hana to a woman hunched over a skillet, dipping her fingernail into a pouch, and bringing it to her nose for a strong sniff before flipping the sizzling meat. Another man and woman sat quietly at the kitchen table wearing heavy chain-link leashes fastened at the neck, blank-eyed. Both looked like they've seen better days.

"Who's that, creepin' in my kitchen?" The woman

spoke in a sing-song tone but kept her eyes to the stovetop. She dipped her finger into the pouch and sniffed again.

"It me, Aunt Tali, just lil ol' me." Hana sang back.

Tali looked over to the kitchen entrance wide-eyed and smiling. "By the Fath-- Hana is that you?" She snapped her fingers towards the man sitting at the table and pointed to the stove, causing him to wordlessly get up and go over to tend. "Don't let it burn." She didn't wait for an answer. X'i watched as Hana and Aunt Tali held each other and kissed cheeks before Hana broke down and told her about Rac'. Tali said a prayer for him, knowing he was with C'elia again. She knew how much Ceeli worried about him when he left for the War and if she would ever see him again. Tali didn't know if she ever did.

Tali pointed to X'i, "This one yours?"

"She was Rac's. He Turned her."

Tali looked X'i up and down a few times, taking an overt interest in the clouded eye that stared back. "She's pretty, but a little tall for you, don't you think?"

"I think he had a thing for tall girls."

That made Tali smile. "Y'all hungry?" She asked after another sniff.

Hana looked to X'i and answered for them both; they had a large meal already but will get something a little later. She just wanted to put her stuff away and rest. Tali nodded and gave her the keys to the guest house and to only use the upstairs or first floor bathrooms. The basement toilet ain't been flushing right, but they had a friend coming to work on it in a couple days. Hana kissed her aunt on the cheek and said she'll talk to her and uncle later.

CHAPTER 2
Monday. Present day.

Returning home on a Sunday turned out to be a good idea. Not telling anyone about his return was a better one. Part of him anticipated someone recognizing his car and starting a foot chase of people cheering his return. He drove to Mesa, blending in with the midday Sunday traffic, and cleared his work area of the maps and notes. The Tabine case was closed; for now. He used his barely touched landline to call his servicer about getting a new mobile call-chip, preferably for his previous number, and texted Penny to tell her he was back. It didn't go through, and he found that someone turned his TechAir router off. Once he reset it and connected the mobile, multiple rapid-fire texts came back in return. Dom wasn't happy about her being zero-dark for over a week but after receiving context, he came around. Now, he wasn't happy with Flip. She said that her canines felt and looked longer, but still hadn't found a way to tell Dom about her "gift" from The Father. That made him go examine his own in the bathroom mirror. He wondered if Penny was given a warning similar to his before she left.

He took the downtime to clear his contacts of old numbers and the voicemails that weren't usable. He called to check in with Wallace, then another with Monroe. Both congratulated him on his work in Monarch and gave their condolences about Ronnie. Wallace admitted he hadn't talked to Ronnie in a long time, but he knew they were still best friends. They just fell outta touch, that was all. Flip felt obligated to tell him a fuller version of what had happened that day. He still didn't remember a few spots, but he could clearly recall the look on Rac's face as he stood over him.

It was as if he didn't even see Flip, he kept looking of next him, like there was someone else. Wallace told him that like Cheryl Shockley, he couldn't let Rac' dwell in his head longer than he needed and told him to get some rest but felt hypocritical in his words. He himself still couldn't shake the image of Flip shooting a downed man; the anger on his face. Wallace wasn't sure how many were left in the clip, but if Flip hadn't collapsed, he knew he would've kept firing until it was empty. Wallace couldn't say that that he'd be able to let that image go away any time soon.

An hour and a half later, there was a series of knocks at the door. Flip cautiously walked over, gifted dagger in hand and stood a foot from the door. "Who is it?"

"FTNComm delivery."

I'm trippin', Flip thought. "Give me a second." He unlocked the door after sheathing the dagger behind his back. "Sorry about that, forgot you guys were stopping by." The delivery rep was a now wide-eyed teenager, just finishing their afternoon shift at the local Fountain Communications retailer before going home to finish a history paper. They also happened to be a huge Flip Stokton fan but did their best to hide their surprise. He heard Founder Stokton died in Monarch protecting Matriarch Elena Starks from a vampyr. Flip looked at him and instantly recognized the frame of a ballplayer.

"Oh shi—Sorry, Mr. Stokton, they didn't tell me who it was at the address. He- here you go, one field call-chip." The rep was pulling out a small tablet from his waist. "Can you sign here?"

Flip used his finger and traced along the screen, "It's all good, lil bro, what's your name?"

"Xartis. Xartis Cro." Xartis still couldn't believe he

was talking to a dead man.

"Nice meeting you, Xartis, and thanks for the chip. You're really helping me out with this. Hold on a sec." Flip closed the door for a few minutes. When he came back, he had a small fold totaling 300 scril. "Not a lot of people know I'm back, mind keeping it that way for a little while?"

"Yeah, man, of course. Thank you, Founder Stokton." *I'm talking to Flip Stokton right now.* This was the first time Xartis was thankful he took a delivery right before his end of shift. He even got a week's worth of scril out of it.

"Just call me Flip, man. Who you play for? You look like you ball." Flip had already put the small box holding the call-chip in his pocket.

"Fountain Fifth District Academy. My family moved to the 2nd District from Redwater when they gave a scholarship. Man, my cousins and I grew up watching you and Elena Starks play. We still play the UBL Tonight from your rookie year sometimes. My dad got me the one with you on the cover of Regional Edition East."

"You and me both, man." Flip responded, thinking about how somewhere in the condo is his own unsealed Regional Edition copy of UBL Tonight. Xartis laughed, but not too hard; gotta keep it cool. He didn't want to come off as a suck up. Then again, he was making a last-minute delivery to a dead Founder. It was still possible Xartis was still sleep in the breakroom. That also means he didn't just receive that huge tip.

"For what it's worth, sir, my family doesn't believe that trash of you jigging games. We were pretty bummed watching your retirement."

"Thanks man, I appreciate that. Don't worry, I still get a pension, so somebody knows it was bullshit, but their loss."

Flip held-out for a fist bump. "Feel me?"

Xartis met it. "Hell yeah. Is it true you're an Investigator now?"

"I just work with the 'tecs sometimes. Just getting' back from a case, actually."

Xartis thought about his next move. He spoke cautiously. "Can I ask if it was that guy they been talking about? The vampyr?"

"Yeah, you can say that."

Xartis' eyes were about to leave his head, "That was you!?" He looked around the empty hallway and lowered his voice, "Sorry. Was that you? People sayin' you died out there."

Flip shrugged his shoulders but let the Stokton Smile speak for him. "People will say a lot of stuff, man. My mom says to believe my eyes more."

Xartis nodded and dapped him up. Flip gave him an autograph, hoping to sweeten the request of discretion. When their hands met, there was a spark and Flip Saw Xartis talking to what looked like friends or coworkers, likely telling them about the coolest work story any of them heard, with evidence to prove it. When he was back, Flip told Xartis he had a headache coming on but to swing by the Fountain City Community Center and introduce himself to the Director. She was a very close friend of his. Flip mentally sized Xartis up again and thought he might also be a good addition to the rec team. He'll see on Thursday.

Later, after his quasi-recruitment of Xartis C'ro and his mobile restored, there was another sound at the door: two deliberate knocks. Flip waited a few seconds before he

620

got up for the door and opened it, just in time to see the elevator doors closing. He looked at the floor and found a black duffle bag with an envelope sitting on top. There was a familiar smell coming from the bag as he picked it up. He opened the envelope and laughed upon reading the message:

Unc said it's on the house. Welcome back home, Stok. Fuck a vamp. - Cal

Flip was about to send his thanks when an incoming call beat him. The caller had an UNREADABLE number. He went back to his living room and flopped onto the couch, putting the mobile on speaker before unzipping the duffel. The odor was so welcoming, even having a hint of fruit to it; must've been a new strain. He took out one of big heavy-plastic sacks and placed it on the coffee table.

"What's up, Sata?"

"'What's up'?" She didn't hear the phrase enough to grasp the meaning. "What's up?" was such a vague question. Humans were always humorously creative in the realm of linguistics, particularly with their greetings.

"Nevermind, what's goin' on?" He heard the door unlocking and saw Elena walking in. He waved, "I'm about to eat dinner."

"Then I will not keep you, but I thought you should know two things that I think will interest you. Unless you are alone, I wish to speak privately."

Flip picked up the mobile and switched over. "Go."

"I was recently informed about the Hhal settlement. Are you familiar?"

"I think so."

"Are you aware it rests in the outlands between Tar'Kuur and the Sovereign 'Chilo Territory? Natives and locals call it Little 'Chilo."

"Nah."

"I see. A black Torina V'ago was seen using its sole fuel station, its occupants being two women who checked later into a motel, staying for at least two full days but possibly three."

"Sata, I told you I don't like the riddles. What happened?"

"I will let you theorize on the details, but all of its citizens are either dead or unaccounted for. Many of the found victims bore the markings of my kind. Others appeared to have been broken."

A whole town? "How do you know what happened?"

"A young elven man left for 'Chilo the day of the women's arrival. I am a close friend of the Ruler's daughter and she spoke his account. He does not know if anyone was killed by the time he left, but he, quote, didn't have a good feeling about them. From what I am told, he is an upstanding man and honest to a fault, though he is said to be 'touched' by whatever deity he adheres to, thus many do take him seriously outside of his labor. He says that It told him he needed to leave Hhal."

"Sata, I just got home, are you serious about this?" Flip saw Elena look over with inquiring eyes.

"To quote your people's fondness for analogies, I am as 'serious as a heart attack'. Will you be here?"

"When you havin' him brought up?"

"I will talk to Sissy and see when they plan to be finished with him."

"Can we trust him?"

"Like I said, he is reputed to be an honest man and

does regular business in both Hhal and 'Chilo, but he will be Questioned should any recorded detail differ from what he says here."

"Aight."

"Flip, this was done out of anger, as she well knows her brother will not be rejoining her in this life. No matter the preceding circumstances, His Ways requires seeing a blood-feud to completion. I pray that The Father stands with you when she returns."

"Just let me know when he's in Monarch."

"Very well. Enjoy your supper and pass my greetings to Matriarch Starks."

Flip hung up and yelled an expletive chain that'd make even his mother object. He gave the current situation to Elena, positing that if this town is just outside Tar'Kuur, Hana's already in her family's protection and unlikely to turn around so soon. Custom says be obligated to settle the "blood-feud", but Sata didn't sound like she felt Hana's return was imminent. Whether it was or wasn't, he'd be ready.

"Aight, well if she ain't coming tonight, then can we forget it for right now?" Elena said with a smile. She understood the situation he was facing, but they just got home and need something of a normal afternoon and evening. "It doesn't help that almost everything in here is either bad or about to go."

"You ain't been here while I was gone?"

"I came by and unplugged your router. Cleaning your fridge must've slipped my mind while I was worrying about you dying. Please, forgive me, Master Stokton." She curtsied, "But seriously, you need to hit the store soon. Like tomorrow, soon."

"Aight, I'll do it in the morning."

"You better."

Flip called and ordered two baked shellcrawler platters from the Hole's new menu. A lot has changed in a week and a half. Was he sure that it's only been that long? 20 minutes after placing his order, Hazel texted him a welcome home and to not to worry about his meals for tonight. He responded that he'd give it to driver if it was all the same. Another 15, and Flip was trading with the delivery girl, despite her stating that she was explicitly told to not accept any scril from him or Elena Starks. She reluctantly gave in and agreed to pass along a message of thanks to Hazel before putting the scril into her waistline.

After setting the table, the two sat in the kitchen and ate their shellcrawler, talking about any and everything that wasn't Monarch, the Tabines, or Sata. That can wait for tomorrow. Right now, they were two people that have been through a crazy 10 days and needed a reprieve, if only for an evening.

In the middle of their meal, Flip reached out and interrupted Elena's side of the talk about the bust of a recent Redwater trade to hold her hand, "Hey."

"What's up? Everything ok with your food?"

"Elena, I ain't afraid anymore."

"What do you mean? Afraid of what?"

"Of It. My Sight is going to be with me for as long as I'm here, and I might end up passing it on. What happens to me when I'm older, it happens. Are you good with that?"

"We having kids? You know something I don't?" Elena shifted in her seat. She tried to keep her voice humorous, and steady.

"I'm being forreal, now, c'mon." Flip kept her eyes in his.

Elena didn't need to think about it. "Yes."

"Are you ok with our kids having it?"

"I don't know," She turned her face away playfully. "they ain't gonna be tryna touch on everything, are they? Tryna see what mommy's got planned for them on their birthday? What kinda *K'dsthajh* gifts daddy's getting everyone?" She couldn't tell if he truly didn't find the joke funny or really intent on getting his point across. "What about Bloss? I'm being forreal, now."

"Fuck Bloss, she got a man."

"I'm serious, Flip."

"You think I ain't?"

She looked at him, at his eyes. She could see a low burn in their new clarity. There was no hitch in his voice. Whatever he was getting at, he was serious. Part of her hoped he wasn't about to impulsively ask for her hand in the middle of their meal, but if he was, she knew her answer. She always knew her answer when it came to Flip.

"Maybe it took losing Ronnie and almost my own life. Twice, if we're being real. Maybe it started after the Shockley situation, but I'm ready for what's coming. Whether it's Hana and her people, or me becoming my mom. I'm at peace with both." Flip continued. He really needed to get everything off his chest. It was now or never.

Elena didn't expect it to be over baked shellcrawler and wine, but she had been waiting for him to say everything he did for a long time. In a dark recess of her, she wondered if this had anything to do with the late-night rendezvous with Sata the other night. Whatever they talked about, it stuck with him. She had a single question left, since they were getting all sappy with each other. It's been on her mind since Sata's feast. "What about your new 'gift'? You seem to be pretty popular up above. Where does that leave me?"

He didn't know, only that he planned to be with her for as long as K'd kept them.

"And I'm always going to be next to you. I'm yours, Flip. I always have been, and always will."

Flip retreated his hand. "I know, and I love you, Olga. I couldn't do any of this without you."

"Yes, you could, but I love you too." Elena returned to her plate, now tasting better than it had previously. She stopped to briefly dab her eyes. "I'm still not moving in, but the offer is open for you."

"I don't remember asking."

They shared a laugh and resumed eating. When they finished, Flip situated the couch to face the TV and they searched for a good movie. After a debate on waiting for an old faithful for Flip to come on or taking a chance on something that was new to them both, they agreed to give the stranger a chance. They got 20 minutes in before switching over to the movie they both admitted was their silent preference. It was a few minutes in, but they didn't miss anything important. The real story didn't unfold until the 30–35-minute mark. Elena curled up to him as they watched in relative silence, smoking the new strain from BLDHnd and quietly talking about Elena's upcoming work week and Flip's conversation with Xartis C'ro.

During a lull, Elena looked up from her pillow, "When're you going back to Monarch?"

Flip took her hand and kissed it, keeping his eyes on

the TV. "Probably a couple days."

"Well, if you have to go out there on Thursday, let me know if you are gonna be late getting back or staying out there. I can't cancel a second week in a row on your kids. They're asking enough questions as is."

"You wanna run 'em for me? You said there were a few girls interested in joining, right? Let them come work out, make the guys sweat a lil bit."

A smile creeped, "Think they can handle me?"

"Do your worst."

There were a few minutes of silence before another call came in. "How many people know you're home?" Elena quipped.

"Fuck, come on." Flip said under his breath before he answered. "Sata, you really need to get a text plan or something." Elena looked up from her pillow, hearing the annoyance in his voice.

"I am familiar with this 'texting', but it is so boring, Mr. Stokton, so mechanical. Besides, you appear to answer whenever I call. Sissy told me we should expect our witness in a *fo'reda'y*."

"A what?"

"I apologize, old language, he will be here in 3 to 4 days. Sissy says he was very distraught when he arrived and wants him to have a proper rest before his transport. I believe she fancies this young man and has taken pity. She's always a special affection for injured creatures, a trait I believe to rubbed off on me."

"Nothing more specific?"

"I'm sorry, but no."

Flip cursed under his breath and went back to the

phone, "Ok, just keep me updated."

"Of course."

CLICK.

He waited until the end credits before telling Elena that she may need to be ready to lead for him this week. This mystery witness should be in town either Thursday or Friday. Elena only nodded and took the remote, hoping to find something else on Monday night programming. She settled on Territory SportsCast X, the main hub for the obscure, and often hilarious "sports" played around the world. A game of dokuball was already going and only in its first few minutes but it looked intense. She always wondered how people in these kinds of sports could manage successful lives, especially when they're basically the same games they played as children, like dokuball; fascinating. She coughed out a subtle laugh as she remembered a similar observation made by Missy Blaskow.

CHAPTER 3
Thursday evening. Present day.

Flip took in the silence of the condo as he finished packing his, feeling a building swell of energy cut through the thin haze of his half-smoke. He rubbed his tongue over his canines, trying to soothe the low throbbing that began earlier in the day. Popping in a piece of Stim, he zipped his bag close and checked his mobile, *6:45PM,* before looking around for his car keys. He felt wired beyond the effects of the stim. It felt what he imagined being *hyper-*aware felt like. As the stim began to dissolve he went to the bathroom and spat into the sink; getting a glass for himself to chase the residue left behind. He went for his bag and then downstairs, texting Elena and Penny that he was leaving and should be back tomorrow. He told Penny to take some time off until he knew what this witness had to say. If it turned out to be some bullshit, at least he didn't drag Penny out with him. He did a final check on Birdie and strapped it to his thigh, before locking up.

Walking through the garage, he sighed as he thought about how he was just getting back home good before he's already going back out Monarch. He hadn't even had his new round of sessions with Dr. H'al'a yet and he was already back into the shit; just more to address on the couch. He heard Joy's welcoming chirp and got in, putting his bag in the front passenger seat and Birdie in the center console. He started her up and got into gear, waiting a minute for his 4th floor neighbors to walk past and to her own car. They were a quiet, middle-aged couple that were said to have been the real hippie types back in the day. He didn't see them much, but they were always nice and spoke to him whenever he did.

This time was no different. The wife looked over and waved with a smile. The husband looked over and nodded. They both were dressed up, or what they considered dressing up. They were either going to a dinner party among friends or a restaurant that don't care about your attire as long as you could afford your bill. Flip laughed to himself as they got into the car and pulled out of his space, filled with anticipation the entire drive out to Monarch.

◆ ◆ ◆

"Hana!? What'cha eating tonight, honey? Want some steak?" Tali called up from the bottom the guest house stairwell. She'd gotten used to seeing more of X'i around the main grounds more than her niece and was getting worried. X'i followed closely but stayed out of sight.

"I'm not hungry!" A hoarse voice yelled back.

"Honey, you need to eat something."

A door opened and closed. What followed were slow and heavy footfalls on the stairs. Standing in the red-tinted window, flooded with early afternoon sunlight, stood a shadow. Hana sniffled and wiped her face with her shirt. It was one of Rac's service shirts, medals and all, now stained heavy along the sleeves with blood.

"Hana, please eat something." Tali's mind went to a particularly bad temper tantrum Hana had as a child the very last time they came to visit. She thought it was about a toy she and Rac' couldn't agree on sharing, or something like that. Hana hadn't even been Turned yet, and it still scared Tali. The anger felt too raw to be over something so petty. She should've talked Ceeli into coming back home like she intended to that night. "I'm comin' up there, ok?"

Silence, besides a short sniffle.

Tali made her way up, slowly. When she got to the landing, she held Hana's face by the chin and lifted it. "Making an old woman climb stairs ain't nice, you know?"

Hana tried at a laugh, but it was tear cloaked and came out as a soft croak. "I'm sorry, I just miss Rac' so much. I left him behind."

"You should be thankful, not here crying."

"But I am thankful, and that's what hurts. I should've stayed behind, not him. I was the bigger sibling..."

"And I'm sure I'd be having this same talk with him and his girlfriend down there. I know he loved you very much. Why else would he do it?"

Silence.

"Come here," Tali held her as she heard more tears. "it'll be ok, but you got a choice, now. Either you go and take care of that PI that did him, or you move on."

"I can't go back now, but I will. I promise."

"I believe you." Tali kissed her forehead, "Now, come and eat before this damn food gets cold. You ain't say your girl here knew how to cook. By the way she been eating, you'd think it was for two." She then took her by the hand before Hana pulled away.

"I need to change."

Tali took a sniff. "And bathe too. I wasn't going to say anything, but honey..." She looked back down the stairs. "X'i, get up here and get Hana cleaned up."

"Yes, Madame." X'i came from behind the wall and met them on the landing, taking Hana by the hand and walking her up the stairs. "Come, let's take a bath."

Hana didn't say anything and allowed herself to be led back upstairs and to the bathroom. As the bathwater ran, she began undressing before, "Please, let me." X'i took over for her. After re-dressing her in a robe, X'i let the water run for a little longer; almost ready.

"You've been a really good girl, X'i. Rac' would be really proud of you."

"Thank you, Mother."

X'i tested the water again as steam gathered. It was ready. She held Hana's hand and let her in, observing the progressing look into a husk. Her skin was not its usual flawless complexion, and in the steam, began radiating the musk of dirt and death. Her hair was no better, with it having taken on a constant wet look and straggly. In the short time they've been here, she's seen the little spare weight Hana had fall away. A careless slip, or carefully timed push on the stairs, would break something, or worse. X'i blinked away her thoughts, Mother might see them on her face. She walked over the table cart with a washtowel and multiple vials of oils and soap on it. "Anything else, Mother?"

"No."

"Should I tell your aunt to bring your food here?"

"No."

Before X'i could turn around completely, she felt a grip around her wrist followed by the puncture of skin. Her body instinctively tensed. Did she do something wrong? Was the water not hot enough? Was it too hot?

"Please, join me, X'i. I won't hurt you."

X'i turned around and looked at Mother, and then the tub. It might be a tight fit, but there was enough room. The grip on her tightened and she felt a slow roll down the inside of her hand.

"Don't make me ask again." Hana sounded winded.

She undressed and noticed Hana inch to the front of the tub. "Mother?"

"Get in, X'i."

X'i did as told without another word and slowly used the washtowel to clean Mother before working on her hair; the water going from a clean milky hot to a faded pink. She added oil and soap into a lather and silently cleaned. It felt weird being behind Mother. She could sense the lower level of watchfulness. She could almost smell the vulnerability under the musk. Mother was powerful, but she was exposed right now. With her back turned, she wouldn't see anything coming. A quick swipe across her throat would--

"Is everything ok, X'i?" Hana asked.

"Yes, Mother."

"Not having any naughty thoughts, are we?"

X'i didn't realize she stopped. "N-No, Mother." She went back to Mother's front, working on her right arm in particular, easing the flaking skin off, shedding it. Hana took X'i's hand into her own, lowering it into the water; closer to her.

"I know you wouldn't try hurting me, would you, X'i?" Hana was bringing X'i's hand to her waist, and then lower. *"After everything we've done for you? What my brother sacrificed for you? I know you wouldn't even think about hurting me, right?"*

X'i let Mother guide her hand as she felt; still in control, even now. Suddenly, she didn't feel right and wanted to get out of the tub as quick as possible. But she didn't. Something told her that would be worse than if she stayed and let whatever was happening play out. Deep down, she knew she would never hurt Mother. No, she couldn't. She was good for Master, and in his absence, been a good pet for

Mother. She couldn't have hurt either of them. Hana went to pour the remainder of a vial with blue liquid into the bath and ran more water. The scent that rose smelled of blueberries with an undertone of spice.

"You wouldn't hurt me, would you X'i?" Hana repeated softly, returning to her place, and leaned back, eyes closed and breathing airily as she rested on X'i.

"No, Mother." X'i responded.

Hana leaned until her face was to the ceiling and opened her eyes, looking directly into X'i's with fire. "*Good girl.*" Her right hand clenched around X'i's forearm until her hold turned into a clawing. X'i saw how the pink water was growing redder from where her hand was but continued. She continued as she saw how her own blood dripped and ran down her arm, mixing into the cloudy water. She continued even as she felt Mother's body seize and then shutter. She continued, softer, because Mother never told her to stop. She continued because she wanted Mother to know she would always be a good girl. She continued because she knew she wouldn't hurt Mother. She continued because couldn't even think about doing such a thing. Not anymore. Not when she was going to make her a real mother. If she really wanted to hurt Mother, she should have done it already.

CHAPTER 4

Flip was met at the compound's edge by a horse-mounted escort. Hait'een held the lantern as Ter'frejr dismounted. What he didn't expect was to see was Viium getting off with her. He walked over and led Flip by the hand to Aunt Tefie and Ms. Hait'een. Between Viium's expressionless face and the dim glow in his eyes, Flip felt like he was being led to the gallows by the hangman himself. Ter'frejr said that Princess Siska proved her word and that their witness was healthy, well-rested, and wanted him returned the same way. Flip agreed and walked, listening to Viium talk coldly about his combat training with Aunt Terfie.

They found Sata in the main hall talking with two domestics, dismissing them when she saw the trio and Viium walking towards her. She saw his eyes ignite as he walked over and was greeted with kisses before she—

"Don't touch me! *Don't touch me!*"

The domestics appeared to all freeze in place as Master Viium thrashed and flailed in Sata's arms while she herself appeared unfazed. Flip could recognize the face that said this wasn't the first time she's dealt with this from him.

"Good evening, Mr. Stokton." She stroked Viium's hair and whispered into his ear and held her forehead against his before returning her attention. The change from Viium was as instant as it was uncomfortable. "Our witness will be here soon." She put a calmed Viium down with a final kiss and told him to go with Hait'een in the back field. They should play Catch the Fox, and there would be something nice for him after supper if he won. "Do not go easy on him, Hait'een. I suspect he is going to be a much more competitive adversary than usual today. The barrier has been established, and the fox will be let loose after you've changed. Just tell M when you are ready. He will be your GameMaster."

"Yes, Your Highness." She bowed, "Alright, Viium, think you can beat me this time?"

"Yes." He responded lowly. Hait'een was frighteningly good at Catch the Fox, no matter how much she said Skein was better. She'd sometimes already be there, even when Viium thought he tracked and caught it on his own. His eyes made her rethink how tonight's game would go. He looked at her as though she was the fox, but she stayed calm.

"Alright then, I don't wanna hear any complaining this time. No head starts, either." Hait'een took his hand and led down the hall, "Let's get changed."

Viium turned around and waved. "Bye, Mr. Stokton."

"See ya later, Viium." Flip waved back. His stomach dropped as Viium walked away, eyes now glowing brighter, and focused on him.

"Terfie, would you leave Flip and I? In fact, please take an early night off. The gentleman at the Landing you hold the eye of is working tonight, I hear. I suggest you not be late for your reservation."

Blush came over Te'rfrejr's face and she smiled coyly. "Thank you, Your Highness. What about the elf?"

"Mr. Stokton and I can handle him, but you will be called upon should he need Questioning. There's something nice in your bedchamber, waiting for you to put it on. I apologize in advance that it's lighter and more revealing than you're accustomed to, but I'm sure your *chal'ikra* would appreciate your show of vulnerability. As your Queen, I implore you to take advantage of his curiosity."

Te'rfrejr's face went completely red, and she quickly walked away with little more than another hushed thank you. Sata let her pass and watched as she went for her room until she bumped into a domestic, who then escorted her the rest of the way. When they turned a corner, Sata went back to Flip, who was feeling his canines with his tongue.

"How are you feeling, Mr. Stokton? Are you hungry?"

"Nah, I had something earlier. My teeth just been hurting a little bit today. Is Viium ok?"

"Ah, they are still getting used to you. Viium is perfectly fine, just a little moody today." She reached her hand out, "Come, we can have tea in my bedchamber. It will soothe the discomfort."

Flip felt the pull and took her hand. Sata wrapped her arm into his as they walked. "No Ms. Starks tonight?"

"Nah, she had to work and cover me with the kids I coach."

"You are quite the humanitarian, Mr. Stokton."

"I just like basketball, that's all. Plus, it helps keep some of some of those kids out of trouble."

"Are these children those of Founders, like yourself?"

"Not at all. Some of them live in the nicer parts of Fountain, but most of 'em ain't what we'd consider wealthy."

"Interesting."

They continued until they reached a dead-end. "This is one of few things your movies get correct about my kind." Sata pressed a stone and caused the dead-end to part, revealing the base of a winding staircase leading up, "As your people say, 'ta-da'." and they walked up. After going through another door, Flip found himself in what reminded him of the lower-level condos at Cloud Mesa: one level, but spacious. There were flowerbeds everywhere and the accessory furnishings were more modern than he expected; modern in the sense of within the last 30-odd years. Flip saw a movie-tape player that looked similar to one he had as a child, connected to a TV that looked just as old. At the time it was one of the newest models available, but now, though Sata's was in pristine condition, it was laughable to think this hunk of metal was seen as cutting-edge.

Rose-tinted dusk filtered in and covered the bedroom as Sata went to her kitchenette to prepare their tea. The entire room felt more like a habitable greenhouse than a bedroom. Going over to sit at the only table, Flip looked across the bed and saw three floor-length portraits against the opposite wall: two men on either side of a woman. Even across the room, their eyes looked as though on him, like the portrait of Hana's mother. He noticed the younger of the two men and himself shared the exact same eye color.

"My parents, and G'jon." Sata said as she placed his mug on the table and a rolled stick of spearflower next to it. She sat and took a sip from her own before striking a match for the table candle.

"You have an amazing painter."

"Thank you. I had to do them each from memory. It took a great deal of time."

Flip turned around, mostly to escape the gazes he was positive were focused on him; too creepy. "You paint, too?"

"No, but I like to think The Father guided my hands. My older sister was blessed with a natural talent for the brush."

"I get you." Flip sipped and saw it was the same tea from the feast, metallic aftertaste included. "How long before what's-his-name gets here, again?" He shifted in his seat.

"A couple hours. Are you nervous, Flip?"

"Should I be?"

"Not unless I make you so. Do I make you nervous, Flip?" The hazel of her eyes began to slowly take on a red that was noticeable even against that of the room.

His mind told him there *might* be nothing to worry about, though he felt even if there was, Sata was the type that got a kick in playing the long game. He felt at his leg and for the first time, Birdie wasn't trying to talk to him. "Nah, I trust you, Sata. You saved my life."

"Trust has nothing to do with it, but I like knowing I have yours. Would you like to smoke before we talk to our witness? Entertain some friendly talk?"

"Sure." Flip lifted the candle to the joint and got it going. "How was your day?"

CHAPTER 5

What. The. Fuck.

Walking along the dark central corridor of the basement-- dungeon being more apt-- of the compound, Flip didn't know a more appropriate summary of what he saw behind the block of cell doors. Men and women stood behind many of them, some with a dulled fire for eyes, many without. As he followed Sata, a dank, stomach-churning smell wafted through in waves. In the distance, he could hear a man scream out, calling for help. He didn't belong in here. He was innocent, he swore. He was an innocent man.

"Sata, what the hell is this?"

"*This* is where we hold those before and after Questioning. I apologize that you have to see this."

"Are all of these people vampyr?"

"There are some down here, but many are of your kind. They are the especially bad ones, 'allegedly'." She giggled. "The Father will determine their final guilt or innocence, and I will abide." She took out a key when they came to a blank slab of a door with a tiny square viewer. When she inserted and turned, they entered an equally dark room with candles lining the walls, creating a lining that reminded Flip of the inside of an oven. The Elf from Hhal sat at a small table, facing the door. He was dark and very clean cut. A little on the heavier side but definitely in shape.

"Queen Sata, the Third of Monarch." The Elf from Hhal rose from his seat and bowed. Flip saw the rope around his wrists and how they connected to similar ties at his ankles.

"Sata, do we need the binds? He's not a suspect."

Sata looked over and thought she saw the smallest of a flicker in Flip's eyes. Quite the humanitarian, indeed. Flip saw her smile before her eyes went back to The Elf. "Please sit." The Elf did. She walked over to the table, "What is your name?"

"This one is named Tom'kii Sil. He prefers you call him Tom."

Flip looked from Tom to Sata and back to Tom. *"This one"?*

"Can I trust you, Tom?" Sata asked as she walked towards.

Without missing a beat, Tom held his face to her. "You can trust this one, Your Highness, he is not devious."

Flip walked over to the table as Sata undid Tom's ropes. She explained that she was familiar with his account of two strangers driving into Little 'Chilo. Tom grew excited as he picked up the rest of the story, almost exact to the word as he told Princess Siska and her father. Flip asked about the women's descriptions. Tom responded with exact descriptions of Hana and who he suspected was Alexis. Hana apparently had even longer hair now, ending just below her backside. Both looked as though they hadn't bathed in a couple days.

"So how did you escape, Tom?" Flip asked.

"This one listened to the One Mother. He tried to warn the others that day at the public house, but they didn't heed, as usual. They didn't know those women were of your kind, Queen Sata, and that they have killed many before getting to Hhal. Mr. Stokton, I'm sorry for your personal loss." Tom replied.

Flip looked to Sata and she shook her head. She hadn't told anyone except The Council about her unorthodox choice of a *ha'kiet*, let alone his brother's murder.

"How do you know about Mr. Stokton?" Sata asked.

"This one doesn't, personally, but the One Mother knows everything. She shares things with this one, as she does with only her most obedient children." Tom said as he reached into his pants pocket, pulling out a pack of cigarettes and a matchbook. "May this one smoke?"

Sata receded her hand, "He may." and smirked. Might as well play along.

"This one is thankful." Tom lit a cigarette and took a heavy drag. "It's been a couple days."

"I understand." Sata nodded. "What else do you know, Tom?"

Tom went on to explain that the One Mother told him the women were going to Tar'Kuur and that he needed to leave Hhal before they did. He's done business in Tar'Kuur but doesn't like it there, preferring the people of 'Chilo and their hospitality, in particular that of Princess Siska. Tom found her to be quite beautiful. She even held his hand as he testified to her father's court. "Touched" or not, Sata saw that this one had good taste.

"How old are you, Tom? What do you do in Hhal?" Flip asked, sensing the conversation drifting away.

Tom looked up for a second, as if listening to someone, and nodded. "This one is 33 years old and runs a small-contract business between Hhal and the 'Chilo Territory." He lowered his head. "He's lost friends and employees to the women you seek. The shorter one had anger, deep in her heart. The taller one, only sorrow and fear."

"I'm sorry, man. Got any family around?" Flip asked.

"This one's has not seen his parents since he was a small child, but he has distant relatives not far from 'Chilo. The One Mother has watched over him since leaving the orphanage."

"Fuck."

"Fuck, indeed, Mr. Stokton. Fuck, indeed." Tom replied before taking a drag. He looked up again, nodded, exhaled and took another pull. "This one also brings a warning. For you." He pointed his cigarette to Flip. Sata now saw the previous light begin to flare. Tom did as well and his faced changed. He backed his chair as Flip stepped forward. He looked to Sata and was met with a cold smirk.

"Go on." Flip told him, walking around the table and sitting on its edge in front of Tom.

"She will be back for you. Not now, but she will come. If she cannot get to you, she *will* find those you hold close."

"I'll be ready."

"But will you?" Tom looked him in the eyes and took a final drag of his cigarette before ashing it out against his chair leg. He put the butt in his pocket. "This one has seen the folly of man's assumption in superiority. Humans in particular are the most frequent offenders." The ensuing silence in the room was almost tangible.

Flip held out for a handshake, "Thanks, Tom. Again, I'm sorry about what happened."

"This one is as well. He will return to Hhal and give his friends a proper burial. Princess Siska has already given her pledge of assistance." Tom took out another cigarette and lit it, forgoing Flip's hand with a glance.

"And after that? Are you staying in Hhal?" Flip asked.

"This one has not been given that information yet.

He would like to go back home to 'Chilo proper, but will obey whatever the One Mother determines is best for him. He hopes she takes his wishes into consideration." Tom took a drag and smiled. The One Mother truly has been kind to him. She's been with him for a long time now and has yet to lead him astray.

"Of course. I wish you safety, Tom." Flip went back around the table and stood near Sata.

"As does this one to you, Mr. Stokton." Tom rose from his seat and bowed. "Queen Sata, is there anything else you need this one for?"

"No, Tom, not now. You have lived to your reputation. I'll be sure to put in a good word with Sissy."

Tom's eyes widened. "You're friends with Princess Siska?" His tone reminded Flip of a nervous teenager talking about the girl he's been digging on.

"I believe the contemporary term is still 'best friends'. Our people use the formal phrase, *x'lait th'rahk nu,* my blood is you as yours is mine. She has seen me at my worst, and never wavered in loyalty or friendship. I think you two would get along just fine."

"This one is amazed and thankful." Tom replied. "He has done only a few jobs for Ms. Siska around her castle."

"I will help change that." Sata walked over and took Tom by the hand, "I think Sissy would enjoy seeing you around more often. Tell me, is this One Mother a jealous one?"

Tom scoffed, "The One Mother finds no other's beauty above her own. Jealousy is beneath her." and took another drag. "Some dedicate their bodies *and* spirit, and she rewards them with a sensation storied to be better than one any mortal can bring. Many, like this one, are not as strong-willed in their abstinence but are still devoted, nonetheless. Some, like this one's parents, are married and therefore do not seek comfort in new flesh. The One Mother looks kindly on this one, for she knows what truth lies in his heart. If the Princess is a true fit for this one, she will allow."

"Interesting." Sata replied simply. "Would you care to stay for dinner, Tom? I invite you to join Mr. Stokton and myself."

Tom tilted his head upwards for a second and must have gotten the green light. He then nodded, "This one would be honored, Your Highness."

"As you should." Sata responded.

Sata and Flip led Tom from his room back to the main of the compound. Dinner was filled with less work talk that Flip expected, but he kept thinking about Tom's—or the One Mother's, warning about Hana coming back, and how she may come after Elena or his family. It stayed in his mind during dessert, during the after-dinner tea, even during Tom's comedic recollections of his time at the 'Chilo Home for Lost Children until he decided to move to Hhal when the One Mother first spoke to him. His parents always told them She would never leave his side, but they did. The One Mother told them to go and spread her word to further Territories and settlements. Flip asked him did he know where they went off to and Tom responded that he didn't, but when the One Mother felt they should be reunited, she would bring them together. Patience and obedience were two of the One Mother's most important virtues. Before excusing himself for the evening, Tom reached across the table to Flip.

"Mr. Stokton, this one enjoyed meeting you, and hopes to see you again sometime."

"You too, Tom. If you ever plan to come to Fountain,

let me know. I'll make sure you have a good time."

"This one will hold you to your offer." Tom smiled.

Flip met his hand. *Flash.* There was a muted scene with an older Tom, or maybe with his hair grown out. He'd slimmed down, but only for it to turn into muscle, and was walking with an older man and woman. They were all dressed in matching red-orange robes and joining a large group in similar colored gowns, some wearing one of four different symbols on the chest. From their movements and faces, it looked as though the group was cheering as Tom approached them. Then nothing. He was back at the compound.

"--more tea?" Flip heard Sata's voice filter in.

He looked over, "Sorry, what'd you say?"

"Would you like some more tea?" Sata repeated.

Tom looked to Flip with a smirk. "Is everything ok, Mr. Stokton?"

Flip pulled his hand back slowly, "Yeah, yeah, I'm good, just a little headache. My fault, yes on the tea, Sata."

"No need to apologize. You weren't gone for long." Tom replied. He then got up from his seat and politely excused himself for the night, asking for directions to his room. Sata had him escorted and bid him a good night and pleasant rest before moving to the chair next to Flip with the kettle. She refilled both of their cups.

"He is fascinating. I think I see why Sissy likes him."

"He'll see his parents again."

"Is that right?" Sata took a sip.

"Have you heard of this 'One Mother', Sata?"

"Not by that name, but it doesn't surprise me that

there is belief in such a thing. There are many peculiar belief systems practiced out in the deserts, I've learned. My father used to say the isolation either turned its dwellers to something, or away from it."

Flip had a few swallows in silence, thinking about Tom's story and then back to the warning. Sata took him by the hand, "Mr. Stokton, you are troubled."

"Just thinking about that thing Tom said about Hana coming back, that's all."

"I will not allow what happened to your brother occur to you, or your family."

"I know, Sata. I trust you."

Sata lifted her hand and rose from her seat. "I take it you are staying for the evening?"

Flip looked at his phone, *11PM,* "Yeah, I had a feeling I might be out late depending on what Tom had to say. I might talk to him some more tomorrow."

Sata adjusted her dinner-robe. "Should I have your bag brought down, or did you intend to spend the rest of your evening with me?" Her voice took on an inviting tone, as did the now low embers in her eyes.

Flip chuckled, "Nah, you can have someone bring it down. I'll wait for them in here."

"Very well, then I bid you a good night and peaceful rest, Flip. Will you join us for morning-meal?"

"Sure." *Morning-meal? Sounds like a damn old-home.*

"Good. I'll send for you in the morning." Sata smiled. "Terfie's night out must have been successful. Had you noticed she has yet to come home?"

They both laughed at the observation and Sata left for her "bedchamber". Less than 20 minutes later, the same elderly woman from the feast had his bag and placed it on the table before him. She appeared to actively avoid eye contact with him when she gave him a smaller pouch and a tiny book of thin rip-paper.

By a quarter to midnight, he was settling into his room and splitting open the joint he brought with him to mix with some of the spearflower the old woman gave him. Flip wondered how long she had been in service of the Queen. Flip had brushed it off and tested his blend as he laid in bed, finding the heightened feeling mix well with the chill of the spearflower and he casually went through his online presence. Looked like Penny and Dom went to a nice restaurant an hour or so before his dinner. Elena seemed to have a good night at workouts, having made an announcement showing off the four new members, two boys, two girls, of the age 15-17 FCCC rec team. Xartis C'ro stood among them.

By the time he was finished with his smoke, Flip thought about Hana's potential return one last time. Fuck her, and her "blood-feud". As far as he was concerned, the score's been settled. Brother for brother; blood for blood. If she wanted to come and run it back, she was welcome. He had the rings to prove he was used to beating sore losers.

ACKNOWLEDGEMENT

I want to take this space to thank my parents, sister, and closest kept friends. Writing a novel has been quite the experience and having had kept it under wraps for so long was not something I took joy in, but if there is any set of people in the world to understand my process, it's you. The support and respect you've shown me throughout the journey is something that I couldn't put into enough words.

To the residents and establishments of Takoma, specifically Olive Lounge and Republic, I can only say thank you. Being able to call myself your neighbor and friend has and always will be an honor I wear proudly.

ABOUT THE AUTHOR

Jamal Donte Childs

There are a few things that the DC native would describe himself at one point or another in life. While "published author" had never been a serious consideration, the want to attempt something wholly new is what changed that. Finding the pen at a young age and following the path to being a visual artist, the secondary loves of both film and reading (especially the scary stuff) bored its way into the foundation of what became not only an artistic aesthetic, but a connecting necessity between each work; every piece needs a full story. Though not a visual piece in the traditional sense of the word, Jamal would still tell you that writing a book doesn't make him an author but an "artist of a couple different mediums". This book, and any others that may follow, are merely new additions to the portfolio.

Made in the USA
Middletown, DE
05 September 2022

73271252R00390